FISHING
for STARS

BRYCE COURTENAY

FISHING *for* STARS

McArthur & Company
Toronto

First published in Canada in 2009 by
McArthur & Company
322 King Street West, Suite 402
Toronto, Ontario
M5V 1J2
www.mcarthur-co.com

This paperback edition published in 2010 by
McArthur & Company

Library and Archives Canada Cataloguing in Publication

Courtenay, Bryce, 1933-

    Fishing for stars / Bryce Courtenay.

ISBN 978-1-55278-895-0

    I. Title.

PR9619.3.C598F58 2010   823'.914   C2010-903934-3

Text design by Tony Palmer © Penguin Group (Australia)
Cover photographs: lights © Corbis; fisherman © Paul Loven/ Getty Images
Author photograph: Graham McCarter
Typeset in Goudy Oldstyle

Printed in Canada by Webcom

10 9 8 7 6 5 4 3 2 1

For the Corroboree frog

PART ONE

CHAPTER ONE

'Frogs are one of our early-warning systems; when they
start to be endangered it's time to take notice.'
Nick Duncan, Port Vila, 1993

SOME THINGS FROM THE past stay fresh in the mind
of an old man: the curve of a young woman's breast, the sheen
of suntan on her legs. A look, a sidelong glance, so beautiful
your mind takes a snapshot to retain it forever, images in which
the colours never fade. Out to sea on a pristine morning on the
gaff-rigged cutter *Madam Butterfly* with the ocean spray hitting
your face, when you were young and strong and anything was
possible. Friends, partners, business deals, government bribes,
drink, fortunes to be made and lost, islands, women, children,
hope. Anna and Marg, especially Anna and Marg, the yin and
yang of womankind. They're all there trapped in the brilliant
blink of a flashlight, then stored as a lasting image. Mine as long
as the lens in my mind remains clear.

I am sitting on the verandah of my home in Vanuatu
looking over Beautiful Bay. It is near the end of the wet season
and the morning air carries a vague hint of crispness. As I seem
to be doing more and more these days, I'm recollecting the past.
When almost everything that is going to happen to you has
already happened, memories occupy more of your time.

Sitting in this large comfortable old cane chair, mentally

meandering, flicking through mindscapes, I am attempting to banish what I have called 'The killing-of-Anna dream'. I woke at dawn again this morning clutching the pillow and bawling like a little kid, choking back my grief, thinking the pillow was Anna. If I don't exorcise this dream, cast out these demons, the dark shadows of the night will linger throughout this sparkling day in paradise.

Welcome to Paradise; another time, a different pace. I'd read that recently on a large poster as I left the airport after picking up Saffron, my goddaughter, who was visiting me from Port Moresby. Beautiful Bay is about as much paradise as anyone can take; add a little phoney Hawaiian music, frame up, roll camera and let *Tales of the South Pacific* begin.

Mine has been a fortunate life in so many ways, but in the end we live more in our head than we do in a place and lately there's some alarming stuff happening in my head. More and more I seem to be recalling the blood, sweat and tears of my life in the islands. Nick Duncan. Billionaire? Sailor? Lover? Soldier? Killer? Dreamer? Pioneer? Nice guy? Bastard? Adulterer? What?

Saffron disturbs my thoughts in a lap-lap sarong and bikini top, looking every inch a beautiful young woman. 'Uncle Nick, the phone. It's Great Auntie Marg.' She giggles. 'And she's talking green.'

'What else,' I sigh, then laugh, rising from my chair. 'It's morning, and her morning calls are always a dark shade of green.'

Saffron, brought up in the islands where the pace of life is relaxed, asks, 'But why is she always in such a hurry?'

I shrug. 'It's her way. Yesterday is a lost opportunity, a list of tasks not completed, so today all *must* be recovered. Marg is always running to catch up with herself.'

'She's seventy-seven! When I'm her age I won't be jumping around like Jiminy Cricket.'

'You mean jumping around *saving* Jiminy Cricket,' I retort. 'May we be spared from all zealots, religious or green, God-botherers or self-appointed custodians of all creatures great and small.'

'What about frogs, Uncle Nick . . . and butterflies?' Saffron asks mischievously.

'Ah, that's different,' I grin. 'If you kiss a frog he may turn into a prince, and butterflies are born to become princesses.'

'You're not *really* a cynic about the environment, are you, Uncle Nick?' Saffron asks.

'No, but there's a big difference between being concerned and being a zealot. Frogs are one of our early-warning systems; when they start to be endangered it's time to take notice. Old man trees must be respected not turned into chopsticks and cardboard cartons. Moderation in all things, my dear.' This last remark I recall coming from my Anglican missionary father when, as a child, I'd excitedly captured half a dozen of the same species of butterfly.

'Better hurry, you know how cranky she gets when she has to wait,' Saffron cautions, seemingly satisfied with my reply. Some of the kids today really seem to care and don't think nature is confined to the strip of grass beside the pavement where the dog takes a poo.

Marg Hamilton's morning calls from Sydney are always a machine-gun barrage of words, and usually I'm hit with a request. This time it's 'Nick, I need your help! Have the Japanese secured the fishing rights to your Marine Exclusive Economic Zone? Has that corrupt government of yours already signed away their rights? We've got to do something, darling! Did you know the Pacific tuna fishery is the last fishing resource not to be decimated by factory fishing!'

That's our Marg, straight to the point, no opening niceties, strictly business. Some item or other needs to be ticked off her inexhaustible list of crucial green issues, something that invariably involves my time or money or both.

I'm in inter-island shipping, though she's aware that I would, of course, know about the tuna resources in this part of the Pacific. She also knows damn well that nothing whatsoever happens swiftly in an island government department.

'Good morning, Marg. And how are you? Lovely day here on the island.' I glance through the large picture window overlooking Beautiful Bay and then further out to the harbour. 'Not a cloud in the sky, the bay is sparkling, God's thrown a handful of diamonds into the water, the harbour beyond is like a millpond. Unusual weather, even for this late in the wet season.'

The irony in my voice is lost on her. She's probably got the phone tucked between her shoulder and chin the way women seem able to do, freeing both hands to make notes, fish in her handbag for the car keys, check her make-up in the mirror. How do they do that?

'Nick, is there any way you can find out quickly? I thought Anna might have been mixed up in it. These things usually take a year or two to resolve,' she says, silently acknowledging that her agitation was merely for effect.

I feel an involuntary pang of guilt at the mention of Anna's name. Had she still been alive, she would almost certainly have been part of negotiations with the Japanese. And a small but significant percentage of the licensing fees would have been skimmed off the top as 'Ongoing Consulting Fees' or some such euphemism for appropriating the island people's money. As well, you could bet your army boots there would be a significant backhander from the Japanese for facilitating negotiations; 'smoothing' is the common word.

Marg Hamilton and Anna Til are the two women who have been equal halves of the whole of my loving, the greater part of my frustrations, probably the bulk of my infuriation and certainly most of the happiness and abundant love I've been blessed to receive. No man on earth, least of all myself, is sufficiently strong to manage two such beautiful, intelligent, articulate, stubborn and determined women who are opposed to each other in every conceivable way. Philosophically, in their aesthetic and gastronomic tastes (Marg eats pretty bland vegetarian; Anna, a contradiction as always, Japanese and French), in the movies, entertainment and music they love, I cannot imagine two people more at variance.

Anna, in her day a superb example of the work of the Big Craftsman in the Sky, passed away four months ago at the age of sixty-six, so I would have welcomed a soupçon of tact from Marg, also once a finely chiselled edition of the Maker's art. But even so soon after Anna's death, Marg's forthright opinions of the other woman in my life are unlikely to be tempered by mealy-mouthed niceties. She is too well bred to say so, but not only has she endured the ambiguities of her relationship with me, she has also outlasted her opponent and must feel that she therefore deserves certain rights. Women are by nature predatory creatures and I have long since understood that any influence I might have had on either Anna or Marg was based entirely on the constant threat that the other might gain the upper hand. Marg has waited a long time to have me all to herself again and she will make the most of it.

'No, I don't believe Anna was involved,' I say, deliberately keeping my voice matter-of-fact, abiding by the old rules even though there is no longer any need.

'Nick, it's important we know the very moment they sign. The media will give it a big run. Bob Brown may be able to get some sort of brouhaha started in the senate and that's very good for us.'

'Sweetheart, isn't it about time you threw in the towel, put your feet up?' I tease, mixing my metaphors. 'Let the youngsters save the planet. Come to Beautiful Bay and live with me all the days of your life. God knows, collectively we haven't got that many left. An insurance bloke told me recently that at my age they could estimate on average the number of minutes I could expect to live!' I chuckle. 'Minutes, mind you!'

Marg laughs politely, ignoring my deliberately insensitive invitation. I already know she'd find it unacceptable, not only because of the too recent death of Anna, but also because it's difficult to save the planet from Port Vila. 'All the more reason to use one's time productively,' she replies primly.

'Please, Marg, not the schoolmistress,' I tease. 'It's the least attractive aspect of your personality.'

'Don't be ridiculous, Nick. I'm an old head and old heads are hard to find in the movement. There are plenty of marvellous young people prepared to throw themselves in front of a whaling ship, and while these confrontations are very important for the movement, of equal or even greater importance is the silent force, the behind-the-scenes work. The kids don't know who to badger, threaten or compromise in Canberra.' Then she cleverly gets back on track, 'As I know you do in the islands.'

'I don't know about this fishing business,' I reply. 'I don't have the pull, the influence I used to have.'

'Nonsense!' Marg cuts in. 'You're the grand patriarch and, unlike us, the islands still respect the wisdom that comes with age.'

'It's changing fast, new generation, cocaine, piercings, youth culture.' Despite myself I'm flattered that she has referred to me as the grand patriarch, even if it is a bit of an exaggeration. However, I am aware that it isn't like the old days. Many of the new breed of politicians in the Pacific possess law degrees and almost all are university trained, a bequest to the youth of the various Pacific Islands from Australia, New Zealand, Britain or France. It doesn't make them less open to corruption, only smarter at it.

'I'll see what I can do; I can't promise.'

'Good boy,' she replies. I imagine her crossing the item off her list. Good ol' Nick, always comes through. But I know from experience Marg usually has two requests. I have come to think of this tactic as the 'double tap'. Moreover, she always makes the less important request first. A right jab followed by a vicious left hook. Suddenly she announces, 'Nick, I hear you've been giving away money . . . a lot.' A slight pause. 'Is it Anna's?'

'Would it matter if it was?'

Another pause. 'Well not now, I *suppose*,' she says, drawing out the last word.

'*Don't* go there, Marg,' I say.

'Nick, will you help the zoo?' Marg asks, ignoring my caution.

'Help? With what?'

'A frog. I know you're rather fond of frogs.'

'You'll need to be a bit more specific, darling.'

'The Southern Corroboree frog. It's facing extinction.'

Marg knows how to get my attention. 'Ah, *Pseudophryne corroboree*, unique to Australia, habitat – Snowy Mountains. What, the amphibian chytrid fungus?'

'Yes, amongst other threats. Guy Cooper, one of the directors with me at Taronga Park, estimates there are less than two hundred left in the wild. We want to begin a recovery program.'

'Hmm, how much?'

'For the Corroboree only?'

'Oh, I see. There's more?'

'Nick, you know there is! At least forty-seven Australian species face extinction, hundreds more worldwide.'

'Pliny the Elder said, "Out of Africa always something new".'

'Nick, you're changing the subject.'

'No I'm not. Some authorities suggest the fungus has spread across the planet from Africa in the last twenty years.'

'Well yes, Nick, thank you. The point is, frogs are dying. May I say you're good for a hundred thousand dollars?'

I pause deliberately to make her work for her money. 'That's a big ask.'

'She can afford it!'

'She? Watch your step, sweetheart. You and Anna – it's time to stop. Anna is no longer here.'

Marg doesn't know how to watch her step, or how to take a backward one. 'Darling, let's face it. Anna only liked frogs for their legs, lightly sautéed with fresh garlic and a sprinkling of truffles.'

I don't take the bait. The antipathy between the two women was always going to continue beyond the grave. If the situation had been reversed and Anna had outlived Marg, she would probably have been even more vituperative. Nevertheless, Marg can't have it both ways. I allow the silence to grow, then say, 'Pity you disapprove so strongly of Anna. After all, it was her money, and as far as I'm concerned still is. I rather like frogs – frogs and butterflies; both so wonderfully diverse. But you're right, frogs are having a terrible time. I tell you what I'll do. I'll send the money to the Bronx Zoo; they have an excellent frog conservation program underway.'

'You bastard, Nick! You're being a deliberate shit! It's different now!'

'What, now that Anna's dead? Why is that?'

'Anna!' Marg comes down hard on the name so that it seems to crack into two equal pieces, both parts whacking into my ear. 'The *only* thing Princess Plunder ever did was rob the environment! You name it – fish, old-growth forests, animal habitat – she contributed in no small way to their degradation!' Marg's voice is filled with righteous anger. 'It's time to make restitution, and charity begins at home!'

It's one of the things I love about Marg; she's not just tough and stubborn, she's got a good mind and the courage of her convictions, not to mention a whiplash tongue when she's riled. I know I'm defeated; she'll get her money. But nevertheless I attempt to regain the upper hand. 'Like you, Marg, Anna had a mind of her own. As a matter of fact, she made a number of significant bequests.'

'What, to the Institute of Chartered Accountants?'

I laugh despite myself, so she knows she's won. In the past I survived the invective of either of them by staying neutral, perhaps reflecting an ambivalence that has been the key to my relationship with both of them. 'Enough,' I say quietly.

I wait. Usually there's a fair bit of growling before the purring resumes, but Marg's dulcet tone catches me off guard. 'Nick Duncan, I've loved you for most of my life. I continued to love you even after I married the admiral. But at eighteen you were too young and at twenty-six I was too old for you. We started out as lovers and here we are, still the dearest friends.'

I'm not fooled for a moment. She's got what she wants and she's much too intelligent to have another crack at Anna, for now. But I'm not fool enough to think the donation of the money will lead to a modicum of respect for Anna's memory. Marg simply wants to keep a foot in the door in case she needs access in future. Yet, despite everything, I know she loves me and always has.

I've often mused about how I could have loved and continue to love two such completely dissimilar women, both utterly convinced they were right in all matters. Absolute conviction must be a nice thing to possess, but it's hell on everyone else.

'Nick, I have to go. I have a meeting this afternoon with Macquarie Bank. They're still young – unlike the others who are all ruled by old men with paunches – and they're considering throwing their support behind renewable energy. It looks very promising.'

I glance at my paunch. 'I see, and their money *isn't* tainted?' My voice is still a semitone too sharp.

She ignores this. 'I'll call you in a couple of days, darling.'

'Yeah, righto, I'll look forward to that. Morning business or evening pleasure?' I ask, a touch acerbic. While Marg calls me often enough from Sydney, her *'Lovely to speak with you, darling!'* calls always come in the evening when she's through with her daily lists and is feeling mellow after a regulation gin and tonic.

'Bye, darling, love you!' The phone clicks in my ear. Corroboree frog will be duly ticked off as business completed. It is something I had wanted to do anyway. When you mention that frogs are endangered, people are at best only vaguely concerned. Frogs are not a priority on the endangered species list, yet they are often the canary in the coal mine, one of the warnings that our environment is changing, usually for the worse.

Despite the humidity outside, I walk back onto the front verandah and flop into the cane chair; the view over Beautiful Bay never fails to calm me. It's too early for a drink, although I'm almost tempted. That's yet another thing that has changed: the level in the Scotch bottle seems to be dropping more quickly since Anna died.

I am becoming dismayed at my despondency, a mood that in truth has little or nothing to do with Marg's call, but obviously has something to do with my recurring dream about killing Anna.

I've always been a loner, content with my own thoughts, but never moody or churlish. I've observed such weakness and self-indulgence in other men and thought less of them for it.

Now I know that if I should allow the small dark cloud of despair hovering above my head to envelope me, at the very least I will destroy this gorgeous day and be tempted to open the Scotch bottle far too early.

In an attempt to dispel my gloom I try to dismiss the Marg Hamilton of Japanese fishing licences and recall the stunning twenty-six-year-old WRAN in Naval Intelligence who stole my virginity in March 1942, a month after I'd turned eighteen.

By sailing *Madam Butterfly*, a twenty-nine-foot gaff-rigged cutter, across the Pacific from Java to Fremantle, I'd escaped the Japanese invasion with only hours to spare. It had been in Java that I'd first met Anna, the illegitimate daughter of a wealthy Dutch businessman and a Javanese woman who had died in childbirth.

Anna was my first love, a young girl so beautiful that my heart still pounds at the thought of her at sixteen.

Upon my arrival in Fremantle after a difficult and eventful month at sea, I was questioned by a Naval Intelligence team, which included Marg Hamilton. She took me home and joyously bedded me less than a month after Anna and I had said a tearful farewell, promising to be mutually faithful and to 'wait' for each other until we could consummate our love, however long that might take.

Alas, at eighteen, the one-eyed snake is king. Marg snapped her fingers and I was halfway through undoing my fly buttons before the snap had echoed round the room. She taught me everything a boy should know in the limited time we enjoyed before I left for Melbourne to join the navy. Whereas Anna made my heart pound each time she appeared, the WRAN with the beautiful breasts and long legs gave me a hard-on every time I looked at her. Duplicity had come early in my long life of loving these two women.

Later that year, on the 12th of December 1942 to be precise, while I was at Guadalcanal with the Americans fighting the Japs, Marg wrote to say she'd become engaged to a naval officer. In fact, to Commander Rob Rich who had been my commander at HMAS *Cerberus*, the naval training centre in Victoria I had attended as a recruit. While I'd been in the islands, Marg had been promoted and transferred from Fremantle to Melbourne, where she'd met him and fallen in love.

I recall feeling cheated, deeply hurt and sorry for myself. In fact Marg had always been very careful to point out while I'd been with her in Fremantle that the privilege of sharing her bed was subject to her approval and should always be regarded as temporary. She was eight years older than I was and she announced in her practical way that this was an emotional chasm too large for either of us to leap.

Nonetheless, battle-weary and suffering from malaria, I was shattered by the news of her impending marriage. I felt unloved and entirely on my own. My mother had died when I was five years old; my father, a missionary in New Britain, had declined to leave his flock and had almost certainly been captured by the Japanese and was probably dead. Anna had failed to arrive in Australia, so I told myself I had every right to assume she too was captured or dead. Now the only other person in the world I loved had jilted me.

The fact that Marg was perfectly at liberty to share her affections with whomsoever she wished and that, in turn, I had barely given a thought to my absolute vow of chastity to Anna on the first occasion I had been seduced by Marg never occurred to me at the time. I recall that months later, when eventually it did, I explained my infidelity and settled my conscience by a process of retrospective reasoning.

I'd seen Anna off at the quay in Batavia when she had escaped with her family on a merchant ship. But upon arriving in Fremantle I was to learn that the Japanese were sinking ships on the high seas whether they carried troops, civilians or refugees. So, I'd conveniently made myself believe that Anna had been a victim of such bombing, leaving me free to jump into bed with Marg. My logic, both belated and dodgy, was neat as a three-button suit.

In fact, when I met Anna in Melbourne five years after the war ended and once again fell head over heels in love with a very changed and emotionally damaged woman, I was to learn that her ship had broken down on the south coast of Java, where she'd become a prisoner of the Japanese, forced to spend the war as the consort of the Japanese commander of the region, or to put it more bluntly, as a comfort woman.

After leaving Marg in Fremantle, I had not been entirely faithful to her either. Shortly after I'd arrived in Melbourne to attend the officer training course at HMAS *Cerberus*, I had met a lovely little Irish Catholic redhead named Mary Kelly who, while assiduously preserving her virginity for her marriage bed, had been sweet enough to relieve me in other pleasant ways.

In my mind this meant that I had technically remained faithful to Marg Hamilton. So I was filled with righteous anger that the woman I loved was going to marry a naval officer with a desk job, while I, weak with malaria, was risking my life almost daily in bloody hand-to-hand combat with the enemy to keep her safe so that she could fornicate with anyone she fancied.

I had written to her every week while I'd been in the islands with the marines, and while her own letters never promised fidelity or suggested a shared future, I nevertheless had taken it for granted that she would be waiting for me, that I had matured sufficiently to jump the emotional chasm.

The dreaded letter telling me the bad news had crossed one of my own telling her I was being repatriated from Guadalcanal; that the umpteenth dose of malaria had finally done me in; that

I was to be sent to a military hospital in Victoria.

I had lain naked in my tent under a mosquito net, drowning in my own sweat, teeth chattering, shivering from the fever raging through my body, imagining my homecoming. *Boy soldier, broken by malaria, returns home a hero to claim his faithful love. She sits tearfully at his bedside holding his hand in the military hospital. When he finally recovers they walk together into the sunset.* In my fevered imagination I could practically hear the violins in the background.

Commander Robert Rich, Marg's husband, was and always had been a great bloke. He subsequently welcomed me as a friend, and in the twenty years that followed he rose to the rank of admiral. Pretty bright in his own right, with the added advantage of Marg – a charge of dynamite in his life – there was no stopping his climb up the ladder. Together they raised two intelligent and thoroughly delightful children, John and Samantha, and appeared to be very happy. Alas, he was killed in a freak accident in 1965. While on a routine inspection at the Cockatoo Island Dockyards in Sydney, he was hit by a steel beam that fell from a crane.

In the five years that followed, Marg grew weary of tea and sympathy, garden parties and official dinners, which she attended alone wearing her husband's medals. While she'd enjoyed being the admiral's wife and raising a family, she'd been a captive of her husband's career. Now she found herself trapped in her new role as the admiral's widow, expected by the naval establishment to do good works within the navy family.

Marg is a woman with the energy of a buzz-saw and she was slowly rusting away in a corner of the work shed. At fifty-four she was a highly articulate and still extremely attractive woman who craved a new start, longing to walk out of the shadows cast by her former life. Finally, fed up to the teeth with fetes and charity functions, she resumed her maiden name and went to live in Tasmania.

She joined the Australian Conservation Foundation and she became actively involved in the rolling battles to save the Tasmanian wilderness. She was among the first members of the United Tasmania Group, the world's first green political party, which was formed in 1972. This led eventually to membership of the Tasmanian Wilderness Society, where the Tasmanian Greens were born as a political party and ultimately to her election as a member of the Tasmanian Legislative Council.

Marg knew how to get things done, and quickly became a bloody nuisance in Hobart and as a lobbyist in Canberra where both Labor and the Coalition thought her political party at best temporary and at worst a bad joke.

Always the closest of friends, she and I returned to a somewhat peripatetic though more intimate association after she went to Tasmania. I'd visit her in Hobart or Canberra when I was in Australia or she'd visit me at Beautiful Bay. It seemed I had finally managed to jump the emotional chasm.

When she retired from the Tasmanian Legislative Council in 1985 she returned to live in Sydney. By that time she'd earned the sobriquet 'Madam Termite', for her ability to undermine the halls of conservatism and complacency that seemed particularly common in Tasmania, especially the Tasmania Club, which she regarded as the greatest single assembly of silly old farts in the land.

Now, at the age of seventy-seven with all her marbles very much intact, she's the Martin Luther King of climate change, preaching the hot gospel of global warming and the cold logic of melting icecaps. She's the old woman and the sea, relentless defender and spokesperson for all creatures great and small, those that swim, fly, run, crawl, slither, hop, burrow or simply exist.

When Marg began her crusade she lived in a lonely world

where most politicians thought of her kind as tree-hugging ratbags. She and they have come a long way, but not without suffering the slings and arrows of the environment sceptics. Last year she was invited as a non-representative speaker to the Earth Summit, the United Nations Conference on Environment and Development in Rio de Janeiro and the very first conference to be held on the subject of environment and sustainable development. Her talk followed that of British explorer Robert Swan, the first man to walk to both Poles, who warned the world that the Arctic and Antarctic were showing alarming signs of change and drew attention to the size of the hole in the ozone layer over the Arctic. Her podium-thumping talk caused several representatives from the larger nations to walk out and the remainder to give her a standing ovation.

Marg completed her speech by saying: '*As the twentieth century totters to a close, one despotic oil-producing Arab nation has attacked another equally deficient in human rights. The organisation sponsoring this conference went to the defence of one of them in order to protect the flow of oil from the Middle East.*

'*Despite the pious rhetoric, this was the cynical protection of a cheap source of the material appropriately named "crude" that is destroying our planet. The road to Basra is not only littered with Iraqi dead but also with the hastily forsaken principles of nations whose politicians claim to care. This self-serving rescue mission is a clear indication of what the so-called forces for good will do to protect their right to continue to pollute the world in the name of progress.*

'*It is time to reclaim a world once beautiful but now slowly dying as we stand by and let these internal combustion bullies have their way with our planet. May they burn in a hellfire fuelled by an everlasting oil well!*

'*Green is a silent force; it is not a nation, it is you and it is me. It is every individual who loves and cares about the future of our planet.*

Our only weapons are our voices, but we will be heard! You cannot destroy, in the name of human progress, what God provided as necessary for all life on earth.

'Thank you.'

I don't suppose that anything Marg said was new or hadn't been said by others. But the passion with which this seventy-six-year-old woman stated her convictions carried the audience. A minister in the federal Labor government brandishing a copy of the *Sydney Morning Herald* containing her speech called it a disgraceful diatribe by an ageing ex-Greens agitator who in her day was known to be a mischief-maker. To the general mirth of the House, a member of the Queensland National Party brought it up in Question Time, where he referred to Marg's speech as a direct attack on democratic rule and a threat to the ANZUS Treaty.

If I am beginning to sound like a fellow traveller, then I must confess that my conversion, like that of so many others, is only very recent. Anna's world had no time for the climate debate and, to be fair, I gave the subject almost no thought until the advent of the Earth Summit.

I guess we were all simply too busy kicking and clawing our way up the ladder to question our ambition or the morality of our actions. We may never have used a phrase such as 'Greed is good', but we also never questioned our right to have what we wanted, whatever the cost. While I loved Marg Hamilton, I thought her views a bit far-fetched at times, in fact most of the time, while Anna simply dismissed her as a raving fucking fanatic.

I guess I'd always accepted that humans are by nature greedy and that altruism is rare in our species; enough is never enough and we cannot be too rich. Or, as Anna would say with an impatient sigh, or a naughty giggle, 'Nicholas, if I don't, someone else will.'

If Marg saw the Iraq–Kuwait war as a disaster, Anna had very different views. In the early stages of her cancer, when she wasn't so ill from the chemotherapy, she and I watched the bombing and the carnage on the road to Basra as American aircraft bombed the retreating Iraqi soldiers. I recall her saying with a shrug, 'Well, at least it is good for my oil shares.'

'Isn't it rather a risky time to be investing in oil?' I suggested. While she never consulted me on money matters, and often dealt in big numbers, I was shocked when she told me the size of this particular transaction – a million dollars US.

'No, the price of oil was bound to go up,' she said calmly.

'Was it worth risking so much?' I asked.

'Nicholas, I was lucky to get them in the scramble to buy on the New York and London stock exchanges.'

'But surely the greater the price of raw material, of crude, the less profit to the buyer?'

Anna laughed. 'Not with oil; without it the world would grind to a halt.'

Anna loved explaining the intricacies of a financial system that had made her perhaps the richest woman in the southern hemisphere. 'They buy the crude from the supplier country and then add a percentage, predicated on all the costs they incur right up to the moment you use the bowsers, and with a good solid profit margin included.'

'Sure, that's what we all do. I do in the shipping business. What's wrong with that?'

'Nothing, but you don't own the docks, the cranes, the passengers or the freight you carry, the terminal at your destination, the transport to the retailers or the retail outlet itself, as the oil companies do.'

'They own everything? I've never thought of it like that.'

'Yup, the entire distribution system, the six or seven stages it takes to go from a barrel of crude to the petrol pump, and each of these stages is a separate profit centre.'

'You mean they've already made a profit on the first stage, buying the crude and adding their mark-up, then they add an additional profit at each stage? Seven stages, seven additional profits . . . Wow!'

She grinned. 'Nicholas, you're improving. I'll make a financier out of you yet.'

'But that's double dipping, it's cheating the customer!' I exclaimed.

'Cheating? If it is, it's legitimate cheating. It's capitalism and the joy of profit centres.' Anna sighed heavily. 'Nicholas, whatever is going to happen when I'm gone? These days you're sounding more and more like the Green Bitch.'

'Steady on, darling. I won't have you calling Marg that!' I reproached her.

Anna sniffed, ignoring my reprimand. Faced with a possibly terminal illness, she didn't give a shit and the gloves were off between the two women. She openly called Marg the 'Green Bitch' and Marg in turn referred to her as 'Princess Plunder'. I knew there wasn't going to be any reconciliation.

'Nicholas, if I'm not here when the price of oil drops below twenty dollars a barrel, you must sell immediately,' Anna instructed me.

I recall laughing and protesting, 'Darling, I'm in the shipping business. If it doesn't drop soon the company will probably go broke – diesel fuel is our greatest expense.'

'Try to understand, the higher the price of a barrel of crude the greater the profit to the oil companies.'

Anna pointed to the screen, where as far as the camera eye could see, thousands of mangled trucks and piles of ordnance lay scattered along the road to Basra. The dead lay sprawled in their thousands in the fierce Arabian desert sun, many roasted and blackened, or grotesquely welded together in the back of still smouldering Iraqi army trucks. 'This little war is eventually going to make me a lot of money, Nicholas,' Anna asserted. She'd seen too much death and destruction in her life to take much notice of what was happening on the television screen.

I shrugged, deeply saddened by her desire to make a killing in the market, because all the money in the world wouldn't save my beloved Anna, yet she couldn't let go.

I guess Marg Hamilton represents the new, emerging, untried and inexperienced *good* of the new century soon to be upon us while Anna typifies the careless greed of the one coming to its end.

I still think the odds are probably stacked against Marg as the wealthy countries maintain their voracious appetites for profit despite the cost to the plundered planet and the emerging nations become increasingly industrialised and demand their share of the goodies. But try telling Marg this. She, like Anna, is a poor loser, determined, even if single-handedly, to pry our tottering planet from the clutches of greed, capitalism and pollution which are causing the extinction of so many species that have no immediate economic value to humans.

'The last generation belongs to Princess Plunder, the next generation to our young people and their children,' Marg claims optimistically. I hope she's right. I lived through the sixties when flower power was going to change everything. I can only hope green power is more effective.

As I sit ruminating over the Misses Yin and Yang, Princess Plunder and the Green Bitch, each possessed of the same fanatical desire to destroy the values of the other, I am unaware that Saffron has walked onto the verandah until she coughs politely to catch my attention.

'Where will you take your lunch, Uncle Nick?' she asks.

I remind myself that while she didn't mention it earlier she represents yet another female issue I have to contend with.

Saffron wants permission to get a tattoo, a butterfly on the point of her shoulder. Joe Popkin, her grandfather and my partner in the shipping company, has refused his permission and she's working on me to convince him.

Joe Popkin, who runs the Port Moresby shipping office, is a Black American married to a Tahitian woman, the delightful Lela. Their son, Joe Junior, married yet another, the fiery and beautiful Frances. The gorgeous Saffron, who has recently completed a Bachelor of Economics at Sydney University, is the result. 'Would you kindly fetch me a Scotch and water, please, darling?' I ask.

She nods. 'Uncle Nick, have you spoken to Grandfather Joe?' Her eyes remind me of a starry night at sea.

'No.' My bloody memory isn't what it used to be. But then I suppose nothing is, in particular the area immediately below the belt line. One of the tragedies of growing old is that pretty is still pretty, the roving eye still takes in what it sees and the imagination is just as active, but alas, for most of us the one-eyed snake can no longer raise its head. I guess in theory this makes me a dirty old man.

'Will you?'

'No. Your grandfather is right; you'll only live to regret it.'

Saffron pouts and makes no move to get my whisky.

'Put one of those studs through your tongue instead,' I suggest. 'At least it goes largely unseen and you can remove it when you're mature enough to realise that you're a beautiful woman and don't need any of that trendy crap.'

She looks shocked. 'Uncle Nick!' she exclaims, dark eyes as wide as saucers.

'What?'

'Do you know what those are for?'

I don't, but instantly realise I'm in some sort of trouble.

'Fellatio,' she says calmly and starts to giggle.

'Oh, gawd!' I laugh to hide my embarrassment. It seems only yesterday she was a little girl holding my hand as we visited nature's fairy lanterns, the ripe persimmons hanging from the bare branches of the trees lining my driveway.

Her one-word explanation of the stimulatory use of a tongue stud together with her giggling has completely stolen my resolve. She knows I'm done for, mere putty, an old-man pushover. 'Very well, I'll have a word with Joe,' I say gruffly. 'But I suggest you think about it carefully; tattoos don't rub off.'

Saffron pecks me happily on the cheek, turns and wiggles her tight little bum triumphantly as she leaves to make my drink. 'It's called a tongue bar and there's even a version that vibrates,' she calls back, laughing. 'I'll bring your lunch out on a tray.'

I don't ask her how she knows all this. The kids these days seem to know everything and nothing very useful.

Next evening Marg Hamilton calls. I'm relaxed, two stiff glasses of Scotch under my belt. I tell myself it's an evening call, so no harm can come.

'Nick darling, I'm worried about you.'

'That's very nice to hear but quite unnecessary,' I laugh. 'Saffron and I have been out on *Madam Butterfly*; it's been a lovely day, good strong breeze, I feel ten years younger.' Saffron's a damn good sailor and does the hard work on board while allowing me to appear to be the skipper.

'I mean generally,' Marg replies, not listening. 'When we last talked you didn't sound yourself. What's wrong?'

I've been unable to keep anything from her for as long as I can remember. It's something about her tone of voice and the strength of her character. Even a casual question demands an answer. Maybe it's because she listens with her eyes, and despite this being the telephone, I can sense her gaze fixed upon me. I clear my throat. 'Old man's dreams, nothing more,' I reply, attempting to make light of the matter. 'And I'm up and down all night.'

'Well, have you had a prostate examination lately?' she asks in her practical way.

'No.'

'When was the last time?'

'Never. Marg, stop fussing!'

'And the dreams . . . What kind of dreams? Good ones? No, they couldn't be, or you wouldn't be complaining. I read recently that ex-servicemen often start having dreams as they grow older. They may feel guilt—'

'I'm *not* complaining!'

'Well of course not, not directly. But I can sense you're distracted. Something's wrong. What is it? The war? Anna?'

'Both,' I reply lamely, knowing she isn't going to let go.

'You're grieving, Nick. Hardly surprising,' she adds in a rare albeit offhand acknowledgement of her departed rival. 'These war dreams . . . *do* you feel guilty?'

I sigh. 'God knows I have reason enough to feel guilty. Though probably least of all over what happened in the war. The Japs had it coming to them and I've never felt any remorse. Although I don't suppose one ever quite gets over the business of killing.'

'Ah, then it's *Anna*,' Marg announces, as usual coming down hard on the name. 'Is she in your dreams, these war dreams?'

'Yeah . . . somewhat,' I mumble.

'Well, we're going to have to do something about them,'

Marg says firmly.

'Like what exactly?' I ask, slightly impatient. 'I imagine it's all a part of the process of grief and growing old. The past revisited. Elephants going to a predestined place to die.'

'Nonsense, you're eight years younger than I am. It's probably PTSD.'

'Huh? I beg your pardon?'

'From the war. I told you, I've recently read about it – Post-Traumatic Stress Disorder.'

'The war! You mean like the Vietnam vets?'

'No, our war, the Burma Railway, Changi, Sandakan, the Middle East, New Guinea, the Solomons. We didn't give it a fancy name then.'

'Do I need to remind you our war ended forty-eight years ago?'

'So?'

'So I haven't had a sleepless night thinking about it from the day I was demobbed and exchanged my naval uniform for a cheap government-issue suit. That is, until about four months ago. It's a bit bloody late for Post-Traumatic Stress whatever, don't you think?'

'Nick, that's when Anna died,' Marg says patiently. 'I think you should see someone. And you should definitely get that prostate checked.'

'What, a shrink? Nah.'

'Darling, it's nothing to be ashamed of. I'll ask around. I'll be very discreet.'

'Marg, leave it alone!' I protest. 'It's only started recently. I daresay it will pass.' I laugh. 'It's probably the after-dinner glass of Scotch catching up with me . . . the years of after-dinner Scotches.' I don't tell her that my nightcap has turned plural three or four times over.

Marg isn't listening. 'Don't worry, I won't use your name.'

'Wouldn't matter if you did. Who'd know?'

'Oh, I see, feeling sorry for ourselves are we? The navy doesn't forget its war heroes, darling.'

'Ha, ha. All those invitations to mess dinners must have been lost in the mail.'

Marg's voice grows concerned. 'Should I come over to the island?

I could help with your inquiries about the fishing rights.'

Despite myself I burst into laughter. 'I couldn't think of a quicker way to scuttle your plans. As soon as the Department of Fisheries learned you were on the island, darling, they'd close everything tighter than a duck's bum.' I hope my mirthful outburst will distract her attention from me and bring it back to matters green, but I should know better. She's tenacious. 'You can trust me, Nick.'

'Marg, no quacks!'

'Nick, I'm only going to make a few inquiries. Bye, darling.' I hear the click at the other end.

'Yeah, yeah,' I mumble to myself. Marg Hamilton is on the warpath and somewhere along the line someone closely resembling Dr Strangelove will be tapping the end of his fountain pen on a desk and asking me a bunch of questions intended to reveal my innermost mind. X-rays and brain scans are certain to follow, with a urologist in the wings waiting to probe my arse with a surgical glove.

A week later, with a couple of nightmares thrown in for good measure and five empty bottles of Scotch, I pick up the phone to hear Marg Hamilton on the other end. I groan; it's a morning call. As usual there's not so much as a greeting. 'Nick, very exciting news. I've found just the chappie.'

'Chappie? What chappie? By the way, good morning, Marg.'

'Your Post-Traumatic Stress Disorder, of course!'

I sigh. 'Why, of course! It's confirmed then. Good. Now, may I get on with my life?'

'Don't be ridiculous! Nick Duncan, you're damaged . . . possibly severely damaged. You're going to need help.'

I'm certain she must feel the weight of my impatient sigh all the way down in Sydney. 'Forget it, darling. I'm past repairing. Let it go, it will sort itself out.'

'No it *won't*!' she says emphatically. 'You'll simply have to fly over and see the psychiatrist I've found. Lovely man. You'll enjoy him.'

'Enjoy him? I can well imagine.'

'Now, Nick, don't start! Dr Freeman is one of the best in his field.'

'*Free man*, is that a pun?' I say, in a feeble attempt to be clever.

'Of course not! He's Jewish.'

'Well then, he's probably got deep psychological scars of his own to attend to.' Suddenly angry, I find myself shouting. 'Bloody oath, Marg, will you leave me alone!' And I slam down the receiver.

But, of course, the phone rings again moments later, finally stops, then five minutes later starts to ring again. Somewhat calmer and ashamed of my childish tantrum I answer it. Her voice is triumphant. 'See, I knew it! You're in trouble, Nick. You can hang up all you like, but I'm not giving up on you. You need help. Now get Saffron to pack your bag and drive you to the airport and I'll meet your plane on arrival. You can stay with me. Ring first and tell me the number of your flight.'

I grin despite myself. 'I have to be over next month for Saffron's graduation, we'll discuss it then. But if you don't mind we'll stay in a hotel.'

Marg doesn't take umbrage. She's too busy to care for guests anyway. 'Don't disappoint me, Nick. It's hard to get an appointment. I'll have to pull strings; he's top-drawer.'

'I'll call from the hotel when we get to Sydney.'

Silence, then her voice suddenly grows tender. 'Nick, you do know that I love you, don't you? I don't want anything bad to happen to you, darling.' She pauses and then gives a despairing choke. 'I . . . I couldn't stand it!' I'm surprised to hear that she is crying.

Christ! Anna and Marg! What must I have done in some previous life to deserve such an infuriating duo? Whatever it was, I am being punished for it in this one.

'Oh, by the way, your prostate is fixed as well,' she sniffs.

As it turns out Dr Freeman seems a decent sort of a cove, not at all as I'd imagined: in his early fifties I'd say, lean as a whippet, easy manner, no Sigmund Freud, very Australian. We're seated facing each other in two club chairs, a large glass-topped coffee table between us. To one side, so as not to obscure his seated patient, is a vase of Easter lilies. Several competent watercolours and a large oil painting by Ken Johnson of a wild cliff-top and low cloud hang on the surrounding walls.

His receptionist enters with a flat white for me, straight black for him, brought up from the coffee shop downstairs. I point to a framed photograph of a helicopter on his desk to my left. It shows him as a young army captain standing under the motionless rotor blades with four medics and the pilot.

'Vietnam?' I ask. He nods. 'What – evacuating wounded from the jungle?'

With a dismissive flap of the hand, he grins. 'Yeah, long time ago.'

'That's scary stuff,' I remark. He doesn't reply. 'I've done a fair bit of that myself,' I volunteer.

'What, flying helicopters?'

'No, no, jungle work. Solomon Islands, Guadalcanal, then New Britain.' I feel I'm talking too much. I don't want him to think I'm trying to compete. You know – *my war was harder than your war, so stop whinging, son.* Vietnam vets have had enough of that old-fart RSL bullshit.

'Mr Duncan . . . ' he begins.

'Nick,' I interject. 'Call me Nick, doctor.' I'm a tad more nervous than I thought I'd be. It's a great many years since I've been nervous during an interview. Having money breeds a certain self-confidence.

He grins. 'Ah, thank you, Nick. Please call me Tony.' He looks directly at me. 'Nick, why have you come to see me?'

Somehow I'd expected him to know why I am here. Of course, his is an obvious opening question, yet I'm thrown by its directness. I stall for time, take a measured sip of coffee, put the cup down slowly. 'I'm not sure where to start,' I say guardedly, my tongue brushing the coffee from my top lip.

Tony Freeman grins sympathetically. 'That's always the hard part.'

What the hell, I think to myself. *Psychiatrists are supposed to be interested in dreams.* 'I've started to have bad dreams, Tony.'

He nods. 'As we age, a lot of stuff may bob up. These dreams, what are they about?'

I'm not going to tell him about Anna. 'The war, fighting the Japs.'

'You said *started* – you've not had them before?'

'No, only in the past few months.' I'm still not going to tell him about Anna. I don't want to be hit with any of the grief shit people like him carry on about.

'Ah, this can be true of older war veterans who have functioned normally, never had problems for most of their adult lives, then during retirement things start to unravel.' Tony Freeman pauses. 'Frankly, we're not sure why.'

'Unravel?' I repeat. 'You've got the wrong bloke, Tony. I think that's highly unlikely in my case. Strictly speaking I'm not retired; as chairman of an inter-island shipping company I'm still busy and interested. Until four months ago the war was simply something that happened to me almost half a century ago. I occasionally talk about it over a few beers, but certainly not because I find it stressful. I was young and at the time I guess I regarded it as a rite of passage.'

'You said four months ago that changed?'

Bastard's got me! 'Well . . . yes, Anna died . . . passed away.'

'Anna . . . your wife?'

'Personal partner, but much, much more than that.'

'I see. Then what happened?'

'Well, that's when I started to dream, have nightmares.'

'Combat nightmares?'

'Yes, you could call them that, other things as well.'

'Such as?'

I find myself becoming annoyed by his probing, each question leading me inexorably into what seems like a trap, some sort of admission of personal weakness. It only took him half a dozen questions to get to Anna. He's good at this and I'm not. I don't think I want to continue answering his questions.

I am prepared to admit to myself that Anna's death, despite my being prepared for it, has been a terrible shock, but I'm not ready to share it with anyone. Her memory is too precious, too private . . . too raw. He waits for my answer. It's all too complicated – her imprisonment by the Japanese, her subsequent heroin addiction. She's gone and I don't want her judged, her memory sullied.

Tony Freeman wants to dig into my past, and while I understand why he needs to do so, I don't like the process one little bit. He seems to sense my reluctance and doesn't press the point but asks instead, 'Has your sleep pattern changed since your partner died? Do you wake at night more frequently?'

I grin. 'You mean to take a piss?'

'Yes, or just wake up spontaneously?'

'Are they connected? The dreams and my over-active bladder?'

'Whatever the cause, sleep deprivation can have a pronounced effect on the unconscious,' he replies.

'My need to take a piss several times a night started well before Anna's death,' I protest.

'Ah, the two things are probably not connected.' He pauses. 'Do you find yourself increasingly grumpy, impatient . . . even exasperated for very little reason?'

I laugh, despite myself. 'You've noticed.'

'And do the dreams in some manner include your lifetime partner?'

I feel myself frowning; he is back again with the same question. 'Yes.'

'You mentioned earlier that you'd been involved in jungle warfare in the islands. Does this feature in your nightmares?'

'What, in a general or specific sense?'

'Well, for instance, does the dream experience take place at the same location?'

'Not always, though mostly it's Guadalcanal; I'm on Bloody Ridge with the marines.'

'You fought with the American marines at Guadalcanal?' he asks, obviously surprised despite his calm manner. 'I thought you'd mentioned Guadalcanal earlier, but I'd always imagined Bloody Ridge was strictly an American battle.'

'It was. I was seconded from Australian Naval Intelligence – the coastwatchers section – where I worked as a Japanese translator for their Radio Intelligence Unit.'

'You speak Japanese?'

'Yes, I was born in Japan. My father was a professor of English, later turned missionary in New Britain.'

'Bloody Ridge? Radio intelligence? You said earlier that you *fought* in the battle?'

Christ, is he trying to trap me? 'I was present at Bloody Ridge manning the radio, listening in to the enemy field transmissions. Towards dawn on the second night, with the Nips coming at us from every direction, things got a little difficult. I had my Owen with me and fired at them as they advanced.' I grin. 'It was either that or a Jap bayonet in the guts.'

Tony Freeman looked at me doubtfully. 'Owen? Are you sure? I thought the marines were using Springfield rifles then. I always understood the Owen submachine-gun was exclusively used in battle by *our* forces. An Australian invention, isn't it?'

Fucking smart alec; now he doubts the veracity of my story. Suspects it's bullshit. *Stay calm, Nick, don't pop your lid.* Attempting another grin, I say, 'I see you know your weapons history.' I think twice – will I or won't I bother to straighten him out? What the hell, let him think what he wants. He was in Vietnam and ought to know the drill.

'I received my training from the Special Forces Unit in Queensland where the Owen was my instructor's preferred submachine-gun. We were trained to double tap, two shots, head and chest, in less than two seconds and, used correctly, deadly up to twenty-five yards. When I was seconded to the Americans I took my Owen along with four hundred rounds. Good thing I did as it turned out – there's no better weapon for fighting at close quarters, or wasn't at the time.'

I am jabbering, anticipating, over-explaining, saying too much, in my own mind losing control. Freeman is obviously trying to get some sort of overall picture, threading the bits and pieces together to learn about Nick Duncan's personal war. Not doing a bad job either and I have no reason to be angry with him. It isn't that I don't want to cooperate. It's just that it is all so very bloody personal. I can't see how spilling my guts to a psychiatrist will help, telling him how I wake up in the dark screaming and blubbing like a baby. I'm not prepared to share the whole fucking catastrophe with a stranger, even if he is a doctor.

I hate the nightmares, hate revisiting the battlefield in the phantasmagoria of a dream, double tapping my Owen as the bastards advance, a Jap soldier getting close enough to lunge at me with his ridiculously long bayonet, parrying his thrust, reaching for the blade I keep secreted in my boot, coming in under his heart, seeing him sink to his knees, me staring down at the surprise on Anna's beautiful young face as my wrist twists and the knife slices through the main artery from her heart. Then waking in the dark screaming, clutching the pillow, thinking I have Anna in my arms with a trickle of blood running from the corner of her mouth.

'And Guadalcanal is where, for the most part, these nightmares take place?'

'Look, doctor,' I say, addressing him formally. 'I'm grateful that you agreed to see me. I'm told you have a very busy practice, so I'm sure you won't mind if we leave it there.' I rise from my chair. 'I'm grateful for your time, but after the graduation of my goddaughter – my primary reason for coming to Sydney – it's back to the island.' I take a breath. 'There's work to do before the dry season begins.'

Tony Freeman shows no surprise. 'Nick, it's hard, very

hard.' He remains seated and starts talking in a quiet, steady voice. 'A soldier never cries. If a mate is stitched up by a burst from an AK-47, dismembered by a mine blast or ripped apart by shrapnel, you don't have time to grieve over him. The chopper comes down and you scoop what's left of him into a plastic bag on the jungle floor or rice paddy and whisk the bits to Long Binh. A unit memorial service will be held before the end of the tour.' He pauses momentarily. 'But the feeling of numbness, emptiness, never goes away. You can't tell your wife how you feel about your mate. The politicians who sent you over there don't give a shit.' Tony Freeman glances up at me briefly. 'But sooner or later there comes a time to cry – for your mate, certainly – but also for yourself.'

The feeling of numbness, emptiness, never goes away. His words strike hard, like a punch in the guts.

On the night of my eighteenth birthday, after the first day's sailing from Batavia, I'd pulled into an estuary along the coast of Java at sunset. Throughout the night I could hear the big guns as the allied battleships faced the Japanese navy in the Sunda Strait. I didn't know at the time that USS *Houston* and HMAS *Perth* were sunk in the battle that followed. The next morning I'd witnessed the slaughter of nine Australian sailors from HMAS *Perth* who'd come onto the lonely beach in a Carley float. I watched helplessly as the natives hacked them to death with *parangs* in a killing frenzy.

After the murderers departed, I was too afraid they might return to take the time to bury the dead, so I laid their mutilated bodies in a row on the beach, attempting in one instance to replace the head of a decapitated sailor. Using scraps of driftwood and string I fashioned a crude cross for each, placing it above their heads. Stricken with panic and frequently glancing over my shoulder, I recited an appropriate part of the burial service, a prayer I'd remembered from countless native funerals where I'd stood beside my father at the grave.

I try to stop my thoughts, tell myself that Freeman as a young doctor working a chopper in Vietnam will have witnessed just about everything, and judging by what he's just said, his experiences will have been hugely traumatic. I know I should pull myself together, but I can't. Instead, I am consumed by sudden rage. For over fifty years I have buried the murders of those nine sailors so deeply, wrapping them in layer upon layer of pain and guilt, that I thought them safely gone, expunged from my memory. Now, in just eight words, he has resurrected that brutal morning on a lonely beach.

'You fucking bastard!' I yell, then stumble blindly from the surgery. I stop at the reception desk long enough to fling a handful of fifty-dollar notes onto the desk of the surprised receptionist.

Rushing into the corridor, I press the lift button and the indicator shows it is five floors up. I am shaking like a child, lips trembling. If anyone follows I know I will attack. I am six feet three inches tall, big-boned, heavy-set. Even at my age I pack a fair wallop, which many a lazy or drunk member of a native crew has felt to his regret. I look about me wildly, see the exit to the stairs and make for it. It is three storeys down to the street, and the sound of my boots echoes in the stairwell like the clappers of hell. I arrive, bursting straight onto the pavement, where I am forced to stop, to bend over, panting heavily, my hands gripping my knees. The adrenalin that fuelled my flight is now all but spent.

I glance up, deciding where to go next. Across the street is a small park. Still panting furiously I start to cross towards it, not realising the traffic lights are against me.

Later I don't recall the squeal of brakes or even the thump as the courier van hits me. I come to in the emergency ward of the Prince of Wales Hospital with Marg Hamilton sitting beside the bed.

'We're having you moved to St Vincent's Private,' she says calmly. 'Food's much better.' Then she adds, 'While you're mending they can do your prostate examination. I'll make enquiries.'

'What? Where? How?' I ask, looking about me, confused.

'Broken left leg – the doctor says you'll probably be left with a limp – severe lacerations to your hip, dislocated left shoulder, possible concussion . . . this is not the jungle, Nick, you really ought to be more careful,' she remonstrates.

I wonder fleetingly if she knows about my spitting the dummy and running from Freeman's surgery. Knowing Marg, she'll keep that for a proper brouhaha at a more appropriate time when I'm capable of absorbing the full force of her displeasure.

I sign myself out and I'm placed on a gurney and taken by ambulance to St Vincent's Private in Darlinghurst where, unsurprisingly, I discover that Marg is a good friend of Doctor Light, the general registrar who attends me. They put a plaster cast on my leg and generally patch me up. I'm wearing more bandages than you'd find wrapped around a mummy. The drip into my arm must contain morphine because I don't feel any pain. Exhausted, I fall asleep quickly and don't remember Marg leaving.

I wake up stiff as a board and bloody sore. It's 6.30 a.m. and I press the buzzer to have a nurse come and hopefully slip me a painkiller and prop me up in bed. I think about yesterday and feel myself colouring . . . *bloody silly old fart.*

Several hours later, sitting up in bed with my leg hoisted in the air, I look up to see Saffron enter my room. It's a private room, so they allow her in this early. She takes one look at me and bursts into sobs, running over to kiss me, then she starts blubbing and talking at the same time. 'Uncle Nick, Great Auntie Marg wouldn't let me come last night,' she tosses her dark hair mutinously, then rushes on, 'so I got the *Yellow Pages* and called every hospital in the metropolitan area starting with the letter A and . . . and S for St Vincent's was near the end of the list.' She's forced to catch a breath before continuing. 'I called the public section and they checked and said you were in private. By the time I got through again it was nearly midnight and they told me you'd been given a sleeping pill and shouldn't be disturbed.' She pauses at last. 'I'm so sorry . . . I'm so sorry,' she repeats tremulously, fresh tears glistening, looking too beautiful for words.

'Ah, I was pretty zonked from the painkillers; probably a good thing you didn't see me yesterday, you couldn't have woken me with a baseball bat,' I say, comforting her. Then add, 'But I'm proud of you for trying. For taking Great Auntie Marg's smack square on the chin then slamming her back with the *Yellow Pages*. She can be a very formidable old lady. Now, let me see your artwork, darling.'

Saffron draws back, grabbing at the sleeve of her T-shirt. 'No, no, Uncle Nick, you're not allowed to see my tat until it's finished!' She rubs self-consciously at the point of her shoulder.

I laugh. 'What? Is it bad luck or something?'

'Could be,' she says, wide-eyed. 'No, not really,' she laughs. 'It's just that I want you to see when it's beautiful. In a couple of days it will have scabbed over, but it should have healed in a week or so.' She winces, indicating my leg and the various bandages. 'Does it hurt a lot?'

'Nah, probably not as much as your tat did.' I abbreviate the word as she did, thinking it sounds friendlier.

Her pretty face grows suddenly distraught. 'Oh, Uncle Nick, you won't be there! At my graduation!' Then her hand flies up to cover her mouth. 'Ooh, ah, I shouldn't have said that! It'll be fine, I promise,' she cries, attempting to recover.

While I live in Vanuatu, Joe lives in New Guinea and runs our shipping and transport business there. Joe Junior and our general manager are in America on a buying trip. Fiery Frances, Saffron's mother and an accountant by profession who worked for Anna, has had her passport temporarily revoked pending an inquiry into alleged bribery, concerning several local politicians and the Ok Tedi mine. While it's all show-trial stuff and as usual won't come to anything, it means she too cannot attend. Marg has, of course, been invited, but she has to speak at a protest rally against Gunns, the timber-milling giant logging old-growth forest for woodchips to export to Japan. Saffron will be alone if I don't attend.

I laugh and reach for her hand with my good arm, taking it and holding it to my cheek. 'There's life in the old boy yet, my sweet. I wouldn't miss your graduation for quids.'

'No, no, you mustn't!' she cries. 'It'll be too much for you.'

'Two days is a long time; I've always been a fast healer,' I joke. I release her hand in case it seems mawkish. Joe Popkin's grandchild is special, has been since she was a small child, bright as a polished button. At last count I am godfather to eighty children, their parents all employed by the company. Many of them are smart kids. All will be or have been educated by the shipping company. If they choose to work, they'll have sound careers, some in government departments (Anna's idea), but this one, Saffron, is the jewel in the crown. 'Princess Saffron,' I say quietly, then immediately regret my sentimentality, thinking it may embarrass her.

'Would you like a coffee, Uncle Nick? There's a cafeteria in the foyer. I would have brought you one, but I wasn't sure if you'd want it.' Clever girl, she's moved to keep the ship on an even keel.

'Love one, Saffy, flat white, no sugar, large and strong.'

Saffron kisses me and hurries towards the door.

'Money!' I yell.

'Got some!' she yells back, not turning.

Marg Hamilton appears seemingly moments after Saffron departs.

'Good morning, Marg,' I say, not sure I'm thrilled by her arrival.

Marg makes for the chair beside my bed, slightly breathless, clasping her large handbag. She bends over and kisses me. 'I can't stay long. After your unfortunate peregrinations yesterday, you've given me more than enough to do without having to play catch-up.' She smiles, dropping into the chair. 'How are you, darling? I couldn't sleep a wink worrying about you.'

'Fine. Well, a bit sore, but I can't complain. I'm lucky – it could be a hernia.' It's a feeble enough joke and she doesn't respond. 'Thank you for taking care of me yesterday, Marg. Did you pass Saffron on your way here?'

'Saffron? But she doesn't even know you're here. I phoned the hotel this morning to say I'd pick her up in the taxi on the way, but she didn't answer.'

'She told me about how you'd banned her coming last night. She checked every hospital in the *Yellow Pages*.'

Marg's right eyebrow arches slightly as she prepares to defend herself. 'When I called and left a message at five, she was still out gallivanting. She called me well after six, just as I was leaving for a dinner engagement and I told her you'd had a *small* accident, just so she wouldn't be alarmed. You were out like a light even before I left, so I refused to tell her where you were.' Marg attempts to further justify her action. 'She's always been a strong-willed child; she'd have ignored my advice and been over to see you in a flash.'

'She wasn't gallivanting; she was at a tattoo parlour,' I explain. Then realise what I've just said.

'A what?' Marg's eyes almost pop out of her head. 'Did I hear you correctly, Nick? Did you say *tattoo* parlour? Why that's . . . well I'm shocked. Deeply shocked! What on earth has she had done?'

'Got a butterfly as a tattoo, on her shoulder,' I say calmly, trying to hide my amusement. 'It's her graduation gift from me.' *Please don't let this stop now, God!* I beg silently.

Marg's throat is wobbling like a turkey cock's. Mid-wobble she senses my amusement. 'It's not true, is it, Nick?' she exclaims, relaxing.

I don't want Saffron to be castigated over her tattoo. Marg has known her since she was a child and has always believed she has full reprimanding rights, earned when Saffron attended boarding school at the Presbyterian Ladies' College here in Sydney. In a half-fib, I chide, 'Just getting my own back, darling.' Then add, 'Saffy had every right to know where I was when she called you last night.'

To my surprise, Marg apologises, a very rare event. 'I wasn't myself, Nick. I was worried and upset about you. I now realise I should have told her your whereabouts.' She lifts her chin slightly, making up her mind. 'I shall apologise to Saffron . . . although I wish you wouldn't call her Saffy. Saffron is such a nice name.'

She really is a grand old dame; always has to have a comeback. I guess at seventy-seven with all her marbles and with a burning desire to save a world from which she will soon enough be departing, she has to be admired, despite her sometimes overweening manner.

'That's very gracious of you, Marg.' Then thinking it's probably better to delay the shock, I say, 'By the way, do keep my little joke about the butterfly tattoo to yourself when Saffron returns. She's gone to fetch coffee. Don't want her getting ideas, do we?'

'I wasn't fooled for a minute! As if she would go to a place like that!' Marg snorts, her confidence in Saffron and her expensive education at PLC Pymble restored.

Saffron bursts excitedly into the room, takeaway coffee in

one hand and the *Daily Telegraph* clutched in the other. 'Uncle Nick, you're in the paper, on the front page! Look!' She props, clutching the *Telegraph* to her breast. 'Hi, Great Auntie Marg,' she says tentatively.

'Saffron, it was quite wrong of me not to tell you the name of this hospital. I apologise without reserve.'

If it's not an effusive apology, Saffron has probably never seen Marg Hamilton contrite and I'd have to go back a fair way, too. I expect Saffron to accept gracefully, pretty eyes averted. No such thing. 'That's all right, Great Auntie Marg. No problems. I found out for myself,' she says without rancour, cool as a cucumber, eyes fixed directly on Marg. The kid, like her mother, has plenty of fire. Then she remembers the newspaper and holds it out to me, crying, 'You didn't tell me you were a war hero, Uncle Nick!'

'Gawd! Spare me! What now?' I accept the newspaper with my good hand, then, turning to Marg, ask suspiciously, 'You have anything to do with this?'

Unusually, she doesn't look at me directly. 'All accidents are reported to the police,' she allows obliquely, 'that's how the reporters get onto these things.'

'That doesn't answer my question. It's almost a column on the front page!'

Marg sniffs, then in a haughty voice says, 'Well, ten days ago, Nick, you were complaining on the phone that you'd been forgotten. I simply mentioned it to a friend.'

'I wasn't bloody complaining!' I tap the paper. 'This friend, he wouldn't be the editor of this scurrilous rag, would he?'

Marg Hamilton looks up, her chin thrust forward. 'Well, at our fundraising dinner at Taronga Zoo last night I was sitting next to Guy Cooper, telling him about your offer to sponsor the frog-breeding program and he must have overheard. He's also one of our directors . . . and well . . . it just slipped out about the accident.

It was an upsetting day, and what with you lying here in hospital close to death . . . '

Saffron's eyes dart from one of us to the other, taking it all in. She is receiving a gratis lesson in female manipulation from Marg bloody Hamilton.

Billionaire Butterfly Collector & War Hero in Traffic Accident

Sydney: Mr Nicholas Duncan, DSC, was injured in a traffic accident yesterday while crossing Macquarie St. Mr Duncan, 69, sustained a broken leg and multiple lacerations and is recovering in hospital.

As Lieutenant Nick Duncan, RANVR, he served first with the Australian Naval Intelligence Services in New Guinea during the Second World War. Later he served as a radio intelligence operator with the American marines at Guadalcanal in the Solomon Islands. There he was awarded the Navy Cross for valour by the Americans after the famous Battle of Bloody Ridge in 1943.

Recovering from malaria

and battle fatigue, Duncan received the Distinguised Service Cross from General MacArthur.

Bloody Ridge was the first major American land offensive against the Japanese and, together with the battles at Midway and the Australian victories at Milne Bay and Kokoda, it is credited with turning the tide against the Japanese in the Pacific War.

Widely reported to be a billionaire, Mr Duncan lives in Vanuatu, a popular tax haven for the very rich. He has shipping and transport interests in several Pacific nations.

Perhaps surprisingly, Mr Duncan possesses the world's finest and most valuable collection of butterflies from the Pacific region.

Mr Duncan was intimately involved with the international financier, Ms Anna Til, until her recent death. Ms Til was also known as Madam Butterfly, the name of an infamous house of bondage she established in the 1950s in Spring Street, Melbourne.

I slam the paper down and glare at Marg. 'I don't imagine you've read this arrant crap?' I snort angrily.

'No, well yes, but I don't *usually* read the *Telegraph*,' she protests. 'Don't be angry, Nick. I mentioned your philanthropy and the fact that you've bequeathed your butterfly collection to the National Museum but they chose to ignore it. There will be harsh words to the editor, I promise. Although I don't think at heart he's a frog person.' She hesitates momentarily. 'By the way, darling, are you *really* a billionaire?'

'And the drop of acid about Anna at the end. Your doing?'

'Nicholas, how *dare* you! They must have dug up that part about the brothel from the newspaper archives. And I haven't told them why you're in Sydney.'

'Oh, for Christ's sake, woman! That's *not* why I'm here. When will you get it into your stubborn head that we're here for Saffron's graduation; the rest, including looking up my arse, is purely incidental!'

'Well, I do say!' Marg exclaims, eyebrows taking off, expression suitably shocked, nose twitching. She glances over at the wide-eyed Saffron then announces, 'Poor darling, your Uncle Nick most certainly won't be there to see you receive your degree.' She smiles sweetly. 'Would you like me to come?'

'No! You'll be in Tasmania!' I cry, too loudly and too quickly. Saffron has turned away so neither of us can see her expression, which I dare say isn't too difficult to imagine.

'Nick, you *can't* go in your condition and the child should have someone there.'

'Just you watch me,' I yell. I point to my goddaughter. 'Saffron has arranged a wheelchair with a plank for my leg!'

'Clever girl,' Marg sniffs. Glancing at her watch she adds, 'Dr Light hasn't been on his rounds yet. Who gave her permission? The cleaning lady?'

I ignore the fact that she's caught me out in a fib. Instead, exasperated, I sigh. 'I don't need permission. I'm just going! Okay?'

Lips momentarily pulled tight, she doesn't argue, then at last she smiles. 'Well, I must be off; busy, busy, busy. I'll see you tonight, Nick.'

Saffron turns towards us, her face full of concern. 'Great Auntie Marg, you *must* go to Tasmania, the old-growth forests are much too important.' Then she adds, 'Those Gunns people should be shot!'

Marg looks pleased. 'I'm glad you think so, dear. Obviously you're not a protégé of your Aunt Anna.' She reaches into her bag and removes a tissue and pats her lips. 'Lipstick. Don't want people talking, do we?' She laughs then kisses me lightly on the forehead. 'Well, it seems your Uncle Nick is to disregard all medical advice and have his own way as usual. Very well then, I'll go to Tasmania with your blessing. You have my very best wishes, Saffron. We are all very proud of you.'

Marg rises from the chair. 'Thank you for the frog money.' She stoops and pecks me on the cheek this time, whispering, 'I do love you, Nick,' then she kisses Saffron, slings her handbag over her shoulder and walks towards the door, at seventy-seven her step still light and her back ramrod straight. I think to myself, *she must have inherited bloody good genes because she's still a nice-looking woman.*

Marg turns at the door. 'Oh, by the way, I spoke to Dr Freeman, and he may pop in to see you after he's completed his rounds this afternoon. He's the honorary at the clinic across the road, you know.'

After she's gone Saffron starts to giggle. 'Thank you, Uncle Nick,' she says, kissing me.

'Go on, Saffron, be off with you. You don't have to hang around an old man.' Then I remember. 'Fetch my wallet, Saffy.'

I indicate the drawer at my bedside.

Saffron retrieves my wallet. 'Uncle Nick, I don't need any money,' she says, adding, 'I've saved up the money for the tat.'

'Open it, I can't with one hand,' I explain. She opens the wallet. 'See the Visa card in the first pocket? Pull it out and read it.'

Saffron does as she's told and her eyes grow large. 'Uncle Nick!' she exclaims. 'It's in my name!'

'It's your combined twenty-first and graduation gift. The credit limit should be high enough for a good time, and low enough to satisfy your family. Every year we'll add a little until you're thirty-five. If you can't support yourself by then your mother will be thoroughly ashamed of you.' I know Joe Popkin hasn't spoiled his grandchildren and Fiery Frances and Joe Junior have been equally careful not to indulge them.

Saffron is trying hard not to cry.

'I can't take the credit for it, Saffron. It was Anna's idea.'

Then suddenly she claps her hands. 'I know just what to do! I'm going out to hire one of those electric wheelchairs and have a man fix a plank on it for your leg.'

I feel a sudden lump in my throat and I'm damned if my eyes don't start to lose focus. I point to the wallet. 'No, no! It's a lovely idea, but take my money for that, sweetheart.'

Saffron looks directly at me. 'Uncle Nick, how *could* you!' A flash of something like anger momentarily crosses her pretty face.

I laugh, trying to recover. Serves me right, it was arrogant of me. 'Extremely generous, Saffron,' I say quietly, suitably chastened.

'Oh Uncle Nick, I love you so much!' she cries suddenly.

Relieved that I've been forgiven, I say, 'G'arn, give me a kiss and then be off. Come and see me tonight and show me your butterfly tat.'

'No!' She laughs and then kisses me. 'It will be all red and sore from the needle. You should have seen it last night! My arm was like one of those sausage balloons. You'll have to wait for my graduation; the tat artist says it will be perfect by then.'

'Okay, then tonight we'll share our pain, and commiserate with each other. Be sure to bring me a large flat white; a good cup of coffee is better for pain relief than a shot of morphine.'

She too turns at the door. 'Oh, by the way, Uncle Nick, I'm thinking of getting a tongue bar. Don't worry, it's only for decoration.' She giggles. 'I promise I won't get one that vibrates!'

'Over my dead body, girl!' I yell, grinning like an ape.

'See ya!' Saffron flicks her dark hair away from her face and departs, her laughter echoing down the hospital corridor. That young woman is learning too much too fast, I conclude happily. Oh, dear, how much I love the mere thought of women. Marvellous creatures.

Tony Freeman's head appears at the door shortly after four in the afternoon. 'Got a moment, Nick?' he asks, as if nothing has happened between us.

I shrug my good shoulder and grin, slightly embarrassed. 'As you can see, I'm not going anywhere.'

He points to the chair beside my bed. 'May I sit down?'

'Sure, go ahead.'

He seats himself and says, 'Nick, I saw the piece in the paper this morning. Bloody *Telegraph*! Nobody needs that sort of gratuitous muckraking.' He pauses then looks at me directly. 'Your visit yesterday morning . . . it's pretty clear that you're not yet ready to talk. In fact, you may never be. But if and when you are, I'd like to think I could be of some help.'

'Tony, I apologise for what occurred . . . '

Tony Freeman raises his hand. 'Stop, Nick, there's no need. But may I make a suggestion?'

I grin, pointing to my leg in the air above me. 'No way I can run from you this time.'

He laughs. 'You're obviously a very articulate man. Sometimes it helps to put things down. Of course, it may not.'

'What, write?' I ask, surprised. 'Where do I begin?'

'Anna, write about Anna.'

And bloody Marg Hamilton, I think to myself after he's left. The yin and the yang, Princess Plunder and the Green Bitch, the two impossibly infuriating, frustrating, remarkable and totally loving females in my life!

CHAPTER TWO

'Nicholas, bondage is all I know how to do,
and fortunately it is something
that is always needed by those
who can afford to pay.
Besides, heroin is expensive.'
Anna Til, Port Vila

THE SUN GOES DOWN early and quickly in the tropics; one moment it is a great fiery ball on the horizon, the next it plunges sizzling into the sea leaving a tincture of brilliant colour that quickly smudges to dusk and as soon darkens into night.

All this happened as we left Beautiful Bay and motored around Iririki Island, where I pointed out the British High Commissioner's residence and the British Hospital to Anna. By the time we could no longer see the harbour lights, a full moon was rising out of the darker line that indicated open sea. Navigation was going to be easy in the moonlight and I cut the motor and hoisted the mainsail to catch the strengthening land breeze.

Anna stood in the stern of *Madam Butterfly* leaning into the light wind that lifted her long dark hair from her shoulders so that it flowed behind her. Her slim silhouette, silvered in the moonlight, reminded me of the Spirit of Ecstasy, the mascot on the radiator of a Rolls Royce Silver Ghost I had once seen.

My heart started to beat faster as I realised that I had been thinking of Anna as an innocent sixteen-year-old, whereas at twenty-four she was not only a sexually and intellectually mature woman but a damaged one, way beyond my mental grasp and experience. During the war I had been blooded and had fought and killed the enemy at close quarters, but what I had seen as a young warrior in the heat of battle was quite different from her experience of the mindless cold-blooded slaughter of prisoners and perceived enemies by the Japanese.

As a captive she'd been forced to become the consort of the regional commander, Konoe Akira, the scion of a famous Samurai family, a frustrated professional soldier and a highly complex personality. Like many privileged Japanese men of his generation he was an aesthete as well as a sexual aberrant. Struck by Anna's extraordinary beauty and the idea that she was still untainted – new clay to mould – he took her as his own possession and began with great care to instruct her in his peculiar proclivities and aesthetic.

He employed the services of two retired geishas to instruct Anna in the ancient art of *kinbaku*, a highly sophisticated form of erotic bondage. Under their instruction she proved a fast learner and soon began to partially satisfy the needs of Konoe Akira. Gradually she mastered the divine rope and with it the subtleties of erotic massage so that she could meet his stringent requirements and completely satisfy and, more importantly, gratify him, her natural talent for sexual domination confirming in his mind that he had chosen well.

The two geishas had initially been brought from Japan to establish and supervise the running of a Japanese officers' brothel known as the Nest of the Swallows. It was here that only the most comely Dutch women and girls, some as young as thirteen, were forced to become comfort women. Upon arrival and for several days thereafter, heroin suppositories were forcibly inserted into the anus of any recalcitrants to make them compliant. They soon became addicts and the threat of withholding the drug kept the girls working and willing to service even the most perverted and bizarre needs of their officer clients.

Konoe-san was too much of an aesthete to resort to such crude tactics. He saw Anna as a part of the order and perfection he craved in his life and set about carefully and slowly coercing her so that it became her desire to please him.

Anna was by nature strong-willed and not easily influenced. She had been brought up in the Dutch Calvinist tradition and possessed a strong sense of right and wrong. This conditioning may have presented an even greater challenge to the Japanese colonel. Even so, he made no improper demands or threats. She lived separately and away from him, and outwardly seemed to have a freedom of movement denied to any of the other Dutch women prisoners of war. His demands, while absolute, took into account her intelligence and natural desire to learn, and he cultivated in her an innate sense of beauty, discipline and perfection, so that this unfamiliar tuition quickly transcended any sense of morality. If she were forced to comply with his demands, then he would later assuage her feelings with a fresh insight into the nature of his arcane discipline or some exquisite aesthetic pleasure. He was always careful to bend this young and pliant twig slowly, taking great care never to snap it or inhibit the flow of young sap.

After nearly three years of conditioning and constant reinforcement Anna willingly became mistress to his needs, incapable of separating her personality from his commands and bizarre desires. His sudden vitriolic reprimands when she failed to meet his exacting standards would cause her great distress and as a result she would become even more determined to please him. Never for a moment did she think she was handmaiden to his perversion, but only that his ultimate gratification was her most ardent wish.

Moreover, she came to believe that his insights into self-discipline and unyielding will were well worth the price of her bondage. More importantly, Konoe Akira instilled in Anna the idea that losing her virginity would mean the destruction of her perfection, that she would be impure and tainted forever, a beautiful portrait brutally slashed and destroyed. So graphic was this imagined sense of emotional and physical violation that it was to have repercussions throughout her life.

I have since learned that it is not unusual for victims of a kidnapping to grow to identify with their captors. When I suggested to her that she was the innocent victim of her captor's nefarious influence and that she had no alternative but to submit to the Japanese colonel's authority, that she was truly, if unknowingly, motivated by a deep sense of fear and the need to survive, Anna was quick to disabuse me.

'No, Nicholas, this is *not* true! *Ja*, perhaps in the beginning, maybe it is so; I do not remember because from *mijn* mind all that is going. But later, this is not so. I want always to please him. I cannot fail. I will do *anything* to please him.' She looked directly at me and shrugged her shoulders helplessly. 'If now he walks in the door it would be the same.'

In the five years Anna had been in Australia, she had perfected her English and spoke with almost no trace of an accent. Naturally gifted with languages, she had a sound grasp of grammar, but when she became overwrought with me, and *only* it seems with me, she reverted to the slightly accented and syntactically incorrect English she spoke when we first met in Java. Thus I always knew when Anna was upset, whereas to others she appeared enigmatic. This helped her to become a formidable negotiator and opponent, someone who could risk everything while appearing to be completely calm, or punish a miscreant or avenge a betrayal without raising her voice.

However, Anna's war was not to end in the company of her patron. Konoe Akira was recalled to Japan three months before armistice to run a military academy in Tokyo and was replaced by the regional head of the *kempeitai*, the fearsome Japanese military police, as ruthless and efficient as the German Gestapo but even more brutal. They were a force separate from the regular Japanese army, who feared these vicious enforcers almost as much as their victims did.

The new commander, Colonel Takahashi, felt a great malevolence towards his predecessor and had made it his business as head of the *kempeitai* to be informed about his private life. A commoner of no breeding, he resented Konoe Akira's Samurai ancestry and privileged upbringing. His aestheticism he regarded scornfully as mere pretension, an excuse for his highbrow perversion. Learning that Konoe Akira's beautiful young bondage mistress remained a virgin, Takahashi determined to deflower her so he could have the pleasure of informing the previous commander that he had personally ravaged her.

Shortly after Konoe Akira's departure Takahashi sent a squad of six *kempeitai* to bring Anna to him. She fought like a tiger to resist them and, when finally subdued, was battered and badly bruised. The new commander, infuriated by her temporary disfigurement, could not bring himself to have his way with her until she was once again as flawless as she had been for his predecessor. She was imprisoned in private accommodation in the Nest of the Swallows, where the two retired geishas were ordered to oversee her recovery and administer heroin to make her more biddable.

With the loss of Konoe Akira's patronage Anna's safety was

no longer guaranteed. She knew Takahashi planned to despoil her. She also knew she would rather die than submit to him and so he would be forced to rape her. Afterwards he would almost certainly kill her or, even worse, send her to become a prostitute in the common soldiers' brothel, where she would be expected to service up to thirty men a day.

Nor did her enforced addiction to heroin help to overcome her fear of the psychological consequence of losing her maidenhead. Anna told herself that everything she had become with the help of *Konoe-san* would be destroyed: her self-esteem, willpower, sense of unyielding discipline and inner strength (the core of the persimmon tree), and the aesthetic appreciation he had inculcated; the fires he had lit in her psyche would be reduced to ashes. Without these gifts from the master Anna saw no point in continuing with her life. Whatever happened afterwards, she would, in her own eyes, be dog shit (her words).

The day had finally arrived when she was completely recovered from the bruising and lacerations she'd received at the hands of the *kempeitai*. For the following two days she was denied her suppositories, so by the time Colonel Takahashi arrived to perform his long-anticipated defilement, it took all the resolve and discipline *Konoe-san* had taught Anna for her to hold herself together.

He made her strip naked then stand to attention in front of him while he examined her closely to ensure she was unblemished. Then, seated at a desk, he offered her two glycerine suppositories containing the pure heroin and crystal amphetamine that her body craved, on condition she willingly gave him the pearl of her virginity. Anna affected compliance, feeling the relief and euphoria of the two drugs coursing through her bloodstream. She seemed to understand that she was beaten, the pain of withdrawal overriding her previous resolve. Meekly she invited him to partake of the traditional tea ceremony prior to sharing her futon. But first she offered, in the traditional geisha manner, to massage him.

Anna had been well trained by the two geishas in this preliminary to seduction, and she felt the *kempeitai* colonel flinch as her pliant fingers worked deep into the muscles of his back and neck. She noted the tension under her kneading fingers and realised that despite his bombast and bullying Takahashi was feeling the strain of his new command. The first massage, known as *unwinding the roots*, was intended to relax his tension; it would be followed by the therapeutic massage, *growing the lotus bud*. Anna worked steadily, relaxing the tightly bunched muscles, her oiled hands eventually beginning to play *the slippery eel*, the transition from therapeutic to erotic massage.

Soon she could sense his erection growing. 'It is time to turn onto your back now, *Colonel-san*,' she instructed quietly. Takahashi, his inhibitions overcome by her clever hands, rolled onto his back. Anna did as she had been taught by the geishas, working with the pads of her first and second fingers and thumb down the length of his erection in *the finger dance*, moving lightly from the exposed head to the scrotum, gently massaging his testicles, then back again with the ball of her forefinger in *dragonfly dancing* where she pressed, rubbed and released the pronounced veins that run the length of the penis, teasing, building, anticipating his climax. 'Careful!' Takahashi cried suddenly. 'Oh, oh, oh! Oh, no!'

He was horsemeat, no class whatsoever, his premature ejaculation no better than that of an over-anxious schoolboy. She grabbed him in *the turtle's neck*, stroking firmly with her fist to maximise his pleasure. She could hear *Konoe-san*'s words instructing her on how to defend herself against rape: '*Any object that is sharp and at hand will do. You can do it with a chopstick.*

Directly under the sternum, push it in and twist, it doesn't have to go very deep.'

Takahashi had shut his eyes, overcome by the ecstasy of release. Anna reached under the futon where she had concealed the razor-sharp crystal sliver she'd retrieved from a broken ashtray and, doing as she had been instructed, shredded his heart.

Hunting through the dead commander's uniform, she found the key to the private room in the Nest of the Swallows that led directly to a small enclosed garden, dressed quickly and hurried through the garden into the outer grounds. Avoiding the guards in the dark, she managed to climb over a concealed section of the surrounding wall.

Anna hid for the remainder of the night and the next day, terrified of capture, little knowing that the second atomic bomb had fallen on Nagasaki and the Japanese had already surrendered. Anna had miraculously made it through the war.

At the time we set sail on that glorious moonlit night, I knew that Anna had been a comfort woman and mistress to Konoe Akira, for whom she had learned the art of *kinbaku* bondage from the two retired geishas. The remainder of Anna's story, apart from her addiction to heroin, was unknown to me. It would be some considerable time before Anna trusted me sufficiently to confide in me.

I had invited her to come to Beautiful Bay, Port Vila, after meeting her again in Melbourne under what may seem less than fortuitous circumstances. She was the madam of a house of bondage called Madam Butterfly, in secret partnership with a lawyer named Stan McVitty and the wife of a senior police officer. McVitty was a partner in the law firm we used to help establish our war salvage business and owned the building and the majority share of Madam Butterfly, the remainder being split between Anna and the police officer's wife. But to outsiders, Anna appeared to be the sole owner.

Janine de Saxe, a lawyer in the same firm who took care of our company's legal affairs, came upon the contract between the three partners by chance. Aware that I had been seeking the whereabouts of Anna van Heerden, a.k.a. Madam Butterfly, since the termination of the war in the Pacific, she discreetly mentioned the coincidence of the name Anna and the sobriquet Madam Butterfly, but pointed out that the surnames were not the same.

Sufficiently intrigued by the two out of three matching factors, I caught a plane to Melbourne to discover it was indeed Anna van Heerden. She had been accepted as a refugee by Australia several months after the surrender of the Japanese and, having no documentation, she had acquired forged papers in the name of Anna Til. She later explained to me that the name Van Heerden carried too much baggage and she wanted a new identity. This was not entirely true, as I would later discover. As the killer of the Japanese commander, she was endeavouring to cover her tracks.

What can I say? These things don't usually work out, but as I had done on the first occasion, I fell almost instantly in love with this now astonishingly sophisticated and beautiful woman, the new Anna. I was well aware that having anything further to do with her may have been inadvisable, but there you go; in the affairs of the heart there are few logical decisions. I was in love with the madam of a house of bondage who was a heroin addict. It probably doesn't get more potentially calamitous than this.

When Anna eventually told me of her experiences as a prisoner of the Japanese she hadn't broken down and wept as I might have expected. Nor did she seem in the least self-conscious about her new vocation. 'Nicholas, bondage is all I know how to do, and fortunately it is something that is always needed by those who can afford to pay.' She'd shrugged and added, making no apologies for her addiction, 'Besides, heroin is expensive.'

'But aren't you afraid of getting caught? Isn't what you're doing illegal?' I'd asked.

Anna had laughed. 'Nicholas, if you ever have a problem with the law you must let me know. I can *rope* in at least two judges, half a dozen magistrates, a well-respected clergyman and God knows how many prominent lawyers and politicians, while a high-ranking police officer's wife owns a share and several other officers are regular recipients of a brown envelope.' She'd grinned mischievously. 'So you can see, my profession *ties up* all the right people.'

During this time in Melbourne we had discussed her addiction and she'd admitted that she would like to give up – *become clean* is the expression – but claimed she had attempted to do so in the past and had always succumbed to the drug. At the time I was unaware of Anna's formidable will, but as I grew to know her I realised how powerful the addiction must be to have so completely mastered her. I rather naïvely took her at her word and immediately set about learning all there was to know about withdrawal from heroin.

My advice was that if, and only if, the addict wishes sincerely to kick the habit, it would take a period of up to three weeks for the acute craving to subside and then another unknown period to overcome the psychological addiction, although another three weeks would probably be sufficient. Six weeks in all. It was also highly desirable for the addict to be away from her normal environment and her usual supplier. It was explained to me that heroin addiction has a psychological component that is very difficult to overcome: the addict believes implicitly that after one more hit they will be able to give up permanently. This conviction is unshakeable and overrides both willpower and logic. This is why it is important for the addict to be away from their normal environment and out of reach of any regular substance supplier.

Anna finally agreed to come to Port Vila and attempt to get clean, although she stipulated that she could be away for no more than two weeks. My advice was that this would not be sufficient time to kick the habit and so I hatched a plan to kidnap her and to sail around the islands for six weeks, by which time she would likely be clean and sufficiently grateful to forgive me for taking her prisoner.

She arrived on the noon plane from Brisbane, having first flown up from Melbourne. I was delighted to see her, fearing she might have changed her mind. I'd been warned that this was likely and could occur even when she was on her way to the plane. As I drove her from the airport Anna had only just thanked me for inviting her to Beautiful Bay when she produced a small box tied with white ribbon from her handbag. 'Inside are eighty persimmon seeds. I have no suitable land in Melbourne. Will you help me to find a place to sow the seeds? Only five seeds now, because I am five years behind. Then, even if I am not here, you must sow one seed each year on my birthday.' She turned and gave me a stern look. 'You must promise me, Nicholas.'

I smiled, taking the box and placing it in the pocket of my khaki shirt as I drove. 'I promise, Anna, but why persimmon seeds?'

'I will tell you some day, not now,' she answered quietly.

After a light lunch at home I suggested Anna take an afternoon nap to recover from the eight-hour flight beginning early that morning in Melbourne. Then I proposed an evening sail, a picnic at sea on *Madam Butterfly*. The yacht had once belonged to her father, who had suggested I sail it from Java to Australia in 1943 to escape the Japanese, otherwise he would have been forced to leave it behind when he and his family fled the country. There was a tacit arrangement that it would be ours, Anna's and mine, when we were reunited in Australia.

Anna was thrilled at the prospect of seeing the beautiful cutter she had sailed in her childhood and which was known as *Vleermuis*. I had renamed the yacht *Madam Butterfly*, the nickname I had given Anna at sixteen, so very long ago when we had been out hunting butterflies and life had been so simple. Ironically, Madam Butterfly, in a bizarre twist of fate, had transmogrified into Anna's professional name and that of her nefarious house of bondage.

Anna, rested and smiling, had appeared at five o'clock wearing white shorts, a light blue shirt and, hanging from her shoulders, a white sweater, the arms of which were tied loosely below her neck. We'd talked at some length, over an afternoon tea of sponge cake cook had baked, about my need to live in the islands to run our shipping and war salvage business and she asked, 'Is it to be forever? Will you not eventually return to Australia, Nicholas?'

'There would have to be a damn good reason,' I grinned, looking directly at her. 'With the exception of boarding school in Brisbane, you will recall I was brought up first in Japan, then on the island of New Britain, the son of an Anglican missionary. I am more familiar with the jungle than Queen Street, Brisbane. I guess I'm an island person.'

Anna sniffed. 'When there is no more scrap metal what will you do? This doesn't seem a place where you can make *real* money.'

'Ah, it depends on how much,' my hand swept over Beautiful Bay, 'and what you want in life.'

Anna's English deteriorated and I could see she was upset. 'Life? *Ja*, I have already two lives, Nicholas. One is *goed*, when I was growing up in Batavia. Then come the Japanese . . .' She didn't complete the sentence, jumping to the next. 'Now I am lucky so I have another life, another chance, I must be sure.'

'You mean security? If we stay together, there is always going to be enough, Anna. After the war salvage scrap runs out, Joe Popkin, Kevin and myself are starting a small inter-island shipping line, people, parcels and produce.' I laughed. 'What Joe calls "freight and fright"! The leaky and unseaworthy vessels doing this now are always overloaded and carry twice the passengers they're laughingly licensed to take on board. If a big storm happens out to sea it usually spells disaster. There's a great need for a decent service and we already have a small fleet of vessels, and they're a damn sight better than most of the leaky tubs sailing between the islands right now.' I admit I said all this in an attempt to impress her, show her we were not sitting on our hands and were seriously planning for the future.

Anna seemed to deliberately ignore or dismiss what amounted to an informal proposal from me . . . well, a toe in the water anyway. Her speech was slowly reverting to normal. 'Property? It is expensive here?' she asked.

'No, not really.'

'And when Port Vila grows, will property values increase?'

'Who knows? The natives are beginning to talk independence, though it's years off yet, more a whisper than a demand. That is, if it *ever* happens. The various colonial powers are doing a pretty good job of keeping them in the dark.'

'*Ja*, the Dutch also, but in the end it happened there.'

'Yes, perhaps, maybe, who knows? The New Hebrides is a condominium, jointly ruled by the French and the British. This island is a bureaucratic nightmare; for a start, there are two sets of rules regarding property and that's only the beginning of the complications.'

'What about industry? Cheap labour? This is a tax haven?'

'Nah, too far from anywhere, but you're right, real-estate development is usually connected with industry and in terms of exports here on this island, as on most of the others, it's coconuts and coconuts, coffee, cocoa and a bit of mining, with Nauru and its deposits of bird poo the exception. Although Port Vila as a tax haven has some small attraction to overseas buyers.'

'*Ja*, Java is also an island. After three hundred years it was still coconuts and coconuts.' Anna spread her hands. 'Then independence came and we, the Dutch, had nothing, not even coconuts. But it was okay, the people were free.'

I chuckled. 'Three hundred years is a pretty good innings, don't you think?'

'*Ja*, but most of the islands are still ruled by white men. They should also be free.'

'There is some talk about New Guinea in the United Nations, but I don't think it's going to happen tomorrow.'

'Do you think it will happen? Do you *want* it to happen, Nicholas?'

'I must admit I haven't given it a great deal of thought, but now that you mention it . . . yes, I think I do.'

'So, to buy property in the islands, not such a good long-term prospect, eh, Nicholas?'

'For investment purposes, I dare say, no,' I grinned, 'but as our own slice of paradise, a way of life, *definitely* good.'

Anna cast me a scornful look immediately disguised as a smile. '*Tush!* Paradise? Paradise I know already! Java was paradise! The *only* paradise is security and money, Nicholas.'

'Anna, where does all this come from? Property? Security? Money? You're twenty-four years old, there's lots of time for those later. I know things have been pretty tough, in fact ghastly for you, but don't you deserve a little fun?' I laughed. 'We could take *Madam Butterfly* and sail around the world!'

Anna looked genuinely horrified. 'No! I cannot! I must not! I must start now! Property, it is safe.'

'C'mon, Anna, what do you *really* know about property? Safe as bricks, but also slow as bricks, crumbling as bricks. Real estate sits in one place slowly decaying, it just isn't a good proposition.'

'Like a yacht?' Anna interjected, pointing at *Madam Butterfly* in the bay below. 'My rich clients tell me to own a yacht is to make a hole in the water to throw money into. Ha, you are wrong, Nicholas! Future development!'

'And you know this for sure?' I asked.

'Not me, my clients, they know. Only the very rich or influential come to enjoy my services at Madam Butterfly. They talk and I listen. The Olympic Games is coming. You'll see, Melbourne will change, Sydney also. I have rich clients who come down from Sydney. They are all buying property to develop later.'

'Anna, that takes money, property development takes *real* money.'

Anna smiled proudly. 'Madam Butterfly is not cheap. I have already bought two workers' cottages in Abbotsford, near the brewery. It is slums now and cheap and I think a good investment.'

My heart sank. If Anna had aspirations as a property

developer, no matter how small, it meant she'd hang on to Madam Butterfly as her main source of income and information from her rich clients. This was not the scenario I had in mind for us. 'Near the brewery? Can't see that area improving much in the years to come,' I said dismissively.

'It's a start,' Anna said quietly. There followed an awkward silence between us. I sensed she was aware of my unspoken disappointment. Then she said suddenly, 'Nicholas, we can do this together.'

'What, buy slum houses?' I said somewhat disparagingly.

'Property. My rich clients call it from rents to riches, buying at teardown prices and selling at skyscraper rates.'

'In your dreams, Anna! We're in scrap metal merging into the shipping business. My two partners will think . . . well I don't know what they'll think, but it won't be about property development, that I can assure you.'

Unaware at the time of the training she had received at the hands of Konoe Akira, I simply regarded Anna's determination to succeed as the result of her appalling experiences under the Japanese. Now as a single woman in a dog-eat-dog world where nobody seemed to care what happened to her it was hardly surprising that she wanted financial security; something more anyway than the income, uncertainty and associated problems that I felt sure would be involved in running an illegal high-class whorehouse. But what the hell did Anna know about buying rundown houses for future property development?

Even if I thought it a good idea, and I didn't, I couldn't ask my two American partners, Kevin Judge and Joe Popkin, to get involved. They'd think I'd popped my lid. I smiled inwardly. In my mind I could hear Kevin saying in his Chicago slum accent, 'It dat cockamamie island, Nick. Too much fuckin' sun, baby!

Put some ice inside'a yer hat, wear dem dark glasses and take a aspro!'

Joe, on the other hand, would listen carefully, then shake his dark head slowly like the swing of a pendulum. 'I don't think so, Nick mah man. Dis prop-o-zee-tion ain't for such as me. Nosirree! Did you say dis chick, she got herself a *heroowin* habit, like she a smack queen? If she bin chasin' da dragon she gonna burn, man, burn!'

I dismissed the idea of Anna's property dreams more or less out of hand, but if I didn't want to lose her from my life, I'd have to think of something else to capture her imagination. Although I was beginning to realise that I wasn't really all that close to possessing her.

Increasingly, Anna struck me as the kind of woman one could never take for granted. Beautiful as she was, she was never going to be someone's handbag. Still, romance wasn't what this visit was all about. It was about helping her. While I was certain Anna would not take kindly to being kidnapped and so forced to go through the long and painful process of heroin withdrawal, in the end she would understand. I even saw myself as a bit of a hero, although I wondered if I possessed the strength of mind to persist when things got really bad, as I had been told they assuredly would. This was, I realised, a test for both of us. It might even decide whether we had a future together. I was risking the loss of any affection she may have felt for me.

Whereas my passion had been rekindled almost immediately, Anna appeared hesitant and unable to recover the spontaneous affection she had shown when we'd first known each other. Despite my declaration of love, she had not yet expressed any feeling for me. I recalled my churlish and self-indulgent assumptions when Marg announced she was going to marry Rob Rich, and told myself I had learned my lesson and had no right to expect anything simply because we'd shared a relationship in the past, although I was fairly confident something good, something close, remained between us. I convinced myself that, at the very least, she had decided to trust me, even though her experience may have taught her to trust no one else. She had come to Beautiful Bay with eighty persimmon trees to plant, trusting me enough to charge me with planting one each year on her birthday. Eighty seeds adds up to a long time. I decided rather arrogantly perhaps that she would eventually learn to love me again. It was a chance I had to take.

When we had finally finished our tea I rose and took Anna's hand. 'Come,' I instructed, 'the gardeners have prepared the soil; you have five persimmon seeds to plant.'

Anna became strangely excited. 'Where will we plant them, Nicholas?'

'Well, eventually there will be eighty trees. I've measured the length of the driveway, and planting them ten feet apart would take the last tree almost exactly to the front gate.'

Anna planted the first five seeds, carefully smoothing the soil over each with her palm. I handed her a watering can then moved a short distance away so that she could baptise each seed in what seemed to be a private ceremony of grief. As she completed the last one I heard her sob, 'Sayonara, Konoe-san.' It would be many years before I knew the story behind the seeds.

Which brings me back to the moment when I stood watching Anna, the wind lifting her hair and her slender body reminding me of the Spirit of Ecstasy. Although she was patently nobody's mascot, in the short time we had been reacquainted I realised that she had become a woman with an iron will, and a quick, clever and inquiring mind; a woman who backed her own instincts. The next six weeks would not be easy.

I had provisioned, fuelled and taken on board sufficient

water, bought all the toiletries, creams, cleansing lotions, unguents, whatever she might need, with the help of the little French assistant at the chemist shop. We'd blushed mutually when she'd thoughtfully included a packet of sanitary napkins and I'd stupidly asked her what they were. I'd purchased a dozen knickers from La Petite Boutique owned by a very large woman with a mole on her nose, petite as a female elephant. I bought six pairs of shorts and the same number of tops, two sets of ladies' pyjamas, two sweaters, two sunhats in case one blew overboard in a sudden breeze, a weatherproof jacket and bad-weather gear. In each instance I guessed her size, erring half a size larger and hoping for the best. I knew nothing whatsoever about female clobber, so stuck to shorts and shirts, skirts and dresses being well beyond my grasp. As an afterthought I even purchased chopsticks from one of the Vietnamese shops in town, thinking that while she was accustomed to knife and fork she might prefer the chopsticks she would have used under the Japanese.

The decision about when to tell Anna was easy enough – after the moonlight picnic when hopefully she'd had a couple of glasses of champagne and felt relaxed. If Anna was a little sozzled it might be easier for her to accept what I had decided to do.

While Anna had agreed to go cold turkey for a week, the expert advice I had received was that she would almost certainly have brought a secret supply (a stash) with her to Beautiful Bay in case her withdrawal became unbearable. However, I reasoned that she wouldn't have brought any heroin on board, surmising that she would not have the privacy to give herself a fix. If she'd brought any with her she'd *chase the dragon* before we left, wanting to be at her best for the evening picnic and knowing we'd return before midnight. Chasing the dragon is a way of imbibing heroin by smoking it so that there are no outward signs, no needle marks to reveal addiction. As I previously mentioned, all this apparent expertise I had acquired was second-hand and I had no way of knowing what might happen. I was, as the saying goes, flying blind.

Dinner was simple enough: cold roast chicken, new potatoes and a mixed salad. At the suggestion of a French chef I knew on the island I'd purchased an expensive bottle of French champagne named *Cristal*. He assured me it was a great drop and, in the name of *l'amour*, he'd presented me with two champagne glasses and lent me an ice bucket. Dessert was a gooseberry mousse bought from a French patisserie in Port Vila.

The open sea was calm with the breeze persisting and I tied the tiller to a fixed course that would take us to a small island. I spread a cloth on deck and we sat on cushions. Anna, I noted, knelt quite naturally in the geisha style with her feet tucked under her, back straight, so that she was balanced on the back of her heels. I confess I thought nothing of this at the time, nor the fact that she assumed control of the food, serving me personally, completely attentive, seemingly waiting for my approval with each mouthful. She placed no food on her own plate until I was forced to remark, 'Anna, you are not eating?'

'It is a pleasure to watch you,' she replied.

'Hmm, I'll have to watch my table manners,' I grinned, then added, 'Perhaps a little chicken . . . a small glass of champagne to keep me company?' I added casually, hoping like hell I remembered the instructions my mate the chef had given me on how to pop the cork without it flying off into the sea. ('This is not professional,' he'd sternly advised me.) I reached over and lifted the bottle from the ice bucket, removed the foil and untwisted the loop of wire, then eased the cork out of the bottle with a small and professionally perfect pop. A wisp of gas escaped from the bottle before the fizz of white bubbles appeared and started to pour spontaneously from the spout. I panicked. Grabbing frantically for a champagne glass, I filled it to the brim with froth and bubbles.

'Shit, what now?' I exclaimed involuntarily.

'Let it settle,' Anna laughed, adding, 'You did that very well. Add a little more when the bubbles have settled.'

So much for Mr Suave. 'We must drink to the good fortune that brought us together again,' I said, trying to recover my poise while handing her the now settled and half-filled glass.

Anna's expression suddenly saddened. 'Oh, Nicholas, I hope it will be nice for us.'

My heart skipped a beat knowing what must come when we'd completed the meal at about the time we reached the small island, which Anna would expect us to sail around before heading back to port. I knew I could no longer delay telling her of the plan to keep her captive at sea. 'Anna, there has been a lot of water under the bridge, but it is still the same bridge, same bricks, same railings to hold onto so that we don't fall; it has two ends and meets in the middle.' I held up my glass. 'To us . . . to meeting in the middle.'

We clinked glasses and Anna took a tiny sip, her eyes cast downwards. *Oh, God, what is she thinking?* Then she looked up at me directly and to my relief her eyes, clearly seen in the moonlight, were smiling. She waved her glass so that her gesture seemed to encompass *Madam Butterfly*. 'Oh, Nicholas, it was like this when I was a child, in this same boat, Papa and me, we would go out and have a picnic on board and find a small island and make a fire and sleep there for the night. In the morning we would sail home.'

'We can do that!' I said with alacrity. 'There is a tiny island called Hat Island, less than an hour away to the north-east.

It's only a narrow strip of beach but the tide is out and we'll be awake before it comes in again. I have sleeping bags on board.'

I saw a hesitant look appear on Anna's face before it was masked by a soft smile. 'I am not ready yet, Nicholas.'

'What? To sleep on a sandy beach and wake up in paradise?' I grinned. 'I'll wake you up with a cup of coffee, condensed milk, hot and sweet as early-morning sunshine.'

Anna looked directly at me. 'You know what I mean, Nicholas. I cannot now sleep *mit* you. I have kept myself for you, always you, but now it is not yet the time.'

Anna's grammar had deteriorated, she was upset, though I couldn't help wondering whether it was because she knew she would wake up needing a fix or because she wanted more time for our renewed relationship to develop. I reached out and took her hand. 'Anna, there's plenty of time. It's not why you've come and I understand. I promise you will be safe.' I grinned, adding a little lamely, 'Safe from my clumsy clutches on the beach.'

'No! No! You are not clumsy, Nicholas! Some other time I would love to stay on this island, but tonight we go home.' She squeezed my hand. 'I want to wake up in Beautiful Bay where I have planted the seeds for the persimmon; that is enough for now; I cannot want more.'

'Anna, it's only twenty minutes' sailing. We'll go ashore and I'll make a fire and you can have that coffee tonight and not in the morning.' *Oh shit, what now? Should we stay on board? Should I tell her now? Face the consequences? Get it over with?* The island wasn't much more than a jumped-up coral reef. In profile it looked like a hat with a strip of beach and a tuft of jungle at its centre, but if Anna was going to resist me, there was less chance on shore of her falling overboard or getting knocked about. A yacht of just thirty feet is all bits and pieces, awkward angles and it's very easy to fall and hurt yourself. If I needed to restrain her it would be a lot easier and safer to do so ashore. I had no idea what to expect or how she might react when I told her what was in store for us.

'Yes, that will be nice, darling,' she replied, her voice once again relaxed, syntax perfect.

Anna hadn't called me 'darling' very much in the few weeks we had known each other the second time around and I confess I ached to hear it as an endearment, no matter how casual. Now, knowing what I was about to do, the trust it implied filled me with dread.

We reached the island not long afterwards. Bathed in the moonlight, the strip of white sandy beach gleamed against the dark backdrop of the silhouetted jungle. If I say so myself, it looked wonderfully romantic. 'Our own desert island,' I quipped as we reached the shallows and I dropped anchor close in.

We waded ashore, the water not much above Anna's knees. The sou'-westerly had almost dropped away and the humidity, always present at this time of the year, was somewhat alleviated by an offshore breeze.

I quickly collected sufficient driftwood for a small fire. The tinder was somewhat damp from the receding tide and so I removed my shirt and used it to flap the curl of smoke to fire, casting it aside as the kindling licked into flame. I boiled the billy and tossed in a couple of tablespoons of coffee from a jar, then pouring the dark liquid into two tin mugs stirred in a generous portion of sweetened condensed milk. 'Nothing nicer than this after a good dinner,' I said, the moonlight so bright that I could see the blue rim of the white enamel mug and the steam rising from the surface of the coffee as I handed it to Anna. 'Careful, it's very hot,' I cautioned. Reaching for my own cup, I placed it on the sand

and sat on my haunches facing her.

Anna blew at the lip of the mug and then took a tiny, cautious sip, drawing back. 'Hmm, hot . . . delicious,' she announced. She looked at me through the steam rising from the surface of the mug. 'We must do this more often.'

'Anna, there is something . . .' I began.

Her expression was immediately cautious. 'Something? What is it, Nicholas?'

'Please understand it is for your own good,' I stammered.

'What?' she asked sharply, lowering the mug. 'What is for *mijn* own good?'

'Coming clean, the heroin, your addiction.' I was making a hopeless mess of explaining.

Anna glared at me. 'So?'

'So, well, we are not going home tonight. We'll be at sea six weeks, then you'll be cured . . . clean.'

'You bastard! You fucking bastard!' I managed to jerk my face away just as the scalding hot coffee hit. There followed a moment when I felt nothing and then an excruciating pain spread across my chest and the side of my neck. I jumped to my feet, rushed across the narrow beach and dived into the shallow water.

When I emerged, I turned and stood facing the beach, water dripping from my hair and body. Anna had reached the shoreline and was stepping into the water holding my own mug of coffee. In the bright moonlight I could see the rage in her eyes and the curl to her lips. 'Come, there is more, you bastard!' she snarled, then furiously splashing towards me she hurled the contents of my mug at me, the coffee splashing harmlessly into the surf a foot or so short of where I stood.

'Anna! Anna! Please,' I cried, arms spread wide, palms open as I started to walk towards her.

'Dog shit!' she screamed and hurled the empty mug at me.

I rushed forward and grabbed her. Lifting her out of the water, I held her tightly against my scalded chest. She managed to get one arm loose and I felt her long fingernails rake the side of my face and down across the section of burned skin on my neck. The pain was so intense I gasped and for a moment lost it. 'You bitch!' I yelled furiously, then lifted her across my shoulder and ran splashing onto the beach. I couldn't think what to do next except perhaps to hurl her angrily onto the wet sand. But then suddenly I started to laugh, and carrying her towards a coral rock worn smooth from the constant pounding of the tide, I sat down and placed Anna across my knee. Holding her down with one hand, with the flat of the other I gave her a damn good spanking. She jerked, cried out, then realising she couldn't escape my grasp, she started to whimper and moan with each whack, but when she let out an anguished cry I immediately stopped spanking and removed my restraining hand. It was to be the first and last time I would ever raise my hand in anger to a woman.

Anna lifted herself from my knee, sobbing and panting. I was surprised to see that her beautiful blue eyes were no longer angry, her expression seemed contrite, almost loving. 'Oh, Nicholas, you are bleeding!' she cried. 'Your beautiful face!'

'It's not my face, woman! It's my bloody neck and chest!' I yelled, attempting to show that I was still upset.

'Oh, Nicholas, you are hurt so very bad. We must go home, to the hospital. There is a hospital, *ja*? You showed me when we were going out from the harbour, the British Hospital.' While she was attentive and sympathetic as she examined the burns to my skin, she appeared to take no responsibility or show any regret for her action.

I had a couple of tubes of paraffin-based salve on board, but realised the burns covered my neck and most of my chest. The ointment, if it helped at all, wouldn't last me two days. I'd treated a few burns on board our salvage vessels where crew had been injured in the engine room. You did the best you could at the time but got them to the nearest port where there was a mission clinic or hospital. A bad burn in the tropics festers quickly and can lead to the direst consequences. I recall on one occasion I had watched helplessly while a young boy, a member of the crew from Pentecost Island, died as a result of burns received when a valve in the boiler room had broken and we were three days out from the nearest port.

I was hurting like hell and knew just by looking down at my chest that I was badly burned across most of it. I could feel the skin on my neck starting to tighten. 'Come, let's go home,' I announced quietly. Then, attempting a grin, I turned to Anna and pointed to the outcrop of jungle. 'From now on this will be named Coffee Scald Island.'

Anna had defeated me. We would try many more times to beat her addiction, but she was destined, despite almost yearly visits to clinics in Switzerland and the Betty Ford Clinic in America, to chase the dragon for the remainder of her life. She was the most disciplined person I would ever know, her strength of character and determination as an opponent were legendary, her independence often infuriating, but in this one thing she was a slave to the dragon.

What's more, while she was attentive and loving during the week she remained on the island while I was treated for second-degree burns, she never apologised or ever mentioned the incident directly again. My chest and neck healed well but a small white scar that refused to suntan remains on my neck from the scratch to remind me every morning as I shaved that I was in love with a damaged, dangerous and unpredictable woman.

Oh yes, and one more thing. In the months that followed Anna started to visit Beautiful Bay for a week each month but we still did not make love. I confess I was growing impatient. 'Give me a little more time please, darling,' she would plead.

The first few times we'd gone to bed together I had attempted to caress her. I'm a big bloke with big hands, but I was not inexperienced in the art of pleasuring a woman and I don't believe I was clumsy or rough. But instead of the warm welcome with which these preliminary explorations had been received from partners in the past, there had been with Anna a compulsive tightening and flinching away and great emotional distress. It was obvious that I was having quite the opposite effect from the one I had come to expect. Anna had not resisted me; the spasms brought on when I touched her vulva, let alone her clitoris or vagina, appeared to be totally beyond her control.

On the third occasion my forefinger had gone exploring the situation had ended in tears. 'Anna, what is it? Am I hurting you?'

'No, Nicholas . . . it's . . . it's . . .' She broke into fresh sobs.

'It's what, darling?' I persisted gently.

'I don't know! I don't know!' she howled, her abject misery almost palpable. 'Oh, Nicholas, I want always to please you so much! Only you, I have kept myself for you and now . . . I . . . I . . . am no *goed*!'

'*Sshh*, sweetheart, it will happen, give it time, you've been through a lot, darling.'

But it didn't. It was obviously psychological and beyond her control. Eventually I was forced to give up.

In every other way except penetration Anna proved wonderful – her hands were magic instruments, her mouth generous and she would leave me sated while never allowing me to reciprocate. I could kiss her and fondle her breasts and try in every other way I knew to satisfy her without being allowed to go near the forbidden region I had termed, for the sake of my own sanity, the *Grotto of Not*.

The paradox was that while I was undoubtedly in the hands of an expert at pleasing a male, I still longed to consummate our relationship, to truly possess her and bring us to a mutual climax, in order, I told myself, to remove the terror I could see in her eyes.

As I had done with her heroin addiction, I set out to discover all I could about any psychological cause for Anna's seemingly pathological fear of penetration. It should be remembered that this was at the beginning of the 1950s when psychiatric therapy was not as commonly used or symptoms as correctly diagnosed as perhaps they are today. Furthermore, in those days the stigma of mental illness made a visit to a psychiatrist almost unthinkable.

I went to Melbourne University Medical School, where I contacted a psychiatrist named Dr Denmeade, a man in his mid-forties who had qualified in medicine here and then taken his psychiatry degree and practised in the United States, recently returning to take an associate professorship at Melbourne University.

I learned from him that Anna's condition, or what *might* have been her condition, had a name. It was termed vaginismus and is defined as the involuntary spasm of the pelvic floor muscles surrounding the vaginal opening. This involuntary contraction occurs in anticipation when a partner attempts to penetrate or even in some cases touch the vagina.

Professor Denmeade pointed out that unconsummated marriage is probably a condition as old as human existence, the first recorded diagnosis of vaginismus being in the eleventh century. 'It is common in arranged marriages and in women who have been sexually assaulted in childhood or brutally raped. It is the vagina in panic,' he went on to explain, 'where typical intercourse becomes physically impossible. This is estimated to occur in up to fifteen per cent of the female population,' he'd concluded.

However, I couldn't be certain I was on the right track because Anna was emphatic that she wouldn't see the professor, and no amount of persuasion could convince her. 'I am not mad or psychotic, so why do you want me to see this professor, Nicholas?'

'Well, it may help, darling. He may be able to explain why this happens to you. Don't you think its worth a try?'

'*Agh* . . . It's all mumbo-jumbo, those guys are nuts!' she exclaimed. I argued further but got nowhere, Anna stubbornly resisting any attempts to get her to the professor.

On one occasion I'd even said, 'Are you secretly frightened of a cure?'

'What do you mean by that?' she'd replied dismissively.

'Well, sometimes I feel that by giving yourself to me something will change in you.'

Anna laughed; it was a clumsily put question. 'Don't talk crap, Nicholas!' She had risen and abruptly left the room. I recall feeling at the time that I'd nevertheless touched on something.

Anna, while seeming to enjoy my advances in bed and my caresses above the waist, still involuntarily resisted even the slightest dalliance below it. The *Grotto of Not* was effectively out of bounds.

While I had been prepared to kidnap her in an attempt to cure her heroin addiction, I certainly wasn't going to attempt to overcome her fear of intercourse by forcing myself into her.

That I didn't persist may well be a sign of weakness on my

part, but on every occasion I had attempted the preliminaries, it had ended in copious tears. Our closeness was being placed in jeopardy and, I told myself, love isn't only about a well-dipped dick bringing her to a climax. Anna was otherwise doing everything in her power to please me and took obvious delight in doing so. Sometimes the smaller picture becomes the more valuable in the gallery of human experience. Or so I attempted to convince myself.

Had I known at the time about Anna's three years of conditioning by Konoe Akira, which ultimately led her to the absolute conviction that the loss of her virginity meant the destruction of her perfection, her intellect and aesthetic appeal, I would have been much closer to understanding her fears.

The carefully inculcated sexual complex the nefarious Japanese colonel had planted in Anna's mind meant that no man could be permitted to enter her. She had already killed to defend this absolute belief. The blood and horror of killing Takahashi when he'd attempted to force her to disobey her master's instructions seemed the perfect reinforcement needed to bring about the condition of vaginismus.

Professor Denmeade stressed that it was the patient herself who must effect the cure with the help of a practised psychiatrist, and until Anna was willing to embrace both factors, acceptance and treatment, it was unlikely that she would recover from her deeply entrenched fear of male penetration. 'But she will still be capable of enjoying clitoral stimulation,' he concluded.

I then explained that Anna had *also* resisted my attempts at clitoral stimulation. Denmeade then suggested this might be an additional psychological factor and until Anna was willing to undertake therapy her rejection of my attempts to touch her was also likely to be permanent.

'Have you tried oral sex?' he asked. 'It may well be that your finger represents the male phallus while your tongue doesn't.'

I hadn't, and while today this would seem a curious omission, I should point out that in the early fifties most women thought of oral sex as somehow perverted, almost never performed out of marriage, and even within only under duress.

If women avoided fellatio, it was absolutely taboo for any decent, self-respecting middle-class male to engage in cunnilingus. This was the preserve of heavily pomaded gigolos with dark sideburns and pencil moustaches who spoke with thick Spanish accents. Putting it into crude male parlance, a cock was clean, a woman's fanny wasn't. This was a belief held not only by males but also by many women at the time.

I was fairly sure that Anna, despite her background as a captive of the Japanese and as a comfort woman in the Nest of the Swallows, would not have experienced a male using his mouth to bring her to climax. She may well never have climaxed to a Japanese soldier during penile penetration either.

But, of course, this was all speculation on my part. All I possessed was a smattering of knowledge concerning her captivity; what had actually happened to her I was yet to learn. I had no idea, for instance, that Anna was still a virgin. While she had told me she'd kept herself for me, that I would be the first, I had taken this to mean the first lover she would accept of her own free will.

As a comfort woman, I incorrectly surmised that she had been raped daily, that in her mind she couldn't yet separate the loving act from the brutal one and hence the involuntary vaginal resistance. I convinced myself that with time, gentle handling, love, patience, tenderness and trust, I would eventually prevail.

I truly loved Anna; moreover, in a much more basic way, I craved a mutual sexual experience and the sense of sharing that comes with two lovers coupling, being as one, generous with the sheer joy of knowing and exploring each other's bodies.

But I was getting absolutely nowhere. Anna rejected my tongue as she had my finger, sobbing as she tried to accept me, but failing, her tears and her flinching expressing the depth of her distress. *'Please, a little more time, darling,'* followed as usual.

After the fourth time she had rejected cunnilingus I finally lost patience. 'Christ, Anna! How long is a little more time? Don't say that! I'm sick of hearing it! Fucking sick and tired of hearing . . . *Please, a little more time, darling,'* I cruelly mimicked.

'Oh, Nicholas, I am so sorry. Maybe I can go away. I am no *goed,'* she said tearfully. Anna, so strong in most things, trembled like a child.

Despite my frustration and eagerness for the ultimate satisfaction of possessing her, I felt a right bastard for being so impatient. If I'd known what the Nips had done to her in captivity I'd have gone out and killed a few more of the little yellow bastards.

I also couldn't bear the thought of her leaving me a second time. 'Anna, I love you!' was all I could manage just then and even this was said with a lack of gallantry or graciousness.

Anna continued to care, to leave me physically satisfied, and her tenderness went some way to appeasing my ardent desire to please her sufficiently to at least bring her to a spontaneous orgasm. As the weeks merged into months it became apparent to me that she was damaged, possibly beyond recovery.

I hadn't ever thought of finding the ultimate pleasure I sought from another woman, even though in moments of stress Anna had begged me to do so. 'Nicholas, I understand, we can still be together!' Then one evening sitting on the verandah watching the moon coming up over Beautiful Bay and enjoying a glass of what had now become Anna's favourite champagne, she turned to me and said, 'Nicholas, do you remember the first night, when we sailed to the small island in the moonlight?'

'Anna!' I exclaimed, jabbing my forefinger to indicate my neck. 'You mean I'm supposed to forget?'

'No, not the coffee! What happened next.'

Was there no end to this woman's lack of remorse? For a moment I thought to chasten her further. But her gorgeous smile and show of wide blue eyes was all it took to forgive her clumsy question. Despite myself, I was forced to chuckle, recalling Anna across my knee, her wet shorts stretched tight across her dear little bottom. Whack! Whack! Whack! 'You got what was coming to you, Madam Butterfly, a damn good spanking.'

She pointed across the bay to the glorious, impossibly big moon. If there had been a string attached to it I would have described it as dangling just above the arched rim of the ocean. 'Tonight it is a full moon, Nicholas. Would you do it again, please, darling,' she asked softly, eyes demurely downcast. Then she looked up and grinned wickedly. 'I haven't had a decent orgasm since that night.'

CHAPTER THREE

'Dat you, Nick? Dat cockamamie nigger,
he's costin' us all our profits!
You gotta pull him into line!
We ain't in the fuckin' soul-counting business.
We in the fuckin' scrap-metal business.
No more tithe fer da Pope; he got plenty already!'
Kevin Judge, Brisbane

THE DECADE FROM 1950 to 1960 may be described as a slow walk down to the village garden for the various islands in the Pacific. Some periods are like this; you think you're making progress but it's basically more of the same, each year much like the one preceding it. However, in the early 1960s there seemed to be a new sense of urgency and the people of the Pacific took their first true leap forward into the modern era.

Having employed a lot of islanders in our war-surplus scrap reclamation, we were well accepted by the locals. We were also on good terms with the colonial administration and the churches, for similar reasons. Different churches predominated in different areas – Catholic, Anglican and Seventh Day Adventists, known commonly as the SDAs, who ran the best schools. The Mormons, or the Church of Jesus Christ of Latter-day Saints, arrived on the scene a little later.

From the beginning Joe, who came from Chicago via Alabama and had been brought up in the Southern Baptist tradition, seemed to know exactly how to handle the various denominations promulgating their particular version of Christianity to the local people.

'Brother Nick, it the same God, only He got Himself a house a different style in many neighbourhoods. They all want souls; they in the soul-countin' busi-ness. So what we gotta do is bring dem souls, man!' He'd clap his hands and laugh, 'Then they gonna cooperate big time!'

It was clear to us that for the indigenous population of any island there were two main European authorities as well as the underlying tribal system, the most powerful of all: one was the colonial administration and the other was whichever church controlled the area where we worked. It became my job to deal with the various arms of the colonial administrations and Joe's to deal with the churches. Both were important, but the denominations competing for souls were often more important to our daily operations than the sporadic visits of a district officer attempting to supervise the remote jungle areas where some of the largest dumps were located. Our profit margins depended on working salvage sites seven days a week and this brought us up against the Catholics, Methodists and Anglicans on Sunday and the Seventh Day Adventists (or SDAs) on Saturday.

Joe used the church or mission as a labour-recruiting centre, and a condition of employment was that the labourer's children, should he have any, must attend the mission school. Joe would then reward every child with an Uncle Joe Scholarship. This involved the recipient being supplied with slate and stylus, textbooks, writing paper and pens, and if a school uniform of sorts was required, that too.

Joe explained. 'The church dey know der neighbourhood and dey do the recruitin'. Naturally dey in the soul-countin' business.' He spread his arms. 'But, hey, it don't cost nuttin' but peanuts to send dem village kids to mission school. An' every worker don't have fifteen children, so who's countin', man? The mission dey gonna see-lect only the best workers, 'cos dey don't want their soul count to go tumblin' down. If the worker he screw up on the job, then his kids don't have no Uncle Joe Scholarship no more and the numbers drop at the school. Ever-one o' dem young souls saved for Jesus gonna stay forever wid· dem. So, you see ever-body they gonna win! The souls dey gonna be counted. The kids dey gonna get some itty bitty schoolin.' And the workers dey gonna bust their sweet ass for yours truly or the Lord Jesus he gonna want to know why dey screw up.' He'd laugh and show his large palms. 'The ree-sult, we ain't got no recruitment problems. We can work on Saturday and Sunday 'cos we got special dispensation. We ain't got no bad labour relations. The Church, dey gonna take good care of us 'cos we labouring in da jungle for Jesus.'

As the sweetener for the SDAs, Joe Popkin would pay our workers a fixed daily rate then add a tenth as a tithe to the local mission. Joe got me to organise black school caps for the kids – boys and girls alike – with a white cross on the front. 'Ever-body countin' souls dey got the same cross for Jesus.' On every island and every mission station Uncle Joe Scholarship kids could be identified, the cap amongst their proudest possessions. Years later, when some of these kids were grown men and women, you'd see them sitting in the congregation with their Uncle Joe Scholarship caps perched on their heads.

We would soon become responsible for the rudimentary education of two or three thousand island children, some among them no doubt future leaders in the governments they would eventually control.

Kevin Judge was our third partner. Chicago Irish, diminutive and fiery, he was the financial brain behind our war salvage business. He worked out of Brisbane, but would call me from time to time, steam practically hissing from the receiver at my end.

'Dat you, Nick? Dat cockamamie nigger, he's costin' us all our profits! You gotta pull him into line! We ain't in the fuckin' soul-counting business. We in the fuckin' scrap-metal business. No more tithe fer da Pope; he got plenty already! After what I bin through wid da Church I don't owe dem fuckers nothin'! You tell Joe, you hear? No more numbers for Jesus! The only big numbers I wanna see are in the fuckin' profit margin. What we got in the Uncle Joe Scholarship column is nuttin' but a shitload o' debt!'

'You tell him, Kevin. You're sitting on your arse in Brisbane running things. Catch a plane and come and tell Joe Popkin what you think about us educating these island kids.'

'Nick, wassa matta wit you? You crazy or sumthin'? Joe "Hammer-man" Popkin, he's my brother. We bin buddies since way back! He took care of me when we was in the kid clink upstate Illinois. The Hammer-man ain't gonna take no profit-and-loss shit from me! He's gonna tell me to jam my profit column up my ass. From you, Nick . . . dat's different . . . he got respect.'

On paper it must have seemed an unlikely partnership and it had certainly come about in an unusual manner. I have already recalled the horrific murder on the beach in Java, when I'd observed the nine sailors from the *Perth* being slaughtered by the Javanese islanders. What I didn't mention was that the USS *Houston* had been sunk in the same battle and that the nine Australians had rescued an American, hauling him from the sea onto their life raft where he collapsed unconscious. Coming ashore they'd laid him, still unconscious, under some bushes at the top of the beach to keep him out of the sun. Shortly after, the Australian sailors had all been killed while the Yank had gone unnoticed by the murderous mob. The American was, of course, Kevin Judge. We'd sailed together to Fremantle or, perhaps more correctly, as he proved more of a hindrance on board than an asset, I sailed and he recovered from severe concussion and told me his story.

The little street-smart Irish–American brought up in a tough Chicago Catholic orphanage and later reform school had been given an ultimatum by a judge. 'Da judge says to me, "The US Navy or prison, son. Make up your mind."' Kevin explained, 'So, I'm stupid ain't I . . . I chose the fuckin' navy and next thing *boom-boom* and I'm swimmin' fer dry land! Nick, I want yer ta know, I ain't no fuckin' hero!'

There was very little that was stupid about Kevin. After his basic training, which built on what he'd learned when he'd worked in the library as well as the loading bay at Illinois State Reformatory, he'd put in a request to join the quartermaster's division. This meant that he was assigned to the ship's quartermaster every time he was posted to a new ship. 'Nick, a man gotta be on the influence end o' the supply line, that way you gonna make a buck an' earn a little respect.'

When we had arrived in Fremantle after our escape from Java on *Madam Butterfly*, Kevin had been repatriated to the States to recover and several months later had returned to Australia with Purple Heart and Bronze Star ribbons on his chest and a petty officer's chevrons on his sleeve. Situated in Brisbane he was a part of the vast organisation supplying the US Navy's requirements in the South Pacific region. His job was to assist US Navy Chief Petty Officer Bud Lewinski to issue contracts to the locals for navy supplies. Kevin, under the guidance of this navy veteran, was in business at the sharp end of just about everything. He thought he must have died and gone to heaven.

Now in a position of enormous influence on the navy supply line, he'd somehow managed to get Joe Popkin transferred from the Negro unit in San Diego to become his personal driver at the Brisbane depot where they'd spent the remainder of the war together, linking up with me again in the process. Kevin ensured that a small percentage, in cash, was added to every supply contract and secretly deposited in my father's missionary bank account, where I was a signatory, so that by the time the Pacific War ended, Kevin was worth over twenty thousand pounds, in those days a king's ransom.

It would have been impossible for Kevin to take the money back to the States without risking an investigation from either the navy or what he referred to as the 'eternal revenoo'. 'Nick, unnerstan, buddy, if I take dat stash back Stateside dey gonna lock me up in San Quentin twenny years!'

With Joe Popkin, he returned to America without the funds to be demobbed. Before they left, Joe and I had attended several US Army war-surplus auctions in Brisbane and, with a bit of jiggery pokery, had purchased most of the basics needed to start our scrap-metal business in the islands. Before I'd been demobbed I'd also hit the jackpot in Rabaul where a friendly US officer, Captain John Tulius, had allowed me to buy a small landing craft for next to nothing and in a moment of generosity had thrown in a second one. 'That's a small thank-you from the US Marines,' he'd said at the time, then added, 'Nick, if you're half smart you'll drop into Luganville. Our boys are being repatriated States-side to be demobbed so quickly they're short of labour to dismantle the infrastructure and move the equipment. Should be an item or two you could usefully pick up.' He'd given me a written introduction to his superior officer,

General Lachie Urquhart, and another to a certain Sergeant Bill Moss. 'See Moss first,' he'd advised, 'it's the non-coms in Supply that run the army and navy supply lines.'

I'd also picked up two wooden coastal vessels for a song, probably for half a chorus if the truth be known. With some difficulty I'd managed to get the four vessels to Australia to load up our auction gear.

Now our little convoy had left Brisbane, the two wooden vessels loaded with our purchases. I'd decided to take the advice of Captain Tulius and visit Espiritu Santo, the largest island in the New Hebrides, and go to see the huge US military supply and support base at Luganville. We still had a wish list, in fact we were probably starting our salvage operation on the smell of an oily rag, Kevin as usual being the tight-arse.

'Buddy, we don't wanna land in dem islands wid a heap of crap we cain't use,' the ever careful Kevin had cautioned when Joe and I had wanted to buy one or two more items at auction.

On arrival I'd gone to the general's office to make an appointment, handing the grizzled senior sergeant in the front office the letter of introduction from Captain Tulius. 'You a civilian?' he snapped, pushing the unopened letter aside and not bothering to introduce himself or to ask me my name. He was clearly unimpressed.

'Yes, sergeant, now I am,' I replied. Then hoping to use more influence than I had, I added rather diffidently, 'Before that I was with the US Marines at Guadalcanal.'

He looked at me sharply. 'What you say your name was?'

'I didn't, it's Nick Duncan, sergeant.'

'The Australian lootenant? Navy?'

'Yes, sergeant,' I replied, surprised.

He pointed to the letter addressed to the general. 'Who that come from?'

'Captain Tulius, salvage officer, Rabaul.'

'Yeah, okay.' He opened a file that seemed to include the rest of the day's mail and telexes and dropped it in. Then his demeanour changed and he grinned, sticking his hand across the desk for me to shake. 'Bill Moss, Nick. Pleased ta'meetcha. You know a good buddy of mine, Chief Lewinski, in Bris-bane.'

Chief Lewinski was Kevin's boss at the Navy Supply Depot in Brisbane. 'Yes, of course, we became good friends. But he's in the navy. How would you . . . I mean, how did you get to know him?'

'Lieutenant, how do you think we won this war? Departmental cooperation, it's the American way. We all know each other, army, navy, air force, we all have the same understandin' with Uncle Sam, if you know what I mean.' I nodded. It seemed skimming off the top was standard procedure in supply. 'Chief Lewinski sent me a signal to say maybe you'd be calling in aroun' these parts to say howdy.' He rose. 'I'll tell the general you're here.'

He was back in less than two minutes and ushered me in without the formality of a salute to his superior officer.

To my surprise General Lachie Urquhart rose from his desk and shook my hand. 'Lieutenant Duncan, I'm proud to know you, son,' he said in a booming voice. He appeared to be straight out of a Hollywood movie – a big man, going a little to fat; leathery face, pale blue eyes, snowy white crew-cut hair and a ham-fisted grip on him like a gorilla. A cigar seemed permanently positioned at the corner of his mouth.

'Nick, please, sir,' I said hurriedly.

When we were seated he came right to the point. 'I like what you did at Guadalcanal, Nick. Navy Cross, eh? That ain't for beginners. What can we do for you, son?'

I was somewhat taken aback – I hadn't mentioned being decorated by the Americans – but then realised he'd been briefed by Moss, who'd been briefed by Lewinski. 'Well, sir, I was hoping to buy some equipment.' I went on to explain to him that we wanted to get into the war salvage business, tidying up the islands.

He laughed. 'Well, Nick, when can you start? Tomorrow?'

I explained that it might be a year or so yet before my two partners were finally demobbed from the US Navy and were able to return to the islands. 'It's my job to set things up, sir.'

'Pity, I haven't got a year, Nick. More like three or four months, and the goddamned Frogs and Limeys are trying to screw me!'

'I beg your pardon, sir?'

General Urquhart explained that he'd offered the French and the British a twenty cents in the dollar deal for every US military item on Espiritu Santo. Lock, stock and barrel, the whole goddamned shooting match! 'Those bastards came back with a counteroffer – they'll take it off my hands for nothing, not even one cent in the dollar! Jesus H. Christ, what kind of bullshit offer is that! *They want a whole goddamned city, the whole shebang, for nothing!*' he shouted, the cigar hanging on for grim death in the corner of his mouth. 'Uncle Sam ain't goin' to stand for that kind of blackmail crap!'

'Well, yeah, it does seem rather mean-spirited, sir,' I said, not quite knowing how to react to his outburst.

'It's greedy, son, that's what it is, greedy! Sons of bitches thinking they can exploit Uncle Sam! Battle of the Bulge, America's saved their prissy Frog asses more than once, invasion of Normandy, Yankee know-how, the last time the goddamned Brits saw that coastline they escaped from it in dinghies at Dunkirk! I'm going to leave the four electricity plants for the island people, then give every island family anything they want. Put a refrigerator in every goddamned hut, diesel generator in every village! Then I'm going to dump the rest straight into the goddamned sea. Two hundred yards beyond the surf the island shelf drops near two hundred feet, that's where it's all going, son, off the point into Davy Jones's goddamned locker!' He'd said all of this seemingly without drawing breath.

'You mean you'll . . .?' I wasn't sure I understood. Surely he was just kidding, wasn't he?

'Trash the lot, every goddamned nut and bolt, groundsheets to grenades, shit paper to Sherman tanks. Nobody screws Uncle Sam, leastwise not a jerking-off Frog or a goddamn Limey swallowing his consonants!'

It was all so outrageous I thought General Urquhart must be drunk, but it was only a few minutes past nine in the morning and there was no smell of grog on his breath. 'I guess it isn't much of an offer, sir,' I stammered.

'Goddamn right it ain't. We've already reduced everything. If they'd offered me one cent in the dollar, then maybe I'd have gone along. That would mean you could have bought a Jeep still in its goddamn packing case for three bucks.' He removed the cigar from his mouth and, as if he'd pulled a cord from the plug, seemed to instantly calm down. 'So, have you brought your list, Nick?' he asked, smiling.

'Well . . . er, yes, sir.'

He looked at me. 'Navy Cross, eh? Well I reckon that deserves a small tribute. You've got two American partners did you say?'

'Yessir, US Navy.'

'Well that's real nice, son, shows fraternity and brotherhood. I like that. Now you go into Sergeant Moss's office, sit yourself down real quiet and think. Think about every goddamn thing you're going to need – *everything!* You take all day, all week. Take a jeep, look around. Bill Moss will give you an all-areas pass. Then give the sergeant your cheque for ten bucks . . . ' He thought for a moment. 'That's five pounds, just so we can give you a receipt, make everything kosher.'

I wasn't sure I understood. Was he asking me to give him five quid to look around and make a list or was he . . . ? No he couldn't, surely not. 'Sir, we don't have unlimited finances, but I've worked out a budget, and we'd be happy to pay 20 cents in the dollar.'

'Son, ten bucks, that's the deal. Anything you want. You going to help me to kick Frog ass and British butt? Anything!' he repeated, then added, 'You put your life on the line at Bloody Ridge for our American boys. Marines don't award a sailor the Navy Cross for picking his goddamn nose. Now Uncle Sam wants to show a little appreciation. Don't be shy. Either you take it, or we dump it. The Frogs and Limeys can go screw 'emselves.'

I spent the following week in Luganville with my three skippers and ships engineers and the supercargo, a drunk from Auckland, to organise the loading. We ate in the officers' mess and slept in a Nissen hut equipped like a luxury hotel with clean sheets and towels and hot running water, all of it compliments of General Urquhart.

By week's end, with the help of Sergeant Moss and one of the engineers, who made sure I got the right gear in top condition, I had scored an almost new landing craft and sufficient equipment to run four separate salvage operations with an entire workshop and spares for everything we'd purchased. In one fell swoop we had become the best-equipped small salvage operation in the Pacific. Our equipment manifest, if it were to be bought on the open market, was worth at least one hundred thousand American dollars! Remember, this was 1945; in today's money that would be over five million dollars.

We left for Rabaul with Gideon, a Gilbert Islander crew member from one of the other landing craft, handling the new one. The Gilbertese are the great seamen of the Pacific, undertaking major sea voyages on their *bauruas* – large outrigger sailing proas – long before Europeans arrived on the scene. They had developed a unique navigation system over vast distances by not only using the stars, but also sitting naked and cross-legged on the deck to 'feel' the direction of the swell through the movement of their testicles (fortunately the weather is generally warm in the Pacific).

Gideon, who would be in my employ for the next thirty years and would eventually become a certified skipper in our fleet, told me a story that, given that he grew up in the islands, I was inclined to believe, even though it seemed incredible.

He had been working on an inter-island freighter moving heavy equipment to another island when a bulldozer and other heavy machinery broke loose during a sudden squall one night and shifted to one side of the deck, flipping the ship in less than a minute. By dawn he was alone in the water, where he stayed all day, flayed by the hot sun. That night, exhausted and ready to die, he closed his eyes and he believes he actually dozed off. He awoke suddenly to find that he was being lifted, and realised it was a large tiger shark buoying him up. He grabbed at the dorsal fin and was carried on. That night he was attended by three large sharks, one on either side to cling to and the other swimming beneath him. Every time he was too exhausted to stay awake or even to hang on and started to sink, the shark beneath him would hold him up. All night and the next day the sharks remained with him. On the morning of the third day he saw land, whereupon the sharks started to nudge and pull him towards the shore. Then, guiding him to the opening of the reef where he would be carried ashore by the current, they finally abandoned him.

I recall asking him, 'Gideon, the sharks . . . did they not frighten you at first?'

'No,' he replied. 'I am a member of the shark totem on my home island. When they first appeared I knew they were members of my totem, brothers who had come to help me.'

I readily admit that having been brought up for a part of my formative years in New Guinea I may well have picked up, almost by osmosis, a certain susceptibility to superstition. But this was only one of a number of strange stories I had heard over the years and found myself, in many instances, inclined to believe. Whereas we Caucasians tell untruths as easily as we breathe, this is not the case for islanders, who have little or no reason to conceal their motives. For instance, Gideon's story would have been far more heroic had he struggled manfully and survived three days at sea on his own, rather than claiming to receive the assistance of three tiger sharks.

However, I later checked and discovered that the freighter had indeed been lost at sea on the date he had given me and that Gideon was listed as crew but was not the only survivor. Two women clinging to a wooden crate were picked up after twenty hours at sea. Of thirty passengers and crew only the three of them survived.

We eventually arrived in Rabaul and I organised four permanent moorings and a lock-up warehouse for our gear, leaving Gideon behind as caretaker.

General Urquhart was true to his word. After allowing the islanders to take what they wanted, and under the direction of Sergeant Bill Moss, he dumped tens of millions of dollars of US Army ordnance over the island's lip to the ocean bottom from what is still known today as Million Dollar Point.

As a postscript to what the *Paris Match* termed 'The biggest act of vandalism in the history of the Pacific Islands', the local French administration, calling it the property of the French Government, confiscated all the equipment given to the islanders, down to the last kerosene-powered refrigerator.

With all our equipment warehoused in Rabaul, the French couldn't confiscate it, and besides, I had receipts to cover everything. So, in the nearly nine months before my partners, Kevin Judge and Joe Popkin, returned to this side of the Pacific, I set about negotiating contracts to remove the veritable mountains of valuable scrap left by the defeated Japanese and the victorious allies. We were ready to begin work by the time Kevin arrived in Australia to marry Brenda O'Shaunnesy, his wartime sweetheart, nicknamed Bren Gun because of her rapid-fire speech. Joe Popkin, an African American, was not permitted to live in Australia under the White Australia Policy, and came to work with me in the islands.

Kevin ran our business affairs from Brisbane. As usual he'd selected the cushy job while Joe and I did the blood, sweat and toil in the jungle. This was just as well. The slightly built Kevin was both physically and mentally unsuited to island life. Joe Popkin, on the other hand, had the ideal looks and personality for work in the islands. He was everything the white commercial expatriates and administrators were not. Not only did the colour of his skin match the local people's, but the way he handled them soon earned their admiration and respect. He bore no grudges, took no bullshit and was generous to a fault. Eventually, as a sign of their respect, they named him Uncle Joe, even though he was still a young bloke.

When it came to leadership, Joe had no peer. His colour was an immediate advantage and his size precluded trouble among the workers. Joe Popkin could laugh and knock two kanaka heads together and the other workers would laugh with him. If I did the same thing, they might see the swift justice as fair, but I would still be a white man dishing out punishment. 'Uncle Joe, hem blong mifella,' they'd say about Joe Popkin. Then to emphasise the difference, they'd add, 'Masta Nick, hem blong white masta.'

Joe would never ask any of them to do what he wouldn't do himself. Usually he'd strip to the waist and help with the heavy loading, but he also ensured that the older and smaller of the island men were taught how to drive our bulldozers, cranes, winches, jeeps and forklift trucks, thus enabling them to be gainfully employed.

Joe loved the island kids and they followed him in a whirl of dust and noise whenever he went into a village. Sometimes he had some difficulty keeping their mothers, with or without the approval of their husbands, from taking him into the jungle for a bit of extra-connubial bliss.

There were literally hundreds of children named Joe on the islands, although this was almost certainly due to his popularity and not to his fecundity. We worked in a very big backyard and Joe was reluctant to piss on his own doorstep.

By the mid-fifties we'd largely cleared the islands of war-surplus scrap, and in order to switch to our long-term plan to run an inter-island shipping business we'd converted the original wooden vessel to general cargo and passengers and bought three more similar vessels for the same purpose. Despite Joe's increasing education expenses, we were pretty cashed up. The three ex-US

Navy vessels, now also converted, earned their keep shuttling general freight between Australia and New Zealand and the main island ports. Thus the Pacific Island Shipping Company, registered in Port Vila, was born and we seemed to have moved almost seamlessly from salvage to freight and then to carrying passengers as well.

We had earned a small reputation as reliable and fair employers in the war-salvage business. The way the various other scrap merchants conducted their labour relations had allowed the islanders to make comparisons very much in our favour. Now, contrary to our expectations, we were to learn that the advent of a reliable inter-island passenger and freight service that didn't exploit the locals wasn't going to reward us with the same loyalty.

We'd made a few enemies in the scrap-metal business, but this was nothing compared to the hostility we encountered from rival shipping companies. While we'd been shifting from salvage to freight they'd left us alone. We weren't carrying passengers and there was plenty of freight available for all of us. When we refitted to take passengers as well, the shit hit the fan. Many of them were running ships that were barely seaworthy and in an attempt to put us out of business they dropped their ticket prices, then carried up to twice the numbers of islanders allowed on the ship's manifest. Understandably every penny counted with the impecunious islanders and race relations and goodwill came a poor second to saving a quid. We still carried whatever white passengers were travelling between the islands, but there weren't sufficient to make a difference. We couldn't match the competition's prices without resorting to the same tactics, and for Joe and me that simply wasn't an option.

For a while we looked like going under and Joe became really worried. One of our vessels would come into port with a load of copra and with only a handful of paying passengers on board. 'Nick, dose cocksuckers, dey winnin', man! How long we gonna be in business this keeps up? Ain't no money in haulin' copra. Kevin's goin' crazy, man. You know how he says we gonna go broke in two more months. Is dat true?'

'Joe, touch wood, all we have to do is stay in business until the wet season comes,' I assured him. 'That's next month. If the competition continues overloading their passenger manifest, then the first big storm that comes along is going to mean trouble. The bastards know this and so they'll be forced to pull way back when the dirty weather arrives. Then our prices will be competitive and our reliability and service should make the difference.'

But it didn't happen. The cyclone season arrived and the competition continued to overload their ships. Two were caught out at sea during a violent storm and both went down. All 229 islanders drowned.

A great uproar followed and at the hearing to investigate the disasters it was discovered that the two shipping companies, one French and the other Australian, had both registered their vessels in Panama and carried no disaster insurance. Both companies simply declared themselves bankrupt and walked away scot-free, with none of the islanders, most of whom had lost family members, receiving any compensation.

Curiously, a rumour circulated among the commercial expatriates that we were indirectly responsible for the disaster because we had forced our competition to resort to overloading in order to remain in business. Only in the islands! This was the beginning of the ill will that would be directed at Joe Popkin and me for years. Throughout the sixties and early seventies, as our allegiances became increasingly clear, the hostility deepened. We had regarded ourselves as permanent island residents from the beginning, which stood in marked contrast to the colonial service personnel posted to the islands by their various governments. The other Europeans were usually on short-term work permits or saw their stay as an opportunity to earn a nice solid nest egg before returning home. Thus, exploitation of the locals was commonplace and the largely transient white population earned a dubious reputation. Our island way of life was often referred to as a place in the sun for shady people.

This wasn't entirely fair, there being of course many people, government and otherwise, who made a remarkable contribution – my father, the Anglican Bishop of New Britain, being one of them – but the average white resident put very little back and enjoyed a way of life few if any could have afforded in their own countries. The high salaries they received, together with the 'hardship allowance' for living away from home under 'difficult circumstances' with as many lowly paid servants as they wished to retain, allowed them to enjoy a splendid and privileged way of life.

The two disasters at sea put an end to the overloading of commercial ships, but the mission ships, trusting to God, continued to load passengers until people virtually hung from the ship's rails and the draft was within a few inches of the waterline. With every wet season they would lose more ships and more people. This loss of life was often caused by inexperienced captains who left port in bad weather and, unfamiliar with navigation equipment, were lost at sea, never to be seen again. On one occasion several years later, with a cyclone threatening and the possibility of a tidal surge on one of the islands, the Seventh Day Adventists loaded their barge to evacuate only the members of their faith, leaving the Catholics behind to perish. The cyclone arrived while the rescued congregation was barely out to sea, overturning the barge and driving it back onto the island with all hands lost. The tidal surge failed to arrive and the Catholics remaining on the island were unharmed. From that day onwards the local priests at the mission used the disaster as proof to their congregation that God is most definitely a Catholic. The SDAs buried the dead, then, stripped of their influence with Him upstairs, left the island, never to return.

From the outset of our operations we employed European captains on the larger ships that travelled between the mainland and the islands. For our smaller inter-island vessels there were plenty of qualified ex-naval Europeans with a taste for adventure willing to work as skippers and engineers. One of the conditions of their employment was that they train any promising native crew members as second mates, the idea being that the more promising islanders would be given the opportunity to advance. One of Joe's proudest achievements was when we sent ten promising island lads to Marine Training School to qualify as masters and engineers. Our first two local skippers were Gideon of the tall tales but true and Ellison.

Ellison had been the leader of the small gang of native scouts who had fought with me in the jungle during the war and had subsequently worked as our foreman on salvage locations. He also served from time to time as my personal assistant and I trusted him. In fact, during the war I had often trusted him with my life. A member of the Tolai, a New Guinea coastal tribe, he was completely at home with the sea and he eventually became the respected senior captain in our fleet.

Joe and I spent a lot of time on these island vessels and we both studied and eventually took our masters ticket. Together we saw to it that the captains ran the vessels the way we wanted. No drunks, and no liquor to be taken on board by passengers or crew; a clean ship properly loaded according to the cargo manifest; passengers, including the islanders, treated with respect by crew. Stowaways smuggled on board by crew in return for sexual favours led to instant dismissal. The myriad details that make for a smoothly run operation were practised as a matter of routine. These vessels were not exactly the *Queen Mary*, but we earned a reputation for running a tight passenger ship and a reliable freight service.

With Joe and me riding constant shotgun we were able to see at first hand what was needed to transport copra and other produce to the market, and kids to and from high schools. With self-government now inevitable on many Pacific Islands, we were also transporting an increasing number of junior public servants being trained in local-government work. Reliable inter-island transport had always been a problem for the local farmers and the European plantations and businesses, and as our fleet grew we eventually covered most of the commercially viable routes.

Grumble-bum Kevin, living the life of Riley in Brisbane, would complain every time we requested a new vessel. 'How many cockamamie islands you got, Nick? I got eyes! I got a goddamn atlas! Las' count there was nine worth a crock a shit! One big one, lots a small ones! You got nine fuckin' ships. What you want? A fuckin' armada? You ain't Francis goddamn Drake! Now we not only got Uncle Joe Scholarships suckin' us dry, we got half the fuckin' population goin' ter navy school!'

Kevin, of course, went looking for freight business in Australia, too, where he would refer to our operation as 'The fleet'. In Brisbane on one occasion I heard him on the phone to a would-be exporter. 'We got us a big operation, a fleet dat kin go everywhere you want, ain't no place in the goddamn Pacific we cain't cover. Sir, trust me, you wanna crap in a seagull nest on a coral atoll, we already got a seagull egg freight franchise from dere. Ain't no place we don't go, man!' Coming from someone who got seasick on wet grass it was outrageous bullshit, but it worked. Kevin was highly respected in Australian and New Zealand export circles.

'Now don't let me down, Nick,' he'd say when a near impossible contract was being discussed. 'Yeah, I heard yer good. It ain't possible. So? You want we should lose all da government business? Tell me so I can pick up da phone and cancel a twenny grand contrak! Send us broke. Da fucking bank dey screaming at me tree, four times a day, I cain't eat breakfast before da first motherfuckin' manager he's yellin' down my ear. Now, you tell Joe Popkin we gotta do dis, yer hear? Tell dat nigger to get one a dem Uncle Joe Scholarship and navy school captains to bust his black ass. Dey eatin' us outta house an' home! Dey gobblin' up the profit margin! Fuckers owe me big time!'

With our reputation for reliability growing, Kevin was obtaining more and more contracts from the Australian, New Zealand, British, American and French governments and even the UN. Our international freighters could transport just about anything to the various islands, then our smaller vessels would complete the delivery: demountable school buildings, administration offices equipped with typewriters, machinery for power stations, food for fridges, in fact everything a potentially self-governing nation might need to create a modern society.

All this meant that we were in constant contact with the local movers and shakers around the island coastlines, many of them the likely leaders of the future. All politics are local, especially in the islands, so we set about making permanent friends. We would perform small favours for island politicians or be seen to be looking after the needs of their constituents. It was impossible to sit on the fence, and Joe and I decided that as our future lay with the islands, so must our loyalty.

This didn't always go down well. By the late sixties we were known in some white island circles as kanaka-lovers, coconut cobbers or *meri* fuckers – *meri* being local slang for a native woman. This overt racism was most openly expressed in Rabaul where the exclusively white membership of the New Guinea Club, the New Britain Club and the Yacht Club produced the most outspoken white supremacists.

Joe Popkin, even in the late forties, was only admitted to these clubs by special dispensation because he was an American, although he was still made to feel distinctly unwelcome and subjected to racist remarks. In the late fifties, with the dawn of nationalism, this bad-mouthing had become more frequent, and by the early sixties Joe finally refused to enter any of the three clubs.

Unfortunately, a lot of island business happened over a beer at the club and Joe, ever the pragmatist, wouldn't hear of me resigning as well. 'Nick my man, busi-ness is busi-ness. Don't matter what dem cocksuckers call me. In da end we gonna chew 'em up and spit 'em out, flush da toilet. Who you think gonna still be here when da freedom bell rings? It ain't gonna be dose motherfuckers. Meantime we gonna take der loot, man! You gotta do the busi-ness. So you gotta stay a legit member o' dem hokey white-boy clubs.'

I recall on one occasion overhearing a conversation between four ruddy-faced European men indistinguishable from most others in the islands with their short back and sides, dressed in the white man's tropical uniform – white shirt, white shorts, white socks neatly turned back at the knees and highly polished black shoes. I walked up to the bar of the Yacht Club to wait for a government official to arrive. The conversation appeared to be well underway, and the only part I heard of what seemed to be an animated discussion was as follows:

First man: 'Yeah, the place is going to the fucking dogs. Mark my words, it'll end up like the Mau Mau in Kenya, a bloody uprising with the kanakas raping white women and murdering Europeans in their beds.'

Second man: 'Too right. What really pisses me off is that the dumb bastards don't realise how bloody hard we work to keep things running for them.'

Third man: 'Spot on, mate! They wouldn't last a month. Soon as the lights go out, no more fuel at the BP depot and they can't buy a bag a' rice at the Chink shop, they'll finally realise things don't happen by themselves.' He looked around, lifting his empty beer glass. 'Whose shout? Mine, is it? Righto.' He nodded to the barman. 'Boy! Same again.'

Second man: 'It's the new uni in Moresby – commo lefties stirrin' them up.'

First man: 'These kanakas are rock apes, ferchrissake! Climbed down from the trees day before yesterday and now we're givin' them a fucking university! You don't need a fucking PhD to cut copra!'

The islander barman placed the drinks down in front of them. Chorus of 'Cheers!'

First man continued: 'Did'ya read where this white bitch from the uni married a local? What sort of a slag would let a kanaka screw her? Hey? I mean, fair dinkum, it's just not on, is it? In the old days we sorted things out quick bloody smart – you got caught with a *meri*, straight off, *bang*, you're onto the BP steamer back home in disgrace.'

There were nods all round, then the fourth member of the group smiled and piped in: 'Hey! Fair go, Mack! If they brought that regulation back, there'd be a lot fewer members in this club for a start.'

General mirth followed.

First man (Mack): 'Steady on, mate, that's *totally* different. White women have to set a standard, that's always been the rule. You don't see any of us paradin' down the street with the house girl on our arm.'

Fourth man: '*Ha ha*, yeah, mate, sure . . . we've all heard about your little *Tolai* house girl!'

Mack: '*Bastard!* That's not the same!' (Knowing laughter from the other three.) 'Look . . . when a single bloke lives with a *meri* everyone knows he needs a bit of company in bed, somebody to cook and clean – there's no harm in that. It's not the same for that commo bitch at the university. There'd be no shortage of white blokes linin' up to screw the arse off her, unless she's a real crook sort.'

Second man: 'She'll be digging in the garden with a wooden stick, a piccaninny on her hip, another in her guts, carrying firewood home on her head.'

Third man: 'Oath! First time she opens her mouth when he comes home pissed, she'll lose her front teeth. In three years you won't recognise the stupid bitch.'

At that moment my business appointment arrived and we moved away from the bar to a table. As a longstanding islander, a coastwatcher with a couple of reasonable medals, and the son of the local Anglican bishop, I was more or less accepted, mainly out of deference to my old man, who'd survived the Japs and was considered a hero among both the white and native populations. But I knew I was being privately condemned for my so-called radical political views.

My father, John Duncan, held similar views to my own, but as a man of God, he refused to get mixed up in politics. 'I dare say the locals will win in the end,' he'd confided. 'Good thing too, but it won't bring them closer to the kingdom of heaven. Alas, for some, the devil will have his way. Corruption is colour-blind, an affliction to which few men are immune. Black men suddenly catapulted to power will be easily tempted.'

During the quarrels, enmity, hyperbole and earnest discussion between the various colonial governments and the indigenes of the islands and, in the case of Australia, with the United Nations over the future of Papua New Guinea, Anna, like ourselves, had been getting on with her own increasingly successful business.

Madam Butterfly was becoming the improbable headquarters for business gossip, know-how, information and advice among some of the biggest movers and shakers in the city, to all of whom Anna listened with a growing sophistication, charm, attention, mock incredulity, and genuine admiration. Add the allure of a beautiful woman, and the combination was irresistible.

CHAPTER FOUR

'I try not to cheat and not to lie,
which I find is almost impossible
in the world of business.
But I've also discovered
it's futile to feel guilty.
He technically steals from me
and I claw back what I can.'
Anna Til

ANNA IGNORED MY ADVICE and prospered by listening to her wealthy clients in the privacy of her rope and whip boudoirs; more than prospered. She owned real estate at the Paris end of Collins Street, and although it wasn't the most salubrious area in the fifties and sixties, it was one that seemed to be ripe for redevelopment. The centre of the city was just a sniff away from a makeover – a new metropolis of ugly skyscrapers replacing the old Victorian-style buildings that made Melbourne so attractive. Whelan the Wrecker was going day and night with his great steel wrecking ball, and if it all went to plan, Anna the speculator looked like being amongst the city's new elite – the developers.

Our relationship did not change; she continued to cherish me in every way but one. During this period she didn't expect to be, nor was she, the only woman in my life. The islands were awash with attractive young women. In Port Vila they might be

French or British, and on the other islands there were Australian, New Zealand and United Nations personnel. With the peripatetic lifestyle of a shipping executive, and as the owner of a magnificent home at Beautiful Bay, I was initially the fortunate recipient of many an amorous overture, and in the years that followed I settled for long-term casual relationships with several lovely women.

Though it is easy to say in retrospect, I never gave up on Anna and the hope that she would one day decide to seek help. Besides, she was one of only two women I had truly loved, and Marg, married with two kids, was unavailable. Being a male I could have found a hundred reasons why Anna wasn't suitable, why I should settle down with a more compliant woman, have three or four kids and get on with my life. But whereas lust and desire make easy accommodations, love doesn't. I learned to live with the cards I'd been dealt and hung on to the only single woman who truly mattered to me.

Over the years I gradually pieced together the story of Anna's life under the Japanese and in particular under the influence of Konoe Akira. Although it seemed incredible to me, eventually I was forced to accept that Anna believed her virginity was the source of all her other powers. Her inner strength – what she referred to as the core of the persimmon tree – would fail if she were to lose her virginity, and she would become, as she herself put it, a nothing and a nobody.

On one of my frequent trips to Rabaul I brought up the subject of virginity and the notion of its invested power with my father the bishop. As I had expected, he proved a fount of knowledge on the subject.

'Ah, well, of course there are the brides of Christ, the nuns, as the most obvious example of the role of virginity in the Christian faith,' he began.

'But isn't their virginity predicated on devotion and service rather than personal power?'

'Well yes, it may manifest itself in that way, but it emanates from the Virgin Mary, who is among the most powerful symbols in Christendom. No greater power can exist than the immaculate conception, the ability to spontaneously give birth to the Son of God.'

'I hadn't really thought of the Virgin Mary in terms of personal power; she's blessed, tranquil, motherly, but hardly dynamic, is she? She doesn't seem to have made much use of her power.'

He laughed. 'See how you unthinkingly speak of her in the present tense? That is how millions of people see her, as a living presence. Wouldn't you see that as evidence of a dynamic character? Her personal power can help people to change or bring about change, her presence can be taken into battle or used around the hearth.'

'Immaculate conception – isn't it . . . I mean, a bit of an excuse to create a *symbol* of power rather than *actual* power exerted through personality, will, determination, intellect, whatever?'

'Close to a billion Catholics wouldn't agree with you, son,' he gently argued. 'In the mind a symbolic reality and an actual one are often the same thing. The Mother of God lives just as surely as God Himself and is an omnipotent presence in the lives of around one in five of the world's population.'

'Clever idea,' I remarked.

'But not an original one.'

'Oh?'

'Virgin birth as a symbol of power is not the preserve of Christians. Athena the Greek warrior goddess, believed historically to be the forerunner of our Virgin Mary, gave virgin birth to Erichthonius according to some of the sources,' he told me.

'Clever people, the Greeks.'

'Ah, yes, they realised that virginity, as a symbol of purity, swaddles naked power with the notion that it has no motive other than good or what's right. That's a pretty powerful and compelling idea, don't you think?'

'Sure, the Greeks, Romans, Christians – classical antiquity; but what of the rest of the world, the Asians? Japan, for instance. Is virginity self-empowering within Japanese culture and beliefs?' I asked him.

As usual he had the answers. 'Whosoever *chooses* celibacy is seen to have mastery over body and mind; moreover virgin power is also a concept found in the Buddhist and Hindu religions. The idea that women, when virgins, remain autonomous and independent seems to be a universal belief, and the association of virginity with power is widely accepted.'

'But in the end it's not a rational view, is it?' I asked.

'Ah, there we have it, the cynic's viewpoint. Religious beliefs are not sustained by logic. They are all the more powerful because they come from our emotions, because they are accepted as a matter of faith and with the promise of ultimate salvation. Humankind, it seems, must have faith. Finally, the virgin is a pure, unadulterated vessel in which God resides at His most powerful. Ergo the virgin nuns, the Brides of Christ, to bring us back to where this conversation started.' My father sat back in his chair.

If her virginity was what Anna believed to be the source of her power, I was to learn that the persimmon tree was the template for her character. The Japanese commander had given her a seed to plant every remaining year of her life so that she could constantly renew within herself the metaphor the tree represented. It was a classic case of reinforcement. While Anna explained the characteristics of the persimmon tree to me, she did not admit that Konoe Akira had inculcated the virtues of the tree into her inner being. She stated that he had once merely addressed her, next to a small specimen he'd planted in the tropical garden in Tjilatjap, where he had enumerated its virtues.

'Nicholas, it is a tree that can accept great hardship. It will survive the coldest winter and the hottest summer, too much rain and no rain at all. In the summer its leaves are glossy and catch the sun. Its blossom feeds the bees. Its shade is so dense all may seek shelter from the heat under its verdant canopy or protection from the fiercest summer storm. In autumn its leaves turn the colour of flame then drop, a blanket that will turn to pulp and feed the earth in spring. In the winter its nourishing fruit hangs abundant, great golden orbs the size of a geisha's fist attached to pliant, artfully twisted twigs dark against the snow. Thus, when times are hardest, it is at its most beautiful. The outer bark is springy, supple, resisting, it will accept great punishment from roaring gales, yet will not snap. But its greatest virtue lies deep within, a secret core of black ebony, the hardest of all wood; nothing in nature can break it. When all the trees on earth have been destroyed by the furious elements, only the persimmon will still stand, proud and undefeated.' She paused in what was obviously a soliloquy, each word placed carefully as if in a poem. Then she added in a quiet voice, 'Only the biting blade of man can penetrate it, reduce it to nothing, wilted, broken, utterly destroyed.'

The words she had recited were obviously too close to her heart for me to question at the time and I decided to wait for another occasion when I would attempt to make her see that the characteristics of the persimmon she had attempted to personify, her inner core of strength, would not disappear if she relinquished her virginity.

Lust as a symbol of temptation and temporal life has long been contrasted with discipline, the inner self and divine inspiration. Sex is what we deny ourselves in order to become more resolute, stronger in mind and spirit – the mythical warrior.

Konoe Akira was playing a very old tune on a young, ingenuous and intellectually vibrant instrument when it was placed under abnormal stress. I would have been a fool to think I could counter his effect on Anna by simply using logic. Anyway, I have long since realised that when it comes to humans, few things in this world are wrought by logic alone. So, I decided to attempt a different strategy and to take Anna to Japan to confront Konoe Akira, assuming he was still alive. He was the key to solving Anna's delusional fear of losing her virginity.

Anna and I shared a knowledge of Japanese culture and an intense interest in Japan that kept us together despite what I thought of as 'our problem'. Apart from what I had gleaned during childhood and later war experience, my knowledge of Japan had benefited from my father's deep understanding of Japanese life and culture.

We were also both fluent in Japanese and often spoke it together, Anna refining or correcting my grammar or usage. In a language that depends on nuance and exquisite politeness, every word must be placed with infinite care; just as in a game of checkers, the wrong one in the wrong place can lead to disaster. Anna, with three years' tutelage from a language instructor appointed by Konoe Akira as well as the pressure of his exacting standards, spoke a fluent and more refined Japanese than did I. My knowledge of the language had begun in early childhood and then continued in a scholarly manner with my father, but it had been coarsened by my exposure to the argot spoken by the Japanese field-radio operators I'd listened to and interpreted during my stint with Intelligence at Guadalcanal and later as a coastwatcher.

Once I'd made up my mind about visiting Japan it seemed completely logical. Our business needed another ship, and now we could afford a brand-new one. The Japanese shipbuilding industry was back in business, their prices more than competitive and their technology up to the minute. I'd take Anna along and we'd seek out her Japanese mentor and confront him. I'd use the ship as an excuse for a bit of a jaunt.

In addition to buying a ship and attempting to track down Konoe Akira, there were two other people of interest I hoped to find. The first was Gojo Mura, a Japanese radio operator who had lived alone on a cliff face high on the mountain overlooking Henderson Field, the American airport at Guadalcanal. He had been relaying American aircraft movements to the Japanese headquarters in Rabaul and proved difficult to dislodge. As someone trained in jungle warfare, I volunteered to get him out of his mountain eyrie.

I'd finally found him half-starved in the jungle at the base of the high cliff where he had lived. He'd climbed down from his cave and was seated in a sunny glade painting butterflies using a battered tray of watercolours. The paintings were both accurate and beautiful, and instead of killing him as I had been ordered to do, I struck up a conversation with him and he showed me his sketchbook filled with drawings and paintings of jungle insects, moths and butterflies.

A less likely soldier than Gojo Mura never existed. In fact, he explained that he had been seconded to the navy after training at the Telegraph Department of the College of Engineering in Tokyo and had never received a single day's military training. When he led me to his cave I discovered that the bolt on his rifle had rusted up and the barrel had deteriorated so much that it would never fire another shot. He had subsisted alone for months on a bag of rice and the few jungle plants and roots he'd discovered, through trial and error, that he could eat.

After he'd been interrogated as a prisoner of war I managed, through the inestimable Marg, then in Melbourne, to have him assigned to a civilian Japanese internment camp near Hay for the duration of the war. I had always intended to keep up our friendship but he had unexpectedly been repatriated to Japan, leaving me the address of a friend of his who, like me, collected butterflies. I had duly contacted Iko Fuchida, but he had written briefly to say that he too had lost contact with Gojo Mura, who had never in fact turned up.

Over the years that followed I had sent butterfly specimens from the jungles of New Guinea to Gojo's butterfly-collecting friend and he had reciprocated with specimens from Japan and the surrounding islands. Apart from these carefully named and mounted specimens and his notes on habitat and species, I knew nothing about Iko Fuchida. This is often the way with passionate collectors whose shared interest is only one aspect of their lives. Now I hoped to make contact and had brought him as a gift twenty-four splendid specimens mounted in a rosewood and glass tray to ensure my welcome.

Apart from Konoe Akira, Anna knew nobody in Japan except the two retired geishas who had instructed her in the ways of bondage and later cared for her at the Nest of the Swallows. The likelihood of tracing them seemed pretty remote. As two of the four madams supervising the officers' brothel, they could have been prosecuted for war crimes and gaoled.

While I had fond memories of the effete but certainly delightful Gojo Mura, Anna's associations with Japan were less pleasant. She may have benefited from her intensive education in Japanese culture and willingly embraced the values, aesthetics and philosophy of a distinct and rarefied version of the Japanese way of life, but she had paid a tremendous price in psychological damage.

Colonel Konoe had shaped her to his own ideal of womanly perfection, which included an aristocratic appreciation of Japanese art, the exacting disciplines of ikebana and formal manners. In fact, Anna was a throwback to the pre-Meiji ideal of courtly behaviour, almost certainly unique outside the small remaining Japanese aristocratic elite of which Konoe Akira had been and perhaps still was a part.

In so many ways she was intrinsically more Samurai than anything else, despite the fact that she functioned as a contemporary woman with a sharp mind, ready wit and formidable will. I was to learn that she continued to live by many of the intellectual tenets of Samurai philosophy, for example, their formal politeness in addressing an enemy and the exquisite manners involved in the creation of an insult.

In doing business, Anna was said never to lose her politeness or gentle and courteous manner, even when faced by daunting male opposition, or by taunts or improper remarks designed to upset her. Even when she had her opponent thoroughly beaten, she would allow him to leave the contest with his head held high. If she was herself defeated, she would bow and smile politely without any outward sign of anger, frustration or remorse. If someone lied to her or cheated she would wait. 'Nicholas, as long as you remain in the game, those who play it will return and you will not have forgotten.' It all added up to a redoubtable opponent who many an arrogant male had cause to remember after assuming she was just a pretty face and could be taken for a ride.

When I put to Anna the notion that we should visit Japan together she was so quick to respond that I knew the suggestion did not come as a surprise. I also knew that we had both thought about Konoe Akira, but perhaps she imagined a different outcome from the hopes I entertained.

'Nicholas, that would be wonderful!' she enthused. 'I know so much and yet so little about Japan and the Japanese. Now you can show me where you were born and share your experience of the people with me,' she added gracefully.

'Anna, the pre-war Japan of my childhood is long gone, as is the autocratic and esoteric world of your Japanese colonel,' I added somewhat slyly, watching her carefully.

But if Anna had plans to meet Konoe Akira she gave no indication of this. 'It will be fun to be with you when you buy your ship, Nicholas. I too would like to do business with Japan – it would be a pity to waste my knowledge of the language – but what form that business might take I'll have to wait and see.'

She was in so many ways smarter than me. Besides, I'd long since discovered that second-guessing Anna Til was an exercise in futility. I am ashamed to say that I thought she might well use the trip to enlarge her knowledge of sadomasochistic techniques by visiting places whose reputations she had learned about from her clients.

On the jet to Japan, one of those new 707 Boeings that made flying long distances a damn sight more comfortable than the lumbering Super Constellations, Anna and I had a conversation that I recall to this day with total clarity.

Her establishment, Madam Butterfly, a source of constant disagreement between us, was now being used by many of the Japanese businessmen who were once again allowed to trade with Australia. Public hatred of the Japanese was slowly fading, no doubt due to passing time and, more importantly, the desire to make a big quid. Our inestimable leaders plainly saw that exports of raw materials, coal and iron ore in particular, to a rapidly growing Japanese economy could balance the books, and our new-found prosperity would soon assuage the national conscience.

Like many of us involved at the sharp end of the war, I had come to accept that the average Japanese soldier was almost as much a victim as we had been – mere cannon fodder. Our wartime propaganda had turned them into bestial torturers, whereas this description more often fitted the *kempeitai*, selected for and trained in brutality. As well, it described many in the officer ranks, such as the beasts who had ordered the murder and torture of our prisoners of war at Changi, Sandakan and the Burma–Thailand Railway. These were the vile creatures who deserved to be exterminated and I would have been the first to volunteer to give each and every one of them a double tap from an Owen submachine-gun.

Against vociferous opposition from returned-services organisations and labour unions our pragmatic government issued residential permits for Japanese businessmen lasting seven years. This allowed the establishment of Japanese companies in Australia and granted them equal rights to shipping and transport. It also meant that Anna had additional Japanese clients for Madam Butterfly who appreciated that she spoke a very good style of Japanese and observed the courtesies of their culture. I am not implying that most Japanese businessmen are sadomasochists, but there is perhaps a greater predilection for formal sexual punishment in some circles of Japanese society than in most Western societies.

Anna's new clients proved to be a marvellous source of information and opportunity for her, and not surprisingly she was unwilling to give up Madam Butterfly, despite my pleading and argument.

'Nicholas, I own only thirty-nine per cent, a police commissioner's wife owns another ten per cent, Stan McVitty has the majority. He would continue to run Madame Butterfly alone. I have personally trained sufficient girls for there to be dominatrices who can carry on without me.'

'Well then, sell that sanctimonious shit the rest of the joint. You don't need the money.'

'Ah, but I need the information, and the girls don't understand business, so they can't stand in for me, nor do they speak Japanese. Nicholas, the big Japanese banks and investment companies are anxious to buy into Australia. They need a go-between to broker partnerships and facilitate introductions with the local big-money players.' She laughed excitedly. 'Fortunately some of these movers and shakers are among my customers and they trust me. Who better than little Madam Butterfly to flutter in and skim off a small introduction fee or brokerage percentage?'

'Anna, how much is enough?' I cried in frustration. We were the only couple in first class so it didn't really matter if I raised my voice. 'You already own – how many? – nineteen lots surrounding Madam Butterfly, each, as you've told me, worth a potential fortune when the Paris end of Collins Street is eventually redeveloped. Several of your other projects have already made you a tidy profit. How much more do you need?'

'More! Lots more!' she said in a low urgent voice. 'Nicholas, Stan McVitty's brother, Peter, is a senior public servant in Canberra and a section head in the Department of External Affairs. He's responsible for dealing with the Pacific Islands . . .' She paused, leaving the sentence unfinished, then asked, 'Wasn't Peter McVitty your commander in New Britain?'

Anna's memory was prodigious. I had mentioned Peter McVitty to her almost ten years previously. 'Yeah, when I was a coastwatcher, towards the end of the war. He was a major and pretty senior in the Australian New Guinea Administration Unit. Then after the war he was responsible for issuing the contracts for war salvage in the islands.' I grinned. 'Good guy. He was the lucky break for me, I guess.'

'Nonsense, Nicholas, it's wheels within wheels, it's who you know and *exactly* what we've just been talking about. Anyway, he has told Stan that the British Phosphate Commission can't hang onto the rights to mine phosphate in Nauru much longer and are being pressured by the UN to hand the rights back to the people. The BPC has been paying the Nauruans next to nothing for phosphate and selling it to us and to the New Zealanders at an artificially low price.'

'Yeah, the Brits are well known for their altruism,' I observed wryly.

Anna, whose sense of humour still suffered a little from her Teutonic past, missed my irony. 'Yes, well, they've made a pretty sum; now it's our turn.'

'Our turn? What precisely do you mean by that?' I asked.

'Well, McVitty, Swan & Allison have been appointed as the lawyers to oversee the establishment of the new Nauru Phosphate Company. Stan is the lawyer chosen to personally represent the company in Australia.'

'Poor bloody Nauru! How very convenient. Brother Peter certainly doesn't miss a trick. Take my advice, darling, have nothing whatsoever to do with fat, unctuous brother Stan.

There isn't a straight bone in his smarmy, larded body. A snake doesn't turn into a tortoise even though they're both reptiles. Anna, don't get involved a second time with the fat bastard. I fear for you, darling. In the long run, whenever it's convenient or there's a quid to be made, that slimy bugger is going to drop you like a hot potato. He'll dob you in to the police for possessing heroin or some other trumped-up charge where his name won't come up. The best day in the life of our company was when Kevin fired his law firm and we stole Janine de Saxe as our personal lawyer.'

'Don't think he's forgotten that either,' Anna warned. 'Nicholas, I've dealt with worse than Stan McVitty.'

'It depends what you mean by worse. How can you trust a man who presents himself as a moral beacon in society, church deacon, assistant magistrate, chairman of the Save the Children Fund, on the board of the Yooralla Children's Home . . .'

'Nicholas —'

'You probably don't listen to Sir Irving Benson on the radio, do you. "Pleasant Sunday Afternoons" it's called.'

'Sir Irving Benson? Stan McVitty once mentioned his name. He said he's a great friend, and that Sir Irving is a confidant of Mr Menzies.'

'Yeah, he'd say that. The point is that McVitty sometimes goes on Sir Irving's Sunday radio program, where he invariably rails against the evils of gambling and prostitution, and advocates harder sentences for crims and drug traffickers. The bloody sanctimonious hypocrite is your partner in Madam Butterfly! And he did a lot of legal work for John Wren, the city's biggest illegal gambling operator! It wouldn't surprise me if he came creeping into Madam Butterfly to be bound and whipped, and no doubt to check the take in the cash register. Didn't you say he is partial to a snort of cocaine? And he owns those two brothels in North Melbourne —'

'Nicholas! You must never say a word to anyone. I told you that stuff about the brothels and cocaine when I was discussing Stan as a partner. My client list is secret and that would include him, *if* it were relevant. The names of the people who come to Madam Butterfly I'll take to the grave with me. Besides, we don't have a cash register!'

'Ha, you don't have to be Einstein to know he'd like being tied up and whipped!' I snorted. Anna, who can disguise her feelings perfectly, allowed herself a smile, so I knew my guess was spot on, although she'd never openly admit it.

'Besides, there's a financial killing to be made,' she announced, changing the subject.

'What? With the odious Stanley?'

Anna laughed. 'Yes, but not in a partnership. Once is more than enough.'

'What then?'

'Nauru. When they assume control of their phosphate, ultimately worth billions, Nauru will be the richest of the islands by far.'

'Until it runs out.'

'Precisely! How clever of you, Nicholas. So, the plan is to invest as much of their cash flow from phosphate as possible in income-earning assets overseas. In Australia and America, and Honolulu, for a start.'

'And you can be the skimming butterfly again?'

'Well, kind of.'

'How are you going to do it? Stan's law firm is entitled to its legitimate fees from the Nauruans. What else is there?'

'The Australian report, written largely with the help of Peter McVitty, has suggested the erection of a major building in the Melbourne CBD. It will be Melbourne's tallest building, fifty-two levels above ground, five parking levels below. The reasons are compelling,' Anna continued. 'Melbourne needs the space, the income from rents is ongoing and the asset has long-term potential.'

'So where's the money to be made, other than from lawyers' fees?' Then it struck me. 'Anna, this isn't the American Navy's Supply Department and you're not Kevin Judge and there isn't a war going on, where anything goes and nobody is looking! Taking a percentage from would-be contractors as a front for Stan McVitty is insane. Don't do it! You're going to get caught!'

'Nicholas, Nicholas, don't get upset, darling,' Anna cried. 'As you say, why would I do something as stupid as that?'

'Anna, listen to me! Stan McVitty is not under any circumstances to be trusted!' I continued despite her reassurance.

'Nick, will you *shut up* and *listen*!' Anna hissed. She only uses 'Nick' when she's cranky or impatient with me.

'Yes, well . . .' I grunted, only partially mollified.

'Nicholas, you forget, he's been my partner for nearly twenty years.
I know him far better than you do. I agree he's a snake, a greedy one and a sly one and certainly not to be trusted. He unabashedly charges nearly five times the going rental rate for Madam Butterfly and increases it every year. Technically that takes his fifty-one per cent ownership to almost eighty per cent of the profits, leaving the shareholders of the remaining forty-nine per cent actually receiving only about twenty per cent of the profits.'

'So, by owning the building he's got you between a rock and a hard place. Bloody typical of the sly bastard!'

Anna shrugged and nibbled on a canapé. 'It's a cash business and while Stan's fifty-one per cent has done very well, my thirty-nine per cent has done a great deal better and the cop's wife's ten per cent has shown a nice regular little income, sufficient to pay the mortgage on a new double-storey house in her brother's name on the beachfront at Brighton. Over the years we've been in business my *slightly* augmented portion of the profits has gone into the surrounding real estate. As soon as a building has come onto the market at the Paris end of Collins Street, or Little Collins or Exhibition streets, I've snapped it up, although snapped isn't quite the word. I've mortgaged, borrowed, begged and, as I've just explained, technically stolen the cash from Madam Butterfly.'

Anna sighed. 'I try not to cheat and not to lie, which I find is almost impossible in the world of business. But I've also discovered it's futile to feel guilty. He technically steals from me and I claw back what I can. Now I own most of the immediate area – nineteen lots.'

'But, darling, why haven't you talked about any of this?'

Anna gave a tiny sigh and said quietly, 'Nicholas, you were never interested in my property developments, remember?'

What could I say to that? After a moment's silence I asked, 'But surely somebody was bound to notice you buying up on such a scale? Stan McVitty for a start. Property sales are pretty public affairs; they all have to be registered with the Titles Office.'

Anna smiled. I know she sometimes finds me a bit backward, but she tries to conceal her impatience. 'Each of the buildings is owned separately by a two-dollar shelf company via nominees owned by my umbrella company registered in Port Vila.'

'Anna, you didn't tell me that,' I said, surprised.

'Didn't I? Never mind, now you know. Perhaps the islands will never prove a good investment, but there are distinct advantages to this one being a tax haven.' Anna took a sip from her gin and tonic, her eyes shining and a grin forming at the corners of her mouth. 'The total area I own at the top of Collins Street forms one of two possible sites for what is to be known as Nauru House.'

Despite myself I lifted my glass in a toast and said, 'Well done!' Then quickly added, 'Hey, wait on. What if the Nauru government chooses the other site?'

Anna grinned. 'Here comes the real fun.' She looked at me and put down her glass. 'Nick, I think I'll change to champagne. Can you ask the hostess? Perhaps some blinis to go with it?'

I had no idea what blinis were. The air hostess brought a bottle of French champagne, poured it and apologised that they didn't have any blinis. A plate of smoked salmon appeared instead.

'Pity,' Anna remarked. 'I love those tiny pancakes with smoked salmon.'

So now I knew, small pancakes. 'What's the real fun?' I asked after the hostie had departed.

'Fun?'

'You said, "Here comes the real fun".'

'Oh, why yes . . .' Anna took a breath. 'Well! Stan McVitty has formed what he calls a secret consortium to buy the properties he doesn't know I own. In fact, the only building he owns in the immediate area is Madam Butterfly. You know that's how he originally got his fifty-one per cent share in Madam Butterfly. I tried to rent the building when I first arrived and he offered to fit it out and turn it into a high-class establishment. We agreed I'd pay him rent by cheque each month and he'd take fifty-one per cent of the profits as well, but in cash, of course.'

'Didn't you move from the original building in Spring Street shortly after I met you in Australia?'

'Yes, it became too small, so he bought our present place in

Little Collins Street.'

'*He* bought it alone? Why not be partners in the building as well?'

'He wouldn't hear of it.' Anna shrugged philosophically, then as an aside, added, 'I have since learned that in life, real estate always beats know-how. In the long run bricks are more permanent than tricks,' she added cleverly. 'I should be grateful. He taught me that.'

'Stan's secret consortium,' I reminded her, anxious to get back to the development site.

'Yes . . . well, quite obviously, the Nauru government can obtain a loan from any major bank backed by their phosphate assets to buy the real estate they need to erect the building, so there's no need for a consortium to buy it. McVitty, Swan & Allison are responsible for overseeing the sale so they can't be seen to be double-dipping. It would amount to what the law calls a secret commission, to say nothing of the legal ethics regarding conflict of interest. You can't be seen to be making a profit by exploiting confidential information from your own client.'

'Which is what Stan McVitty hopes to do. Isn't he taking a tremendous risk?'

Anna nodded. 'Yes. If he is discovered it would destroy him, as well as his brother in Canberra.'

I had a sudden thought. 'Hang on, what's to stop you doing the same thing? You can't be accused of insider trading.'

'Go to the top of the class, Nicholas. But there's one catch. Stan McVitty owns the Madam Butterfly building. *And* that just happens to sit in the heart, almost in the dead centre, of the development site.'

'Damn! What will you do?'

Anna giggled. 'He may call it a secret consortium, but

that's a euphemism for greed. Stan wants to keep all the profit for himself.'

'Why are you grinning?' I asked, somewhat bemused.

'He wants me to front for him, be his straw man.'

'Good God!'

'He told me after almost twenty years in partnership he knows he can trust me. But what he's really saying, or believes, is that he's always got the heroin thing, and the fact that I am the madam of a house of ill repute, to keep me in line.'

'But you've got his partnership with you to throw right back at him. Imagine what such exposure would do to his sanctimonious public image. It would ruin him!'

Anna looked at me somewhat scornfully. 'Nicholas, you really are a babe in the woods. He'd simply say he rented the building to Madam Butterfly without knowing how it was being used. The rent was the only thing that wasn't cash. He's a bastard, but he's not a fool.'

'Yeah, you're right. I can hear him saying it, *sotto voce*, on Sir Bloody Irving's "Pleasant Sunday Afternoon" radio program. Probably have Bob Menzies following, saying what a sterling chap he is, pillar of the establishment.'

Anna laughed. 'It's the Melbourne Club. They stick together.'

'Okay, if he isn't going to offer to share the profit he hopes to make, what's he offering?'

'Well, thank God he didn't!' Anna exclaimed. 'I would have been hard put to explain that I didn't want to make what would otherwise amount to an enormous killing.'

It was getting complicated.

'Greed, it can be a friend.'

'Anna, what sort of money is involved? I mean, what did you pay for the properties in the first instance?' I then realised that I might be prying into her private business, something I'd never done. 'Don't tell me if you don't wish to, darling.'

Anna laughed. 'How much? It's not always about money. Mostly sweat, sometimes blood and occasionally tears. Every property was paid for with endless lengths of bondage rope and a great number of carefully tied knots. I'd work on a client for two hours and when he was both exhausted and satisfied, I'd say to myself, "Well, that paid for half a kitchen or possibly the outside toilet." In dollar terms? I've paid around half a million dollars in our new decimal currency for the nineteen lots I own at present. Not too bad. I've been lucky – nobody wants property at this end of the city. We are not the only brothel on the block, even though Melbourne sees itself as a choosy and refined city.'

'The brothels, they still going?'

Anna shrugged. 'I don't own them, it's rent.'

'And now, what's the whole shebang worth as a development site?'

I knew I was prying, but Anna didn't seem concerned.

'How long is a piece of string? If a high-rise developer comes along, possibly more than ten times what I originally paid.'

'*Phew!* Nice work. And now one *has* come along – Nauru House!' I paused. 'Hang on, how are you going to overcome the little matter of the Nauru government choosing your site, and further, the problem of the Madam Butterfly building?'

'By accepting Stan's offer to be his straw man.'

'But you already said that didn't make sense.'

'No, I said a partnership sharing the potential profits didn't make sense. Stan has agreed to pay brokerage fees of five per cent for the use of my name on the contract. And, because the assistant police commissioner retires from the police force this year, in addition he's offered me a forty-nine per cent share of a new Madam Butterfly to be established elsewhere in Melbourne. "A nice tidy little package, Anna," is how he put it to me.'

'Oh, Anna, you wouldn't. Please say no to continuing in the business.'

'Don't be impatient, Nicholas. As it turns out, a relocated Madam Butterfly won't be possible.'

'But by agreeing to the deal, you now *only* get five per cent when you own all the properties but one. That's bloody crazy.'

'I agree, it would be crazy, insane. But I wouldn't work like that. My only reason for agreeing is to have the Madam Butterfly building included. That guarantees that McVitty, Swan & Allison will nominate the site I own for the Nauru House development. If I went in alone and tried to buy the building from Stan he'd make me pay a ridiculous price for it, or out of sheer spite he'd simply nominate the alternative site.' Anna spread her hands. 'No Madam Butterfly building, no deal – simple as that. Stan McVitty holds the key but he doesn't know it.' She took a sip of champagne. 'But there's another way.'

'Oh?'

'I'll agree to be his straw man and set up a company in my name, buy the nineteen lots I already own in the name of the new company for exactly what I paid for it, not a cent more except for the legal fees and stamp duties. This is going to take a period of at least a year. So every month or so, one or another of my properties will appear as sold to the new holding company, including the premises Madam Butterfly occupies, which will naturally be the first to be sold at Stan's insistence.'

I frowned. 'Anna, I don't get it.'

Anna ignored me. 'Then, I'll sell the whole parcel to the Nauruans for roughly ten times as much.'

'And only get five per cent of the value? That's bullshit, you said so yourself.'

'Shush, Nicholas, listen. I keep *all* the money. Around four and a half million dollars. All I give Stan McVitty is the $500 000 he gave me to buy my own properties for the new company plus the money the new company paid for the Madam Butterfly building. He hasn't lost a cent. I've even allowed his money to earn bank interest, which is what we agreed. He has his entire original investment back, plus the money he made on the Madam Butterfly building. A nice safe little profit on the money invested. Or as I will put it to him, "A nice tidy little package, Stan".'

'Holy Moly! And there's no contract between the two of you? That right?'

'Right. Not a single scrap of paper to interfere.'

'Anna, he's a lawyer, a smart one according to you. Is he going to buy this?'

'Buy what? It's his suggestion, not mine. He made me a loan at current bank interest. I have a piece of paper, a loan agreement, to prove it. It's the only documentation in the entire project between us. He demanded it in case something unforeseen went wrong.'

I chuckled, not sure I approved. 'And something unforeseen did happen?'

'Darling, as W.C. Fields once said, you can't cheat an honest man.'

'Do you think he'll kick up a fuss when all this comes out in the wash?'

'Nicholas, the operation has been going for a year. I'm supposedly frantically buying up the properties I already own and the investment company in my name is duly registered and already has ten lots in its portfolio.'

'Anna, the McVittys are Melbourne establishment! Aren't you afraid of what he might do? These people, they stick together, you know. Besides, you mentioned the heroin and the madam thing.'

Anna shook her head. 'Of course you can't be too careful, but as I told you once before, it's who you know, and I feel sure that the VIP list I've roped in over twenty years with never a whisper of impropriety is enough goodwill – that will go further than any influence he may have. A quiet word here and there, an exposure in the *Herald* or *The Age* and the attempted scam will be all over town.'

'Nice work, darling.'

Anna was more than a little elated and I realised that she'd told no one up to now, that letting off steam in the plane to Japan with a glass or two of good champagne was exhilarating. 'The arrogance of males never ceases to surprise me,' she went on. 'Stan McVitty is so smug he hasn't even taken into consideration his personal reputation. Besides, there's Peter McVitty in Canberra. I'm told he's a candidate for a safe seat in a coming by-election, that they want him to be the new Minister for External Affairs. He certainly isn't going to allow a family scandal of such proportions. Can you imagine, the scion of one of Melbourne's most respected families and a principal in a leading law firm being implicated? What's more, there's the implied nepotism Peter showed towards the family law firm appointed to broker the building of Nauru House. Then the inside knowledge of the deal his brother attempted to exploit. It all adds up to a huge mess.'

I grinned. 'Even the law wins. Stan McVitty would most certainly have to retire from his law practice, the Nauru government business would leave the firm, removing a source of future profit, both honest and suspect.' I shrugged. 'Anna, what can I say, you seem to have worked it all out, but you're getting in awfully deep.'

Anna shrugged in turn. 'Nicholas, gold is a heavy metal and it sinks to the bottom of the harbour. But there is another small matter.'

'Aha, and what does that mean?'

'Well, I added another element to the deal when I agreed to be the straw man for Stan McVitty. I asked for the lease of the five floors of parking in Nauru House at a price always to be competitive with that currently charged for inner-city parking space. It was a contract that had to be signed by the Nauru government, a legal document, or I wouldn't agree to the rest of the deal.'

I looked at Anna strangely. 'Parking space? Are you sure? What's wrong with the street? Melbourne has these big wide streets . . . besides, most people come into the city by tram or train.'

'Stan McVitty said the same thing. He laughed and agreed immediately and got the paperwork done with the Nauru people.'

'But car parks. Why?'

'My Japanese clients tell me that Nissan, Toyota and Mitsubishi are planning to flood the market with cheap motorcars, and there is General Motors Holden of course. This will force down car prices. It seems logical. With people owning cars they'll not only use them for Sunday picnics.'

'Nah, public transport, that's the Australian way. You'll never get rid of the buses and trams,' I said, dismissing her observation. Anna was smart, but I reckoned in this instance she was way out of her depth. Cars are a man's business after all.

'Perhaps, perhaps not . . . Anyway, I have given Stan McVitty fifty per cent of the twenty-five-year parking franchise in Nauru House.'

'I'll bet he was impressed,' I said with a good dollop of

sarcasm. 'Anna, let me assure you, if you and he hope to make a quid out of inner-city car parks you've got Buckley's.' I shook my head. 'Underground parking? No way.'

Anna had hitherto been polite about my criticism of the car-parking idea. But now my rude rebuttal prompted her to protest. 'Why, Nicholas, it makes perfect sense. All the architects and planners are building car parks in excavated space under the new high-rise buildings going up in Sydney. They must know something we don't. Think about it for a moment. All a car park is . . . well, is space, lights and concrete. No upkeep, no painting, no depreciation, no fixtures, no windows, no people to complain about the neighbours, a few yellow lines, a power bill once a quarter, exit and entry signs and an attendant at the gate. And every month, rent from the tenants and cash from the casuals.'

Anna would one day own the parking franchises for twenty per cent of Australia's high-rise buildings, worth millions of dollars annually, and the odious Stan McVitty did eventually get the profit he'd hoped to make on the site for Nauru House, without it costing him a penny beyond his fifty per cent share of the maintenance costs and painting a few yellow demarcation lines on the concrete. As for smart arse, bloody good thing I lived in a place in the sun for shady people, where you didn't have to think too hard to make a buck.

Anna also took out twenty-five-year leases on the plan on seven prime locations within the Ala Moana Shopping Mall in Honolulu, another major asset the Nauru Government acquired and the largest mall in the world at that time. Then she flew to Paris and signed up Chanel, Dior, Yves Saint Laurent, Louis Vuitton, Charles Jourdan and Pierre Balmain, then over to Italy to visit Gucci.

And, of course, she got away with the redevelopment scam without a breath of the near scandal reaching the Melbourne establishment. Moreover, she went to see Peter McVitty, now the Minister for External Affairs, and briefed him on what she'd done. He was to become a grateful and firm friend in the years to follow.

You could say that, for Madam Butterfly, this was her first really big flutter. To give you some idea, in today's property values, the five million or so dollars paid in 1971 for the development site where Nauru House now stands is the equivalent of a profit of seventy million dollars.

Madam Butterfly, the establishment, closed with the sale of the building site. A year or so later several of Anna's girls, her dominatrices, opened another house of bondage in St Kilda named Moths to a Flame.

I recall we were sitting on the verandah at Beautiful Bay watching the sunset, Anna with a glass of her favourite French champagne, when she told me about the new house of bondage.

'How would they obtain the finance? Do you think Stan McVitty is up to his old tricks?' I asked.

'I shouldn't think so,' she answered. 'They loathed him.'

I hesitated. 'You? Anna, you didn't . . .?'

Anna gave me a wide-eyed look. 'Nicholas! Don't be ridiculous! I don't know what you could possibly be thinking.'

'Oh, Anna, Anna! Shame!'

'Nicholas, a little more bubbly, please.'

Relationships are built on trust and yet the dichotomy between Anna and me meant that there were some things she admitted to me and some things she didn't. It wasn't duplicity. It was just that she lived a part of her life where I simply could not go. The fact that she'd told me about the McVitty incident and other aspects of her business life showed that she wanted me to know some of her secrets. But by not admitting to financing, perhaps even owning, Moths to a Flame, the new house of bondage, she excluded me from other areas of her life.

But there was one exception. Anna, born and raised on an island, was fascinated by island politics. She never wearied of hearing the 'who, what, how, why and when' about the prospect of self-government for any of the various Pacific nations.

I guess she'd been brought up under an oligarchic colonial island regime and suffered under another even more despotic one with the Japanese. She longed to see something good happen for the islanders, so people would no longer be under the dictates or whims of a nation other than their own. 'Nicholas, they need to make their own decisions, their own mistakes, follow their own customs, govern in their own right – that is the only true freedom.'

Anna, to my knowledge, never lied to me; she simply didn't tell me everything. I admit, from the beginning of our re-acquaintance we agreed that the so-called nefarious aspects of her life were not brought into our shared life. But when you love someone, knowing there are secrets can create tensions and cause you to speculate, fear the worst, without being able to resolve those fears.

I imagine it is like being the partner of a crime boss. You don't ask questions and you try to live your life as normally as possible, bring up the kids with all the right values, pretend everything is hunky-dory when you know it isn't, know that at any moment something horrible might happen. In my case, of course, there were no kids and I was a male, but my anxiety about Anna's covert life was much the same.

The fact that we lived in different countries and saw each other for one week every month probably made the relationship possible. For three-quarters of the time we lived separate lives, in some respects as strangers. When I wasn't at sea we phoned each other almost daily, but we couldn't question each other's routines too closely. Plying between islands carting copra, coffee, cocoa and people had its conversational limitations for Anna, and there were also the other women she affected not to mind, while in her life there were many no-go areas for me.

I wished my life lacked those no-go areas, but we had openly discussed my need to have normal sex and I had made it clear to Anna that this was desirable on two counts: first, I spent three weeks a month away from her, and second, she was unable to have penetrative sex.

Faced with reality, she'd finally agreed to see Dr Denmeade, the Melbourne psychiatrist I'd first consulted about her problem, apparently without any positive result. Because we weren't married and Anna was now his patient, he wouldn't discuss her case with me other than to confirm that she most definitely suffered from vaginismus. So I'd brought the subject up with Anna and she'd merely shrugged. 'It's *still* mumbo-jumbo, Nicholas,' was all she would say.

'Okay, then will you see a gynaecologist? Maybe it's physical and not something in your head.'

'Okay, you find one and I'll see him, that way you'll know I'm not cheating,' she'd added unnecessarily, indicating how fraught with difficulties the issue had become.

Unbeknownst to Anna, I'd found a specialist in Collins Street with the help of Marg, who at the time was still married.

Marg and Anna hadn't exactly taken to each other, which was hardly surprising. Both were strong, organised, independent, and differed in almost everything they believed.

Anna, of course, knew about my original relationship with Marg. At that time, Marg's husband was still alive, so there was no question of anything going on between us. Over the years she and the children had spent several holidays with me on the island and we had simply remained the best of loving friends. Now, with Anna's problem, I knew I could trust her to find the right physician.

Marg, as usual, wasn't willing to fly blind. 'What is it, Nick?' she wanted to know.

I replied in the clumsy manner of a bloke, even though I could probably have addressed a roomful of doctors on the subject. 'Um . . . er, you know, something down there.' Then added by way of further clumsy explanation, 'Women's stuff.'

'Hardly a clinical description,' she sniffed. 'C'mon, you can do better than that. If I have to find the right chap I want to know what the problem is.'

'I think it's vaginismus,' I replied, grateful for the word because it avoided going into further detail.

'Think?'

Not wishing to go into graphic details with Marg I feigned impatience. 'God, Marg, how would I know. It's difficult for her to, you know . . . have sex.'

'Sex? Could be lots of reasons, Nick,' she said sympathetically. 'Anna's been through a lot.'

'Yeah, but let's start with the physical side,' I said, putting a stop to any further probing, if that's the right word in this context.

Marg was as good as her word and found, she assured me, exactly the right chap if it was vaginismus. 'If it isn't we'll see about somebody else I have in mind.' Marg was always pretty thorough, if formidable, in pursuit of a solution to any given problem.

I travelled to Melbourne to be with Anna on the day of her appointment, but when I volunteered to attend with her she refused. 'Nick, I'd feel more comfortable on my own.'

'You'll tell him everything, won't you, darling?' I begged. She nodded, but I knew she wouldn't or, more specifically, probably couldn't.

Later, back at my hotel, I asked her what the gynaecologist had said.

'There's nothing wrong with me physically, Nick. He found nothing specific,' she answered.

'Found? You mean he was able to do an internal examination?'

'No, not at first, then he gave me a local anaesthetic.'

'Now what?'

'He didn't say. He agreed it probably is vaginismus, but said there was no apparent physical cause for my condition.'

'You mean the spasms?'

'Yes.'

'What, that's all? He didn't suggest anything?'

'Only that I should keep trying to have sex.'

I sighed. 'And will you?'

Anna drew back. 'No, Nicholas! We've tried already, a *hundred* times. I can't. I just *can't*! That's all.' I realised then that Anna wasn't generalising, that she'd actually decided to make a hundred separate attempts to allow me to enter her and now she had given up.

'Anna, you're not alone in this,' I said evenly, trying to rally her a little.

'What do you mean?'

'Me. I'm a man, I have needs; we're partners,' I replied, trying not to show any emotion, to keep my voice matter of fact.

Anna started to cry. For once I said nothing, waiting, not

drawing her to me. 'But you're allowed to have other women,' she sniffed. 'We agreed.'

'Yes, but I don't love *them*. It's simply getting rid of my frustrations.' I paused, upset as hell. 'Anna, I don't want *them*! Just fucking is not enough. They mean nothing to me. I want *you*! Okay, you didn't like Dr Denmeade. Can't you see another shrink? Maybe next time you're overseas? Swiss doctors are supposed to be good at all that psychological stuff.'

'Nicholas, I love you more than my life. But we have tried a *hundred* times. I can't!' Her voice kept rising. 'I simply am unable! I spasm! Tighten! Lock up! It isn't you! It's me! If it's in my mind there's nothing I can do about it!' she shouted. Then as suddenly she grew calm again, took a deep breath and shrugged, her blue eyes glistening with tears. She looked directly at me and said quietly, 'That's all.'

What I wanted to say was that while my need for proper sex hadn't diminished, it was becoming less and less meaningful to me. I wasn't sleeping with whores, but I might as well have been. It wasn't fair to these other women, who were pleasant and loving, but sex without love does something to the male psyche, or at least it did to mine. I was trying hard to be decent to these generous and, I think, often caring women, but was finding it increasingly difficult to fake something I didn't feel. Intimacy is complex and the notion of getting rid of a build-up of semen is macho bullshit; wanking can do this just as efficiently with no complications.

And so the years passed. Good years. In every other way Anna was a delight and the week each month we spent together was heaps of fun. Of course we quarrelled on occasion, but never for long, except for one momentous occasion I will mention later and which, surprisingly, had nothing directly to do with the *Grotto of Knot*, which was how I had amended the expression.

Relationships, let alone with the kind of complications Anna and I faced, are hard enough to sustain and it was difficult to believe that twenty years had passed since we'd been reunited. I don't know how this is going to sound, but the sex thing and the addiction to heroin we somehow eventually managed to put aside. She controlled her habit so discreetly that I was almost never aware of it. If you'll forgive a bit of a lecture, the popular conception that heroin leads to physical ruin simply isn't always correct. Alcoholism is infinitely more dangerous to health than a well-managed addiction to good-quality heroin. The complications with heroin are caused by social factors. If it were as readily available as tobacco, and had similar quality controls, it would have a far less disastrous effect on community health and bring about fewer tragic repercussions.

Life is about making accommodations and Anna gave me more, much more, than she denied me. She could afford her habit, she didn't inject and she acted with the utmost discretion. I tried to be equally discreet about my physical needs, and the various island liaisons I enjoyed over the years were never mentioned between us. For my part, while I found that they were not emotionally fulfilling, nor provided the intimacy I desired, I tried to make up for my lack of closeness and commitment by being generous to each of them in other ways. It was a peculiar situation: I wasn't cheating on Anna yet I didn't think of myself as entitled to look for an alternative to her. I never entered a room filled with eligible women, say at a party, and told myself, 'Maybe tonight I'll meet the complete woman with whom I can share the remainder of my life.' I had only ever truly loved two women: Anna almost from the moment I'd set eyes on her, and Marg since a brief and passionate encounter during the war. I couldn't bring myself to imagine a third who might possibly replace these two in my affections.

I guess if friends had known about Anna and me it would have seemed pretty bizarre, but I saw very little to envy in the enduring conventional marriages I observed. Many seemed pretty dull and mundane. They were settled at best, most couples in a rut but reconciled to their lot: the devil you know, some companionship better than none, separate lives lived out under one roof, not sufficiently bad for a divorce, staying together for the children. And when the children had finally flown the coop, career prospects were limited, jobs routine, retirement ten years away, bowls, bingo, barbecues, boats and too much booze. There was nightly snoring, and weekly sex on a Saturday, or even worse, the mandatory birthday and Christmas naughty – *Oh, Gawd! Here he comes, his little willy trying to stand to attention. It must be Christmas morning, or has he remembered it's my birthday?*

However, as so often happens in life, you turn a corner, all unsuspecting, to discover your world has changed. Five years after the death of her husband, Marg was a regular visitor at Beautiful Bay, staying several days at a time. At fifty-four she was still a magnificent-looking woman, and to my mind still dead sexy. In the mathematics of love, a forty-six-year-old male and a fifty-four-year-old female form a better ratio than an eighteen-year-old male and a twenty-six-year-old female, which is how old we were when we first met in Fremantle.

One moonlit night at Beautiful Bay when Marg had been visiting and when, unusually for her, she'd had two or three G and Ts beyond her usual limit, she'd turned to me and said, 'Nick, how are things with Anna? Did you ever sort out the problem?'

In all those years she'd never brought up the subject of Anna's visit to the gynaecologist, a tribute to her discretion, but now the gin and tonic had done the trick.

I pretended not to understand her question, playing the dumb male. 'What problem were you referring to, Marg?'

'Nick, don't take me for a fool. Her vaginismus of course!'

'Oh, that,' I said, still pretending innocence. 'Yeah.'

'Yeah? What does that mean?'

'Yeah, she still has it,' I admitted, taking a sip of Scotch.

'And you? How do you manage?'

Marg had her eyes fixed steadily on me. She may have been a tad inebriated but it was the old Marg interrogation technique that brooked no platitudinous replies. She still had the ability to make me feel like a schoolboy caught with a mouthful of stolen pie. 'I . . . er . . . have several generous female arrangements.'

'Several?'

Generous female arrangements? Jesus! I winced inwardly at the clumsiness of my answer. 'Marg, I'd rather not —'

'How many?' she asked. 'Two? More?'

'More, but not in the same place . . . not here, living on the island,' I said, feeling foolish. Now that I was being questioned it seemed a bit boastful, but it wasn't, nor was it (what's the latest term for a testosterone-loaded sexual athlete?) macho! That wasn't at all how it was. Or how I felt. The number, I often reminded myself, was for my own safety, to stop me doing anything foolish, like committing myself when I was already committed. I'm pretty easy to force into a corner when it comes to women. I love the female gender for its own sake and their peculiar logic invariably defeats me. But how could I explain all this to Marg?

She suddenly dropped her gaze. I became conscious of her breathing, her splendid bosom moving – 'heaving' is the usual unavoidable expression. 'It's been five years since Rob died and I am no longer the admiral's wife, I'm Marg Hamilton again.' She looked up directly at me. 'Nick, you are the only other man I've ever loved, *still* love, care about,' she corrected quickly. 'I don't want to interfere with you and Anna. That's special.' She paused, grinned, swept back her hair with a defiant swing of her hand. 'But I don't think I'm over the hill and five years is simply too long!'

Drunk or sober Marg never let innuendo stand in the way of making her meaning clear. I was being propositioned and how I answered would affect our future.

The two of us together again in an intimate way had obviously been playing on her mind for some time, as, I confess, it had on mine. While I had been absolutely circumspect and had never brought up the possibility in the years after her husband died, I'd often enough lain in bed when she visited Beautiful Bay and thought of her sleeping two bedrooms away and had real difficulty restraining myself from getting up and tapping lightly on her door. I had never stopped desiring her and now I found myself lost for words.

'Marg, this comes as a bit of a surprise,' I ventured, stalling for time.

'Nick, don't talk nonsense, it's been on my mind and yours ever since Rob died. I've admired your restraint.'

'Even if that's true, and I don't deny it, it's still . . . well, it's bloody awkward.'

'Of course it's awkward!'

'It's being, well . . . duplicitous.'

'You mean unfaithful to Anna? What about the other women, your scattered regulars? What do you call that?'

'It's hard to explain. They ensure that I'm not unfaithful to Anna.'

Marg threw back her head and laughed. 'A second is duplicitous, five is safety in numbers? How very male!'

'Okay, would you like to be the sixth?' I asked suddenly.

Marg looked horrified. 'Of course not! I don't wish to be a member of anyone's harem!'

'See what I mean? I do not love them and they always knew it was an arrangement, one that benefitted all of us. That's pretty crude, I admit, even unfair. They are not harlots and probably deserve better. Anna knows about it without my being explicit.' I was getting in deeper and deeper and, I daresay, wasn't all that sober myself. 'Besides, with the impending Japanese trip I ended all of those "liaisons", call them what you may, several months ago.' I didn't add that this parting of the ways was much to the tearful and confessed disappointment, even chagrin in two cases, of these lovely and certainly blameless women, each of whom knew of the existence of the others. Nor did I add that in the islands my behaviour was considered neither unusual nor reprehensible. The ability of the white man to justify scattering his seed around the South Seas is the stuff of legends.

Marg had the grace to pull up at this stage and stop what was obviously a conversation that could only end in disaster. 'So, it's just you and Anna again. Is that what your trip to Japan is all about?'

This was a perceptive and difficult question. While Marg had some knowledge of Anna's past under the Japanese, she didn't know the story of Konoe Akira and the murder of the *kempeitai* colonel Takahashi. All I'd ever confided in her was that Anna had been a prisoner in a comfort women's establishment named the Nest of the Swallows and that her vaginismus was a result of the trauma she'd suffered under the Japanese.

'Marg, you were instrumental in having Anna see a psychiatrist several years ago. She's seen several since. You also know it obviously hasn't worked. There is a Japanese general who had a major influence on her, not a good one, I might add.

It was he who introduced her to *kinbaku*, the Japanese art of bondage. It has been suggested . . . no, that's not entirely true . . . we have come to hope that by confronting him there may be a resolution.'

'A cure?'

'Well, who knows, perhaps the beginning of one. By facing her demons there may be something tangible to work on.'

'So you've decided to be celibate?'

'I feel that she should know that I am no longer living a compromise, even one that is relatively harmless and would never challenge our relationship.' How pompous this all sounded.

'And you've told her this?'

'No, of course not; she would be put under additional pressure. It's something in my own psyche, knowing that I'm not having a bet each way. I don't need to tell her.'

'So you're saying if you and I . . .?'

'Marg, you know how I feel about you, always have, probably always will. I've never quite recovered from you and Rob Rich, and that's the problem. An affair with you right now – if Anna were to find out – would be a disaster. Japan may work, it may not, but if she were to find out we were having an affair, then any chance she has of living a normal life, of being cured, would be gone. And as you know, Anna is an extraordinarily perspicacious woman. She knows how I feel about you; she'd know it wasn't like the island women. She'd understand at once that you would be competing with her for my love and affection and she'd consider you had the advantage over her. I can't let her feel that. It would be terribly cruel, terribly destructive.' I knew I was rambling on, over-explaining, saying too much, but nevertheless I added rather sanctimoniously, 'She knows there has been nothing between us since Rob's death and that's important to her as we are about to embark on our first trip to Japan.'

Marg may have been a little sozzled, but her good mind was still working. 'And you've discussed all of this together?'

'All of what?'

'The reason you're going to Japan. The hope for a cure?'

'Obliquely, yes. Ostensibly we're going to Japan to buy a freighter. She's coming along for the ride, so to speak. The other is not something you can discuss in much detail. It's not like going to Lourdes and expecting a miracle cure; no psychiatrist she's seen will venture an opinion. It's all happening in her head. Our heads.' I shrugged. 'I have to play my part as well.'

Marg rose and put her half-finished gin and tonic on the rattan coffee table. 'It's high time I went to bed,' she said. Then she came towards me, stooped and kissed me lightly on the forehead. 'I've always loved you, Nick, almost from the first moment I set eyes on you, a sunburnt, barefoot, unshaven, long-haired boy in ragged, dirty shorts, without a shirt, who had sailed virtually single-handed across the Pacific Ocean to escape the Japanese.'

I laughed. 'Marg, you're being overly romantic. As I remember, I'd showered, shaved, and changed into clean gear. We first met upstairs in an office building in Fremantle where I was waiting to be interrogated by that dreadful little Australian Customs bloke, what was his name?'

Marg laughed, remembering. 'Mr Henry.'

'That's right, Mr Henry, who thought I might be a Japanese spy cunningly disguised as a six-foot three-inch, blue-eyed Australian. You were there supposedly to take notes. You were simply gorgeous, wonderful breasts, long legs, you wore a blue cotton dress and your hair was in a bun as if you were trying – unsuccessfully I might add – to look plain. You were sexy as hell and, I knew, well beyond anyone I could ever aspire to kiss, not that I'd dared to dream.'

'That's not where I first saw you,' Marg persisted. 'When you docked in Fremantle you were met by the police and Lieutenant Commander Rigby as you stepped off your little yacht, *Madam Butterfly*. You may not recall, but as a matter of routine an official photograph was taken for our Naval Intelligence files. It arrived in my in-tray a couple of hours before your interrogation took place. An eight by ten black-and-white print, but that's all it took. I knew then that I had to have that cheeky grin all to myself.'

'Marg, you've never told me this,' I cried in surprise, knowing the immediate crisis between us was over.

'See you at breakfast, Nick.' She turned and left, then halted at the verandah screen door. Holding it open she turned again to face me. 'When I might even show you the photograph. Goodnight, Nick, darling.'

PART TWO

CHAPTER FIVE

*'Ask the stupid gaijin who insults us
by bringing his whore and robbing us
of a night out eating and drinking
what type of vessel he wants to buy.'*
Fukuoka-san, Mitsubishi executive

A CHILD DOES NOT judge the people surrounding him
unless they affect him personally. I had spent the first seven
years of my life in Japan, but I had forgotten the experience of
day-to-day living, and besides, a great deal had changed since I
had left with my father to travel to New Britain in 1935.

Paradoxically, although Anna and I spoke the Japanese
language with commendable fluency, we knew very little about
the people. My knowledge was almost entirely based on my
father's reminiscences and his academic interest in Japanese
culture. Putting it crudely, as an adult the closest I had come
to the Japanese in any numbers was when they'd charged me
in battle with fixed bayonets and, in turn, I had mowed them
down with an Owen submachine-gun.

Anna's exposure to Japanese culture was, to say the least,
problematic. Her mentor, Konoe Akira, had instructed her only
in the things that interested him. These were mostly to do with
how she deported herself, the niceties of language, her manners
and appearance and the appreciation of art. The remainder of
her experience had been deeply traumatic.

Ours was therefore a mishmash of theory, practice and trauma and we may well have been better off starting from scratch with no knowledge whatsoever. Very little of what we thought we knew manifested itself in the Japan in which we landed in the northern spring on the 13th of April 1970, the same day that Apollo 13, on its way to the moon, developed a problem that seemed certain to result in the lonely death of its crew in space. The entire world was glued to their televisions as the crew prepared for the end. It seemed an inauspicious omen, for in a small way, Anna and I had launched ourselves into an alien environment where we too could very well come unstuck.

At Anna's insistence we'd ordered a limousine to take us from Haneda Airport to the new Imperial Hotel, one of the grandest hostelries in Tokyo and yet another Anna request. 'Nicholas, for the sake of my self-confidence I must arrive in style. I will observe the courtesies they expect, I will not seem brash or demanding, but I will not bow to any man as a subservient being.'

This was Anna-speak for a fearful inner disquiet. Outwardly there was almost no sign of the frightened little creature who still lingered within, the teenager who had faced the Japanese invaders alone and somehow survived but had never fully recovered from the experience and was again going to face her demons. Japan was to be a test for her, and my hope, of course, was that the ghosts that still haunted her from the past would finally be laid to rest.

The Anna arriving in Japan seemed to exude natural confidence and poise. At forty-four she looked ten years younger and remained an astonishingly beautiful woman who, upon entering a noisy boardroom, would often bring it to sudden silence. Everything about her was understated, yet redolent of class. Her dress, jewellery, make-up and deportment all accentuated her natural beauty. She had perfected Konoe Akira's concept of less is more, that one exquisite detail is more powerful than flashy ostentatious show. While she made no demands to be noticed, she simply couldn't be ignored.

However, I sensed that, while she had agreed with alacrity to accompany me, she felt deeply apprehensive about visiting Japan; it had been a decision requiring a great deal of courage. By insisting on all the trappings of wealth, she was, in effect, maintaining her distance. She had learned that an elegant and beautiful woman stepping from the rear seat of a Mercedes-Benz is not as accessible as one, equally elegant and gorgeous, stepping from a taxi, train or bus.

We had entered a country where women had no presence or power. Japan had practised the diminution of the female for centuries and few heroic female figures had ever featured in its history. Despite the changing times, there had been little improvement in the status of the female sex, except perhaps in their appearance, where the deliberate constraints of the kimono had often been replaced by Western dress, including the miniskirt and platform-soled shoes, popular with bar girls and secretaries.

Later I came to realise that by maintaining a quiet aloofness Anna was signalling that she was not subservient to businessmen. She even grew to enjoy the attempts of the Japanese businessmen to hide the acute discomfort and even anger they felt when she trapped them with a question on finance or framed an answer indicating an astute insight that clearly surprised them.

At first sight the Tokyo we entered seemed to be a Western paradigm, but we were to discover that this was not the case, despite the contemporary architecture. Tokyo remained unmistakably a Japanese city. Nestled seemingly in the cracks and crevices of the myriad high-rise towers would be a Shinto temple, a restaurant, home, traditional market or even a lamppost that was uniquely Japanese. These were the familiar touchstones of the city, its creature comforts and quiet assurances, lacking in Western cities, where the people appeared undaunted by the bland anonymity of the structures surrounding them. Tokyo was not only quintessentially Japanese, more than anything it was a city of and for people.

We'd arrived after sunset and the Ginza district seemed to be pumping out sound and light. Facing one side of the Imperial Hotel was the world's most dazzling light show, an explosion of neon colours that twinkled, spat, arched, zigzagged, spiralled, leapt and blinked, the colours singeing the edges of the towering buildings and tinting the clouds. The roar of the Ginza traffic, added to the visual shock, made me think that all colour and all sound coalesced in one place. Yet, somehow the major feature of the place remained the people. Looking down from our hotel window onto their dark heads, I thought they resembled an army of ants, teeming over the lighted pavement until it appeared to be an endlessly moving platform.

We were to learn that in Japan nothing is what it seems to be. Even though we understood many of the subtle nuances of language, we simply never knew quite where we stood, and even the most formal conversations seemed to contain dark shadows we couldn't penetrate.

It might have been simpler if Anna hadn't accompanied me to Mitsubishi, but we'd decided to do everything together for the added experience it would bring us, and although I said nothing, I felt it might prove that we were quintessentially a couple and diminish the ever-present spectre of Konoe Akira.

We'd also agreed to speak English until such time as we both believed the people we were talking to could be trusted not to be duplicitous, which, I suppose, indicates duplicity on our part. We were instinctively arming ourselves in anticipation of the two deadly conversational *m's*: mistrust and misunderstanding.

By the standards of the giant shipbuilder, my purchase was small beer. They didn't as a rule sell second-hand ships, but they possessed a small fleet of inter-island freighters they'd accepted as part of a deal to build four larger ships for a client in the Philippines. Anna had been informed of the existence of these freighters by a Japanese client who had been transferred from the Mitsubishi shipbuilding division to Sydney to drum up business in Australia and who had visited her on his frequent business trips to Melbourne. He had given us a letter of introduction to his head office, sending a copy on to them. It was normal procedure to deal with a broker who was usually retained by the larger shipbuilders to act on their behalf, but we hoped to use the introduction to avoid the middleman's percentage and so secure a better deal with the shipbuilding giant. I was hoping to obtain one or even two freighters at a bargain price.

It was the first time that I had stood to benefit from business conducted privately in a house of bondage, a world Anna never spoke about in detail and one I had never entered even to meet her. I must admit I initially felt a little uncomfortable briefing Anna on our requirements when she'd mentioned a client who seemed anxious to help. As the son of an Anglican missionary I was clearly still something of a prude, but somehow that letter of introduction felt dodgy, or even illegitimate. I could hardly say we had conducted our island business with the utmost propriety when it had begun with the money Kevin had made skimming his illicit commissions off the top of navy supply contracts. Still it felt strange and so I had spoken to both Kevin and Joe Popkin about the matter.

Kevin didn't blink an eye. 'Nick, whatcha saying? Der sumthin' wrong? You crazy! Business don't need no office, don't matter if it happen in da shithouse or da White House. Be grateful, grab it wid both fuckin' hands. Then thank God or da devil for tappin' you on da shoulder. Opportunity it like free pussy – you ain't gonna ask too many questions when it come yer way.'

Joe as usual thought for a while. 'Nick, my man, it ain't no problem of ours dat dis Japanese he like himself tied wid a rope so he all truss up and den he want to have himself some sweet conversation wid Miss Anna. We don't pay him no bribe and all he wanna do is show his appre-ci-ation, be helpful. Ain't no crime I can see in dat. You all go to the club, get pissed wid somebody, make a deal, and everthin' gonna be all right, only contrak you got is a bottle Scotch whisky you done drink together.' He spread his hands. 'So what da difference?'

In the foyer of the executive building at the Mitsubishi shipyard we were met by a young bloke wearing a merchant navy uniform with the Mitsubishi logo on his cap holding up a sign with our names printed on it in English. After making ourselves known, we were escorted to a small boardroom where we were met by two executives and a translator. 'You are most welcome to Mitsubishi, sir,' the translator said, bowing.

'Thank you. My name is Nick Duncan and may I present Miss Anna Til,' I said, indicating Anna.

The translator looked unsmilingly at Anna, then turned and removed one of the chairs from the small boardroom table and placed it against the wall. Standing at rigid attention he gave a sharp nod of the head. 'Please . . . you sit here,' he instructed.

I immediately realised that he thought Anna was my secretary, but explaining to him that she was my business partner would cause him to lose face. So I stepped forward and took a second chair and placed it beside the one intended for Anna. 'Thank you,' Anna said politely to the translator, and then, smiling at the two young executives, sat down. I joined her in the vacant chair making it appear that we thought this was correct Japanese business procedure. Whereupon the yet to be introduced executives, both of whom now wore decidedly bemused expressions, each removed a chair from the table and placed it beside me and sat down. Moments later the translator followed suit.

The five of us were now seated in a line against the wall with the unoccupied boardroom table some two metres away. It wasn't a propitious beginning.

'You have not introduced us, you fool,' one of the executives said to the translator in Japanese.

Whereupon the seated translator, looking thoroughly confused, jumped to his feet. 'This Mr *Nakamura-san*,' he said, indicating the Japanese executive seated beside me. With a stiff nod of the head he then turned and repeated the gesture. 'This Mr *Fukuoka-san*.'

Both men jumped to their feet and snapped their heads forward in a simulated bow and grunted, '*Hai!*'

'Also I . . . Mr Bando,' the translator said, bowing a little more formally. All three had studiously avoided eye contact with Anna or any other form of recognition for that matter. Now they returned to their seats against the wall.

'Ask the stupid *gaijin* who insults us by bringing his whore and robbing us of a night out eating and drinking what type of vessel he wants to buy,' *Fukuoka-san* instructed Mr Bando.

'Whatever it is, sir, we should make him pay dearly for our disappointment,' *Bando-san* said, meanwhile leaning forward and smiling at me.

'*Duncan-san*, Mitsubishi have many ship, what kind you want? Mr Fukuoka he ask you.'

'A small freighter suitable for inter-island work, about fifty metres long, in good condition, no more than fifteen years old. It is all in my letter of introduction,' I answered.

The translator passed this on and the two Japanese conferred. Then one of them, *Nakamura-san*, stood up and went to the boardroom table and retrieved a manila folder and handed it to the second executive, obviously his senior. *Fukuoka-san* opened the folder and after riffling through several pieces of paper and what appeared to be a contract, the government purchase permit we'd obtained, survey certificates and a brochure, he finally extracted our letter, written by Anna's client in Japanese. He looked at the document carefully to give the appearance of seeing it for the first time and when finally he'd completed reading it he placed it back in the folder and handed it to *Bando-san* who returned it to the table and then sat down again. Ignoring our presence *Fukuoka-san* spoke directly to *Bando-san*.

'As you know the letter says they want a freighter, or if the price is right they may take another. Of the twenty-eight such inter-islanders we have laid up, eight of them are rust buckets equipped with short-range fuel tanks. Let's make the *gaijin* settle for one of these. We'll tell him we can't keep up with the demand and have only two vessels for sale at present. If he's prepared to offer us a good price he may take them off our hands. By the way, you'll have to cancel the restaurant tonight. We can't have him bringing the Chinese whore. Pity, there is a bar girl just around the corner who promised me a nice surprise – only ten thousand yen for fifteen minutes of her valuable time . . . You'd think they were queuing up outside for her favours!' He smiled and then collected himself.

I realised that they thought Anna was Chinese, which would have added greatly to their chagrin. Except for the Koreans, no people are less worthy in the eyes of the Japanese, who had committed bestial atrocities against helpless victims in the wars in China and Manchuria, among other things using Chinese civilians for live bayonet practice. We were to be punished for not only ruining their plans for an all-male night out at company expense, including a visit to a love hotel with a bar hostess, but also for the supreme insult of bringing a Chinese woman into the premises to negotiate with them. I guess it was three strikes and you're out; a woman, a Chinese and an all-male banquet denied.

'What if he knows his ships and isn't fooled?' *Bando-san* cautioned. 'Didn't his letter of introduction say he owned a small fleet?'

Fukuoka-san was unimpressed. '*Pfft!* This *gaijin* who brings a woman with him to buy a ship can't know much about ships or men. Take my word for it. He is an *ōbaka* [a big idiot]. Besides, all eight vessels have had a lick of paint to cover the rust. There is a broker who wants six of them for an African buyer, a Nigerian, who can't afford more, that's why they're not included in the brochure. He has offered sixty thousand US dollars each, a fair price. That leaves two of the eight leaky tubs.'

'We don't want to be too greedy, sir. The Africans want those six for short trips to load the bigger ships lying out to sea off Lagos. All the other prospective buyers have rejected them because of their limited fuel capacity – their cruising range is too short.'

'This *baka* [fool], who brings with him this *hafu* [this

half-breed], won't know that.' He turned to Mr Bando, the translator. 'Tell the *gaijin* that unfortunately we have only two ships available, but even they are in demand. We are only talking to him because he has come a long way from Australia, and out of courtesy for our representative in Sydney. Tell him we regret, but he must take it or leave it. The two ships we hope will prove to be ideal for his purposes, but he will need to make up his mind in twenty-four hours and the cost is one hundred thousand US dollars each.'

Bando-san looked momentarily doubtful, realising that *Fukuoka-san* had added a premium of eighty thousand US dollars for the two freighters. As Anna was sitting beside me I couldn't see her face, which I knew would be perfectly composed while inwardly she'd be a raging inferno. But then Anna always looked coolest when she was fired up. I'd have to tread carefully. Anna had insisted on being thoroughly briefed on every specification. It was her way. No matter how small the business transaction, she did her homework so that she wouldn't be caught out on some small neglected detail. On the plane, despite my insisting that I knew ships and how to buy one, she'd laughed, glancing at me with her blue eyes wide. 'Nicholas, I couldn't sit in a meeting and not understand every aspect of the negotiations. I *must* know, I must be able to think, to plan the next move. Knowledge is power!'

'But, Anna, I will do all the negotiations,' I insisted.

'Yes, of course! But, Nicholas, you said they would take at least three days – our first meeting with them, our visit to the harbour to inspect the freighter the following day, then back for the final negotiations. We will need to discuss things each day when we get back to the hotel. If I don't understand *everything*, then how can I be useful?' she said appealingly, then added, 'We have never done business together. I must not let you down, darling. My client told me about these two ships and the possibility of buying them in good condition for less than a new one would cost. I could never forgive myself if something went wrong. You must brief me, please.'

Now, seated in this ridiculous row against the wall we listened to the ultimatum *Fukuoka-san* offered us. I sensed that Anna ached to have a go at them – they were small fry and not in her league but nevertheless needed to be taught a lesson. They'd fondly believed they'd set a trap for us and I'm sure she wanted to extract the cheese from it, leaving it unsprung and her would-be assailants totally bewildered.

While I could handle myself in any boardroom and usually knew what I wanted to achieve, Anna was and always would be the better negotiator. She simply had the patience, cunning and intuition I lacked. Furthermore, she enjoyed the process immensely and needed to win for too many reasons in her past to discuss. This would be especially true against the Japanese. These two clever dicks conspiring to cheat us because of 'the insult' of her presence in the room she would regard as simply too good an opportunity to resist.

For my part, I would have enjoyed nothing more than to stand up, grab both of them by the lapels of their cheap blue serge suits, lift them bodily off the floor and bang their heads together while castigating them in Japanese. I could even think of the precise phrase to use – *baka wa shinanakuya naoranai* [a fool is only cured by dying]. Alas that pleasure would have to wait.

Fukuoka-san gave me an ingenuous smile as the translator announced the offer, stressing that we must make up our minds quickly.

I returned the smile, almost neglecting to wait for the translator to finish. 'Ah, thank you, *Fukuoka-san*.
We would be greatly honoured to discuss this generous offer with

you and your esteemed colleague,' I said in the exaggerated formal Japanese manner while still speaking in English.

Mr Bando, the translator, looked pleased, no doubt relieved that we hadn't understood the previous conversation between the two executives. He quickly translated, retaining the formal style of my reply. *Fukuoka-san* and *Nakamura-san* smiled broadly, nodding their heads, both looking extremely pleased with themselves.

I turned to Anna and smiled. 'Whacko, Anna, over to you, give bib and bub their comeuppance.' This was a sentence Mr Bando had no way of translating and he looked totally confused.

Only the tiniest flicker in Anna's eyes registered her surprise. 'Thank you, Nicholas, however did you guess?' she said, rising from her chair. She carried it to one end of the boardroom table where she seated herself. 'Mr Bando, would you kindly bring your seat to the left side of the table. Mr Nakamura and Mr Fukuoka on the right side if you please and Nicholas at the other end.'

Mr Bando was too astonished to react and stood looking at Anna and then at the two executives. I grinned and jumped up with alacrity, taking my chair and placing it at the opposite end to Anna and sitting down. The translator, overcome with apprehension as well as confusion, pointed wordlessly at the right side of the table then stammered, 'She wants you to sit there.'

Both men turned to look at each other, their expressions just as surprised as Mr Bando's had been. It struck me that they hadn't yet understood that somehow the tables had turned and the advantage no longer lay with them. They were both small men and now seated in front of them was a six-foot three-inch Caucasian male and a slim, incredibly beautiful female who seemed perfectly composed and completely in control. She was also in the process of ordering them in the politest possible manner to do as she required, there being no way they could resist without remaining seated like supplicants against the wall of the boardroom.

The two men brought their chairs over and positioned them at the table as they had been instructed, *Fukuoka-san* collecting himself enough to mutter 'Kusatta gaijin! [Stinking rotten foreigners!]'

Anna waited until they were properly seated then she pointed at the manila folder. 'I noticed that you have a brochure in that folder. I would be grateful if you would tell us which of the two ships of the twenty it features are the ones not yet sold, Mr Fukuoka.'

Bando-san translated and *Fukuoka-san* nodded his head vigorously. 'No, no, those are all sold, we have two others.'

Anna waited for the translation. 'These two others, what is the survey status?' she asked.

The answer came from Mr Nakamura. 'The vessels are from the Philippines; we have not yet translated the information.'

'Oh, that will be no problem. Ship surveys in the Philippines are conducted in English. If you will let us have the papers we can read them ourselves,' I said, as Anna wouldn't have known this detail.

'Not possible,' *Fukuoka-san* said.

'Confidential information,' *Nakamura-san* added quickly.

The tedium of translation proceeded.

'Oh? But, of course, we would need to see the current survey certificates if we are to purchase the vessels,' Anna insisted quietly.

Fukuoka-san thumped the table. 'This is Mitsubishi. You will trust us – we will not be insulted by you!'

Anna did not react. 'Can you tell us the cruising range, the capacity of the fuel tanks?' she asked calmly.

'Not available!' *Fukuoka-san* yelled at Mr Bando. 'Tell the *kyabajō* [cabaret girl, ergo prostitute] we want a decision today or the vessels will be sold. We have a buyer waiting!'

Anna waited for the translation, which *Bando-san* modified. 'Unfortunately there is another buyer. You must give Mr Fukuoka your decision today.'

It was a mistake. 'Ah, then if you have a buyer who is so careless he will buy two vessels without a current survey certificate and no idea of the cruising range of the fuel tanks, then you must let him take them.' Anna smiled. 'With the greatest respect, Mr Fukuoka, there is also more information we would need as well as the right to inspect the ship, possibly with our own engineer.' Anna paused and gave the Japanese man a brilliant smile. 'Please permit me to list the additional information required from Mitsubishi if we are to proceed.' Whereupon Anna, not waiting for his reaction, reeled off the information we would need: 'When was each ship launched? Who built them? What are the displacement weights, including cargo? We need to know the cubic capacity of the holds. Refrigerated cargo capacity? Draught-depth? The type of engines they have? Hours run and their maintenance history? Fuel consumption – gallons per hour at cruise? Can you tell us the number of generators on board and their respective voltages? Navigation equipment and cargo-handling equipment?'

I admit, I was totally gob-smacked. Anna had sailed on *Madam Butterfly* since she was a child but in terms of a cargo vessel, she would struggle to tell the prow from the stern. She had simply memorised precisely what I had told her on the plane from Hong Kong to Tokyo.

All this enumeration took some translating and *Bando-san*, obviously familiar with the nautical language from previous negotiations, made a fair fist of it. By the time he was finished,

Mr Nakamura's head was in his hands and Mr Fukuoka repeatedly banged the boardroom table with his fist. The corners of his mouth spittle flecked, he yelled, 'No negotiation! Tell the *kusatta gaijin* [stinking rotten foreigners] it is over! No more talk! No inspection! Go away!' He waved his hand towards the boardroom door.

Mr Bando translated this as: '*Fukuoka-san* regrets we cannot continue to negotiate. Mitsubishi cannot sell you these ships.'

Anna rose from the table and stood quietly waiting for *Fukuoka-san* to calm down, whereupon she said evenly in Japanese, '*Kako o mizu ni nagasu.* [Let the past float with water.]' The consummate negotiator was giving the Mitsubishi executives a chance to begin again. Later I would realise that by remaining calm and seemingly reasonable she had exacerbated their loss of face.

For my part, now that we'd let the cat out of the bag, I was furious. '*Baka ga ate rikō ga hikitatsu.* [In the presence of fools wise men stand out.]' I pointed to Anna and said, 'You are unprofessional and have insulted my honourable partner. *Nō aru taka wa tsume o kakusu.* [The hawk with talent hides its talons.] You would do well to be less smug and more attentive. As shipping men you are a disgrace!' I turned to face *Fukuoka-san*. 'You should be more careful in future. Not all *gaijin* should be taken for fools, nor should all Japanese be seen as honourable men. My hope is that we have both gained from this experience.'

Anna's hands rested flat on the boardroom table and she raised the index finger on her right hand to indicate that I should say no more. Then leaning forward slightly she bowed her head formally and looking up at the two executives she smiled. 'We thank you for your honourable presence and your valuable time, *Fukuoka-san* and *Nakamura-san*. We have appreciated your openness and your sentiments.' Then turning to Mr Bando she continued, 'Bando-san, your most honourable translation was very discreet and you are to be congratulated. Furthermore, it is customary in the West for women to sit at the same table as men, but I want you to know I respect your ways and took no offence whatsoever. Will you do us the great honour of personally escorting us to the foyer where we have a limousine waiting for us?' Anna's spoken Japanese was of a class above that spoken by the three Japanese men and so formal that they would have been even further humiliated.

In the back of the limousine on our return to the Imperial, Anna apologised. 'Nick, I am so sorry!' she said, plainly distressed.

'Sorry? What for? It wasn't your fault. Bastards!'

'I shouldn't have been with you,' she exclaimed.

'What! And missed all that? We learned more in that hour than we might have in a week or a month.' I smiled. 'You were very clever, darling.'

'Not clever enough; we failed.'

'Ah, don't worry. There are dozens of brokers. Besides it was probably too good to be true, getting two vessels in good shape for the price of a new one was always going to be a big ask. We'll revert to the original plan to buy a new ship and contact Mitsui at Chiba and IHI shipyard at Yokohama. It'll be fun to see how *they* go thinking we don't understand their lingo.'

'No! Not yet. We're not through with these bastards yet.'

'Don't let it get to you, Anna. We have a lot to learn about Japan and that was lesson number one.'

'I'm a good learner but a very poor loser, Nicholas,' she said somewhat primly.

Back at the hotel Anna made a phone call to her Japanese client who'd provided the introduction to Mitsubishi. She spoke to him for over an hour while I had a beer at the bar downstairs and then went into the dining room for lunch where she joined me halfway through my main course.

'How'd you go with *Kobi-san*?' I asked.

'Lots of tut-tutting and glottal sounds, I imagine a fair bit of head shaking, and an abject apology every two minutes. He said all boardroom business meetings are recorded.'

'Bugged?'

'Yes, he explained it was for future reference if things went wrong and for review by their senior executives. When I suggested the record of our conversation might be destroyed he said that wasn't possible, it would lead to instant dismissal. It seems paranoia is universal in Japan.'

'So?'

'Well, he said he'd call head office and alert them to the meeting.'

'Bit late, isn't it? I'm not inclined to go back.'

'Fine, but let's at least wait and see.'

Anna once explained to me that winning wasn't always about reaching the top of the mountain; sometimes whoever clung longest to the cliff-face without falling was the ultimate winner. 'Business seldom has a formal start and definite finish but is more like a constant cliff climb,' she'd said. 'After you've won, you keep climbing.'

'Righto, we'll wait. But as far as I'm concerned, stuff 'em. Plenty more ships in the sea.'

The following morning just after nine the phone in the hotel suite rang. 'Mr Duncan, the contingent from Mitsubishi has arrived,' the concierge announced, adding, 'We have booked a private lounge for you. Is there anything else you will need?'

Accustomed to rising early I had dressed and had returned from a walk in the Hibiya Park that directly faced the hotel and was looking forward to breakfast. But Anna had only just bathed and was still drying her hair in the bathroom. I thanked the concierge, and replaced the phone. 'Better hurry and get dressed, darling, we have visitors!' I shouted above the racket the hairdryer was making.

The hairdryer ceased and moments later Anna called, 'What? Did I hear you say visitors?'

'Yeah, Mitsubishi!' I exclaimed.

Anna laughed. 'Now what?'

'Who knows? They've booked a private lounge. How long will you take?'

She walked into the bedroom wearing an oyster-coloured silk dressing-gown and fluffing her hair so that it appeared to fall to her shoulders in slow motion. I was reminded that even without make-up she was a beautiful woman. 'Wait ten minutes, darling . . . then go down,' she advised. 'We don't want to appear too anxious. I'll be down soon. Order coffee, juice, whatever.' Then as a sudden afterthought she giggled, 'Speak Japanese, we don't want to get off on the wrong foot.'

Downstairs we proceeded to go through the introductions, exchanging our calling cards in the two-handed manner of the Japanese, bowing formally.

I apologised and said that my partner Anna Til had been delayed and sent profuse apologies but would join us in half an hour. This was received with some warmth and it was at once obvious that the group had been well briefed.

'We are honoured by her presence, *Duncan-san*,' said *Hashimoto-san*, who appeared to be the head honcho. He was a man already slightly greying who appeared to be in his late fifties. His business card indicated that he was senior vice-president in charge of sales. Two of the others were vice-presidents, one in the shipbuilding department, the other from the engineering department. The fourth was a senior translator in English and French from customer relations who wore the thickest lenses I had ever seen in a pair of spectacles. I guess this time they weren't taking any chances. All, with perhaps the exception of the translator, were senior to the two ingrates we'd met the previous day.

We sat down on the two lounges facing each other, the respective business cards we'd been given laid out in front of us on the low table separating the couches. They seemed pleased that I had greeted them in Japanese and we continued to converse in their own language. *Hashimoto-san* congratulated me on my fluency and expressed surprise when I said that I had been born in Japan. I then explained that my father had been headmaster of the International School in Tokyo. The Japanese have great respect for scholars and as the bishop's offspring I sensed I'd gained a little more status in their eyes.

It was strictly small talk until Anna arrived wearing a coffee-coloured Chanel suit, sheer stockings and brown alligator-skin Charles Jourdan stiletto-heeled shoes. She wore a single diamond in each ear. Nothing more, not even a bangle or a wristwatch. Fashion wasn't exactly my strong point, but we'd been shopping the previous afternoon at Mitsukoshi, one of the grandest department stores in Japan, where she'd bought both the suit and the shoes. When I'd exclaimed at the outrageous price she'd given me a short lecture on Coco Chanel's famous haute couture ensemble and Mr Jourdan's piss-elegant shoes. 'It's standard boardroom chic,' she'd explained. 'Men don't need it and can look like a dero and get away with it. Like the proverbial book we are definitely judged by our cover.

The woman who doesn't present well in everything doesn't get a hearing.'

The four Japanese jumped to their feet as Anna approached. '*Anna-sama*,' *Hashimoto-san* said bowing deeply, and showing by his use of the title '*sama*' his respect for her status. There was another round of introductions and the meeting finally began.

No apology was offered, in fact no mention was made of the previous day, for which we were both thankful. Instead *Hashimoto-san* said that Mitsubishi was glad to welcome us as honoured customers and that they had looked carefully at the letter of introduction stating our needs. He then 'humbly suggested' that the best of the freighters in the brochure be sold to us for one hundred thousand US dollars and combined in a package with a brand-new ship. He explained that a small island shipping line in Ceylon had gone bankrupt and had forfeited a twenty-five per cent deposit on a new vessel. If we wished to purchase this vessel as well, they would consider deducting the deposit they held and, as a gesture of goodwill (read, apology), another twenty-five per cent, which was the profit margin.

I did the sums in my head and immediately accepted. It meant that I would be getting two freighters, a brand-new one and a second one in excellent condition, for close to or slightly more than the market price for the new ship. Even Kevin would be pleased.

I signed the contract subject to an independent engineer's inspection of both ships. Then, in the Japanese tradition of handing out gifts at the conclusion of a meeting or negotiation, we were both presented with elaborately wrapped parcels and, among copious assurances that we would remain customer friends for the future, they departed with everyone's 'face' still intact and Mitsubishi's honour restored. Anna, looking ravishing, hadn't opened her mouth other than to greet them.

The Shinto gods were in their temple and all was right with the world.

Back in our suite we fell into each other's arms and danced around the room, then we opened our gifts. Mine was an inlaid cherry-wood box decorated with a sprig of cherry blossom and fastened with a beautiful brass clasp that resembled a dragon. When I opened it, displayed inside were two dozen of the finest Havana cigars together with a solid silver cigar cutter. Kevin and Joe would be the recipients of the cigars and the beautiful box would remain with me as a memento of the time Anna and I had spent together in Japan.

Anna gasped as she opened her gift. 'Oh my God! Look, Nicholas!' She held up a double string of Mikimoto cultured pearls. Although Anna could, or would eventually be able to, buy just about anything she wanted, that string of cultured pearls remained among her most cherished jewellery; eventually I would bury her with it.

'I see what you mean by being the last to cling to the cliff. Well done, darling. If it had been left to me I would have waited outside the gates of Mitsubishi for those little Nip bastards and knocked their heads together, biffed them on the nose and sent them on their way with a kick up the arse. Bloody good thing you came along.'

But that evening after dinner and a bottle of French champagne, Anna said to me as we retired to the lounge for coffee, 'Nicholas, I must go out tonight and I don't want you to come.'

'Anna!' I exclaimed, more than a tad surprised. 'What is it?'

'I need heroin,' she said simply.

'Oh shit! You didn't bring it?'

'I did, but I was too afraid of Japanese customs to bring much.

I bought a pair of those ghastly platform-soled shoes and had the heel hollowed out, but now I've run out.'

'When?'

'Yesterday. The last I used before going into the meeting at Mitsubishi.'

'But that was, let me see, thirty-six hours ago.'

She grimaced. 'Don't know it!'

'Wherever will you get it? And how? You don't have any contacts here in Japan.'

'Yes, Nicholas, I do. I have an introduction to a very exclusive bondage house in Roppongi. I will be quite safe. I've ordered a limousine.'

'They'll sell you heroin?'

'They will know how I may obtain it.'

'I'll come. I'll wait in the car.'

'No, Nick! I go alone there!' I noted the 'Nick', and Anna's abrupt change of syntax; she was plainly upset.

Suddenly suspicious, I asked, 'Anna, promise me you're not meeting Konoe Akira.'

'Nick, I am not your wife! I am going now *mit* a driver. No, there is no *Konoe-san* there at that place. I am going two hours, maybe also more.' Her battered syntax and irritable tone indicated clearly that she was undergoing withdrawal. She clasped her arms about her chest, hugging herself, rubbing the surface of her upper arms unconsciously.

'Anna!' I protested. 'Just give me the name of the place, just in case . . .'

'No!'

'Why?'

'Nick!' she cried in exasperation. 'You cannot come inside that place!'

Anna turned and left, walking rapidly across the foyer

to where the limos were parked. Feeling like a weak shit, not knowing what to do, I followed and watched from the steps of the hotel as she entered a big black car. A taxi drew up and two Japanese girls in miniskirts and the now almost mandatory platform soles came up the steps laughing. 'Taxi!' I shouted on a sudden impulse. Halfway towards the waiting cab a young Japanese man in a black suit and sunglasses ran up and opened the rear door. 'Excuse me, that's my taxi!' I shouted in Japanese, moving quickly towards him.

The doorman stepped directly into my path. 'No, sir, *yakuza*!' he warned.

'Bullshit!' I said in English and, pushing him roughly aside, reached the cab just as the bloke in black was closing the rear door. I yanked it from his grasp, flung it wide then grabbed his arm and pulled him out of the cab. It wasn't difficult; I was furious and twice his size. He landed sprawling on the pavement and I jumped into the taxi. 'Roppongi!' I shouted to the driver, then pointing to the tail lights of Anna's limo added, 'Follow that black one.'

He didn't move. '*Yakuza*!' he exclaimed, leapt from the cab and ran around to my side to help the doorman lift the bloke to his feet.

I got out of the cab and stood over them. I seemed to be bigger than all three put together and suddenly I started to laugh. The bloke I'd pulled from the taxi was only a skinny kid and I could see from the scared look in his eyes that he was out of his depth, anticipating a good belting from the giant *gaijin* looking down at him. I stooped and picked up his sunglasses, lost in the fall. 'I'm sorry,' I said, handing him his glasses. 'You may take the taxi with my compliments.' I handed the driver a handful of yen. 'Take this *kobun* wherever he's going.' It was too late anyway. Anna's limousine had long since disappeared into the endless flow of Ginza traffic.

The fact that I spoke Japanese and referred to the *yakuza* kid as *kobun* (the lowest member of a *yakuza* 'family') seemed to do the trick. The kid climbed back into the taxi, vigorously brushing the sleeve of his black suit and avoiding eye contact. The driver, not knowing what to make of the big *gaijin* who spoke fluent Japanese and didn't appear respectful of the *yakuza*, bowed and then moved quickly to the driver's seat and pulled away.

As I watched, the rear window of the taxi was wound down and the kid shouted, '*Kusatta gaijin!*' It was the second time in forty-eight hours I had been called a stinking foreigner. I laughed as I returned to the hotel entrance. The kid had been flexing his muscles, assuming authority that in this instance it turned out he didn't have.

I handed the doorman a tip which he accepted without looking down. 'Sir, you must be careful, the *yakuza*, they are not like us.' Then, glancing at his hand and seeing the generous gratuity, he jerked his head in acknowledgement. 'Even the young ones, they are dangerous,' he warned.

'Ah, just a cheeky kid,' I replied.

My knowledge of the *yakuza*, like so much else about Japan, was from my father, which was why I had known the term to use for the youngster. I knew I was fortunate that he hadn't been a senior member, though I had been so preoccupied by and frustrated with Anna that had he been an *oyabun* I would probably have done the same thing.

The *yakuza*, like the mafia, are formed into families, the *oyabun* [godfather] taking in or adopting youngsters, usually from poor and disadvantaged families, who begin as *kobun*, advance through *wakagashira* to *oyabun* if they are able and lucky.

The *yakuza* pride themselves on being followers of *bushido*, the Samurai code of honour that involves the concepts of *giri*, honour, and *ninjō*, compassion, though both characteristics appeared to be seldom present in *yakuza* in the seventies. Nonetheless, despite being little more than organised thugs for hire, in the eyes of Japanese society they still retained something of the aura of Robin Hood.

Like so much in Japanese society that is inexplicable to Western minds, the *yakuza* played a very real, public and even recognised role in society. For instance, they acted as *sōkaiya* to banks and organisations. This involved terrorising shareholder meetings where their presence encouraged shareholders to agree with the decisions of the board. They were often used by these same organisations to frighten small landholders into selling their property for large-scale developments. They also had and still have all the usual criminal involvements with standover and protection rackets, transport, gambling and labour unions, and they owned or controlled many of the thousands of *pachinko* and pinball parlours and hostess bars, as well as running most of the brothels and street prostitutes.

There was very little that was covert about the *yakuza* in the seventies, when they were at the height of their power. They maintained close and open ties with senior political entities, as well as the corporate giants, and were an integral part of the post-war power structure. Some went as far as maintaining offices with signs advertising their services to the public as openly as any legitimate organisation.

The personal appearance of individual *yakuza* was striking, too. Most were heavily tattooed with elaborate designs and mystical symbols, usually covering one shoulder and upper arm but sometimes the entire body. They wore only black suits and white shirts, cropped their hair short, wore dark sunglasses and walked with a calculated swagger and pronounced gait, arms slightly bent at the elbows, like a boxer patrolling the ring prior to a fight. Their peculiar code of honour required them to sever a finger at the joint each time they made a mistake that might lead to repercussions or harm their organisation. It was not unusual to see older *yakuza* with several fingers missing joints.

It was almost ten in the evening when I returned to our rooms. I turned on the television, preparing for a long and anxious wait for Anna. The program was about the crew of Apollo 13, who had miraculously managed to bring their craft back into the earth's orbit and were about to plummet into the Pacific in their capsule. Despite my concern for Anna I watched fascinated as the greatest rescue in space history reached its climax, the three red and white striped parachutes seeming to allow them a soft landing at sea. Hooray! Elated by the rescue I told myself how much more difficult their mission had been than Anna's. But the euphoria didn't last long. The Apollo crew hadn't had to deal with drug pushers and criminals, and in my mind I saw Anna being raped, robbed and left for dead in some dirty needle-strewn alley. It was going to be a long night.

I had arranged a morning meeting with *Fuchida-san*, the collector with whom I had been corresponding about butterflies for twenty-five years. He was to pick me up at the hotel at 11 a.m. to go to his home to view his butterfly collection but I told myself I ought to try to cancel the meeting. It was too late to call and I decided I'd have to ring first thing in the morning if Anna hadn't returned and I was forced to go looking for her. Though how I would go about doing so I had no idea.

The fact that Anna was out there somewhere alone in Tokyo trying to make a connection with a heroin dealer while I cooled my heels in our hotel was getting to me and I wasn't all that far from panicking. I'd never thought of myself as the nervous type. I'd been through one or two hairy experiences in my life and had managed to stay more or less calm. But the difference then was that I was proactive; this time I was twiddling my thumbs, unable to do anything except wait.

An hour later, when the crew of Apollo 13 was clearly safe and the world had breathed a collective sigh of relief, the program changed to a review of the upcoming Cherry Blossom Festival. We'd booked a bus trip to an outlying village to witness a ceremony at a Shinto shrine in two days' time, but in my mind I now saw myself visiting Tokyo's mortuaries instead, asking if they held the body of an unidentified woman.

It was ridiculous, I know, but I couldn't help it. I kept reminding myself that this was the first time her habit had ever interfered in our life, that she must know what she was doing, must even have done this before when she'd been in a foreign country. But all the self-chatter didn't make the waiting any easier.

I cursed her addiction a dozen times over, told myself I must try to do something to help her overcome her dependence on heroin. I felt guilty that I had long since come to the convenient as well as erroneous conclusion that it was pointless trying to help her kick the habit, accepting as gospel an adage on heroin from the famous American jazz saxophonist Charlie (Bird) Parker: 'You can get it out of your body, but you can't get it out of your brain.'

I had accepted that heroin was a part of Anna's life. She obviously had a regular supplier in Melbourne and finding the money to finance her addiction wasn't ever going to be a problem, but she kept these details intensely private. Anna had always realised that her addiction would have enormous consequences in her business life if it were discovered. She was in this matter, as in all others, completely organised, and it wasn't for me to interfere.

Her years as a madam and dominatrix in a house of bondage were equally private; it was a clandestine world I never entered. We discussed it rarely, and then only if a client mentioned a business opportunity that might concern me. I was simply locked out of her world of drugs and bondage, which in many ways made her a stranger to the person who loved her the most.

Even Anna's almost annual visits to some famous American or Swiss drug rehabilitation clinic were always referred to by both of us as business trips. It was cautionary shorthand in case the true purpose inadvertently slipped out and was discovered by the media, who, as the feminist movement gathered momentum, were becoming more and more interested in the beautiful, though unapproachable, lone-wolf entrepreneur said to be amassing a private fortune. I also formed the impression over the years that Anna's client base consisted solely of the rich and powerful, the kind of people who were as fanatical as she was about avoiding publicity and who could quickly put a stop to an overzealous reporter.

But now, away from home, I told myself all the discretion and careful attention to detail meant nothing. This wasn't a Western country where the pusher and the user were familiar with street procurement procedures. Anna, like any other addict, was out there in the middle of the night in a city she didn't know in a country that seemed to do everything differently. Earlier in the evening I had thrown a *yakuza* lad to the pavement and right now she might be begging another such low-life for a deal in some dark alley smelling of piss and excrement. Or so I imagined.

I had no idea whether she was telling the truth about the house of bondage in Roppongi or if this had simply been a lie to reassure me that she understood the world she was entering. Anna never lied to me; if she didn't want to answer a question she simply ignored it. But now, facing the pain of withdrawal, she was probably as capable of barefaced lying as any other heroin addict needing a fix.

As the night wore on I grew more and more apprehensive. Earlier I'd attempted to calm myself with a logical analysis of the situation. Anna, I told myself, wouldn't leave such an important aspect of her daily life to chance. She *must* have faced this predicament before on her various overseas trips. But now, in the early hours of the morning, when my emotions had taken over and I kept telling myself that this was Japan where nothing is ever as it appears to be, these assurances carried little or no weight.

At 4 a.m. Anna arrived back bright-eyed and bushy-tailed. After promising myself not to say a word I immediately began to shout, more from relief than anger. 'Where the fuck have you been?' I yelled, throwing up my hands and pacing around her.

'Nicholas, *shush!*' she said, calm as you like. 'I went to Topaz. It is the oldest and most respected BDSM house in Tokyo. You could not come; *gaijin* are not normally admitted. Now remove your pants at once and allow me to apologise.' She grinned wickedly. 'You may spank me if you wish.'

'You've got Buckley's,' I answered, attempting to calm down. 'I'm completely buggered and *bloody* angry.'

'You can sleep in tomorrow, when you can also apologise for shouting at me,' she replied mischievously. 'Now, Nicholas, kindly unzip, unbuckle and unwind!'

Of course I was wrong. Maybe intense anxiety heightens one's sex drive, because Anna was extremely successful at channelling my anger elsewhere. Afterwards I fell asleep almost immediately and woke a few minutes before 10 a.m. the next day with Anna asleep beside me looking positively angelic. She'd obviously chased the dragon and finally caught it, rewarding herself with a long and blissful slumber (maidens who associate with dragons never sleep, they only slumber).

My appointment with my butterfly-collecting Japanese swap mate, Iko Fuchida, was at eleven. I decided to have a Japanese bath. This is a process in two stages and in our suite there were two small bathrooms adjoining each other. In the first stage I thoroughly soaped and rinsed myself using a handheld shower, although water can also be scooped from the bath with a dipper. The second stage involved a deep bathtub filled with steaming water, where I immersed myself, relaxing, ridding myself of the effects of my all-night vigil, an altogether reinvigorating experience. My only problem was the size of the towel. I'm not a small bloke and the towel was no bigger than what we would refer to as a hand towel. The idea is to put on a *yukata* while the skin is still damp to further relax and unwind.

But there wasn't time to do this so, still damp in parts, I dressed in grey flannels, sports jacket, shirt and tie, my shoes polished to a military brilliance. It was about as formal as I ever got, with the exception of funerals, where I wore a blue serge suit the government had issued when I'd left the navy to resume life as a civilian, the buttons, alas, no longer partnering the buttonholes. My fellow collector I was almost certain would be wearing the ubiquitous blue serge suit, the national uniform for all Japanese office workers from messenger boy to chief executive.

I was ready and waiting, seated in the foyer with ten minutes to spare, the rosewood and glass tray of rare Pacific butterflies I had brought as a gift perched on my lap. I'd had it wrapped at Mitsukoshi when I'd previously shopped with Anna, and the shop girls had gathered around *ooh-ing* and *aah-ing* and exclaiming at the beauty of the specimens. The elderly lady wrapping it took positively ages, but I must say when she'd completed the task it looked rather swish. She'd wrapped it in handmade paper of milk chocolate brown flecked with genuine gold leaf, every fold precise, the whole a brilliant example of the ancient Japanese art of making and folding paper.

In fact, I became a little concerned that the wrapping might be a bit ostentatious, and that I might look like a show-off, that it might embarrass my fellow collector if he should prove to be a man of modest means. I'd made the original phone call mid-afternoon, and the person on the other end had said she'd have to contact my friend and could I leave my name and number, that he would return my call in three hours. I'd thought then that he might live in a lodging house or some such place and get the message when he returned from work.

I'd positioned my chair so that I could look out through the hotel entrance, ready for his arrival on foot from the nearby subway or by taxi. A *gaijin* my size with a large gift-wrapped box on his lap wasn't going to be too hard to spot, but we'd agreed on the phone he would carry a butterfly collector's catalogue.

I guess it's natural to feel a little anxious when you meet someone for the first time with whom you've been sharing a passion for twenty-five years but, in fact, about whom you know very little. I guess I was preoccupied with just such a notion when there was a squeal of brakes beyond the entrance. Moments later, two bellboys rushed past me towards the glass doors, holding them open and standing as stiffly as a pair of wooden figures. The doorman, I observed, had also sprung to rigid attention, and I could hear people outside crying out.

Two black Toyota motorcars had drawn up, burning rubber and halting seemingly inches behind each other, horns blaring, almost immediately followed by a black Mercedes Grosser, the first of these huge German cars I had ever seen. Then two more Toyotas slammed to a halt behind it. Men in black wearing sunglasses spilled from the four Toyotas and formed a guard around the Grosser 600.

By this time everyone in the foyer, hotel guests and staff, appeared frozen to the spot and the place had fallen completely silent. The desk clerks at reception were standing rigidly to attention, ignoring a telephone that suddenly sprang to life within arm's reach.

As I watched, the driver opened the rear door of the huge square-rigged monster of a car and a tall, slender Japanese man dressed like the others in a black suit and wearing sunglasses stepped out, took two steps away from the car and paused. The men divided and ran to either side of him. He advanced a couple of steps towards the entrance then stopped again and retreated to the car, opened the rear door, stooped and half disappeared into the interior. By this time I'd partially gathered my wits and realised, some time after seemingly everyone else had made the connection, that the entire entourage as well as the bloke reaching into the rear of the big car were *yakuza*. And the guy rummaging in the back of the big Benz was obviously a very important gangster.

My immediate thought was, *Shit! It's about the kid I humiliated on the pavement last night . . . They've come to get me!* All this happened in a matter of seconds and then the tall slender gangster turned back towards the hotel entrance, whereupon the six *yakuza* on either side of him formed an escort as he moved through the open plate-glass doors. It look me several seconds more to realise he was carrying a butterfly catalogue.

Fuchida-san entered the hotel, ignoring the doorman's salute, and seemed to recognise me immediately, although this may have been because I appeared to be the only person still seated and a *gaijin* to boot. He advanced, smiling, his entourage drawing back. I rose to my feet, placed the butterfly box on the chair, and went to greet him.

'Welcome, honourable *Duncan-san*, master of all butterfly collectors!' he announced loudly so that all could hear his tribute to me, then he bowed deeply.

'I am not worthy, *Fuchida-san*, it is you who surely deserve such a title,' I answered, bowing in return. He seemed pleased with my reply and the men around us smiled and nodded. 'I have brought you a small gift. It is unworthy, its only virtue is that it is almost unique – the twenty rarest Pacific Island butterflies.' I bent to retrieve the parcel and handed it to him, knowing that in theory the gift should be handed over at the conclusion of our meeting. But I decided to do it the Western way.

I had expected him to accept it politely in the enigmatic manner of the Japanese and put it aside for a private appraisal. But no such thing happened. His eyes shone with excitement and he immediately called for another chair. When it was brought he sat down and, placing the butterfly box on his lap, untied the parcel. I noticed the top two joints on one of his little fingers were missing. His hands were slim and tattooed, each finger sporting a gold ring, one of which was set with a large ruby, the others crusted with diamonds. He carefully separated the folds in the paper, unconcerned about the time this took. Finally, without the tiniest tear in the wrapping, the tray of butterflies within was revealed. 'Hiee!' he exclaimed, clasping his hands tightly. 'It is a treasure beyond the imagination!' He scanned the tray. 'Twenty, and I have only three of them!' Then showing off outrageously he pointed to each and recited its Latin name. Laughing, he turned to face me. 'You honour me, *Duncan-san*. I cannot repay your generosity.'

'Twenty-five years of friendship between collectors is sufficient repayment, *Fuchida-san*. I am grateful to you for this alone without your own generosity in sending me specimens in return.'

'And now, at last, we meet.' He seemed to hesitate momentarily, then, seemingly on an impulse, removed a gold ring set with a large yellow diamond from his forefinger. 'It is a small token of our butterfly brotherhood,' he said, thrusting the ring at me.

It was a gift of ridiculous proportions. I knew better than to refuse, but enough to protest. 'You pay me too much honour! How can I accept?'

'As a brother,' he exclaimed. 'In twenty-five years you have given me great pleasure. It is but a small token.'

'I accept, because to refuse would deny the pleasure of meeting you at last,' I said, surprising myself with my grasp of the idiom of compounding compliments. While I am not the ring-wearing type and would choose to wear a diamond least of all, I slipped the ring onto my pinkie, it being too small for any of my other fingers. I have always been self-conscious of my hands, which are the size of boarding-school soup plates. 'I shall wear it always as a sign of our fraternity. It is my turn to be overwhelmed by your generosity, honourable *Fuchida-san*.'

I suddenly became aware that nobody in the lobby had moved, that the *yakuza* surrounding us had now turned to watch every corner of the foyer. I wondered what they possibly thought might happen on an early spring morning in one of Tokyo's most prestigious hotels and concluded that their vigilance was a show of power and an indication of the importance of their *oyabun*.

Fuchida-san, who can't have been anything less than an *oyabun*, saw me looking at the reception desk where three telephones were ringing while the clerks ignored them, standing rigidly to attention. I glanced over at the entrance where the doorman and the bellboys stood like statues. 'Get on with your business!' he called out. 'This is not a zoo, even if you all behave like frightened monkeys!' This caused a burst of fraternal laughter from the *yakuza* and a few nervous titters from the patrons still in the foyer. 'Come, *Duncan-san*, we shall go to my home,' *Fuchida-san* said. 'I would be greatly honoured if you would give me your worthy opinion of my unworthy butterfly collection.'

CHAPTER SIX

'No, Nick, I cannot continue!
I must go away from you.
I cannot be your woman. I am useless!
I must let you go.
You must find another woman to love you.
But only understand,
no one can love you as much as I do.
It is not possible.'
Anna Til, Coffee Scald Island

SEATED IN THE BACK seat of the big Mercedes with the four Toyotas front and back we merged into the Ginza traffic. I'd left instructions at the front desk that Anna wasn't to be disturbed by either the phone or the maid, and asked them to slip a note under the door. Not wishing to worry her, I didn't mention the *yakuza* surprise in my note, but simply said my butterfly swap mate had invited me home and that I expected to be back by late afternoon. I added that the Apollo 13 capsule had splashed down and the crew were safe, adding several XXXs so she'd know I was no longer angry about the previous evening.

Our Toyota escorts added to the traffic noise with their constantly blaring horns, which did nothing to speed us up. The Ginza seemed locked into an unvarying pace, perhaps because the traffic congestion appeared to remain constant, even in the small hours when, waiting for Anna to return, I had stared disconsolately down at the swarming vehicles from my hotel bedroom window.

Though the constant din was muffled in the interior of the big automobile it was still difficult to talk, and it was not until we'd left the Ginza strip and moved into a comparatively quieter street – Tokyo has few quiet streets – that *Fuchida-san* did more than simply point out landmarks and features.

'*Duncan-san*, you will now realise I am *yakuza*. I hope you are not too surprised.'

'Very,' I answered. 'How else should I be?'

'Ah, an honest man,' he laughed. 'What do you know about the *yakuza*?'

'A little. My father is a Japanese scholar and amateur historian. I was born here, so he kept up my language and we often discussed Japan. Although the little I know about the *yakuza* is mostly from before the war.'

'Then you are Japanese!' he joked. 'I also like to think I am the historian of the *yakuza*, but only since the war. Is there anything you wish to know about us, *Duncan-san*?' He grinned. 'Some things I cannot tell you, but others . . .' he shrugged, 'it's okay,' he said, using the English word to add a casual, throwaway and, perhaps to him, sophisticated effect.

'Well, you personally, you are obviously not *wakagashira*, a lieutenant.'

'No, I am *oyabun*. I run the Kanto, the greater Tokyo district and the area surrounding it.'

I whistled. 'But not just *oyabun*?'

He laughed. 'I control many *oyabun*. I am like the godfather of lots of mafia godfathers. There is only one *oyabun* above me,' he explained. 'In your country I am a criminal boss; in Japan, no . . . *yakuza* are part of our system.'

I was conscious of not wanting to question him too closely,

but my natural curiosity and the fact that I would probably never again be as close to a senior *yakuza* made me persist. Besides, he seemed willing, almost anxious, to talk to me. 'In what ways are the *yakuza* different?' I immediately qualified this by saying, 'As I mentioned, I am aware of the Samurai origins, the tradition of honour and compassion, *giri* and *ninjō*, and of noble deeds. Do they still pertain? Is that what you mean?'

He laughed, although I sensed a slight embarrassment. I was to learn that *Fuchida-san* laughed a lot to cover a multiplicity of circumstances and evasions. When his twelve lieutenants – his *wakagashira* – were with him, they would echo his laughter, even when plainly they hadn't been able to hear the cause of his mirth or follow his conversation. It was a Japanese version of canned laughter, sycophantic cackling. 'We are more like a service business today,' he replied.

'Business? What, based on helping people?'

Again the laughter. 'More often persuading them, calming them down,' he said with surprising honesty, then added, 'The war . . . the Americans, they taught us a lot.'

'By bringing democracy to Japan?'

This time *Fuchida-san*'s laughter seemed genuine, but he thought for a while before answering. 'No. They organised the *yakuza*. Before, we were just rival gangs fighting each other for territory, but they turned us into a united force.'

'The Americans organised the criminal element? You mean, like the mafiosi?'

'Exactly.'

'But why?'

'Well they not only wanted to introduce democracy to Japan, they also wanted the Japanese people to understand and embrace it. At the time the various *yakuza* gangs were making huge profits on the black market by hijacking aid supplies handed out by the Americans. The Americans saw us as the enemy; they thought the people would associate democracy with criminal activity, making us rich while Japan starved. So they attempted to use conventional means to stop us – police, their own forces, the FBI,' he shrugged, 'but without any success.'

'They didn't stop the black-market activity?'

'No, it didn't stop. Not at first. But they realised then that while we were separate gangs we shared a Samurai tradition. They saw the potential of a covert unified force and they needed one to fight communism. The Communist Party was growing in leaps and bounds among the Japanese working classes. It was backed by the Soviet Union and the Americans saw this as a major threat to a young and, to the Japanese, alien democratic system. They needed a force that could,' he smiled, '*discourage* communist and leftwing activity, a force that wasn't directly associated with a democratic government, because democracy is supposed to embrace competing ideologies. Remember, Russia had recently been America's ally in the war and it wasn't so easy to paint communism as an evil force to a defeated and hungry Japan.'

I was beginning to realise that *Fuchida-san* wasn't simply a thug who had risen from the ranks of the *yakuza* by brutal force. Despite the comic-opera scene in the Imperial Hotel, I was dealing with a clever, informed and articulate man.

'How did they go about this unification?' I now asked.

'Well, they needed someone who would work with US Intelligence, the rightwing political parties and big business, and they found Yoshio Kodama who, at the time, was in prison as a Class A war criminal.'

'Why this man, Yoshio Kodama?'

'He had all the right connections to all the forces that needed to be united. He was imprisoned before the war by the Japanese government for his involvement in several ultra-nationalist assassination plots. But he was too valuable to keep in prison, so they released him and he started working for intelligence in Korea, Manchuria and in Japanese-occupied China as a spy.

'After this he worked freelance for the military industrial complex that was running Japan and preparing for war. He organised raw materials from other countries, China, Korea, any neutral country willing to trade with Japan . . .' *Fuchida-san* laughed. 'Also, before your war with Germany, pig iron from Australia.

'The military government paid him commissions on all purchases and turned a blind eye to his control of the drug trade between Japan, China and the remainder of the Japanese empire. When we declared war he joined the navy, and by its end, at the age of thirty-four, he was a rear admiral. He had continued to control drugs in Japan and to all the regions throughout the Greater East Asia Co-prosperity Sphere, where the Japanese forces used them to calm the local population. At the time of his arrest by the Americans as a war criminal it is said that he was worth one hundred and seventy-five million dollars US!'

'Thirty-four! He was still a young man. Is he still alive?'

'Certainly.'

'Do you know him?'

'He was my mentor when the *yakuza* were brought together. He chose me and some other young *kobun*. I was twenty-three years old and just making my way in the *yakuza* when he made me one of his *wakagashira*, his lieutenants. Later he sent me to Tokyo University. I didn't have the necessary qualifications, but he had influence and I studied logic and political science.'

'I'm interested – how did Yoshio Kodama go about it?'

'It wasn't all that difficult. Yoshio Kodama was a longstanding member of a powerful *yakuza* gang, although he was too young to be the *oyabun*. We, all the gangs, had great admiration and respect for him. He was the one man in Japan who could unify us by promising us a share in *kuroi kiri* [black mist].'

'*Kuroi kiri*? What is that?'

Fuchida-san spread his hands. '*Duncan-san*, there are aspects of every society where the government and the army cannot be seen to be involved. They are necessary and practical aspects of government influence such as paying bribes to ensure the right result, making sure that politicians see the national interest in the right way, making sure the right company gets the government contract. Sometimes a certain amount of *persuasion* of one kind or another is needed. That is the meaning of the black mist. Apart from violence, *kuroi kiri* is what gives us our power. We, the various *yakuza* organisations, agreed to unify and, through Yoshio Kodama, to work with the US Army Intelligence arm, G2.'

'To do the government's dirty work?'

The *yakuza* boss nodded. 'Of course. But first we had to be trained. The Americans are very thorough, and to let us loose against the communists and some of the new unions would look too obvious. I was chosen with Yoshio Kodama's other lieutenants and taught how to find locally plausible excuses to break major strikes, to disrupt leftwing party meetings and to use violence to the best effect.' He grinned. 'To break all the right heads or kneecaps, to hurt without leaving marks. It was a natural progression for the *yakuza* – we have always been ardent nationalists. We were serving our country and we were proud patriots.'

'And now?'

'Now?'

'Do you believe you're serving the best interests of Japan?'

He thought for a moment. 'Yes, but now perhaps it isn't so clear-cut . . . things have changed, the Americans have gone home. It is 1970. Japan begins to prosper as a democracy and is becoming a world power. Its government no longer faces imminent danger from leftwing forces.'

'So, how have you adapted to these changing circumstances?'

'You said your father studied our history. Then you will know that Japanese society has always done everything by strictly observed rules of behaviour. Traditionally there is a way to behave in every situation. But that is *old* Japanese history and now there is *new* Japanese history. We are a people who have had to adapt to new ideas, those that our *old* history may not have accommodated.'

'No doubt *old* history includes your social mores?'

'Yes, traditional behaviour has developed throughout our history. Since the defeat of Japan by America, traditions have changed more quickly than at any other time in our history and so the old ways have been replaced with new rules that have no historical basis and have not yet stood the test of time.'

'I guess most people are slow to embrace change.'

'Ah, to understand the Japanese it is important to realise that we *must* have a set of rules to follow in our daily lives.'

'Do you mean morality? What is regarded as right and wrong?'

He sighed. 'You see this is precisely what I *don't* mean. Japanese society doesn't have a concept of individual morality or guilt, only collective behaviour that has evolved over generations. What one does, all do. Morality is a group experience and so is guilt. In the West you talk much about

Japanese atrocities during the war. To us these were not individual atrocities. They were a collective way to wage war, common practice against any enemy. There was no individual conscience or guilt. When you hanged our leaders for war crimes you were punishing all of Japan, you were challenging our entire belief system. You were threatening us with change we did not understand, change without the benefit of practice or precedent.'

'What about the young people? They are always the ones prepared for generational change,' I suggested.

'Not in Japan. Our young men were exhausted by the war; they thought of themselves as a collective failure.'

'Are you saying there is, or was, mass confusion? People, even the post-war generation, didn't know how to respond to the new world they inhabited?'

'In the West it is the individual who has a set of behavioural rules. Guilt, morality, ethics are all personal standards, the individual is responsible for his own behaviour. Our religion does not teach individual guilt or morality. In Japan collective behaviour is safe behaviour and correct behaviour, whereas individual behaviour is dangerous and leads to trouble. So the people collect into groups and it is these groups that make the rules and teach them, especially to the young, about how they must behave. And so we are able to embrace the new ways necessary to prosper and compete with the outside world while maintaining the essential character of our own culture.'

'And the *yakuza* as a power group is not alien to Japanese society, but a part of it.'

'Yes, you have it. For instance, the *yakuza* group I belong to is part of the *Yamaguchi-gumi*. We are the *Inagawa-kai*, part of an alliance created by the honourable Yoshio Kodama. When we speak it is not one voice but four thousand voices in my region alone, and in all of Japan, many, many more. In this way we are seen as a legitimate power group by other power groups – banking, industry, manufacture, politics, agriculture, fishing and all the other sections of Japanese society. If there is a legitimate need for violence we supply it, or the threat of violence, then we prevent it. We will act in the name of the *yakuza* power group for whichever organisation requires our services.'

'Legitimate need for violence?'

'If one power group feels it has the need to discipline or exert its authority over a section of its own group, and it does not possess its own disciplinary force, it calls on us, the *yakuza*, to act on its behalf.'

'But what if the section of the group that is being "disciplined" by you still feels aggrieved and wants to retaliate? Who do *they* call upon?'

'Us.'

I laughed. 'But now you are acting for both sides? In effect disciplining yourselves?'

'Ah, that is a good Japanese question, *Duncan-san*. That is my job, or the job of my honourable leader. He or I will decide which section of the group is to be supported.'

'And that decision will be accepted by the disaffected group?'

'That is the Japanese way. If they continue to object we will "persuade" them that it is pointless to resist.'

I was receiving a valuable insight into the *yakuza*, but perhaps more importantly into Japanese society. We, that is the West, always assume that democracy is a logical idea and its ways can be grasped without effort, particularly the rights of individuals, whereas this simply isn't the case. The concepts of individual freedom and equal justice for all can seem quite bizarre to the Japanese.

'But what about the conventional justice system, does it not play a part?'

'It is there to interpret the law. We will always cooperate with it.'

'As a criminal organisation, isn't cooperating with the law a contradiction in terms? For instance, what about conventional crime – prostitution, sex bars, pinball and *pachinko* parlours, drugs, extortion?'

Fuchida-san shrugged. 'Those things, yes, they are always with us. They are a part of any big city. We control them. Crime is not for amateurs; we are professionals and the police are professionals. We negotiate. There is room for both.'

I must have looked puzzled because he went on, '*Duncan-san*, we try to maintain what you in the West would call the status quo, only it is more complex than that.'

'But what if the status quo is not to the advantage of the group as a whole?'

'Ah, another good question. If the status quo is not going to benefit Japan, the government must bring about change. The *yakuza* do not get involved at this level.'

'But government and industry, it seems to me, are closely entwined. We have just negotiated a deal with Mitsubishi, and I understand that the present government has a strong working relationship with the shipping industry, almost a controlling influence.'

'Yes, shipbuilding is a vital national industry.'

'So, if there was a strike in the shipyards, would the *yakuza* be brought in?'

'At the beginning, under the Americans, yes, that would happen, but not now that we are a strong democracy. The government will send the police or the military, unless it does not wish to be seen to be involved in limiting the democratic right of unions to protest, then the shipping company would call on us.'

'With the government's approval?'

'Unspoken.'

'And government and opposition parties, do the *yakuza* play a part in deciding who will be in power?'

Fuchida-san seemed alarmed by such a notion. 'No, *Duncan-san*, we are now a democratic nation! Of course, we have influence in every political group and do them many favours in return, as long as they are not communists or leftwing parties who encourage disruptive labour unions and cause strikes and interrupt our national progress.' The *yakuza* boss paused for emphasis. 'Japan *must* be competitive with the rest of the world. Every power group *must* accept this. We would *never* interfere with responsible and progressive government. But it is our duty to control those disruptive forces that want to endanger our prosperity.'

'But labour unions are meant to be the free voice of the workers, their way of being heard.'

'Legitimate unions are acceptable, but if we had allowed the communists and their followers to control the unions, Japan would never have risen from its knees. If you receive a scratch or a cut you treat it immediately, you do not allow it to fester and make you sick.'

'And rightwing groups such as your present government?'

'Rightwing? That is just another term for democracy, *Duncan-san*.

I am a patriot. Japan needs continuity, *not* disruption.'

I grinned. 'In the West we would not agree with this definition of democracy.'

It was the wrong thing to say and I realised it was time to

stop asking questions. It is commonplace in life that no matter how bizarre any group in society may be, it will find a way to justify its existence. Clearly my butterfly swap mate believed that his criminal organisation of thugs and standover men played an essential, influential and beneficial role in Japanese society.

I was also reluctantly forced to admit that, while everything he believed in was in direct opposition to my own political beliefs, nevertheless, a Japan with a regulated labour force and without industrial strikes was beginning to flex its industrial muscle and was already on its way to becoming one of the world's leading economies. In fact, the early influence of the *yakuza*, heinous as it was, probably helped post-war Japan to recover and prosper. I was learning that pragmatism was the linchpin in Japan's industrial success. But then, of course, pragmatism is not unknown in the West either.

I had one more question to ask. 'Fuchida-san, if *yakuza* have such an accepted place in Japanese society, then why is it necessary for you to be so heavily protected . . . er . . . escorted?'

Again he laughed uproariously. 'In the West it is called public relations. The people need to see that there is a *yakuza* presence, a *powerful yakuza* presence,' he repeated. 'It is like your Western politicians who must be seen to be out and about.' He grinned. 'Only we do it with a display of power and you do it by kissing babies.'

I laughed at his clever analogy. 'But, in the hotel, people seemed to be genuinely fearful.'

'No, no!' he insisted. 'Not fear, respect! Respect is very important; it is *everything* in our society.'

We had arrived at one of the more impressive high-rise buildings I had seen in Tokyo. Preceded by the two Toyotas, we passed through an electronic gate into the underground parking lot, the big Mercedes driving up to a private lift where the six lieutenants had disembarked. Three had already gone ahead and the others waited for it to return, carrying one of the original three riding shotgun to ensure it contained no surprises. The remaining two escort vehicles blocked the entrance to the underground car park.

If the extroverted public display in the hotel lobby was a perverted type of public relations, then why the elaborate measures involved in entering this building?

'There is no need for public relations here, so why the precautions?' I asked.

'The Shield Society,' he said, just as the lift arrived. 'They want to bring back the *old* Japan. I tell you, all Japanese, myself included, are paranoid.'

While none of this made sense to me he explained no further and we entered the lift and rose in silence.

Fuchida-san occupied the penthouse and, I was later to learn, the apartment immediately below that as well, converted into two dormitories and used as accommodation for his lieutenants.

The two *yakuza* lieutenants who had preceded us to the penthouse met us at the door of the lift. With a nod they immediately re-entered the lift and the doors closed behind them. We'd stepped directly into a large room where a *mama-san*, an elderly woman in a working day kimono, waited to greet us. She was an elderly, dumpy, flat-faced, crinkle-eyed woman without make-up, who from her general appearance seemed to be of peasant stock, except that hanging from her ears were what appeared to be diamond pendants of considerable worth, assuming they were genuine.

Fuchida-san seemed to read my thoughts, or otherwise was accustomed to guests commenting, although I hadn't remarked on the earrings. 'Yes, diamonds,' he pronounced. 'I gave them to her for her seventieth birthday.' He laughed. 'At least we guessed it was her seventieth.' He turned to address her. 'You weren't sure, were you, *Mama-san*?' The old woman covered her mouth and giggled, shaking her head. 'She has not taken them off since that day five years ago,' he laughed. 'Sometimes in the morning, when she brings me green tea, the shape of one of them is imprinted into her cheek.'

Turning back to me he said, 'She has been with me since I was made *wakagashira* with Yoshio Kodama, when I was twenty-three. He sent her.' He gave her a hard stare and said, 'I think she was *really* a spy on the American payroll!' She giggled again, this time shaking her head vigorously in protest. This was obviously a routine they often performed. 'Come, *Duncan-san*, let me show you,' my host volunteered. 'Bring green tea,' he ordered the *mama-san*, who it appeared was to go without either a name or a formal introduction to me, yet it was obvious the crime boss was fond of her.

I must say the penthouse was impressive, although I had expected *tatami* floors and paper screens, low tables and silk cushions. I was surprised by the immediate impression of smoked glass and chrome. The furniture – chairs, settees and low tables, with their framework of tubular chrome, plus the pristine glass surfaces – looked like a spread from an interior-design magazine. Even the floor appeared to be of polished black glass tiles. The whole effect was as formal as the foyer in a modern New York skyscraper, except for several antique Japanese silk screens, each of which blazed in yellows and reds, peacock blues and browns to warm and humanise the fashionably minimalist decor.

'You like it?' *Fuchida-san* asked proudly. 'It is American. The best interior decorator from Dallas, Texas.'

'Yes, very nice,' I replied.

He grinned. 'It is the *new* Japan.'

We walked from the large room into another that was in complete darkness, the light from the open door penetrating no more than a couple of feet. '*Duncan-san*, you must walk twelve steps slowly towards the centre of the room.' He hesitated momentarily. 'No, you are too tall; for you only ten steps, then feel for a swivel chair, where you must be seated. Tell me when you are ready.'

I did as I had been told, not knowing what to expect. At nine steps I bumped into the leather swivel chair and sat down. 'Do I face the door?' I called out.

'No, any way but that,' he replied.

I swung the chair away from the direction of his voice and called out, whereupon the lights came on and I was dazzled by his astonishing collection of butterflies. Under single sheets of glass, from floor to ceiling on three walls of a large room, were literally thousands set out in family groups and regions. I would someday boast one of the world's finest collections of the butterflies of the Pacific, and even then I had an impressive collection, but this was something else. There are around eighteen thousand species of butterfly, and on the walls around me there must have been butterflies from at least five thousand species. I grinned then laughed and clapped my hands. 'Remarkable! Stunning! Impossible!' I exclaimed. 'I have never seen so many in a private collection!'

'Ah, it is a beginning, *Duncan-san*. There are ten thousand or more I do not have!' He laughed, stepping into the room, obviously delighted by my reaction. 'The ones you gave me, I told you, I have only three of them.' He pointed to the centre of the wall on my right where he had the butterflies of the Pacific region. I immediately recognised the Magpie Crow, the rare butterfly found only on the Indonesian islands and the

Malayan Peninsula. It had been this butterfly that had taken me to Java where I had first met sixteen-year-old Anna and shortly after escaped the Japanese invasion by sailing away in *Madam Butterfly*. He was right. Seventeen of the twenty specimens I had brought him were not in his collection. How he could possibly have known this and recited their Latin names, given the tens of thousands of butterflies displayed, was a remarkable feat of memory.

We spent the next hour discussing his collection, many of which I had never seen, not even in a catalogue or book.

'Do you travel much? This collection is from all over the world,' I said at one stage in the conversation.

'No, I have been to Manchuria as a soldier, also China, the islands of Japan and Korea, but that is all. Most are sent to me, swapped for Japanese butterflies. My network of collectors is vast, but yours also I think, *Duncan-san*? Your own collection must be very impressive.'

'Not like this one,' I said, indicating the walls around me. 'I collect only those from the Pacific region and, since we have been swapping, the butterflies of Japan. But only those specimens you have sent me. I like to catch them myself. I am in shipping,' I explained, 'in and out of the various islands. It is a hobby and good exercise. Do you hunt much yourself?'

'Alas, no, it is hard for me to leave Tokyo. I have another system for collecting the Japanese species I use to swap with other collectors.' He held up his hand to show me the pinkie with two joints missing. I had already noticed this in the hotel. 'Two joints, two mistakes, it is a *yakuza* punishment. Mistakes are unavoidable and I have four thousand *yakuza* under me, so there are many mistakes. Now it is known amongst my people that if you fuck up you have two choices – cut off a finger joint or go hunting for butterflies.' He laughed. 'In other parts of

Japan the Tokyo *Kanto* is known as "The Butterfly Mob"!'

'No! Really?' I exclaimed in disbelief.

He laughed. 'A guilty man must wait until it is the butterfly season, then he is given a butterfly net, a map and a picture of a particular specimen. He must return within thirty days with six specimens or remove a finger joint. He also takes an oath that he will not pay someone to obtain them. If he does and we discover this, then he loses two entire fingers and is demoted.'

'What a bizarre solution, but obviously effective,' I exclaimed, chuckling.

'Not always,' he replied. 'These guys are mostly from the city slums and know more about cockroaches than butterflies. They don't know the countryside. The specimens they must catch are always rare and so are difficult to find. The area they are given may be difficult. Sometimes it is rugged mountain terrain or swamp land. Some come back exhausted, three have died – two were lost in the mountains overnight where they froze to death and one drowned in a swamp. Here in the Tokyo *Kanto* butterfly hunting is regarded as very severe punishment and, if a miscreant still has all his fingers intact, he may even opt to lose a finger joint rather than go on a butterfly expedition into the vast unknown.'

'I can understand that,' I laughed. 'I have had more than one narrow escape in the New Guinea jungle and on some of the islands. A. S. Meek, the greatest of Australian butterfly collectors, suffered malaria, yellow fever, dysentery and various other tropical diseases. At that time in the early 1900s there were also headhunters and cannibals and so he hunted with a butterfly net in one hand and a revolver in the other. Most of his porters died of fever and pneumonia and he barely survived himself. But it was he who found the Queen Alexandra's Birdwing. The female's wingspan can reach 31 centimetres.

Hunting butterflies is not a sport for wimps or city boys.'

Fuchida-san whistled. 'I would very much like to see that big butterfly, *Duncan-san*.'

'Then come and visit me and I will show you one,' I replied.

'In your collection?'

'Yes, when I was fourteen years old. I have never caught another.'

'If you do I will pay you a great deal, *Duncan-san*. I would treasure it.'

'*Fuchida-san*, if I find another you shall have it as a gift, a gesture of our friendship.'

The *mama-san* had knocked several times to say that tea was ready but had been dismissed with a flick of the wrist, then finally dismissed to prepare lunch. Now she announced that lunch was ready and we repaired to a small room decorated in authentic Japanese style, *tatami* floor, cushions and a low black lacquered table only large enough for two people. The old woman, who had changed into a formal silk kimono, served us *sake* on her heels, diamond pendants shining.

'*Duncan-san*, your gift is of incalculable value to me,' *Fuchida-san* began. 'To know that you have hunted these butterflies yourself adds greatly to their worth. We are now friends who drink *sake* together and face each other across the table and not across the seas.' He smiled. 'If you were *yakuza* we would exchange blood.' Then a serious expression crossed his face. 'If I can do anything to help you while you are in Japan you need only ask.'

'We have been swap mates for twenty years,' I replied. 'It is a pleasure just to meet you at last, and a privilege to be permitted to see your remarkable collection.'

'It is so long ago that I have forgotten how our swap

friendship began,' he observed.

I was immediately alerted. Any person who could remember the Latin names of seventeen Pacific butterflies in his vast collection would remember Gojo Mura, the little Japanese radio operator I had befriended during the war. 'You will remember that I was given your name and address by your friend Gojo Mura. I hoped to contact him through you,' I reminded him.

The *yakuza* boss feigned a look of surprise. 'Ah, yes, now I recall it.'

'At the time you wrote to say you had lost contact with him,' I added.

Fuchida-san paused. 'There cannot be lies between good friends, *Duncan-san*. At that time it was difficult. I wanted to help but it was not possible. Gojo Mura was a traitor to Japan.'

'Traitor? Impossible!' I exclaimed. 'He was the *worst* soldier I have ever known. He had no treachery in him, no interest whatsoever in fighting. When I captured him, his rifle bolt and barrel had rusted up and the cartridges and magazines were green with mildew.'

'It was not that, *Duncan-san*. He *returned* to Japan having been taken a prisoner of war and put in a concentration camp. At that time it was still *old* Japan. If a warrior is captured he must commit *seppuku* – *harakiri*; this was our way then, collective guilt. When I received your letter I did not know who you were, only that you were in my mind still the enemy, one of Japan's conquerors. But then I found out you were a warrior of great distinction awarded the Navy Cross, America's second-highest medal for bravery.'

My surprise must have been apparent. I obviously hadn't mentioned my role in the war, other than to say in the original letter that I'd captured Gojo Mura while fighting with the

Americans and had subsequently got to know him well while he was interned in Australia, where we had become good friends. 'How? How did you know of my war record?' I asked, amazed.

'When your letter arrived just after the war I had already been recruited by Yoshio Kodama. I thought it might be a trap to plant someone close to me, so he could spy on my boss. I told him about your letter and he said he would check you out with the FBI. They came back and told us you were a great warrior and worthy of the highest respect.'

I laughed. 'The FBI credited me with too much honour, *Fuchida-san*. At that time the Navy Cross was only the third highest American award for bravery. It is not a big deal; many were much braver than me in battle.'

'Also that you got another medal for bravery, the Distinguished Service Cross, which you received personally from the hands of MacArthur! There can be no higher honour for a warrior on your side!' he said, his expression close to awestruck. 'It would be like the Emperor awarding a Japanese soldier a medal. Such a gesture from the Chrysanthemum Throne would not be forgotten in his family for ten thousand lifetimes.'

'Ah, MacArthur gave out a lot of medals. He was the world champion at giving medals. I think I got it mostly for having malaria.' I glanced up and grinned. 'The FBI didn't tell you I was in an intelligence unit?' I asked. It was clear to see why the young *Fuchida-san* had been recruited by the notorious Yoshio Kodama. He had been careful and circumspect even as a young man. His apparent respect for my war record also explained his openness and the candid discussion we'd had earlier.

Fuchida-san looked momentarily horrified, then burst into uproarious laughter. 'It is my luck then,' he said finally. 'If the FBI had told us you were in Intelligence at the time, I would not have become your butterfly swap mate. I would have regarded it as too dangerous to be associated with you. As I said, we Japanese are by nature paranoid.'

'This affirmation from the FBI, it didn't change your mind about helping me find Gojo Mura?'

'At the time, I still thought it better to do nothing about finding him. To let, as you say, sleeping dogs lie. Although we came from the same village and were childhood friends, I knew he would not return to the village because of his shame. The village people would not have tolerated it. Besides, he was officially dead. Officially there were no Japanese prisoners of war.'

'But many did return to Japan?'

'That was the *haji*, the disgrace. They had dishonoured the Emperor's *Senjinkun* military code, which laid down that no surrender was possible for the individual soldier. They had not only disobeyed the instructions to commit suicide if they were captured, but now they were refusing to be officially dead. Their reappearance in Japan would cause great disgrace to their families who had received a small box supposedly containing their ashes, so they knew their beloved son or father had died an honourable death fighting for the divine cause. Their names were listed at the Yakusuni Shrine as honoured dead and their families received a small government pension. They were also removed from the national family register as, clearly, dead men cannot continue to be Japanese citizens.'

'And that is what would have happened to Gojo Mura?' I asked. I had, by alluding to the fact that I had captured him, in effect condemned my little Japanese friend to a future of shame. He was a dead man walking. 'I am to blame for telling you of his capture,' I lamented.

Fuchida-san sniffed and then shrugged. 'No, he would have

been on a repatriated prisoner of war list. When he got back he changed his name. He was clever but, like me, came from a very poor but honourable family. He would not want them to lose their pension and, much worse, be forever disgraced in the village for a son who brought them *haji*, shame and humiliation.'

'Wait a minute, if he gave me your address did he not contact you?'

Fuchida-san hesitated momentarily. 'Yes.'

'That's how you know he changed his name?'

'Yes.'

'And did you see him again?'

'No. I was in the *yakuza*, it was not appropriate to know a traitor.'

'But all the Japanese prisoners of war were exonerated and the *Senjinkun* military code abolished by a dictate from your emperor.'

'Ah yes, but that is the *new* Japan. The shame is not abolished in the mind. The shame is *old* Japan, and it will not go away so easily. It will only die when the soul of the last captured soldier who returned to Japan is enshrined at *Yakusuni*.' *Fuchida-san* suddenly paused and frowned as if a perplexing thought had occurred to him. 'You don't *still* wish to find him, do you, *Duncan-san*?' he asked.

'Do you know his name?'

'No. I advised him to change it but not to tell me. What you don't know cannot harm you . . . or him.'

'So, it would be impossible to trace him?'

The *yakuza* boss seemed to think for a moment. I sensed he felt he was being challenged. 'Not impossible; we can try. If he is alive there are fifteen thousand *yakuza* in western Japan who can make enquiries. But it will be *very* difficult. I will have to think if there was anything about him that would identify him.'

'He was a brilliant artist, a painter of butterflies and jungle insects,' I volunteered.

'It is a start. There are probably ten thousand such unofficial artists in Japan.'

'You mean unofficial because he has changed his name?'

'No, like myself he was a poor boy and could not afford to be formally trained as an artist. He received a scholarship to the College of Engineering to study radio and we were very proud of him, the whole village received prestige from this. But he will not now be accepted into any artists' colony. He cannot become recognised without the correct qualifications. It would not matter how skilled he is, he cannot make a living as a teacher or an official artist without the proper qualifications.' *Fuchida-san's* recitation of these strictures revealed more of the complex layers of Japanese society. Even artists formed a collective, a power group that required formal qualifications rather than naked talent to enter its portals.

Poor little Gojo Mura, the non-soldier, dreamer, painter of nature, original innocent, harmless participant in a savage and brutal encounter, had copped the lot. He was trapped in an *old* Japan which, despite the *new* Japan, would never forgive him for being a man of peace who would rather paint a fly than kill it. I realised that despite the efforts of my host, the likelihood of finding him was practically zero.

Mama-san had prepared a small banquet obviously on my host's instructions and in my honour. Anna was a superb Japanese cook so I had learned to appreciate a great many foods. *Fuchida-san* seemed impressed that I could recognise the various dishes and was able to comment on them with some small authority.

'You are not what we Japanese expect from a *gaijin*,' he laughed. 'If you stayed here for long you would soon become civilised!'

It was a joke he would never have made if he hadn't decided that I was to be a close friend. I confess I wondered to myself if, in the long term, this friendship was a good idea. Being known as a personal friend of one of Japan's most powerful gangsters might not go down too well in Canberra. I imagined myself trying to explain to ASIO that we were simply fellow butterfly collectors!

But I had no reason not to like him and friendship doesn't require social equality or the opinions of others. Even so, I decided never to talk about him in the context of *yakuza*, even to Anna. I would tell her only that our meeting had been pleasant, that he was a cultivated and considerate host and his butterfly collection was impressive.

There were two reasons for this. Anna would see him as an irresistible opportunity for business in Japan and perhaps *Fuchida-san* would want a reciprocal arrangement in Australia. I hated myself for thinking like this, but knew my girl too well not to take precautions. Anna saw business as the ultimate solution to most of the world's problems and would often quote an axiom from a Presbyterian clergyman, William Boetcker, wrongly attributed to Abraham Lincoln: '*You cannot help the poor man by destroying the rich.*'

The second reason was more practical. If Anna's efforts to get heroin led to trouble, I would need the *yakuza* boss to help. Blackmail was always a possibility, so was arrest; a stranger looking for a fix in a strange city was easy prey. I was, as the saying goes, covering her arse in the event of an emergency.

In my own mind I had given up any idea of finding Gojo Mura. It was patently an impossible task and I wasn't going to hold *Fuchida-san* to it. Obligation is taken seriously in Japan and I didn't wish to compromise him. Besides, with his identity changed, Gojo Mura would have created a new life for himself and probably had no wish to be reacquainted with his past. It was no different to Anna trying to find the two retired geisha who had trained her in *kinbaku*, rope bondage, and had later cared for her in the Nest of the Swallows. Of course, she hadn't suggested that we attempt to do so, stressing that they would be in their early seventies now if they were still alive.

Lunch was finally concluded with a dish of eel, one of the great Japanese delicacies, and quite clearly a compliment to me. In Japan eel is very near the top of the culinary list, whereas it is plentiful in Vanuatu, where the eels from the southern hemisphere come to breed. Anna, discovering this abundance, had often prepared the dish I was now being served. I had acquired a taste for it and was able to discuss the subtleties with my host. The dish served by the *mama-san* was of excellent quality.

Japanese people take their food very seriously. Their diet is mostly fish, so the subtle variations of taste are often completely lost on European palates accustomed to stronger flavours. But in Japanese society the smallest differences in taste and texture are often the subject of lively discussion. Preparation is everything and a compliment is taken seriously; no comment indicates either a culinary disaster or simply bad manners.

I recall explaining the natural miracle of eel migration to Anna, though not without some incredulity on her part, as the facts truly defy belief. Eels only breed in two or three places. In the southern hemisphere, they breed in the deep waters near Vanuatu and New Caledonia, and in the northern hemisphere in the deep waters of the Sargasso Sea in the West Indies, although Japanese eels spawn on the west Marianas Ridge in the Pacific.

The eels in every dam, stream, rivulet, river and municipal

drain head for one or other of these breeding grounds, often travelling miles overland to reach water. Once they have arrived at their destination they spawn and die, but the leptocephali – the tiny hatchlings no bigger than a gumleaf and still translucent – are carried on the ocean currents where they eventually turn into elvers and begin the migration back to dams, rivers, creeks, ponds or drains of fresh water, some travelling thousands of kilometres from where they were spawned. I recall telling Anna on the first occasion she served eel to me, 'That poor sod worked very hard to get onto our plates. It has travelled further than Marco Polo, so let's enjoy it!'

I left *Fuchida-san* at the door of his penthouse lift, having told him that I had decided to, as we say, let sleeping dogs lie, and asked him not to try to trace the whereabouts of Gojo Mura.

After a moment's silence he said, a small smile playing at the corners of his mouth, 'We shall see, *Duncan-san*. I will think about it. It could be a good exercise for my younger *wakagashira*. Perhaps we could add a missing persons service to our special skills.'

I returned to the Imperial Hotel alone in the Mercedes accompanied by only one of the black Toyotas containing the driver and three *wakagashira*. Upon arrival, thankfully without the mandatory squealing brakes and burning rubber, I quickly realised that things had changed for me. The doorman rushed to open the rear door of the Mercedes, but not before the three black suits in sunglasses had reached it, one standing on each side, while the third headed towards the main door of the hotel to ensure my way into the foyer was unimpeded. Again the two hotel pageboys stood motionless holding the plate-glass doors open and the five desk clerks had turned to stone.

Climbing from the car I said to the doorman, 'Please, this is *not* necessary, I am *gaijin* and have no authority here.'

But he remained rigid, his eyes fixed unblinkingly on some spot beyond me. 'Yessir!' he barked in the manner of a sergeant major taking instructions from his company commander.

Anna was still asleep, my note from the morning lying on the floor where it had been pushed under the door. She lay clutching her pillow, looking so beautiful I almost wanted to weep. I longed more than anything else to possess her. How could I love someone so much and not be permitted to make love to her?

I have often wondered since if I would ever have taken up with Marg again had Anna been other than the way she was. I don't know; I can never know. I loved them both, the yin and yang. I was aware that it wasn't moral or in some eyes even decent, and it certainly wasn't fair to either of them. But both acquiesced while remaining totally antagonistic towards the other. Some perverse competition was going on between them, though not only for the sole possession of the Nick Marg knew and loved or the Nicholas Anna knew and loved, but for the two entirely opposing points of view they represented. They were competing for two different future worlds, each strong and determined to win, both possessed of fine intellects, both playing out their emotional convictions and using each other as a yardstick to measure their success. It was a mind thing and I was, at best, the whetstone on which each sharpened the blade of her personal ambition.

Then again, perhaps that was crap. It was quite possible that Anna, ever the pragmatist, saw Marg providing intimacy she couldn't provide herself and realised that it was better coming from someone with whom she had nothing in common, an enemy she knew, than from someone who might ultimately replace her.

Marg, on the other hand, was the true enigma. If it wasn't

for the yin and yang reasons, then, I asked myself, why did she tolerate this time share? Still an extraordinarily attractive woman, she had been pursued by men far more politically and socially powerful than I was who came with the promise of marriage, security and respectability. Her explanation, unsolicited, was simply, 'Nick, I love, want and need you. But tomorrow I may not!' Marg was always scrupulously honest. She was warning me that she had accepted Anna but that was it. There would be no infidelity, no other women.

It had been a strange and unexpected day and I rather badly needed a Kirin, the excellent Japanese lager, and a few moments alone to think things out. I left a note to tell Anna I was downstairs at the bar and to call me when she wakened. When she had returned from her successful journey into the Tokyo night, I had been too overwrought and angry, and also too relieved at her safe return to get a blow-by-blow description of her search for dope.

Her cool, calculated and confident persona had been falling apart even before she'd left the hotel and, although it had been years since I'd witnessed her in such a state, I told myself it was the one time she was completely vulnerable and couldn't disguise her feelings. In the world she had entered the previous night this would be commonly recognised; heroin withdrawal is a universal experience amongst addicts, and can easily be exploited.

Now I was worried that she might not have obtained sufficient heroin to last the duration of our stay in Japan, which could be potentially disastrous. For several years after the coffee-scalding incident on the island I had begged her to seek help and she had certainly tried. Her regular 'business' trips overseas to try to kick her habit always ended in failure, as did her efforts to overcome her vaginismus, and my insistence – demand might be a more precise word – that she continue to seek professional help had produced a growing tension between us until Anna had finally broken down completely.

We had been out sailing on *Madam Butterfly* on our way for a picnic lunch on Hat Island, the actual name for the island we had laughingly come to call 'Coffee Scald'.

Anna had arrived the previous day for a week's visit after one of her 'business' trips, this time to a Swiss clinic. I had met her at the harbour airport after a prolonged liquid lunch with a customer.

I wasn't big on the proverbial business lunch, alas all too common in the islands, but he was a regular client and he believed I'd done him a favour, so he was being insistent. The favour consisted of my agreeing to load machinery between the hours of twelve and two to ship to New Guinea. This was when the country, including my loading crew, normally stopped for lunch. It was a small concession and didn't require an invitation to lunch.

I'd finally agreed, thinking I'd get away before two-thirty to meet the Sandringham flying boat, which was due to land on the harbour at three o'clock. But when I phoned the port terminal to check the time of arrival they told me takeoff had been delayed in Brisbane and the seaplane was expected in around five o'clock. My business associate was a bit of a booze artist, but I'm big enough to take a fair amount of grog. However, by the time the plane landed I'd had a skinful, though nothing I believed I couldn't handle. The delight at seeing Anna and the hope that this time she might be clean after her trip overseas should have been reason enough to stay happily sober.

As had become her custom, she'd brought two bottles of Cristal, her favourite champagne. One we called our 'joyous bottle', traditionally intended for her arrival, and the other our 'melancholy bottle', consumed the evening before her departure. After dinner on her first night home we would sit on the verandah looking over Beautiful Bay and quietly drink our joyous bottle, delighted to be together again.

On this particular visit I recall it was a beautiful evening with just the sliver of a new moon showing, the stars so numerous and the air so clear that they seemed to suffuse the sky with a constant glorious glitter. It was close to midnight when the joyous bottle stood empty and we foolishly decided to follow it with the melancholy one, which proved to be a salutary lesson that one should not interfere with tradition. Anna lifted her melancholy-filled champagne glass to indicate the stars, and began to recite in Japanese.

> 'Look up, up . . . up there, at the midnight sky
> At the game of chance within the firmament
> Saturn's rings, mooned Jupiter, planet Mars
> All yours if you hoist ambition's sails and set
> A galactic course, then cast a wide-flung net
> To fish for the brightest stars in all creation.'

'Anna, that is beautiful!' I exclaimed.

She laughed. 'Too much champagne. I have never recited it aloud to anyone before, although I do so in my head every morning the moment I wake and every night before I go to sleep.'

'Does it have a name, the poem, and what does it mean to you?' Like a lot of poetry, you don't always get the meaning first off, but I was curious about it because it was obviously very important to her.

'It is called "Fishing for Stars". It urges me to dare to seek my fortune everywhere and not to be afraid to take the risks involved in the truly big ventures,' she replied.

'It's lovely. Where did you learn it? Is it Japanese?'

Anna hesitated. Had I been sober I would have stopped as soon as I noticed her hesitation, knowing she could only have learned it in one place at one time. I daresay, had she too been less inebriated she would have reminded me of her request and in turn my promise never to ask questions about her experience under the Japanese unless she volunteered the information herself. 'Just something I learned long ago, Nicholas,' she replied.

'Him?' I asked stupidly, knowing.

'Yes.'

A voice in my head yelled, '*Stop! You've had too much to drink.*' But I couldn't. The champagne, added to what I'd drunk earlier, had tipped me over the edge and a blinding resentment fuelled my tongue. 'And you repeat it twice daily? Must be pretty important to you.'

'Yes,' Anna replied, not backing off.

'Why is that?'

'Nick, stop it! I don't want you to know. It has something to do with the silver cigarette case you found here in my bedroom.'

It was the wrong thing to say, another unspoken resentment that gnawed at my pathetic heart. A year or so back I had gone to fetch Anna's suitcase and had seen a silver cigarette case on the table beside her bed which she had obviously forgotten to pack. As Anna didn't smoke I thought it curious and before returning it to her I had briefly glanced at it, then inexcusably opened it to discover it contained just a dusting of a dirty white powder that I realised must be heroin. She had chased the dragon and no doubt intended to clean the cigarette case before she went through customs in Brisbane. On the lid of the case was inscribed in Japanese script a line that made no sense in that language.

It read: *Nyuwun pamit ratu.* I returned the case to her without commenting on the contents, but asked casually what the inscription meant, as it was clearly not Japanese.

'It is Javanese,' Anna replied, accepting the case and putting it into her handbag, 'a small joke.'

'A joke in Javanese written in Japanese? That's funny in itself,' I remarked at the time. 'Does it translate?'

'No' she replied. 'Some other time I will tell you, Nicholas,' she said, smiling and attempting to sound casual.

I have a half decent memory and it was only three words. To satisfy my curiosity I'd had it translated and found it meant *Goodbye, Princess*. It didn't take a lot of imagination to realise it had been presented to her by Konoe Akira. Anna had never mentioned the cigarette case again, nor had I, nor that I knew the meaning of the inscription on the lid; that is, until this starlit night when I had too much French booze in my belly.

'Ah, the famous silver cigarette case *Konoe-san* presented to you. The one in which you keep your smack; inscribed, no less, with the words,' I laughed, 'Goodbye, Princess'.

'Nick!' Anna said, her voice sharp yet tinged with dismay.

But it was too late. Five years of sexual frustration, childish resentment and jealousy of her Japanese mentor turned into verbal vomit, which I was unable to prevent spewing out of me. 'And it came with a lovely little poem about the stars?' I chuckled. 'Go on, darling, recite it for me again, will you?'

A moment's silence followed, then Anna rose and placed her glass on the bamboo table between us and reached for the melancholy bottle. She lifted it from the ice bucket in a clatter of melting ice cubes and upended it over my head. I could hear the gurgle of champagne and felt it fizz as it poured over my head, neck, chest and shoulders. 'Get fucked, Nick,' she said, then she dropped the empty champagne bottle, retrieved her own glass and jerked my waistband away from my waist and poured the contents down my trousers. 'That's the only French love you're going to get from me tonight, you bastard!' Without another word she walked calmly from the verandah into the house.

'Where are you going?' I called, suddenly sober, soaked, and feeling desperately ashamed of myself.

'To chase the dragon, arsehole!' Anna called back.

I wakened the next morning lambasting myself, using every unsavoury epithet I could think of, wincing at the thought of my behaviour the previous evening. I spent the first half of the morning preparing *Madam Butterfly* to sail and instructing cook to roast a chicken, bake a canary cake, Anna's favourite, and pack a picnic hamper. Sailing to Coffee Scald on the morning after her arrival was another of our traditions, although, like the melancholy bottle, I wasn't at all sure we would now be following it.

Anna appeared on the dock at about eleven and I was somewhat relieved to see that she wore white shorts and a sky-blue shirt, another tradition; it was the outfit she'd worn when I'd disastrously attempted to kidnap her and she had tossed scalding coffee over me. It suggested that she might agree to come along.

'Morning,' I called. No answer. I waited until she came closer and said with a shrug, 'What can I say? I was drunk and out of order. I apologise.'

'Accepted,' she replied crisply, though without even the hint of a smile.

'Anna, I *really* am sorry. It was a beautiful poem and it obviously means a great deal to you; to belittle it was unconscionable. We have an agreement that I don't pry into your past and I broke it. What can I do to make it up to you?'

'You can stop this longwinded and pathetic apology, Nicholas!' she said sharply, then added, 'And you can start looking for another girlfriend, one with a less unfortunate past.'

'You're back on the smack then? You never intended to give up, did you?'

'What do you think?'

My father had once counselled me as a teenager, when he'd caught me arguing vehemently with a friend over a matter of no consequence: 'Nick, most emotional arguments have one of two obvious conclusions: you either win or lose. So, before you open your big mouth, ask yourself: if I win this argument will it change anything, and what are the likely consequences? You will discover that, except in very rare circumstances, nothing positive will come from it either way and you may have lost a friend and changed very little else. Emotional altercations rarely have great potential for turning out well. Argue emotionally only when there is a deeply held belief at stake that you would only forsake if God required you to do so.'

Sometimes having a bishop as your dad becomes a bit tedious. 'But then I would appear to be weak in the eyes of my opponent,' I recall protesting.

'Ah yes, peace and goodwill always demand compromises. War occurs when we are no longer able to accommodate an adversary. True strength is knowing when that moment of principle arrives and our sense of truth has been betrayed.'

I was sober and contrite and I wasn't going to pick a fight, even if Anna used every foul imprecation known. 'Are we sailing to Coffee Scald?' I asked quietly, not looking directly at her and pretending to thread a length of rope through a brass eyehole in a sail.

'Yes.'

'Fifteen minutes?'

'Okay.'

'Good, I'll fetch the picnic hamper. Cook's baked your favourite canary cake.'

A tiny smile. 'You're pathetic, Nicholas!'

The wind had been fairly strong and changeable so that I was kept busy with the sails while Anna manned the tiller. There hadn't been much conversation between us on the way to Coffee Scald; in fact, apart from calling out the odd instruction, we had exchanged not a word.

Anna splashed ashore lugging the picnic hamper and proceeded to prepare lunch in the shade of a large coral outcrop while I tied sails and set the shallow-water anchor. She was waiting for me, seated on the beach and holding out a glass of white wine. I dropped to my haunches beside her to accept it. 'Fair wind. I think that was just about a record run,' I said, as a throwaway opening gambit, then, extending my glass, 'Cheers.'

'No, Nicholas, it was an ill wind and it brings no good,' she said, her glass un-clinked.

'Anna, please . . .'

'No, Nick, I cannot continue! I must go away from you. I cannot be your woman. I am useless!' She looked forlorn. 'I *must* let you go. You must find another woman to love you. But only understand, no one can love you as much as I do. It is not possible.' Then, heartbroken, she started to cry in earnest. It was the first time I had witnessed her howl. The usually self-contained Anna was now an abjectly miserable creature bawling her heart out, the wine glass abandoned, its contents spilled into her lap.

'Anna! Anna!' I threw my glass aside and dropped to my knees, holding her to my chest as she continued to weep, her breast and shoulders shaking against me. 'Darling, no! Not ever!' I cried, close to tears myself. 'Don't you understand, I love *you*. I don't *want* anyone else. They, the others, mean nothing!' I kissed the top of her head, her forehead, her hands covering her face, her ears. 'Sweetheart! Darling! Please!'

In an adult storybook I would have held her, comforted her and then made love to her on the lonely island beach, waves lapping at our feet, Deborah Kerr and Burt Lancaster in *From Here to Eternity*. But of course no such thing happened. Anna eventually quietened down then pulled away from me, brushing away her tears with the fingertips of both hands, regaining her dignity with this one small gesture. 'No, Nicholas,' she said quietly, 'we cannot continue.'

The next day Anna caught the DC-4 leaving for Sydney via Noumea. No tears and a peck on the cheek at the airport. 'Nice, Nicholas,' she said softly, and turning, walked across the tarmac to the waiting aeroplane.

My final view of her, seen through a blur of sudden tears, was of a perfectly contained Anna, the dark sheen of her hair, her trim figure in a beautifully cut grey business suit, the skirt just above the knees, nylon stockings and the click, click, click on the tarmac of the six-inch stiletto heels of her black leather shoes. The little Anna I'd seen on Coffee Scald was safely tucked away deep down where hurt couldn't reach.

The next month I was in turn angry, remorseful, tearful, drunk and belligerent. I picked fights, screwed around, paced the bedroom floor in the small hours of the morning, stopped myself reaching for the phone to call Melbourne on a thousand occasions, was consumed by self-pity and generally made a bloody idiot of myself. Until one night Joe Popkin, who must have heard about my pathetic carryings on, arrived by boat from Port Moresby and found me pissed as a newt in *Le Club Français*. Lifting me bodily (I weighed round 190 pounds) he carried me over his shoulder to a waiting taxi. Once home he dumped me under a cold shower then threw me, still wringing wet, into bed.

The following morning, bleary-eyed and hideously hungover, I stumbled onto the verandah where cook was serving Joe breakfast. 'Nick, mah man!' he exclaimed cheerfully. 'Sit you down, Champ. Take yoh'self a chair, boy. We got ourselves good news. Yeah, man . . . real *good* news!'

'You've arranged to have me shot? Put me out of my misery,' I muttered, plonking myself down heavily in the wicker chair, the smell of eggs and bacon causing my stomach to turn.

'Juice.' He handed me a glass of orange juice then turned to the cook. 'Cookie, bring masta Nick coffee. Head blong hem sore tumas.'

I sat with my chin on my chest, my head thumping like the clappers from hell, orange juice in my hand. 'What good news, Joe?' I ventured at last.

Joe cackled. 'Well you jes about alive ee-nuff for me to tell you, son. Las night I called Mel-bourne.' Joe laughed and clapped his hands, sending a jolt through my head. 'Hallelujah! Tomorrow she's comin' back. Dat Sandring-ham, it bringing yoh lover back to yoh arms! Now maybe we can do some shippin' busi-ness and Kevin, he gonna get offa mah back.' His voice changed and he mimicked Kevin. 'What's wrong wid Nick? The whole goddamned Pacific is crawlin' wid free pussy and he wants dat screwed-up junkie widda black leather corset, widda thigh-high boots!' Joe laughed, 'That's our partner, partner.'

Anna had once told me that she worked in a silk evening kimono and I would later question Kevin about the bondage uniform he imagined. 'Where you been? You ain't never seen no porn movies, Nick?' he asked, clearly astonished. 'Dem punishment dames, dat da standard uniform. Every Joe Palooka know dat, man!'

In fact, Kevin liked Anna a great deal and moreover

respected her for her acuity in business, constantly suggesting that they go into ventures together. Out of politeness Anna had asked me what I thought and seemed relieved when I told her I regarded it as a truly bad idea. Nevertheless he would seek her advice, often making a killing because of it. 'Soon Bren Gun, she gonna be wearing Gucci from Paris,' he'd promise after a successful venture, unaware that Bren Gun had been wearing fashion labels for several years and that Gucci was an Italian label.

The fifteen years that followed Anna's return to the island were not without their ups and downs; she would spend one week of every month with me and I would see her when I occasionally went to Melbourne. Anna was two people, the loving and generous woman who visited the island, and the businesswoman who ran a house of bondage. In our twenties and thirties, when most couples are building careers and having families, she was slowly making a small name as a property owner. She had speculated and gambled on the development of a post-Olympic Melbourne and done nicely without being noticed by the big developers. Her foresight in acquiring the properties around Madam Butterfly was unknown at the time, and she was lumped in with other small speculators under the collective title of slum landlord, those bit players who hoped to gain from the city's rapid expansion by buying in some of the right locations and making a small killing.

In fact, she was laying the foundations of a huge fortune. In the male business world of the sixties and seventies, nobody saw her coming. Her often rich and powerful clientele, many from the establishment and propertied elite, were generous with their advice, often boasting or confiding inside information. By slowly placing each building she bought into separate dollar shelf companies to protect her name, she quietly and discreetly built her property portfolio. Anna, for all her beauty, never glittered in public. She remained intensely private and low-key, crouched for the kill, ready for the Nauru property development site.

However, during the week she spent each month on the island, she let her hair down and soon became immensely popular, not only with the ex-pats but also with the local people, in particular amongst those who would eventually assume the mantle of leadership.

As a shipping company we clearly knew that ultimately our loyalty lay with the natives and self-government, but we had to appear to be neutral. Anna, who travelled with me around the islands, was investing in the future by supplying funds for education, overseas study and the development of political organisations whose members and leaders could be trained in basic leadership skills, politics, and recruitment techniques. She claimed the brightest kids on every Pacific Island, usually ferreted out from among the most gifted of the initial recipients of Uncle Joe scholarships. They were funded through the various indigenous political organisations she'd helped to create, to take accountancy and economics degrees in Australia, New Zealand, France and the United States. She would chuckle when the white rightwing elements on the island, which was almost everyone, would mutter darkly to one another in the clubs or at private dinner parties, 'They're being funded by the Communist party, you know. China and Russia are very involved. Moscow University is chock-full of Africans and Islanders. Jesus, some of the buggers have only just climbed out of the trees and they're supposed to be taking economics degrees.'

Anna went to great pains never to accept credit for her largesse. 'The people who will count in the future know who I am and those who have no future in the islands never need to know,' she'd say, happy to keep a low profile in these matters.

On the surface she appeared to be an extroverted, fun-loving, uncomplicated, witty young woman, a gracious hostess, a loving partner, and, everyone assumed, my beautiful mistress. I lost count of the number of times I heard, 'Nick, you lucky bugger!' when I was taking a piss in the club toilet. On one occasion in Rabaul it was the police commissioner, and I wondered what he'd say if I told him the beautiful woman he'd been ogling all night was a heroin addict and a murderer.

Now sitting in the bar in the Imperial Hotel in Tokyo nursing my second Kirin and waiting for Anna I wondered if the halcyon years were over. We'd been together for twenty years, most of them very good. We'd sailed and laughed and cried and shared each other's misfortunes. It had been my idea that we try to contact Konoe Akira, but Anna's obvious keenness to do so now concerned me.

I knew that she loved me in every way it was possible for her to love, but he had owned her in a manner I never could, or would wish to. He had been a part of the enormous damage done to her, although she could not accept this. In Anna's mind, he was responsible for everything she had become, and she knew with certainty that without him she would be dead.

The difficult part for me to accept was that this was probably true. He had given Anna sanctuary within the tyranny of the Japanese occupation, while extracting a bitter and selfish toll that denied her the ultimate entitlement of her womanhood.

However, in the process he had furnished her with a set of finely forged intellectual weapons to survive and even to prosper in a hostile world. Anna couldn't see that he had warped her mind and stolen the gift of absolute intimacy, the eternal way of a woman with a man.

Instead, I suspected, while he had no use for her body,

she still believed he owned her soul, and that this was a higher state of being. If we located him and they met, I was taking the chance that they might renew their relationship, and come together again to create a far stronger bond than the unconsummated love between the two of us. By now he would be a man in his early sixties and probably at the height of his intellectual powers. Anna, with her own hard-earned, practised and disciplined intelligence, would make a worthy acolyte.

While I had believed it was necessary for her to face her demons by confronting Konoe Akira, I was taking a gamble with our relationship. I tried to tell myself that if Anna discovered that the bond between them had long since been broken, she might eventually recover. Now, sitting in the bar waiting to hear of her exploits of the previous night, I wasn't feeling quite the clever Nick I'd thought myself to be on the verandah overlooking Beautiful Bay when I'd suggested the reunion.

Anna arrived wearing knee-length high-heeled boots, jeans and a white cashmere polo-necked sweater, her hair catching the light as she entered the bar. The barman, mixing a martini for another guest, stopped mid-shake and came over to us.

'*Sake tokutei reishu* [sake served specially cold],' Anna requested, smiling, unaware of our newfound notoriety. Pointing to the cocktail shaker resting on his mixing bar she added, 'Please, serve your honourable customer, I am in no hurry and do not deserve prior attention.'

'Sleep well?' I asked as she leaned over to kiss me on the cheek.

'Like a baby.' She glanced at her watch. 'Ten hours. I needed it. A long night,' she said in a staccato manner.

'So, tell me.'

She glanced around quickly. 'Not here, Nicholas . . . later.'

'We can speak in English,' I laughed. 'We *are* speaking in

English!'

'I have to go back tonight,' she said quickly in a low voice.

'Back? Where?'

'Topaz.'

'The bondage joint in Roppongi?'

'Yes.'

'Why?'

'I left my silver cigarette case behind.'

'What, forgot it? Phone, tell them to put it in a taxi.'

'No.'

I was losing patience. 'Why not?'

'It was deliberate, a calling card.'

'Shit no! Anna, don't tell me . . .'

'I have to go alone.'

'Bullshit! That's not what we agreed.'

'I know, but he won't come otherwise. I told you, they don't allow *gaijin* and I am allowed *only* because I have a special introduction and am a fellow professional in the art of *kinbaku*.'

'Okay, then we'll give it a miss. Go home.'

Anna's violet-blue eyes looked at me, unblinking. 'No, Nicholas, I can't do that.'

CHAPTER SEVEN

'You have killed before, Nick-san.
We both know only the first time is difficult.
Come, we must prepare.'
Oyabun Fuchida, Tokyo

I HAVE WRITTEN EARLIER about the futility
of pursuing an argument when the outcome won't change
anything, but I was furious. I saw myself as Anna's
protector, but now she wanted to face Konoe Akira alone.
I hadn't any idea what the outcome might be, but I convinced
myself that it wouldn't be good, that he could even harm her. *If*
she'd mentioned me on her previous visit to Topaz, the house
of bondage – and I realised it was a big *if* – why was her former
mentor insisting she come alone?

When I imagined the confrontation, Anna always saw
Konoe Akira in a different light, not as the immaculately clad
and all-powerful commander of the Japanese forces in Tjilatjap
that she had known but as a civilian in his sixties with a severe
limp. In my mind I had rehearsed her reaction to him after
twenty years. First would come the slow realisation that the
greying man in her presence was no longer in control of her
mind, then the understanding that she was free from the horror
of the past and of his power over her. I imagined standing at her
side with a foolish grin on my face, trying not to show too much

emotion in front of the bitter, disillusioned old man leaning heavily on his walking stick.

'Anna, you could be walking into a trap!' I cried angrily.

'No, Nicholas, he has sent *his* calling card.'

'And what's that supposed to mean?'

She reached for her handbag. 'I went to the porter's desk on my way here, and . . .' From the interior of her bag she lifted a gold fob watch and chain. 'He sent me this.'

I took the magnificent chronometer, weighing it in my hand, the heavy gold links settling in my palm. 'So you were expecting a message?' I asked pointedly.

'Yes, of course. They said they would contact me if he responded. When I woke up an envelope had been pushed under the door,' Anna pointed at the watch in my hand, 'to say there was a parcel waiting for me.'

'Just this, the watch?' I asked.

'No, it came with a note.'

'From him?'

Anna nodded. 'It's very friendly.'

'May I see it?'

Anna hesitated momentarily then reached into her handbag and produced the note. It was carefully written in Japanese on handmade paper, set out in four widely spaced columns of exquisite kanji as if each was a separate message placed on paper after considerable thought.

Honourable Second Vase,
I am deeply honoured that you
wish to renew our acquaintanceship.

These flowers they want to dance
and you are making them stand

to attention. They are not an
orchestra, they are a jazz group.

We will meet tomorrow night at
six o'clock, when it is essential
that you are alone.

I look forward to seeing
the photographs of the
persimmon trees
you have planted.

Sincerely,
Konoe Akira

Anna, I felt sure, could see my frown increasing as I attempted to absorb the meaning hidden within the note: the address, Honourable Second Vase; the allusion to the vase of flowers made no sense and was obviously some kind of code between them. 'The flowers as a jazz group?' I asked. 'What's that all about?'

'It is a small joke about flower arrangements,' Anna explained, slightly flustered. 'He is reminding me of the first day we met. It's meant to tell me that I may come on my own terms and that our meeting will be a friendly one.'

'Oh, you know this, do you?' I returned the sheet to her and noted how carefully she folded it, holding it a fraction too long and close to her chest before placing it back in her handbag. Anna, I could sense, was excited. 'I see. A joke about flowers to tell you that you're safe?' I said without humour. 'Well, *Blossom*, I will nevertheless wait outside Topaz until you return from discussing your mutual flowery arrangements.'

Anna ignored my sarcasm and the not very clever and needlessly disparaging play on words. She threw up her hands in a gesture of impatience. 'Ha! I can just imagine! A six-foot three-inch *gaijin* with his arms folded across his chest waiting outside the entrance like a nightclub bouncer. You are sure to go unnoticed!' Anna tossed her head, always a sign that she was nervous and thinking on her feet. 'Nicholas, I'll be fine, quite safe. Sending the pocket watch . . . the flower joke . . . it's obvious he wants it to be a cordial meeting.'

Clutching at straws I said, 'Yes, but can he be trusted? Didn't you say he was a heroin addict?'

'What's that supposed to mean?' Anna said, indignant. 'Yes, he uses heroin, or he did. So do I. It doesn't make us potentially violent or untrustworthy.'

I didn't much care for the virtuous coupling of the two addicts. 'Anna, it's a trap. I just know it! My instincts in such matters are rarely wrong.'

'That's total crap, Nicholas! Your instincts are no better than mine. Besides, I've made up my mind and I'm not jeopardising our meeting because he thinks I've brought along what he'll see as a personal bodyguard. As it is, he could well believe that *I'm* the one setting the trap.'

'What's that supposed to mean?'

'Well, for instance, he could be afraid I've come to Japan to report him for war crimes.'

This had occurred to me, but I hadn't mentioned it to Anna. I should have known the thought wouldn't have escaped her, although almost certainly a case such as this wouldn't be reopened. The War Crimes Tribunal might have charged him, but a hearing was unlikely. Konoe Akira was from a leading family and, like so many important families, his had probably allied itself with one of the large vertically integrated industrial groups usually organised around a bank, groups such as Mitsui, Mitsubishi, Yasuda, and many others. The War Crimes Tribunal had finally come to the conclusion that these groups, and the individuals within them, were essential to Japan's post-war reconstruction. Hearings, unless they concerned the more heinous crimes, were postponed and eventually the charges were dropped. There were few trials after 1950.

'What do you mean? He'll think I'm some big *gaijin* policeman from Interpol? You obviously didn't make any mention of me when you left your calling card.'

'No, I'm afraid I didn't.'

'Why not?'

Anna sighed, sipped her drink then looked at me directly. 'Why? Because I never intended for you to be at our first meeting. I have things I need to say . . .' Anna shrugged, blue eyes wide. I had seen that look before, her eyes challenging me, telling me her mind was made up.

My father was right – our argument wasn't going anywhere good and I'd pushed Anna into a corner, making her explain her motives and, in turn, forcing her to offend me.

'Right!' I said, getting to my feet, managing, though only just, to keep my voice more or less civil. 'I need a shower. Will I see you upstairs before you go?'

'Of course . . . I have to change.'

I turned and walked to the entrance of the bar.

'Nicholas!' Anna called.

I stopped and looked back, scowling. 'What?'

Anna smiled and held out her hand. 'The watch, please.'

I looked down, surprised that I still held the gold watch and chain, the calling card with its unspoken message to her across the years. Suddenly, unable to contain my fury, I hurled it at the bar, its chain trailing through the air behind it and whipping past the barman's head to crash into a stand of bottles on the counter, the heavy gold chain snaking around a Johnny Walker bottle and preventing it from falling to the ground. 'Good luck!' I cried furiously.

While I instantly regretted my fit of jealousy and the vulnerability it exposed, I lacked the guts to apologise in public. Instead I fled the cocktail bar like a petulant schoolboy, the surprised drinkers no doubt watching my angry departure, then staring at a mortified Anna.

When I walked from the shower back into the bedroom Anna was seated at the mirror brushing her hair. She was dressed in the Chanel suit, the outfit she'd worn to meet the Mitsubishi executives, and was wearing the two solitaire diamond earrings. 'I wish to apologise. I only hope the watch can be repaired,' I said, shamefaced.

'It isn't broken,' she said crisply without looking up at me. Then placing the brush on the dressing table with a small, deliberate bang she rose from the chair and reached for her handbag. 'Well, I'll be off. The car will be waiting downstairs.' She glanced briefly at me, her expression deadpan. 'Blossom mustn't be late now, must she?'

'Kiss?' I asked with a rueful grin.

Anna had already moved several steps from where I stood and now halted and bent over slightly with her derrière facing me, and in a voice far from amused snapped, 'You can kiss my arse, Nicholas Duncan!'

'Gladly,' I returned, but by this time she'd reached the door and moments before it swung shut I heard the click-clack-click of her expensive stilettos on the Italian marble foyer leading to the lift. 'Jesus, what now?' I said aloud, plonking myself down on the edge of the bed, aware that I'd screwed up big time.

The 'what now' turned out to be another long, vexing

and sleepless night as I waited for Anna to return to the hotel. My imagination ran riot – Anna in a silk kimono attending to Konoe Akira's perverted needs, showing him how much more she had learned over the years, helping him to inject heroin, seated at his feet, her blue eyes fixed on him, drinking in every word he said, even modestly telling of her success and giving him the credit for it. My febrile imagination knew no bounds. I even pictured Anna naked with her worshipful master fucking her, his tiny cock happily accepted, vaginismus free, as she moaned in ecstasy.

By 7 a.m. I could contain myself no longer. I dressed and went downstairs to hail a taxi. 'Roppongi – take me to a place called Topaz!' I instructed.

The taxi driver hesitated. 'I don't know this place in Roppongi, sir. Do you have the address?'

I pointed to his radio. 'Call your base,' I snapped. He did so and moments later the operator answered to say they couldn't locate a place of that name. 'Shit!' I exclaimed in English. Then in Japanese I instructed him to wait. I jumped from the taxi and ran up the steps, entered the hotel and, with my newfound *yakuza* notoriety, interrupted a clerk on the telephone. He immediately hung up and stood to rigid attention. 'Topaz, in Roppongi!' I barked. 'I need the exact address.'

'Immediately, *Duncan-san!*' He reached once more for the telephone and instructed the hotel switchboard to find the address, then waited nervously for the reply. A minute or so later he shouted down the receiver, 'Look again!' Finally, his hand shaking, he placed the receiver back into its cradle. '*Duncan-san*, we regret there is no such address,' he apologised.

I guess I was exhausted and overwrought. 'This is bullshit!' I cried, my fist thumping the desk so that the clerk jumped backwards and brought his hands up to protect his face, anticipating a punch. I shoved my hand in my pocket and withdrew two notes, a thousand yen and a five-thousand yen. Placing the thousand on the counter I said, 'Here, give this to the taxi driver. Tell him I no longer need him.' I handed him the second note. 'For your assistance,' I growled.

I returned to my room, then decided on the spur of the moment to have breakfast, realising that I hadn't eaten since I'd left the penthouse apartment of my butterfly-collecting mate the previous day. I told myself I needed coffee, food and a little time to calm down.

I couldn't yet grasp the fact that Anna had lied to me, deliberately concealing the whereabouts of her assignation with Konoe Akira. Christ! What was going on? Was this a conspiracy hatched between the two of them? Our trip to Japan organised long before we'd left? Was my suggestion that she come along with me a carefully cultivated thought planted by Anna, when I'd imagined it was all my own idea? Had I been suckered into the whole thing?

Over a couple of cups of strong black coffee, toast and a ham omelette – I couldn't stomach the thought of salted salmon or dried horse – I calmed down somewhat and realised that I was exhausted and not thinking straight, asking myself too many emotionally charged and unanswerable questions. Anna was a big girl, travelled frequently, spoke Japanese fluently – she wouldn't have needed an excuse to come to Japan alone to sort things out with Konoe Akira. She could have done so by travelling via Japan on one of her trips to Europe and I would never have known the difference.

I needed to understand Anna's reason for deliberately concealing the place of assignation with Konoe Akira, after we'd agreed that we'd meet him together. Something must have occurred when she'd gone looking for drugs. Was she attempting to protect me if things went wrong? It seemed unlikely. Did she, as she claimed, want to confront her one-time mentor on her own, believing that this was the only way she could lay the ghosts of the past to rest?

What was becoming clearer was that she'd gone looking for heroin and, using the letter of introduction she'd brought with her, entered the house of bondage (whatever its name), arranged for a source of heroin and, furthermore, been accepted as a fellow *kinbaku* bondage mistress by the proprietors. Then having earned their trust, she'd consequently asked about Konoe Akira. Anna was smart enough to realise I would probably insist, as we'd previously agreed, on attending any meeting, and even if she refused to allow me, I would nevertheless follow her to be at hand should things go wrong. So she had deliberately concealed the true name of the establishment. Of course, this was pure conjecture on my part, but it seemed more probable than the phantasmagoria and nonsense that had previously run through my stupid head.

However, there was one factor I couldn't disregard, the simplest and only real fact in all these speculations – Anna hadn't returned to the hotel. I had known her intimately for twenty years and while I realise one can never completely know the mind of another, I felt certain she would, despite our acrimonious parting, have called to say she was safe but delayed and told me when she would be back.

Anna never neglected even the tiniest details, let alone something as important as this. She had no possible reason to disappear and had much to lose by doing so, for example, the impending McVitty payback that would establish the basis for her fortune. If she had wanted to change her life, this was not the place or the time to do it. Anna, I decided, was undoubtedly in trouble.

I called the *yakuza oyabun Fuchida-san* just after nine on the number he'd given me, only to be told by Miss Sparkle, his *mama-san*, that he was unavailable and that he'd call me back. Just before eleven he called and I explained that I had a problem. I was about to expand on it, saying, '*Fuchida-san*, I think there has been an abduction —'

'No more!' the *oyabun* yelled. 'Hotel telephones are not reliable. There are too many ears listening to foreign guests. I will send someone to fetch you in half an hour and we will have lunch at my apartment.'

I realised after I'd replaced the phone that I should have volunteered to take a taxi, that another hotel invasion by the *yakuza* in half an hour would further confirm my fearsome reputation among the staff. However, it also occurred to me that if, as *Fuchida-san* suggested, phone tapping was commonplace, then his first visit to the hotel would certainly have been reported to the authorities and, as a consequence, the telephone in our suite would have received more than a little attention from the First Intelligence Division, Japan's equivalent of the FBI.

To my enormous relief, only a single black Toyota with a driver and two black-suited foot soldiers in dark glasses turned up. But it seemed to make little difference: the doorman turned to cement, the staff at the reception desk froze and the bellboys appeared to be afflicted by rigor mortis.

Once in the *oyabun's* apartment, with the *mama-san* Miss Sparkle serving us green tea, I explained what I suspected had happened to Anna, or at least enough for him to understand the relationship between her and Konoe Akira. His first question, of course, was to ask the name of the bondage house, and when I shrugged and said I didn't know, he rose and went to the phone in his office and returned a few minutes later. 'They are all under *yakuza* control. We will know soon enough. There are not so many houses of bondage – it is a rich man's diversion.' He laughed. 'The poor can't afford a rope that isn't attached to something they are required to pull.'

'Do you think your own people may have been hired to abduct Anna?' I asked.

'It is possible; the one answer will supply the other,' he said. 'If so, our problem is solved. But it is unlikely. *Yakuza* are not happy to abduct a foreigner. It is bad for Japan and the government, and the First Intelligence Division will not tolerate it. If it *must* be done then I must know about it, so I can make sure the forces of law will not intervene.' It was yet another example of the interconnectedness of the *yakuza* and the formal law-enforcement authorities.

'But what if she's harmed, even . . .' I couldn't complete the sentence.

'Killed? *No*, that will not happen. She is a foreigner,' he said with emphasis.

Lunch was a simple affair. Traditionally, towards the end of April, Japan swaps from warm *udon* noodle soups to cold *soba* noodles topped with sesame seeds, grated ginger, dried seaweed, chopped green onions and wasabi served with dipping sauces. Miss Sparkle had been given the task of calling his five *oyabun*, the senior *yakuza* who ran Tokyo under his overall control, and throughout lunch my host was constantly being called to the phone. At 1.25 p.m. a call came in to say his men had located the house of bondage that Anna had visited. I couldn't give her marks for originality; she'd simply switched semi-precious stones. It was called Jade House.

'Have you news of Anna?' I inquired anxiously.

'This Konoe Akira must be very powerful or very rich, or both. The Jade Mistress will not talk and denies seeing *Anna-san*.'

'Oh? Then how do we know we have the right place?'

Fuchida-san grinned. 'In all *yakuza* interests there is always someone planted – they are known as "caretaker's eyes and ears". It is how we know what's going on and are not cheated of our share of the profits. Our informer says Anna was present last night and that she demonstrated some *kinbaku* techniques they didn't know. She says Anna is very skilled and earned true admiration from the other professionals, but later when *Anna-san* was abducted, she personally was with a patron and so didn't see who abducted her.'

'How then will we find out?'

The *yakuza* boss laughed. 'I will personally ask the Jade Mistress. Her denial tells me that the abduction is not simply a criminal gang looking to kidnap a *gaijin* for the ransom money she might bring, but involves either herself or one of her patrons, otherwise she would have immediately reported the incident to our people, to whom she pays protection. We also know she was instrumental in arranging the meeting last night at the Jade House between your partner and Konoe Akira, presumably a valued client and certainly a very powerful and influential person. She would be foolish to risk his retaliation by attempting to gain personally from the abduction. By not informing us in the first place she no doubt hoped to hide the information so that if the police made inquiries she could deny ever knowing your partner or Konoe Akira, which is standard practice in a place such as that. Now that she knows that the *yakuza* are asking questions she also knows that she has been exposed and cannot deny being aware of Anna. To do so would put everything at risk. So now she will plead loss of face by being asked to inform a mere *wakagashira* of the incident. This will be her excuse for not contacting us earlier. She will claim that she *must* be seen to have demanded someone of equal stature to her client in order to inform us correctly, otherwise, if the incident becomes known among her other patrons, the reputation of her establishment and herself will be diminished in their eyes.'

These intricacies of Japanese social protocol were way beyond me. 'So she will tell us who was involved?' I asked.

Fuchida-san jerked his head back, momentarily hurt by my lack of faith. 'Of course! She requires someone with the status of an *oyabun*, but I will bring her extra honour by attending myself.'

'May I come?' I said, anxious not to be left behind to wait.

The *yakuza* boss hesitated. 'Nick-san, in Japan there are eyes everywhere. Are you sure you want to be seen to be involved?'

'What? With you . . . the *yakuza*?'

He nodded. 'Sometimes it can be difficult, the authorities . . . you are *gaijin*, a foreigner,' he explained.

'It is already too late. Since your visit to the Imperial Hotel the staff turn to stone every time I appear. I imagine the "eyes" you talk about are already well aware of our friendship and have alerted the "ears".'

'That is true. Come with me then. Have you ever been into a house of bondage, Nick-san?'

I shook my head. Anna had never allowed me to enter the Madam Butterfly premises. 'No, I have never felt sufficiently guilty to want to pay to be punished,' I joked.

'Then you are definitely not Japanese,' he grinned. 'In Japan, guilt and shame are just as much a part of our national and individual personality as love and joy. Their ultimate expression is *seppuku*, ritual suicide.'

This time the flying *yakuza* circus contained six black Toyotas with four men to each car and *Fuchida-san* and myself in the big Mercedes. 'We will block the street outside the premises so that the people in the immediate area will come to watch,' he explained. 'In this way the Jade Mistress will gain a great deal of face and prestige from my visit, her honour will have been satisfied and her rich patrons suitably mollified.' He chuckled.

I was slowly beginning to grasp the extent of the subtleties and intricacies of Japanese society, although I realised I would never be able to understand them all. When manners, mannerisms and meanings have such delicate nuances that one word placed or emphasised in a certain way in a perfectly proper statement can corrupt it and give it quite the opposite meaning, then only one who is born and raised in a particular class or section of the society can interpret it.

We turned into a narrow cul-de-sac, the six Toyotas making an appropriate amount of noise with squealing tyres and blasting horns. 'Noise is essential to create fear and anticipation in the public,' the *yakuza* boss shouted above the din. 'A proper entrance is everything.'

We came to a halt in what seemed like a synchronised squeal of all twenty-eight tyres with the smoke of burning rubber rising from the surface of the road. 'Excellent!' *Fuchida-san* exclaimed with a satisfied smile. The three leading Toyotas had halted one behind the other at the end of the narrow cul-de-sac and directly in front of what appeared to be a small three-storeyed apartment building occupying its entire width. The only distinctive feature to separate it from the surrounding buildings was its jade-green door, at which two older black-suited *yakuza* stood guard.

'I guess we've arrived!' I exclaimed.

'We will wait, *Nick-san*. First let the people come. An entrance without an audience is pointless.' *Fuchida-san* laughed. 'Unless it is an assassination.'

We waited as the foot soldiers piled out of the black vehicles to surround the Mercedes. The noise of our arrival subsided and I could hear the sound of running feet as the street rapidly filled with onlookers who began to line up on either pavement, each selecting a position and then standing silently at polite attention. In almost no time, more than a hundred people appeared to have gathered from nowhere. The *yakuza* boss, watching them arrive, suddenly made up his mind. 'There are now enough people; the Jade Mistress will gain face. We can go in.'

We stepped out of the large black car surrounded by *yakuza* to a buzz of excitement from the crowd. There was an almost palpable feeling of fear in the crowd mixed with a sense of delicious excitement, as if they were being permitted to take part in an exciting public event. *Fuchida-san*, stern-faced, bowed in a perfunctory way to acknowledge them, whereupon the onlookers on both sides of the street immediately inclined their bodies in a deep formal bow. It reminded me of primary-school classes when we all greeted the teacher with a resounding chorus of 'Good morning, Miss' as she entered the class. This crowd, as excited as schoolchildren, were unabashedly saluting the crime chief of Tokyo. They maintained the bow until we reached the jade-green door and entered to the equally deep bows of the two *yakuza* guards.

The *wakagashira* and foot soldiers, arms folded, remained outside, lined up across the width of the building, facing the crowd in a menacing display intended to heighten their sense of occasion.

Fuchida-san turned to me. 'If you will permit me to talk, *Nick-san*?'

'Of course.'

'There is a manner to be observed,' he added gratuitously.

The Jade Mistress, dressed in a formal kimono, met us in a small reception lounge. She was kneeling, geisha style, with her weight on her heels. The *yakuza* boss bowed politely, saying only a single word, '*Mama-san*'. I wasn't sure whether this was an insult or the correct way to address the mistress of a house of bondage.

The woman appeared to be in her forties, though it was difficult to tell under the heavy make-up, her face a flat, white, powdered mask punctuated with dark black-rimmed eyes and brilliant red Clara Bow lips. If she was the senior dominatrix, her get-up was in marked contrast to the black leather thigh-high boots and bikini of Kevin's pornographic movie fantasies, and I wondered briefly about the traditional *kinbaku* kimono Anna wore while working at Madam Butterfly. The *mama-san* bowed deeply in the *saikeirei* manner, her forehead touching the floor in the highest form of salutation to a feared superior. 'Welcome, *Oyabun*, to the Jade House,' she said in a voice hardly above a whisper.

'Thank you, *Mama-san*. My visit is intended to honour you and your house. I have with me a *gaijin* of great importance and it would give me great distress if the answers you are about to give me are not the ones I require.'

In a gesture reminiscent of a gangster movie he'd taken

a gold Dunhill lighter from his suit pocket, and as the Jade Mistress came out of her bow, he flicked it alight so that her eyes were attracted to the flame and to his hand with the missing pinkie. He would continue throughout the ensuing conversation to flick the lighter on and off. Like a bird in front of a snake she was mesmerised, unable to take her eyes off his mutilated hand, her mind I felt sure very aware of what it signified.

'I am servant to your wishes, *Oyabun-dono*,' the Jade Mistress replied. The suffix *'dono'* means 'lord' and is used as the ultimate mark of respect. Quite clearly the Jade Mistress wasn't taking *Fuchida-san's* visit lightly, or, like the true actress she was trained to be, she was playing the role of humble compliance to perfection.

'You must allow me to leave with the satisfaction of having pleased my honourable colleague, thus enabling me to reward you by allowing the Jade House to maintain its integrity and its reputation in the eyes of your esteemed patrons.' This sentence was punctuated by three flicks of the lighter flame.

The formality of the language, delivered in an even monologue, sounded like an actor's first reading of a play, but then I realised that this was precisely the intention. The threat to the continuation of the Jade House, buried in polite and formal language delivered without emotion, informed the *mama-san* that she would have only one opportunity to come clean, the implication being that, if she refused, she would cause the unthinkable – a loss of face for *Fuchida-san*. The consequences were unimaginable.

The Jade Mistress bowed deeply once again. 'It is not possible to refuse your request, honourable *Oyabun-dono*. The abduction was carried out by the writer of books.'

'Thank you, you have been most courteous, *Mama-san*. I will now ask a question to which you will merely nod your head so your lips may remain sealed. Was this abduction at the request of someone whose approach can be recognised by the tap, tap, tap of his cane?' The Jade Mistress, in an almost imperceptible gesture, lowered her eyes and nodded her head. 'I honour your house,' *Fuchida-san* said softly, then bowed and added, 'We will trouble you no further.' The *yakuza* boss paused. 'But for one more question . . . the whereabouts of the mistress of *kinbaku*?'

Her head touched the floor. 'I do not know, *Oyabun*, it was not revealed to me.'

'We will leave now, Jade Mistress,' *Fuchida-san* said, giving her finally her correct title.

'It will always be an honour to welcome you to our humble house, *Oyabun*,' the Jade Mistress answered, bowing as deeply as before.

But the *yakuza* boss had one more trick up his sleeve. Producing a small notepad and then a gold Parker pen, he handed them to her silently. She read what was written in the note that *Fuchida-san* would later show me. As I remember it, the note said: *Write the name of the people who kidnapped Anna-san and the name of the person who ordered it to be done. Then sign it.* I recall how the Jade Mistress could barely control her hand sufficiently to write, but I later saw she had written the four words, *Shield Society, Konoe-dono,* and signed it, *Kanako Nariko.*

I'd thought the performance with the Dunhill had been a little over the top, but it was nothing compared to the extroverted display when the *yakuza* boss had first come to meet me at the Imperial Hotel. Then *Fuchida-san* had openly flaunted his power, even though there seemed no need to do so, whereas in the Jade House he had concealed it, in the first instance brandishing the metaphorical sword, in the second deliberately leaving it in the scabbard, thereby emphasising the menace behind his calm words. The note at the end, confirming that both parties had understood the oblique dialogue, demonstrated the thoroughness of *Fuchida-san*'s interrogation method.

Neither Konoe Akira's name nor Anna's had been spoken, and Yukio Mishima, novelist, leader of the Shield Society, and a declared enemy of the government, had only been alluded to obliquely. If the room had been bugged, the exchange was open to conjecture and easily denied or otherwise explained away.

Back in the big black car we reversed the entire length of the narrow road in a furious whine of engines. I waited until we had turned into a major thoroughfare before asking, 'Do we know how to get to the Shield Society?'

'Oh, you know about them?' *Fuchida-san* asked, surprised.

'My father again,' I confessed. 'He likes to keep informed.'

The Shield Society was an extreme rightwing post-war militarist secret society founded and led by the brilliant and famous Japanese writer, Yukio Mishima. Later, in November of the same year we were in Japan, he attempted a futile *coup d'état*, and after its disastrous failure he committed *seppuku* – ritual suicide.

'You are fortunate to have such a scholar for a father, *Nick-san*. Your country should make him a diplomat to Japan.'

'Thank you, I will tell him of this compliment from you, *Fuchida-san*. But with these fascists . . . Will Anna be safe?'

He thought for a moment. 'They are crazy romantics and very dangerous, but there is no political point to make in harming her. This is almost certainly a paid kidnapping, or one done as a favour to Konoe Akira. From what you have indicated he is just the type of old-guard rightwing militarist who would secretly provide them with finance and logistical support.'

I was only partially satisfied with *Fuchida-san*'s answer. 'You don't think they may want to use Anna's kidnapping for propaganda? You know, drum up some support for the Shield Society among the common people, the poor and deprived who blame the Western world for their misfortune?'

The *yakuza* boss shook his head. 'There is no strong feeling against Westerners, even among the disadvantaged. Japan had been at war off and on since 1931 and by the end of 1945 we were destroyed and broken as a nation. Our people were starving, our cities burnt and the working class in particular was thoroughly disillusioned. The warmongering rulers had brought them nothing but death, defeat, misery and empty bellies. I don't think the common folk want to see the return of those days. Those pre-war times, when the Emperor was regarded as a god and had complete control of the state, are long past. Only extreme rightwing romantics like Yukio Mishima and diehards such as Konoe Akira see the old Japan as better than the new society we now live in. The government would like nothing more than to learn of such a kidnapping; it would be the perfect excuse for them to interfere directly.'

'You mean that right now we could go directly to the First Intelligence Division or the police?'

'Of course.'

'But —'

Before I could continue he interrupted. 'Then the crazies would almost certainly kill *Anna-san* in retaliation.'

'And that won't happen when the *yakuza* come calling?'

'*Hai!* I have a plan,' he said. 'You must wait until the meeting I have arranged with my people.'

'Do you know of Konoe Akira?' I asked, thinking *Fuchida-san* might be able to bring me up-to-date with his post-war career.

'I know of him, but I do not know him, which is not unusual. These old-guard families often keep a pretty low profile.

I have put three of my best men on the job and by the time we meet with my five *oyabun* I expect we will have a complete profile on him and also know where Konoe Akira lives. We have been watching these fanatics for some time. Like the government, we see them as a distinct threat to the harmony of our nation. If we can prove Konoe Akira is heavily involved with this group it will earn us the gratitude of the authorities.'

'But if Konoe Akira is a member of one of the powerful family groups, will he not have a lot of influence . . . protection?'

'*Hai*! If it becomes known that he is involved in this lunacy he will have dug his own grave. His powerful friends will desert him.'

'Your plans to get to Konoe Akira . . . I would not like them to put Anna in any danger.'

'*Nick-san*, I cannot deny that she is already in some danger. Our plan is to attempt to rescue her. Konoe Akira will stand to lose too much not to respect our wishes, just like the Jade Mistress. This is Japan and sometimes a woman may have a certain value, but it is never greater than the scandal she may bring if her tongue is loosened. From what you have told me, Anna would look very beautiful on the television explaining the past and exposing the scion of a noble family. In this case shame is our most powerful weapon.'

'No violence then?'

He laughed, this time a real laugh. 'Violence comes when you least expect it. We will prepare for a battle and hope the enemy comes out carrying a white flag.' *Fuchida-san* clapped me on the shoulder. 'You have done me a great service, *Nick-san*. I feel young again, and it will do my men good to see their *oyabun* leading them in a patriotic cause. Intimidation is essentially a boring pastime; it has been too long since we did something for the honour of the new Japan.'

'But only after Anna is freed,' I begged.

'*Hai*! Of course, but afterwards perhaps we will be less passive.' He turned and grinned at me. I made no reply, unsure whether 'we' included me. Once Anna was safe I had resolved that come hell or high water we'd be getting out of Japan; I wasn't going to become involved in putting down some fanatical uprising. As Kevin would have said, '*What I want yer to know, buddy, I ain't no fuckin' hero.*'

We arrived back at the apartment building and once we reached the penthouse after the shenanigans with the cars and the lift, I asked if I might use one of the numerous phones that were keeping Miss Sparkle running around like the proverbial blue-arsed fly. I couldn't help being puzzled that the *yakuza* boss didn't have a young whip-smart lieutenant or some such to do his phone work, note-taking and administration. The old woman with her hair styled in the manner of a geisha wearing the ridiculous sparkling ear pendants simply didn't fit my image of personal assistant to the most powerful crime boss in Tokyo.

Of course, my most ardent wish was that Anna had returned to the hotel, and a situation that was becoming a little complicated would then be resolved. Just to be sure, we'd take an almost immediate taxi ride to the airport.

The hotel switchboard dialled our suite and after a small delay told me that there was no response. I had felt constrained for too long. 'Get reception to send someone up to my suite and take a look!' I yelled down the phone. Then using the newfound influence they didn't know I didn't have I shouted, 'Or there will be more trouble than any of you monkeys can handle!' using *Fuchida-san*'s term for them. I seemed to wait for ages only to be finally told in a trembling voice, prefaced by a thousand stuttered apologies, that Anna was not in the suite.

I returned to the chrome and black room to discover

five older *yakuza* men seated around the highly polished circular table – all of them *oyabun* as I was later to learn – in earnest discussion with *Fuchida-san*. They were all sporting the mandatory black suits and cropped hair, some of it greying, although they had removed their sunglasses. The chrome pendant lamp etched shadows onto their faces, giving them the appearance of a group of stern-faced generals, which, in a manner of speaking, I suppose they were. A chair had been placed in the circle for me, and the *yakuza* boss indicated that I should occupy it, barely pausing in his briefing.

'It is essential the woman *Anna-san* be rescued without violence and we must obtain some leverage of our own in order to do so. We will abduct the mother of Konoe Akira, who I am informed is of a venerable age.' He turned to one of the *oyabun*. '*Saito-san*, this is your area of expertise. Do you have four young men who cast no shadows who will take her from her futon without disturbing the sleeping house?'

'I have three such who are as good as *ninja* and I ask permission to be the fourth, so I may lead them personally.'

Fuchida-san hesitated. '*Saito-san*, in the old days, yes, of course, you were greased lightning and could step on dust without leaving a footprint . . . but now? Are you sharp enough . . . sufficiently fit?'

'I am older and wiser, a little slower, but my footfall is as silent, my breath as even and my strike as swift. I will not let you down, *Oyabun*. But we will need time to study the house, maybe enter the grounds tonight and then go back tomorrow night.'

'There is no time, it must take place tonight!' *Fuchida-san* insisted.

'Impossible, honourable *Oyabun*, if we break this egg too soon we cannot put it back in the shell for tomorrow's omelette.'

'The egg *must* be broken tonight!' *Fuchida-san* insisted. He turned to another of his *oyabun*. '*Kato-san*, send a technical man in with *Saito-san*'s people. Have him cut all the phone wires. When you have reconnoitred the house and the immediate area, guard it while the abduction is taking place, and invade if things go wrong. I still want the old woman. Have an ambulance concealed close by with one of our doctors in attendance in case she is in shock. Is this understood?'

'Yes, *Oyabun*.' He glanced briefly at *Saito-san*. 'We have a plan for entering. It is an impressive compound with high brush walls, all of it completely rebuilt in the traditional manner after the Great Earthquake. There are not many like this left in Tokyo,' he said, obviously impressed. 'I will arrange for everything, but where will we take the old woman?'

'I will let you know the name of a private hospital,' *Fuchida-san* said. 'In the meantime you will also arrange for the capture of a female servant on her way home, so she will not be missed until the morning. She can explain the internal layout to *Saito-san* and his *ninja*, from the best entrances to the last footstep needed to reach the old woman's futon.'

'What if *Anna-san* is also in the house?' I asked.

It seemed to me to be a reasonable question, but now they all looked at me and then at each other as if I'd just made a fool of myself. '*Nick-san*, it would not be possible for a foreigner to enter a traditional Japanese home.'

'But I am here in your home, *Fuchida-san*.' I protested.

'*Hai!* That is different. I am the new Japan. This is *Japanese Cosmopolitan*, a new-style Japanese home,' he declared somewhat smugly. I was in no doubt that the name for this chrome and black minimalist extravaganza had been supplied by the Texan interior decorator as part of the justification for his whopping bill. 'The house of Konoe Akira is old Japan, it is not the same.

It carries the burdens of the ancestors and must be furnished accordingly and someone from an alien culture should not be allowed to enter or they will feel uncomfortable,' he concluded, while everyone around the table nodded their agreement. 'You will enter the house of Konoe Akira after midnight, *Saito-san*. There will be no more phone communication with me until then, unless there is a leak and the First Intelligence Division hears of the raid and stops it. Then you will call the operation off, use the night number and I will decide then what to do. We have an understanding with them regarding the Shield Society and I will square the matter with their divisional chief in the morning. If all goes well, call me, but *only* after the ambulance has departed.' He turned to *Kato-san*. 'Remember, the old woman must have the best of geriatric care.' He grinned. 'I don't want to negotiate with a corpse on my hands. The doctor must give her a sedative as soon as she is in the ambulance. Tell him she must remain conscious in case I need her to talk on the phone.'

'But if she dies?' *Kato-san* asked. He was the oldest of the men around the table and seemed to have a little more authority, or at least sufficient to question the leader.

The *yakuza* boss thought for a moment. 'If she dies almost immediately after her capture, then she must be returned to her futon; if later in the hospital, you will use a contact at the morgue and leave her there.'

'Would it not be preferable to abduct some other member of the family? We could simply wait and snatch a younger member off the street?' *Saito-san* suggested.

'No! An abduction performed in public doesn't leave the right impression. We must demonstrate our power and show Konoe Akira and the Shield Society that we can reach them anywhere, that nowhere is safe for them and that we will stop at nothing.'

One of the other three *oyabun* who had remained silent up to this point now spoke. 'Only Konoe Akira and the old crone are in residence at the moment; the three spinster sisters and a widowed daughter with his three grandchildren are in the country attending a cherry-blossom festival at the family shrine in a small fishing village on Hokkaidō. After that they are going to the World Exposition in Osaka.'

'Well done, *Oyabun* Fukuda!' the *yakuza* boss cried. 'You have been very busy since I called you earlier.'

Fukuda-san smiled. 'I cannot take the credit, *Oyabun*; it comes from the school the grandchildren attend, the brother of one of the teachers' assistants who is a *kobun* with me. He is a poor boy, but bright and will someday make a good *wakagashira*; he has appointed his sister as caretaker's eyes and ears on his own initiative.'

'You have always been a modest man, *Fukuda-san*. But it seems the gods are with us in this. With the rest of the family absent, *Konoe-san* will be left alone in the house.' He turned to me. '*Nick-san*, did you not say his leg gives him great pain?'

'That's what Anna told me, yes.'

'Then he probably takes a sedative to sleep.'

'He is, or at least *was*, a heroin addict when she knew him,' I added.

'*Hai*! Better still; he will be accustomed to using it for the pain.'

'Is it not possible there will be a servant or nurse who sleeps near the old woman?' I suggested.

'Damn! You're right, I didn't think of that!' *Fuchida-san* cried, deliberately overreacting in order to make my contribution seem more important.

He turned to the two *yakuza* bosses, Saito and Kato, who were to be involved directly in the action in and around Konoe

Akira's residence. 'As soon as the abduction is successfully completed call me, Saito-san, and Nick-san and I will join you at the location. Kato-san, you and your men will be responsible for the ambulance and for transporting the ancient one to the private clinic.' He handed Kato-san a small card. 'This is the address; they are expecting you. Two of my personal wakagashira will be waiting to let you through the main gate. Your men will also secure the immediate area up to three hundred metres from the residence in every direction.'

Next he addressed Saito-san. 'The compound and the interior of the house are your concern. All the gates to the property must be manned so that nobody can leave.' He paused. 'Thank you. I have complete trust in you both. You must leave now to make preparations. Saito-san, get the doctor to give you a needle to use if there is a nurse – chloral hydrate so she remembers nothing when she wakes up.'

I was practically dead on my feet, having not slept at all the previous night and only four hours after Anna's eventual return the night before. I wanted badly to be on hand when Fuchida-san went in after midnight to confront Konoe Akira, but had no chance of doing so if, in the meantime, I didn't get some shut-eye.

Despite my protests that I should take a taxi, the yakuza boss called Miss Sparkle to arrange for one of the ubiquitous Toyotas to return me to the hotel. 'It is too late for anonymity, Nick-san, and now it is expected that you be given the correct status. The Intelligence "eyes" must not be disappointed nor their "ears" put out of a job.' He walked me to the lift, probably grateful to have me out from under his feet for a few hours.

'I am putting you to a great deal of trouble, Fuchida-san, as well as taking you away from your normal business,' I apologised, adding, 'I owe you a considerable debt.'

'Hai! Yes, you will incur a debt. That is our way. When one's hand clasps another's, both carry obligation, but, in your case, not as much as you may think. I am young again and it is like old times. These lunatics have been a growing thorn in our side and now we have an opportunity to pluck it out. The First Intelligence Division's policy is to do nothing until they attempt to harm the state. We do not agree. You do not wait to remove a weed from a bed of flowers until after it has thrown its seed. Now we have the chance to act first. This will bring the yakuza great honour and restore our prestige as partners in the peaceful democratic progress of the new Japan. My wakagashira want action and this is a way to show our young men what it means to inherit the ways and obligations of the Samurai.'

I didn't much like the sound of this last statement. If my wartime experience counted for anything, young Turks let loose with automatic weapons seldom remained quiet. If there was going to be open conflict with the Shield Society, then my most ardent desire was that it would happen when Anna and I were roughly thirty thousand feet in the air with the sound of four jet engines humming in our ears as we sipped champagne in the first-class section of a Qantas Boeing 707.

While I still used a rifle fairly frequently to shoot wild pig or an occasional shark for the crew, both considered delicacies among the natives, I hadn't fired a shot in anger since the Pacific War ended. I had no idea whether ASIO carried a file on me, nor could I think why they should, but now in my imagination I could see the one they would open on our return from Japan.

Nicholas Duncan: a known associate of the Japanese yakuza *and a personal friend of* Oyabun Fuchida, *crime boss of the Tokyo region. Known to have been involved in the fighting between the Shield Society, a fanatical rightwing organisation, and the* yakuza *crime syndicate for control of the lucrative . . .* It didn't bear thinking about and I felt sure Anna would have reacted quite differently had she known where all this would lead.

I regretted ever coming to Japan. It had been my idea for her to confront Konoe Akira, but now the notion that by doing so she would exorcise her demons seemed like romantic pop-psychobabble. There was a good chance that she would have to pay for my bright idea with her life. I realised that all I had achieved was to grant the nefarious Konoe Akira the power to decide once more whether she lived or died.

The lift, accompanied by two *wakagashira*, arrived and I thanked *Fuchida-san* again. 'We will call for you at ten-thirty tonight, *Nick-san*.' As the doors of the lift closed he shouted, 'Wear warm clothes! The nights are still cold at this time of year.'

Joined by two other foot soldiers, I was driven in silence back to the Imperial where a dozen spines stiffened at my approach. Going up in the hotel lift I tried to think how I would react if I discovered Anna asleep on the double bed. Would I feel relief, anger, joy, what? Would I shake her, kiss her or break down completely? At least one thing was certain – my second reaction would be to phone the airport and my third would be to start packing.

But, of course, she wasn't there. I was suddenly too weary to feel very much of anything and I barely had the energy to remove my shoes and jacket and loosen my tie, then call reception to wake me at 9 p.m., before flopping onto the bed.

When my wake-up call came I lay in bed for a while wondering what the night might bring, then showered and dressed. I thought about ordering room service but suddenly felt the need to be with normal people and went downstairs to the dining room just in time for last orders, although I feel sure that, had I arrived even later, the kitchen would have remained open to midnight or beyond. It isn't hard to see how people get hooked on power. My entry into the dining room was met with a frenetic scurrying of waiters and the clatter of dishes being hastily cleared. It was as if the inspector of kitchen hygiene had arrived. The maître d', short and stout, came trotting towards me, clicking his fingers for a waiter to follow him. It seemed every eye in the room was drawn towards me, so I guess notoriety must also have its downside.

Once in the Toyota, which thankfully arrived with a minimum of fuss, the *wakagashira* kept a respectful silence, except for the perfunctory grunts and monosyllabic affirmations that usually accompany servile attention, as we drove back to the penthouse apartment. They treated me as they would an *oyabun*, while the young *kobun*, one of whom was usually in a car for training purposes, avoided eye contact and squirmed constantly in his seat beside me, obviously nervous in my presence.

To my surprise, once we reached the apartment building I was taken directly to the floor where the *wakagashira* on duty were based, along with the brightest *kobun*, orphans and boys from the slums who showed promise and were being groomed to be more than standover men, riot breakers and guards.

I was escorted to a small and very austere reception room. The *tatami* matting on the floor was old and frayed, and four canvas cushions surrounded a low and much-scuffed table in the centre. The premises were scrubbed and clean but redolent of a boy's boarding school, Japanese style. I was served green tea from a chipped enamel pot by a *chinpira* – a young *yakuza*, not yet *kobun* – who held the pot in both hands to fill my cup while avoiding my eyes. My head almost reached the level of his own when I was seated on the cushion and I felt sure he must have wondered what the giant *gaijin* was doing amongst them. I reached over and touched the side of the teapot to discover it was almost too hot to hold. The lad was burning his hands rather than allow me to see they were shaking. He had already begun the long and disciplined road to fortitude. The only sign of pain was that he kept nervously lifting one foot then the other as if he needed to urinate.

'Put the pot down at once!' I ordered. He placed the enamel teapot on the table and immediately hid his left hand behind his back. 'Let me see,' I said gently. He produced the damaged hand with the palm facing downwards. 'Turn it over,' I instructed. He did so and I noted that his palm had turned almost scarlet from the burn. 'Ouch! That hurts, eh?' I said, sympathising.

'No,' he said, tears welling.

'To be strong without being foolish is the hardest lesson of all to learn. You have kept your pride but made yourself unfit for battle.' I grinned in an attempt to put him at ease. 'Next time bring a cloth, worthy *chinpira*.'

'Yes, *Oyabun*,' he said, barely above a whisper, still avoiding my eyes.

'I will tell your superior of your courage.'

A look of dismay crossed his face and he glanced up fearfully, meeting my eyes for the first time. 'Please! No, *Oyabun*!' he begged. 'I will lose my rice bowl!'

His fear of being expelled from his *yakuza* family and finding himself back on the streets was palpable and his small frame shook visibly. 'I understand,' I said hurriedly. 'Now run to the bathroom and splash cold water over your hand, it will take away the immediate pain. Tonight go to the kitchen and ask them for a little honey to heal the burn.'

'Yes, *Oyabun*.' He reached for the teapot.

'No, leave it. I may require a second cup.' The child bowed deeply, then turned and scurried away like a small rodent.

Shortly after the boy's departure *Fuchida-san* arrived carrying a red Moroccan leather box roughly the size of a double-layer cigar box. He placed it on the table and with a small sigh lowered himself onto a cushion, whereupon a young bloke three or four years older than the first little guy appeared with a fresh teapot, and placing a cup in front of him, poured green tea into it, bowed deeply and left. Unlike the previous lad, his hand didn't shake. He was, I thought, a little further along the road to being trained in the art of fearlessness.

'*Nick-san*, I have a gift for you,' *Fuchida-san* said, nodding towards the box.

'You have been too generous, honourable *Fuchida-san*. Already I am unable adequately to repay your kindness.'

'Ah, *Nick-san*, between true friends kindness is always repaid and accepted without a sense of obligation.' He laughed. 'But ah . . . perhaps one day the Queen Alexandra's Birdwing . . . ? Imagine a butterfly with a wingspan of 31 centimetres!' He leaned forward and pushed the box towards me. 'Open it, *Nick-san*,' he instructed, clearly excited.

I reached out, lifted the brass clasp, and opened the lid. Inside, resting in a black felt-covered mould, was a Belgian Browning Hi-Power 13-shot automatic, arguably the finest handgun made at that time.

'Jesus!' I exclaimed.

'The best!' *Fuchida-san* laughed. 'I have one myself. Now we not only have butterflies in common; tonight we are partners in this operation.'

I confess I wasn't quite as pleased about his comrades-in-arms notion as he seemed to be, but I tried not to show it. 'I am speechless, *Fuchida-san*,' I said, beaming, but feeling somewhat the hypocrite. I loved the gun but not how it might come to be used in the next few hours. The last time I had used a handgun was in New Guinea as a coastwatcher. The standard issue for officers was the Webley Mk IV revolver, although I had chosen to use the American issue 1911A1 Colt Automatic because I regarded it as a better weapon. Although I wasn't a bad shot, I had never fired it in anger. And in combat I preferred the Owen submachine-gun.

'You have killed before, *Nick-san*. We both know only the first time is difficult. Come, we must prepare. We have a firing range, it is soundproof and only fifteen metres, but it will make you familiar with this weapon.'

The pistol range was obviously in frequent use, judging from the black human silhouette that was so perforated it seemed to consist of more bullet holes than metal. My first few shots were far from accurate until I recalled the wartime training I had received from Special Services. Adopting the front-facing two-handed method I began to feel in control and after twenty or so shots I was able to create a reasonable grouping, although with all the bullet holes already around the heart area of the target it wasn't easy to tell. In my overlarge hands the Browning seemed to almost disappear but the kickback of the 9-millimetre was nothing compared to the solid whack of the .45 calibre Colt. This was a precision weapon that could do a lot of damage in the hands of a good marksman.

I had obviously impressed *Fuchida-san*, for as we cleaned our weapons he said, 'You have the steady hand of a killer, *Nick-san*.' He grinned, placing his own hand on my shoulder. 'I would trust you at my side in a fire fight.'

'I have big hands and it is a small gun,' I laughed. *Please*

God let these practice shots be the only ones I fire while I'm in Japan, I silently prayed.

At twenty-five minutes after midnight Miss Sparkle called *Fuchida-san* to the phone and after a short conversation he returned. His expression was deadpan and my first thought was that something had gone wrong. *Fuchida-san* was a naturally exuberant character and surprisingly apt to display his feelings for someone in his line of business. I had regarded the even tone of the Jade Mistress's intimidation as a performance, but now I saw that it was simply a different aspect of the *yakuza* boss. I was now witnessing the cool-headed leader completely in possession of his emotions. 'It has been done. *Saito-san* and his three *ninja* have brought the old woman out. The remainder of the household is still asleep. It is time to go, *Nick-san*.'

'*Saito-san* was true to his word then? He has not lost his touch,' I said admiringly.

'*Hai!* I should not have questioned his powers. In public life he is one of the three great kendo masters in Japan but is also possibly the most deadly practitioner alive of the art of the *katana*. The old texts teach us that to have at your side one such sword-master is equivalent to thirteen lesser swordsmen. I should not have been surprised that even now his footsteps leave no mark in the dust.'

For once we arrived quietly with only one Toyota accompanying the Mercedes. We drew to a halt in a side street close to Konoe Akira's residence in the diplomatic quarter of Tokyo and quite close to the imperial palace, then walked a few yards and turned a corner to see a large compound directly facing us. *Fuchida-san* checked the address. 'It is this one,' he said quietly.

I would return to this area again in daylight and observe that, judging from the high stone and brick walls surrounding them, there were perhaps a dozen compounds of similar size in the immediate area. All, with the exception of Konoe's family residence, were embassies. In Tokyo space is at such a premium that only the truly rich can afford what I would have estimated was an area no bigger than a third of an acre, not much more than the land occupied by the average middle-class outer-suburban home in Sydney or Melbourne and about a twentieth the size of the grounds of Beautiful Bay. I was amazed to see that the wall surrounding Konoe Akira's residence was made of brush.

'The brush wall . . . ?' I said, my implication being that it wasn't the greatest protection from intruders.

'We are lucky again. It is a traditional fence.' *Fuchida-san* pointed to the wooden shingles on the roof, visible in the city lights reflecting from the low cloud cover. 'You will see, every detail is as it has always been. I do not think Konoe Akira is a man who is prepared to compromise on anything.'

So far we had not seen a single person. This was surprising as we were close to the centre of the city, and while it was well past midnight, Tokyo, like most great cities, never sleeps. 'My men have done a good job; the immediate area is clear,' the *yakuza* boss observed. The only sounds were our own footsteps and the distant hum of traffic a city block or so away. A soft call came suddenly from directly behind us. I turned, surprised to see *Saito-san* and the three other *yakuza* who had performed the abduction standing no more than a couple of metres away. I swear I hadn't heard a single step other than our own; absolutely zilch. One moment we were alone and the next they were standing large as life directly behind us, barefoot and dressed in what appeared to be heavy black cotton karate uniforms. *Saito-san* carried a *katana* tied to the belt at his waist.

Unlike myself, the *yakuza* boss didn't seem surprised at their sudden appearance. 'It went well?' he asked.

'As you requested, *Oyabun*,' *Saito-san* replied.

'The ambulance?'

'It left without the need to use a siren.' He chuckled softly. 'The old crone didn't need sedation. She remained asleep even in the ambulance. If it wasn't for her snores we would have thought she was dead.'

'Was there a nurse in the house?' *Fuchida-san* asked.

'Yes, but she too remained asleep. We gave her the needle anyway.'

'*Kato-san*'s man has cut the phone connections?'

Saito nodded. 'Yes.'

'And you came out immediately?'

'Yes, but we await your instruction to go back in to fetch —'

'No, he is mine. Konoe Akira belongs to me,' I said quietly, not knowing what had suddenly possessed me to make such a demand, but equally certain that I should be the one to bring Konoe Akira out.

The *yakuza* looked at me, waiting for *Fuchida-san* to speak. '*Nick-san*, it is not wise. *Saito-san* knows the layout of the house.'

'*Fuchida-san*, I have waited twenty years for this moment. Do not deny me now,' I pleaded, forcing myself to keep my voice and my breathing even.

The *yakuza* boss looked at me steadily. 'This was not in my original plan. It is a long time since the war, since you were an active warrior. Now you must go into his home in the dark and find him and bring him out alive. It is much too risky, *Nick-san*.'

'That is what you implied with *Saito-san*, that he was too old, that his footsteps would show in the dust.'

'*Hai!*' he expostulated, momentarily caught off guard.

'I have lived much of my life in the jungle. I am accustomed to measuring my footfall. I will bring him out alive, I promise.'

'And if you don't?' The *yakuza* boss glared at me. 'Understand, they will retaliate by killing *Anna-san*. Will you take such a risk?'

I hesitated momentarily. 'If I don't succeed, then nor will your people. The consequence will be the same. It is my duty and responsibility. My honour will be insulted if you do not allow me, *Fuchida-san*,' I persisted, playing the ultimate card. I had got myself in a position where Anna's life was possibly threatened but where there was no turning back: *heads you win, tails I lose, the old Nick dilemma*.

Far from pleased, *Fuchida-san* shook his head slowly. '*Nick-san*, you make it impossible for me to refuse without dishonouring you.'

I attempted a grin. 'I have a weapon,' I said, patting the Browning concealed by my coat. 'A very good one a friend recently gave me. It will be okay. You will see, *Oyabun*,' I answered respectfully.

'We will give you fifteen minutes, then we are coming in.'

'Twenty?' I asked. 'I have to learn the interior of the house.' I turned to Saito. 'Did you get a plan of the layout from a servant?'

He nodded and removed a slip of paper from inside his black kendo robe. Then he turned to *Saito-san*. 'Show *Nick-san* the gate you used to enter.'

'No gate, *Oyabun*, we used a butterfly cut,' Saito replied, touching the *katana*. A butterfly cut I was to learn is an X-shaped slash traditionally used by the Samurai to dismember an opponent, but in this case it proved to be a convenient way to make a hole in the high brush fence.

I removed my jacket so that my movements wouldn't be restricted, revealing the automatic pistol stuck in my belt.

'Your white shirt makes you an easy target even in the dark,' *Fuchida-san* said. He turned to the tallest of the men. 'Give the *gaijin* your jacket,' he ordered. By using the term for a foreigner rather than my name he was expressing his barely contained anger. The *wakagashira* removed his heavy cotton fighting jacket and I put it on. Traditionally a loose fit, it proved not nearly big enough, a fact that seemed to anger the *yakuza* boss even further. 'You will be a large white elephant and very easy to kill!' he said.

'Perhaps not so easy, *Oyabun*. You people have tried without success to do so before!'

'*Hai!*' Fuchida exclaimed. Then suddenly his expression changed. He grinned and shrugged his shoulders. 'Okay, *Nick-san!*'

Saito-san led me to the fence which, in the near darkness, seemed entirely undamaged. By pushing it inwards it opened up but proved too small for me to enter. He laughed. 'I will make another larger cut for the elephant,' he joked.

I pointed to the opening. 'How did you get the old lady through there?'

'We didn't, we took her through a gate.'

'So why . . . ?'

He realised what I was implying. 'It is not an honourable entry, *Nick-san*,' then he added, 'even for elephants.'

I took out the piece of paper showing the layout of the house and grounds. 'Where is the gate, so that I can bring Konoe Akira out through it?'

He pointed to the gate on the roughly drawn plan. 'You wish to enter through it as well?' he asked.

'No, we will enter the honourable way, *Saito-san*.' If all this carry-on seems ridiculous in retrospect, it was not to *Saito-san* and his men, for whom the observation of ritual is essential if the gods are going to be with you in your endeavour.

Removing the *katana* from its scabbard *Saito-san* moved several feet away and in two lightning-fast strokes slashed open the fence. It was hard to imagine how sharp the blade must have been, but, taken together with the precise technique he used, it slashed through the thick plaited twigs like a knife through butter. Very few things in Japan are haphazard or spontaneous, and even this method of entry had become an art and a tradition, perhaps over centuries. Like most things Japanese it was tidy, and when the thick twigs were pulled back into place it was difficult to see where the cut had been made.

'I will come with you to show you the door to enter. We left it unlocked, thinking we would be returning.' He led the way along a path composed almost entirely of moss and slate, yet another Japanese contradiction – the path made of moss, and the garden of rocks and raked gravel. It led to a rear door in the large wooden house. 'It may be best to remove your shoes,' *Saito-san* whispered. He waited until I did so and then slipped away noiselessly into the night.

I took the Browning from my belt and entered the darkened house, waiting a couple of minutes to allow my eyes to grow accustomed to the interior. I realised then that I was standing in the kitchen where I could make out an electric kettle and an electric rice cooker. Not everything in Konoe Akira's home adhered rigidly to tradition, I decided.

Fortunately the house beyond the kitchen proved to be classical Japanese, the spaces left uncluttered, wooden floors covered with *tatami* mats, low tables displaying vases or other objects, a few embroidered silk screens, cushions and very little other furniture. Unlike the West where quantity matters, a rich person's house in Japan is defined by the quality and age of the objects and not by their number. Though it was too dark to see anything clearly, I surmised that the furniture and various decorative objects in the central room where I stood would be expensive antiques.

The interior walls were of rice paper so that the direction of any noise was easy to identify. I moved towards the centre of the room and stood waiting. It was not dissimilar to the jungle where at first there is only silence, then slowly you begin to pick up the sounds around you until eventually it becomes a virtual cacophony of clicks, buzzes, hums, croaks, ticks and knocks. Within perhaps thirty seconds I could hear snoring coming from two directions, the first in the northern corner of the house and the second, lighter, from the eastern side, which I surmised must be from the drugged and comatose old lady's nurse. The other snores were more sonorous, coming fast and in a cadence where every second snore seemed to be at a slightly different pitch. Either Konoe Akira suffered from severe breathing problems or there was more than one person asleep in the northern section of the house. I decided after listening a little longer that this was the case. I was going to have to contend with two people in close proximity to each other.

By this stage my eyes had grown accustomed to the dark so I was able to see objects and doorways quite easily. I returned to the kitchen and, finding a knife, I removed the plugs of the kettle and rice cooker from the wall sockets and cut them off to give me two lengths of electrical cord each approximately two and a half feet long. Then I found a dishtowel, and wiping the handle of the knife carefully, I returned it to the rack and stuffed the dishtowel in one trouser pocket and the flex in another.

I returned to the centre of the house, stopping to listen and ensure that the snoring duet continued before moving in the direction from which it came, padding down a fairly broad passageway, the walls of which were made of rice-paper panels. I passed the sliding doors to three rooms and then saw a dimly illuminated form asleep on a futon at the end of the passage. A tiny nightlight stood on the *tatami* matting beside him. I approached very slowly, pausing after every carefully placed step, realising that I probably only had one chance at surprise. I finally reached the foot of the futon and saw by the nightlight that a high-powered torch and a Japanese Type 26 service revolver lay on the *tatami* inches from the man's head. He was lying on his stomach with his face turned away from me so that I could see only the back of his head. I noted his hair – grey. Konoe Akira's nightwatchman was clearly not a young man.

I silently thanked my lucky stars that he wasn't supine. Lying as he was on his stomach he was going to be a lot easier to subdue. Disarming a sleeping enemy sentry when attempting to get behind enemy lines was fundamental stuff I'd learned in Z Force. Fundamental then, but that was more than twenty years ago. I'd never come across a sleeping sentry in combat conditions and not all that many times during practice. I lowered myself to my haunches and picked up first the torch, the more dangerous of the two weapons, for if it were to be suddenly shone directly into my face I would be blinded for at least thirty seconds. This would be more than sufficient time to empty the chamber of the service revolver at point blank range or to bludgeon me unconscious with the heavy torch. I placed it well out of reach and then took up the revolver and laid it beside the torch.

I was no longer young; at forty-six my breath wasn't as even as it should have been. Anxiety is the opponent you carry within you, so I waited a moment to calm down, assuring myself that I wasn't dealing with a *ninja* or any of the other kinds of Japanese unarmed combat specialists, none of whom would dream of using a gun, least of all an ancient and clumsy wartime Japanese service revolver. Besides, if my adversary had been any of these trained killers I would certainly not have been able to approach without his becoming aware of my presence.

What I did next would probably decide whether I succeeded or failed in bringing Konoe Akira out without having to kill him. I placed the Browning automatic down near the sleeping man's feet so he couldn't reach it if anything went wrong. Then, taking a short, sharp breath, I straddled the futon and the man's torso and knelt down hard, my knees slamming into his ribs. Two hundred and thirty pounds of concentrated weight just under the lungs will blow the air out of the Michelin man. I heard a loud exhalation as the air was forced from his lungs and then some strangled gasping as he struggled for breath, unable to cry out. I half rose and turned to face his feet, seated on the back of his thighs so he couldn't move his legs. In a few moments I had his feet crossed and tied at the ankles, knotting the flex sufficiently tightly so he could not struggle free, but not so tightly that I prevented the flow of blood to his feet.

I turned to face his head again, this time sitting astride his buttocks while I pulled his arms behind his back and tied them with the second piece of electrical cord, again not sufficiently tightly to restrict the circulation. I rose to my feet and stepped to the side of the futon and flipped him onto his back, softly kneading his stomach so he could regain his breath. He did so with a gasp, gulping hard, desperate for more air. Satisfied that he could once again breathe, I used the dishcloth to gag him then rolled him back onto his stomach. I was gratified that my training in Queensland all those years ago had come back to me. I would probably have been a bit slow and clumsy for the likes of Sergeant Major Wainwright, the Geordie Z Force instructor. ('Clumsy and slow, Duncan! You've wakened the whole *fooking* enemy guard room and you're halfway to hell by now!')

'If you attempt to move I will kill you,' I said quietly to the frightened little man, whom, I now realised, I could probably have knocked unconscious with a single cuff behind the ear, or better still, simply found the right pressure points in his neck. I was also surprised at how rapidly I was breathing. I guess I didn't have what it takes to be a James Bond.

I thought about clocking the little bloke, a solid tap with the torch, but he was no longer in a position to endanger me, and as the bishop sometimes said, 'Sufficient unto the day, Nicholas. One shouldn't overdo things.'

I emptied the chamber of the Japanese revolver into my trouser pocket and wiped it clean using my shirt, stooping and dropping it onto the futon so it didn't make any noise. Taking up the torch and regaining my own gun I gently started to slide back the door to what I hoped might be Konoe Akira's bedchamber. It opened with hardly a sound, a credit to the carpenter and *Konoe-san*'s insistence on perfection in all things.

I know this is beginning to sound a bit like a scene from a comic opera, but he simply continued to snore. Remembering that morphine is also a powerful sedative, I switched on the torch, directing the light against my chest then adjusting the glow with my fingers so I could look for the switch that didn't seem to be beside the door. I scanned the room and discovered the light switch a foot or so above his head. My heart jumped as I saw a cane leaning against the wall beside the switch. I had my man.

I walked slowly over to the bed and lowered myself until I was resting on my haunches, then turned on the light, the barrel of my Browning automatic held against the side of Konoe Akira's head.

He woke up with a start, emitting a loud grunt. 'What? What is it, Staff Sergeant?' he asked. Then his eyes focused on me and grew wide with surprise. He closed them again, thinking perhaps that he was dreaming, blinked several times then opened them once more. This time he appeared to be truly afraid. 'Who . . . who are you?' he asked, trembling.

'I have come to fetch Anna,' I said evenly.

'Anna?' he asked, confused.

'Second Vase! Where is she?'

Konoe Akira began to shake. 'Oh,' he said.

'Come, get up, *Konoe-san*.' I reached for the walking stick and handed it to him. 'We have to leave. My twenty minutes is almost up.'

'Please, let me get dressed,' he said, an old man frightened and shaken, but still conscious of who he was. You had to respect that.

CHAPTER EIGHT

*'You must understand
that it is the public prosecutor alone
who has absolute discretion
to decide if you will be charged with any crime.
If he finds there is a case to answer, then it is
extremely unlikely that a judge will overrule this finding.'*
Kinzo-san, criminal lawyer, Tokyo

I SOON REALISED IT was going to be far from easy getting Konoe Akira dressed. Firstly there was the matter of his gammy leg and then, even though he was in his early sixties, there was every possibility that he was dangerous. Anna had finally told me the true story of the Nest of the Swallows and her murder of Colonel Takahashi, and I remembered that it had been Konoe Akira who had told her how she might kill a man using a chopstick.

'You're going to have to help me,' Konoe said. His initial fright had passed, and although he was still trembling from the unexpected shock of waking with a gun at his head, his voice was reasonably steady and his breathing even. 'My name is Konoe . . . Konoe Akira. I regret I cannot bow unless you help me to my feet.'

Jesus! Either he was a very cool customer and wanted me to put down my weapon so we'd be on equal terms or he was simply a very civilised man who wanted to make light of the indignity of being caught in a red flannel nightshirt by a stranger and then having to be helped to get into his clobber.

Allowing him to dress would be a foolish decision. I could clearly hear Sergeant Major Wainwright's words in my head: 'Nudity is maximum humiliation, boyo. The frog march with bollocks bouncing is the next best weapon to a gun held to the back of the *fooking* head.' But then there were also my father's words. During the hot tropical nights in New Britain, he had slept in the nude, and when the Japanese had come to the mission station in the dead of night to take him prisoner they had marched him naked with his hands on his head through the mission compound and the adjacent native village, forcing the inhabitants to witness his humiliation. 'It was a bright moonlit night of the kind that allows one to read the small print in a newspaper and my parishioners were made to line the road and then assemble in the centre of the village to witness my humiliation. I shall always be grateful to the chief for his probity, for while nudity is not shameful among the heathen, he made all the women turn their backs in defiance of the Japanese.' While my father was considered a hero among the native people for remaining with his parishioners when the other Europeans escaped the Japanese invasion, there was one aspect of this heroism that stamped him unique among the natives. The small size of his penis had so impressed them that forever afterwards and until this day, if a native male appears to be less endowed than average the people say, 'Hem goddem wan Jesus prick.' It was Wainwright or the Bishop of New Guinea and very foolishly God won. 'How do you usually get dressed?' I asked suspiciously.

He pointed towards the door, 'Staff Sergeant Goto, my driver and batman.'

'Staff Sergeant?'

'Yes, my driver during the war,' he explained. 'He simply stayed on,' Konoe added with a shrug. 'He is also supposed to be my bodyguard.' He gave me a wry grin.

I wasn't having any of his old soldier shit or charm or whatever it was he was trying to pull. 'You don't need to know my name just yet, and I've known yours for twenty years,' I said, stern-faced, then asked, 'Where are your clothes?'

He pointed to a small open-faced cupboard with three shelves. A blue serge suit jacket and trousers on a coathanger were suspended from a brass hook on the side of the cupboard, while the bottom shelf contained a pair of highly polished black shoes, the second held underpants, vests and socks, the top a neatly folded shirt, belt and plain navy-blue tie. 'I don't think I can get up,' he said, apologising again. 'Perhaps if you allow me to use my stick?'

Time was running out and I didn't much care for the idea of *Fuchida-san* and *Saito-san* and his men storming through the house supposedly on a mission to rescue me. In fact I was rather pleased with myself and wanted to bring out Konoe Akira, making light of the task at the same time. I also told myself that while he was tall, I was at least twice his weight and twenty or so years younger than him, and as well, I was supposed to know how to take care of myself. Still it would be embarrassing if the *yakuza* entered to find me unconscious or dead, unable to subdue an old man.

Leaving him seated on the futon I moved the stick out of his reach, then crossed the room and removed the trousers from the hanger, grabbed the shoes, underpants and shirt from the shelves and dumped them beside him on the futon. He reached over and picked up the shirt and started to unbutton it, working slowly. 'Here, give it to me,' I instructed, taking the shirt from his grasp. Placing the Browning into my belt I quickly unbuttoned the shirt and handed it back to him. 'Put it on first, you can do that seated. I'll help you with the rest,' I said.

He pointed to his underpants and then indicated his stiff leg. 'Please?' I went down on my haunches and pushed the underpants over his ankles and up to his knees where he pulled them further, but was then unable to lift his buttocks, so I stood and lifted him from behind. With his underpants on he seemed much relieved and pulled the red flannel nightshirt over his tall, skinny frame. I noted that the broad purple and white scar on his leg ran in a jagged line from the base of his right quadriceps down through the smashed kneecap. He put his shirt on and I repeated the process with his trousers, and while he laboriously tucked in his shirt I slipped his shoes on minus socks and tied the laces. Finally I rose and, standing behind him, put my hands under his armpits and pulled him to his feet where he immediately grabbed the waistband of his trousers. 'Belt. I need my belt, please.'

Still standing behind him I handed him the cane. 'No belt,' I snapped.

'My trousers, they will fall down,' he said, appealing to me.

'Then use one hand to hold them up.' It was standard procedure when taking a prisoner into custody when handcuffs were unavailable. With one hand using the walking stick and the other holding up his daks he was rendered more or less harmless. At least some of my Special Services training was being observed.

'You pay me too much respect. You have nothing to fear, my leg prevents me from using the ability I once possessed,' Konoe Akira said, attempting to salvage some of his pride.

I glanced at my watch; my twenty minutes were up. 'Start walking,' I commanded. 'We go out via the kitchen.'

'I am not sure where it is. I have never been into the servants' section. Let me take you through the front of the house,' he suggested.

'The kitchen!' I insisted, not believing him. 'I'll direct you.' Paranoia, once it's taken possession, is hard to control and I couldn't bring myself to believe he had never entered his own kitchen, deciding he must have some devious reason for taking a different route, perhaps a weapon concealed somewhere or a burglar alarm to be tripped? 'Switch on the lights as we go,' I commanded.

We paused at the prostrate Staff Sergeant Goto, who had managed to roll onto his back. Moments later Konoe Akira switched on the light to illuminate the passageway. The trussed and gagged batman stared at us wide-eyed, emitting small grunts, drawing up his knees and kicking out in a gesture of defiance. 'Will he be all right?' Konoe Akira asked, examining him without a smile as one might a trussed chook.

'Sure. What time do the servants arrive?'

'Six o'clock.'

'They can release him then.'

'I have an aged mother who will be alone in the house,' Konoe now said, moving down the passageway.

'Ah, I am sure she is all right. When the servants arrive they will care for her,' I said, deciding to play dumb about her abduction. It was a card we would need to play at a later time.

'Where are you taking me?' he asked, seemingly less afraid or at least resigned to his immediate fate.

'The real question is where are you going to take *me*, Konoe-san. Now would you please remain silent and turn on the lights as we go?' We reached the centre of the house where I could now clearly see the elegant furnishings that were obviously a part of a traditional and very wealthy family home.

It denoted a different world to the *Japanese Cosmopolitan* style of *Fuchida-san's* penthouse pride and joy and once again supported his remarks about the two Japans existing side by side.

Konoe Akira gestured towards a beautiful melon-shaped vase with a clear light-green glaze over black and white inlaid decorations. It stood about eighteen inches high and rested on a cherry-wood base. 'It is twelfth-century Korean, made during the Goryeo Dynasty. It has "Best Under Heaven" classification and is beyond price. If you free me I will give it to you together with the provenance. Without me to care for her, my esteemed and aged mother will not continue to live.'

'I am only interested in Second Vase, *Konoe-san!*' I snapped. 'Take me to her and you will save your mother's life as well as your own.' His deliberate delaying tactics were beginning to annoy me; I should never have allowed him to dress. Any minute now *Fuchida-san* and his cohorts would burst in thinking they needed to rescue me. They'd catch me with a gun pointed at the back of a scrawny, ageing Japanese cripple, hardly a courageous or impressive capture.

Konoe Akira appeared to be showing less and less fear for his personal safety, completely disregarding my order not to talk. How bloody imperious can the Japanese elite classes be? Or did he guess that there was no way I was going to harm him until I knew where Anna was being held?

Konoe Akira sighed. 'I do not know her whereabouts,' he replied.

'We'll soon see about that!' I snapped impatiently. 'Let's go!'

But he didn't move. 'You may shoot me now but spare my esteemed mother. I cannot take you to Second Vase. I don't know where she is, I *really* don't.'

'This is bullshit!' I cried in English, suddenly feeling

furious. 'Move!' I shouted in Japanese, conscious that he was making a fool of me. I struggled to regain my poise. 'No more talk,' I snapped. Then suddenly I heard *Fuchida-san* and the others running down the passageway from the kitchen.

Konoe Akira shook his head. 'No!' he shouted. His cane fell to the floor and he lost his balance as his trousers dropped to his ankles. He staggered towards me, threatening to crash into me, but I swung my left arm around his neck, my forearm across his throat, and held him, preventing his fall while still holding the Browning. Moments later four police officers burst into the room carrying submachine-guns. Had I not held Konoe Akira against my body I feel certain they would have gunned me down. He had obviously also heard the arrival of what he correctly surmised was a rescue team.

'Drop your gun!' one of the police officers, a sergeant, shouted. 'Put both hands on your head.'

They were dressed in black, wearing bullet-proof jackets and hard helmets and were obviously the Japanese equivalent of a SWAT team. If I took Konoe Akira hostage I was stuffed. The *yakuza* had either been arrested or had escaped in time. I had nowhere to take him and in the open I could easily be gunned down from the rear.

I very slowly lowered Konoe Akira to the floor, still holding the Browning. If the police sergeant intended shooting me he was taking the chance I would get a bullet away in time. All I could think was *Fuck, what now?*

One of the policemen retrieved Konoe Akira's cane and held it, while two others lifted him to his feet and pulled his trousers up. He accepted the cane, steadied himself, and without even glancing at me, he set off down a passageway, his free hand holding up his trousers and the tap of his cane on the wooden floor increasing in tempo as he began to hurry. I dropped the

Browning at my feet and the sergeant took a step forward and kicked it out of my reach. I then placed my hands on my head, indicating that I wasn't going to resist. The two policemen advanced, one on either side of me, and each grabbed a wrist and pulled my arms behind my back. The third handcuffed me while the senior police officer held his submachine-gun pointed at my chest. I was suddenly very frightened.

'What is your name?' the cop with the submachine-gun asked me.

'Nick Duncan.'

'*Hai!* From the Imperial Hotel. You are *yakuza*!'

'No.'

'Yes!' he declared, contradicting me. 'What is your association with *Oyabun* Fuchida?'

'We both collect butterflies,' I replied.

'You are under arrest, Nick Duncan. I am taking you into custody and charging you with attempting to kidnap a Japanese citizen.' He pointed to the Browning. 'As a foreigner do you have a permit to carry a weapon?'

'No,' I replied. 'I neglected to bring the licence with me to Japan and did not declare it to your customs,' I lied, avoiding a reference to the *yakuza*.

'Smuggling a weapon into Japan – that is yet another charge in addition to possessing an unauthorised weapon, Nick Duncan,' he said, staring at me steadily. I could see why he was in charge of a SWAT team. He was a consummate professional who, with the exception of shouting at me to drop my gun as they'd burst into the room, hadn't raised his voice once. At another time in another place he was just the sort of bloke you'd want beside you in a fire fight. A few more like him at Guadalcanal and things might have turned out differently for the Japs in the Pacific.

He stooped and picked up the Browning, holding it by the tip of the barrel to protect my prints, then he dropped it into a plastic bag one of the police officers held open.

I could hear the tapping of the cane growing louder as Konoe Akira returned. He appeared at the entrance to the passageway, then crossed the room to stand directly in front of me, forcing the bemused police sergeant to step aside. He'd found a means of holding up his trousers – the waistband was now bunched and turned over, lifting his trouser legs and exposing his bare ankles. Akira was tall for a Japanese, six foot, perhaps a little less, though he was still obliged to look up at me. Grim-faced, shaking, his lips spume-flecked with rage, he yelled, 'Where is my esteemed mother?'

I shook my head and then shrugged, trying to keep my voice steady. 'What? I don't understand. But you said . . .' I replied, hoping the feigned innocence was convincing.

I had decided that if *Fuchida-san* had escaped arrest or even if he hadn't, I wasn't going to betray him or the *yakuza*. While this may at first seem chivalrous, it was no more than commonsense on my part. If, as the *oyabun* of Tokyo, Fuchida possessed the influence with the authorities he claimed, then he was going to be my only possible chance of avoiding a very long stay in a Japanese prison. If he thought I had betrayed him after he had set out to help me reach Anna, he would obviously make no attempt to intervene on my behalf.

Konoe Akira turned to the senior cop. 'He has abducted my mother!' he cried. 'She will not live! It is murder!'

'Your mother is missing? You're saying she has been kidnapped by this man?' the sergeant asked.

'Who else?' Konoe spat, still furious.

He turned back to me. 'Where is she?'

Obviously Fuchida, Saito and the three others had not been

arrested. Somehow they must have been warned and left before the police arrived on the scene. I shook my head. 'As you can see, I am on my own, sergeant.'

'Hai! We will soon find out, Nick Duncan.' He turned back to Konoe Akira. 'It is only you and your mother who live in the house?'

'She has a nurse, but I cannot wake her up.'

'She sleeps in the same room?'

'Yes, but she has been drugged.'

'You know this for sure?'

'I cannot wake her!' Konoe Akira repeated.

The sergeant nodded to one of his men, indicating he should take a look. 'No servants, just the nurse?'

'Oh, also my staff sergeant.' He pointed at me. 'He has tied him up. He is lying outside my bedchamber.'

'This woke you up?' the sergeant asked.

'I beg your pardon?'

'The noise – tying your . . . er . . . staff sergeant up?'

'No, this man is well trained, a professional. I heard nothing. I pressed the alarm when he crossed the room to fetch my clothes.'

'Professional?' the sergeant sniffed, glancing at me. 'And he allowed you to get dressed?' Then he added, 'How very considerate.'

I don't suppose you can blush when you're shitting yourself, but I'm sure I did; I certainly felt my face burning. The old bloke had outsmarted me and pressed the alarm virtually under my nose.

I would later learn that because most of the foreign embassies and the Imperial Palace were in the same vicinity, they had all been wired up, alarmed directly to the *Keishicho*, the Metropolitan Police Headquarters in Central Tokyo. Konoe

Akira had been permitted to avail himself of the system, a buzzer or some such at his bedside, which he had pressed to alert them. The cunning old bastard knew if he delayed me sufficiently they'd arrive in time to arrest me. It said something for Saito and his men that they'd moved the old crone without waking anyone, and Nick Duncan on his own had made a bloody great hash of things. I should have marched him out barefoot in his red flannel nightshirt; chivalry has no place in today's world.

'Are you sure he was responsible for your honourable mother's disappearance?' the sergeant asked. 'Old ladies sometimes go wandering. They can be senile and confused. It is not uncommon.'

'But there is the nurse to mind her,' Konoe Akira insisted. Then glancing malevolently at me he spat, 'Of course he did it!'

'With their help . . . the yakuza, it is possible,' the policeman replied.

'As you can see there are no yakuza. I am on my own,' I said unnecessarily.

The sergeant shook his head slowly and then, with the beginnings of a smile, asked me, 'Do you expect me to believe that two unrelated incidents, the one a kidnapping and the other an attempt to kidnap, took place coincidentally in the same home almost simultaneously?'

I held his gaze knowing he was right and that there was no other way to explain things. 'I can only answer for myself. Perhaps you should ask Konoe-san why I entered his home and attempted to abduct him. It obviously wasn't in order to rob him – I could have done that easily enough.' I pointed to the green vase. 'It belongs in the Goryeo Dynasty and is near priceless. Why would I not take that and leave well satisfied?'

'Because you are a professional and knew the vase was alarmed and you want a ransom for my esteemed mother!'

Konoe Akira shouted. Which explained why he'd offered the vase in exchange for his life.

I had to hand it to him, he was resourceful.

'If I had kidnapped your honourable mother, which I haven't, why then would I kidnap you if I wanted to hold her to ransom?' I turned to the sergeant. 'Perhaps you should ask *Konoe-san* why he thinks I have attempted to kidnap him. My partner and I are *gaijin* and strangers in a foreign country.' I pointed to Konoe Akira. 'He has kidnapped her for reasons that will soon become apparent. It is he who is the kidnapper and who forced me to enter his home to discover where she is!'

It was the first time I had admitted knowing more of Konoe Akira's background than he might have supposed and he blanched, crying, 'He lies!'

'Enough!' the sergeant said, finally running out of patience. 'Why did you not report this alleged kidnapping to the police? Kidnapping is a serious offence.'

I sighed. 'It seemed at the time to be a matter I could clear up on my own.' I pointed at Konoe Akira. 'My partner and this man have a long association. They are not strangers. This man has a personal agenda.'

'I am taking you into custody, Nick Duncan. Anything further you say may be used in evidence.' He turned and dipped his head in a cursory bow to Konoe Akira. 'You may be required to give evidence, sir. I would request that you inform the police if you intend to leave Tokyo.' The sergeant handed Konoe Akira his card in the two-handed manner of the Japanese, bowing slightly.

The two policemen sent to find Staff Sergeant Goto now appeared with him in tow. He was rubbing his wrists, his expression totally distraught. He broke away from the two officers and went to stand in front of Konoe

Akira, bowing deeply. 'I have let you down, Colonel. I must be punished,' he said.

'*Hai!* I will deal with you later. Fetch my belt!' Konoe Akira snapped.

The thoroughly dejected Goto turned to obey and, suddenly observing me, let out a sharp cry, then pivoted on one foot and karate-kicked me high in the chest, obviously aiming at my throat. With my hands handcuffed behind my back I had nowhere to go but backwards, knocking into the green vase and sending it crashing to the floor, where I joined it moments later, coming down on my arse, then my back, my head finally knocking hard against the wooden floor. I lay dazed among the shards of porcelain with the ear-piercing racket of the alarm filling the room. It took only a few seconds for me to realise that I was bleeding, but how badly I couldn't say. I attempted to rise, but with my hands secured behind my back I had no way of getting to my feet. I looked up to see Konoe Akira standing over me, weeping like a small child.

I left the Emergency Department of the University of Tokyo Todai Hospital in a police car just after dawn. Whilst I wasn't severely injured I had multiple cuts to my backside and the back of my arms, most fairly deep, and one just below the right shoulderblade, in all requiring fifty-seven stitches. I was told once the painkillers wore off to expect a bit of a headache from the bump on the back of my head, but I wasn't concussed and while my sternum felt bruised where Goto had kicked me, an X-ray showed nothing was broken. I was probably carrying the most expensively acquired sutures the hospital would have performed in a long time. Years later in New York I saw a similar vase for sale in a Fifth Avenue antique dealer's for two million American dollars. I recall how Anna wanted to buy it for me. Laughing, I'd quickly refused. 'It gives me a pain in the bum just to look at it,' I'd remarked, kissing her for the generous gesture it undoubtedly was.

I was taken to the huge Metropolitan Police Department Complex located in the Kasumigaseki district of Central Tokyo, the biggest in Japan with five hundred police officers operating from it. Here I was brought to the charge desk where a sleepy sergeant, no doubt looking forward to the completion of the night shift, started the paperwork, charging me with attempted kidnapping, assault, breaking and entering, and possession of an unlicensed and prohibited firearm. He explained in a bored voice that later in the morning I might have to undergo an interview by the public prosecutor who would decide whether I was to be indicted, but that the police could hold me for forty-eight hours without charge.

After my belt and shoelaces were removed, I was escorted to the holding cells. Prison cells in foreign lands are usually depicted as filthy holes with blood, gore, urine and vomit on the floor, the toilet in one corner overflowing with faecal matter. These were clean and smelled of strong disinfectant, and were arranged in a semicircle with the bars facing the guard station so that the occupants were under twenty-four-hour surveillance. The nocturnal sounds issuing from the cells reminded me of the islands where passengers sleeping on deck emitted the same snores, grunts, snuffles and cries in their sleep. The only sound missing was the cry of an infant. I suddenly felt very far from home and very alone.

My cell, better described as a dog box, had *tatami* flooring, slightly less than half of which was occupied by a narrow futon on which lay two blankets, two small towels roughly the size of dishcloths and a toothbrush and miniature tube of toothpaste. There was no washbasin, but at the far end was an open semi-squat toilet. It seemed that even the process of defecating was under observation. The entire cell was about three metres long and one and a half metres wide. I was to learn that the lights were perpetually on, though dimmed at night.

For a bloke my size it was a tight fit, my head either up against the open bars of the cell door or resting against the toilet. I was dog tired. Over the last two days I'd managed to snatch only a handful of hours in the hotel after the meeting with *Fuchida-san* and the other *oyabun* at his penthouse apartment. It felt like several days ago but was in fact only yesterday afternoon. Forced by my various wounds to lie on my stomach I chose to sleep with my head against the toilet, burying my nose in the blankets, rather than look through the bars at the guards.

However, try as I might, I couldn't sleep; my mind was racing wildly. I'd screwed up big time: Anna was no nearer to being rescued and I now found myself incarcerated, wounded, exhausted and beyond desperation. I tried to look at each of the problems separately, to see if I could find a way out of our predicaments, otherwise I might end up rotting in a Japanese jail, and Anna could possibly be physically harmed or perhaps even killed. By ordering her kidnapping, Konoe Akira had potentially implicated himself with the Shield Society. This could soon become public knowledge and the honour of his noble family and his personal and professional reputation would be deeply compromised. So, I reasoned, he might be prepared to organise Anna's release as soon as possible in return for keeping his association with these extreme rightwing fanatics from the public and his business associates. This seemed initially a positive thought. At least Anna would be free.

But, almost immediately, it occurred to me that there wasn't anyone to plausibly implicate him or link him to the organisation. My own evidence was hearsay and would probably be regarded as entirely specious. The only confirmation that Anna's kidnapping had been the work of the Shield Society under orders from Konoe Akira came from the Jade Mistress. Furthermore, the likelihood of her confirming this fact, or even that she knew Konoe Akira, was negligible. That is, unless she was forced to do so by *Fuchida-san*, the *yakuza* boss who had her written and signed confirmation. Without that document, Konoe could refute the accusation and, for that matter, deny knowing Anna. The only tangible proof that he'd known her in the past was the inscribed silver cigarette case he'd given her all those years ago as a parting gift, and it was now back in his possession, since Anna had used it as her calling card. My mind was going round in circles, but I couldn't stop. This meant that *Fuchida-san*, with the cooperation of the Jade Mistress, was the only possible link between him and the extreme rightwing society, and with Anna.

I was forced to ask myself why the *yakuza* boss would want to help me. I was not a part of his organisation. In fact I was a relative stranger to whom he owed no loyalty. While we had swapped butterflies for twenty-five years we had only known each other in a personal sense for a few days, during which time I had caused him and his people nothing but trouble. Putting myself in his shoes I could see that there was yet another compelling reason why he should distance himself from Anna's kidnapping. He held Konoe Akira's ageing mother captive, and rather than merely using her as a bargaining tool to gain Anna's freedom, he could use her to turn a handsome profit. A nice little ransom payment would see her restored to the comfort of her home with additional assurances that the *yakuza* boss would not reveal Konoe Akira's patronage of the Jade House; if any inquiry were instituted, the Jade Mistress would deny ever knowing him. To make it even more attractive for him to pay up and shut up, the Jade House *mama-san* could quash all speculation about Anna by declaring that she had come to her establishment late at night looking for a job as a *gaijin* bondage mistress. Apart from proving incompetent, she had been discovered to be a heroin addict and so had been escorted off the premises and put back onto the streets where she belonged. The authorities of course would be well aware of what might happen to an attractive and desperate junkie in the sleazy nightclub area of a strange city at night. This little conspiracy between the *yakuza* boss and Konoe Akira would effectively discredit as well as dispose of Anna, who in the minds of the police and the authorities would be human trash, not worth bothering about. They'd duly notify the Australian Embassy and post a missing-persons bulletin and get on with the more important work of providing protection for honest law-abiding, tax-paying citizens.

As for my personal predicament, as the saying goes, I was done like a dog's dinner! With his undoubted connections in high places, Konoe Akira could make it impossible for me to prove that he had a case to answer for crimes committed in the dim and distant past, and without that, how could I link him to Anna, or to her kidnapping? All my evidence was purely hearsay. It would be a lot easier for him to suggest that I was an opportunist and a con man with a junkie partner. And then there was my war record. To the Japanese authorities, I was a highly decorated killer of the sons of Japan's grieving mothers. Like my own country's hatred for the Japanese, here too I was sure there would be no love lost for an old enemy.

By the morning shift change, I finally concluded my own trial.

I hadn't slept a wink, the hospital painkillers had long worn off, I had a splitting headache and my lacerations were stiff and sore. As self-appointed judge and jury I found overwhelmingly for the prosecution and duly sentenced myself to a minimum of twenty-five years hard labour in a Japanese prison, a just sentence, given that I could well be responsible for Anna losing her life. All this because I'd allowed a scrawny old man time to put on his underpants!

Breakfast consisted of a tin mug of weak green tea and a bento box, a small cardboard container of fried fish and boiled rice. I was to learn that the fare never changed. After breakfast I was escorted to a washroom and allowed to wash my face and clean my teeth – a hugely gratifying experience.

At ten o'clock I was escorted into an interview room where two uniformed policemen and a plainclothes guy who may or may not have been a cop sat on one side of a large desk alongside a vacant chair. Each had pads and pencils (not pens) in front of them and a large tape recorder rested on the table. All three men were smoking and the plainclothes bloke reached over and offered me a cigarette. When I declined he seemed surprised; virtually every male smoked in Japan at that time.

I was motioned towards a chair on the opposite side of the desk. 'Sit please, *Duncan-san*,' the plainclothes bloke said in a friendly voice. I was to discover that he played the good guy in the good-guy bad-guy routine that was shortly to begin.

'Thank you, but I prefer to stand. I have a problem with some cuts on my bum,' I said, which caused them all to laugh.

'Very expensive cuts I hear,' the plainclothes bloke said, grinning, which indicated he had been briefed on the events of the previous night.

Moments later a second plainclothes guy entered the room,

scowling at me. 'Why is this man standing?' he asked one of the policemen. The bad guy had arrived. The policeman explained and he grunted and took the vacant seat.

The good guy (I was never given any of their names) then explained that the interview must by law take place in Japanese regardless of how proficient I was in the language. 'We cannot speak your language and no interpreter is permitted.' I nodded and he continued. 'No public prosecutor is present today and so you will not be formally charged. We simply wish to get all the facts down and we hope you will cooperate.'

I nodded again, determined to say as little as possible. I was unaware at the time that in a Japanese court only a judge presides and all evidence is written. Then, and even today, ninety-nine per cent of cases that go before a judge lead to a guilty verdict. Therefore, if the public prosecutor decides that a case may be heard, it is tantamount to a conviction. The interrogation I was about to undergo was clearly designed to make me admit my guilt. I was also to learn that there were no rules of engagement and no right of appeal against foul play.

'Let us begin,' the good guy said quietly. 'Please state your name and nationality.'

'Nicholas Duncan, Australian.'

'Do you have any formal identification?'

'My driving licence is in my wallet, which you have already taken from me.'

'It has no photograph,' one of the police officers said accusingly.

'No, it is not required in my country.'

'What country is that?' the bad guy asked.

'I told you, Australia.'

'But you don't live in Australia?'

'No, I live in the New Hebrides.'

'A tax haven?' again from the bad guy.

'Yes, I run an inter-island shipping company.'

'Why did you come to Japan?'

'To purchase two trawlers from the Mitsubishi Shipping Company.'

Good guy, smiling: 'See, it is not all bad. We honour you for contributing to the prosperity of the Japanese people.'

Bad guy: 'Where is your passport? When you were arrested you had no passport. It is an offence for a foreigner not to carry his passport.'

'I was not told that.'

Bad guy: 'Where is it?'

'In the safe in my hotel suite.'

Bad guy: 'What hotel?'

'The Imperial.'

Bad guy: 'You must give us the combination!'

'No,' I said quietly. 'If you will contact the Australian Embassy I will give an embassy official the combination and he will fetch my passport and give it to you.' Also in the safe was nearly six thousand American dollars in Thomas Cook traveller's cheques and possibly Konoe Akira's calling card, the gold fob watch, as well as the receipt for the two trawlers. I wasn't going to let these buggers indulge in a lucky dip and then later find myself unable to prove that anything was missing.

Bad guy: 'What are you suggesting? We are not the criminals here! It is required that you hand in your passport.'

'Yes, an embassy official will do that.'

Bad guy: 'I see, you do not wish to cooperate?'

There isn't any real answer to a question like that. 'I am trying to answer your questions, sir.'

'Did you fight in the recent war?'

'Yes.'

'In what capacity?'

'I was a radio operator.'

'Did you carry a rifle?'

'No.' Strictly speaking this was true as I used an Owen submachine-gun.

'You lie, you are a killer!'

I guess you get the idea. I was asked about my childhood in Japan and New Britain, how I came to speak Japanese and a host of other seemingly irrelevant questions, the bad guy always suggesting something fishy, the good guy smiling and asking me to cooperate as they were only trying to build a profile of me. It was all pretty ingenuous from the good guy and pointed and direct from the bad guy and I guess it was meant to get a pattern of questions and answers going so that I would become accustomed to the rhythms of speech and become less cautious with my answers.

When we got to the subject of the *yakuza* and *Fuchida-san* and I explained that we swapped butterflies and had done so for twenty-five years they clearly didn't believe me. It only started to get really rough when they began to question me about Anna and her past. This was a story I was prepared to tell as it implicated Konoe Akira directly and gave us a further reason for coming to Japan.

But from this point there was no more good-guy bad-guy routine. 'Thank you for coming to Japan,' the original good guy suddenly shouted. 'You give us an opportunity to pay you back for killing our fathers and uncles. You were not a radio operator! You are a murderer! You are going to die. Do you hear me! We are going to kill you!'

It was sub-standard interrogation technique, what not to do, almost the first lesson I'd been taught in naval intelligence. The threat of certain death usually achieves nothing in an interrogation. The alternative of sweet and sour, hope and despair, is the only technique that works in the psychology involved in obtaining a confession. If no carrot exists the stick won't do the job on its own. Hope springs eternal, remove it and the subject closes down. Individual survival is largely built on choosing one or another outcome. In interrogation, threat only works when physical or psychological punishment, not death, is the consequence. The interrogator's mantra has always been 'Dead men tell no tales.'

'If you intend to kill me, then there is no point in my answering your questions,' I said. I had been standing for nearly two hours, and with no sleep and the aggravation of the cuts I was in pretty poor shape, dog tired and hurting like hell. There wasn't much more they could do to make things worse than they were. I decided to say nothing more.

'Sit!' the original bad guy commanded. I remained standing. 'Sit!' he shouted again. Again I refused to comply. The bad guy turned to the two policemen. 'Make the murderer of our fathers sit,' he instructed.

The two uniformed officers rose from their chairs and came to stand on either side of me and the original good guy came around the table and placed the chair behind me. The two policemen then pushed me down hard onto the chair. The pain was excruciating as my lacerated buttocks crashed down onto the seat. 'Stand!' The cops lifted me partially from the chair. 'Sit!' I resisted by pushing down on the desk in front of me, making it impossible for the two small policemen to force me back down. 'Handcuff him!' came the order. I was handcuffed and at the same time the chair was pulled sufficiently far from the table to be out of reach. Then they crashed me down again. The command to sit or stand went on for a good twenty minutes with the result that first the dressings aggravated the wounds, then I felt the thirty or so stitches in the cheeks of my buttocks begin to tear apart. The seat of my trousers was soon soaked with blood, which ran down the back of my legs into my socks and shoes.

The effect of lifting me and crashing me back down meant that my shoulders often met the back of the chair, which caused the large cut behind my right shoulderblade to open up, and soon I could feel my blood-soaked shirt sticking to my back. 'Confess! You murdered the old lady! Confess!' my tormentor shouted each time I crashed down, his face no more than an inch from my own. Up I went and then down again, the command to confess becoming a mantra screamed into my ears. I lost count of the times I was lifted and dumped – the two policemen were plainly exhausted – then suddenly the seat of my blood-soaked trousers met the blood-covered chair and I slid off it and crashed to the floor, hitting the back of my head on the edge of the chair. I rolled onto my stomach and lay on the floor with my handcuffed hands tucked under me and my eyes closed. The dozen or so stitches on the back of my forearms were the only ones that still seemed intact. I was dazed, bloody and close to passing out from sheer exhaustion, or possibly loss of blood.

'Get up!' the second plainclothes guy commanded. I lay still, eyes closed, feigning unconsciousness. 'Lift him!' came the command. The policemen were not big men and attempting to lift a bloodied and inert body weighing two hundred and thirty pounds was not easy. They tried rolling me over onto my back to get at my arms but the back of my shirt and trousers from shoulders to ankles was blood-soaked and the task proved well nigh impossible for the two men. They made several attempts and must have been pretty bloodied by the time I heard the command, 'Leave him!' Then moments later, 'Call an ambulance!'

I must have passed out on the way to the hospital because I came to in Emergency where two nurses were swabbing me with iodine, the sting of the antiseptic excruciating. They then set about removing the broken stitches, another very painful experience, and finally a doctor attended to me, re-stitching the wounds, all of which was done without giving me any anaesthesia. I confess I didn't handle the process at all well. While the police were torturing me I managed to contain the agony with grunts and winces and an occasion cry of pain, but released from the need to remain stoic I sobbed and shouted and pleaded like a child for them to stop. I was finally given a blood transfusion and spent the night in a private room in the hospital with a police officer outside the door.

To my surprise, the following morning a police officer arrived with a full set of clothes, clean undies, shirt, trousers, socks and jacket, all obviously obtained from the hotel, including a spare pair of shoes, as the ones I'd arrived in were blood-soaked and beyond cleaning. I'd asked a nurse for a painkiller during the night but she'd refused, saying that the police had left strict instructions that I wasn't to receive any. Then she'd smiled. 'But they said nothing about a sedative.' She'd returned shortly and soon afterwards I was able to sleep, although I awoke very sore, battered and doubtful that I had the fortitude to get through another chairing session. I was unable to shower, but with the help of a nurse I was washed down completely, my wounded bum and shoulder again painfully dressed.

Clean linen always helps and I felt a little better when the police car came to fetch me. I speculated about whether I had brought sufficient shirts and trousers on the trip to last the torture sessions that possibly lay ahead. The Japanese police had found the ideal way to torment me: either they'd repeat the chair dump or simply demand that I be seated. The latter would be less painful than the former, but nevertheless it would be a very unpleasant experience.

I had been expecting to be brought in front of the public prosecutor and formally charged. Instead my belt and shoelaces were confiscated and I was taken to a cell and left alone all day with only the mug of green tea and the bento box of fried fish and rice at noon and again in the early evening.

I was attempting to sleep, despite the noise and the lights, when around 10 p.m. the original plainclothes bad guy arrived with two police officers in tow. 'Get up. Put your shoes on!' he snapped. I did as I was told, the cell was unlocked and I walked out to stand between the two policemen. 'March!' the bad guy ordered, giving me a hard punch on the back, right on my wounded shoulder. Pain stabbed through my shoulderblade at the unexpected punch and I reacted instinctively. Turning, I grabbed him by the throat and lifted him off the ground. A look of surprised terror flashed into his eyes.

Before the two cops could react I lowered him to the ground, knowing he'd be wearing the bruise of my thumb for a couple of weeks. 'Sorry, sir, you caught me by surprise,' I said, then added, 'I was not expecting to be attacked from the back.' A roar of approval came from the surrounding cells and the prisoners started to clap.

The bad guy's hands were clasped around his throat. 'Hand . . . cuff urrr . . . him!' he cried, his voice squeaking and breaking.

I held out both hands to one of the police officers, but they pulled my arms behind my back then handcuffed me, whereupon the plainclothes guy kneed me hard in the groin and I pitched to my knees in agony. The booing and shouting from my fellow prisoners became deafening.

I attempted unsuccessfully to rise and was finally dragged to my feet with the help of the two policemen and frogmarched down a long passage to arrive, panting and biting back groans from the pain between my legs, at a different and much smaller room. A tall slender greying man almost my own height sat on a corner of the desk, immaculately dressed in a plain grey tailored suit, striped shirt, the starched cuffs of which sported gold monogrammed cufflinks, blue silk tie and black expensive-looking shoes polished to a military shine. He politely thanked the two cops and stood and turned to the plainclothes guy. 'May I have your name please?' he asked in a formal manner.

The plainclothes guy came to attention and bowed. 'Special Services Officer Razan.'

'You are with the First Intelligence Division?'

'Yes, sir.'

'I would like to speak to my client privately, *Razan-san*,' he said quietly, with only the semblance of a bow.

The plainclothes guy who now had a name bowed more formally. 'As you wish, *Kinzo-san*. Only five minutes is permitted, then I am authorised to return.'

'That will be quite sufficient time, thank you,' *Kinzo-san* said, his forefinger flicking in the direction of the door. Then suddenly he said, 'Oh, send one of the police officers in to remove *Duncan-san*'s handcuffs,' adding, 'This is not included in the five minutes.'

Razan hesitated, his eyes suddenly angry. 'He is a murderer and a kidnapper. It is best that he is restrained! He has shown recent violence,' he warned.

'He is none of those things until he is formally convicted, and in my experience, men in custody seldom show violence towards their lawyers,' *Kinzo-san* said without raising his voice. 'Send in the officer, please.' He smiled. 'My sympathies, none of us like being called out at night after a hard day's work. I'm sure you will be able to go home shortly.'

Whoever this tall Japanese was, it was obvious he commanded respect. The police officer arrived, removed my handcuffs and left. It took all my resolve to prevent myself from clasping my hands to my scrotum as *Kinzo-san* bowed formally and introduced himself as my lawyer.

'But I have yet to be permitted to request a lawyer,' I said, puzzled.

'Well then your request is granted, *Duncan-san*. It seems you have friends who ask to be permitted to appoint me.'

'Thank you, I am grateful to them and to you,' I replied, bowing to this exquisitely polite man who seemed to know his way around. My hopes rose that I might get through the day without having to undergo another bout of chair exercises.

'This violence he talked about, when did it take place? Was it in the home of Konoe Akira?' he asked, concerned.

'Hardly,' I said. 'An incident occurred on our way here to see you. *Razan-san* unexpectedly punched me in the back on the wound to my shoulder. I reacted instinctively by turning and grabbing him one-handed around the throat, but then I released him immediately.'

'That's serious; he is a special intelligence officer.'

'I'm afraid it was instinctive. My reaction to a totally unexpected punch from behind.'

'Then he handcuffed you?'

'Yes, then kicked me in the testicles.'

'Once you were handcuffed?'

'Yes.'

He grinned. 'Ah, a cowardly gesture in public,' he said, obviously pleased with my answer.

'Are you in pain?' he asked, suddenly solicitous.

I tried to grin, though it came out more as a wince. 'It all adds up.'

'I'm sorry I was not available yesterday to prevent what occurred during your interrogation, but there were other aspects of your case to attend to.'

'Oh, then you know what happened?'

'Of course, we even have photographs of your back and . . . er . . . buttocks.'

'Photographs? I don't recall . . .'

He indicated a fairly large brown manila envelope on the desk. 'A conscientious ambulance attendant when you passed out on the way to hospital, then again another in hospital, these second ones in colour,' he explained. 'Very useful. Your harsh treatment may have saved us a great deal of trouble. Westerners still think we Japanese are barbarians, but we have been a civilised race since Emperor Jimmu ascended the Chrysanthemum Throne six hundred and sixty years before your Christ, when your people were still living in caves and painting themselves blue. This is the new Japan; our government puts great store in our justice system and they do not like photographs like these to appear in the newspapers and on the television or to be sent to a foreign embassy or distributed worldwide by Reuters International News Service.'

This turn of events was all rather sudden and I was having difficulty comprehending that *Fuchida-san*, the *yakuza* boss, whom I had virtually written off, had stuck by me when he stood to gain handsomely by walking away and negotiating directly with Konoe Akira. I silently thanked him for his caretaker's eyes, in this case taking photographs of my re-opened wounds.

'Will they not simply say it was caused by an accident?' I queried.

He quickly brought his finger to his lips and I realised

he was telling me the room was undoubtedly bugged. 'Ah, "accident" is a useful word. In my experience it seldom carries its true meaning when it relates to obtaining a confession. We must thank the gods for stupid policemen. The two plainclothes men should be ashamed of their inept and brutal performance yesterday. I have in my possession a copy of the report at the time of your re-admission to the University Hospital Emergency Department shortly after the interview session, and the nurse's and doctor's report on your condition.'

I was suddenly aware that Kinzo was giving me all this information in a clear and carefully enunciated manner for the benefit of the secret listening device. 'What will happen next?' I asked in an attempt to avoid any more leading questions.

'You will be arraigned, taken before the public prosecutor who will decide whether to charge you for the four offences – kidnapping, attempted kidnapping, breaking and entering, and possessing an unlicensed gun brought into Japan without a permit.'

I groaned. 'I've really screwed up. That bastard Konoe Akira wins again.'

'Ah, maybe not. I have some good news. *Konoe-san* has agreed to drop all the charges. His mother, who suffers from dementia, was most fortuitously found wandering in the street by the great kendo master, Saito Miro, and naturally the charge of kidnapping her has been dropped. It is a strange and remarkable coincidence. The nurse responsible for looking after the old woman took a strong sedative by mistake, thinking it was a headache tablet, and that is how the old woman was able to wander off into the night.'

Realising that I was required to play the game of stating our case before I went in front of the public prosecutor, I merely said, 'That is a great relief to me,' then added charitably, 'To think of one's mother wandering the streets alone at night would bring any son to despair.' I immediately regretted this last statement – it was clumsily phrased and I hoped it didn't indicate that I was aware we were being taped.

Kinzo-san grinned, acknowledging with a damping movement of his palm that I understood the game we were playing but should keep it simple. 'I have requested the public prosecutor grant permission to hear the other charges in private here at police headquarters and not in a public court. I am happy to say that he accepts that discretion is required in this particular hearing. I regret the two police officers and the two plainclothes officers who interviewed you yesterday are required to be present, along with the arresting officers.' He paused and pointed at me, perhaps to emphasise what he was about to say. 'You must understand that it is the public prosecutor alone who has absolute discretion to decide if you will be charged with any crime. If he finds there is a case to answer, then it is extremely unlikely that a judge will overrule this finding. I ask only that you allow me to do the talking, and if you are personally addressed, you are permitted to bow deeply and then to say, "I ask permission to consult my lawyer before answering your question, your honour." Do you understand?'

'Yes,' I replied for the benefit of the bugging device.

My lawyer glanced at his watch. 'Time's up, *Duncan-san*. Try to get some sleep. I will be present tomorrow afternoon when you will go before the public prosecutor.'

He bowed and I did the same. 'Thank you, *Kinzo-san*, I am honoured to know you. Will you please thank those friends who have greatly honoured me by appointing you to my case?'

He laughed. 'Ah, we lawyers are like butterflies, we like to land where the nectar is,' he said, confirming that *Fuchida-san* was my benefactor.

I was taken back to my cell, this time without the handcuffs, and without plainclothes First Intelligence Division Officer Razan. The two police officers showed a new measure of respect by instructing me politely to move and being careful not to touch me. Most of the prisoners were asleep when I returned but some nut still awake shouted, 'The *gaijin* has returned!' Moments later those awake started to clap, waking all the others, and soon the cops on duty were shouting for silence. It seemed that, like the *yakuza* experience at the Imperial Hotel, I had once again acquired respect for all the wrong reasons.

I guess hope springs eternal, and despite nursing a new frontal area of pain that now made it difficult for me to lie on my stomach, I finally managed to get some sleep.

The following afternoon, no doubt after the public prosecutor had duly listened to the recording of my interview with my lawyer, I was led down a long corridor punctuated with doors, all of them closed. I was surprised to see *Kinzo-san* waiting for me a little further along. As I approached him, he said, 'I have requested three minutes with you before we go into the hearing.' Turning to my two police escorts he asked them politely to stand three doors further down the corridor on either side of where we stood and out of earshot.

'We are going into your examination by the public prosecutor. It is like a court hearing, with many of the powers to compel witnesses to attend, but it is not a sentencing court,' *Kinzo-san* explained. 'You will not be placed in the dock, in fact there isn't one; you are simply required to sit beside me.'

'Sitting might be a problem,' I grinned.

'Better still; standing beside me will do nicely. Now this is important. I don't want you to respond to the prosecutor's questions as I instructed you to do yesterday for the benefit of the tape recorder. This is because it may appear uncooperative. So, this is what we will do. I will have my hands resting on my lap. If I raise my forefinger a fraction on the hand nearest to you, this means you must answer the question directly. If my finger does not move, leave me to answer or to object on your behalf.'

Walking together with a policeman front and back we entered a small court-like area with twenty or so fixed seats facing a platform that occupied most of the width of the room. A stenographer sat at a small table at one end. Three men sat at a desk in the middle of the platform, the one in the centre a small man in the ubiquitous blue serge suit, white shirt and plain blue tie. He seemed to have no distinguishing features except perhaps for his slightly broader, flatter face and the fact that his greying hair was cut very short but seemed to grow in several directions, which was probably why it was kept so short. The two others were roughly the same age as the prosecutor, undistinguished-looking, although well dressed, both sporting expensive silk ties of the kind usually worn by politicians or lawyers.

I remained standing while six other men seated themselves. The prosecutor glanced up from case notes he appeared to be reading and said, 'You may sit.'

Kinzo-san sprang to his feet. 'Your honour, my client prefers to stand for reasons that will be made clear at a later stage.'

The prosecutor sighed. 'Very well, let us proceed. Nicholas Duncan, you are charged under Japanese law to answer on four counts: kidnapping, attempted kidnapping, breaking and entering, and unlawfully possessing a dangerous weapon, in this case an unlicensed automatic pistol. I will hear what you and the honourable *Kinzo-san* have to say before deciding which of these charges are to be proceeded with. This is an inquiry only and you and your lawyer are free to present any evidence you believe contradicts the report I have here and the evidence of your arresting officer . . .' he glanced briefly at his notes, 'Sergeant Yamamoto. In the presence of two police officers you have undergone an interview with Special Services Officers Razan and Tanaka and their written evidence may also be taken into account at this hearing. Do you understand?'

'Yes, your honour.'

'Is there anything else you wish to say before we proceed? There is the matter your lawyer promised to explain, of your need to stand . . .'

Kinzo-san rose to his feet. 'Your honour, I ask that this matter be presented at a later time, but there is another I would wish to present immediately.'

The prosecutor nodded. 'Proceed, please.'

'Your honour, it pleases me to inform you that the supposed kidnap victim has been found. Apparently she suffers from dementia and rose from her bed and left the home, wandering the city all night. She was discovered by a young kendo pupil next afternoon in a state of near-collapse in the vicinity of the Kyumeikan Kendo Dojo.'

'Dementia? What is this condition?' the prosecutor asked, then added, 'There is nothing of this in my case notes.'

'Your honour, the term "senile dementia" has only come into recent use in the medical profession and describes a form of brain disorder marked by mental deterioration that is irreversible and is known to affect some people, most often those over the age of sixty-five years. Progressive loss of memory inevitably occurs. We would previously have lumped it all together under the term senility,' *Kinzo-san* explained.

'Oh, I see. If she suffers from memory loss, how then could she tell whoever found her where she lived or even her name?' the prosecutor asked pointedly.

'Ah, in the case of her address she didn't know where she lived. But I am informed that those elderly people who are afflicted have moments of clarity, and only in the final stages of senile dementia do they usually forget their names. It was most fortunate that she was brought to the notice of the honourable *Saito-san, kendo hanshi,* who recognised the noble name of Konoe and escorted her home in his limousine. I therefore ask that the charge of kidnapping be struck from the list of charges against my client.'

'Very well, let us proceed with the hearing of the charge of attempting to kidnap Konoe Akira.'

Kinzo-san was already seated but immediately jumped to his feet. 'Your honour, I am pleased to inform you that I received a telephone call from the honourable *Konoe-san*'s lawyer this morning dropping the charges of attempted kidnapping as well as breaking and entering. I have his instructions with me and if you wish him to attend he is standing by. It seems that *Konoe-san* has received an explanation for the purpose of *Duncan-san*'s visit and is satisfied that no threat to him or to his property was intended.'

The prosecutor sighed. 'I am obliged, though reluctantly, to accept *Konoe-san*'s decision, although I feel sure a judge would be unwilling to let it pass without further cross-examination. Please tender your colleague's instructions.'

Kinzo-san handed in the written statement from Konoe Akira's lawyer. '*Konoe-san*'s instructions are without equivocation, your honour.'

The public prosecutor looked at *Kinzo-san*. 'I feel quite

sure Sergeant Yamamoto, the arresting officer, would see it differently, but I am prepared to accept that the complaint has been withdrawn. With regard to property damage, I see here that there is the matter of a broken vase that I believe was of great value and was destroyed by your client.'

'Your honour, as this is not within the framework of the charges laid in this hearing, but may well be the subject of another such, I have been instructed by my client to charge the manservant of Konoe Akira, known as Staff Sergeant Goto, with assault and battery. I intend to subpoena Sergeant Yamamoto as a witness. My client was attacked by a vicious karate kick aimed at his throat while his hands were handcuffed behind his back. This caused him to be knocked backwards and into the vase in question, which resulted in serious wounds from the porcelain shards.'

'I anticipate you, *Kinzo-san*. No future assault charges against Goto in return for ignoring the matter of the accidental loss of the very valuable vase. It is well known that the courts are overworked. I am happy that you so diligently endeavour to make it easier for the law to cope with the pressure.'

'Thank you, your honour,' *Kinzo-san* said, sitting down.

'This brings us to the extremely serious business of the unlicensed weapon you were carrying, *Duncan-san*. How do you explain its presence on your person?' He glanced down and turned a page. 'Ah, here it is, a Browning Hi-Power 13-shot automatic. Not even our police or members of the First Intelligence Division are equipped with such an effective weapon.' He paused, then continued, 'Can you tell me how you acquired this weapon?'

I glanced down at *Kinzo-san*'s hand to see that his forefinger was slightly raised. 'I brought it from my home in the New Hebrides, your honour. I have an inter-island shipping fleet and it is judicious to carry such a weapon when on board ship.' It was a careful lie to protect *Fuchida-san* and I was prepared, if I needed to make my lie more convincing, to build a story around the homicidal instincts of primitive people fired by alcohol on board ship.

'Did you obtain a permit to import a weapon into Japan?'

'Foolishly not, your honour. It is always in my luggage when I travel to the various islands, and I neglected to remove it when I was packing. I used the same valise as part of my luggage and most regrettably only discovered the pistol when I unpacked in the hotel.'

'So you thought to use it when you paid what now seems to have become a cordial visit to the home of Konoe Akira?'

Kinzo came to his feet. 'Your honour, there is a matter of another kidnapping of my client's partner by the Shield Society and his belief that Konoe Akira instigated it with this fanatical rightwing organisation. *Konoe-san*'s involvement is yet to be established but my client had reasons to believe that he was in danger. At the time, rightly or wrongly, he believed he needed to protect himself.'

'Protecting a foreigner is a matter for the police. This is not a primitive land, we are not primitive people, we do not take the law into our own hands, *Kinzo-san*.'

'Your honour, you are quite right. But in the matter of primitive people and their behaviour I submit these photographs and copies of the hospital report on the physical condition of my client after being interviewed by the metropolitan police and two special officers from the First Intelligence Division.' He handed the manila envelope to the public prosecutor who opened it and took from it several ten by eight inch photographs and a single document. 'I have of course in my possession the black-and-white and colour negatives, as well as the hospital report.'

The public prosecutor looked at the photographs briefly then said, 'As you well know, the so-called kidnapping of your client's partner is not a matter for this hearing, honourable counsel.' It was the first time he'd addressed *Kinzo-san* formally. He divided the prints and passed them to the pokerfaced men beside him. To this point in the proceedings neither had said a word.

After a minute or so of silence the man seated on the left scribbled a note on his pad and placed it in front of the prosecutor who glanced at it briefly. 'We will adjourn for ten minutes,' he announced. 'Please do not leave this room.'

Ten minutes later they returned and the public prosecutor requested *Kinzo-san* to stand. Then he announced, 'The weapon in question has been confiscated and as it has done no harm in the possession of your client we accept, as a courtesy to our visitor and as a foreign-relations gesture, that he may have overlooked the weapon in his luggage. All charges against *Duncan-san* are dropped.'

Kinzo-san bowed deeply. 'Thank you, your honour.'

'You are all dismissed with the exception of counsel and his client,' the prosecutor said.

We waited until the room had cleared of all but the three men on the platform and the stenographer. 'Now I have one final question to ask you, *Duncan-san*,' he said. I waited while he seemed to think about how he might phrase the question, but when it came it was simple enough. 'Are you satisfied with the treatment you have received from the authorities?'

I glanced down at *Kinzo-san* who raised his finger very slightly. 'Yes, thank you, your honour. I have been treated with care and great respect and have no complaints,' I replied.

The public prosecutor picked up the papers lying on the desk, quickly collating them. Then he looked directly at me.

'There are no charges I wish to make against you, *Duncan-san*. You are free to leave this hearing and need not return.' He turned to the stenographer and instructed her to leave, then reached under the desk. We heard a soft but distinct click as he turned off the tape recorder.

Still standing beside me *Kinzo-san* waited until the stenographer had left the room, then he withdrew a small envelope from inside his jacket, stepped forward and placed it on the desk. 'The negatives, your honour,' he said.

One of the men reached over and took the envelope and, speaking for the first time, said, 'We request that you do not bring formal charges in the matter of the kidnapping of *Til-san* as other arrangements have been made to secure her release.'

My heart leapt. Unable to contain myself I said, 'You have discovered the whereabouts of Anna Til, sir?'

He paused and looked at the second man, who nodded. 'There are arrangements to find her. That is all I wish to say.'

'Is she safe?' I persisted.

'We cannot answer that question,' the second man said.

'Come, *Duncan-san*, we must go to the charge office to sign your release and obtain your personal effects,' *Kinzo-san* urged, anxious not to prolong the conversation.

We both bowed deeply and left the room.

CHAPTER NINE

'Of course I can walk!
I don't need anyone to carry me!
And, by the way,
I'm not a tearful little lady!
Now, will you kindly return
and fetch my handbag and shoes!'
Anna, Tokyo

WE STOPPED OFF AT the charge office, where *Kinzo-san* left me to sign for my personal effects while he made a call from the phone booth in the foyer. 'Count the money in your wallet before you sign, *Duncan-san*. It will all be there, but it shows they have not broken your spirit,' he'd instructed me on the way to the charge office.

We finally left the huge Kasumigaseki Metropolitan Police Department Complex. *Kinzo-san* hailed a taxi and watched as I entered it and sat down very gingerly. 'At least the seat is a little softer,' he said sympathetically. 'You must have the dressings looked at as soon as possible.'

'I have a great deal to thank you for, *Kinzo-san*, and cannot think how I can possibly repay you or those who came to my aid.'

'Ah, *Duncan-san*, you have powerful friends and I will be paid twice over, in money and in assistance from the same powerful people if at a future time I should need it. *Fuchida-san* is a man of great character who values friendship and loyalty above everything. The fact that at no time did you implicate the *yakuza* confirmed his trust in you and your friendship. To a man like him that is perhaps already repayment.'

'I will send him my Queen Alexandra Birdwing,' I said, suddenly deciding.

'Birdwing?' *Kinzo-san* asked as the taxi pulled into the traffic.

'I'm sorry, I was thinking aloud. The Queen Alexandra Birdwing, the female, is the world's biggest butterfly, with a wingspan of over 30 centimetres. It is very rare and *Fuchida-san* has expressed the wish to acquire a specimen for his collection.'

'Ah, that is very nice,' *Kinzo-san* said doubtfully, the habitual 'Ah' preceding the statement. 'I am aware that he collects butterflies and that his men fear above all else the punishment of being sent into the wild to find them.'

'Have you not seen his collection?' I asked, surprised, then added, 'It is *very* significant.'

'Ah, very few have been allowed that privilege and I am not one such,' he replied formally, nodding his head in a small bow, telling me at once that he wasn't an intimate associate of the *yakuza* boss and that his defence, which led to the dismissal of the charges against me, was strictly business. 'I have never been invited to his apartment,' he added.

This gave me the courage to say to him, '*Kinzo-san*, I find myself in somewhat of a predicament.'

He smiled. 'Ah, I thought I had just got you out of several, *Duncan-san*. Now you have found yet another?'

'I have the means to pay you well,' I explained clumsily.

'You see, now the charges have been dropped I have yet to resolve the matter of the kidnapping of my partner, Anna Til. I am no nearer to finding her than I was before my arrest and all the consequent trouble I caused. The prosecutor indicated that I must *not* bring her kidnapping to the attention of the authorities and that other arrangements to free her have been made. Whatever these are, will you allow me to engage your services to guide me? I am totally confused and out of my depth.'

Kinzo-san scratched his forehead, thinking. 'Ah, the Japanese way of resolving problems is sometimes difficult for Westerners to understand. There is no legal way of effectively finding your partner as you have agreed not to bring the matter before the authorities. Nor do the authorities wish to move against the Shield Society until they are sure that they will not upset the balance of power, or do something that challenges our new democracy.'

'But a foreigner has been kidnapped! Surely that is reason enough?'

He shrugged. 'Evidently not. Your partner is a drug addict. It would be easy to leave the Shield Society out of it entirely and blame her kidnapping on criminal activity.'

'But if the Shield Society decided to publicise it?' I asked, then realised that this was a stupid question and corrected myself. 'No, of course not. If Konoe Akira has paid them for the kidnapping there's no point. So then *he* is obviously the key to her release.'

'Exactly.'

What was once again clear was that my rashness had led to this entire mess. By going to the *yakuza* for help I had made a monumental stuff-up of the whole thing.

'What now, *Kinzo-san*? How will I free Anna?'

Kinzo-san cut to the chase. 'As you say, Konoe Akira is the linchpin. He ordered the kidnapping, and may even have paid for it. Either way, as you say, he is the key to her release. Before the prosecutor's hearing it would not have been in his interest to let her go. But now that the whole thing has been hushed up and his mother restored to his home, he may agree.' *Kinzo-san* smiled, thinking. 'Of course, *Anna-san* will have to sign a legal document promising not to talk or indict him.'

'Oh, she wouldn't do that! *Definitely* not talk, and we've seen enough of the public prosecutor! We'll be leaving Japan on the next flight home,' I assured him. 'But in the meantime, what do I do?'

'You go to the *yakuza*.'

'Shit! Not again! Will you not represent us, *Kinzo-san*? See if you can make a deal? Money is no object,' I added hastily.

'I would very much like to, *Duncan-san*, but I am under instructions from *Oyabun* Fuchida.'

'Fuck!' I said in English.

It was evidently an expletive he recognised because he laughed. 'Ah, do not entirely despair, *Duncan-san*. Perhaps there are other ways. I made a phone call while you were collecting your personal effects. The taxi will drop me off at my office and then take you on to see the *oyabun*. I was informed that later today I have an appointment with *Saito-san*, the *kendo hanshi* who, you will recall, found Konoe Akira's ageing mother wandering in the street. This suggests there are further developments afoot. I daresay I will be involved. In the meantime, you would do well to save yourself a whopping legal fee and speak to *Oyabun* Fuchida.'

By the time I'd dropped *Kinzo-san* off and was on the way to see *Fuchida-san* I seemed to be aching everywhere. The wounds on my bum and back were throbbing, and without fresh dressings they would soon become infected, if they already weren't. The backs of my arms felt a little better, though they still stung and itched, and when I had last gone to the toilet my swollen and bruised scrotum showed that my testicles would take a fair while before they were free of pain. Despite all this, I was almost entirely preoccupied with Anna. I would have gladly suffered ten times the pain – no, a hundred times – if I could have secured her release. I kept telling myself that if I had done nothing except wait in the hotel room, then the problem would have resolved itself in a short time without her being harmed.

Having met Konoe Akira, even under the most trying circumstances, I did not believe he would want Anna killed. It was much more likely that he simply wished to warn her that he still possessed the power to retaliate if she decided to bring charges against him for his wartime activities. But his plan, thanks to my personal interference, had gone badly wrong. Then another thought struck me. Anna wasn't silly, nor would she panic; she would try to bribe her captors to secure her own release. She would ask them to contact me by phone to negotiate, but of course they would have been unable to locate me. The hotel desk would report that I had not returned for the past three nights. Yet another Nick Duncan superior fuck-up!

Like all imagined outcomes it immediately sounded plausible and I felt buoyed by the idea that Anna would handle herself calmly and intelligently. Money, as Anna so often said, makes everything possible. We would offer money, heaps of the filthy stuff.

When I arrived at *Fuchida-san*'s, I was met by two *yakuza* and they escorted me in the usual manner up to the penthouse apartment. The lift door opened and *Fuchida-san*, smiling broadly, met me, with Miss Sparkle standing several feet behind him alongside an elderly Japanese man. 'Welcome,

Duncan-san!' he cried, and to my surprise stepped forward and hugged me, then slapped me on the back, smack on my wound. I'm not sure how I restrained myself from crying out, though I could feel my eyes watering.

I smiled, bowed deeply, then said, 'I owe you a great debt, one I cannot possibly repay, *Fuchida-san.*'

'Nonsense!' he bellowed happily. He turned and indicated the elderly man. '*Kinzo-san* phoned to tell us of your need for a doctor. This is Dr Honda. He will dress your wounds.' He looked at Miss Sparkle. '*Mama-san*, take our honoured guest to the room where he can be treated.' He bowed slightly towards the doctor, indicating he should follow us. 'We have much to discuss, *Duncan-san.* I must know everything, and I have news of my own. *Mama-san*, bring our guest green tea. Maybe something to eat?'

'No cold fried fish and rice,' I grinned.

'You do not like fried fish and rice?' *Fuchida-san* exclaimed, surprised.

'Not eight meals in a row delivered through the bars of my cell in a bento box.'

He laughed. 'I see! For me, it has been a long time since I have suffered the delights of holding-cell food. I had forgotten.'

Dr Honda did not question how I had obtained such a peculiar set of wounds but simply dressed them and tut-tutted briefly over my swollen testicles. 'It is too late for ice,' he remarked, then wrote a prescription for painkillers and another for antibiotics. With his bag repacked he bowed. 'I will visit you at the Imperial Hotel if you wish,' he said, bowing again and handing me his card.

'I haven't paid you, *Honda-san*. What do I owe you?'

'That won't be necessary,' he replied.

I thanked him and he departed. Turning, he bowed yet a third time as he left the room. One would not want to suffer from lumbago in Japan.

Seated on two cushions, I ate a light lunch with *Fuchida-san* (I admit I could have eaten more), who seemed to know all about the incident in Konoe Akira's home and apologised profusely for the existence of the secret alarm. 'We had a technician cut the phone lines; he should have checked for the alarm. You may be assured he will be sent away to collect a butterfly specimen in a very remote region,' he promised darkly.

He then explained that they'd had barely sufficient time to get away before the police team arrived. 'When those SWAT bastards get called out in that embassy area and in the vicinity of the Imperial Palace they are trigger-happy. It is not the time to stand and argue. My greatest relief came when I discovered you were not dead.' He then made me tell him of my experience at the Kasumigaseki Police Complex, questioning me in detail, often making me go over some minor matter. In particular the good-guy bad-guy routine during the interrogation. '*Hai!* You did well, *Duncan-san*, you told them nothing. You would make an excellent *yakuza oyabun*.' He laughed. 'You were a hero to the other prisoners, *Duncan-san*.'

Puzzled, I asked him how he knew this. I'd mentioned the punch in the back and the subsequent kick in the scrotum but not the reaction of the prisoners.

'Caretaker's eyes, the same as with the photographs,' he replied with a shrug. Finally he asked, 'Did you get the names of the two special agents who interrogated you?'

'Yes, Razan and Tanaka.'

'Good!' he said. 'They did their job well.'

I looked at him somewhat bemused. 'Yes, it wasn't pleasant.'

The *yakuza* boss looked at me steadily. '*Duncan-san*, I apologise, it was necessary.'

'What, you had me roughed up?' It wasn't possible to conceal my surprise.

'We had everything covered except the possession of a firearm by a foreigner,' he explained. 'Japan has very severe penalties for any unauthorised or unlicensed possession of a firearm. Those convicted of an offence usually receive from one to ten years. We had to ensure that the prosecutor and the two government officials appreciated the need to keep the existence of the gun secret. To ensure this, it was necessary to have leverage – photographic evidence of a foreign prisoner being tortured by the Japanese First Intelligence Division – which we could threaten to release all over the world if necessary.'

'You could have spared me the kick in the balls!'

'I assure you that was not in the plan. Those two are not *yakuza* eyes or ears but had to be bribed. Razan is a nasty piece of work, a bully and a scoundrel; Tanaka is weak.'

There seemed no point in asking him how they had persuaded two special service officers to cooperate. I had long since realised that the inter-relationships of organisations in Japan, honest and otherwise, were beyond questioning. 'I find myself *painfully* aware that I am greatly in your debt once again, *Fuchida-san*. You must allow me to repay you the bribe money.'

'That was very cleverly said, *Duncan-san*. You are not in my debt, painfully or otherwise; it was a matter of honour. It was I who gave you the Browning pistol in the first place.'

I then asked if I might inquire about the matter of Anna's release.

'Of course,' *Fuchida-san* replied. 'What is your understanding of the situation?'

'I understand that Konoe Akira would have refused to ask the Shield Society to release Anna while his mother was still missing and the hearing was still underway. But now that the old lady is returned and the case has been hushed up and won't cause him any embarrassment, will he not simply request Anna's release?'

'*Hai!* I hope so. There is no reason to hold her any longer. But there is more. *Kinzo-san* and *Saito-san* are visiting Konoe Akira later today. Let us see what comes from this afternoon's meeting, eh, *Duncan-san?*'

'There may be one issue,' I replied.

'What?'

'The vase. It was evidently very valuable, but I am prepared to pay despite the deal not to bring charges against Staff Sergeant Goto in return for my release from having to pay compensation for the vase. *Kinzo-san* says it may help him to save face.'

Fuchida-san burst into laughter. 'That is a very good idea, but also a very bad waste of money. I do not think it will be necessary. First let us see what comes from today's meeting.'

'Yes, but if I offer to pay – for the vase and for Anna's release – this will save everyone a great deal of trouble.'

Fuchida-san looked shocked at the suggestion. 'I would like nothing more than trouble with the Shield Society. It would allow us to clean out the bastards.'

'But this way Anna will be safe,' I said, adding, 'The money doesn't matter.'

'That is a very honourable sentiment, but money always matters, *Duncan-san.* I hope she is worth it, this Anna who is a heroin addict. Does she have something over you? We can always —'

'No, no . . . please! To me she is worth everything I possess.'

'*Hai!*' He clapped his hands, delighted. 'At last we discover your weakness!'

Despite myself, I grinned foolishly, then tried to explain.

'As a matter of fact, Konoe Akira is indirectly responsible for her becoming an addict, among several other destructive things I've previously explained to you.'

'Then he should not be rewarded. Leave everything as it is. *Saito-san* will call me after the meeting this afternoon. Then we will know more. We know already that Konoe Akira is not necessarily a member of the Shield Society.'

'How can we be sure?' I asked, then added, 'And if so, why then did he use them to kidnap Anna?'

'*Hai!* Funny you should say that. The *mama-san* asked me the same question. So I told her to call the Jade Mistress to see what she could discover. According to her, Konoe Akira's original plan was to hire us, the *yakuza*, to do the kidnapping. It was only when he learned about your friendship with me from the Jade Mistress – no doubt thanks to information from *Anna-san* herself – that he turned to the Shield Society. It was a better option than employing freelance criminals, low-lifes who couldn't be trusted.' He grinned. 'I think maybe the Jade Mistress belongs to the Shield Society, but we can never be certain. If so, I feel sure a generous donation was encouraged and forthcoming.'

I sighed. It all sounded increasingly complicated.

Fuchida-san continued. 'It is highly unlikely he could arrange any of this without someone's help. Konoe Akira knows the Jade Mistress can be trusted – he is an old and valued customer. *Mama-san* tells me he has a special room in the establishment he paid for himself. These places never talk about their clients. As you saw, the Jade Mistress told me nothing about him when we visited the Jade House, only about the kidnappers. But it appears he wanted *Anna-san* held for several hours to demonstrate his power and to caution her not to try anything. He professes to be very excited about meeting her again after all these years.'

'How do we know all this?'

'*Kinzo-san*, when he negotiated the deal with him to drop the charges in exchange for the return of his mother, and then the matter of the vase in return for not charging . . . what was his name . . . the manservant?'

'Goto,' I said.

'That's right, Staff Sergeant Goto, who could have been charged with grievous bodily harm. Also *Oyabun* Saito learned a little when he returned the old crone. Konoe Akira seemed anxious to talk, to attempt to make amends.'

'So, you are in a position to make a deal this afternoon?' I asked anxiously.

'No deal! No money! But, yes, now that *Konoe-san* knows he's in the clear it is most likely, *Duncan-san*. You mentioned the private talk you and *Kinzo-san* had had with the prosecutor and the two officials this morning at the hearing. Well, I received a call from a contact I have in the First Intelligence Division shortly afterwards. We are free to see Konoe Akira and get him to okay the release of Anna. That is the reason for this afternoon's meeting.'

'Thank God!' I exclaimed, hugely relieved.

'Pity though. Those Shield Society bastards get a big donation when rightly they should be severely punished.' He hesitated momentarily. '*Duncan-san*, we had to guarantee that neither you nor your partner would ever reveal any of the details once she is freed. You must understand, you will tell everyone who asks that you attended the Expo in Osaka.'

'Of course, I will say nothing, nor will Anna. I give you my solemn promise.'

'*Hai*, your word has been tested, but a woman's tongue is designed for spilling secrets!'

'Not in this case, *Fuchida-san*. It is the secrets she refuses to tell that are destroying our lives.'

'I will accept your word, *Duncan-san*. I trust you as I would one of my *oyabun*. Thank you. I would lose my credibility with the authorities if you ever spoke about what has happened.'

'Thank you for your trust, *Oyabun* Fuchida, it is not misplaced.'

'You must stay here until *Anna-san* is released so you can go back to your hotel together. Perhaps you would like to rest. The room Dr Honda used to treat you is ready. I will call you if I receive any news.'

Miss Sparkle received a call from *Saito-san* at four o'clock and called *Fuchida-san* to the phone, then came to my room to ask me to go to *Fuchida-san*'s study. He was waiting for me, wearing a grim expression, and moments later Miss Sparkle brought in green tea. 'The news is not good, but also not bad,' he said. 'The Shield Society wants an additional ransom to release *Anna-san*. They have doublecrossed Konoe Akira. If he doesn't pay, they have threatened to kill her.'

'Jesus no! We'll pay! How much?'

'Twenty-five thousand American dollars.'

'I will arrange it. I will have to call my bank in Port Vila.'

Fuchida-san began to laugh. 'That is the bad news, you haven't heard the good.'

'Oh yes I have, she's going to be freed!'

'Whoa, steady on! Konoe Akira has agreed to pay the ransom.'

'What? Why would he do that? He's in the clear with

the authorities. We are forbidden to do anything to him.'

Fuchida-san smiled like the godfather I suppose he was. 'Nevertheless, *Duncan-san*, there is no need for you to pay the ransom. Konoe is very wealthy. His family have been prominent in the fishing industry for five generations. He is a veritable giant in that business, but it is one with many vendettas where memories are long and old conflicts persist. He has been persuaded that if he doesn't pay up, a leak here and there, a rumour circulated, a slip of the tongue in the right place and he will lose credibility in the business world. Any suggestion that he is a rightwing fanatic will harm him, and there is proof that he gave a donation to the Shield Society for kidnapping *Anna-san*. As he will not wish to be accused of kidnapping a Westerner, it can easily be made to look as if it was a large gratuitous donation. It is much better that it is his own money.'

'This is *Kinzo-san*'s doing?' I asked. 'He is a genius!'

'He is not too bad,' *Fuchida-san* agreed. 'You must not be so eager to pay, *Duncan-san*. If you had persisted, I would have been forced to keep your money so you didn't lose face,' he laughed.

'When will the ransom be paid and Anna released?' I asked.

'Tomorrow morning.'

'Will Konoe Akira himself make the payment?'

'No.'

'Who then?'

'*Kinzo-san*. He is a much respected lawyer, acceptable to the Shield Society.'

'Will Anna be present when the payment is made?'

'No, they may be rightwing fanatics, but they are not stupid. She will be hidden elsewhere and released *only* when the money is paid.'

'Cash?'

'Yes.'

'But do we know we can trust them?'

It was obvious the *yakuza* boss was not accustomed to being closely questioned, but I told myself I couldn't take any risks with Anna's safety, despite knowing I wasn't in control and that there was nothing much I could do to affect the result. Fuchida frowned. 'Kidnapping is always risky; things go wrong, plans don't work, people panic,' he explained. 'But, fortunately in this case everyone wants it to go well. There is no point in attempting another doublecross. The only danger to the Shield Society is if the police are involved and it is for this reason they will be taking such precautions with the handover. They are, of course, unaware that they are completely safe from police involvement or that we are involved.

'The plan they have agreed to with *Kinzo-san* is simple, and simple plans are the ones that work. He will appoint someone both sides can trust to take custody of Anna. This person will be given the exact location where Anna is being held an hour before the ransom is exchanged.'

'Isn't an hour too much time? I mean, if there was to be any trouble, an hour is plenty of time for a rescue force to act.'

'Good question. The hour's notice tells us that Anna is held captive at an address just short of an hour's drive from *Kinzo-san's* office in Central Tokyo.'

'You say the person who will collect Anna must be trusted by both Konoe Akira and the Shield Society. Will it not be difficult to find someone who fits the requirement and can also be absolutely trusted?' I was being paranoid as usual.

Fuchida-san spread his hands. 'A careful man asks lots of questions, but,' he grinned, pointing a diamond-ringed forefinger at me, 'I don't think you would be good at taking orders. You would be a good *oyabun*, but would find it difficult to come up through the ranks where instant and unquestioning obedience is required.'

I realised that I was much too uptight and tried to laugh it off, but found myself trying to justify my paranoia. 'It was not how I was trained in the war, *Fuchida-san*. I think the difference between the Japanese soldier and the Australian was not courage – your men showed too much of that; it was instant and unquestioning obedience. They never questioned their leaders. It is one of the reasons we won the war. Such unquestioning obedience leaves men unable to think for themselves. In jungle fighting that doesn't always work. I run a shipping line in the tropics, in the islands, where a storm can blow up at any time in an apparently calm sea, so it is necessary to question everything,' I concluded. This somewhat critical analysis of the Japanese fighting man was an attempt to justify my obvious anxiety and my need to double-check that everything had been thought of in regard to Anna's rescue. I shrugged. 'Most big plans fail because small details have been neglected. "For want of a nail the shoe was lost",' I quoted. He looked puzzled. 'It is a proverb,' I explained. '"For want of a nail the shoe was lost. For want of a shoe the horse was lost. For want of a horse the knight was lost. For want of a knight the battle was lost. For want of a battle the kingdom was lost."'

'I will remember that,' *Fuchida-san* said, nodding his head. 'You are right, we Japanese are too respectful of authority. We have our own old saying: "The nail that sticks up will be hammered down". We respect authority, and that is precisely why both sides have agreed to this particular third party taking custody of your partner. He is an outstanding citizen and is known and respected throughout Japan and is not identified with any side or faction. He is the principal of the Kyumeikan Kendo Dojo.'

I laughed. '*Oyabun* Saito! Of course, who else?' I exclaimed, smiling broadly.

'*Duncan-san*, you know too much. I did not tell you about his involvement with the kendo institute, did I?'

'You give me too much credit. *Kinzo-san* used this fact in the hearing this morning.'

Fuchida nodded. '*Saito-san* is not known to be *yakuza* and is only used by us very occasionally when we need a secret weapon . . . or a silent assassin. He is not only a kendo grand master but also Japan's most famous exponent of the *katana*, the sacred sword. His name is known and respected by all. He is exactly right for this job. He brings both sides – the Shield Society and Konoe Akira – the correct prestige. At the same time they will know he leaves no footprints in the dust and cannot be crossed.'

'More and more I find myself in your debt, *Oyabun* Fuchida. If Anna is brought back safely, I cannot imagine how I will ever be able to repay you.'

'We will remain friends, and it is my experience that, over the years, there is always something that needs to be done. Friends are not made for personal gain, but neither are they free of obligation. Friendship involves loyalty and support for each other.'

Finally I asked, knowing already that it was not a very bright question, 'Is there anything I can do to help?'

'Nothing. Everything is in place,' the *yakuza* boss said. 'Now we can only wait until *Saito-san* brings *Anna-san* to the office of *Kinzo-san* where you will be waiting, having arrived back from Osaka and the World Exposition. In the meantime you must stay here in the penthouse.'

'I hesitate to ask, but I need another enormous favour, *Fuchida-san*,' I said.

'What is it, *Duncan-san*?'

'Anna will be in withdrawal – three days at least without heroin. She will be in a bad state. Is it possible you could arrange . . . ? I will pay the street price, of course.'

'How much will she need? Once, twice a day, more? Sufficient for a week?' he asked.

'Yes, a week will be plenty. Will you let me know the cost, please?' He could see my acute embarrassment at having to ask.

Fuchida-san sighed. 'The cost of being a heroin addict is already too much. In the end, this woman will let you down; they always do. I know from personal experience. When I was young and recruited by the great Yoshio Kodama, who, you will remember, united the *yakuza* after the war, he made me one of his *wakagashira*, his lieutenants. He was still a drug lord and many of us became addicted to heroin. It took me nearly ten years to get clean. None of the other *wakagashira* managed to give up and I watched them lose their integrity and honour.' He smiled. 'But, as you wish, it will be delivered this afternoon. There is no cost.'

I kept forgetting that the *yakuza* boss had never met Anna and I was forced to conclude that he must have scant regard for her, questioning the wisdom of my involvement with a junkie. It was even more remarkable that he hadn't thrown his hands up in despair and left us to stew in our own juice. This was particularly true when I tried and failed to think of anything we could do for him, or any use we might be to him or the *yakuza* in the future. All we had in common was butterflies! It was hard to imagine that insects alone might constitute an enduring bond between us. If he had any plans for me to pay him back in the future, they were beyond my imagining.

The *yakuza* boss rose. 'I must go out and will be back very late. The *mama-san* will show you your room and attend to your dinner. It has been a difficult time for you, *Duncan-san*. You must rest now. Is there anything else you might need?'

'You have been a gracious host and wonderful friend, honourable *Fuchida-san*, and I, in turn, have caused nothing but trouble for you. I am eternally grateful and require nothing more except a toothbrush and a razor.'

'*Duncan-san*, trouble is how we make our living. I must say, I can hardly wait to meet your Anna; you have endured a great deal on her behalf. This junkie of yours must be really something for you to have persisted with her!' He chuckled. 'You Westerners have strange attitudes to women.'

Later, resting on a futon in the room set aside for me, I realised that, if I had done absolutely nothing, bugger all, to find Anna, she might have long since been back with me and, to boot, not much the worse for wear. Konoe Akira would have refused to pay the ransom and the Shield Society would have realised she was of no worth to them and, furthermore, that kidnapping a *gaijin* did nothing for their cause.

Also, Anna wasn't the sort to sit in a corner hugging her knees with her bottom lip trembling. She would have negotiated and paid for her own freedom. But, of course, she couldn't do this without contacting me to arrange the ransom money and I had been in a police cell nursing my wounds along with my pride. She wasn't to blame for any of my various predicaments. It had been my own lack of patience and inability to think things through, big-noting myself by involving the *yakuza*. Now she would carry a fresh set of scars for the remainder of her life. Even more bizarre and reprehensible, Konoe Akira would once again be responsible for them. *Whatever possessed you to come to Japan, Nicholas*

Duncan, world-class bloody idiot?! I recall saying to myself before I fell into an exhausted sleep.

Let me declare at once that I did not witness what happened next. Anna described everything to me, except for the incident at the gate with the two guards, later recounted to me by *Fuchida-san*, who had seen some of it and heard the remainder from *Saito-san*.

Arrangements were made for *Kinzo-san* to receive a call from the kidnappers to tell him the place at which Anna would be handed over. He would then contact *Saito-san* and give him the address, then wait the hour it took for *Saito-san* to reach Anna by motorcar. Upon arrival and after ensuring Anna was present and unharmed, *Saito-san* would call him and give him an address the Shield Society had given him that was close enough to *Kinzo-san*'s offices for him to deliver the ransom. After *Saito-san* received an all-clear phone call, he would then take custody of Anna and return her by motorcar to Tokyo. Simple enough.

But, as it turned out, what in fact happened was that *Kinzo-san*, having received the call from Anna's captors with the address at which she was being held, called *Saito-san* who was waiting with *Oyabun* Fuchida at the helicopter terminal in Central Tokyo. They immediately boarded a waiting three-passenger Bell Jet Ranger. Five minutes later it set down in a vacant lot in an industrial site close to the Bay area just three minutes' walk from the address the Shield Society had given. They had arrived forty-five minutes before *Saito-san* was expected by motorcar.

Saito, a man in his late forties, was dressed cheaply in the ragged clothes of a poor old man or a bum. Wearing a straggly grey false moustache and a dirty brown felt hat pulled down hard onto his eyebrows, he gave the appearance of a witless alcoholic. He affected a limp and carried a walking stick made from the ebony core of the persimmon tree, a dense, fine-grained timber that is incredibly strong. Fuchida had encouraged him to wear a bullet-proof jacket, as he himself did, but he'd refused. 'It will slow me down,' he'd argued.

They stopped about a hundred metres from the address they'd been given – a small double-storey warehouse set in the centre of an industrial lot and surrounded by a high steel-mesh security fence about twenty metres from the building. Fuchida waited out of sight while Saito, pecking his way with the stick, limped drunkenly towards the padlocked wire gate, behind which he could see two guards with submachine-guns slung over their shoulders.

Swaying and staggering, singing drunkenly, mumbling and shouting to himself, often gripping the cane with both hands to keep his balance, Saito approached, then outside the gate fell backwards onto his bum, toppling over, his legs flung in the air and the stick flying. Laughing helplessly, he lay for a moment, then rolled over so that he was on all fours from where he tried to get up, failing several times, his arms collapsing under him. Finally he managed to crawl towards the walking stick and use it to climb painfully to his feet. He swayed, waving his free arm and shouting incoherently, then staggered up to the gate where the two bored guards stood watching.

Reaching the gate, Saito leant on his walking stick, grinning, and beckoned drunkenly to them, fumbling in his ragged jacket for a stack of what appeared to be postcards. He hooked the stick over his arm so both hands were free and removed the top photograph from the stack and held it up. 'Only one hundred yen,' he slurred, attempting unsuccessfully to push the postcard through the gap between the gate and the steel gatepost. Both guards moved forward to take a closer look at what proved to be a high-definition, colour, full-frontal photograph of a young big-breasted blonde woman with her legs spread, about to insert a large dildo between them.

'*Phiff!* You ask too much, old man,' one of the guards laughed, pulling the postcard through the gap, examining it briefly then handing it to his companion with a grin, who in turn examined it closely.

'We'll give you two hundred yen for the lot,' the second guard offered, pointing to the stack Saito held.

Saito frowned drunkenly and, shaking his head in exaggerated denial, quickly returned the remaining postcards to the inside pocket of his ragged jacket, grabbing the walking stick just in time to avoid losing his balance. He brought his forefinger up and waved it reprovingly at them, then held it still. 'No . . . no . . . one . . . (hic) only one, one hundred yen!' he stammered. 'Look, very good *gaijin* fucking! Very dirty picture!' He propped the walking stick against his leg and once again withdrew the stack from his inside pocket and removed the top one, holding it up against the wire. It showed two young blondes, sexually entwined in the '69' position. It would have been obvious to the two guards that at one hundred yen each the high-quality photographs were a veritable bargain.

'Let's see them all, Grandpa,' the first guard demanded, indicating that he should pass them through the small gap between the gate and the fencepost.

Saito cackled merrily, shaking his head, indicating that even though he was inebriated he wasn't a complete fool. Then, apparently forgetting he wasn't holding the walking stick, he took a step backwards and lost his balance, flinging the cards in an arc as he attempted to snatch the walking stick. Further off balance, he tottered then fell, striking the back of his head against the roadway, the pornographic cards spread around his motionless body, the walking stick somehow ending up between his sprawled legs.

'Shit! He's knocked himself out!' the first guard said.

'Good! Open up!' the second guard said gleefully. 'The photos are ours!'

The first guard reached into his trouser pocket for the padlock key and moments later the gate swung open. Reaching down they quickly gathered up the photographs. The second guard, seemingly the more dominant, took those his companion held out and placed them all in the back pocket of his trousers. 'We'll share them out later,' he decided. 'Show them to your girlfriend – they'll make her horny. Women deny it, but they love hard porn.'

The first guard grinned. 'I don't think so; not mine anyway.' He pointed to Saito. 'What about him? We've got someone coming in less than an hour to collect the foreign bitch.' He paused, then grinning lewdly added, 'Now that's a piece of quality tail. I wouldn't mind having a piece of her!'

'Their slits are too big; you wouldn't touch the sides!' the second guard laughed, then pointed. 'There's a deep ditch across the road. Here, give me a hand. We'll dump him.' He unslung his submachine-gun. 'You're right, the six of us should have gang-raped her. These foreign bitches are hot. They can't get enough cock.' He placed his automatic weapon against the gatepost.

The first guard did the same. 'I thought you said *gaijin* pussies were too big for us.'

'For your cock, not mine! We'd let you go first while it's still tight,' he teased.

'Shouldn't we kill him, smash his head in? It will look like he did it when he fell; an accident.'

'Nah, poor bastard's harmless. When he wakes up he won't remember a thing.'

'Fuck me dead! What's this? Another drunk?' the first guard exclaimed, peering down the road.

In an instant, the kendo grand master leapt to his feet without using his hands in an astonishing feat of athleticism, and in the same smooth movement drove the end of the walking stick hard into the throat of the first guard, instantly collapsing his larynx. Before he'd hit the ground the stick swung in a two-handed backward arc to drive with enormous force up under the ribcage of the second guard, rupturing his aorta and killing him instantly. The first guard, his legs kicking wildly, lay clutching his throat with both hands, choking on his own blood. The kendo grand master quickly dispatched him with a single blow to the side of the head.

Fuchida-san arrived, panting. He was carrying a *katana* still in its sheath in one hand and a short-barrel Remington shotgun in the other. 'Good! Good work,' he gasped. 'I thought you were a goner. Seeing you lying on the ground with the two of them hovering above you I was sure it was all over, my honourable friend,' he panted. 'I was about to fire when you jumped to your feet. I've seen you before but never witnessed anything quite as good!' He laughed. 'You should audition for the opera. Your drunk act would have fooled me completely.'

Saito smiled. 'Your shotgun would have truly ruined our surprise and at that distance probably missed, *Oyabun*,' he said softly.

'Without you, *Saito-san*, there would be no surprise, we could not have done this without your skill,' *Fuchida-san* countered, his voice edged with sentiment.

Saito, ignoring the compliment, pointed. 'There is a ditch

over there. Help me dump this scum.'

Together they carried the two dead men across the road to the ditch and dumped them into it, where they disappeared under the tangle of weeds.

Returning to the gate Fuchida pointed to the two submachine-guns leaning against the gatepost. 'Do you want to go in with one of those, *Saito-san*?'

Saito drew back, pointing to the *katana* Fuchida had brought and placed against the fence. 'It is an old and trusted friend and much my preferred companion in a fight,' the master swordsman replied. 'You take one to cover me; that shotgun looks too dangerous.'

'Those things are for *wakagashira*; boys' toys. They see them all the time in American movies – dat-dat-dat-dat – they all think they're Al Capone!'

They dumped the two submachine-guns into the ditch. No more than fifteen minutes had passed since they'd landed in the helicopter.

'Let me go in alone,' Saito pleaded. 'It will be quieter.'

'No way!' Fuchida cried. 'I'm coming with you, old friend. You've already made my heart stop once today. Besides, we don't know how many of the bastards are in there.'

'There are only four, it will not be too difficult.'

'Four? How do you know?'

Saito pointed at the ditch. 'They said so.'

'Good. It's been a while since I did something like this; I feel young again.'

Saito slung the *katana* over his back. 'I go in first, *Oyabun*. Follow, but not too closely. I don't want to swing the sword and end up decapitating you with the follow-through, or removing your balls if it's a low strike.'

They proceeded towards the warehouse and entered

through an open loading dock, then shortly after located a cement stairway that proved to be perfect for a near silent approach. At the top they stopped to listen, hearing nothing at first. Saito signalled to Fuchida, three steps below him, not to move. Then through a half-open door they heard voices, someone grumbling that they couldn't wait to get out. Another voice replied, 'Soon. The guy coming to get her should be here in half an hour.'

'Not a moment too soon,' the first bloke replied. 'It's been too fucking long. I have to get back to my job. They said it was only going to be a few hours. For all I know I've been fired.'

One of the guards coughed, and began describing what he was going to have for dinner once they'd left. They were obviously perfectly relaxed in the knowledge that there were two of their comrades on guard at the gate.

Saito signalled for Fuchida to follow and, drawing his sword, erupted into the room. The two men seated at the end of a table in the centre of the room with their backs to the door were seemingly killed in a moment. In a single continuous slash the blade decapitated the first and cut into the back of the neck of the second guard so deeply that his head dropped forward, held only by the tendons in his neck as his spinal cord was severed. Neither body moved at first, then both slowly slumped forward onto the table.

Saito, like a huge bird of prey, seemed to expand to fill the room. He killed the third guard seated further down with a horizontal strike from the left. The fourth guard, on the far left of the table and nearest to Anna, was beyond the immediate reach of the katana. He had just enough time to grab his weapon and step towards Anna, intending to use her as a shield. The explosion of Fuchida's shotgun filled the room, blowing away half the guard's chest and spattering Anna with blood and bone.

The entire action had taken less than fifteen seconds.

'Thanks for leaving one of them for me,' Fuchida laughed. Then he seemed to notice Anna for the first time. She was backed into a corner, her hands covering her mouth and her entire body shaking uncontrollably on the dirty mattress. She hadn't uttered a sound.

Fuchida strode forward, stepping over the corpse of the fourth guard, being careful not to slip on the blood-covered linoleum. 'Can you stand, *Anna-san*?' he barked, realising there was no time for sympathy. 'Now, get up! Go on, up on your feet!' he commanded.

Anna somehow managed to get to her feet, her knees shaking uncontrollably. Saito came over and between the two men they half carried her from the room and down the stairs. Once outside the *yakuza* explained, 'We are here to free you, *Anna-san*. The honourable *Duncan-san* is waiting to welcome you! But you must walk at once! It is only a few minutes to the helicopter. This is no time to play the tearful little lady!'

Something must have penetrated Anna's numbed, drug-starved mind, because *Fuchida-san* forever after held her in high regard for what she did next. 'Where I come from we say "please"!' she snapped. 'Of course I can walk! I don't need anyone to carry me! *And*, by the way, I'm not a tearful little lady! Now, will you kindly return and fetch my handbag and shoes!' she commanded.

For years to come the *yakuza* boss would tell how he meekly climbed the stairs and retrieved her bag and shoes. Anna thanked him briskly, made him hold the bag while she slipped into her shoes, then strode off, click click click across the yard, towards the front gate in her scuffed Charles Jourdan six-inch heels, her Coco Chanel suit soaked and filthy, her face splattered and her hair matted with blood. 'She still managed to look beautiful,' he would always conclude.

Of course, it didn't end quite so neatly. Anna would suffer for years, reliving the kidnapping in recurrent nightmares, often waking in the middle of the night crying out. I would hold her in my arms at Beautiful Bay, where she'd lie, sobbing and shaking like a leaf, until dawn.

CHAPTER TEN

'She is suffering from shock,
her pulse rate is too high, she has a fever.
This is not normal trauma;
it is acute stress reaction.'
Dr Honda, Tokyo

I HAVE BEEN INVOLVED with the sea and boats since I was a child. At sea you learn that you must be constantly alert to any change in circumstances, otherwise the ocean can overwhelm you. Some storms are so severe that all you can do is lower the sails, batten the hatches and hope like hell you can ride them out. Your boat is a bobbing cork and you are a tiny insect, an ant, clinging to it for dear life. When the outcome is beyond anyone's control or influence, good sailors try to find something to occupy themselves, knowing that whether they live or die is no longer up to them. At such times it is the waiting that is the worst part.

Of course Anna's situation was different. I had been assured by *Fuchida-san* that her rescue was a formality – pay the money and fetch the girl; there wasn't any danger. Nevertheless, to extend the marine metaphor, you can be sailing on course in a perfect breeze on a calm sea and run into a whale. Nothing is ever guaranteed where there are possible dangers and, like the sailor sitting out the storm, waiting is the worst part. So I attempted to do what I could to prepare for Anna's return and to take my mind off potential disasters.

First I obtained a square of foil about the size of my hand, heated to melt the thin layer of wax that covered its surface; a drinking straw; a disposable cigarette lighter; and, of course, the heroin – all the necessities for 'chasing the dragon'. At least I hoped I had all of them. I had never been present when Anna had prepared or smoked heroin, and she had only once, years previously, described the equipment she needed when I'd asked her why she didn't use a needle like most addicts were reputed to do. She'd explained that injecting the dissolved heroin directly into a vein with a hypodermic syringe was the Western way of obtaining a more intense rush. Inhalation, while less efficient, is the Asian way, absorbing the drug into the bloodstream via the lungs and nasal passages. I guess it's a natural progression from the opium pipe and has the advantage of requiring no specialised equipment. I recall her explaining that needles often lead to infection, collapsed veins and blatant evidence of heroin usage. 'Nicholas, when you inhale, the hit is perhaps not as immediate, but there is no chance of infection, no evidence and, more importantly, if the heroin isn't pure you have an early-warning system. You know from the first tiny intake of smoke if it is good quality.' Heroin, I'd learned, can be pure or mixed. To make it go further, dealers often cut the heroin with various other powders: dextrose, talcum powder, quinine, even castor sugar, but it could be almost anything and it is the 'almost anything' that can often do more harm to the user than the junk itself.

The *wakagashira* who had delivered the heroin had assured me it was purest quality, referring to it as 'China White', then looking up to see if I was impressed.

Because Anna's rescue was a covert operation in which the *yakuza* could not be seen to be openly involved, *Fuchida-san* was reluctant to return Anna and me directly to the hotel. Furthermore, Konoe Akira, the wily bastard, wanted to cover his arse, and so it was decided that Anna would be brought to *Kinzo-san's* office for a debriefing where she would sign an affidavit in the presence of his legal representative that there had been no attempt to molest or harm her, indemnifying him from any future legal action.

I knew one thing for sure: no matter how distressed she might be, Anna would never allow herself to appear bedraggled in front of Konoe Akira's lawyer. In her mind this would signify defeat, and Anna would wish to convey her contempt, I felt sure. So the second thing I did was to go shopping. Anna would obviously be in need of a good scrub-down as well as a change of clothes and undies.

In this last matter I had appealed to one of the secretaries at *Kinzo-san's* office, a delightful young lady named *Muzi-san*, who was clearly the office extrovert. *Muzi-san* appeared to be the only one of the eight young women in the firm permitted to wear Western clothes and also, it seemed to me, granted permission to laugh. All the others were required to wear kimonos in deference to *Kinzo-san's* largely establishment clientele and do a lot of serious formal bowing with lowered eyes.

Muzi-san, always polite but never obsequious, was a thoroughly modern young lady with a quick smile, not in the least afraid to meet my eyes. Therefore it came as something of a surprise when she immediately indicated her reluctance to visit Mitsukoshi Department Store to purchase a spring dress, a pair of sandals and, of course, all the necessary underwear.

Her chin dropped to her chest and her eyes were downcast.

'I do not have the courage, *Duncan-san*,' she said softly.

'Courage? What, to go shopping for someone else? It shouldn't be too difficult, *Muzi-san*. Anna is perhaps one size larger than you. What size are you?' I asked.

'Eight,' she replied.

'Ah, then Anna is a size ten. I also have her shoe size.' I spread my hands. 'But I have one problem. I can purchase a ship, a crane, a freezer or an automobile, but I have no idea how to shop for a dress and shoes.' I paused, affecting a thoroughly helpless expression. 'As for underwear . . .' I left the sentence incomplete, hoping to appeal to her better nature.

She glanced up. 'It is not the shopping, *Duncan-san*, it is the shop. I do not have the status to enter such a place as Mitsukoshi. It is the grandest shop in all of Japan, some say even the whole world. I am too young and not worthy.'

I laughed, relieved. 'C'mon, *Muzi-san*, it's only a shop.'

But clearly it wasn't. 'No, it is not for someone like me,' she said, shaking her head vehemently. 'They will not allow me to enter. I am not correctly dressed.'

'Would you like to?' I asked.

'Like to what?' she asked, clearly not sure what I meant.

'Go into that shop, into Mitsukoshi.'

She looked down at her plain black jacket and the matching skirt that ended just above her knees, the white blouse and black flat-heeled shoes. Heels, while not openly forbidden, were frowned on by height-obsessed and insecure Japanese males. 'They are cheap, my clothes. They will know immediately that I am only a humble office worker,' she said, clearly embarrassed at having to make the admission.

I glanced down at my own gear. '*Hai!* Look at me! I'm not exactly dressed for showing off either.' I was still wearing the now somewhat rumpled clobber that had been produced for me the previous day at police headquarters and my shoes were scuffed and in need of a shine. I glanced at my watch. I had arrived at *Kinzo-san*'s chambers early, having been dropped off by *Fuchida-san* who had business in the city to attend to. At that time, *Kinzo-san* had not yet received the call to tell him where Anna was being held, so at the very least I would have two hours, the time it would take to journey to the hostage location and return. 'Come, let's go together.' I laughed. 'Then they can kick us both out.'

'No!' *Muzi-san* cried, horrified. 'Then you will lose face!'

'*Hai!*' I grinned. 'I will have gained so much face from having a pretty girl like you accompanying me that whatever face I lose will not be sufficient to remove my smile.' I was not sure whether such blatant flirting was permitted in Japanese society, but *Muzi-san* seemed to like it.

She smiled. 'Do all *gaijin* have such nice ways?' she asked shyly, giving me back some of my own medicine. She appeared to be thinking. 'I will come,' she decided suddenly. 'When I tell of this to my girlfriends and my honourable parents they will not believe me.'

'I am most relieved and grateful,' I said sincerely. 'I truly know nothing of women's dresses and shoes. Once in the islands I attempted to shop for *Anna-san* – just shorts and tops – and a kind lady helped me with underwear.' I shrugged and laughed. 'As it turned out I made an awful hash of it. Without you I would have found myself in heaps of trouble,' I grinned, 'especially when it comes to the little things worn underneath!'

It was a glorious, warm late-spring day, and as the Ginza branch of the three-hundred-year-old grand emporium was nearby, we walked, which was probably quicker than taking a taxi. As we approached the entrance to Mitsukoshi I saw the doorman hesitate momentarily. 'Take my arm and stick your nose in the air,' I instructed out of the corner of my mouth. 'Swing your hips; try not to laugh.' This caused her to bring both hands to her mouth in a highly unsuccessful attempt to smother a giggle.

I guess a slightly dishevelled six-foot three-inch Caucasian in rolled-up shirtsleeves wearing an insouciant expression forced the diminutive doorman to decide that discretion was perhaps the better part of valour. He swept off his top hat and bowed deeply as we sailed through the glass and polished brass doorway to the grandest department store in Asia.

When Anna and I had last visited the grand emporium, she had asked to be taken to the *haute couture* department, but I wasn't sure whether spring dresses were regarded as high fashion or whether Mr Charles Jourdan made sandals, high-heeled or not. I try to understand these nuances of women's shopping, but after nearly fifty years of sitting outside changing rooms clutching Anna's handbag, and twenty-something years of Marg's, feeling like a right ponce, I'm still not sure how it all works, except that there's a great deal of getting dressed and undressed and a fair bit of parading in front of me with gear that has labels attached with at least three zeros after the first number. The only certainty in all of this is that if I express the slightest preference for an outfit, shoes, jacket, skirt, dress, jeans ('Do they make my bum look big?'), whatever, this is a definite sign to either woman that they are headed entirely in the wrong direction. My job, sitting outside changing rooms clutching a handbag, is simply to indicate what *doesn't* work. If I like it, then that becomes the benchmark of bad taste. God cannot dwell in this garment, even if it is made from superfine Australian merino wool. The two women in my life opposed each other in everything except their certain knowledge that

Nicholas or Nick Duncan's taste in female attire ended roughly with the lap-lap on a hula dancer. I recall once hearing Marg say to a girlfriend, 'I never buy anything to wear without Nick being present.' There wasn't a hint of sarcasm in her voice. She was simply acknowledging the fact that being consistently wrong is just as good an indicator as being consistently right. Anna, who never accepted my advice on anything involving the making or spending of money, was more direct. 'Nicholas, it is very reassuring to know that you are always wrong; that's why you must always come with me, so I can buy the right thing.' It must have worked, because although they dressed somewhat differently, I always thought they looked great. Now I needed *Muzi-san* to play Anna's role to give me half a chance of buying something Anna might like.

We had hardly entered the temple-like atrium that formed a part of the ground floor when an elegantly dressed assistant rushed towards us. 'Smile,' I whispered to *Muzi-san*, but it wasn't necessary. We found ourselves being welcomed with a bow and then a pleasant formal greeting followed by the universal enquiry, 'May I accompany you? And how may I help?' Put like this I wasn't quite sure how to begin.

'*Pret a porter*, please, Miss. We'd like to see the spring range,' *Muzi-san* instructed in a completely assured voice. Then turning to me she inquired about Anna's age. We were duly escorted to the right department where *Muzi-san* selected a teal-blue pure silk spring dress. 'It's a shirtmaker, for day wear, but it can be worn formally or informally,' she said, holding it against her body. I had assumed my usual handbag position seated on a large chair hurriedly brought by two female assistants and placed close to the changing rooms. I guess Japanese husbands don't do a lot of shopping for women's apparel in the company of their wives.

'I can't tell,' I confessed. 'You'll have to put it on, *Muzi-san*.'

'It is a ten, *Duncan-san*. I am an eight.'

'Do you personally like it?'

'Oh, it's gorgeous, very sophisticated.'

'Yes, but would you wear it . . . I mean, personally?'

She pouted. 'For me, it is a bit too sophisticated. When I am older . . . but then, I will never possess such a beautiful dress.'

I hesitated. My universally rejected opinion was always formed about a piece of apparel that was being worn. I had no way of judging a garment on the rack or held against the body as *Muzi-san* was now doing. 'I don't know . . . Can you get a size eight and try it on? It's the only way I can tell,' I didn't add the words, 'if I like it and therefore Anna won't'.

Muzi-san appeared in the shirtmaker and I thought it looked rather dull, although the colour would suit Anna's skin tone and dark hair. *Muzi-san* was right – it was a bit too sophisticated for someone in her early twenties but probably right for Anna. What's more, I *definitely* didn't like the dress. 'Okay, that's the one. Can we have it in a size ten?' I said to the assistant. Then addressing *Muzi-san*, 'This time I want you to choose the spring dress you would like above all others. I feel sure that is the one Anna would like. Get a size eight and try it on. Maybe a party dress or a cocktail dress to wear in the evening, something glamorous, eh?'

Muzi-san looked pleased and returned wearing an off-the-shoulder silk dress with ballerina skirt festooned with tiny pink roses set against a cream background. She had nice legs and it looked terrific, a knockout, making it absolutely worthless for Anna. 'Wonderful!' I said. 'We'll take it!'

Muzi-san looked slightly doubtful. 'Perhaps it is not wise,

Duncan-san. You asked me to choose what I personally most liked, but I am a younger woman, maybe it is too . . .'

'Nonsense, you have wonderful taste!' I interjected, nodding to the assistant to confirm that we would take the dress. When *Muzi-san* had returned to the changing room I instructed the sales assistant to select a size eight and not a ten.

The next stop was the lingerie department and here *Muzi-san* hesitated. 'Lingerie, it is a very personal thing, *Duncan-san*. How can I choose?' Then she brightened. 'But, of course, you will know yourself.'

But, of course, I didn't. I guess I'd seen Anna in her underwear literally hundreds, maybe a thousand times, but like all men my mind was always on something else and all I'd ever registered was lace and semi-transparency in black, pink or white. Or was that Marg? Come to think of it, it probably was Marg. Moreover, off the body it simply looked like a handful of satin and lace and I hadn't a clue what to choose or even what to look for. I shrugged. '*Muzi-san*, pick what you would wear on your wedding night,' I suggested.

She blushed furiously then giggled. 'That is for taking off, not for putting on. Maybe something more practical?'

'No! Anna has been through a tough time, she will want to look pretty. The wedding night ones will be perfect.'

Our final stop was at the shoe department where it turned out the two women wore the same shoe size. *Muzi-san* selected a pair of strappy Italian sandals for the teal blue shirtmaker and a pair of impossibly high-heeled cream French courts to match the background of the party dress.

The five separate parcels were then elaborately wrapped, and with the congratulations of our personal shop assistant and much bowing we departed.

We were back in the office in slightly over the hour, and I

had scarcely thanked an astonished and overwhelmed *Muzi-san* by presenting her with the party dress and court shoes, when to my surprise *Fuchida-san*'s phone call came to tell me Anna was safe, though covered in blood.

Perhaps you think me insensitive, and wonder how I could go out shopping with one of the girls from the legal firm when things were so very fraught. Of course, I knew nothing of the *yakuza* plan to 'take out' the Shield Society guards, and if I had, I would have rejected it as much too dangerous.

Fuchida-san, probably sensing this and knowing that I was overwrought, had wisely kept me in the dark, assuring me that *Kinzo-san* would hand over the ransom money and Anna would be released into the custody of *Saito-san* without incident. This assurance had, to a large degree, kept me moderately calm, and without it I feel sure I would have completely flipped. I recalled the wartime words of Sergeant Wainwright: *'Boyo, in times of crisis, if we allow our imagination to dictate the state of our disposition it becomes a one-way street to a crack-up.'* So, rather than sit on my hands biting my bottom lip, I had kept myself busy procuring the heroin and buying new apparel for Anna. It felt as if I were doing something for her.

The four nights and days that had passed since she'd left the Imperial Hotel in high dudgeon had been, to say the least, bizarre. Anna's kidnapping, my abortive attempt with the aid of the *yakuza* to rescue her, the debacle at Konoe Akira's home, the accident with the vase, my arrest, the apparently necessary torture during my interrogation and my extremely fortunate but nevertheless harrowing session in front of the state prosecutor – what an unholy fuck-up, and most of it of my own creation.

Shopping with the cheerful and intelligent *Muzi-san* was almost the first bit of normality since we'd stepped off the

Qantas jet at Haneda Airport. To my mind, the small gift of snazzy shoes and a pretty dress didn't begin to thank her.

Fuchida-san phoned from the heliport to tell *Kinzo-san* it would not be necessary to pay the ransom, then asked to talk to me. '*Hai! Duncan-san*, your junkie is safe.' He giggled excitedly. 'But she will need a good wash; she is covered in blood.'

'Blood!' I cried, alarmed. 'Is she injured?'

He laughed. 'No, *Duncan-san*, it is not her own. Have you no faith in me? We will be there in half an hour. *Hai!* That one, she is a veritable tiger!' Then, as I was about to question him further he abruptly hung up, leaving me completely confused. Anna covered in blood? *Please, God, no more mental scars!* I prayed silently, feeling acutely the burden of being in large part to blame for the whole humungous screw-up. Something had obviously gone badly wrong. How? Why? *Saito-san* could scarcely have reached the place where Anna was being held. How then could he be back in half an hour?

Now I was once again up to my eyebrows in excrement, about to face a bloodied, distraught Anna, who was quite possibly even more severely damaged psychologically and enduring the throes of drug withdrawal. The short shopping excursion with *Muzi-san* was all I had to anchor me to what laughingly passed for normality.

Anna, her head covered with a large towel, arrived in the big Mercedes and was taken up in the lift to *Kinzo-san*'s suite of offices. I had been instructed to wait for her in the conference room, no doubt because the prestigious legal firm didn't want a messy emotional scene in the foyer, which, like the lift, had also been cleared for Anna's arrival. Led by *Muzi-san*, who had been delegated to meet her, she entered the small room with the towel still draped over her head.

I rushed to greet her. 'Anna! Oh, oh! My darling!' I cried, snatching the towel from her head and embracing her, holding her close to my chest before I'd even had a chance to get a good look at her face. Anna wrapped her arms around me and wailed, not as a woman in her forties might have done, but like a small, distraught child. I must have held her for three or four minutes, my hand almost enfolding the back of her head, the only part of her hair I would later observe that wasn't crusted with dried blood. Finally her weeping turned to serious sobs. It was a long time before she drew away from me.

'Nicholas, I am so sorry!' she sobbed.

'Christ, I'm going to cry,' I gulped and then grabbed her again as we sobbed in each other's arms. 'My fault,' I choked. 'It was all my stupid bloody fault!'

'No, no, Nicholas! *Fuchida-san* says you were wounded and tortured and put in prison!' Anna burst into fresh sobs. 'They could have killed you!' she wailed. She drew back and looked at me; her weeping had left two clear tracks down her blood-crusted cheeks. She knuckled the fresh tears from her eyes. 'Then, I would have killed myself!'

All I could do was laugh. 'Darling, you're safe, that's all that matters now.'

My words triggered an entirely new reaction from Anna, who began to shiver, hugging herself, teeth chattering. Until now her extreme distress had masked her need for a hit. 'Nicholas, I am not well,' she stammered.

I produced the gear she needed but had no idea how much heroin she would require. 'Ferchrissake, don't overdose!' I cried, not knowing how much was too much.

Her hand trembled as she measured the dirty white powder onto the square of foil but then she couldn't manage to trigger the cigarette lighter, whimpering in frustration. I took it from her. I had never done this before and it seemed deeply wrong, despite the fact that I had procured the heroin for her in the first place. I guess the Puritan in the child dies hard in the man. I held the flame under the foil, heating the powder until it began to melt, immediately giving off a thin coil of smoke. Suddenly my nose was assailed by the most dreadful smell and I realised why in some parts of the world heroin is referred to as 'shit', for that was a distinct part of the stench, along with the acrid smell of fresh vomit. Anna, oblivious to the foul smell, grabbed the straw and, sticking it up her nostril, inhaled as if her very life depended on the effusion.

I had no idea how quickly heroin reacts in the bloodstream, but as the last traces of smoke disappeared Anna looked up. 'Oh God! That was wonderful!' she exclaimed, the stress gone from her face and her expression clear. 'Thank you, Nicholas. I love you very much.'

'The smell! Jesus, Anna, how ever do you put up with the smell?'

Anna looked slightly bemused. 'Smell? What smell?' she asked.

I gazed at her, dumbfounded, and for the first time took in her appearance. 'You look a mess, darling. There's a bathroom and facilities in this office. *Muzi-san*, one of the office girls, will escort you. She has also arranged for a hairdresser to come up to the office to do your hair.' I picked up the receiver and dialled *Muzi-san*.

'*Mushi mushi*,' she answered. I asked her if she'd take Anna to the bathroom. '*Hai! Duncan-san*, there is nothing I would not do for you. I will be there in a moment.'

I have always known that Anna is made of sterner stuff than most mortals, but a little over two hours later when she emerged, it was difficult to believe the transformation. Her glossy hair was washed and perfectly styled, her make-up was faultless, and her gorgeous violet-blue eyes were clear and shining. Moreover she looked perfectly stunning in the blue dress and elegant sandals. Just short of reaching me she propped and posed. 'Nicholas, this outfit is perfect,' she said in English. Then added in some surprise, 'How very clever of you!'

Muzi-san had prudently neglected to mention her involvement in the matter. I knew I was going to chicken out and my only hope was that my shopping companion wouldn't think any less of me. Then I realised that, of course, *Muzi-san* didn't understand English, which, in turn, made me feel doubly guilty for not giving her the credit she deserved for selecting the outfit. I grinned. 'All the years of sitting outside changing rooms clutching your handbag have paid off,' I said, lying smoothly. I imagined that asking another woman to go shopping with you to pick an outfit for the woman you love just isn't *de rigueur*.

Anna looked at me quizzically, her right eyebrow slightly arched. 'And you learned how to pick exquisite lingerie where?'

'Anna! That's not fair!' I protested. 'I've seen you undressing hundreds of times.'

'Oh? Strange. I almost always do so in the dark,' she replied.

I suddenly remembered this was true. Though never afraid for me to see her naked, Anna always undressed in the dark or entered the bedroom completely nude. 'Anyway, I asked the young lady assisting me to choose what she'd wear on her wedding night,' I said, explaining.

Anna smiled, forgiving me. 'Well, she has very good taste.'

She pointed at her feet. 'And in Italian sandals, too.'

We were ushered into the main boardroom where we found a very short greying Japanese man not an inch above four feet ten. He appeared to be somewhere in his sixties and possessed all the comedic characteristics loved by wartime propaganda cartoonists – spectacles as thick as the bottom of Coke bottles, behind which his eyes, despite the gross magnification, were hidden by the narrow slits of his lids, teeth jutting alarmingly and skin the colour of iodine. He wore a black suit, white celluloid collar on a light blue shirt, a polka-dotted red and white bow tie, and, like Dr Honda, white spats and shiny black shoes with pointed toes. He bowed deeply as we entered and *Kinzo-san* introduced him as the honourable *Miyazaki-san*. 'Delighted to meet you, Madam, Sir,' he said in an almost flawless upper-crust English accent. 'Miyazaki Tono, first-class honours in law and philosophy, Magdalen College, Oxford, 1936.'

I admit I was taken aback and only just recovered enough composure to say, 'Pleased to meet you, sir.' Which wasn't the cold, hostile greeting I had intended to give this individual.

Anna remained stern-faced and composed. 'I believe you wish me to sign something. I should like to read it first, thank you,' was all she said.

'My dear, of course, always wise, though I'm sure you'll find it isn't too onerous, just taking care of the details, tying up the loose ends, what? Haw-haw-haw!' The tiny man who barely came to my waist seemed entirely in control as he withdrew two copies of a document from a scuffed old-fashioned leather briefcase and handed them to Anna, who flicked through the dozen or so pages of each of the two legal missives.

'There must be ten pages or more,' Anna said, surprised.

'Load of rubbish, my dear. Ignore all the First Party, Second Party gibberish. Just read the first and the last pages.'

'If it's not pertinent, then why is it included?' Anna asked.

The question seemed to surprise *Miyazaki-san* for he paused and scratched the side of his head. 'Damned if I know. Ah, yes, it's because the law is an ass! Haw-haw-haw! Confounded nuisance, what? Shouldn't worry, harmless jabberwocky.'

'First and last pages did you say?' Anna repeated with a hint of a smile. She sat at the boardroom table and took a fountain pen from her handbag, read the first and last pages, and wrote her initials after the full stop at the end of both pages to prevent anything being added, then signed her name to both documents, handing the four pages to *Kinzo-san* to witness. Once he'd done so, she slowly tore the remaining pages into several smallish pieces, gathering them into a neat pile.

I waited for the explosion but instead Konoe Akira's tiny lawyer chuckled, a look of genuine admiration on his face. 'I say, jolly good! Well done! Bravo! I've been simply *dying* to do that for thirty-five years! I shall tell my client that he was very foolish to trifle with a woman like you. I don't suppose you'd care to have lunch with me, would you?'

Despite herself, Anna laughed, though I could see she was close to breaking point. 'Thank you, not today, *Miyazaki-san*,' Anna said quietly, refusing in impeccable Japanese.

'Then I live in hope,' he replied, still in a genial voice, signing the documents and then tucking his copy back into his briefcase. Instead of bowing we shook hands all round, and as he took Anna's, he declared, 'I say, you are a simply splendid specimen of a woman! Haw-haw-haw!' Then, thoroughly pleased with himself, he turned abruptly and marched out of the boardroom.

Comic opera though this proved to be, I wanted to pick the arrogant runt up by the scruff of the neck, dangle him from the window, spats gleaming in the sunshine, and drop him onto the pavement ten storeys below. I was simply confounded by the little man's astonishing sangfroid. Though he couldn't have known about the multiple murders Anna had witnessed just a couple of hours before, the fact that she'd endured three days in captivity should have alerted him to her acute distress. I will forever admire her for her extraordinary self-control. If I hadn't realised before, I now knew Anna was capable of achieving anything.

'I'm sorry, darling. I should have straightened his teeth or at the very least thrown him out of the boardroom window.'

'Thank you for abstaining, Nicholas. It's been a very strange day. I'm not sure I could have handled another murder.'

Kinzo-san, who spoke no English, seemed to think all had gone well. Pointing to the pile of paper on the boardroom table he started to chortle then to laugh. '*Hai*, *Anna-san*, that was very amusing. You are a strong woman.'

'Thank you for your help, *Kinzo-san*. We are greatly in your debt, but I must now ask permission to leave,' Anna said firmly.

'Your suit, with the ... er ... stains, we will have it cleaned and sent to the hotel?'

'No, please, throw it away!' Anna cried, her expression suddenly changing. 'Nicholas, let's get the hell out of here, I've had my fill of gauche Japanese males for one day. Isn't there a park near the palace? I need to sit in the sunlight,' she said in English.

We bought two expensive bento boxes and cartons of iced green tea, then took a taxi to the small park beside the Imperial Palace. Seated on a bench we ate lunch and Anna, in a calm, almost dispassionate voice, recreated the scene of the beheadings and the shotgun blast. I kept glancing at her to see if she was all right, reaching for her hand, trying hard to control my emotions, worried that she appeared rather too calm. But she looked fine, totally in control, occasionally stopping to chew or take a sip of tea. I listened as much as possible without comment, wincing at some parts, but trying my best to conceal my shock and horror at what she'd so recently endured. Finally she rose and placed what remained of her lunch in a nearby rubbish bin. 'Let's go back to the hotel, Nicholas. I think I need a rest,' she announced in a voice she might use after a busy morning's shopping.

I rose and took the three or four steps to where she stood, the sun silvering her dark hair. 'Oh, Anna, Anna!' I put my arm around her.

I sensed her resistance. 'Nicholas, please, can we go back to the hotel now? I need to lie down.'

'Yes, of course, darling. While you rest I'll pack and phone the airport. Let's get the hell out of this bloody country.'

It was as if an electric shock ran through her body. She pushed me from her, crying, 'No! No, Nick, I have unfinished business!'

'Anna, what are you talking about?' I said, shocked at her sudden reaction, then all my pent-up emotions burst from me in angry protest. 'Ferchrissake! Haven't you had enough? Let's get out of this godforsaken fucking city! The shit hasn't stopped hitting the fan since we got here!'

'No, Nick! I've waited too long. I'm not giving up now!' she said, her voice cold.

I struggled to stay calm. 'Anna, you've been through a torrid time. Take it easy, darling. We'll talk about it further when we get to the hotel.'

'Nick, I won't change my mind. Never! You understand? Never!'

'Wait, I'll hail a taxi. Wait there!' I repeated, running towards the park gates. Three Nicks in a row – she was in a bad way. Shit, what next? She was going to collapse! Gotta get her back!

Despite my attempt at small talk Anna remained stubbornly silent on the way to the Imperial Hotel, her arms crossed and her head turned away from me while she steadfastly gazed out of the taxi window.

I knew, of course, what her 'unfinished business' meant; she was determined to front Konoe Akira, and I didn't know how to persuade her to drop this absurd notion, to walk away, let sleeping dogs lie, bury the hatchet and all the other clichéd metaphors for giving up. I trembled to think what might happen next, and for a moment I thought of asking *Fuchida-san* to use his influence to have the authorities deport us, frogmarch us onto a plane and ban us from entering Japan forever and ever and ever! Until hell froze over! But I reminded myself that I'd already screwed up big time by using the *yakuza* without first thinking things through.

There had to be another way to persuade Anna to abandon her plan to confront the man who had so perversely affected her life over the past twenty-five years. Konoe Akira was slow poison and now I knew, or rather, felt certain that more of the same wasn't going to be therapeutic. So far he had compounded her problems. Despite her almost detached description of what had happened to her kidnappers in the warehouse, I was soon to discover that witnessing such horrific violence had further damaged her psyche.

On our return to the hotel we were greeted with the usual subservience by the doorman and the instant petrification of anyone in hotel livery we passed. Anna marched ahead to the lift in silence, we rose in silence, and walked to our suite in silence. Anna went directly to the bathroom, washed off her make-up, creamed her face and slipped into her nightgown. I realised the heroin was acting as a powerful sedative and that was probably why she had seemed so calm in the park.

I began to sense that her sudden anger wasn't only a reaction to her kidnapping; she'd made up her mind to go through with the assignation with her former mentor and simply wouldn't tolerate being thwarted. Despite or perhaps because of the fact that she now knew for certain Konoe Akira was behind the kidnapping, she was determined to face up to him. It was going to take much more than my most determined efforts to change her mind. With the silent treatment continuing she slipped into bed, adjusted the covers, and within a couple of minutes fell into an exhausted sleep.

The following morning I woke with a start to find Anna sitting up in bed beside me howling like an infant. I reached over to embrace and comfort her but she resisted furiously, then threw herself onto her stomach and began to sob uncontrollably. I switched on the bedside light, then got up, opened the curtains to let the first of the sunshine in and walked around to sit beside her, feeling pathetically redundant and not knowing what to do next. Each time I attempted to touch her she pulled away. 'Please, Anna, tell me what happened again, tell me everything. Get it off your chest properly, darling,' I begged, but all to no avail. Two hours passed and still she sobbed and wailed and resisted every effort to comfort her.

Finally I grew impatient, stood up and shook her shoulder. 'Come on, enough!' I urged. 'Sit up!' Instead she lashed out blindly, her arm catching me square in my already injured and plum-coloured crotch. I leapt backwards clutching my manhood with both hands, gasping and biting back the agonised tears. Anna continued sobbing, her face buried in the monogrammed hotel pillow. If she heard my anguished groans she ignored them.

It took several minutes before I could hobble from the bedroom to the lounge to get to a telephone where Anna couldn't hear me. I dialled the number on the card Dr Honda had given me the previous evening, and asked him in a loud whisper to come to the hotel as he had previously advised he would and to bring a strong sedative or sleeping potion with him, explaining that my partner, I think I said my wife, was severely traumatised by the sight of my injuries and needed to sleep. I would wait for him in the foyer, I said, and rang off.

Dr Honda, in full morning suit minus top hat, appeared half an hour later, although this time a blue and white polka-dotted silk handkerchief spilled from the breast pocket of his coat. In addition, a gold chain, presumably attached to a fob watch, stretched across the ample expanse of his waistcoat. Either I hadn't noticed it previously, or he'd neglected to wear it the previous day. I immediately thought of Anna's calling card from Konoe Akira, the fob watch given so generously to her mentor so long ago, which had been the beginning of all our recent trouble.

I stood to greet him. 'Thank you for coming, doctor. I hope I didn't take you from your breakfast?'

He replied to my greeting with a '*Hmmph!*'.

'It was good of you to come at such short notice,' I said in a second attempt at amelioration.

He responded to this with a further '*Hmmph!*' then added, 'It is of no importance,' reminding me that in Japan all decisions are based on fear or respect. The rules of precedence were so rigid that, with my supposed *yakuza* connections, Dr Honda would possibly, had he been a surgeon, have left the operating theatre mid-incision to attend to me.

'Do you have the sleeping tablets . . . er . . . the sedative, doctor?'
I anxiously enquired.

On the previous occasion we'd met he'd hardly said a word. Whether this was because he was intimidated by the surroundings and the presence of *Fuchida-san*, I couldn't say. This time, in the neutrality of the hotel foyer, he replied, 'As far as I am concerned I have come to treat you, *Duncan-san*. With this in mind I have brought the necessary dressings. The sleeping potion is quite another matter and I will need to see the patient. If you please, can we proceed to your hotel room?'

'My partner is deeply distressed, doctor. Perhaps you can attend to me in the male toilet here in the foyer and leave me to give her the tablet?'

Dr Honda turned slowly, looking down at the shiny caps of his black shoes protruding from his white spats. He said firmly, 'I must remind you that I am a medical doctor and the answer to your question is no! We will proceed to your room please, otherwise I must return immediately to my half-eaten breakfast.'

I had quickly grown so accustomed to authority, so infected by my own self-importance, even though it was merely borrowed from my association with the *yakuza*, that I found myself unjustifiably angry. I had learned in a matter of days how to dish it out (how easily the characteristics of the bully are acquired), and now I was being disobeyed, challenged, or more truthfully, my bluff was being called and I didn't like it. Then, almost immediately, I felt ashamed and then grateful that the little doctor, with his sartorial taste fixed firmly in the 1930s, was using his authority as a conscientious medical practitioner, regardless of who I might be or the threat I might present to his welfare.

'Of course, immediately,' I replied, suitably chastened.

He examined Anna by turning her onto her back after she had ignored his request to do so herself. He took her pulse, peeled back her eyelids, took her temperature and put his stethoscope to her breast.

'She is suffering from shock, her pulse rate is too high, she has a fever. This is not normal trauma; it is acute stress reaction,' he concluded. Then squinting up at me he said, 'You say she went to bed quite calm, then woke early this morning weeping because she'd seen your lacerations?' His expression indicated that he very much doubted this explanation.

'Doctor, I was not free to explain on the phone. She has been kidnapped and witnessed three men being killed. But as you can see she has not been beaten or physically harmed. She is not normally a neurotic woman and if she could only sleep and be given a chance to calm down, I feel sure she will eventually recover.'

'Nonsense!' Dr Honda exclaimed. 'She is suffering from exhaustion and almost unendurable stress. She woke possibly after a bad nightmare, her heart rate is elevated, her breathing shallow and rapid.' He pointed to Anna, who was still weeping. 'This is symptomatic of a panic attack. I am surprised it has taken so long. Did you give her a strong sedative last night?'

I reluctantly explained that Anna was a heroin addict.

'And she received heroin shortly after she was freed?'

'Yes.'

'That is why she was calm last night. The effects of the drug have worn off, and she is now acting as one might expect. I will give her an injection to put her to sleep. When she wakes up she may feel calmer, but you need to understand, this is not something that can be cured overnight with a sleeping pill.'

Anna had not stopped sobbing and seemed oblivious to the little doctor's presence. She barely reacted when he injected her, but soon after, her breathing steadied and in twenty minutes or so she was asleep.

'Now let me attend to your dressings, Duncan-san. Have you taken the antibiotics? If your wounds become infected you will not be able to take care of your wife,' he scolded.

It was nearly ten o'clock by the time Dr Honda had finished attending to me, packed his medical bag and prepared to leave, advising me to remain with Anna until she awakened and then to call him. 'She could possibly sleep for twenty-four hours and may develop a fever and break into frequent sweats. Put a cold compress on her forehead or bathe her body with a wet towel.'

'What if she wakes and needs . . . heroin?'

'Is she a long-term addict?'

'Yes, twenty-five years, doctor.'

'Then give it to her,' he said brusquely. 'If she wakes, give her water. She will probably fall asleep again and when she finally wakes may not remember very much of this assault on her system.' Then bowing formally he left, turning back at the door and bowing a second time. '*Sayonara!*'

I left a message with reception blocking any incoming calls and asking for messages to be taken and slipped under the door. Every time the phone in the suite rang it sounded like the clappers of hell. Anna slept the whole of that day, then through the following night and was still asleep when I noticed a message had been slipped under the door. It was from *Fuchida-san* who'd called half an hour previously and asked me to return his call. I went down to the foyer and called him back, assuming he was inquiring about Anna's condition. Miss Sparkle answered, then moments later *Fuchida-san* came to the phone. I'd hardly greeted him when he declared in an ebullient tone, '*Duncan-san*, I have the most excellent news! We have discovered the whereabouts of Gojo Mura. I will send a car for you immediately!'

'Why, *Fuchida-san*, you never cease to amaze me,' I exclaimed, trying to reciprocate his enthusiasm so that he wouldn't think me ungrateful.

'We must go now! I will send a car!' he repeated excitedly.

'*Fuchida-san*, I regret I cannot come immediately. I must wait with Anna. I am advised by the doctor to wait until she wakes and to check her condition. I may have to call him. She is suffering from shock – acute stress reaction,' I corrected myself.

It wasn't what the *yakuza* boss wanted to hear. '*Hai!* She is a woman. They are by nature hysterical and they also like to sleep late. You will see, she will be just fine when she wakes up. Now we must go, the car is on the way,' he said yet again.

'I must obey the doctor's orders,' I insisted.

'*Hai!* That one, he is a syphilis doctor!'

I was in an awkward situation. *Fuchida-san* had found Gojo Mura, no doubt after considerable effort and the unprofitable use of *yakuza* manpower. Furthermore, there was no possible gain in it for him except re-acquaintance with an old village friend. Now I was refusing to leave Anna to share his triumph and, I imagine, pamper his considerable ego. I was aware that for him, our relationship had been a one-way street – give, give and more give. Whilst he may have ultimately profited from Anna's kidnapping and, in the process, increased his influence with the First Intelligence Service, this had not been his original reason for coming to my aid. He had done so generously and without any hope of personal gain. My sole contribution in return had been a box of butterflies, excellent specimens certainly, difficult but not impossible for a man of his means to obtain elsewhere.

I told myself that, as a confirmed bachelor, *Fuchida-san*'s views on women were understandably ill-informed. On a previous occasion he had questioned my attention to and concern for Anna, suggesting it was inappropriate because she was 'only a woman', a gender whose needs were subservient to those of men. Now, by refusing to leave Anna for a reunion with Gojo Mura, I was causing him to lose face. *Christ, the sooner we get out of this macho bloody country the better!* I silently swore.

'Honourable *Fuchida-san*, you are making it very difficult for me. I cannot leave her,' I began.

'*Hai!* You carry her handbag and her shoes!' he snapped.

Anna had not mentioned the shoe and bag incident during her rescue and I took this as a Japanese metaphor for a wimp and a wuss. The *yakuza* boss was not accustomed to being rebuffed and plainly wasn't happy. No doubt he had every right. I was abusing the rules Dr Honda had so carefully observed when he'd come directly to the hotel after my call. I knew I was being tested, and that I was about to fail. 'Honourable *Oyabun Fuchida-san*, I would happily carry her shoes and handbag if I could undo what has been done to Anna. As I cannot, I must wait until she wakes and if necessary attend to her or call Dr Honda. I most humbly crave your indulgence in this matter.'

A lengthy silence ensued and I was about to ask if he was still there when he said coldly, 'As you wish, *Duncan-san*. Call *Mama-san* when you are ready. She will send a *wakagashira* to fetch you. I have tried to please you in this matter but now have more important matters to attend to,' and he hung up.

I am ashamed to say I felt a curious sense of relief, and while I didn't like the way it had ended and was sad that I wouldn't meet little Gojo Mura, this was yet another reason to get the hell out of Japan. My hope was that a rested and calmer Anna would see things more reasonably and would abandon the idea of confronting Konoe Akira. But I knew it to be a forlorn hope.

I settled down to wait. Mitsubishi Shipping had sent around numerous regulatory forms to be filled in for the two freighters I'd purchased. I'd spent the previous day dealing with them and now I busied myself attending to the last of them while Anna continued to sleep. Halfway though this tedious paperwork and much to my annoyance the phone rang. It was a frightened voice from reception begging a thousand pardons to say that I had a visitor. Frowning, I immediately assumed it was the *wakagashira* who'd been on his way to fetch me for the cancelled appointment with Gojo Mura and had not received the message to return. 'Tell him to return, that I will not be going with him,' I instructed reception.

'It is a woman, *Duncan-san*,' the receptionist announced, then added, 'I don't think she will leave.'

'A woman?' I exclaimed, surprised. Then, recovering, I said, 'Ask for her name, please.'

I waited a few moments before he spoke again. 'She says to tell you it is the *mama-san* with the diamond earrings.'

Miss Sparkle! I was suddenly more than a little bemused and asked myself what on earth was going on. 'Will you show her to a meeting room and bring her tea, please. I will be right down,' I instructed. I left a note for Anna on the bedside table, telling her to call reception to alert me if she woke up and needed me.

Miss Sparkle rose and bowed deeply, earrings sparkling, when I entered the small private lounge. She was dressed in a formal kimono with her grey hair combed and swept up in the geisha style, and she wore the stark white make-up, delicate black and red shading around her eyes and the brilliant red over-painted bow lips. 'A thousand apologies for calling on you without formally requesting your permission, *Duncan-san*,' she offered.

'It is a pleasure to receive you, *Mama-san*, though I am curious as to why you have come. Is there something I can do for you?'

She did not reply immediately. Dropping to her knees and leaning back on her haunches in the geisha style she poured green tea for me. 'No, *Duncan-san*, it is I who hope to be of service to you,' she said, handing me the tiny cup. 'I have come to ask if I may attend to *Anna-san*. I understand she is not well.'

'*Oyabun Fuchida-san* told you?' I asked, surprised.

'No, I listened to your conversation on the phone. It is required of me to listen to all telephone calls.'

'But you have not yet met Anna.'

Miss Sparkle paused, the teapot still held aloft, her own cup not yet poured. 'Ah, but I have,' she said, smiling.

'Oh?' I asked, puzzled. 'How can that possibly be?'

'My geisha name is Korin. I was the seventh *okami-san* in the Nest of the Swallows. We, *Anna-san* and I, first met in the service of the Honourable Colonel Konoe Akira in Tjilatjap more than twenty-five years ago.'

'You know Konoe Akira?' I asked, astounded.

'No, I was merely sent to his house to train *Anna-san*. I only met him to take his instructions.'

'On training her in the art of *kinbaku?*'

'Oh, she has told you?'

'Yes.' I felt it unnecessary to explain further. Anyway, if she was privy to all the calls to and from *Fuchida-san*, *Korin-san* would have known that Anna had visited the Jade House and that she continued to practise the art of the rope. 'Then you know about her kidnapping, that it was instigated by *Konoe-san?*'

'Yes, it is deeply to be regretted.'

'And of her need for heroin . . . you know about that also?'

Korin-san averted her eyes. 'I had hoped she might have conquered the dragon. I am ashamed, *Duncan-san*. It was I who, at the Nest of the Swallows, tricked her into taking heroin suppositories to calm her. I did so to spare my own unworthy life.'

'Then you know what happened to the *kempeitai* colonel?'

Korin-san nodded her head. '*Anna-san* is the bravest woman I have ever known. She has courage beyond that of any man.'

'*Korin-san*, I do not wish to be disrespectful, but does *Fuchida-san* know you have come here to see Anna?'

'Yes. After your phone call I remonstrated with him.'

'You remonstrated?' I asked surprised.

Korin-san chuckled. 'Perhaps, because I am a Japanese woman and a retired geisha, you think this is not possible?'

'I have come to think that *Fuchida-san* is . . .' I tried to think of the appropriate word, '. . . *indifferent* to a woman's opinion. I do not believe he has a high regard for Anna.'

'You are quite wrong.'

'Oh?'

Korin-san then told me of the shoes and handbag incident and added, 'This morning, after the phone call, I told him *more* about Anna . . . when I scolded him.'

'More? You told him about the Nest of the Swallows?'

'Yes.'

I knew better than to show my annoyance at this. 'Was that wise, do you think?'

While polite it was nevertheless a reprimand and the fact that I didn't address her by name would have been obvious to her. 'Yes, it was necessary,' *Korin-san* replied without hesitation. 'He is a powerful man and does not take kindly to having his authority challenged. It is easy for him to think that his decisions, like those of the Emperor, cannot be disobeyed. His friendship with you is important to him. It is, other than his relationship with *Saito-san*, the only proper friendship he has made, one that presents no threat to him, is not a challenge to his power, one that is based on nothing more than your mutual love of butterflies. He is a proud man and this morning he couldn't bring himself to accept that you would cater to the needs of an "hysterical" woman instead of obeying his command.'

'Anna is not an hysterical woman!' I interjected, misreading her emphasis.

'Of course not! I above anyone know this. But it was necessary for *him* to know also. To know that *Anna-san* is not just a woman, but also a person he must respect as he would any brave and courageous warrior. Respect her as he does you. He knows you have been a great warrior and have many medals for courage. Now he knows that she is also such a one, but her medals are the scars she wears on her heart.' She sighed. 'I regret, *Duncan-san*, that like most Japanese men he has difficulty apologising.' She paused and sighed a second time. 'But he is *oyabun*, he finds it impossible to admit he was wrong.'

'So he sent you?'

'Yes and no. He suggested I should come to take care of Anna.' She smiled. 'He is softening the ground. I am glad he asked me, but it was not my request. I did not ask his permission to come or volunteer.'

'Before, when you realised who she was, didn't you wish to be reacquainted with Anna?'

'It would have been a great privilege, but it was a long time ago. Those were bad times. My hope was that she had put them behind her. I did not wish to open old wounds.'

'But if Anna had come with me to visit *Fuchida-san*, would she not have recognised you?'

'That would not be possible, *Duncan-san*. No woman, other than myself, has ever been in the penthouse of *Oyabun Fuchida-san*.'

I was not at all certain that in her present state, or any other for that matter, Anna should be reacquainted with *Korin-san*. 'But now you have changed your mind and wish to help her?'

Korin-san looked dismayed. 'I would *always* wish to help *Anna-san*! She is the finest woman I have ever known. She has the courage of a lioness. But, as I said, I am associated with bad rice, times she would not wish to remember. I thought it better to stay away.' She paused. 'That is why I have come to see you.'

'Me?'

'Yes, *Duncan-san*! *You* must decide what is best. If you wish me to go then I shall do so.'

I spread my hands and sighed. '*Korin-san*, I don't know. I *really* don't know. Until Anna wakes up I cannot possibly decide.'

'Of course! I understand, *Duncan-san*. I have taken too much of your time as it is. You must go to her.'

'No, it is all right, I have left a note. If she wakes up she will call reception and they will inform me,' I said. 'Now it is my turn to ask about you. I am curious, *Korin-san*. Your knowing Anna is an amazing coincidence. How did you come to work for *Oyabun Fuchida-san*? Anna has spoken about you. I know that you were a retired geisha brought to Tjilatjap to train the comfort women. But what happened to you after the war?'

Korin-san sighed. 'When the Americans dropped the second bomb and the armistice was declared I was instructed by the *kempeitai* to poison the six other *okami-san* at the Nest of the Swallows and then to take my own life. I was told that the Americans would immediately hand us over to the Dutch who, because we had enslaved their daughters and wives as concubines, would take their terrible revenge and torture us and we would die slow and agonising deaths. They insisted that poisoning was much the better way for us, the more respectable and honourable way to die. But the fifth *okami-san* and I, who had cared for *Anna-san*, "preparing" her for the *kempeitai* colonel, Takahashi, were witness to her extraordinary courage and tenacity and she gained honour in our eyes. As a result we decided to disobey our instructions. We were consequently captured by the British and repatriated to Japan where we were prosecuted for war crimes. The others received prison sentences of five years and I, as the senior *okami-san*, received seven years.'

'You spent *seven* years in prison?'

'No. The Americans needed comfort women for their soldiers during their occupation and asked the Honourable Yoshio Kodama, who was reorganising the *yakuza* into a single force, to establish clean and safe places for their forces to visit. He had access through the American Army Intelligence, G2, to the records of war criminals and, discovering my past, negotiated my freedom and asked me to organise six comfort-women establishments near the US military bases, then more during the Korean War, until we eventually controlled the military brothels throughout Japan.

'He installed the honourable Dr Honda, who was also imprisoned for work he did as a junior army doctor at Harbin in Manchuria, where they used prisoners of war as guinea pigs in the army's germ-warfare program. He had only a minor part, but as most of the senior staff, the real experts, went to America to continue their research, the young, inexperienced doctors were put on trial to satisfy the War Crimes Tribunal. There was much venereal disease around and the Americans were very strict.

'To help me organise the comfort houses *Kodama-san* sent twenty of his young *wakagashira* to learn the business. *Fuchida-san* was one of these but at the time he was also studying at the university. They were all heroin addicts and were not always reliable, with the single exception of *Fuchida-san*, who was hungry to learn, with a terrible energy and ambition and strict principles. He soon learned the concubine business and also how to control the *kuroi kiri* [black mist], doing the awkward and dirty jobs for the government that gives us our real power. With his own determination and strength I would eventually help him to give up the white powder, to get clean.

'The brothels proved very profitable. Then when the Americans left we expanded, until today most of them and the sex, gambling, nightclub, and *pachinko* – pinball parlour – businesses in Tokyo and in all the big cities are owned by *yakuza* or are under *yakuza* control. It is how *Fuchida-san* first came to prominence. He has a tremendous flair for organisation and eventually gained sufficient power to become the *oyabun* for the Tokyo region. When I retired he took me in as his *mama-san*.'

I had not interrupted while she told her amazing story. 'And now you act *only* as his *mama-san?*'

'Yes,' she replied. 'I have become a feeble old woman who answers the telephone and serves green tea.'

I laughed. 'I don't think so.'

She smiled, her powdered face a study in wrinkles. 'Every man, even the Emperor, needs a mother. Perhaps also I am still a bit useful to him. My memory is good and that is why I must listen to the phone calls. Sometimes the lesser *oyabun* will argue that they didn't say something or that something else was intended, then *Fuchida-san* will call me in and I will tell them in their exact words and inflections what they said. It is part of my geisha training and it has not forsaken me.'

But I had the feeling that Miss Sparkle was much, much more than a human tape recorder and dispenser of green tea, although, because of the outwardly off-hand and dismissive treatment by men of women in Japan, I would probably never know the true extent of her influence. I decided to confide in her.

'*Korin-san*, I have a problem.'

'With Anna?'

'Yes. She wishes still to have the original assignation with *Konoe-san*.'

Miss Sparkle showed no surprise. 'She is strong. She cannot be defeated.'

'Stubborn!'

'It is her way.'

'She must not. It will harm her further. We must go home.'

'You have told her this?'

'Yes.'

Miss Sparkle cackled. 'She is a woman who takes her own advice; not many women do.'

'Always,' I returned. 'But this time it is *wrong*!' I insisted with some emphasis.

'Does she listen to you?'

'Sometimes, but not often; in most matters she is better than me.'

'That is a difficult thing for a man to admit.'

'But it is nevertheless true.'

'And she is successful?'

'Enormously. But there is much more to come.'

'Business?'

'Yes. She is very good. Already a millionaire . . . I think.'

'So, why does she wish to confront *Konoe-san*?'

'I don't know, some sort of revenge maybe? Close the books? I don't really know or care, except I do know that it will damage her – has already damaged her, and that's all I care about.'

'*Duncan-san*, I was a geisha and I think as an old woman I can now say I was a good one. My job was always to anticipate the wishes of a man, to think like him, to know him intimately, instinctively. When Anna was incarcerated in the Nest of the Swallows, my instructions were to prepare her for Colonel Takahashi. I told her what every geisha knows – that if she pleases a man beyond anything he may have anticipated, she acquires power. It is the soft power of a woman. When he is satiated, when every pore of his body is fulfilled, satisfied, when he believes he is the only one, the true satyr, the person of absolute primary importance to a woman's craving for satisfaction, his arrogance weakens him and he becomes vulnerable to her power, her influence. I carefully and assiduously trained Anna in how she might do this with Colonel Takahashi. I taught her the *soft* power of a determined and patient woman. She listened, she appeared to obey my every instruction, she became skilled in the ways of pleasuring a man, and then when she faced *Takahashi-san* she used all I had taught her to disarm him so that he trusted her and foolishly believed he controlled her, whereupon she killed him before he could take her virginity. *Duncan-san, Anna-san* has the hard power every woman wishes she possessed, but doesn't.' Miss Sparkle now looked directly at me. 'Tell me. Is she still a virgin?'

I coloured furiously, my face burning with shame. She had pinned me as surely as if I had been a butterfly on the wall in *Fuchida-san*'s collection, where, by the way, I would probably find myself next to a brown spotted butterfly called 'Satyr'. 'Yes,' I admitted.

'*Hai!* And you think the confrontation with *Konoe-san* will further damage her?' she said doubtfully. 'She has never submitted to the one disadvantage every woman suffers, that we are the mortar, the receptacle, not the pestle, and not only physically, but also for the male ego. We try therefore to make it our strength, an enticement, a spider web, to trap the male. If we are patient and skilful and gifted with beauty, often the soft power is successful. But to be beautiful and desirable in every way, then to refuse to be the receptacle, to refute *soft* power in preference for *hard* power, that is what Anna has done.'

There wasn't any point in trying to pretend to this wise and world-weary old geisha. '*Konoe-san* is different. As you know he never used her as a man does a woman, so soft or hard power was not the issue. He simply captured her mind and took possession of her soul. I love her as much as a man can love a woman, but I believe he controls her still.'

'And what then do you believe you bring to her?'

I shrugged. 'Who may know a woman's mind? Certainly not me. I know she loves me and perhaps I am the stable force in her dangerous life. Dependability may be seen as a virtue, so may consistency, though neither is exciting or compelling. I think my world and the life I lead in the islands is without the complications or the malice that exist in the competitive business environment in which she operates. Perhaps she comes to me to rest her mind and to renew her spirit.'

'That is well spoken, *Duncan-san*. Then *you* are the soft power. That is unusual in a man, but greatly to be cherished. It is also the only way with someone like *Anna-san*.'

I laughed. 'In business, as in choosing clothes, she asks my opinion only so that she can do the opposite.'

'Have you not thought, *Duncan-san*, that perhaps you possess the greater qualities of tolerance and goodwill?'

'Hmm, I don't know about that. With Anna there is always the pain of not possessing her completely. But it is manageable, I have learned to compromise.'

'Manageable? Compromise?' Miss Sparkle chuckled. 'Ah, I see, there is another woman! You want Anna, but also everything else?'

'Yes,' I grinned rather sheepishly, taken aback by her perspicacity. 'I cannot help it.' I spread my hands in an attempt to seem casual. 'I am a man.' In retrospect it was a ridiculous remark, and thankfully she ignored it.

'To possess, then, only the greater part of Anna, is it worth it?'

'Yes,' I laughed, 'well worth it.'

'Then why do you fear her reunion with *Konoe-san*? He cannot harm her now.'

I was stymied. I had never thought about it like that. What Miss Sparkle was telling me was that nobody ever possesses someone entirely, that people are free to apportion their love. I saw suddenly that there might be a need, a hunger in Anna, that I could never fulfil, but perhaps Konoe Akira possessed those qualities that could. I also saw that we were not necessarily competitors.

'What do I fear?' I pretended to be thinking while knowing full well what she was suggesting. 'Okay, I fear that her need for him will be greater than her need for me,' I replied with some uncertainty, surprised by my own reply. Miss Sparkle had made me see it clearly for the first time, made me realise that true love is giving freely of those things you can share while accommodating, accepting, those you can't. Loyalty and trust are two of the most important components of the many that make the whole of love. Put this way it sounded eminently intelligent and simple, providing always that you didn't involve your emotions.

Miss Sparkle rose. 'I will go now, *Duncan-san*. Please call me if I can help. In the meantime I will think about what you have said. You are a fine man and Anna is very fortunate.'

'Thank you, *Korin-san*. Will you please allow me to be the judge of Anna's immediate welfare? I am not certain that I will inform her of your visit. But I would like to think that I may call on you, on your wisdom.'

She cackled at the compliment. 'In Japan only men possess wisdom; women make suggestions. Of course, call on me when you wish.' Then, as if she'd read my previous thoughts, she said, 'I am an old woman who has been trained since a young *maiko* never to make emotional decisions, and the strict observance of this rule robbed my life of real meaning. Reason is why we survive, but without emotion there is very little quality to our existence. True love is about forgiveness and there is no logic in forgiveness.'

With these words Miss Sparkle departed. I noted with some amusement the big Mercedes parked in a no-parking zone directly outside the hotel. Miss Sparkle's appearance resulted in a great deal of bowing as she crossed the hotel foyer, a bellboy rushing to open the rear door of the big black auto even before the driver could leap out of his seat.

CHAPTER ELEVEN

*'Bravo! If you'd stayed in the hotel
to arrange the ransom rather than galloping off
on your white charger to rescue me,
I could have bought my way out
unharmed in a couple of hours.'*
Anna, Tokyo

WHILE SHE HADN'T COME out directly and advised me on what to do about Anna's determination to see Konoe Akira, the meaning of Miss Sparkle's final words was nevertheless unmistakable. I needed to, in her opinion, allow Anna to see her mentor without opposition. I had to trust her strength and her love – our love – to survive whatever might come of that meeting.

I wasn't at all sure that this was sound advice or that I was able to cope with it emotionally. I told myself that I knew a great deal more about Anna's psychology than anyone else, that by giving in and not resisting I would, potentially, be partly responsible for more harm and a fresh set of problems.

However, I also knew that whether or not I was able to stop Anna from seeing Konoe Akira, I was risking our future together by my vehement opposition. After all, it had originally been my idea she visit him. If she went ahead despite my resistance, there would be no way I could back down gracefully.

It had all seemed so neat. In my fevered imagination she would confront a pathetic old pervert of no substance and instantly slough off his influence; before my very eyes, she would be miraculously restored to health.

This was classic Nick Duncan mind-shit. The events of the past few days had proved how ridiculous and inappropriate this excremental notion was. *Here I go again, heads I lose, tails you win*, I thought, feeling a tad sorry for myself.

When I arrived back upstairs Anna was showered, dressed and sitting at the mirror brushing her hair. 'Good morning, gorgeous boy!' she called. 'Where you bin? I've missed yah,' she quipped.

I walked over and she kissed me warmly. 'Downstairs,' I said, surprised at her ebullience. 'Sleep well?'

She grinned. 'Like a log . . . sorry about last night.'

I wasn't sure whether this was an apology for the fight we'd had or for her panic attack. 'That's not necessary. You were under a fair bit of strain. I'm glad you're feeling better, darling,' I said, in this way accommodating either possibility.

She continued brushing her hair. 'Who was downstairs?' she asked casually.

'A messenger from *Fuchida-san* – they've found Gojo Mura,' I said, putting one and three together.

Anna turned. 'Oh, Nick, how exciting for you! When can we meet him?'

I hesitated momentarily. 'I'm not sure. It was arranged for this morning, but I postponed it.'

Anna was not fooled. 'Because of me?'

'Well, yes. Unavoidably. Doctor's orders.'

Lowering the hairbrush she turned to face me. 'Doctor? What doctor?'

'You don't remember?'

'Remember what? We had an awful row. I remember that. I'm awfully sorry, Nicholas,' she repeated, head to one side, her beautiful violet-blue eyes regretful.

'Darling, you had a panic attack during the night . . . early morning,' I corrected. 'Yesterday morning actually. I called the doctor and he gave you an injection,' I said, trying to minimise the seriousness of the event. 'He said I should stay with you and . . . well, call him if you woke up distressed, but you've slept for hours.'

'Really? A day and a night? I woke up with a headache, but even that's gone.'

As I'd entered the room I'd caught the now unmistakable whiff of the dragon, even though Anna had opened all the windows under the pretence of letting in the spring sunshine. She would probably be okay for the next eighteen hours. 'Good, now what about some breakfast?' I glanced at my watch. 'Brunch?'

'Have you eaten, Nicholas?' she asked.

'Not yet.'

'You must be starving. I am. Let me put on some lippy. How about scrambled eggs . . . something that's not Japanese, with toast and coffee, yum!'

But over breakfast Anna seemed preoccupied. 'What's wrong, darling?' I asked, sensing she wasn't happy.

'Nicholas, when I went into the bathroom, I found a woman's clothes – underwear, a pair of sandals . . .' She looked at me steadily. 'Perhaps you'd care to explain?' Before I could say a word she added pointedly, 'I can't say much for your taste, my dear. Her underwear was sluttish!'

'Anna! Surely you remember?' I laughed helplessly. 'They're yours, darling, I bought them at Mitsukoshi.

Your suit was ruined.'

She looked at me uncertainly, then reached over and grabbed my hand. 'Oh I'm so sorry, darling, now I've hurt you.'

I grinned. 'Well at least it proves I'm consistent in matters of taste.' I hadn't personally liked the shirtmaker so I'd assumed Anna probably would. If she didn't, it meant I was losing my bad-taste touch, but the rebuke over the undies restored my confidence. 'I actually thought the undies looked pretty good.'

'The sandals are really quite nice,' she comforted me, ignoring my remark about the underwear.

It was obvious that she could recall very little of what had occurred after her rescue and the helicopter ride to freedom. Kinzo-san's office, the trip to the bathhouse and her new clothes were, it seemed, forgotten. Perhaps, strangest of all, she'd forgotten our lunch in the park and the fact that she had told me of her rescue and the murder of the three guards in great detail. Only our argument seemed to have stayed with her.

'Nicholas, can we meet Gojo Mura?' she now asked excitedly. 'You have such fond memories. It would be good to know how it all turned out for him. It's such a lovely day and I feel completely rested.'

I grimaced. 'Not sure about that, darling. Had a bit of a row with Fuchida-san.'

'Row? What, over Gojo Mura?'

'I told you he wanted to go this morning and I said it wasn't possible. He didn't take my refusal kindly. I guess blokes like him don't expect to be rebuffed.'

'Oh, then it was Fuchida-san downstairs?'

'No, he phoned earlier to tell me he was sending a car. I told him then that I couldn't come. That's when he had a shitty.'

'So, if it wasn't him, who was downstairs? You said it was someone from the yakuza?' Anna as usual had picked up the fine print.

'Someone sent by *Fuchida-san* on a different matter,' I said, prevaricating.

Anna leaned back in her chair, her beautiful mouth in full pout.

'I see. You're not going to tell me. Let me guess . . . it has something to do with me?'

'Yes, I can't deny that.'

Her smile when it came was not intended to charm me. I was headed for trouble. With an impatient flick of her head she said, 'Then surely I am entitled to know?'

'It was *Fuchida-san*'s *mama-san*, the one I told you about, Miss Sparkle with the diamond earrings. He sent – well no, that's not strictly true – she came over to see if she could care for you, you know, after the kidnapping. The shock and all that.'

'Well, what a very nice thing for him to do. Surely allowing her to take care of me was his way of apologising?'

Anna was slowly wearing me down. If I agreed, it would constitute an apology in her mind and I'd have no reason not to call *Fuchida-san*, whereupon he'd promptly make a damn fool of me by refusing to take the call. 'Well not really, as I said, it was her own decision to come.'

'And you sent her home?'

'Yes, of course. I was here to take care of you. She wasn't necessary.'

'That will *really* help to patch things up between *Fuchida-san* and you, Nicholas.'

'Does it matter?' I said defiantly. 'We're getting out of this place anyway!'

Anna's right eyebrow shot up. 'Oh, are we?'

I caught myself in time. I realised my next remark was crucial or we'd be back where we'd been in the taxi coming home from the park. 'She came to see me to ask if it was okay to see you. It was perfectly amicable – the Japanese way. I didn't flatly refuse. I simply said I'd like to think about it. I didn't want you to wake up with a strange Japanese woman at your bedside.'

'Oh, by thinking about it, you mean you were going to ask me. See how I felt. Was that it?' Anna suggested, smiling sweetly, knowing she was on to something.

'Well, yes . . . I suppose.'

'All right then, yes, I'd like to meet Miss Sparkle. I'm fed up with the whole damn business of the *yakuza*. It's been a one-way street, you and *Fuchida-san* making decisions about my welfare. The whole thing has turned out to be a monumental mess!'

'Hey, wait on! We got you out. Rescued you. Shit! Is that the gratitude you show?' I cried.

'Look at you, Nick. You're cut to ribbons, you've been tortured, spent two days in a police cell. Three men have been brutally murdered in front of my eyes, two more I am told at the gate!'

'But you're safe!' I interjected.

Anna laughed bitterly. 'Bravo! If you'd stayed in the hotel to arrange the ransom rather than galloping off on your white charger to rescue me, I could have bought my way out unharmed in a couple of hours. Christ, Nick, I make my living negotiating. The Shield Society was simply a bunch of opportunists.'

'Rightwing fanatics!' I cried. 'They are capable of anything.'

'What? Even killing the golden goose? Don't be ridiculous! Fanatics maybe, but not bloody stupid.'

'Well, I offered to pay your ransom,' I said self-righteously.

'When? After you'd kidnapped Konoe Akira's aged mother, broke into his home, held a gun to his head to teach him not to cross the great war hero, Nick Duncan, and ended arse-up in a thousand-year-old vase and ultimately in police custody?'

'Ouch! You know about that part?'

'Yes, your gangster friend told me with some alacrity in the car from the heliport . . . the whole sense-defying fiasco from start to finish.'

Anna was only confirming what I myself had come to think. Defending my actions any further seemed pointless. 'Anna, you're right. I was stupid; things got out of hand. But you're safe and I'll mend.' I hesitated then reached out and put my hand over hers. 'Darling, can we kiss and make up and get the hell out of here? *Please!*'

'Stupid boy!' Anna cried out now, seemingly more frustrated than angry. Then she sighed and seemed to relax and when she spoke again it was in her normal quiet voice. 'Nicholas, it was entirely my fault. I got us into this jam. I wanted to see Konoe Akira alone initially and I refused to allow your involvement. But, just as I was responsible for getting myself kidnapped, I was also responsible for my own welfare, and able, I felt sure, to have myself freed. You simply acted too quickly and, may I say, without thinking it through, so I was unable to contact you to arrange things.'

Anna paused for a moment. 'The art of negotiation is patience and the ability to win your point with reason, although you can usually rely on good old-fashioned greed. Money solves most things and, as the saying goes, "revenge is a dish best eaten cold".' Anna appeared to be thinking. 'Had it all gone to plan and I'd paid my own ransom, I daresay I would have licked my wounds, kicked myself for acting stupidly in the first instance and decided to go home with my mission unaccomplished.' She paused again. 'But not now. Now I want to face him, to see him.'

'I don't understand. *Why?* What can you possibly gain?'

She frowned. 'Self-respect.'

'But he won't agree to see you. Not now, after all that's happened. Besides, he's had his comeuppance, it's cost him twenty-five thousand dollars.'

'You're not listening, Nicholas!' She looked at me knowingly. 'Self-respect, not just for myself.'

I shook my head. 'I've made a complete dickhead of myself. Sometimes you can't believe your own stupidity.'

'We all know that feeling,' Anna said softly.

'And how do you propose to get to him? Impossible, I should think.'

'You've just helped me to do that, Nicholas.'

'Oh, how?'

Anna gave a cryptic little smile. 'Now it's my turn to use the *yakuza*. I will invite Miss Sparkle over for afternoon tea. You will formally introduce us and then you will be kind enough to leave us alone.'

'You already know her,' I replied, realising I was utterly defeated.

'Oh?'

'Her name is *Korin-san*. She is, or was, the seventh *okami-san* in the Nest of the Swallows.'

Anna looked at me, her expression almost beyond amazement. 'Oh my God!'

I wasn't privy to the meeting Anna had with Miss Sparkle, but when she returned she announced that she would be spending the next several days at the Jade House. This provoked yet another row. When I objected to her returning to the scene of her kidnapping, she replied, 'Nicholas, please don't ask. I'm working at the Jade House, that's all.'

'So who do I call if you don't come back to the hotel?' I asked, feeling helpless.

'*Korin-san* . . . er, Miss Sparkle.'

'The *yakuza*! I thought you said you'd had a gutful of them?'

'It's not the same. We're old friends. This is strictly girls' stuff.'

'So what do I do? Sit on my arse all day waiting for your instructions?' I asked, repaying her for her reproaches over my leaving the hotel when she'd been kidnapped.

Anna didn't bite. 'You said Mitsubishi called, didn't you, and wanted approval for the modifications to the freighters you requested?'

'Well yes, but it isn't strictly necessary, and then we decided to leave Japan immediately.'

'No, Nicholas, *you* decided to leave Japan. I need a few days, so why don't you spend them checking your freighters?'

'Like I said, it really isn't necessary. I've seen the drawings, that's all that's needed,' I replied sulkily.

'Nicholas, stop it!' Anna yelled impatiently. 'What's got into you?' She sighed deeply. 'We were always going to visit the World Expo at Osaka. Why don't you spend three or four days there? You'll be better on your own looking at things that interest men. Besides, the break will be good for us both.' She gave me a look that clearly suggested I should get out of her goddamn hair.

I sometimes think I must be a weak bastard. A man ought'a take her and put her over his knee and give her a bloody good spanking. Then, despite myself, I was forced to grin. I'd tried that once, with surprising results. Between the two of them, Anna and Marg, even the biblical Job with his Old Testament patience would have been forced to throw in the towel. 'Expo? Okay, good idea,' I said, accepting defeat. 'I'll go today.'

'Call me in the early evenings when you can. I won't leave until 8 p.m.,' Anna said.

'Just because I fucked up the kidnapping! I get the message, I'm not needed,' I joked.

Anna came over and hugged me, then kissed me properly, deeply, meaningfully, lovingly, knowingly and insincerely on the mouth, then pulling back she grinned wickedly. 'Sometimes a woman's gotta do what a woman's gotta do!' she said. 'Trust me, Nicholas.'

But I wasn't fooled for a moment. If Anna was preparing to restore her self-respect, then I almost felt sorry for the poor bugger. Konoe Akira was in for a bumpy ride.

I called Anna from Osaka the next evening, and knowing she wasn't going to talk about the Jade House I jabbered on about the Expo and in particular the American pavilion where, after the recent Apollo 13 moon mission abort and rescue, the space exhibition was by far the most popular exhibit. The model of the Apollo 11 spacecraft could be seen towering against the skyline a kilometre away, which was also the length of the queue to enter the pavilion to see samples of moon rock gathered by the Armstrong-led first moon landing. A guide informed me that people slept in the line at night.

I decided to give it a miss, instead visiting the near-deserted Russian stand to see the Sputnik. I recall yakking on to Anna in a somewhat disparaging tone. 'Despite Yuri Gagarin being the first man in space in 1961, the Russians have been left out in the cold. I now know why it's called the Cold War! As far as space is concerned the fighting for superiority is over. The Sputnik is a tin humpy and the Apollo, a Hilton Hotel. Believe you me,' I said with some conviction, 'the Ruskies are not in the race, space or otherwise!'

So much for Nick Duncan's sagacity. As I write this, the Russians in their cramped Soyuz TMA spacecraft and padded silver spacesuits have for several years been, and still largely are, the leaders in space science and technology. As an aside, I recently heard a story, whether apocryphal or not I can't say, regarding the Americans boasting about their space pen at an international space conference. It had taken a great deal of money and years of research, but they had finally cracked the technology required to create a ballpoint pen that would write in space. A Russian space scientist in the audience stood up and asked, 'Why didn't you simply use a pencil, comrade?'

Anyway, we chatted on, talking about nothing very much, the subject of Konoe Akira and the Jade House studiously avoided. Anna told me how Miss Sparkle had taken the afternoon off so that they could visit several small markets together, which she found fascinating, and how, at the crack of dawn tomorrow, she was being picked up by a *wakagashira* to visit the Tsukiji Fish Market, the largest in Tokyo.

'Since when have you been remotely interested in fish?' I asked.

'Nicholas, did you realise that the Japanese constitute two per cent of the world's population and eat ten per cent of its fish?'

'Never was a great fish eater,' I replied. 'Though I'm not surprised. Have you ever seen a bento box without a lump of fish?'

'It's a commodity and the seas are full of the stuff,' Anna said in an equally off-hand manner. Then, laughing, she said, 'I recall you saying once that bricks sit in one place and grow old. I didn't agree, still don't, but maybe I should think beyond bricks and mortar to commodities like fish, tuna, shark fins . . . who knows?'

'Shark fins!'

'There are a billion Chinese in the world and they make a lot of soup.' Anna laughed.

'Is that why you're going to the fish market tomorrow?'

'Well, no, but it should be fun. Why not?'

How stupid was I. Anna never did anything in her life unless she had a good reason. She was a planner, a long-term thinker, but not a gambler. She was up to something but it was pointless asking, so instead I said, 'Glad you're enjoying Miss Sparkle's company. I'm surprised *Fuchida-san* lets her onto the street with that small fortune dangling from her ears. Who'll answer the phone?'

'She's an enterprising woman.' Anna laughed, then changed the subject. 'How are the cuts and bruises?' she asked.

'Itchy, but the good news in the bruise department is that I woke up this morning feeling reunited with my libido.'

'Good, you'll get the attention you deserve when you return,' she promised, a smile in her voice. 'Have you seen a doctor, had the cuts dressed?'

'Yeah, there's a clinic around the corner from the hotel. I had to wait an hour. The place was full of people wearing cotton masks. You wouldn't know it was spring – everyone's got the sniffles. We'd call it Asian flu, but here they're blaming it on all the *gaijin* visiting Expo, calling it Australian flu. Lots of Australians here. The stitches are due to come out in four days, but I'll wait until we get back to Australia.' The small talk was intended to tell her I understood she wasn't ready to talk about Konoe Akira.

'Four days, that's good,' she said abstractedly, then there was a short silence and a deep breath. 'Nicholas, I need at least another week, probably ten days here.'

I could tell she was waiting for the explosion to follow. In fact, it took some restraint on my part not to react. I'd allowed her the four days she wanted and now she was demanding even more. 'What's another week when you're trying to reverse twenty-five years of psychological damage?' I answered coolly.

Anna wasn't fooled. 'Please, Nicholas, don't be angry,' she begged.

'I'm *not* angry!' I protested, because of course I was.

'It's not what you think, Nicholas,' she said, her voice on the edge of tears.

'Think? You asked me for four days more in Japan and I agreed. Now you want another week after that? What am I supposed to think? You haven't told me what you're doing at the Jade House and you haven't mentioned the dreaded you-know-who!'

'Please, Nicholas, I can't say. Please trust me, darling, this is for both of us!' she cried.

'Well thank you very much! Leave me out of it! If you can't trust me with ten . . . eleven days of your life, I don't want to know!'

'Oh, Nicholas, you simply don't understand, do you?' and she promptly burst into tears.

I sighed loudly, fairly confident that the tears were not entirely genuine. The problem with fights on the phone is that you're on automatic pilot. You can't read the body language, an essential guide when quarrelling with a woman – well, with Anna and Marg, anyway. I'm not saying Anna couldn't conceal her feelings, because she was a master at doing so in a business context, but up close and personal she was less successful. A voice choked with tears is auditory manipulation, but I needed to be able to see her to know how upset she really was and what thoughts she imagined she was hiding from me. After spending much of my adult life with two difficult and complex women,

I'd picked up most of the flicks, ticks, clucks, sighs, gestures and signals that indicated what was really going on. Now I heard Anna's lachrymose gulp, then the shift down to more serious tears, then a moment's pause before the double declutch as she shifted emotional gears. 'You bastard, Nick! Piss off! Go home! Leave me alone! Bugger off! I hate you, I hate you!' Then there was the crunch of rough gear changes ending in a roar of sobbing.

I was flying blind. 'Right then! I'm on tomorrow's flight home,' I said, my voice crisp. I was calling Anna's bluff, taking the chance that I was reading her correctly, that this wasn't the same as the panic attack at the Imperial.

Bang! Down went the receiver. I lay back on the bed in my hotel room and began to count. At one hundred and fifty-three the bedside phone rang. I let it ring six times before reaching for it. 'Hello?' I said, my voice icy calm.

'Nicholas, I want to apologise. Can we start again? Please . . . don't go home, darling. I love you! It's just . . . it's been such a stressful day.' All of this was delivered in a carefully modulated and deeply sincere voice, punctuated with one or two nice little half-tearful gulps.

I confess I was tempted to ask what was so stressful about visiting a series of traditional markets with Miss Sparkle, but I thought better of it and then capitulated as usual. 'I've been here one and a half days, which is enough Expo for any man, but I've always wanted to cycle through the Japanese countryside, stay in the traditional inns, eat the regional food, get out of the urban sprawl and have a good look around in the countryside. Might even buy a butterfly net . . . why not? Should take around ten days . . .'

'Oh, darling Nicholas, thank you, thank you!' Anna cried, as I well knew she would. *Weak bastard!* I thought. Moreover,

I wasn't at all sure Anna hadn't orchestrated the whole thing, or at least extemporised brilliantly and assumed control early on in the argument. So much for my perspicacity; I was armed only with a penknife, fencing with a master swordswoman. Besides, I've never been much good on the phone – one of the reasons Marg works me over so efficiently on her morning calls to Beautiful Bay.

As it turned out the ten days that followed proved to be personally rewarding. Anna and I were not able to stay in touch by phone, which was probably a good thing.

The fondly imagined dreamscapes of Japanese paintings – festoons of pink cherry blossom, temple eaves and red-painted wooden *torii* [gates], a solitary geisha shuffling in wooden clogs along a cobbled lane – don't exist except in Kyoto, where at festival times the dream delivers, and tradition and the old ways somehow endure.

I was to learn that there are two Japans and that this dichotomy isn't, as might be expected, between city and country, urban and rural, but rather between mountains and bumpy valleys. Japan is chock-full of people. Seemingly countless villages are strung together by rice paddies and small green fields, the whole landscape dominated by the exigencies of human life.

To be fair, where I cycled the country could only be described as semi-rural. One was more likely to come across a *pachinko* hall than a temple. Every village seemed to have one of these glitzy gambling parlours, flashing gaudy musk-pink, blue, mauve and green neon. Gambling, so long forbidden in Japan, had reached epidemic proportions. God had been replaced by greed, atmosphere by avarice, temples by *pachinko* parlours, the white-robed Shinto priests by the black suits and sunglasses of the *yakuza*, the tattooed thugs who own or control these ubiquitous gambling joints.

Cycling through the undulating countryside on the first day proved fairly monotonous, and pedalling caused not a little pain to my patched-up bum. A day later I took the advice of an old man selling almonds at the roadside and abandoned my bicycle for a backpack and two bamboo poles, a stout one to use for walking and a long slender one for a butterfly net. I purchased a length of strong but pliable wire, a couple of yards of fine muslin and a packet of nylon fishing line and, as I had done so often before, fashioned a tolerably commendable butterfly net in half an hour. My final purchase was several dozen sheets of paper to fashion my butterfly envelopes, whereupon I headed for the foothills of the higher mountains, some of which still carried more than a dusting of early-spring or late-winter snow.

Japan has 238 species of butterfly and the Osaka area is conspicuous for its fifty-two varieties, none of them particularly rare, but it gave my ramble in the foothills a sense of purpose. Besides, it would be lots of fun. This late in spring, most of the pupae would have hatched.

It was here in the dark shade of beech forests and winding, moss-covered mountain paths that I came across the second Japan of quiet *ryokan* [traditional inns] and tiny Buddhist monasteries, where at either place I might stop to eat an entirely vegetarian meal consisting of dozens of kinds of mushrooms, tofu, rice and many unidentifiable dried foods, some pushed aside after a tentative taste to be attempted at some future time.

During the sunlit days I hunted butterflies, and during those eight memorable nights I stopped at small *ryokan*, soaking myself in the *onsen* [hot springs] that dot the hillsides. I laughed with the people of the foothills and joked about the absurdly small towels one was given to dry oneself. The fastidious Japanese required that you wash yourself thoroughly before entering a spring to have the aches and pains poached out of you in the mineral-rich waters. Beech trees, hot springs and mossy paths are not unique to Japan, nevertheless there was something quintessentially Japanese about lying alone in these silent mountain pools with the steam rising into the dark skies.

After long days chasing around the countryside with a butterfly net, I soaked and relaxed, then spent the early evenings categorising and storing the day's catch in envelopes. Then I rewarded myself with a feast – plates of steaming *gyoza* [steamed or fried dumplings], bowls of *udon* [noodles] and, as a special treat, *sukiyaki* [paper-thin slivers of meat cooked at the table in a rich broth with vegetables and noodles], all of this washed down with copious amounts of sake. Finally, dizzy with fatigue, good food and too much sake, I crawled into my bed, a futon laid out on a *tatami* mat, where I slept soundly, untroubled by thoughts of the Jade House.

After my experiences in Tokyo, and the melee of foreign tourists and Japanese holiday crowds at World Expo in Osaka, the tranquillity of the mountain forests and the ancient traditions of the Japanese people brought a welcome respite. I hadn't realised just how overwrought I'd been.

On my last day in the higher foothills I caught a splendid specimen of *Vanessa indica*, known as the Indian Red Admiral, an entirely new butterfly to add to my collection, despite *Fuchida-san*'s generosity over the years. For a layperson, it was hardly a triumph after ten days' work, but for a serious collector it was well worth every scrape, bruise and scratch.

Then, on the same evening, a fellow hiker, a greying

Japanese doctor who appeared to be in his sixties, turned up at the *ryokan* and, noticing the stitches in my forearm, asked to examine them. 'These need to come out,' he declared.

I grinned. 'They're not alone, doctor.'

'You have more? Let me see, please.'

Hoping to spare him a busman's holiday, I said, 'There is no need. I can wait another few days until I get back to Australia.'

'*Hai!* If they are all like these ones, no, I must take them out now.'

After he'd seen the extent of the damage he laughed. 'How did this happen, *Duncan-san*? Were you running away from a bomb?'

'I sat on a vase,' I replied.

He looked serious for a moment. 'You must be more careful where you sit in future,' he advised, then began to giggle for a full minute.

He refused my offer of payment, but accepted numerous cups of sake accompanied by mutual toasts and the inevitable cries of '*Kampai!*'.

The following morning, back on my bicycle and noticeably fitter despite my hangover, I spent the final day pedalling over unending hillocks and through ubiquitous villages. Towards evening I reached the outskirts of Osaka and followed a flutter of yellow flags to a tiny *minshuku* [bed and breakfast place] where the owner served me a delicious home-cooked meal while her husband sat glued to the TV watching hours of sumo wrestling.

Having eaten and refused the offer of a cup of sake I retired early to my by now accustomed futon set on a *tatami* mat for the night. The following day I handed in my bike and caught the *shinkansen* [bullet train] for the 200 kilometres per hour, three-hour journey to Tokyo. As if by magic, the elusive perfect cone of Mt Fuji chose to reveal itself as we passed, a familiar image from Japanese art.

Nick Duncan, the intrepid boy sailor, teenage jungle explorer and butterfly collector, now cyclist and hill climber, felt brand-new when eventually he arrived back at the Imperial Hotel. As I stepped out of the taxi I was met by the familiar row of hotel flunkies standing to rigid attention, bowing as I passed with the quick mechanical jerk of a string puppet. Shortly afterwards I took a loving Anna, who seemed more than pleased to see me, into my arms. I had not been sufficiently naïve to believe that her renewed acquaintance with Konoe Akira would lead to a miraculous cure, and I would be welcomed home with the gateway to heaven wide open and welcoming. Psychological scars disappear slowly, if at all.

I guess there's nothing better than a reconciled quarrel or a reunion after a separation to heighten the pleasure of sex, and I had both going for me. We made love in our own accustomed non-penetrative fashion, in which we'd long since perfected the art of simultaneous orgasms. Conventional wisdom would have it that this couldn't be entirely satisfactory, but this wasn't true. Anna was such a skilled lover that I had come to see myself as beneficiary rather than victim of her vaginismus.

Lying back in bed afterwards Anna told me the story of the days I had been away.

Anna was to learn that Konoe Akira was still a man of rigid habits and his monthly appointment at the Jade House and the ritual that followed never varied. He traditionally arrived at the house of bondage at exactly ten o'clock in the evening in a powder-blue 1953 Cadillac with whitewall tyres, finned and over-chromed. This monstrous American automobile was driven by Staff Sergeant Goto, who could barely see over the dashboard and who was attired in chauffeur's livery that might have been taken from a Norman Rockwell cover illustration for the *Saturday Evening Post*. Konoe Akira was a great admirer of General Eisenhower, and the car had been purchased to celebrate the election of Dwight D. Eisenhower as president. When Truman had fired the hated autocrat General MacArthur – surrogate emperor of Japan – the whole nation had rejoiced. But when eighteen months later Eisenhower followed Truman as American president, Konoe Akira believed that order had returned to the world once again with a military man at the helm of the world's most powerful nation. The monstrously flamboyant automobile, a vulgar symbol of American prosperity, signalled to him that peace and opportunity had finally arrived in Japan under the watchful eye of a benign and competent general.

The honourable General *Konoe-san*, as he was known at the Jade House, would be met by the Jade Mistress and his regular dominatrix of some years, Lee-Li, a woman in her early forties, who wore a black shantung silk kimono for the occasion. After the usual bowing and compliments, which Konoe Akira accepted with a cursory nod and a '*Humph!*', he would be led by Lee-Li to a small room decorated completely in black where he would spend the entire night, leaving as dawn began to melt the darker shadows in the neighbourhood.

This room had originally been created at his instigation many years previously and he had paid for it personally, although it had subsequently become a feature of the Jade House and was now, unbeknownst to him, often used by some of its other patrons. It was at the very back of the building where a doorway at the end of a passage led out into a narrow lane. Konoe Akira desired absolute darkness but wanted to know he wasn't trapped, a curious contradiction to say the least, since for the most part he was bound, tied and utterly helpless should he ever need to vacate the small room quickly. But the Jade House had long since learned not to question his desires. While he was a stern and uncompromising patron he paid generously and, providing they met his comparatively simple demands, never caused any problems.

Once every year the black room was refurbished at his personal expense. The decor was simple and strictly functional, and every part of the room, from the paper and bamboo walls and ceilings to the *tatami* matting, was black. The futon, slightly raised to accommodate his stiff leg, and the single cushion on one side of a low ebony table in the centre of the room were of black shantung silk. Where the second cushion should have been was a small ebony stool, a concession to Konoe Akira's stiff leg. Neatly folded on the table was a black tourniquet and a single chopstick carved from the black heartwood of a persimmon tree.

The only concession to colour in the monochromatic room was a crystal ashtray on the table with a slightly raised and sandblasted butterfly motif at its centre, beside which, in the summer, rested a yellow and cream frangipani blossom and in the winter a single persimmon.

Konoe Akira had never explained the significance of the butterfly ashtray, or the flower or the fruit, but one summer night he'd entered the room to find the single blossom missing and the ensuing conniption had practically removed the roof. This incident had become part of the folklore of the establishment and numerous stories evolved about the meaning of the tropical blossom and the celestial winter fruit, though none of them were ever authenticated. After twenty-five years, Anna explained their significance.

Miss Sparkle, her friendship with Anna renewed after they'd caught up on events of the last twenty-five years, became Anna's co-conspirator and quickly used her *yakuza* influence to persuade the Jade Mistress to cooperate and to instruct Lee-Li to comply with Anna's instructions. Not that Anna was in the least assertive or pushy. She took the time to win the confidence of *Konoe-san*'s dominatrix and to learn all she could about his proclivities and sexual desires. It had been twenty-five years since she'd last attended to him – a long time to remember his precise requirements – and she needed to be carefully briefed. In that time she had also greatly increased her anatomical knowledge and skill at *kinbaku* and in many of the other aspects of bondage.

'He is difficult to please, *Anna-san*,' Lee-Li had warned.

Anna smiled. 'Nothing has changed I see. Does he have any health problems, for instance, his heart? Varicose veins?'

'Yes. Three months ago he had a chest pain – it's not the first time – also pains in the neck and upper arms. He has special pills. I put one under his tongue and he recovered quickly, but there has been nothing since.'

'Nitroglycerin tablets. Does he have them with him?'

'Always; they are in the little aluminium case he brings with him. But he will stop you if he is not feeling well. With him it must be perfect. And because he is such a perfectionist, he is sensitive to the slightest difference in pressure, so . . .'

'Are you saying he will know the difference between your touch and mine?'

'It could be a problem,' Lee-Li admitted. 'We have a servant girl, a cleaner who enjoys the rope. We use her sometimes to teach the *maiko* and to practise ourselves. If you wish I will demonstrate my technique and the rope sequences with the exact pressures the honourable General *Konoe-san* requires,' she offered.

Miss Sparkle, whose phone duties kept her in the penthouse, was unable to attend any but one of these practice sessions, but she'd marvelled at the blindfolded Anna's dexterous and fluid way with the rope. 'You know more, much more than ever I taught you, *Anna-san*. You are the empress of *kinbaku*. You can make the rope do anything,' she cackled gleefully.

Anna, with the help of the other dominatrix, quickly relearned the sequences and the peculiar technique Konoe Akira required because of his stiff leg, as well as the different posture needed to work on the elevated platform rather than the traditional futon on the floor. They practised the precise timing of the preliminary knot sequence and the number of steps to the platform so that Anna could silently enter the darkened room and take over from the other dominatrix. 'Does he talk?' Anna asked, remembering that in the past *Konoe-san* had occasionally made a specific demand or required a response from her.

'Only very rarely. Just the usual expletives, moans, groans, sighs and cries of pain, then, of course, the climax, after which you must remain still and silent for a count of two hundred before releasing the ropes and handing him his *yukata*. Then you wait until he grunts permission to turn on the light and begin to prepare the morphine,' Lee-Li replied.

Thus Anna discovered that Konoe Akira still required that Lee-Li personally prepare and administer the morphine needle at the conclusion of the bondage session, as he had all those years before when she had been a frightened teenager in Java. She wondered if it was the same small aluminium box containing the syringe and morphine phial, now also the nitroglycerin tablet, that he'd used when she'd administered the drug to him.

Now Anna, who chased the dragon, a different method of allowing her bloodstream to accept opiates, was once again required to learn how to use a syringe. In all her years as an addict she had never injected heroin or given it to anyone else and she had to appeal to Miss Sparkle for help.

The old lady quickly arranged for an older addict roughly the same height and weight as Konoe Akira on whom she could practise, with Anna using the same equipment – phial, syringe, tourniquet and chopstick – Lee-Li used. It took three days until she felt she had sufficiently mastered the technique, the drug addict on each occasion shaking his head and marvelling at the purity of the morphine the *yakuza mama-san* had supplied. At the end of his three-day tenure as guinea pig, Miss Sparkle had given him a further week's supply and sent him off, happy as Larry.

The next evening Konoe Akira arrived in his powder-blue Cadillac, and Anna, dressed in a formal black silk kimono, was concealed in the room next to the black room at the furthermost end of the establishment. Anna's entry was timed precisely from the moment the light went out, when she was to go and stand in the complete dark in the open doorway of Konoe Akira's black room. She would be required to count in a practised cadence to five hundred, by which time the first of the ropes would be in place and she could enter, Lee-Li giving a short staccato cough as a signal.

From her position in the doorway Anna heard the familiar moans and sudden indrawn breaths as the ropes wound and tightened, and almost as she reached the end of her silent count she heard the slight cough, more a clearing of the throat, from Lee-Li. She entered the room, skirting the ebony table as she had practised blindfolded so often over the past week, proceeding silently on bare feet, counting the number of paces. She reached the raised platform and found Lee-Li's hand to take up the rope. It was a near faultless exchange and in case Konoe Akira picked up any sudden disharmony in movement she pulled the rope a fraction tighter, causing him to wince and focus his attention back on himself.

Anna applied herself steadily for half an hour, her pliant fingers massaging and coaxing, working the rope with such subtlety that Konoe Akira cried out in ecstasy or moaned in despair as she punished and rewarded him and after almost an hour built him up gradually to a shattering climax.

When the last ecstatic moan had died to a whimper she began to count, but then realised that Konoe Akira was weeping. She began to undo the ropes, massaging his joints and working his slack penis intermittently until it stood erect once again. He had stopped crying and was now panting, irregularly gasping for breath. She had almost removed the last of the ropes when she heard the distant siren of the approaching ambulance, whereupon she twisted the rope in a configuration around his left hip and scrotum, twisted it, then jerked it so violently that the sudden stab of pain shot up through his thighs and into his chest, causing agony so intense that Konoe Akira screamed as he ejaculated the second time. Anna switched on the light just as he experienced a second excruciating pain, this one brought on by a severe angina attack. Anna had judged it to perfection. He would believe he was dying, whereas she had simply punished his heart sufficiently to bring on the attack. Outside the ambulance siren died and Anna listened for the sound of running footsteps approaching. The ambulance had been a safeguard in case she had misjudged his medical condition.

The honourable General Konoe Akira stared up at her,

his eyes filled with panic and disbelief. He pointed, his hand shaking violently, to the table at the centre of the room upon which rested the small aluminium box. 'T . . . t . . . tablet,' he stammered.

Anna smiled down at him. 'Ah, *Konoe-san*, such a great pity. You have overestimated the strength of the heartwood, the core within that, come what may, cannot be broken,' she said softly. 'Remember this night when you could so easily have been left to die.'

Moments later three ambulance medics burst into the room. 'He requires a nitroglycerin tablet,' Anna said to one of the medics. Then turning on her heels, she left the room.

'Jesus, a heart attack!' I exclaimed when Anna came to the end of the scene at the Jade House. 'Is he okay?'

'Yes, it was only acute angina.'

'You've talked to him in hospital?'

'Yes, the day after, and every day since. This morning before you arrived I went again, and I will go again tomorrow.'

I waited for her to explain further but she remained silent. 'Is that all? A few days ago you saw the bloke for the first time in twenty-five years, you've seen him every day since the angina attack and that's all you have to say – you're going back tomorrow!'

'Nicholas, he's had an angina attack! He's been wired to a monitor, sedated, he has a drip in his arm, and he's a frightened old man. The first day I gave him back the fob watch and showed him the photos of the persimmon trees.'

'And the other three days? What, catching up on old times?'

'Yes, sort of. I'll see him tomorrow – it's his last day in hospital – then perhaps we can get down to business.'

'Business?'

'You know . . . stuff.'

'Why? Why won't you tell me?' I begged.

'It's not how it must seem . . . it's not like before.'

'Oh?'

'He's profoundly sorry.'

'Jesus, Anna! You're the one who is supposed to take no prisoners! The one who waits, knowing the time will always come to even the score. Remember? It's a central tenet of your business philosophy.' I paused, gathering steam. 'It's been twenty-five fucking years and all you can say is that he's *profoundly* sorry!'

'It's not what you think, Nicholas. It didn't turn out the way it was supposed to. You know . . . revenge. I'm frightened you won't understand!'

My heart missed a beat. Oh Jesus, was she back under his spell? 'Try me.'

'Nicholas, you may not like it,' Anna warned, averting her eyes.

On the morning after Konoe Akira's 'heart attack' Anna woke very early, showered and put on a pair of jeans, a white cotton turtleneck sweater and knee-high stiletto boots. She did her hair in the style she'd worn as a sixteen-year-old, applied a light-coloured lipstick and a smudge of green eye shadow. At a distance she could have been mistaken for a woman no older than twenty.

She arrived at Tokyo's University Hospital and had to wait until eight before they would allow her into the recovery ward where Konoe Akira, still sedated, was asleep. She took the chair beside his bed and sat down to wait. Around mid-morning he eventually opened his eyes and stared at her, momentarily confused and fearful, not sure whether she was real or simply a return of the hallucination, part of the blinding pain of a severe angina attack, when she'd suddenly appeared to him out of the darkness. Then his eyes left hers and travelled slowly around the hospital room as if he were still trying to orient himself, pausing momentarily on the heart monitor, the drip bag above his bed, the tube entering the back of his hand and finally returning to her face.

'Second . . . Vase?' he asked, not yet entirely sure, clearing his throat between the two words.

'Good morning, *Konoe-san*. Yes, it is me, Anna,' Anna said in a cheerful voice, her insouciance deliberate.

'Last night?' Konoe Akira croaked. 'It was you?'

Anna laughed, then looked at him, her right eyebrow slightly raised. 'One kidnapping deserves another . . . don't you think?'

Konoe Akira did not react but instead reached for the plastic cup at his bedside and swallowed several mouthfuls of water, pausing after each, his eyes fixed on Anna. He replaced the cup and when he spoke his voice had lost its gravelly, tentative quality. 'You could have killed me.'

'Yes,' Anna answered in a cheerful voice, 'very easily.'

'Then why didn't you? It would have appeared to be a heart attack.'

'It was an angina attack. There's a big difference,' Anna replied, deliberately avoiding his question. 'All it needed was a little bit of encouragement from me and it could well have been a heart attack. The sublime rope has its dark side. Is that not why you come, knowing that it can kill you as well as serve your atavistic needs?' Although her voice was light, she was determined to maintain the initiative.

'You were marvellous, Second Vase. I could not believe it was Lee-Li, but it was too good to question, to stop and find out. You have progressed remarkably since last we knew each other in Tjilatjap. I have never experienced anything quite like it.'

'Thank you.'

Konoe Akira smiled. 'Come to think of it, it wouldn't be a bad way to die. I have not galloped the celestial plains twice in ten minutes since I was a young man.'

Despite herself Anna was forced to laugh. The fearless old soldier was back in control. 'And nearly died as a result! You must be more careful in future whom you choose as your dominatrix.'

Konoe Akira fell silent, thinking. 'When I foolishly had you kidnapped . . . it was an unfortunate experience,' he said clumsily.

'For whom, you or me?' Anna asked.

Konoe Akira looked surprised. 'I have learned my lesson, it was a salutary experience for me.'

'Do I take that as an apology?' Anna was speaking in the Western way with none of the courtesies that might have been affected by a Japanese woman in her speech to a man of Konoe Akira's status.

'It was remiss . . . yes, remiss of me.'

'Remiss! Five men died horrible deaths, my partner was badly injured from the accident with the vase and spent two nights in a police cell . . .' Anna was lost for further words.

Konoe Akira appeared not to be listening. 'The vase . . . very regrettable. The stitches will heal but the celestial beauty of a thousand years has gone forever.'

'Why? Why did you do it?' Anna asked angrily, then unable to help herself added, 'It was not worthy of you!'

Konoe Akira appeared to be reaching for the right words but then quite suddenly abandoned the attempt. 'Yes, you are correct, it was the insecurity of a stupid old man. I wanted to be sure we met on my terms. I never intended that you be held for more than a few hours. I was doublecrossed by the Shield Society. We had agreed they would hold you only until the morning, but they saw an opportunity to get more money from me. I had seen the whole thing as little more than a warning not to attempt anything that might indict me, but it went horribly wrong.'

'You did it to show me you were still powerful? Could still control me if you wished? Why, that's pathetic!'

Konoe Akira, glancing down at his hands resting on his lap, was silent for some time, but Anna held her ground, insisting on an answer. 'Yes, it was most reprehensible, Second Vase,' he said finally.

'Anna! My name is Anna!' She looked at him scornfully. 'Let me see now . . . we have *salutary*, *remiss*, *regrettable* and *reprehensible*, but we still don't have the simplest word of them all. We don't have *sorry*!'

Konoe Akira looked up and held Anna's eyes. 'Why did you not kill me? It would have been easy – a heart attack during *kinbaku* – you would not have been suspected. I am fairly certain it has happened to someone before. Instead, you had the ambulance standing by.' He smiled tiredly. 'I could have you arrested for deliberately causing grievous bodily harm. It would not be a difficult case to bring to the prosecutor, eh?'

'Would this then be another attempt to show me how powerful you are?' Anna said lightly, refusing to take him seriously. 'I had no desire to see you dead but you placed me in great danger without much thought and now you know how that feels. By the way, I am told you have had angina attacks before. You may need a heart bypass operation. It is a new technique, but very successful; your heart specialist is sure to know about it. They probably perform it at this very hospital.'

'Aha, I see, so you are an expert with hearts then, a doctor maybe? That is why you knew what you were doing!'

'Yes, I knew, but I'm not a doctor in *kinbaku*. At the highest levels it is a matter of knots and pressure. I know about the heart bypass operation from a friend who also suffered from acute angina and has undergone the new procedure with great results. If the ambulance hadn't been so prompt I'd have given you the nitroglycerin tablet myself. You were never going to die, *Konoe-san*.'

'So, why have you come here today, *Anna-san*? Is it to mock me?'

Anna flicked her hair impatiently. '*Titch!* I have brought you back your fob watch and chain and I have the photographs to show you of the twenty-four persimmon trees we have planted up to this time.'

'And that is all?'

'There is something else, but it can wait until you are feeling well again.'

Anna opened her handbag and withdrew the gold fob watch she'd given him as a farewell gift all those years ago. It had been her father's and before that her grandfather's. She placed it on the bedside cupboard beside the empty plastic cup, thinking that this time he might not see it as the loving gift she had bestowed on him all those years ago. After what had transpired between them he might not even want to accept it.

But Konoe Akira surprised her by saying softly, 'Thank you. I have always cherished it. It has a special place in my life, more precious even than the lost vase.' He picked up the watch and chain and laid it on the sheet covering his stomach, then closed his hand around the beautiful old chronometer.

Next Anna took out four colour prints. Selecting the first she leaned over and showed it to him, saying, 'This is the first one. I had to wait five years to find the perfect place on a beautiful island in the South Pacific. See, it is already a mature tree and fruits abundantly – beautiful golden orbs – even though, as you know, there is no winter in the tropics, only the dry season.' She selected the second photograph, a depiction of a seedling no more than a few centimetres tall, standing twin-leaved against the dark soil. 'This is the latest, number twenty-four. It was planted on my birthday last year. I always plant the seed myself and say something in Japanese, then we open a bottle of champagne.' The third photograph showed the driveway at Beautiful Bay with all the trees in leaf in descending size, and the fourth showed the same view but with those trees large enough now in fruit, their leaves having dropped, the branches witch-broomed against a pewter-coloured sky.

Anna avoided looking at Konoe Akira, aware that her commentary was self-conscious and that Konoe Akira might simply be looking at the photographs in order to be polite. After all, the gift of eighty-five persimmon seeds, which he'd given her in the garden of the Dutch brewer's mansion he'd occupied as commander at Tjilatjap in 1945, may have long since been forgotten, at the time a sentimental gesture to a young girl and no more. Although he had made specific mention of his desire to see the photographs in his earlier note sent to the Imperial Hotel, this could have been part of his planned entrapment. But now she glanced up at him to see that silent tears were rolling down his cheeks. 'What can I say, Second Vase?'

Anna did not correct him this time. 'The butterfly ashtray and the frangipani blossom at the Jade House . . . they tell me the blossom is replaced with a persimmon in the winter. Is that . . .' Anna hesitated, 'because of Tjilatjap?'

In a gesture of defeat the old general nodded, sighed, then raised and dropped his hands back onto the sheet. 'I have thought about you most days of my life since the day I sailed from the wharf at Tjilatjap when I knew that I would never again know another creature as perfect. I have bowed and clapped at my family shrine every morning since returning to Japan, burned incense on the anniversary of my sailing away and said your name while asking the gods to take care of you if you remained alive. I later heard what Colonel Takahashi, that miserable *kempeitai* mongrel street dog, did to you before he committed suicide and then, upon later reflection, what I, no better than he, thinking myself infinitely your superior, had already done to you. Then I realised that I deserved no better myself.'

'It was not the same,' Anna protested. 'You . . . he . . .' She did not explain that she had killed Takahashi before he could deflower her.

'Nevertheless, total power corrupts and we Japanese, more than most people, are historically guilty of abusing power, especially in recent times in China and Manchuria, and of course in the Pacific. Arrogance is the handmaiden to cruelty and I pray to the gods that Japan will not go down that path again, although both characteristics die hard with us and the hindsight that is called history turns the ignoble into the justifiable and then ultimately into the noble. At last we are learning that we are not the master race. The Emperor himself has declared that he is not a living god. You could have taken your opportunity last night to kill me without consequences, but you did not and I am grateful, if only for the opportunity to say that of the two of us you are the noble one and I am the one to be despised.'

Now that it had finally come, Anna saw that his apology was profound. 'If I had thought in this way about you I would not have come to Japan, honourable *Konoe-san*,' Anna said quietly. 'While our early relationship has resulted in some difficulties, it has also produced some very good results. Life is chance and circumstance and I have suffered and benefited equally from both.'

Konoe Akira looked surprised. 'You do not hate me, *Anna-san*? My heart was filled with terror that you had come to Japan to expose me, though not to the war tribunal – that shame is long since over – but to my family, to my daughters and my precious grandchildren, to my aged mother, although her time is now also past and she often forgets I am her son. This shame on my family name I would have found unendurable.' He paused and looked directly at Anna. 'That is why I sought to warn you with the foolish kidnapping arranged with those reactionaries and rightwing misfits in the Shield Society.'

'Some stains endure but most come out in the wash,' Anna replied in an attempt to comfort him. 'I am glad we have talked it out. Now you must rest. Will it be convenient to visit you again tomorrow?'

'By all means. My daughters will come and my grandchildren, but only in the afternoon when the children are home from school. Will you come in the morning?'

'Yes, I would enjoy that. We will be leaving Japan soon and there is one more matter I would like to discuss with you, *Konoe-san.*'

'Is it about the past?'

Anna shook her head. 'We cannot undo the past, *Konoe-san.* But maybe we can use the future to try to heal it.'

'What? What can I do? If it is possible I will do it, Second Vase.'

'It is about business. I wish to talk to you about a business matter.'

'Why, I'm intrigued.' He grinned. '*Hai!* You are not a doctor or a dominatrix, you are now a businesswoman. This I can understand.' He bowed his head. 'Goodbye, *Anna-san.* I look forward to tomorrow.'

'You didn't talk about the past, the war, what he did to you, the psychological scarring?' I asked, astonished.

Anna cocked her head and looked at me. 'The lamentation of poor little Anna? And what possible good would that do, Nicholas?'

'Cleared the air! The bastard owes you!'

'Yes, I agree. He owes me. I have a business proposition I don't believe he can refuse.'

'Jesus, Anna, that's crass. This is not about money! What about us?'

'Oh there's definitely something tangible in this for you, Nicholas,' she said, deliberately misconstruing my meaning.

'I *don't* mean fucking business!'

'Nicholas, there are no pieces to pick up, no road to

Damascus, no epiphany. But there is something to gain from all this.'

I sighed, unable to believe my own ears. I'd had too many Anna versus Konoe Akira dialogues in my head for far too long and what I was hearing was definitely not one of them. 'Christ, Anna, can't you see? He kidnapped you, he meant to harm you and all you've been discussing with him for the past four days is business?'

Anna, unruffled, affected a surprised expression. 'Why, Nicholas, you came here to buy two freighters, that's business, isn't it?'

'Yes, but I didn't have a different agenda.'

'Ah, but as soon as those two middle executives at Mitsubishi tried to cheat you, things changed?'

'Yeah, jumped-up little pricks!'

'But, in the end, who won the day?'

'Yeah, we did, and mostly thanks to you, but what are you suggesting?'

Anna ignored the question. 'In the end you got two freighters for nearly the price of the new one?'

'Yeah . . .'

'Why was that?'

'We tricked them. They thought we didn't understand Japanese.'

'No.'

'What then?'

'We didn't react predictably. We didn't lose our cool. When the tape recording was replayed to whomever afterwards, it was obvious that Mitsubishi had lost a great deal of face and needed to make restitution. The rest you know – two ships for the price of one.'

'Anna, this is not the same!'

'Oh? Why not? If I'd screamed and shouted, cried, stamped my foot, accused, threatened, blamed Konoe Akira for everything, what do you think would have happened? No, don't tell me, you know already – an hysterical woman creating a scene in a Japanese hospital room. They'd have thrown me out on my ear then given *Konoe-san* a sedative and that would have been it. I'd have had my say and he'd wake up thinking he'd endured my outburst, I'd got it all off my chest, he'd tolerated my emotional hysteria, it was just women's stuff, a storm in a teacup, he'd repaid any debt and now he could get on with his life as usual.'

Anna looked at me questioningly, expecting a reaction. 'C'mon, Anna, you're not the hysterical type. You might seem to lose your temper, but you wouldn't have lost your cool. You'd have given it to him straight between the eyes, chapter and verse, left him understanding exactly what he'd done to you.'

'Maybe, but with exactly the same result. I'm a woman and he's a Japanese man, that's not an equal contest in this country. I've consoled myself that I've had *Konoe-san* at my mercy and could easily have killed him had I wished to do so. He'll always know that, know that I could have taken the ultimate revenge but chose not to.'

'Hell, Anna, you must have been tempted. I know I would have been.'

Anna paused and shrugged. 'But what would that have done to me? I would have killed another person, this time in cold blood. Try convincing yourself that natural justice has been served, that you had every right to murder him.' She looked at me directly. 'Would you *really* have killed him?'

'No, I suppose not, not in cold blood. I agree, scaring the shit out of him the way you did was a stroke of genius. But is that enough? One visit to the hospital the next morning to let him know you could have snuffed him out and to tell him why you did it, then forget him forever. Isn't that why we came, to remove his power over you and, if possible, humiliate him? He told you himself, revealing the truth to his family was his greatest fear.'

'Confronting my so-called nemesis and humiliating him isn't going to cure me, Nicholas. I'm tired of all the bullshit, the psychological twaddle. "With Konoe Akira's demise I pronounce you cured! Abracadabra, you've got your sex life back, Anna!" There isn't going to be a miraculous cure, Nicholas. But now maybe I can put this whole thing behind me and get on with my life, knowing I had the means and the opportunity to kill him but chose not to do it. My choice this time! My decision. Maybe, just maybe, if my head is in the right place, this knowledge could eventually lead to a cure!' Anna paused for breath before saying, 'But I don't know. In the meantime there may be something to gain in all of this,' she hesitated, 'if I keep my cool.'

I guess there wasn't a lot I could say after all that. 'So, okay, maybe put that way I'm forced to agree, but not with the last bit, the business . . . the something to be gained bit. Anna, you're fraternising with the enemy. Can't you see, having won, you're setting yourself up all over again? Having once beaten the devil you don't sit down and calmly negotiate another term in hell!'

'Oh, Nicholas, don't be so bloody melodramatic, the two things are totally separate. This is fishing for stars.'

'What the fuck does that mean?'

'It means an opportunity so big that you could never, under any circumstances, have achieved it without the planets aligning three ways in exactly the right configuration.' Anna's eyes shone with excitement. 'I have to try and pull it off! If I don't, then I'll never get another chance like this again.'

I sighed. 'You'll have to explain.'

'Yes, of course. While you've been away, Miss Sparkle and I have had a long discussion and a good look around the fish markets in Tokyo. I've also, as you are aware, talked at some length over the past four days with Konoe Akira.'

'Miss Sparkle? How is she involved?'

'Nicholas, please, let me finish. She *is* involved, and there's an opportunity to make something out of this; yes, a *business* opportunity that virtually allows us to control Japanese fishing in the South Pacific!'

'That's why you've been talking incessantly about fish, is it? You first mentioned it when I called from Osaka. This business is about *fish*!'

'Bravo!' Anna replied, not without a tinge of sarcasm.

'You've planned this all along, haven't you? Like the Nauru House building site. Now I see it all. That's why you wanted to accompany me to Japan!'

'Don't be an absolute bastard, Nicholas! No, I *hadn't* planned it all along! No, it *isn't* why I came to Japan with you,' Anna cried. 'That's a *horrible, horrible* thing to say!' She looked at me coldly and said, 'You were kind enough to invite me to accompany you, and while I've enjoyed some aspects of being your handbag there have been other parts of your business trip I can't say have been quite as rewarding for me.'

'Ouch!'

Anna, having punished me, immediately calmed down. In a quiet and reasonable voice she said, 'Nicholas, you agreed that my presence at Mitsubishi was helpful, now I need you to help me.'

'How?'

'Have lunch with Konoe Akira.'

Shocked, but trying not to show it, I said, 'I'll have to think about it.' Then I realised I was being a deadshit and said, 'Anna, gimme a break, will ya? I want us to get out of this bloody country! It's been nothing but bad news from the moment we met those two pricks at Mitsubishi. You've seen Konoe Akira every day since his attack. Isn't that enough fraternisation without us having to have lunch with the bastard?'

CHAPTER TWELVE

'By the way, I have good news.
I know you've been worried,
but I've squared things with the yakuza.
We're quits, we owe them nothing.'
Anna, Tokyo

LYING IN BED THE following morning Anna asked, 'Nicholas, can we go home the day *after* tomorrow? It's only one more day. Surely that's okay?'

'Didn't you say you were having lunch with him today? What's wrong with going home tomorrow?'

'No, the lunch is tomorrow. Konoe Akira comes out of hospital today. You will come, won't you, Nicholas?'

'Whoa, Anna! I've thought about it. I'm not sure it's such a good idea.'

'He wants . . . he's very anxious to meet you.'

'We've already met.'

'Nicholas, don't be a smart arse!'

'More like a sore arse! Still, I'm not sure. Why don't you go alone? As you so often say, I have no head for business.'

Anna raised herself onto one elbow. 'No, really! C'mon, Nicholas, you're being churlish.'

I sat up, pushing the pillow into the small of my back. 'Anna, I've thought about it for half the night. What you did – the way you've handled this whole thing – was remarkable.' I looked over at her. 'I *really* mean that. Bloody brilliant! But it doesn't change how I feel personally about Konoe Akira. I can't stop you being a part of whatever this proposition is, this fishing thing, but I don't have to be involved. As far as I'm concerned it's dining with the devil. You go for your life, darling, but leave me out of it.'

'Nicholas, don't be a bastard. It's important you be there,' Anna insisted.

'Sweetheart, when I think of what he did to you, all I want to do is smash his buckteeth down his throat! This lunch – it's your idea, isn't it?'

'No, honestly, it was his.' She reached out and pushed me with the butt of her hand, '*And* that's racist! He doesn't have buckteeth!'

'Christ, Anna, I don't see the point! He has every reason to loathe me. I've got many more to despise him, including most recently a barely healed arse and bruised bollocks! Why are we having this lunch?'

'I told you! It's an interesting proposition. Besides, I thought you'd be curious.'

'Curious! Jesus! I woke him up in the small hours of the morning with a pistol at his head, dressed him, frogmarched him through his own home, sat on his precious Korean vase and had the old bastard practically spitting in my face! Isn't that up close and personal enough for one trip?'

'He's not like that; there's another side to his personality,' Anna pleaded.

'Christ, I should hope so. What are you saying? That you've come to admire this arsehole?'

Anna didn't answer. 'Please, Nicholas, will you do it for my sake? It's very important.'

'Important? How? As you've said before, it isn't going to lead to a miracle cure. *That* would have been important; the rest is bullshit!'

'You can be a real bastard sometimes, Nicholas. For once it's not personal, not about you and him. It's a business opportunity you'd be a fool to pass up.'

'Then count me a fool. If you lie down with a dog you'll get up with fleas. Business? Fuck business!'

'What's that supposed to mean? Are you suggesting this is somehow shonky?'

'Anna, we've all got to make choices in life, shonky or squeaky clean. I don't want any part of it!'

'Nick! Will you stop being so bloody sanctimonious! You haven't even heard the proposition!' Anna flicked her hair back. She now sat bolt upright, her legs crossed under her. Her use of 'Nick' together with her rigid body language was sufficient to warn me that she was readying for another fight. 'At least come to the lunch, then. If you feel the same way, well, okay.'

I sighed. What we didn't need was another row. Keeping my voice calm I said, 'Anna, honestly, why would I want to go into business with Konoe Akira? For that matter, even have lunch with him? We're never going to be friends.'

'Nicholas, that's not a reasonable thing to say! I keep telling you it's not . . . he's not like that. Don't be such a drama queen! If you don't like what he has to say, well, what have we lost?'

I shook my head. 'Okay, I agree to stay another day in Japan. But you have your lunch with the devil and I'll take the opportunity to see Gojo Mura.'

I could see she was suddenly furious. I'd switched tack and

caught her by surprise. *Here it comes, the shit is about to hit the fan.* But just as suddenly the tears appeared and Anna looked at me appealingly, irresistibly beautiful. 'I need you in on this, Nicholas. This lunch could change my life forever,' she said softly. 'Please, I beg you!'

I sighed. *Perfidious women – how may a man ever hope to win?* 'Okay, we'll have *your* lunch, but I'm not "in" on anything, understand? Assume nothing, bugger all.' I looked at her sternly. 'I mean it, Anna.'

Anna nodded. 'Thank you,' she said quietly, then untangling her legs she rose to her knees and leaned forward and kissed me, then grabbed a pillow and bashed me over the head. 'Come on, big boy, if you're prepared to stand up for me I'll decide if the result merits going down on you.' She giggled.

What can you do? 'As Uncle Joe would say, "Get ready, now, honey! Dat big one-eye snake he gonna give yoh a kiss on yoh sweet sugar lips you ain't nevah gonna forget, baby doll!'

'Nicholas! That's disgusting!' Anna smiled. 'Did Joe really say that?' She'd started to work her magic, using the soft pads of her unusually talented fingers and thumb.

'How the hell would I know,' I laughed, utterly defeated, sensing it had been no contest all along. Anna had long since perfected the means of getting her own way and, as she was now demonstrating, I was mere putty rapidly firming up in her pliant hands.

Lunch with Konoe Akira was at a restaurant that served *fugu*. Only the Japanese could come up with a culinary experience that involves a deadly poison. Let me explain. The speciality of the house was the toxic puffer fish, a species I learned to avoid as a child in New Britain, where everyone knew, *Fish him belong devil*. There is some evidence that the puffer fish contains the world's second most deadly poison, and the Japanese, with their predisposition for dangerous thrillseeking, have made an art of challenging this toxic fish to kill them. The most poisonous variety, and therefore the most expensive, is known as *torafugu*. *Hai!* What fun. Nothing quite as exciting as knowing that your next bite might be your last. What's more, you will not simply die, but die a horrible death, the poison causing paralysis so that you perish from asphyxiation while remaining fully conscious. Every year, several people in Japan die after eating at a *fugu* restaurant, an expensive and potentially fatal experience.

Young apprentice *fugu* chefs learn the extremely complex method of removing the poison as well as the many different ways to serve the fish. The final test of their skill couldn't be simpler. First prepare your puffer fish, then eat it in front of the examiner. If you die, sorry you failed. Next apprentice please.

Eating puffer fish has been a traditional challenge since time out of mind and here is the paradox: it isn't an acquired taste, it is simply a dull one – it tastes like mush. While it can be served up in dozens of different ways, it is the added ingredients that bring flavour to the dish, not the fish itself. The same ingredients added to almost any other variety of fish would give it a more agreeable taste than *fugu*.

I well understood the dangers of eating *fugu* – as usual the information came from the bishop – but I decided to say nothing to Anna and to see if Konoe Akira might drop it casually into the conversation. Perhaps he thought of it as some sort of Japanese one-upmanship, or a test of our courage?

We took a taxi to the restaurant and Anna made no comment as we passed through the door, above which hung the traditional square lantern with a puffer fish etched and illuminated on the glass. No doubt she thought it was simply the sign for a fish restaurant.

We were ushered through the busy public area to a private room where *Konoe-san* waited for us, seated not on the floor, as I had expected in a traditional Japanese restaurant, but on one of three chairs, perhaps a concession to his stiff leg, or perhaps to our stiff Western knees. He rose with some difficulty, propping himself up with his cane and bowing to Anna and then, hesitating just a moment too long, smiled and extended his hand to me. 'Welcome, *Duncan-san*. We meet again,' he said, nodding his head in a semblance of a bow.

'Thank you,' I replied smiling, then added, 'I see you warned them to frisk me at the front door.' It was a bad joke in poor taste, but Konoe Akira didn't miss a beat.

'A Browning automatic – the best,' he chuckled. Love–fifteen to Konoe Akira as Anna's startled look faded when he reacted positively. Love–thirty to Konoe Akira. Afterwards she castigated me, pointing out that I had risked offending him, upsetting everything only moments after we'd met.

'It's establishing terms, male dogs bum-sniffing,' I'd explained.

'Stupid little boys,' she'd replied, unimpressed.

The Konoe Akira who now stood facing me in the *fugu* restaurant seemed very different from the confused elderly man I'd accosted in his flannel nightshirt when I'd held a pistol to his head. Somehow he seemed taller and his crew-cut steel grey hair, sharp brown eyes and straight prominent nose gave him a hawk-like appearance, the look of a man not to be taken lightly. He had the slightly gaunt face I associated with a judge, the headmaster of a famous school, a senior bureaucrat or, I suppose, the general he had once been. He was as slender as *Kinzo-san* and dressed in a similar way, in an expensive light-grey woollen pinstriped double-breasted suit, cream silk shirt and plain navy silk tie, although he hadn't permitted himself the levity of a flamboyantly displayed breast-pocket handkerchief as had Doctor Honda, and the highly polished toecaps of his black leather shoes were straight out of the army officer's dress manual. While he was a man in his mid-sixties, and therefore not considered old, pain had etched lines down from his mouth and from the corners of his eyes to make him look ten years older. Obviously his smashed knee and permanently straightened leg continued to trouble him and the drugs he took to assuage the constant pain had left its mark. Moreover, he'd just recovered from a severe angina attack.

He grunted when Anna impulsively took his arm as he awkwardly seated himself, whether from displeasure at being helped or in recognition of her consideration it was impossible to tell. His composed expression gave nothing away.

Anna, wearing a new navy blue Coco Chanel suit with narrow pink piping she must have bought while I was in Osaka, high-heeled black court shoes, and her diamond earrings, had barely said a word since we'd entered. Now seated, she unfolded her napkin, placed it carefully and silently on her lap, looked up and smiled, saying, 'Well, here we are. [Sigh.] Who would have thought?'

I could sense that the perfectly poised public Anna was very nervous at the thought of her lover and the man who had managed to manipulate her young mind coming together at last.

'I am honoured that you have arranged it so, *Anna-san*,' Konoe Akira said, putting the lie to her claim that the luncheon was his idea.

I'm ashamed to admit that the best I could manage initially was an inane smile, but then just before my silence began to appear sullen I snatched a handful of initiative and signalled, then called to the waiter. 'Sake, please!' I thus indicated that we would be paying for the lunch and avoided the uncomfortable silence that had been developing.

The waiter arrived promptly and poured sake into two tiny blue porcelain cups. Japanese women don't customarily drink alcohol, so he looked surprised when I indicated he should pour a third for Anna. As soon as he finished, I turned to Anna and then to Konoe Akira, saying, 'May I propose a toast?'

'Of course!' They both smiled and the tension seemed to ease somewhat. Then taking up the tiny cups I pronounced, 'To a future less troubled.'

We chorused, 'Kampai!' and swallowed the contents of the tiny cups in one gulp, whereupon the hovering waiter immediately began to refill them. Anna indicated that she was no longer a participant in what was to become a competition between the old bull and the young bull, and which I might be permitted to say I think I won. The practice I'd gained with the doctor who'd removed my stitches in the ryokan where I'd spent my last night among the mountain beeches proved invaluable. Thus, in the age-old manner of man and boy I earned my stripes, even though I hardly qualified as a boy. But I was twenty years younger than Konoe Akira and a foreigner drinking sake in a country where one's capacity to drink large amounts without being rendered comatose is admired. Becoming intoxicated in Japanese society is essentially a masculine pursuit and, like so much other intemperate male behaviour, is tolerated by the society. In fact drunks, provided their behaviour is not too appalling, are treated indulgently. I felt I had to earn some respect for my drinking ability at least.

The multiple courses began to arrive, all of them simply different ways of serving the potentially poisonous fish. With the first, Konoe-san asked, 'Do you know this fish?

It is called *fugu*.'

'Puffer fish,' I replied. 'In the islands it is known to contain a deadly poison. Is it the same fish?' I replied, knowing of course that it was.

Anna looked down at the serving in front of her and then at me, her expression perplexed, chopsticks poised hesitantly.

'It is the same here; one mouthful can kill you,' *Konoe-san* grinned.

Anna put down her chopsticks and looked in turn at each of us. 'What's going on?' she asked.

Konoe Akira seemed genuinely amused. 'It is the reason I brought you here,' he explained, his eyes suddenly alight.

'What? To poison us?' Anna asked tentatively, then as quickly realised that this couldn't be true or he would have let her partake of the poisoned fish before alerting her. 'It's a joke? A dare?' she suggested with a second questioning smile.

'No, it is a symbolic gesture I wish to make.' Noticing Anna's cast-aside chopsticks he indicated her plate. 'Please eat. It is quite safe. It has been thirty years since anyone perished in this restaurant.' Then resuming he said, 'A symbolic gesture of loyalty, friendship and mutual benefit.'

It's a bit early for that, mate, I thought to myself. *You've single-handedly fucked up Anna's life and indirectly much of my own. Friendship? Ha! You can kiss my arse!* But I was here at Anna's behest and told myself this wasn't an appropriate time to be deliberately recalcitrant or even churlish. On the other hand I certainly wasn't going to go out of my way to be charming. *Fuck him! I'll play my part, no more.* Knowing the chances of being poisoned by eating *fugu* were pretty bloody slim I picked up my chopsticks and tasted the fish while waiting for Konoe Akira to continue.

'Please, if you will indulge an old man, perhaps I

may explain?' Konoe Akira indicated to the hovering waiter to fill my sake cup yet again and then his own, continuing to talk while the waiter completed the task. 'When I was a young man at the Tokyo Military Academy,' he began, 'at the end of every month I, together with six of my closest friends, fellow trainee officers, would go to a cooking school close to the academy where they trained the young *fugu* apprentices.' He lifted his sake cup and waited for me to do the same. We downed the contents and the waiter immediately refilled the cups as Konoe Akira continued. 'We would each select a first-year apprentice and have him prepare a particular *fugu* dish for each of us. Then our personally chosen apprentice, who would remain our choice until we graduated one year and seven months later, would bring in his dish and place it in front of whoever had selected him, so that seven variations of *fugu* arrived at the same time. As you see on your plate, each *fugu* variation is divided into seven pieces and arranged in the shape of a chrysanthemum in honour of our emperor and the chrysanthemum throne. Each of us would then keep one section of our fish and the other six would be placed on the plates of each of my six comrades who would do the same until we each had a chrysanthemum consisting of seven different variations of *fugu* fish, a portion of everyone's chosen dish on our plates.'

'The opposite to Russian roulette!' I smiled, the sake beginning to work its magic.

'Exactly! If one of us died, we all died.'

'Oh my God!' Anna exclaimed, then, regaining her composure said, 'Why are boys so stupid?'

'Well, I guess none of you died or you wouldn't be here, *Konoe-san*,' I said, unimpressed.

Konoe Akira chuckled, acknowledging my point, then

said, 'I imagine the supervising chef watched the apprentices very, very closely.' He smiled wryly. 'To lose seven young officer recruits from noble families would most assuredly have closed down the cooking school. Food is important in Japan, but the military at that time was paramount. Notwithstanding all that, having survived and believing we'd undergone a critical test of courage, we felt like heroes in the tradition of the Samurai.'

'Like the three musketeers, one for all and all for one,' I quoted in my newly acquired sake-charged voice. By this time we'd downed our sixth sake and our third portion of the world's dullest-tasting fish.

'Exactly,' Konoe Akira said and, without turning to face the waiter who stood no more than three feet away, commanded in a loud voice, 'Waiter! More sake! At once!' I was comforted by the thought that the rice wine was getting to him as well.

We waited for him to continue, but while we were being subjected to another round he seemed to have temporarily lost his train of thought. Hardly surprising. It was probably insanity for him to drink the day after leaving hospital after an angina attack, another example of foolish masculine derring-do.

'You were saying, you brought us to a *fugu* restaurant as a symbol?' Anna prompted.

'Yes, that's right, of loyalty and friendship,' he said, suddenly recollecting himself. 'It is what I hoped might develop between the three of us today.'

Anna, grabbing the opportunity, now said, 'We, you and I, discussed a business proposition while Nicholas was away, *Konoe-san*. Perhaps you might care to outline its main features to *Duncan-san*?'

Konoe-san turned to me. 'I congratulate you, *Duncan-san*. Second Vase . . . er . . . *Anna-san* has an excellent grasp of business.'

Only in Japan would a man be congratulated for his female partner's business prowess or intelligence. 'Her grasp of business is well beyond my own,' I replied.

Konoe Akira looked at me as if I were being deliberately modest. '*Anna-san* tells me you have a shipping line in the South Seas?'

'Yes, the South Pacific.'

'But that is a very significant business achievement, *Duncan-san*,' he said. 'I think you are being too humble.'

Don't patronise me, you bastard! The sake was overcoming my willingness to restrain myself and I had to make a real effort. 'We are small. Anna calls it "Boys playing with boats". She is a remarkable businesswoman; I am not in her class.' I grinned, then somewhat ambiguously said, 'You are fortunate she is in charge. If you were dealing with me you wouldn't get too far.'

Whether Konoe Akira sensed my hostility I couldn't say.

'So! Let me tell you about us, *Duncan-san*. We are in fishing. It has been a family concern for five hundred years, but of course, now we are a *zaibatsu*, a group. After Mitsubishi, we are the second largest fleet in Japan. We have eighty deep-sea fishing boats, and many smaller ones that operate in the shallow waters off the Southern Kuril Islands.'

'But don't those islands belong to Russia?' I asked.

Konoe Akira sighed. 'They belong to Japan, but were stolen by Russia at the end of the war.'

'And you still fish their waters?'

'It is by arrangement.'

'With the Russian government?'

'It is an arrangement,' Konoe Akira persisted. 'Water must find its own way from the mountains to the sea.'

'Japanese proverb?'

'No, commonsense. Sometimes arrangements work

better than treaties. Governments must consider lots of extraneous factors. Wisely they sometimes allow things to take a natural course.' He paused, looking directly at me. 'Now that many of the Pacific Islands are becoming independent, we would like to make a contribution to their future welfare, *Duncan-san*.'

'Contribution?' I knew what was coming but wasn't willing to acknowledge it too readily. 'That can be done through your government as foreign aid without the river having to change its course.'

'Yes . . . that is *also* possible,' he said, hesitating slightly. 'As chairman of my *zaibatsu* I am honoured to sit on various government boards that control the fishing industry and am not without influence in matters of foreign aid.' He called for another round of sake. 'But what I am suggesting is perhaps something more direct, like the Southern Kuril Islands.'

I had forced him to come out into the open and say it. 'What form would this contribution take?' I asked.

'*Konoe-san* is suggesting a joint venture,' Anna interjected quickly.

Despite myself, I laughed. 'We have eight freighters,' then remembering the two we'd just purchased from Mitsubishi I amended it, 'ten . . . ten freighters. They are all used for cargo and passenger transport – two are mainland vessels, strictly cargo, most are pretty old and none are equipped for deep-sea fishing . . . any kind of fishing for that matter.'

'*Konoe-san*'s *zaibatsu* is interested in establishing three tuna-processing plants,' Anna continued. 'The South Pacific is the next big fishing opportunity – tuna and shark fins. They won't require your freighters. Understand, Nicholas, this is an entirely new joint venture. They want the sole licence to fish within the coastal areas of each of the island nations.'

'But we know nothing about processing fish.'

'You knew nothing about scrap metal, or running an inter-island shipping fleet either.'

'Yeah, true, but we were a lot younger then. I'm not sure we'd be comfortable —'

'Comfortable? Business is seldom comfortable unless you possess a monopoly.' Anna flicked her hair back in a gesture of impatience. 'Don't you see, Nicholas, that's virtually what this would be, a three-way agreement: *Konoe-san's zaibatsu*, the island government concerned and yourselves. You wouldn't have to know anything about processing fish; *Konoe-san's* people will do that. They will run the fish factories – I mean, processing plants.'

'And we'd do what?'

'Build the infrastructure, the port facilities, and operate them, run the local labour force, the things Joe Popkin does on his ear, and your job would be to liaise with the government, be responsible for labour relations, keep in touch with both sides on the ground.'

'And all this will result in a profit for the three of us?'

'Of course. If *Konoe-san's zaibatsu* has an exclusive fishing licence for the fishing zones it will be very profitable for all concerned.'

'And I would be the one required to kick open the doors?'

'Not kick, Nicholas, facilitate,' Anna said, giving me a reproving look.

'I know nothing about "facilitating", as you so nicely put it, Anna. We've always been upfront, what you see is what you get,' I replied pompously.

'Don't be ridiculous! You do it all the time. Isn't that the point? It's open, it's honest, they trust you.'

'I wouldn't begin to know how to negotiate a deal such as this one.'

'You wouldn't have to, I will do the negotiating.'

I looked at her, surprised. 'But you said you'd never go into business with me . . . with us?'

Anna laughed, obviously amused. 'Certainly not. I love you too much, Nicholas.' She turned and smiled at Konoe Akira. 'I will be the independent go-between, negotiate the licences, agreements, protocol between Japan and the governments of the countries involved. All you will do is open the doors for me, make the necessary introductions. Remember, these are new island governments, still wet behind the ears. They'll need guidance and expertise. You've known all the main players involved since they were schoolboys; you and Joe can help enormously.'

'To see they don't get ripped off?'

'No, Nicholas, nobody gets *ripped off*! The whole idea is to create a sound business relationship between Japan and the island nations.'

'I'm not at all sure about this. It sounds like a monopoly, and it seems to me most monopolies end up as greedopolies, taking more than they ever return to any economy. Witness the British Phosphate Commission in Nauru, for instance.'

Konoe Akira suddenly cut in. 'If all the other fishing *zaibatsu* are allowed in, there will be no control, then soon, no fish.' He gave an exaggerated hand gesture and then a shrug. 'We will fish the resources carefully, *Duncan-san*. That way there is always a business for you, for the government and for us.'

I turned to Anna and switched to speaking English. Rude perhaps, but the Japanese do it all the time when they're negotiating through a translator. 'I'm a bit pissed,' I said, 'but I don't know, I'm not at all sure we could finance our third of the business. It looks like a bloody big undertaking. I'll have to speak with Joe and Kevin.'

'No, no, you don't understand, Nicholas,' Anna protested. 'The Japanese *must* have a majority – fifty-one per cent, or at the very least fifty per cent. In return they'll finance the whole deal, down to the last nail in the processing plant, the cost of building the private harbours, slips, cranes, winches, refrigeration, the lot. The local government gets the other forty-nine per cent or, if I can't swing it, fifty per cent.'

'Hey, wait on. I'm not that shickered! And our share is what? Zilch?'

'Nothing of the sort. As I said, you get to supply all the raw material for the factory, all the transport contracts, build the roads and have an agreement to supply local labour. This alone should show you a decent ongoing profit. In addition you also get an overall management contract.'

'I thought you said they would staff and manage it themselves.'

'Nicholas, I thought you understood,' she said a trifle impatiently. '*Only* the interior of the processing plant, you get the rest.'

'I should think the local politicians would want a share of that too,' I remarked.

Anna nodded. 'Maybe. That's your territory, nothing new for you there, Nicholas. But the big money for them is in the renewable tuna and shark-fin licences and their share of the overall profits from the processing and packing plants. Compared to these, anything they could rake off from the factory and infrastructure would be peanuts.'

I grinned. 'In my experience there are plenty of political monkeys scurrying around looking for peanuts. Or, tell me, Anna, is it us – Kevin, Joe and me – who are getting the peanuts?' The sake that kept being poured was turning me decidedly nasty.

'That's not fair!' Anna cried, patently hurt. 'I don't like it when you're drunk, Nicholas. The fish-processing plants are going to make you a damn sight more money than you've ever made lugging people and coconuts from island to island!'

I pulled my addled wits together. 'If the Japanese run the fish factory with their own personnel, who keeps the books?' I asked, glancing at *Konoe-san* who, to my surprise, appeared to have quite inexplicably fallen asleep. Then again, he'd just come out of hospital where they'd probably filled him with all sorts of drugs for which alcohol was contraindicated. I glanced at Anna. 'Should we call someone?' But at that moment he began to snore softly and his breathing seemed normal. Falling asleep in a meeting wasn't considered bad manners in Japan. I knew that older Japanese senior executives frequently nodded off, an accepted and not uncommon practice.

With my concern for Konoe Akira I had forgotten my question, but Anna now answered it in a somewhat trenchant manner. 'Why the hell would the bookkeeping concern you, Nicholas? Kevin will send in your bill and if I know him it will be plumped up nicely. I won't question it unless he's dreaming fairies when it's raining frogs. It will be paid promptly. Your management contract would be fee-driven. *Konoe-san's zaibatsu* isn't going to go broke . . . or hasn't for the last five hundred years. Any profits from the joint venture between them and any of the island governments won't ever be your concern.'

'C'mon, Anna, you know better than that. Joe and I have to live in the islands. If the local governments get ripped off they won't be catching the next plane to Japan, they'll come looking for us. After all, as you say, it's me who has to open the doors.'

Anna looked at me scornfully. 'Nicholas, I'm trying to make a deal that includes you, one that isn't going to cost you a penny and will make you all very wealthy. All you are required to do is facilitate. What are you trying to say?'

Pissed as I was, I knew this to be true. Anna wasn't asking me to do anything I didn't already do, or hadn't done practically every month our company had been in the islands. It was money for jam, but I felt out of control, unprincipled, caught in a web of possibilities, and so I wanted to be difficult. 'Yeah, but we've been in charge of the situation and kept our noses clean for twenty years,' I protested.

Anna sighed. 'Work it out for yourself, Nicholas. Why would the Japanese want to alienate a local government and stand to lose their fishing licences when they come up for review? Anyway, I'll set up an independent audit as part of my negotiations. The Japanese are not going to —'

'Piss on their own doorstep?' I finished for her.

'Oh, charming, but yes, that's about it.' Anna seemed to realise that I was perhaps a little more pie-eyed than I appeared and was spoiling for a fight. She was handing us a business on a plate and I was being recalcitrant. But she sensed she'd pretty well won the day. Glancing across to see that *Konoe-san* was still asleep she abruptly changed the subject. 'By the way, I have good news. I know you've been worried, but I've squared things with the *yakuza*. We're quits, we owe them nothing.'

I was taken by surprise. 'How? What?' I guess one of the reasons why Anna was so successful is that she was astute enough to know when to leave off. I was grateful. I'd been heading towards being stupidly obstinate, the Japanese firewater doing the talking.

'*Konoe-san* needs some heavy muscle at several large city fish markets. So I introduced him to the *oyabun*.' Anna knew of my concern that at some future time *Fuchida-san* might call in a favour that would compromise one or both of us.

'*Fuchida-san* will be pleased; that's right up his alley.'

'Well, actually, it was Miss Sparkle's doing. It seems the *yakuza* are responsible for negotiating the bribes for the local Russian authorities. Very little money changes hands. Payment is with Japanese prostitutes, electronic consumer goods, processed food and all the myriad luxury items the Russians can't obtain. There is a flourishing underground economy run by the island's Russian bigwigs. In return they allow the Japanese fishing boats to use their harbours and fish the local waters.

'But, of course, there is the usual *quid pro quo*. The Japanese government turns a blind eye to all the mischief going on, because the fishing-boat crews spy for them. In fact, the boats are known as *rupo-sen* [report boats]. Miss Sparkle said that the *yakuza* used their considerable influence with the Russians to set up their own fishing fleet in the Kuril Islands but have a great deal of catching up to do as they are comparatively small players compared to the big *zaibatsu*, and simply lack the clout they need in the big local fish markets to achieve the best prices for their own catch. Miss Sparkle was delighted when I suggested she meet *Konoe-san*.'

'Yeah, but why Miss Sparkle? I would have thought this was an important enough issue for *Fuchida-san* himself to be involved, or at least one of his important *oyabun*, rather than delegate it to his *mama-san*.'

Anna looked at me wide-eyed, unbelieving. 'Nicholas! You mean you haven't twigged yet?'

'Twigged?' I shrugged. 'What's to twig?'

'Miss Sparkle is the boss of the Tokyo *yakuza*. *She* is the top *oyabun*!'

'Christ no!' I gaped. 'I always had a suspicion she wasn't quite the humble *mama-san* she claimed to be, but head honcho! Are you sure?'

'Of course. I thought you knew the set-up, how it works with *Fuchida-san* being homosexual, or gay as they say now.'

'No! C'mon, you're pulling my leg. Gay? Jesus! Fair dinkum?'

Anna laughed. 'Don't worry, he hasn't got his eye on you.'

'Bugger!' I said, trying to regain the initiative.

'It's what prevents him being the top dog. The *yakuza* simply won't accept a homosexual at the helm. It would completely overturn the Samurai tradition.'

'Well what about a woman?'

'As long as she doesn't appear to be making the decisions, nobody minds.'

'But that's crazy! That means *Fuchida-san appears* to be making the decisions, which is unacceptable because he's gay, and a woman is *really* making the decisions, which again is unacceptable because she's a woman?'

Anna shrugged. 'That's Japan, I guess. As long as the public don't know and the *yakuza* do, but nobody admits they know, it's okay.'

With *Konoe-san* asleep I stopped drinking. The sake competition had caused me to consume far too much alcohol. The *fugu* variations on a theme kept coming and, as I'd been led to expect, I had a distinct tingling sensation in my tongue which hadn't yet reached my fingers, apparently the next destination for the poison. This tingling of the tongue and the fingers was meant to reassure the diner that the poison still exists in the fish but is no longer present in lethal quantities – a bit like giving yourself a hard backhand then feeling good that while your hand and mouth hurt you haven't broken any teeth. The sensation was supposed to be similar to mild intoxication, but give me alcohol any day.

Anna went on to explain the relationship between

Fuchida-san and Miss Sparkle. 'She is the strength and makes the hard decisions. He is an organisational genius, obsessed with detail. Between them they're a combination that is hard to match, even though there are always challengers. The loyalty of *Saito-san* is yet another factor – none of the contenders want him to come looking for them, and whoever tried to kill a national icon would create a public scandal throughout Japan and almost certainly lose any chance of becoming the top *oyabun*.'

'And Miss Sparkle told you all this?'

'Women talk to each other, Nicholas! Besides I've known and trusted her for a long time, twenty-five years in fact, and she feels the same. It never does any harm to have the same skeletons in the closet and share part of a common history. She is quite remarkable, in fact exceptional. In Japan, for a woman, let alone a geisha, to achieve the status of top *oyabun* is almost beyond comprehension. In fact it can't happen, but it has.'

'She'dhavetobeprettyruthlesstosurviveonthewaytothetop,' I observed.

'More than simply ruthless, that would be the minimum requirement. It must have taken enormous intellect, courage and determination.' Anna laughed. 'She credits me with starting it all for her,' then she quickly added, 'which is nonsense, of course.'

'Oh? What did she say?'

Anna looked up at me, her expression serious. 'It's not stuff I care to remember, but according to *Korin-san*, it was the thing that happened at the Nest of the Swallows.'

'The *kempeitai* colonel?' I refrained from adding the words – *Takahashi, the one you murdered.*

'Yes, him.' Anna then began to relate the conversation between Miss Sparkle and herself at their reunion luncheon.

Miss Sparkle had picked her up at the hotel and taken her to a small inn, part of a traditional marketplace, for lunch. It was obvious that Miss Sparkle was a regular patron and an important guest as they were immediately ushered to a small private room. The meal was ordered and when it came the waiter was instructed that they were not under any circumstances to be disturbed.

It was here that between them they hatched Konoe Akira's comeuppance and also where the following conversation took place. Miss Sparkle, after sampling several dishes and sending one back, put down her chopsticks and looked directly at Anna. 'Anna-san, when the odious *kempeitai* Lieutenant Ito brought you to the Nest of the Swallows covered with scrapes, cuts and bruises we were amazed to hear how you had fought, on your own, the six *kempeitai* soldier thugs sent to bring you to Colonel Takahashi. "How can a single woman do this?" all the *okami-san* asked. It was beyond the possibility of our imagination.'

'*Korin-san*, they had murdered my beautiful friend, Til the trishaw driver, and placed his head on the front gatepost. I was beyond fury, beyond shock. If I had had a machine gun I would have killed them all.'

'But you fought them with your bare hands and we heard later that their cuts and bruises were worse than yours.'

'No, I don't think so, but they were caught by surprise.'

'Ah, surprise. That was the first lesson you taught me,' Miss Sparkle said. 'Then came patience and then sudden and swift punishment. I have used these three in combination many times in the *yakuza*.'

'No, no!' Anna protested. 'It was you who made it all possible, your instruction; you must take the credit, *Korin-san*, not me!'

Miss Sparkle shook her head, having none of it.

'*Anna-san*, I was trained as a geisha. All I could do was teach you submission, the power of pleasing a man and therefore the power to earn some privileges and remain safe, even gain a little power yourself. You used this instruction in a new way. This was a new purpose for patience, one that a Japanese woman would not have considered.'

'I was protecting my womanhood,' Anna explained.

'Ah, yes, the precious pearl. Every Japanese woman knows that it is hers to keep for as long as she wishes.' She chuckled at this observation. 'But she also knows that the cost is much too great, in fact, impossible. In the end it is worthless; she would end up as neither geisha nor wife nor concubine and her own family would banish her; she would have nowhere to go. She would become a slave, a rag picker. To risk your life to remain a virgin, that, to us, was unthinkable. Men are too strong. They will take the pearl, one way or another. That is what I prepared you for at the Nest of the Swallows. How to accept and survive the rape of Colonel Takahashi.'

'The need to maintain my virginity was too strong in my mind to overcome,' Anna said, not explaining any further.

'When you killed him, knowing that you would die as a consequence, I learned the lesson of ultimate strength,' Miss Sparkle replied. 'It is taking a risk that defies and confuses the imagination of men and confounds them with the power of its unthinkable audacity. In a Japanese woman it was impossible.' Miss Sparkle looked directly into Anna's eyes. 'You have been the template for my subsequent life. When I was fortunate enough to be rescued from the American prison in order to open soldier brothels for American troops I knew that I would never get another such chance in life. I decided I would emulate the woman I most admired in the world.' Miss Sparkle leaned forward and took Anna's hand. 'There you have it, honourable *Anna-san*. If not for you I would be an old woman in rags selling my body to fish-market drunks for a bowl of noodles.'

Anna started to sob. 'You were right, *Korin-san*, I should have listened to you. Keeping the pearl intact has ruined so much of what it means to be a woman.' Anna then began to tell Miss Sparkle of the result of Konoe Akira's complete dominance and the effects of his brainwashing, with the result that she had never been able to give herself to a man, even to me, whom she confessed to love more than her own life.

The old woman listened silently and when Anna had completed the whole sorry tale, surprisingly she hadn't attempted to comfort her. 'So now when you have him in the Jade House you will kill him, yes? It will not be hard. I will help you. It will look like a heart attack. I know you have maintained your skill with the *kinbaku* rope. Do you know how to induce a heart attack?'

'Yes, I know the method,' Anna replied. 'But I have not attempted it.'

'I will show you tomorrow when we go to practise with Lee-Li,' Miss Sparkle said.

'No, I do not wish to kill him, *Korin-san*.'

Miss Sparkle looked bemused. 'But he must be properly punished.'

'I will humiliate him, that is sufficient.'

'What do you mean? *Anna-san*, Konoe Akira is a man! It is not possible for a woman to humiliate a Japanese man. This one, he was also a general. They recover from humiliation by a woman without blinking. It is a second-rate humiliation; he will not remember it when he goes to bed that night.'

'I think he will remember me,' Anna said quietly. 'I can bring on an angina attack. In a man of sixty it should not be difficult. But I think we should have an ambulance standing by, just in case.'

Miss Sparkle looked doubtful, even unhappy, but then reluctantly agreed that this could be arranged. 'How will you humiliate him?' she asked.

'If he realises I could have taken his life, but then decided to spare him, will he not be humiliated?'

'*Hai!* He will think you a fool, a woman. Only a woman would lack the courage to go the whole way. A fool, a coward and a woman are all the same thing in his mind.'

'But it still proves that I am stronger than him.'

'True. But is that enough? Surely not, when you consider what he has done to you. He is a Japanese man. The thought of your strength of character will not linger beyond his next bowl of noodles.'

'I don't care, I have satisfied my own pride!' Anna exclaimed.

Miss Sparkle cackled heartily at this. 'Ah, yes, very commendable, like satisfying yourself with your finger – it does no harm and makes you feel good. But, ask yourself, please, *Anna-san*, will this satisfaction now allow *Duncan-san* to possess the precious pearl?'

'I don't know,' Anna said softly, confused and close to tears.

'Then you will have nothing to show for the years you have suffered,' Miss Sparkle said, not relenting. 'You will have shown Konoe Akira that you have character, strength, patience, determination and perseverance, even the ability to kill, all the things you claim he was responsible for teaching you. How then is this going to humiliate him? All it proves is that he still possesses your mind and has every right to be proud of his honourable pupil. What sort of humiliation is that? What revenge? What satisfaction?'

Anna, sipping green tea, thought for a while. She was

not used to a woman who had a stronger mind and more determination than herself and who forced her to examine her own motives. 'You are right, *Korin-san*,' she admitted finally. 'But short of killing him, what else can I do?'

Miss Sparkle chuckled. 'We will cover for you if you wish to kill him. But I think perhaps you are right. You must frighten him out of his wits; he must know you planned and possessed the power to kill him, then spared his life. If you do this properly, show no emotion, behave like a man, the gift of his life can involve his code of honour. It will create an obligation he cannot avoid. There has to be a price for sparing his life; this is the time-honoured way. Konoe Akira is from a Samurai family, he cannot escape this obligation. Then you must put a proposal to him that is big enough to cancel the debt he owes you for sparing his life.' She paused. 'Since your kidnapping we have researched him. He is a very powerful man, the chairman and major shareholder in a fishing *zaibatsu*, the second in Japan. Tomorrow we will go to the fish markets and you will see for yourself.'

Anna spread her arms. 'I guess that's why we're here, Nicholas. This is the payback.' She laughed. 'Though I must say Miss Sparkle has taught me a lesson in both opportunism and business acumen.'

'How is that?'

'Well, work it out for yourself. I get the opportunity to liaise, to be the agent, call it what you may, for Japanese fishing licences with the Pacific Island nations with a whopping great initial fee attached and another every time they need to renew; you get what promises to be a very lucrative business opportunity without it costing you a bean; Miss Sparkle gets a chance to extend *yakuza* influence into the local fish markets; and finally, *Konoe-san*, the ultimate control freak, loses control and potentially loses face. He is forced to do as I say in this deal, which is anathema to someone like him, but face is everything. I will be humiliating him by bringing uncertainty into his decisions, undermining his control. Nothing upsets a large Japanese corporation more than uncertainty. Look what happened with Mitsubishi and the two freighters – they lost face and opened themselves up to criticism. They would have done just about anything to regain control. In fact, they ended up virtually giving us an extra ship.'

I glanced over at the quietly snoring *Konoe-san*. The tiny dose of poison from the *fugu* fish, the sake and no doubt the drugs he'd been given in hospital had knocked him for six. There was no way he was feigning sleep, and anyway, he'd have had trouble following our conversation in English. 'You've learned all this since we came to Japan?' I asked.

'No, of course not. A bit – the deal with Mitsubishi helped – but most of it comes from Miss Sparkle. Remember, she's spent her entire life understanding what goes on in the head of a Japanese man, especially one who is autocratic and powerful.'

'Japanese mind games; I'm impressed,' I said.

'It's not that hard and it's not that Japanese, Nick. If you were a Western corporation about to invest roughly a billion dollars US in a long-term fishing venture, you'd want to be pretty certain that your exclusive licences were secure and under your own control.' She nodded her head at the sleeping Japanese man. 'I have that control, renewable every five years for the next twenty years.'

'You mean you can dictate the terms of the contract?'

'Well, yes, in conjunction with the island governments who grant the licences. I will suggest that they demand a percentage of the gross profits from the catch and the new fish factories to build schools, hospitals, sports facilities, regional medical clinics, that sort of thing.'

'And they'll agree to that?'

'Yes.'

'Why? They're not going to tell you their gross profits.'

'They won't have to.'

'Huh?'

'We'll simply audit the catch and estimate a figure that's around ten per cent of the market price for wholesale fish on the Japanese stock exchange. They won't care. It's not their money.'

'But you said it was a percentage of their profit.'

Anna laughed. 'They'll simply apply to the Japanese government to grant the amount in foreign aid instead of granting it to some other third-world nation. It's a way of jumping the queue and not having to go cap in hand to the Japanese government for aid. Konoe Akira's *zaibatsu* will do that for us. Because it's infrastructure and not money their government is supplying it will be difficult for the locals to extract bribes. Besides, the contracts to build the schools, hospitals and other infrastructure will naturally go to your company and so prevent corruption on the ground.'

I was filled with admiration. 'Wow! That's nice work, Anna. I can see now that the Mitsubishi business was just a warm-up session. To think I very nearly didn't come to this lunch. We have to have a drink to celebrate, but not bloody sake! A Kirin beer for me and for you, what will it be, darling?'

'I don't suppose they'd have a gin and tonic? This isn't the sort of place where Westerners would come to die of fish poisoning. I guess it will have to be a sake. I've never tried Japanese whisky.'

'Hey, wait on! This is a pretty posh joint. I'll bet they have French champagne. The Japanese are at heart awful snobs.' So we ordered a bottle of Cristal that cost damn near as much as the *fugu* itself.

I fondly believed the champagne would sober me up. Can't think why. Some deeply held racist belief that the European alcohol would somehow subdue the Asian. I'd somewhat recovered from the earlier effects of the sake but in the recesses of my skull I could feel a headache creeping like a cat stalking a lizard. We'd finished all seven *fugu* dishes, the number Konoe Akira had ordered in memory of the derring-do with his mates as an officer cadet. I could feel the result – slight dizziness, tingling of the tongue and fingers – but it was nothing a couple of glasses of French bubbly wouldn't chase away with a Gallic flourish, I decided.

Konoe Akira was still asleep, his rigid leg straight out and his head resting on his shoulder and the back of his chair. He was snoring fairly loudly. I guess you could say that at least I'd won the little boy doggy bum-sniffing stuff.

A glass and a half each of champagne later the food waiter came in to say that *Konoe-san*'s chauffeur was waiting outside. I paid the bill and tipped him and the sake waiter, both over-generously, then asked for *Konoe-san* to be allowed to continue his afternoon nap. We remained another twenty minutes to finish the bottle before leaving.

Almost the moment we walked out of the restaurant and hit what passes for fresh air in Tokyo, I was gone, done like a dog's dinner. The effect of the rice booze combined with the champagne went straight to my legs, as well as whacking me on the back of the head with an invisible sledgehammer.

Ignoring Anna I focused on the big American car and walked unsteadily up to Staff Sergeant Goto who stood at the door of the gigantic and outrageous powder-blue Cadillac. Drunk language doesn't come easily off the page so I'll stick to what I said rather than how it was delivered, which was with much slurring of words and frequent hiccupping. 'The honourable *Konoe-san* is sleeping (hic),' I informed Staff Sergeant Goto. 'I did not wish to wake him up (hic). The last time I did so (hic) led to the most regrettable consequences.' I paused and, closing one eye, gave him a withering look, or so I imagined, then, almost losing my balance, I stabbed a blunt and belligerent forefinger in the direction of his brass-buttoned Norman Rockwell chauffeur's tunic. 'One of them,' I pronounced, 'being that yours truly was karate-kicked and landed (hic) on a very . . . valuable vase (hic). So, what do you say to that, my good man?' I demanded.

Anna would tell me the following day that Staff Sergeant Goto's polished boots and leggings came sharply to attention as he bowed deeply without uttering a single word.

'Come, Nicholas, you are very drunk,' Anna said, not entirely sober herself. Then she hauled me off, put two fingers to her lips and sent out an ear-piercing whistle towards the nearest taxi. In Japan this single action instantly placed her unequivocally beyond the pale. Two thimbles of sake, the seven-course *fugu* fish luncheon and three glasses of French champagne, as well as the relief and exhilaration of a triumphant outcome, had left her more than a little relaxed. Nevertheless, a passing taxi almost instantaneously skidded to a halt beside us, and I laughed drunkenly until I practically wept.

During the ride home Anna's high spirits continued, while I began to feel pretty ordinary. The passing streetscape appeared to be running on fast forward. Moreover, the cat had caught the lizard and my head was thumping like the clappers of hell.

'Nicholas, you haven't noticed,' Anna said playfully, then brought her forefinger up to her earlobe and flicked it.

'W-w-what?' I said.

'Can't you see?'

'Your diamonds?'

'Look closely,' she invited.

I was having trouble focusing and squinted at the diamonds on the ears of both her heads. The light in the back of the taxi wasn't extra good, either. 'Yeah . . . same (hic) answer.'

'Nicholas, what's wrong? You usually notice everything. They're pink!'

I looked again, forcing Anna's two heads to become one. 'Well . . . I never . . . so they are!' I pronounced haltingly. 'Anna, did you know (hic) your diamonds have . . . turned pink? How . . . that happen . . . sweetart?'

'They're pink Brazilian diamonds, silly! A gift from Miss Sparkle.' She giggled. 'Our share of the Konoe Akira ransom money.'

When we arrived at the Imperial Hotel, Anna was forced to commandeer two bellboys and the doorman to carry a legless Nick Duncan, the bum-sniffing sake champion Australian wonder dog, up to our hotel suite.

I woke late the following morning with the mother and father of all hangovers. Rice, the staple food of half the world, may appear bland and innocent, but if left around at room temperature it can quickly grow a variety of bacteria that can lead to such a dose of the trots that to be more than twenty feet from the toilet for the next two days is courting disaster. Fermented into wine it can render you comatose as quickly as any alcohol and give you a hangover that is guaranteed to bring you whimpering to your knees in the shower the next morning.

If I'd won the sake contest with Konoe Akira, it was at

a high price. When I eventually managed to drag myself to the phone there were no seats left that day or night on any plane flying to Australia.

'You could have called Qantas when you got up this morning,' I grumbled at Anna.

'I could have, but I had a better idea,' she answered cheerfully, unaffected by yesterday's lunch and her intake of sake and champagne. 'I called Miss Sparkle and asked her to reschedule the Gojo Mura meeting for today and then booked us out on tomorrow night's flight.'

'What time today?' I asked, dismayed. 'Christ, I feel awful!'

'We're seeing Gojo Mura this afternoon at two-thirty, though I could change it to tomorrow morning if you prefer. Although it seems *Fuchida-san* is all set to go today.'

'Nah, leave it,' I decided. 'But could you call the desk and ask them to send out for aspirin or whatever the Japanese equivalent is?'

'Oh how the mighty have fallen!' Anna declared. 'It took two bellboys and the doorman to get you up here yesterday afternoon. I could have killed you when you threatened *Konoe-san*'s chauffeur.'

'Chauffeur? I didn't! Did I? Oh God! What happened?'

'Well, the last time you met he karate-kicked you into *Konoe-san*'s vase. I daresay this time he could have sent you over the hood of his big blue motorcar, but like the gentleman you weren't, he clicked his heels, bowed and remained silent.' Anna paused and looked at me as if appraising the extent of my hangover. 'You were in a terrible state, darling. You seemed perfectly fine until we left the restaurant . . . then . . . *kerplunk!* How much about yesterday do you remember?'

'Most of it – a joint venture in several fish factories in the islands, your payback, schools for island kids . . .'

'Good, that about sums it up. What's your opinion?'

I hesitated. 'Anna, I told you I'd changed my mind. But I'll have to talk to Kevin and Joe; it's not solely my decision.'

'Yes, of course,' she replied. 'But are you happy? I mean personally?'

'Darling, I'd be awfully happy if someone would chop off my head.'

I groaned. 'Could you send out for the local executioner, please?'

'Nicholas, it's important. I need to know I have your blessing. If your partners turn it down, well . . .'

'They won't!' Hangover or no hangover, I could anticipate Kevin's reaction: 'Whaddaya sayin', buddy? Dey gonna get us to make da harbour, run da fuckin' place, labour recruit, management fee, transport rights, and we ain't gotta put in no capital? No bribe to nobody? You sure you got dis deal sewn up real tight, Nick? What you mean ya ain't gonna do da negotiation? Dat she gonna do it wid da government concerned? Nick, now hear me good, sonny boy. I'm gonna make da ultimate fuckin' sacrifice. I'm gonna catch da fuckin' aeroplane to dem cockamamie islands! We gonna make our own deals, man! Cain't have no goddamn junkie doin' da spruikin' fer da biggest fleet in da whole fuckin' South Pacific, ya hear me, buddy? Dem two freighters we got from da Japs, you done good woikin' on ya own. We don't need no fem fatal fuckin' up da woiks. Anyone gonna stitch up dis fish factory it gotta be usselves!'

Joe would think a while then say, 'Nick, I tink yoh got us a gooood one, mah man. Lotsa labour re-quire-ment, and dat good foh da niggers! We can have us a school foh all dere piccaninny, I pro-pose dat be a part of da nego-she-ation wid da Japanese management fee. I cain't see no problem wid doing dat job, man, I can do dat easy. Dem new freighters, Nick, con-grat-u-lation, even Kevin he goin' a be a happy man foh a change . . . dem Japs payin' foh da piccaninny schools and all dem new Uncle Joe scholar-ships dat's gonna come! I's gonna create a great aggri-vation foh dat muth'fucker, mah good brother, bottom-line Kevin!'

Of course, while today our part in the fish factories would be considered pretty reprehensible, it must be said that in 1970 the rape of the seas by Japanese tuna-fishing boats wasn't the issue it has subsequently become. Like North Sea mackerel, codfish and haddock, Pacific tuna was a natural resource that seemed inexhaustible. Whales were perhaps the only endangered ocean species at that time, as far as most people were concerned. Americans had encouraged the Japanese to eat whale meat during the post-war protein shortage. Now the world was just beginning to realise that some species of whale were threatened with extinction due to centuries of whaling.

Many countries, such as Britain, Norway and Holland, finally stopped whaling not because of the threat of extinction, but simply because whales were so scarce that it wasn't worth spending time and money hunting the few that remained. But Japan continued, for complex reasons, even though the economics were decidedly shaky.

While nobody was surprised that it would take a long time for such huge creatures as whales to come back from the brink of extinction, most people thought that tuna and all the other fish of the oceans would be replenished as quickly as they could be caught.

As for restricting the catch of that notorious predator of the seas, the universally dreaded shark, well, frankly, the fewer of them the better for all of us. Thank God for the Chinese and their love of shark-fin soup.

Ouch! Today up to one hundred million sharks are caught each year simply for their fins – that's a lot of noughts, 100 000 000! We are only just beginning to understand that the extinction of the shark could upset the ecological balance of the oceans and eventually threaten humankind. All of this for a bowl of indifferent-tasting soup.

As they say, it's easy to have twenty-twenty vision with hindsight.

I saw no evidence of the plunder of the environment. The jungle I knew so well on the islands remained as it always had, filled with birds, bees and butterflies; the destructive whine of the chainsaw was almost never heard and the giant hardwoods reigned on the silent slopes. As for dams, well, everyone knew that they were needed – the Aswan in Egypt, the Hoover in America, the Snowy in Australia.

Of course, at this stage Marg wasn't involved in the environmental movement and was still doing duty as the Admiral's widow. I'd taken very little notice of newspaper reports of drowning a Tasmanian lake to make electricity. I was a philistine just like almost everyone else. But Marg was about to change all that soon after we returned from Japan.

Forgive my digression.

With the help of headache pills and fizzy drinks I was reasonably okay by midafternoon when the big black Mercedes carrying *Fuchida-san* came to pick us up. It seemed that Miss Sparkle's scolding had had the required effect and he was in an ebullient mood, his demi-tantrum forgotten. 'Hai! *Nick-san*, this is a good moment when old things are forgotten and new things are now possible. Gojo Mura will no longer need to feel shame. I will tell him that the past *must* be forgotten and we will be friends again like we were as boys in the village.'

'Oh, so you didn't see him after you phoned me?'

He looked at me curiously. 'No, certainly not. Without you, *Duncan-san*, it cannot be made to work. We have found him so we can *share* this unifying experience, you and me and Gojo Mura, three brothers long lost from each other, come together at last, the old Japan, the West and the new Japan.'

I now better understood his anger at my refusing to accompany him on the previous occasion. Gojo Mura's predicament was a product of the Old Japan. By allowing himself to be taken prisoner and then afterwards returning to Japan, Gojo Mura had officially became a non-person.

It should be remembered that Japanese casualties in the Pacific theatre were sometimes very high. While most of these men died of malaria, dysentery and starvation in the jungle, they had nonetheless died for their emperor and were rightly considered war heroes. But this was not the case for Japanese soldiers captured and interned. To surrender to the enemy and then to be made a prisoner of war was an unimaginable humiliation felt by the entire nation. In such circumstances a soldier's official duty was to commit suicide. If he failed to do so, the state obligingly did it for him, removing his name from his village register and sending his parents an urn supposedly containing his ashes and at the same time granting them a small pension. So when Gojo Mura was repatriated to Japan, he found that he was considered officially dead.

In Japan, a returned prisoner of war had no official way of proving that he existed, no identity papers to contradict the fact that his name appeared on the list of the Japanese war dead. He was unable to apply for a job or gain any further qualifications because there was unequivocal proof that he was *konpaku* [a ghost]. For many, this technical death seemed far worse a fate than the real thing and many ex-soldiers committed suicide.

However, *Fuchida-san* was now determined to transform

Gojo Mura from being the victim of the intransigence of old Japan to being a beneficiary of the tolerant and democratic new Japan. The most harmless Japanese fighting man ever to be sent to war was about to be brought back to life.

In *Fuchida-san*'s eyes this would need to be done correctly. To resurrect Gojo Mura and restore him to citizenship he would replicate the way the post-war nation had recreated itself: Old Japan (Gojo Mura) + Western influence (me) = New Japan (*Fuchida-san*). This symbolism was obviously very important to him, and so it was hardly surprising that he thought my initial refusal to accompany him, preferring as I did to take care of a woman, was frivolous and unworthy, when I could have been bringing the officially and technically dead back to life.

The number two *oyabun* for Tokyo undoubtedly possessed sufficient clout with the government to ensure Gojo Mura's official restoration – at that time Japan did not have a national census, and births, marriages and deaths were kept in village registers – but *Fuchida-san* was a stickler for detail and insisted that Gojo Mura's return to contemporary life should have a symbolic as well as a practical dimension.

Fuchida-san explained that Gojo Mura had changed his surname to Gekko, retaining his initials and first name. A name such as Gekko Mura was so common in Japan that it would go virtually unnoticed. Even so, finding him had proved less difficult than expected. A *wakagashira* had visited the village where the now officially dead Gojo Mura and *Fuchida-san* had spent their childhood. He had contacted *Gojo-san*'s aged parents who were overawed to hear that the Tokyo *oyabun*, the most famous and powerful scion to ever emerge from any village family tree, wished to locate their son for a most honourable purpose, to submit his name for reinstatement on the village register, so that he could be resurrected from the officially dead.

With this dazzling possibility in mind they admitted that their son had secretly kept in touch with them. Once every year during the Spring Festival, the old couple would travel to visit him for a single day under the pretext that they were visiting the *Yakusuni* Shrine in Tokyo to pay tribute to the name of their officially dead war-hero son. This is not unusual in Japanese society where, because something is officially true, people pretend that it is actually true, while those around them accept the deception even though everyone knows the truth.

We were driven to an impressive building in the downtown area of Tokyo, the home of the giant *manga* [comic book] publishers Skip. We were met at the front of the impressive building by the owner, *Shozo-san*, a short, fat and unctuous man with eyes that all but disappeared behind his plump shiny cheeks. He wore the usual blue serge suit, but surprisingly a pink shirt, pink tie and pink braces. He was sweating – plainly overcome – and more than a little apprehensive about the visit of the *oyabun*, who was purported to run the Tokyo area. He had begun bowing while we were climbing the numerous front steps to the entrance of the building and had repeated the gesture at least six times before we finally reached him.

'Welcome, honourable *Fuchida-san*, to my humble building. Your guests are doubly welcome. This is a great occasion of momentous importance to Skip!' The welcome was shouted and had obviously been carefully rehearsed.

Fuchida-san returned this sycophantic welcome with a barely perceptible bow, more a jerk of the head. 'Ho! May I introduce my esteemed colleagues *Duncan-san* and *Anna-san*.'

Two more bows followed. 'Welcome! Welcome! Please follow.'

We were ushered through a foyer that contained several giant vases, where ten secretaries in bright pink smocks with

Skip embroidered across the left breast stood in line. All bowed simultaneously as we crossed the black marble tiles and walked down a short hallway, lined with more of the grotesque six-foot-high vases vying to out-uglify each other in a grotesquery of design and colour. Finally we were shown into a very large conference room. Space is at a premium in Japan and large by Japanese standards can seem small by our own, but this was a large room by any standards.

Arranged in a circle were ten dark leather club chairs, about three feet apart, each with a low table placed in front of it. At the centre of the circle, standing on a black polished marble plinth, was a twice-life-size bronze image of *Shozo-san*, the founder. In his left hand he was holding a *Man Alive* magazine, the bronze painted red and black, to represent the sexually explicit young men's comic book that was the basis of his considerable fortune. Started in 1959, it was selling over two million copies a week. His right hand was pointing at the ceiling where the garish covers of all his other titles were painted. In Western terms, Skip was a porn publisher, although in Japan pornographic comics were a popular and long-established tradition and raised few eyebrows.

Around the walls stood at least fifty grandfather clocks, averaging between five and seven feet high, all in elaborate burnished steel, polished bronze or carved wooden cases, all with inscribed and decorated faces showing the phases of the moon and other superfluous information and with various and equally complicated brass pendulum designs. Fifty large clocks ticking away made a bizarre sound, like an army of death-watch beetles trying unsuccessfully to match each other's rhythm. All of them were set to the local time.

These, I was to learn, are one of the traditional gifts from large Japanese suppliers to their valued customers. Thus, the supplier for newsprint, the ink manufacturer, the glue supplier, and so on, would send one each year, the size and overall decoration of the giant timepieces indicating the worth of the supplier's annual business. Judging from the display of clocks in the room, the Skip organisation was obviously an esteemed customer to many large suppliers, some represented by more than one of these appalling monstrosities. The vases in the foyer and hallway I imagined were from lesser suppliers, although you never know with the Japanese – they may well have been the premier marks of customer esteem.

Japanese art, with its emphasis on minimalism and negative space, is perhaps the most esoteric of any national art style. But the Japanese predilection for expensive grotesquery in excruciating taste undoubtedly leads the world.

I glanced at my wristwatch, which, in retrospect, seems a curious thing to do. It was just after 2.30 p.m. – we had just thirty minutes to go before what I imagined would be the hourly grand cacophony: fifty grandfather clocks each attempting to out-chime the others in tribute to the statue of fat *Shozo-san*.

I glanced at Anna, who returned a small conspiratorial smile. Later she would remark that it wasn't quite the Japan Konoe Akira had inculcated into her as a girl.

Once seated, six young women appeared, again dressed in the ubiquitous pink smocks, each of them carrying a small pink tray with a pink pot of green tea, a pink cup and two miniature cakes topped with pink icing. Pink was obviously very important to *Shozo-san*, although curiously it didn't form a part of any of the ceiling illustrations. The young women came to stand in front of each of us, bowed in unison and silently placed the tray on the table in front of them, poured the tea, then stepped back smartly, bowed again and departed, marching with arms swinging in crocodile formation out of the conference room.

While we drank our tea, *Shozo-san* stood facing us with his back to his bronze double, and began a harangue on the history and numerous successes of Skip. He huffed and puffed and explained at length, in what soon developed into an overweening manner, the story of his success. While I forgot most of it (years of hardship and travail), what he essentially said, or at least what I remembered, was that his success lay in his being a common man who never lost sight of his common roots and so went out and asked the common people for their opinions through extensive market research. Artists, he pointed out, were nothing but trouble and hadn't the foggiest idea what the common comic-book buyer wanted. Instead, he maintained, he backed his own judgment with market research. 'Listen to the voice of the people is my motto!' he exclaimed, then added, 'Artists are prima donnas, not under any circumstances to be trusted! We do not employ these arrogant impostors, only those who do as they are told by the surveys!' His voice was growing more and more strident and I glanced at *Fuchida-san* who was clearly losing patience. 'Now you will want to know about the colour pink . . .'

Fuchida-san suddenly jumped to his feet. 'I too am a common man and if you want my opinion, with the greatest respect, you are talking shit! No, I don't want to know about pink – it is a colour I detest, the colour of a neo-communist! We have come to see Gekko Mura. Will you fetch him now please.'

Shozo-san's mouth fell open giving him the appearance of a fat toad. 'Certainly, at once, *Fuchida-san*,' he stammered, then turned and peeping around the statue towards the door yelled, 'Come!'

We all expected Gojo Mura to appear, but instead a clerk, wearing a pink shirt and tie, appeared and hurried to *Shozo-san*'s side, handing him a note. The fat founder glanced quickly at the note then, looking at *Fuchida-san*, declared, 'We have eight employees with the name Gekko, honourable *Fuchida-san*.' Whereupon he nodded at the clerk who hurried to the door and reappeared moments later with eight men of various ages who were made to stand with heads bowed in front of us. All wore pink shirts, though only two sported pink ties as well. The ties I surmised must be those of executive staff.

'What is this?' *Fuchida-san* exclaimed angrily. 'He is not here!'

Fat Shozo turned to his clerk, red-faced. 'He is not here!' he repeated.

The clerk, evidently accustomed to being yelled at, answered, 'There is one other of this name, but it is not possible. He has no presence and is a filler artist. He is not even entitled to wear a pink shirt!'

'Bring him!' *Fuchida-san* shouted. 'You who say you are a common man should be ashamed! We are all equal in the new Japan, except for the emperor, and even he is no longer a living god.'

'Yes, but this Gekko is officially dead, he is *konpaku* [a ghost].'

'Enough of that old bullshit!' *Fuchida-san* thundered. 'Bring him here at once!'

The clerk left at a veritable trot and returned some minutes later with an emaciated little man whom I immediately recognised, if only for the fact that he had also been emaciated the first time I saw him in the jungle when he had been painting a Clipper butterfly. His hair had turned almost white and constant malnourishment had made him even bandier and more wizened. He was dressed in a shabby and ill-fitting suit and his tie resembled an enlarged rat's tail; the collar of his shirt was frayed, but his shoes were polished and his clothes were clean. Even in the jungle, living alone in a cliff-top cave, he had been neatly turned out. But now I could see him shaking, his trembling knees agitating the thin material of his oversized trousers so that I thought at any moment he might collapse. Abandoning any formalities I rose and strode over to him, grabbing him in a bear hug. He felt like a small child in my arms. '*Gojo-san*, it has been too long!' I cried. 'But the gods have been merciful and we are together again!' I was very close to tears. I held him away from me, beaming down at the withered little man. 'It is so good to see you!' I cried, overcome, unaware that I must appear a complete hypocrite for, in my anxiety to leave Japan, I had almost decided not to take the trouble to meet him again.

Behind Gojo Mura the fat founder stood, mouth agape once more. 'Leave us at once!' *Fuchida-san* said, then in case he didn't get the message, he indicated the door with a wave of his hand and added, 'Scram! Piss off!'

'*Duncan-san*, it is you?' Gojo Mura said startled. 'Are you a ghost from the jungle?'

Anna laughed and rising from her large armchair came over. Bowing she said, 'I am Anna. I have heard a great deal about you, *Gojo-san*.'

Gojo-san glanced quickly up at her then immediately dropped his eyes, too shy to meet her gaze. He bowed. 'I am honoured,' he said, barely above a whisper.

'This is *Anna-san*, my partner. She knows of you as a great naturalist, a painter of insects and butterflies,' I said.

'No, no, I am nothing, not a painter, just a filler,' Gojo said, embarrassed at receiving such unfamiliar praise.

Fuchida-san stepped up and bowed. 'How are you, my childhood friend?'

Gojo bowed deeply. 'All Japan knows of your stature and fame, honourable *Oyabun Fuchida-san*,' he said humbly.

'Nonsense! We are village brothers. There is no ceremony possible between us. Remember when we would catch tadpoles in the gutter behind the village? We have come to take you away from this shit hole and its fat, pink arsehole who, I have no doubt, pays you a pittance. I have a great need for a painter of butterflies.' He clapped his hands, causing Gojo Mura to jump, startled. 'We will make a book, yes, that is a good idea! We will call it *The Oyabun's Butterflies of Japan*. He glanced over at me. 'Then another, *Nicholas Duncan's Butterflies of the South Pacific*. What say you, *Nick-san*?'

'Leave off the Nicholas Duncan. Just *The Butterflies of the South Pacific*,' I said. 'Great idea!'

'See, already there is five years' work,' *Fuchida-san* laughed.

'I am not worthy. I have forgotten. I will let you down. It is impossible. I am a humble filler of shameful images,' Gojo Mura insisted.

'A little practice is all you'll need,' I said encouragingly, unaware of the depth of his despair.

Gojo Mura shook his head, at once forlorn. 'It is a kindness I cannot accept, because I will surely fail you, Lieutenant *Nick-san*,' he said, remembering how he had addressed me all those years ago.

'Enough depressing talk!' *Fuchida-san* interrupted in a jocular voice. 'There is a wonderful restaurant next to this building. I have caused it to be closed to the public for the afternoon and the staff sent home so that we can have it to ourselves for a resurrection ceremony.'

At that precise moment a whirring filled the room, whereupon the fifty giant clocks started to chime.

Anna was the first to recover. Cupping her hands around her mouth she shouted above the astonishing din, 'See, *Gojo-san*, they chime for you! Now there is no turning back!'

CHAPTER THIRTEEN

'Why? Why do you mock me?
I have done nothing to harm you!'
Gojo Mura, Tokyo

THERE WAS NO SIGN of the fat founder as we left the conference room, passed the vases in the passage and gained the foyer, where this time a lone receptionist stood holding open the plate-glass door. Anna stopped as we reached her. 'Go ahead, I won't be more than a moment or two,' she said.

Approaching the receptionist she said, 'Excuse me, why does everyone wear pink?'

'It is compulsory, madam,' the receptionist replied.

'But why?' Anna knew there must be a reason because the fat founder had been about to explain when *Fuchida-san* had cut him off.

'There was a market survey done three years ago among the readers of *Man Alive* magazine. The young men were asked: "What colour does your mother like best?"'

'Let me guess, pink?' Anna grinned.

The receptionist nodded, still serious. 'Ever since then sales of *Man Alive* magazine have increased. Pink is our lucky colour, madam. It is called "market synergy". Our honourable founder says our readers feel that we respect their mothers.'

'I see. But isn't *Man Alive* a sexually explicit magazine?'

The receptionist looked alarmed. 'It is only a *manga*, madam! It is for young men. Mothers don't read them.'

'If the mothers who prefer pink don't read them, then what is the point?'

'It is called "mind compatibility analysis", madam,' the receptionist said in a serious tone. 'The readers love their mothers and they know we feel the same. It has been tested and completely proven.'

'Oh? How was it tested?'

'For one week last year our honourable founder, *Shozo-san*, decreed that nobody should wear pink. Also, it was forbidden to think pink. We were told if we think a colour it must only be white. Can you believe it! The sales went down for that week's issue.'

'No!' Anna exclaimed in mock horror.

'Yes, madam, it is true!'

'Did the sales go down significantly? I mean, did they plunge?'

'I don't know, madam, we were not told. But *Shozo-san* said it proved that mothers are always right and our future success is tied to thinking and wearing pink. So we are instructed to always wear our smocks in the future. Some girls wear pink underwear so it will bring them extra luck.'

'And you?'

'Yes, of course! Our company motto is "*Kaizen*" – it means continuous improvement. I used to be the second receptionist. Now in only three years I am the first.'

Anna then said in a kindly voice, 'Well done, but take my advice – keep your pink panties on. Taking them off is another way to improve your lot in life, but a great deal of market research indicates that it usually ends badly, in particular for secretaries and receptionists.'

'Yes, thank you, madam,' the receptionist said, still serious. 'Thank you for visiting Skip. I hope you have a pink day.'

Anna met us in the car park a minute or so later, shaking her head in bemusement. I guess Japan will always be an enigma. On the one hand the Japanese are an extremely clever and ambitious people, on the other – well, what can you say – naïve, stubborn, rigid, conditioned, obedient, institutionalised, unquestioning, subordinated, superstitious . . . perhaps all of these things, but still uniquely enterprising and innovative. Japan is a country that has risen from the ashes of war more effectively perhaps than any other in history.

The restaurant was literally next door to Skip. In a back room, a small banquet had been prepared on *Fuchida-san*'s instructions, the dishes ranging from traditional Japanese fare to modern cuisine, rice cakes to thinly sliced beef sashimi. The alcoholic drinks available – sake, beer and Suntory whisky – spanned both eras, and a lone soft drink, Pepsi-Cola, represented the new Japan now eagerly borrowing the bad habits of the West. Japanese teenagers were embracing junk food almost faster than American fast-food companies could build their distinctive outlets. Whereas the national diet of old Japan was possibly the healthiest in the world, the new Japan seemed to be hell bent on swapping it for the worst the West had to offer.

Gojo had never before tasted beef or soft drink and shyly refused both while accepting a cup of sake, though only for the sake of the inevitable introductory toast, afterwards claiming it made him feel quite light-headed and that he hadn't had alcohol for over twenty years. Later I discovered that he was accustomed to eating one small helping of rice and vegetables at night, all he could afford after paying the rent on a room so tiny it resembled a medium-sized wardrobe.

As he was plainly overwhelmed by the sudden and unexpected attention, we all tried our best to put him at ease. He had spent the last twenty-five years of his life making every effort to be invisible and now reacted with a start every time his name was mentioned. He also found it almost impossible to meet our eyes. His replies to our questions always came, like those of a shy child, with lids downcast.

For my part I was ashamed that I had virtually decided to return to Australia without seeing him. Had Anna not asked Miss Sparkle to set up another appointment I daresay I would have left Japan never to see him again. The capture of Gojo Mura while he was painting butterflies in the jungle would have become one of those wartime stories old men tell after a glass of wine too many at a dinner party that has gone on too long.

As it turned out he was to play a not insignificant part in our future lives. But now, overcompensating perhaps for my own intransigence, I was determined to help this dear, gentle and tormented soul who had been so cruelly punished, forced to lead a life he wasn't able to alter in the smallest respect by any effort of his own. It was to his credit that he had survived, if only as a shadow. Suicide among these walking ghosts was so common that it was met with a casual shrug. Again, many of those who didn't take their own lives spent them as alcoholics in the gutter or as beggars outside shrines. Gojo Mura had shown enough character to lead a blameless existence, eking out an impecunious living filling in the outlines of pornographic images rendered by artists probably far less talented than he was. My most ardent hope was that we would be able to restore his confidence sufficiently for him to resume painting the butterflies and other insects he had previously so loved to depict.

I was aware that people like him who are barely surviving

don't always respond well to being rescued. This was evidenced on the Burma–Thailand Railway and at Changi, as well as at other Japanese prisoner-of-war camps, where cruelty, disease and starvation were endemic. When the Australian prisoners of war were finally rescued, some of these hollow-eyed skeletons were dismayed and even furious at the sudden disruption to the pattern of their daily lives. They had worked so hard and honed their survival instincts to such an extent that they became terrified that any sudden change in their routines would sever the tenuous thread which kept them from certain death.

However, *Fuchida-san* was possessed of no such sensibility. This was to be his day as much as Gojo Mura's, and he was determined to perform the resurrection ceremony with the degree of formality he considered necessary to convert the old Japan into the new and paradoxically the new Gojo Mura back into the old one.

I had learned that the *oyabun* was a man with two separate personas. When he was in total control, as he had been during the raid on Konoe Akira's home or during Anna's rescue, he was quiet and measured in his response, but when unsure of the social situation in which he found himself, he became rambunctious, loud and arrogant, flaunting his power as he had on the first day we met in the Imperial Hotel and again in the presence of the fat founder where he had plainly been nervous about meeting Gojo Mura. Perhaps this was another reason why I had become an essential part of the reunion.

Moreover, like myself, I have no doubt he felt some guilt at having neglected his boyhood mate all these years. But now in the restaurant he was entirely self-possessed, and if he seemed insensitive to Gojo Mura's disquiet, this may well have been deliberate. Despite his claim to have embraced the culture and ways of the West, *Fuchida-san* was still essentially Japanese and in his mind the ceremony had to be performed as he'd envisioned it; he wasn't going to allow for any errant behaviour, even from Gojo Mura himself.

'Sit, please,' he commanded, remaining standing himself. '*Hai*! A toast!' he cried, shortly after we'd all lowered ourselves to the cushions on the *tatami* matting. Two of his *wakagashira* were deputising as waiters and served us the means of drinking a toast: a Pepsi for Anna, a beer to chase away the last of my hangover for me and sake for our honourable host and major guest. '*Kampai!*' we all shouted, and the formalities began.

The *oyabun* opened proceedings in the time-honoured way. 'This is a most auspicious occasion,' he said. 'Today, in this restaurant, the old Japan gives way to the new Japan. Feudalism is replaced by democracy, bondage by freedom, dogma by enlightenment, mass obedience by the right to protest, autocratic authority by public debate, government propaganda by freedom of the press.' It was pretty grand stuff, even if it was largely wishful thinking, and had plainly been carefully rehearsed by our host. But it nevertheless demonstrated to anyone listening that the old ways were over and that the new Japan was the only future.

'All of this was brought about by three factors,' the *oyabun* continued, 'our defeat in the war, our willingness to embrace Western democracy, and our ability to suspend group judgment and find a new way to forgive the past and to live in peaceful coexistence with our neighbours.' *Fuchida-san* smiled, obviously pleased with his grandiloquence. 'We are three brothers: two have gone the new way and the third, *Gojo-san*, through no fault of his own, has been trapped in the old way. Now the two brothers blessed by freedom have searched and found the third brother cursed by the dogma of old Japan. Today the three brothers are reunited at last. Welcome, brother Gojo, to your resurrection and your new life!'

Anna and I, together with the two *wakagashira*, clapped madly, while little Gojo Mura looked utterly confused, glancing quickly in the direction of the doorway as if he were about to make a run for it. *Fuchida-san* gestured to one of the *wakagashira* who handed him a scroll. Holding it above his head he let it unroll. 'To the resurrection of Gojo Mura!' he shouted.

'To the resurrection!' we all chorused, whereupon Anna leaned over and hugged the little artist. Years later *Gojo-san* would tell us that it was the first time he had felt a woman's touch since his mother had embraced him before he marched off to war in 1943.

The head of the scroll was decorated with a watercolour scene of the sun rising over the words '*Fukkatsu no hi*', meaning 'The Day of Resurrection'. Hand-lettered under it in large *kanji* were words that I now translate as best I can from the original Japanese into English:

Fukkatsu no hi
****
Gojo Muru has on this day
31st May 1970
been reinstated as the living
son of Gojo Aki and
Gojo Asa in the village of
Hakuba.
This recognition meets the
approval of the council and
the Soncho —
honourable Suyuki-san.
****
This is also to testify that

Gojo Mura
was born in this village on
20th January 1922.
He remains a worthy son
of his honourable parents
and of Japan.

The official wax seals of the village and of the headman appeared on the bottom left side of the scroll to authenticate it.

Fuchida-san gestured for Gojo Mura to rise to his feet, something he did with some difficulty, for his frail body shook. His nervousness was such that he was swallowing convulsively and attempting to moisten his dry mouth.

The *oyabun* handed him the certificate.

Trembling he accepted it and we all clapped again.

It then became apparent that *Fuchida-san* expected the little artist to respond. But it was equally apparent that this was beyond him. Sudden tears welled in Gojo Mura's eyes and ran down his hollow cheeks and chin, and he trembled so much that he dropped the scroll. Stooping to pick it up he fumbled and the scroll fell open once more, though upside down. He was sniffing and trying to regain some self-control but was unable to wipe his tears because, desperate not to drop the scroll again, he now held it upside down in both hands. Despite his best attempts he began to sob, gulping and sniffing then howling, his face crumpled like that of a distraught child. At last he managed to wail, 'Why? Why do you mock me? I have done nothing to harm you!'

I glanced quickly at Anna who was close to tears herself as she jumped up and put her arm around Gojo Mura's shoulders. 'We are not mocking you, precious Gojo, we have come to honour you, to restore your self-respect,' she cried. 'The bad days are over; it is time to begin your life again and we are here to help you.'

Gojo Mura's distress increased. 'But I am dead. How can I begin my life again?'

'As a painter of butterflies,' I said. 'Gojo, I didn't spare your life in the jungle for this to happen. I was ordered to shoot you but I saw immediately that you were a good man. A painter of butterflies is a gentle person with a great soul.' I smiled. 'You were a lousy soldier but a very good painter. It is the soldier who is dead and the painter who has been resurrected.'

'Listen to Nicholas,' Anna urged, 'and you will soon paint butterflies again.'

'I have not seen a butterfly for a long time,' Gojo Mura said. 'My eyes are not meant to see small beautiful things anymore.'

'*Hai!*' *Fuchida-san* announced, missing the poignancy. 'I have thousands! You can take your pick and paint any one you like free of charge!'

Naturally we cancelled our flight and remained in Tokyo another three days, mostly to attempt to get to know Gojo Mura and to help him to become accustomed to his new circumstances.

Fuchida-san allowed *Gojo-san* the permanent use of a tiny apartment rent-free, one of several the *yakuza* owned to accommodate members from out of town. We paid for a place in an art course so that he could regain his painting skills, as he had entirely lost his confidence in the use of a fine brush. Then we took him to an optometrist to discover he was in need of spectacles, which seemed the major reason for his difficulty with fine detail.

He absolutely refused to enter a menswear shop to buy new clothes, explaining that while he had been officially dead he had bought his clothes from the flea market. He could not afford the usual Japanese resistance to anything second-hand which might have belonged to a dead person.

Anna tried to reason that now he wasn't officially dead anymore he was entitled to new clothes.

'You are very kind, Anna-san, but I have learned that the dead wear very comfortable clothes that people can't see, whereas people are always looking at those who wear smart new clothes.' I guess it was his way of saying that he wanted to maintain his anonymity. And so we took him to the best flea market we could find and outfitted him there.

The next stop was an art-supply shop. We had decided not to hang around with him while he made his purchases, hoping that he would be encouraged to buy anything he wanted. So when we reached the art supplier I said, 'Go inside on your own, Gojo-san. Anna and I know nothing about these things. We will go to a tea-house and be back in an hour, but you must make us a promise to buy everything you could possibly need.'

'Nick-san, I am not permitted. A person like me going into a shop like this . . . they will know.'

'Know what?' Anna asked.

'That I am one of those . . . a dead person.'

'Gojo-san, you have nice clean clothes, new spectacles, your hair is cut and neat.' She turned to me. 'Nicholas, give me your watch. The Japanese judge people by the value of the watch they wear.'

Anna had given me an 18-carat gold Rolex which I only wore when I was with her because it somewhat embarrassed me. I definitely felt I wasn't a gold Rolex person, though at a pinch, I might have been a stainless steel one, or so I imagined. Everyone I'd noticed wearing a gold Rolex seemed to possess an aura that I didn't wish to emulate. In fact, with Anna's watch on my wrist and *Fuchida-san's* diamond on my pinkie I was getting into the habit of keeping my left hand permanently hidden within my trouser pocket. I removed the heavy watch and handed it to her. But, of course, *Gojo-san* could have worn it as a collar. Three of his wrists would have fitted nicely within the band. Anna handed it back. 'Here, take mine,' she instructed *Gojo-san*.

I laughed and *Gojo-san* very nearly burst into tears again. While it fitted better, a diamond-encrusted ladies' wristwatch on an emaciated and rather strange-looking Japanese man wasn't likely to inspire confidence in *Gojo-san's* honest intentions. 'Not one of your better ideas, darling,' I suggested.

Anna gave an impatient shrug and promptly marched into the shop to return a short while later. '*Gojo-san*, they are expecting you inside. I have left my wristwatch as security and they have been informed to let you have anything you want. Now, we'll be back in an hour with a taxi to carry all your equipment.' Anna was sounding rather more like Marg, but I think she felt it might be necessary to snap the little artist out of his trembles.

It kind of worked. *Gojo-san* reluctantly entered the premises, looking terrified and glancing back twice to see if we were still outside, perhaps thinking to make his escape the moment our backs were turned.

We duly returned in a taxi within an hour and Anna went in to pay for Gojo's purchases and to retrieve her watch. The proprietor shrugged, returning the watch. 'He is at the back and has bought nothing,' she said.

Anna found him in a dark corner of the shop quietly weeping. Faced with the prospect of being able to purchase everything he'd ever wanted he'd become confused and helpless.

'What's the matter, *Gojo-san*? Are you okay?' Anna asked, alarmed.

'Yes,' he sniffed tearfully, nodding his head.

'What is it then?'

The tiny man reached out and touched Anna lightly on the shoulder. 'It is you, *Anna-san*?' he asked ingenuously, seeming surprised that she appeared to be made of flesh and blood.

'Well, yes, it is,' Anna agreed smiling.

'Then I am still alive?'

Anna was tempted to laugh but it was at once obvious from *Gojo-san*'s tremulous demeanour that he wasn't joking. 'Yes, *Gojo-san*, you are alive and will be for a long time to come, I should hope.'

Judging from his expression he seemed profoundly relieved. Anna realised that finding himself surrounded by art materials of every description he had panicked and thought he must be hallucinating.

'Thank you,' *Gojo-san* said quietly. Whereupon, not having made a single purchase, Anna led him from the shop, clinging to her arm.

We then realised that in our own anxiety to leave Japan we were moving too fast, battering *Gojo-san*'s mind with too many stimuli. In a psychological sense it was no different from giving a starving man too much rich food – he simply couldn't mentally digest the impact of our clumsy albeit eager generosity.

He was due to start art lessons in two days so we phoned the art school and they offered to give us a list of his requirements. 'Make it a generous list, please,' I requested. 'One that will provide him with sufficient art supplies for a couple of years.'

Armed with an officially sanctioned list *Gojo-san* and Anna returned to the original shop, much to the joy of the proprietor who thought she'd lost the sale of the season.

Finally we decided the best way to provide *Gojo-san* with what he needed was to open a bank account in his name, explaining carefully to him how he could access it, as well as writing down the instructions in case he panicked at the thought of possessing not only more funds than he needed to survive for one day, but more than he had ever dreamed of. We ensured the amount was sufficient for him to attend school and eat well for the next year, during which time it was hoped he would start to paint selections from *Fuchida-san*'s butterfly collection.

As it turned out, the *oyabun* was genuinely excited about the prospect of his collection being immortalised in a book, thus allowing him to contribute to the entomology of Japan.

As one of the top figures in Japan's major criminal organisation he seemed to yearn for legitimacy. Of course, he insisted that he would take care of all the artist's expenses. But as Anna pointed out, it was going to be tough enough for *Gojo-san* to be accepted as a legitimate member of society without being totally beholden to the *oyabun* and the *yakuza*, yet another fringe organisation. Our small financial contribution would give him a sense of independence as a member of the larger community, and because we would be absent, he wouldn't feel that he must account to us for every coin he spent.

I guess it's easy to use money as an excuse to simply walk away from responsibility, especially when *Gojo-san* was going to need time, encouragement and friendship to become used to the idea of being treated as an equal in Japanese society. But frankly, there wasn't much more we could do except to promise that we would have him visit the islands when he felt ready to do so and, of course, if he felt inclined, to stay and paint every creepy-crawly or flying insect he could lay his hands on in the surrounding jungle.

Anna had taken a tremendous liking to him, and her liaison with Konoe Akira's *zaibatsu* meant she would need to come to Japan a couple of times a year, so she could check on Gojo Mura's progress and welfare then.

With the extra three days in Japan she managed to arrange a formal letter of appointment for herself as the representative of Konoe Akira's *zaibatsu* in the South-west Pacific. Anna also appointed Miss Sparkle as her Japanese agent with the right to sit in on the quarterly meetings the contract specified, concerning the fishing operations in the territorial waters of those island states Anna represented.

While this may not have seemed a significant appointment to someone of Miss Sparkle's stature, it was precisely what the *oyabun* required, the opportunity she needed to learn a business that had been in the same tightly held hands for centuries.

The *yakuza*, while having fishing interests of their own in the Southern Kuril Islands, were not the big player in the city fish markets they hoped to become, in fact did become, and still are today.

Miss Sparkle was now in a position to learn how the centuries-old system worked within the big city fish markets, and Anna had given her an entree which allowed her to sit in on the quarterly meetings of Konoe Akira's *zaibatsu*. In this way Miss Sparkle had the means of ultimately gaining valuable insights into the Japanese fishing industry. It was only a toe in the door, but one Miss Sparkle needed, and it served to pay back the considerable debt we owed for the help the *yakuza* had afforded us, a debt I had incurred because of my rashness.

In fact so much had happened between Anna and Konoe

Akira in so short a time that I was somewhat bewildered. We'd come looking for the key to Anna's problems, which had damaged and ruled her life for a quarter of a century, although even here there were contradictions – both her failure as a woman and her success in business could be laid at Konoe Akira's feet. We had fondly hoped that she would be cured of the former while maintaining the latter, and Anna believed with absolute certainty that if she surrendered her virginity, she would immediately lose her mental acuity and her power. Of course, this was palpable nonsense and she had openly admitted as much on a hundred occasions, and yet it still held her in its sway.

During one such discussion I'd said, 'Okay, this fear you have that sexual normalcy will only come at the expense of your brilliant mind, let me ask you, in money terms what are you worth?'

'Nicholas, I don't like to discuss wealth as an aggregation,' she said quite sharply.

'Yeah, okay, well let me put it a different way. If you never earned another penny in your life, do you have sufficient to live the rest of your life in your present more than comfortable manner?'

'Yes, of course,' Anna said dismissively.

'Okay, then if you elected to have normal sexual relations and as a consequence found yourself unable to make any more money, then so what?'

Anna appeared to be profoundly shocked by this notion. 'Then I would be a sexual zombie!' she cried.

'But just maybe you would conquer your fear and we would manage to make love normally and successfully and afterwards you would be as brilliant as ever. What then? Isn't it worth taking the chance?'

'Nick! *Ja*, you are now ridiculous!' Anna was plainly upset, her grammar and syntax immediately falling apart, something that almost never happened these days. '*Ja*, also, would you jump into the water in the middle of a deep river only because you have read some instructions in a book how you can swim?'

'If my life depended on it, yes, I suppose,' I said, knowing that no amount of logic was going to make any difference, and that I'd needlessly upset Anna.

'Nicholas, I wouldn't jump in the river,' Anna said firmly, recovering her poise, and I knew that she meant it. She had convinced herself beyond any logic that the chance of drowning was too great, that dying as she was, intact and yet damaged, would be preferable.

'Oh, I see,' I said ruefully.

'It has nothing to do with money or success,' she said.

'What then?'

'I don't know. Maybe he will tell me.'

'He? Konoe Akira?' Anna didn't reply and in a sudden fit of pique I said, 'Go on, say his name. Say it out loud! Shout it! Shout out, scream, KONOE AKIRA!'

'No.'

What was the use? Like her heroin addiction, she'd long since given up seeking psychiatric help, so we had hoped, perhaps forlornly, that coming to Japan and confronting her nemesis might be the solution. But it hadn't worked. Sexually, nothing had changed, although I sensed that something was different. What was it that had changed? I felt I needed to know before we left Japan. I knew I loved Anna and I didn't want to lose her. Now I tried to put all the pieces together, if only to explain things to myself.

Anna had offered no explanation, and yet, despite her kidnapping and the obvious trauma she'd suffered, she seemed curiously happy, even contented. Can one seriously suffer a major trauma and at the same time find contentment? Wasn't this a contradiction in terms? Yet it seemed to be the pattern for Anna's whole life. Trauma = Success = Contentment. I asked myself, was this possible? It was pointless trying to analyse her, or use logic to solve the riddle, which in effect meant that further discussion between us was a waste of time.

Konoe Akira had cruelly kidnapped Anna. She'd brilliantly avenged herself. More than this, she'd shown him how easily she could have been his nemesis if she'd wished. She'd effectively turned the tables, and now it was she who possessed power over him. Why then wasn't she on the way to being cured? If it wasn't about money or success, then what the hell was happening? She'd become involved with him again in quite a different way, and now they were partners in a new adventure.

That was it! I'd cracked it! What's more, she'd tied me into it as if we were an essential threesome, Joe and Kevin included simply because they were inextricably connected to me. And why? There could only be one reason. My inclusion made this new adventure with Konoe Akira both permissible and respectable in Anna's mind. She could maintain her psychological status quo; the threesome she depended on for her life hadn't been destroyed but had simply been reconfigured. Anna needed Konoe Akira's presence in her life as much as she needed mine. I decided to put this theory to her, expecting a denial, if only because I suspected it was a subconscious need which she could not have articulated or even acknowledged. Therefore I suggested we have our final night in Japan alone, so we could talk.

I had booked a secluded table at *La Brasserie*, the newly opened French restaurant on the mezzanine floor of the hotel, and now I was waiting in the living room to go to dinner.

Anna emerged from the bedroom dressed in a magnificent formal kimono with her hair done in the correct manner, and while she hadn't attempted to look like a geisha by whitening her face, she wore kohl to darken the area around her always astonishingly beautiful eyes and bright scarlet lipstick. On her feet were formal *tabi* and wooden toe-sandals.

'You look beautiful, very beautiful,' I said, delighted, beautiful being an understatement in this case. Anna seemed to have the knack of taking on the character of the clothes she wore – a pretty evening dress and all you could think to do was laugh and dance, feeling uninhibitedly joyous in her presence; a business suit and you wanted to sit down and listen respectfully; shorts and a T-shirt and you could smell the ocean and feel the slap of the waves. Now she looked serenely poised and perfectly Japanese.

'I thought just for tonight, our last in Japan, it would be appropriate, don't you think?'

'Brilliant!' I replied, almost lost for words. It was just like Anna. The formal kimono would have cost her thousands but she'd wanted to surprise me, and while most people might think it an atrocious waste of money for an occasion of no significance, I was overjoyed that she had dressed to please me. Had she worn this kimono to Konoe Akira's lunch, he would have been deeply gratified at the compliment, but she hadn't attempted to please him; it had been a formal business lunch and she'd dressed in a beautifully tailored business suit, entirely appropriate and signifying nothing personal.

We emerged from the hotel lift into the lobby and proceeded up the grand stairs leading to the mezzanine floor. It was packed with guests arriving for a wedding reception in the major conference room next door to the restaurant. There was a palpable gasp when the women, and I guess the men also, saw

Anna, then there was a discernable hush as every eye followed our progress up the stairs and into the restaurant.

There have been few moments in my life when I know I have witnessed perfection, of time, place and appearance, but this was one such moment. Here was an object of desire, of such stunning beauty that a hundred and fifty people were likely to carry an image in their minds forever of that rarest of all types of beauty in a mature woman, one that transcends race, colour or conventional perceptions. I couldn't help but wonder what they might have thought had they known the circumstances of Anna's life.

We ordered a good bottle of her favourite champagne and I broached the subject slowly. 'Anna, this is not only our last night in Japan but probably the last time I shall ever bring up the subject of your vaginismus. While you may wish to do so and I will always be happy to listen, after this I will never mention it again.'

'Oh, Nicholas, must it be tonight, on our last evening in Japan?' she asked, her expression alarmed.

'Darling, I've always loved you, but in the time we've been here I've learned to love you even more than I ever thought possible. I want to put this thing between us to rest forever.'

'I'm so glad!' she exclaimed. 'I couldn't bear it if you didn't love me, Nicholas. You do know, from the very beginning, from the age of sixteen, I've never wanted another man – the butterfly collector is the only one.'

'In a roundabout way, that's what I want to talk about. I have given our problem a great deal of thought.'

Anna reached out and took my hand. 'No, Nicholas, it is my problem, it is only our problem because you have suffered as a result of it.'

'Nevertheless, after coming here and meeting Konoe Akira, I now know that things are not going to change, that there will never be an instant cure, an epiphany, and I think I know why it may never be cured.'

'Nicholas, I want more than anything —'

'No, stop there, Anna. Let me speak. You don't need to explain. When I'm finished you may comment, although I expect you won't agree with me.'

'I will try, darling.'

I laughed. 'Shush! It will be quite understandable if you don't. Besides, you never try to agree with me; you either do or you don't, you never prevaricate. So, just hear me out, darling.'

I topped up her champagne and then, hesitating an instant, said, 'Anna, I've been thinking about myself and Konoe Akira. How both of us have been present in your life since you were sixteen.'

'Well yes, I suppose that's true,' Anna replied. 'I've never thought about it in that way.'

'But I think you have, if only subconsciously.'

'And what might you mean by that?' Anna said in a slightly defensive voice.

'Well, to fully complement your personality you need us both, that is, the influences both of us exert or have in the past exerted on you, to make you what you have become.'

'What are you trying to say, that I don't have a mind of my own?'

'Good lord, no! You're about the most original person I've ever known, darling.' I grinned. 'For the most part I don't even pretend to understand what's going on in your mind. But one of us is about loving you and the other is about discipline and success, one is emotion and the other is intellect. You crave both and you're terrified that if you obey the instinct to love completely you will lose the ability to think in an original and disciplined way. Moreover, if you choose not to have love in your life then that will be equally disastrous. We are creatures of both emotion and intellect; take either away and we're totally unbalanced. Perhaps refraining from physical love, yet loving in every other way, is the compromise that allows you to balance both of us in your life. You need Konoe Akira's psychological presence as much as you need my actual presence. We are both a necessary part of your life, and rather than resolve your problem with Konoe Akira, you have, in the last two weeks, gone to extraordinary lengths to keep the trinity intact. Konoe Akira and I are the two parts that make a whole in your life and you have no intention of losing either.'

Nearly ten minutes had passed and Anna hadn't touched her champagne; now she was weeping quietly. I reached for her hand and kissed it. 'Darling, I will always love you, and whether you agree or disagree with what I've said, it's not going to make me feel any differently about you.'

'Oh, Nicholas, I don't know if what you think is right. I just don't know!' she sobbed. 'Perhaps you are right.' She dabbed her tears with her table napkin then, looking at me directly, said, 'There is something I haven't told you about Konoe Akira.'

'Oh?'

'About meeting him again, you know, confronting him, hoping it might solve the problem. Nicholas, your conclusion is right, at least the first part. I had every reason to hate him – my kidnapping, my revenge . . . When I knew and he knew that I held his life in my hands, just as he had done mine in Java, in Tjilatjap, all the ingredients were there to resolve the psychological hold he'd had on me all this time. As you put it, I'd turned the tables. It should have worked, but it didn't.'

'You mean he still holds the same power over you?'

I asked, deeply shocked.

'Oh, God no! That's the whole point. That part worked perfectly! I'm not in the least in his thrall or power.'

'What then?'

'The vaginismus, it's not of his making. He's not the cause.'

'Oh, bullshit!' I burst out. 'Every psychiatrist you've ever seen has strongly suggested . . .'

'I know!' Anna said urgently. 'But it isn't, I just know it isn't.'

'But can you say what it is, what's caused it?'

'No!'

'Great. You know it isn't Konoe Akira, but you don't know who or what caused it?' I thought for a moment. 'Okay, what about the *kempeitai* colonel you . . .' I recovered just in time and changed direction. 'What was his name?'

'Takahashi. No, I had it before him. Definitely.'

'How could you know that? After all, you were a virgin.'

'Because every time I thought of you and tried to use my finger it happened.'

'Anna, why didn't you tell me this before? When did it first happen? Try to think. The very first time . . .'

'It was in Tjilatjap.'

'Before Konoe Akira or after?'

'That's the problem, I can't remember. Can you remember the first time you masturbated?' she asked.

'Yes. I was six, my Japanese nanny did it to me. I can still remember her cackle.'

Anna didn't even smile. 'It was a difficult time, my stepmother had committed suicide, my father was drinking himself to death, the boat was stuck in Tjilatjap. I was effectively a Japanese prisoner of war and Konoe Akira had possibly already taken possession of my life.'

'Anna, it's terribly important, can't you think? Before or after?'

'Nicholas, I knew nothing about sex. I thought the spasm was natural, a sort of protection before you married. I'd heard girls at school say your virginity had to be broken, something to do with the hymen. The cramping when I tried was, I thought, just something like that. You know, natural, it hadn't been broken so my finger couldn't get in and if I rubbed my clitoris it started to cramp. I can even remember that some of the girls had said it was a sin and I thought perhaps it was God punishing me.'

'But it happened round Konoe Akira's time?'

'Yes.'

'But you can't swear?'

'No. But I still feel certain he had nothing to do with it.'

'How long have you thought this?'

'Since the morning I visited him in hospital.'

'So we're no nearer the truth than before,' I said.

'Yes we are, Nicholas. All that clever stuff about the three of us being intimately bound together in a psychological knot can be dismissed.'

'I'm not at all sure about that, but you know more about knots than me, Anna.'

'That crack was entirely unnecessary, Nicholas!'

I grinned. 'Couldn't resist it.'

'Bastard!' she laughed.

'More champagne?'

'Maybe later. I too have something to say to you.'

'Well at least our Japanese sojourn ends with a bang not a whimper.'

'Is that another snide crack?'

'What?'

'Ends with a bang?'

'Oh, I see, that sort of bang. No, it's T.S. Eliot misquoted. What was it you wanted to say, darling?'

Anna took a sip of champagne – more than a sip, half the glass. 'Nicholas, can you remember the terrible row we had at Beautiful Bay fifteen or sixteen years ago?'

'Guilty as usual. I started it.' I pointed to the bottle. 'We were drinking.'

'It was the worst two months of my life, worse than the Japanese, worse than anything,' Anna confessed.

'Can't say I enjoyed it myself. I was drunk most of the time, slept around with any moll I could pick up. "Hello, who are you?" I'd ask in the morning.'

'Then Joe came to the rescue.'

'Thank Christ for Joe,' I said, trying to keep the conversation light. Anna's confession that it was the worst time of her life, especially given the events of her life, was a fairly startling admission, even if perhaps not entirely true.

'After we got together were you faithful to me?' Anna asked.

'No, not until just before this trip.'

'Good. That is the correct answer.'

'What, you've been checking on me?'

'I asked Joe.'

I laughed. 'How do you know you can trust him?'

'Joe never lies.'

It was true.

'So what does all this mean?'

'You have permission.'

'Permission for what?'

'To sleep with Marg.' Anna burst into tears.

I was too shocked to respond except to take a deep breath

and exhale, then to exclaim, 'Oh.'

Anna wiped her tears away and was quickly back in control. 'Since her husband's death she has called you every week. I know you loved her very much, Nicholas. It was her or me and if she hadn't chosen someone else I think I would have lost.'

'Oh, Anna, Anna, what am I expected to say?'

'Expected? You're *expected* to say, "Thanks, but no thanks," but no, I don't really want you to say that. Nicholas, we have tried everything now, and provided we can continue our relationship, because I can't bear to think I will lose you, then I want you to make up your mind. Whatever you decide I will honour it.'

'Phew! It should be easy, but somehow it isn't,' I said, knowing that Anna had read me like an open book. I knew that I still cared deeply for Marg. Knew I wanted her. If ever anything should happen to Anna, I would go knocking on her door. But now, of course, there was that awkward conversation we'd had, just before I left for Japan, where I'd turned down Marg's generous offer. She might well see herself as a woman scorned, and when I came grovelling back be unlikely to welcome me into her forgiving arms. 'How much time have I got?' I asked.

Anna glanced down at her watch. 'One minute, starting now.'

'Hang on, what if Marg says go to buggery?'

'Fifty seconds! She won't.'

'How can you say that?'

'Forty-three seconds! Because I'm a woman.'

'How can it be made to work?'

'Thirty-four seconds.'

'What if I can't make up my mind?'

'Twenty-four seconds! You already have.'

'Anna, I don't want to lose you!'

'Fifteen seconds! You won't.'

'Help!'

'Five seconds!'

'Yes!'

Anna turned and signalled to the waiter. 'Another bottle of Cristal, please, *garçon*,' she said. She turned back to me. 'Now we work out the rules.'

Okay, now somewhere around this time I should have been acting like the stronger sex, being a little assertive, maybe making a few conditions of my own. But, what would they be? I would have felt noble, strong, in control, if I'd said, 'Thanks, but no thanks, Anna. It's lovely of you, darling. Makes me love you even more,' but I would also have been a hypocrite.

I was forty-six years old, and my sexual drive was still strong. Anna was wonderful in bed but men always hanker for what they can't have. I confess to feeling sorry for myself on more than one occasion, even telling myself I had the best excuse in the world to play up behind Anna's back. And I'd tried it, and found that it was just bonking – nice bonking, because the regular women in my life were nice people and I'd be a hypocrite if I said anything else. But sex is sex and love is love, and sex with love is quite a different matter. If what I had with Anna was unconsummated it was still a relationship filled with love and I feel sure, if I'd been forced to choose, it would have been Anna every time.

Now she was offering me her love as well as the opportunity to have sex with the other woman I loved. It was generous almost beyond comprehension. I suppose I should have been quietly joyous at the thought that I could have the two women I loved for myself, that is, of course, if Anna was right and Marg accepted, but suddenly I felt very scared. 'Rules? Maybe Marg won't accept your rules, Anna,' I said, attempting to assert myself, if only a little.

'She will. It's called "The Calendar of Nick's Joy". The first week of the month is mine, the second is yours, the third is Marg's and the last is yours again. For two weeks a month you're celibate.'

'Rule accepted!' I replied, thinking that with two such strong women in my life, a week in between each visit was probably a sound idea.

'The second rule. While *we* may talk about each other, *you* may not talk about us to each other. When we're with you it's one on one. Always.'

'Hey, that's a bit unfair. What if Marg says something nasty about you? Am I not supposed to defend you? Or the other way around?'

'Don't worry, she will and I will, but if you start taking sides we're all in trouble.'

'Any more rules?'

'No, but Marg's bound to have a few of her own.' Anna lifted her glass. 'Shall we drink to "The Calendar of Nick's Joy"?'

'Wait on, you only call me Nick when you're mad at me.'

'I *am* mad at you, Nicholas, but I'll learn to live with it. The Calendar!' Anna said, touching my glass.

And so ended our last evening in Japan, one of the more surprising and unexpected, I admit, of my life.

The following morning we found ourselves on the way to Haneda Airport in a cavalcade of six cars, two Toyotas in front filled with *yakuza* troops, the big black Mercedes containing

Miss Sparkle, *Fuchida-san* and *Gojo-san*, then two more Toyotas behind. Then came the chrome monster, the powder-blue Cadillac driven by Staff Sergeant Goto, where, in the immaculate white leather back seat, thick as thieves, sat Konoe Akira, our new business partner in the South Pacific, Anna and myself.

All the trouble and strife and the one delight (Gojo Mura) of our visit to Japan had come to farewell us. We had arrived weeks previously knowing little and eager to experience everything and we were leaving Japan having experienced too much and eager to depart quickly and quietly.

But I must say, it was a strange and unique experience to watch as the head of the Tokyo *yakuza*, weeping copious tears, clung to Anna, reluctant to let her go, despite final calls for passengers. Miss Sparkle may have been as tough as old boot leather, but it was obvious she loved that girl to bits.

I couldn't help but feel, not without a certain sense of foreboding, that with Miss Sparkle and Konoe Akira once again her bedfellows, Anna was entering a different world, one that, for better or worse, would launch her into the real big time, but which could also possibly return her to the dark shadows she'd experienced in their company so very long ago on a different island. But I also knew that this was a different Anna, stronger than the one who had arrived nearly a month earlier when her ghosts had not yet been laid to rest.

We'd come to Japan ostensibly to buy a freighter, and thanks to Anna's skill and diplomacy I'd ended up with two. But, more importantly, our secret shared purpose – to attempt to assuage the pain of her past by confronting her nemesis, Konoe Akira – had strangely been achieved despite my bull-in-the-china-shop clumsiness over her kidnapping, which had added God knows how much to the sum of her distress.

Anna had obtained her pound of flesh by scaring the living daylights out of her dark angel and, as a consequence, she had gained both his immense admiration and respect and perhaps even deepened his undoubted love for her. She'd also set herself up to profit hugely from a business association with him in the future.

In addition to all this, Kevin, Joe and I stood to become rich men as a result of her brains, guts, effort and, yes, additional suffering. We were all about to get a free ride on Anna's golden goose with me clinging, so to speak, to its tail feathers.

Not a bad outcome when all was said and done, not forgetting that if you hang on to a set of tail feathers too long they're likely to come away in your hands.

But of all of these outcomes, one mattered more to me than all the rest. By the time I'd strapped myself into the seat of the Qantas jet, there was no doubt in my mind that Anna was free of Konoe Akira's influence. If she hadn't been cured of her vaginismus and if its source lay elsewhere in her damaged past, perhaps never to be discovered, most of the other ghosts of the past had been put to rest. Her vaginismus was not due to his influence and had no bearing on the disciplines he had taught her all those years ago. It was this knowledge that allowed her to make the ultimate loving gesture, to share the man she loved with someone else.

While, of course, I had initial pangs of guilt, I also felt enormously honoured that I was still a loving part of this convoluted, mixed-up, damaged, undoubtedly brilliant, unreadable, enigmatic, stubborn, drug-addicted, strong-willed, frustrating, loyal, loving, generous, exciting and beautiful woman. She was also, if you'll excuse the pun, the world's greatest expert at tying a man up in all sorts of knots. Anna, Anna, Anna, how deeply I miss you!

PART THREE

CHAPTER FOURTEEN

'I was simply casting my net for future stars.
They won't all make it.
When you're fishing for stars
even some very bright ones
fall through the net.'
Anna, Solomon Islands

THE FIFTEEN YEARS FROM the seventies to the mid-eighties brought a great deal more wealth for Anna. Everything she touched seemed to turn to gold and it was during this time that the real trouble started between her and Marg, and where the epithets Green Bitch and Princess Plunder evolved as the two women's worlds drew steadily further apart.

After we returned from Japan, Anna turned her business attention to Indonesia, although, unbeknownst to me, the land of her birth had been receiving her quiet attention for several years, more as a result of her time as a prisoner of war under the Japanese than from any fond memories of her childhood in Batavia.

Every year since I can remember Anna would visit Indonesia, but from around 1965 she began visiting at least three times a year, ostensibly to see her Javanese family, as she referred to Mother Ratih and her son Budi and *Kleine* Kiki (Little Kiki).

If asked she would say, 'We have lots of fun, I practise the language and I help them with their restaurant businesses, which are doing very well; they now have two more.' In truth, while she was enormously fond of the two women and, of course, Budi, whom she regarded as her little brother, I would eventually discover the visits were to conduct regular reviews of a rapidly expanding property empire initially based on the money Anna had left behind during the war.

Perhaps a little background is warranted. Anna, her father, stepmother and personal maid, *Kleine* Kiki, had been stranded when their refugee ship the *Witvogel* broke down and limped into Tjilatjap, a river port on the east coast of Java, where it remained for the duration of the war. Her paraplegic stepmother had subsequently committed suicide by rolling her wheelchair over the edge of a wooden dockside; her father died of diabetes brought on by advanced alcoholism; and *Kleine* Kiki, an indigenous Javanese, was apprenticed by Anna to Mother Ratih, the cook and manager of a small kampong restaurant, a widow with a young son, Budi, whom she couldn't afford to keep at school and who worked for a local Chinese merchant named Lo Wok.

Anna's father left her a steel box he'd brought away with him that contained his will, personal papers, several valuable diamonds and a considerable amount of money in Dutch guilders. It was cash that Anna knew would be taken from her as soon as it was discovered, and, furthermore, as a Japanese prisoner of war she had no way of concealing it. She consequently used it to buy the kampong restaurant for Mother Ratih as well as a native house each for her and *Kleine* Kiki, which left sufficient funds to put Budi through high school and then university after the war and independence. Anna had also paid the passage money that allowed Lo Wok to escape to

Malaya when the Japanese were systematically murdering the local Chinese merchants in Tjilatjap. Sadly, he may well have been killed in the massacre of Chinese that took place in that country in the sixties.

In return for her generosity, and perhaps remarkably in those hard times, Mother Ratih and Budi kept the remainder of the money, still a considerable amount, in safekeeping. The diamonds Anna managed to hide in the brass casing of a military revolver shell that she then sealed with candle wax and inserted, whenever necessary, in a very private women's place. She used the precious stones to fund her share of the bondage house, Madam Butterfly, when she got to Australia, and to buy her first three workers' houses in a slum area of the city. I had met Budi and his mother and stepfather – a lieutenant in the police force, now deceased – when, after the war, I went to Java in an attempt to find Anna.

All this seems a rather long way of saying that by the mid-sixties Mother Ratih and *Kleine* Kiki had prospered and Budi had graduated from the new University of Indonesia as a lawyer. When Anna made her big move into Indonesia he was a captain in the army.

Anna had already laid the foundation of what was to become a vast property portfolio, but it grew dramatically as she capitalised on several turning points in the young country's history, the first of which was the demise of Indonesia's first president, Sukarno. Like most resistance leaders who become president, he built a great many monuments in praise of himself and ran the national economy into the ground until the poor were starving and the middle class had become totally disaffected. Many of both classes subsequently joined the PKI, the communist party directly aligned with Peking. With Sukarno ailing and isolated, the PKI attempted a coup in 1965 that was put down by a relatively obscure army officer, Major General Suharto. He then took over the army and the government and subsequently became the next president of Indonesia. It was at this time, in the most disastrous circumstances, that Anna saw an opportunity to truly prosper.

Following the suppression of the coup, in 1966 Suharto went after the communists and the previous president's immensely rich Chinese cronies. The army presided over the murder of possibly a million Indonesians accused of being communists or fellow travellers. In addition many of those Chinese who had grown rich under the founding president Sukarno and who posed a threat to the new regime were either slaughtered or in some cases exiled, their property seized by the army and appropriated by Suharto's followers.

The army's approach to the killing was unsophisticated but very effective: they would enter a town or a village and order the population to round up all the communist party members and sympathisers, while the army detachment set up a cordon around the area. The locals were then ordered to kill all the people who had been rounded up. The wealthy Chinese, traditionally hated by the people, were even easier prey. Victims were hacked, strangled, burned and beaten to death en masse by the frenzied mobs. This complicity in the killings is one of the reasons why most Indonesian citizens were and still are reluctant to revisit the events of 1966, which have been virtually expunged from official records; a truthful version of events at the time has never appeared in the nation's official history books. Many countries have revised, rewritten or ignored the blacker parts of their own history – witness Australia's attitude to the history of the invasion of Aboriginal lands, or the gap in the official records about the massacre of the Chinese in Malaysia in the early sixties.

Budi, a lawyer and a captain in the army, was undoubtedly

heavily embroiled in organising some of the killing, in this way gaining favour with the new Suharto regime. Years later he inadvertently mentioned to me that in 1966 he'd been stationed in Bali, where over 200 000 communists and fellow travellers were killed in that year. It was inconceivable that Budi would not have been involved, especially given his later influence and power in the Suharto hierarchy. Nevertheless, he was too low in rank to get much direct benefit from this macabre bonanza. Still, he was in the right place at the right time, and under Anna's instructions, he was able to use her inheritance to buy for a song former Chinese-owned mercantile properties from the suddenly property-rich but often cash-strapped generals. Moreover, he was able to do his own conveyancing, thus ensuring watertight titles.

Anna sensed that Bali, a tourist resort popular with the Dutch since the 1930s, would take off again, so they bought several sites in Denpasar and Kuta Beach. But most of the properties suitable for restaurants were in the better areas of major cities in Java – Jakarta, Surabaya, Solo, Semarang, Jogjakarta – and Cilacap, the large town, now a city, formerly known as Tjilatjap, where Anna had spent the war.

Anna, as usual, had a long-term plan which she had formulated on her first trip to America in the late fifties when she'd attended a clinic in an attempt to withdraw from her heroin addiction. There she'd noted and been impressed by a Kentucky Fried Chicken outlet. After fish, chicken is the next most commonly consumed protein by the middle class in Indonesia. It also constituted a large part of the cuisines of the four restaurants the two women owned. On her next visit to Indonesia Anna registered the KFC initials and the name Kiki's Fried Chicken for a nationwide restaurant chain.

Suharto and his cronies, having eliminated the

communists and the influence of mainland China, were quick to establish relations with the West, and Indonesia was soon seen as a valuable anti-communist ally of America. Foreign investment poured into the country, the standard of living rose immeasurably and Indonesia became one of the fastest-growing economies in Asia.

As soon as all things American were once more in favour, Anna got *Kleine* Kiki and Mother Ratih to restyle their rapidly growing Kiki's Fried Chicken restaurant chain to resemble a typical American Kentucky Fried Chicken outlet. Foreigners who had visited America and Americans themselves thought of Kiki's Fried Chicken as a quaint imitation of one of America's cultural icons, a form of Asian sycophancy, and smiled indulgently, at the same time often remarking that Kiki's spicy chicken was infinitely tastier than the original eleven herbs and spices of the Colonel Sanders American version.

By the mid-seventies Anna, together with her two partners, had acquired ninety-eight potential restaurant sites and converted forty into Kiki's Fried Chicken restaurants. In each instance Anna owned half the property, *Kleine* Kiki owned a quarter, and since her death in 1970, Mother Ratih's quarter had passed to Budi.

In 1975 Kentucky Fried Chicken decided to enter the burgeoning South-East Asian economy, by which time the rules of doing business in Indonesia were truly set in concrete. To operate in the country you needed to have a local partner, almost certainly drawn from among the ruling army clique, who would also require a majority holding.

By this time Budi had risen in rank and status and was now a colonel and a junior member of Suharto's kleptocracy. It didn't take Kentucky Fried Chicken long to sniff the wind and examine the lie of the land and soon Kiki's Fried Chicken was converted to the real thing, with Anna and her two partners owning fifty-one per cent of the profits. Moreover, they owned outright the real estate of forty of the outlets and sold half of the remaining fifty-seven outlets for a vast fortune to their American partners. Anna, with Budi as her gatekeeper, was now in business as a big-time player in Indonesia.

It stands to reason that Anna must have endured several failures in business over the years. Most great self-made business successes are built on failure, which is where the lessons are learned that ultimately lead to success. Apart from her Indonesian successes, she'd taken the considerable fortune she'd made selling the site for Nauru House and built an international conglomerate. Increasingly she would be referred to in the financial sections of the newspapers as Australia's richest businesswoman, her fortune often compared with that of the wealthiest male tycoons. But Anna seldom talked about business when she was at Beautiful Bay and I knew as little of her successes as I did of her failures. That is, except for the Japanese–Pacific fishing business that had resulted from our trip to Japan.

Today, in the islands of the South-west Pacific, cruise ships deliver tourists eager to pick up bargain bangles, beads, T-shirts and sarongs, as well as a quick dose of island culture, but in the 1970s, which doesn't seem all that long ago, the islands were backwaters. The shorts, white hose and short-sleeved shirts of the perspiring white men and the cotton dresses and sandals of the exasperated and constantly complaining women usually indicated one of the three Ms – missionaries, misfits or mercenaries, the last two categories usually consisting of Australians or New Zealanders, with the occasional American or even European. Pacific Islanders have always had a pragmatic view of white folk. Providing you don't break any tribal taboos they accept you as they find you, angel or bastard or, more commonly, a mixture of both.

I had chosen the Solomon Islands carefully for our first foray into the fishing business. The winds of change were beginning to blow in the islands and, like all change, they brought confusion. New Guinea, the largest of the islands, and the second largest in the world, was five years away from independence, but at the start of the seventies, even the most optimistic supporters of independence, as well as the Australian Government, believed that it was far into the future, despite the fact that Indonesia had been enjoying independence for decades.

My own home, the New Hebrides, with its joint British and French administration, was torn between the British desire for a graceful exit and the French determination to hold onto their Pacific territories come what may. If they caved in over the New Hebrides they felt certain that the valuable nickel reserves in New Caledonia would be threatened and, of course, no government in its right mind was going to give up Tahiti.

The British had already signalled that Fiji was to be granted independence on 10 October 1970, with the Solomon Islands to follow in the not too distant future. In preparation for this, Solomon Islanders were increasingly filling the lower levels of the public service, although British expatriates still clung to the top jobs and headed the government departments.

Every week Joe, who got the weekly newspapers from every island state brought in by ship, sent me clippings mapping the progress of 'his' islanders, the names of recipients of Uncle

Joe Scholarships underlined in red. Joe never lost touch with his kids, many by now adults. People said of Joe that, when independence came, he could choose to stand for president of any of the emerging nations in the South-west Pacific and it would turn into a one-horse race. He had grown an afro – greying at the sides – and at six feet four inches of hard, firm-gutted man, he looked every inch a chief.

'Fuckin' nigger. Dey gonna make him da king! Where our profits gonna go den? You tell me, buddy. Every piccaninny got hisself a scholarship ta Yale!' Kevin would shout down the phone from Brisbane. His last words invariably were, 'Nick, ya gotta do sumthin' 'bout dat nigger! Dem Uncle Joe's, dey eatin' us outa da house 'n' home. Bren Gun gotta ask can she buy another pair a shoes, ferchrissakes!'

Kevin's wife Brenda must have already rivalled Imelda Marcos in the shoe department, and after Uncle Joe, her love of designer shoes was Kevin's greatest worry. 'She live a hunnerd years she ain't gonna wear all dem Froggy an' Wop shoes. Some ain't even outta da fuckin' wrappin' after two years already, already!'

I had made my initial approach to the senior local public servant in the Chief Minister's Department knowing that, strictly speaking, protocol demanded I go through the British expatriate Department Secretary, but I was pretty sure I'd be forgiven my transgression. Gerald Fitzgerald (why do parents do that double-name thing to their kids?) was a good bloke who was doing everything he could to bring the new breed of island public servants up to the mark in the best British tradition. I knew he had high hopes for Joseph Abraham Minusi, whom I'd met on one or two previous occasions on shipping business, finding him both pleasant and efficient. It was common knowledge that he was being groomed for higher office and was a shoo-in for the first local head of the public service.

There are plenty of expatriates happy to tell you that the locals couldn't run a chook raffle. While I admit over the years since independence there have been more than a few disastrous appointments, this certainly wasn't true of Joseph Minusi, who seemed born to be a top administrator and a good one. He was honest, extremely hardworking, loyal and highly intelligent, alas, characteristics that are almost impossible to find today in independent island politicians and civil servants. I expected that Joseph Minusi would get tired of venal and incompetent politicians and would end up as prime minister himself. I trusted him completely.

As the 727 burst through the heavy cloud on its final approach, Anna and I had fastened our seatbelts for the landing at Henderson Field. We swept low over land before our final turn to approach from the sea, the lush green plains of Guadalcanal visible through my left-hand window. 'Look!' I yelled, pointing at a rocky mountaintop sticking up out of the jungle. 'That's where I captured Gojo Mura!' Moments later we came in low over Bloody Ridge, where I could so easily have died in combat and where so many marines gave their lives. I was reminded how precarious is our hold on this planet and that I'd had more than my fair share of luck. Anna and Gojo Mura had also come as close as a whisker to death, Anna at the hands of the Japanese *kempeitai* and Gojo at my own. My orders had been to shoot him on sight and I could easily have done so had he not been seated on a log painting a butterfly. Anna's extraordinary beauty had saved her, Gojo Mura's talent had saved him, but my salvation was just plain luck – the bullet that missed me by a hair's breadth hit someone else's beloved son.

The long contrails of moist air streaming from the flaps as we came over the end of the runway showed that the atmosphere was as humid as ever. I recalled arriving here for the first time and landing on the bumpy marsden matting that had since been replaced with asphalt. I had stepped off the plane wearing the full blue serge uniform of a naval lieutenant and felt as if I had walked directly into a foundry furnace.

We were met by Jimmy, our local manager and a relative of Ellison, who you will recall was once the native leader of my coastwatch gang during the war and still worked as my indispensable right-hand man. Jimmy had attended boarding school in Brisbane, compliments of an Uncle Joe Scholarship. Ellison made sure that all his relatives were educated and employed by the company, a system that worked well because any slack-arse amongst them was dealt with by the family, so there was seldom any trouble. In fact, between Joe and Ellison we probably had the best labour relations in the islands.

We loaded our bags in the Toyota four-wheel drive and I noticed that Jimmy had washed it in our honour. I visited Honiara often enough that the way into town was as familiar to me as the roads around Port Vila, but when you have someone with you who is seeing everything for the first time – Anna had never visited the town – it's as if you see things in a fresh way yourself: Chinatown on our right, a motley collection of buildings of every type of construction with a predominance of corrugated iron and an insufficiency of paint; the pot-holed tarmac; the one-lane Bailey bridge across the Mataniko River built by the Yanks to last a year or so, now unpainted and weary-looking but still doing duty more than twenty-six years later. We approached the sprawling markets, at this hour relatively quiet after the early-morning mayhem where each islander seems to generate twice or three times the noise and laughter that Europeans in a similar environment might create. The morning market is a happy, generous-spirited place, attended as much for its fraternity, laughter and gossip as it is for shopping for food and the miscellanea of domestic life. Groups of locals were still standing around as if reluctant to go home to their villages to tend their vegetable gardens.

Anna knew and loved the islands but had only passed through Honiara and never seen beyond the airport at Henderson Field. She immediately noticed the three distinct racial groups – Melanesian, Micronesian and Polynesian – remarking on the Western Islanders, said to be the blackest people on earth, whose skin was blue-black, almost purple. I explained that there were over eighty ethnic and cultural groups on the island, and Anna, noticing people with light coffee-coloured skin and blond hair, said dryly, 'Yes, and I can see that the Europeans have been having a good time fraternising with some of them, Nicholas.'

'Not so,' I laughed. 'That red-blond hair occurs naturally amongst the Malaitan Islanders; it's a sport, that is a genetic mutation. It's common enough to be accepted as quite normal, even typical.' I pointed to another group of Asiatic-looking people and explained, 'They're Gilbert Islanders, transported from barren and unsustainable islands by the British after the war, who had unsuccessfully attempted to settle them on the Line and Phoenix Group in the mid-Pacific before the war.'

Jimmy pulled up outside the Mendana Hotel on the waterfront, where our bags were taken to our beachside suite.

I could be transported blindfolded from anywhere in the world to a hotel room with the blinds drawn and I would immediately know I was in the Pacific Islands just by the smell of mould and mildew mixed with the sharp taint of a spent mosquito coil. I explained as a matter of no possible interest to Anna that the hotel was named after Alvaro de Mendana, who had discovered the island group and claimed it for Spain in 1568. She sniffed, moving towards the drawn curtains. 'And they haven't opened the windows since then?'

We grabbed what we could find from the smorgasbord counter at the late end of lunch in the hotel dining room and then set off down the street to one of the few two-storey mildly imposing buildings in town for our two-thirty appointment with Joseph Minusi.

'Look,' Anna cried, pointing to the pavement, which was stained with hundreds of red splatters from betel nut, the mild narcotic chewed by Solomon Islanders. 'Must have been a big gathering.'

I looked down at the vivid red blotches on the cement. 'Nah, you see it outside every public administration building, people spitting as they wait outside.'

'It's not a pretty habit, but when it comes to narcotics, who am I to speak?' Anna conceded.

'Damned nuisance, if you ask me. When one of our ships does the Solomon Islands or New Guinea run, the streaks of red running from the scuppers over the white paint make it look as if there's been a massacre on board. Takes some getting off the deck as well.'

We entered the building and were greeted by a pretty light-skinned young Malaitan receptionist who'd taken her fuzzy blonde halo several shades lighter at the local hair salon. 'Mr Duncan, the Department Secretary Mr Fitzgerald wishes to see you before your appointment with Joseph Minusi,' she smiled.

'Uh oh, trouble is it, Olive?' I asked, having met her on several previous visits.

'No, I just think he wants to say hello,' she laughed.

I glanced at my watch. 'Will you let Joseph know where I am?' I asked, not wishing to be late, even though island time is fairly lax and a delay of fifteen minutes wouldn't be regarded as rude.

'Oh, he already knows,' Olive said, thus indicating that Joseph had been circumspect enough to discuss my appointment with his expat superior.

Gerald Fitzgerald was a lanky, freckled Englishman whose thinning ginger hair was peppered with grey. He had an easy smile and, unlike many of the other expatriate civil administrators, was invariably well-mannered and agreeable. He liked the islands and the islanders and they him, and he seldom stood on ceremony; he was just as likely to grab a couple of kids in his arms when visiting a village as not. 'Him belong England also belong Solomon Island,' they commonly said about him.

'Nice to see you again, Nick,' he said, rising from behind his desk, then turning to Anna he said admiringly, 'And you're Nick's partner, Miss Til? Well, well, how nice, welcome to Honiara.' He indicated two chairs. 'Have you a moment or two to spare? Tea?'

'No, no, we've just had a late lunch, but thank you,' I declined. We sat and he took a third chair, crossing his lanky Ichabod Crane legs.

'Mind if I smoke?' He lit a cigarette, leaned back, took a puff, exhaled and said, 'Fish, eh?'

Anna glanced at me and I nodded. 'Yes, Mr Fitzgerald, we —'

'No, no, call me Gerald, and may I call you Anna?'

Anna gave him one of her knockout smiles that leave men's knees rubbery. 'Yes, please, Gerald, I'd like that very much,' she said in a throaty voice, then, 'As I was about to say, we hope to apply for a licence to fish in your coastal waters on behalf of a Japanese syndicate I represent.'

'Yes, so Joseph tells me. Jolly good. Don't see too many problems there. One small thing, though . . .' We waited. 'The island government's share . . . forty-nine per cent?'

'Oh?' Anna asked, smiling.

'We thought it generous,' I said quickly. 'I am aware that no foreign-owned businesses working here have partnerships with the island government – our own shipping line for instance, or Levers with their vast copra plantations and their timber operations at Kolombangara.'

Gerald Fitzgerald took a casual puff, squinting through the smoke as he exhaled. 'A British company, Levers, have been here a long time,' he said lazily. 'Things are changing fast as I feel sure you are aware, Nick. It won't be long before we Brits are gone. First Fiji and then I imagine here. My job now is to lend a helping hand.'

'Of course,' Anna replied. 'That's why we are determined to set a precedent. We have built in a significant share beyond the separately negotiated initial licensing fees so that any future government has a continuing source of income.'

'Extremely generous, my dear.' He paused and looked up at the ceiling, then, as if thinking aloud, 'It's just that one little missing unit, the one per cent difference. In my experience it's small enough to seem insignificant, but on the other hand large enough to cause a great many future problems.' Before either of us could reply he straightened up, seemingly in sections, and rose to his feet, indicating that the interview was over. 'Very well then, I'll leave you in the more than capable hands of Joseph.' He smiled, extending his own hand. 'I feel sure you'll sort it out between yourselves. Perhaps you'd like to join Maggie and me for a drink. The Resident Commissioner has invited us to his home and has asked that we bring you along. Shall we say I pick you up at your hotel at six o'clock?'

We duly agreed and said our goodbyes at the door. 'Well, what was that all about?' I ventured to Anna.

'The forty-nine–fifty-one split in favour of the Japanese, he's gently warning us it's not on. It's equal shares, so that Konoe Akira's people don't have the majority in future if there's a disagreement,' Anna replied.

'And the invitation to the Resident Commissioner's place? Can't say I've had too many of those before.'

Anna grinned. 'That very much remains to be seen, but it's a good omen, I should think.'

We walked the length of the long corridor to Joseph Minusi's office, where his serious-faced secretary rose to greet us. 'Mr Duncan, Madam, Mr Minusi is waiting; to follow now please,' she said formally, indicating to me that she was already rehearsing for independence. It was unusual for island-born secretaries to refer to their native-born boss formally, the friendly islanders usually called their own people, even their superiors, by their Christian names. She took the three or four steps to the door, knocked and opened it immediately.

Joseph must have heard us arrive because he was already halfway to the door. 'Nick, welcome, come in!' he called, his hand extended. Then to my surprise he dropped my hand, looking surprised and delighted to see Anna. 'Missus Anna! I didn't know it was you who was coming with Nick!' he cried enthusiastically.

I glanced at Anna, who looked equally surprised. 'You two know each other?'

'Of course!' Joseph laughed, 'I don't think Missus Anna would remember.' He turned back to her. 'It was fifteen years since you came with Uncle Joe to Noro.' Joseph took Anna's hand, holding it in both his own. 'You paid my school fees through King George School.' He turned to me. 'If it wasn't for her generosity I wouldn't have won a scholarship to university in New Zealand. My brother, Wilson, she paid for him also. He went to Queensland University, now he's Deputy Secretary of Finance.' He released Anna's hand. 'This is a very nice moment for me, Missus Anna,' he beamed.

'And a very nice one for me too, Joseph. I apologise for not recognising your surname. I knew you only as a boy called Joseph, a very bright one as I recall Uncle Joe telling me at the time, but now you're a big man. I'm glad I was able to help you and your brother, although, from what I hear from Nicholas, you'd have got here under your own steam.'

'Please,' Joseph said, indicating two chairs set out in front of his desk. 'Lily, bring tea, hey!' he called, before seating himself behind his desk.

The office was humid and a desultory ceiling fan stirred rather than cooled the torpid afternoon air. The sound of a truck banging over potholes filtered through the dusty pink louvres, momentarily drowning the laughter and the snatches of singing from a group of islanders we'd seen squatting in the shade under the wide eaves of the building.

'You've read the contract, of course, so I'll be brief.' I explained that Anna was representing the *zaibatsu*, the Japanese syndicate interested in procuring a fishing licence and establishing a joint venture, and that she would explain further shortly. Then I proceeded briefly to outline the aspects of the proposed deal we – that is Joe, Kevin Judge and I – would be responsible for, in particular the fish factory.

Lily then brought tea (milky and too sweet), and I sat back and let Anna get on with her presentation and was again struck by her calm, forthright negotiating manner. I noted that her voice had an almost hypnotic quality, assured and convincing without ever appearing overenthusiastic, strident or honeyed. 'The Japanese are keen to be seen as partners rather than as foreign exploiters,' she said evenly, not stressing the last two words so that they passed almost unnoticed, although I knew they wouldn't be. 'They are conscious that their reputation has been damaged by their behaviour during the war and they want to emphasise that they come as friends and equals.'

'Equals?' Joseph said quickly. 'I notice there is a difference of one per cent in the two shares . . .'

Anna smiled. She had been correct about Fitzgerald. 'It seemed reasonable as my client is supplying all the capital to build the infrastructure for the project as well as supplying the pole and line fishing boats and the equipment for the cannery and freezing works.'

'With a general fishing licence this might be reasonable,' Joseph said evenly. 'But did you not request an *exclusive* licence to fish our coastal waters?'

'Yes, that's correct, and if this requires equal shares I feel sure my client will understand,' Anna said in an accommodating voice.

'Thank you,' Joseph Minusi said quietly. 'I will await their decision.'

Later Anna would explain that she'd already settled on a fifty-fifty deal before she'd left Japan. 'It was just a little leverage I built in, a bonus if you can get away with it, but invariably you can't. Everyone wants a little something extra. My grandfather had a Dutch saying about negotiating – I think he claimed it was Jewish – "Always remember to leave a little salt on the bread," he'd say.'

At the conclusion of Anna's presentation Joseph turned to me. 'Nick, what locations have you considered for the harbour and the cannery building?'

'Ah, obviously we haven't made a detailed survey, but several good locations spring to mind, pending your decision of course. Why? Do you have a suggestion?'

I waited. Nothing had changed and I hadn't expected it would. He paused for effect. 'I think Noro would be a particularly good choice for the building of just such a large project.'

I grinned to myself. 'Your people, eh?'

Joseph didn't even look embarrassed. 'Yes, my father is the paramount chief in the area and if you should choose Noro I can guarantee the project will have the government's full support.'

'This will need the support of your Department Secretary though, won't it?' I now saw clearly why Joseph had taken the project to Gerald Fitzgerald.

'Of course,' he said, not batting an eye.

'And you're confident?'

'Extremely,' he assured me with a shrug.

Later Anna would tell me that it hadn't been necessary to ask Joseph if he was confident he had the approval of the Department Secretary. 'You were gilding the lily, Nicholas, and besides, it was almost patronising.'

'Hang on!' I protested. 'What about that friendly hands across the sea bit, remorseful partners and not foreign exploiters? That was spreading it on pretty thick!'

'Nicholas, Nicholas, have you ever heard of James Thompson, the extreme leftwing professor of business studies at Auckland University where Joseph studied? No, of course not. Thompson constantly brainwashed and indoctrinated his island students about the iniquities of their exploiting colonial masters and the rapine of the islands by big business, French, British and Australian. Joseph practically purred when I came out with that little gem!'

'Oh, so you did know who he was when he first greeted us?'

'Of course.'

'And all those years back, with the scholarships? You knew then?'

'Don't be ridiculous, Nicholas. I was simply casting my net for future stars. They won't all make it. When you're fishing for stars even some very bright ones fall through the net. I got lucky with Joseph. I'm also keeping an eye on Wilson, his brother. Not quite as bright, but ambitious and a good accountant.'

'But how did you know he'd gone on to university and was now in the government over here?'

'When you mentioned his name and told me to send the contract ahead, I looked up my list.'

'List? You keep a list?'

Anna nodded. 'I make it my business to follow their educational progress and their careers. Joe keeps me in touch, lets me know what's needed. Who do you think paid his scholarship to Auckland University?'

I guess I'm never going to make the big league. My life has too much immediate action and not sufficient forethought. 'Humph. I personally felt I'd handled it all rather well in there,' I lamented.

'You did, Nicholas, *almost* all of it.'

'Now who's the one being patronising?' I grinned, knowing I was never going to win.

The day wasn't quite over. We were duly picked up at six o'clock by Gerald and his plump, no-nonsense wife Maggie, who was equally loved by the locals. In the car on the way to the Resident Commissioner's house, the Department Secretary said casually, 'Nick, I think the Commissioner and his lady wife would very much like to visit Japan.'

Anna didn't even pause to take a breath. 'Of course! The Japanese Government will be honoured to welcome his delegation, and I do hope you and Maggie can find the time to go, too. Perhaps Joseph? And I daresay there will be several others who are necessary to finalising the negotiations. You may have to put up with a day or two of formal welcoming, but after that, perhaps a week of sightseeing? Though it's starting to be a little cool at the moment. I recommend somewhere around, but not before, April – cherry blossom time. Let me know and I'll make the necessary arrangements with the Imperial Hotel. Any personal shopping will be at your own expense, of course, but I'm sure you can leave the rest in my care. I speak adequate Japanese and I'll enjoy being your guide.'

Well, I guess there's something to be said for negotiating a deal with a man recovering from an acute angina attack who is captive in a hospital bed in Tokyo. Anna would have anticipated all the necessary protocol and negotiated it with Konoe Akira and he, in turn, would have dealt with the Japanese government. By the time we'd returned from the Resident Commissioner's home it was game, set and match; the rights to a five-year exclusive fishing licence for the territorial waters controlled by the Solomon Islands together with an automatic renewal clause appeared to be all but certain.

Now, looking back, I can only sigh wistfully. A few free overseas trips, a couple of posh hotel suites and expensive dinners were all that was necessary sometimes for any agreement. They were the days when basically honest and disinterested administrators would assess a proposal on its merits and always in the interest of the majority of the locals. Now, as I write this, they have been replaced for the most part by a bunch of greedy indigenous political thugs who won't consider anything unless there is a significant cut from any deal for them, be it mammoth or minnow. Today, on any of the self-governing islands in the South-west Pacific, you couldn't hope to open a roadside chicken brazier without a politician or a nepotistic civil servant getting his cut on the chicken, the charcoal and a rent for the shade under the poinciana tree.

The likes of Joseph Abraham Minusi and most of the earlier island politicians who tried to work for the benefit of their own people are all but gone. Joseph, for instance, died on a civil service salary at the age of forty of a stroke, some claimed brought on by overwork and disillusionment.

Perhaps I am becoming reactionary in my old age, but Joe and I were so very keen on independence. In our opinion, with a few honourable exceptions, the islands were full of jumped-up white men earning too much and doing too little for it while they looked down their noses at the indigenous people, who we honestly believed deserved better and would do better on their own for their own people. Nobody has a monopoly on brains and Uncle Joe Scholarships were meant to create a lively and intelligent population. Nobody worked harder than Joe to bring it about. A black bloke born in the South, he knew what it was like to be regarded as inferior. If they ever make a model of a good man, they are going to use Joe as the template.

However, at dinner recently Joe lamented, 'Nick, if yoh converted all da aid and da handouts into cash and loaded it onto one dem landing craft we bought for salvage and left it on da beach, any beach, on any island state, in twelve months all dat money gonna be in da hands of da same folk. Ain't gonna be no paint foh schools, money foh books, food foh kids, med-dee-sin in da clinics, running water in da village, no pay foh nurses, teachers, doctors.' He sighed a special heavy Joe sigh. 'I ain't got no patience lef' for da muth'fuckers running da islands. Saffron, she gonna go live in Australia, ain't no use her stayin' in New Guinea no more. It fucked, man! Da rascals, dey running da streets and da politicians, dey got dere hand in ever' pocket. She cain't make no diff-fer-rence, like she brought up to do. Me, I gotta stay, I'm Uncle Joe. I cain't walk away from mah people. I gonna cry just thinkin' 'bout mah poor kanaka people, man!'

Right from the very beginning Anna had seen little or no value in starting a business in the islands. She had a number of sound reasons for this decision, the foremost being that she didn't want a partnership with me, or the three of us. She also claimed that unless the business was self-contained and earned most of its income on the islands, such as our shipping line and the building and employment company she'd enabled us to create, a venture manufacturing for export simply wouldn't work. The reasons she gave for this were that labour was unskilled, the infrastructure inadequate, the shipping unreliable and the position of any of the islands too remote. While she'd toyed with the idea of mineral exploitation in New Guinea, the big Australian companies such as BHP were already there and she couldn't hope to compete, although, I would eventually discover, she held a large bundle of shares in Bougainville Copper Limited, for many years the world's richest gold and copper mines.

But all this changed in 1975 when Anna finally persuaded Gojo Mura to move from Japan to the New Hebrides. The little artist had kept faith with *Fuchida-san* and painted the two hundred and thirty-seven specimens for the yakuza boss's *Butterflies of Japan*, a major entomological study that brought the *oyabun* a great deal of credit among butterfly collectors throughout the world, as well as legitimate status among the Japanese scientific community and finally a major natural-science award from the Japanese government.

Anna visited Japan at least twice every year on business and after a couple of visits managed to persuade Gojo to visit the island, where he stayed with me for a month at Beautiful Bay, spending each day collecting and painting insect specimens.

Despite being employed as *Fuchida-san*'s resident artist, Gojo Mura had never settled down in his own country. The many years as a ghost had left an indelible mark on him and he continued to feel alienated and a stranger in his own country. The initial visit became an annual event, and when he'd completed painting *Fuchida-san*'s Japanese butterflies Anna persuaded him to move permanently to the island by creating a small silk-screen business producing sarongs, T-shirts and silk scarfs for the tourists beginning to come to Port Vila in increasing numbers.

Gojo's beautiful butterfly designs were an instant success and Anna, never able to leave a good thing alone, initially took a dozen hand-painted butterfly scarves to her designer boutiques in the Ala Moana Mall in Honolulu, where she priced them as couture items under the fashion label Gojo. They sold out almost instantly. She then bought from Germany the machinery to set up a small textile plant to create butterfly prints on silk which were sent to a designer house in Paris to be made up into evening gowns and as the lining of couture garments. These were sold in her Honolulu outlets, initially to wealthy American and Japanese tourists. By limiting distribution to Honolulu and Paris the Gojo label soon acquired a reputation among high-fashion cognoscenti.

It was a lucrative hobby for Anna and gave Gojo an income way beyond anything he could hope to spend with his modest lifestyle, even after maintaining his ageing parents in Japan, and he used it to establish a college for the arts that would ultimately attract students from throughout the Pacific.

Gojo eventually built himself a small but beautiful home hacked out of the side of a cliff, not quite as austere as the one he'd occupied as a radio operator at Guadalcanal, but a place that brought him happiness and the peace and quiet he craved.

For Anna's fiftieth birthday he created a tropical butterfly design to which he added a single exquisite scorpion and then printed a special bolt of silk, sufficient to make her a pair of silk pyjamas and matching peignoir. When he presented this truly gorgeous sleepwear ensemble to her, he pointed to the tiny scorpion and said, 'Anna-san, true beauty always contains an element of danger, and that is what men crave the most in a beautiful woman.' This was delivered with a lovely innocence, and although he blushed as he made this observation, he spoke as an artist expounding on the meaning of art and beauty, without the slightest sexual connotation. Gojo had once confessed to me that while he worshipped the idea of feminine beauty he thought that the sexual act could only tarnish what was truly exquisite. I often wondered if he sensed that Anna's beauty remained untarnished. He also confessed that he had never felt the slightest desire for intimacy with another human; Gojo, it seemed, was one of those rare humans with a profound admiration for beauty but with no sexual drive whatsoever.

Anna was delighted with this beautiful gift, which, as it turned out, was to have surprising consequences. The morning after her birthday she came bouncing out of the bedroom onto the verandah at Beautiful Bay, resplendent in the long, flowing and absolutely gorgeous peacock-blue silk peignoir. 'Nick, I've just had a great idea!' she announced. 'Boys' pyjamas!'

Looking up from the morning paper I remarked, 'Well yes, boys have been known to wear pyjamas.'

'No! You don't see it, do you? Scorpions!'

'No, I'm afraid I don't. Scorpions? What about scorpions?'

'Boys' pyjamas featuring scorpions! Oh yes, and other nasty creepy-crawlies. Little boys love that kind of thing. We could have sheets and pillowslips. That's it! We're going into natural fibres.'

'Cotton bedspreads?' I said, adding my two bobs' worth while gently sending her up.

'Yes, yes, bedspreads as well!' She danced around me excitedly looking very beautiful, the silk of Gojo's butterfly and scorpion peignoir rustling provocatively as she moved. 'I'll order the machinery from Germany as soon as I get back to Melbourne,' she said with the absolute certainty that was so typical of Anna.

And that's how the Kreepy Krawley Klothing Kompany came about. Anna seemed to reserve a special love for what came to be referred to as 4K, and she built a new factory for it on the island, thinking of it essentially as a hobby. But the project was most annoyingly a success from the outset. I say annoyingly because I had expected it to fail. 'Mothers buy kids' pyjamas and bed linen and they're not going to cover little Johnny from head to toe in insects that sting, itch, bite and kill,' I'd declared in an attempt to dampen her enthusiasm for what was patently a foolish idea, adding the immortal words she'd no doubt been hoping to hear, 'Darling, this time you've got it wrong. As Kevin would say, it's a goddamn cockamamie idea.'

But it wasn't. It seemed that there was a readymade market for good-quality children's cotton nightwear and bed linen. Cheap synthetics had come to dominate the market for kid's sleepwear – hot and uncomfortable in summer and dangerous to wear near radiators and open fires in winter. Interesting designs in natural fibres that breathe were avidly sought out by well-to-do parents at the high end of the market. Little boys in every language pleaded and cajoled until their parents or indulgent grandparents bought them Kreepy Krawley pyjamas and bed linen. In an amazingly short time the 4K logo became the measure of success in international children's marketing and was stocked by emporiums such as Macy's in New York, Harrods in London, and Le Bon Marché in Paris.

Poor little Gojo was constantly being forced to comb the jungle for more and more exotic insects. Anna immediately recognised that there was an equal demand for little girls' sleepwear and she already had the artwork for hundreds of butterfly designs, to which, on each garment, she added a single bee and the BBBB logo was born, Beautiful Butterfly & Busy Bee. Using the same marketing template 4B soon captured the imaginations of privileged little girls everywhere.

By the early eighties it became apparent that the island location presented production problems. While neither label was mass market, worldwide sales were nevertheless considerable and supplies couldn't be reliably maintained with the current island infrastructure, freight shipping services and trained factory workers. Anna decided to keep her exclusive boutique silk design business, as well as the silk-screened local business in sarongs and T-shirts, on the island and to take the high volume 4K and 4B labels to Indonesia, where she proposed to build a state-of-the-art factory.

This was how we indirectly became involved in Anna's business affairs. Kevin, Joe and I, as well as owning the shipping line and a project management and personnel company, also owned Inter-Island Constructions Pty Ltd, the largest construction company in the islands. The two new companies were initially formed to build and run the harbour facilities and non-Japanese component of the processing factory as well as provide the staff for Konoe Akira's *zaibatsu* and its Pacific fishing business. Once these were complete, we moved on to the various Japanese foreign aid projects. This, in turn, led to aid projects for other foreign countries who observed that no bribery or corruption was involved and that our projects were generally completed on time and on budget and that our management and personnel company, if required, could staff the facility and get it up and running ready to hand over to the local government. Now Anna wanted us to build her 4K and 4B factory in Indonesia and this was how I came to know about her property investments with Budi and *Kleine* Kiki.

We also quickly came to learn that doing business in Indonesia isn't for the faint-hearted, and but for Anna's extraordinary sagacity, Inter-Island Constructions would certainly have been chewed up and spat out without even a decent burp to follow.

Anna flew from Melbourne to Beautiful Bay to brief the three of us – Kevin, who felt suitably martyred by being forced to fly from Brisbane; Joe from New Guinea; and of course me on the spot. Anna began with a simple statement. 'Nothing happens in Suharto's Indonesia without the military being involved.'

'What? Dey got a war going on?' Kevin asked querulously. 'I want yer to know I ain't no fuckin' hero! Dey got a war, I ain't goin'. No way, man, I done dat once already, already. Da last time I was in dat cockamamie country da Japs shot my sweet ass right outta da water, and Nick, he found me on dat lonely beach where I'm half dead and got me concussion. First I gotta fly to dis cockamamie island, now Anna she want to take me into a fuckin' war zone! Me, I'm a family man, I got responsibility!'

'Kevin, will you shut up!' I demanded. 'I should have left you on that beach. Just shut your trap and listen to Anna.' With Kevin present the meeting was getting off to the usual disastrous start.

'Yeah, well I ain't goin' if dere's a war,' Kevin growled.

Joe cackled, then rolled his eyes. 'Anna, yo-all tell dat dumb-ass Irishman, he gonna use bad words dat ain't respectful in front a lady he gonna have'ta deal with da big niggah, Joe "Hammer-man" Popkin. You tell him dat it don't matter none dat I love him like a brudder, 'cos I gonna have no he-see-ta-shun to crush him like a bug.'

Anna laughed. 'How do you three ever get any business done?' she asked.

'By keeping Kevin in Brisbane, where he's very good at making money and finding international freight business,' I replied.

'Yeah, man. Dat foh sure,' Joe added.

'Lemme tell ya somethin' fer nuttin'. If it was left to dem two muthers, we'd be broke a hunnerd times already!' Kevin retaliated, reminding us all of his business acumen, which, as I said before, was considerable. He was a natural trader and, if not quite in Anna's league, his efforts had ensured that by the early eighties we were all extremely well-off.

'Well you'll be happy to know there isn't a war at present in Indonesia,' Anna told us. 'Business is booming. The generals who helped Suharto come to power are now in charge of everything except for what the Suharto family have kept for themselves. They are setting new standards in venality. The best way to work in Indonesia is to realise that this is a feudal system. From the lowest bureaucrat, traffic cop and railway clerk to the very top, everyone is corrupt and that makes it a highly predictable business environment.'

'So, how will we build a factory in a corrupt environment we don't understand?' I asked. 'It can be difficult even here on the islands where we know the ropes.'

'We know the ropes,' Anna replied simply, adding, 'I'll

guarantee any overrun on your building costs and will personally do the necessary negotiations with my Indonesian business partner.'

With these assurances, Kevin agreed to contract to build the factory, although we were surprised when Anna briefed us on the size she required. While it wasn't my part to question this in the meeting with my two partners present, it seemed to be far too big for Anna's 4K and 4B manufacturing requirements, even if the venture were to prove very successful.

That evening in bed she explained the full extent of her interest in Indonesia to me for the first time and the fact that Budi was her gatekeeper and would have fifty per cent of the business.

'I don't understand,' I said, 'why would you give away fifty per cent when you could locate your factory almost anywhere and own the lot?'

'Skilled labour is intelligent, cheap and plentiful in Indonesia,' Anna replied.

I remained sceptical. 'That would be equally true of Fiji, Malaysia, Singapore or the Philippines, surely?'

Anna laughed. 'I thought we never discussed my business, Nick?'

'Well mostly because we can't. In the first place, I simply never know what your business is. You've just explained that you own half of Indonesian Kansas Fried Chicken and have a very significant property portfolio in Indonesia and I had no idea. But with this kids' pyjamas affair I've seen it grow from the outset with Gojo and I suppose I'm interested. Besides, we're building the factory and while it wasn't my place to say so in the meeting today, it seems inordinately large, even if you achieve enormous international success.'

'Well, that would be true if we were building it only for the two children's sleepwear brands, but we're not.'

'Oh?'

'Budi has negotiated a four-year contract to supply the Indonesian army and police force with uniforms, well over a million units a year. I supply the factory and the capital and we each take fifty per cent of the profits. I run the kids' sleepwear business as an adjunct and take one hundred per cent of those profits.'

'But the capital outlay must be enormous, the factory building, textile plant, raw material. How long will it take to recoup your money?'

'Roughly four years.'

'So what's the point?'

'Well, the kids' sleepwear production uses the same machinery and labour, and the cotton is all part of a bulk order for materials needed for uniforms and in effect is paid for by the discount margins we receive from suppliers. It won't cost me a cent to run 4K and 4B, other than shipping costs. I can produce high-quality natural fibre children's sleepwear and bedroom linen, add a high margin of profit and still sell for less than any competitor who is likely to challenge me in the world market.'

'But what if your army and police uniform contract isn't renewed after four years?'

Anna laughed. 'Silly, that's why we're doing business in Indonesia. While Budi only holds a licence to supply the uniforms for the next four years, he also holds, in perpetuity, the exclusive permits required to import textile machinery into the country, a wedding gift from Suharto when Budi married the president's cousin. At present the uniforms are made in five separate factories and no factory other than our own will be big enough to tender for future contracts. And if any of them plan to expand, they can't import the machinery needed to be competitive. In four years' time we'll be in the black, and the army and the police force are not going to get any smaller . . .'

I had always regarded Indonesia as an unstable business environment but Anna seemed to have anticipated everything. She never failed to surprise me. 'So you're in retailing and manufacturing, army uniforms and food. I guess they're pretty safe long-term bets, but surely you wouldn't want to do much more in Indonesia?' I asked.

'Well, you never can tell what will turn up, Nicholas. It worries me a little that we're not in natural resources, the next great boom. Last time I was in Japan Konoe Akira introduced me to Japan's biggest paper manufacturer and they're desperate for raw product.'

'What, wood?'

'Yes, Borneo has huge potential.'

'Anna, those are old-growth forests, some of the world's best.'

Anna gave me a sharp look. 'You've been speaking to the Green Bitch. I thought we had an agreement, not to discuss each other's affairs.'

'Yes, but . . .'

'Nicholas, the Malaysian Chinese are already bribing the generals; better us than them.'

'What about fishing? You already have vast experience in that while you know nothing about timber.'

'No, no, I've already examined that possibility, but the Indonesian fishing industry has almost exhausted its fishing grounds. Apart from that, it's traditional and run from village centres. Its only future is poaching in northern Australian waters and I don't want to be involved in that. As for timber, you cut it down, haul it out, chip it and load it into ships then send it off. You don't even need a fish factory.' Anna paused. 'Although I may need you to build a harbour or two in remote areas.'

'Don't ask us to do that, Anna! This isn't because of Marg. I was raised in the jungle. As the bishop always said, "The big trees are the lungs of the earth. We owe the very air we breathe to them." With me trees are a personal thing, Marg just happens to have come to think the same way.'

Anna's violet-blue eyes looked unblinkingly at me. 'Nicholas, what do I care what she thinks? To hell with the Green Bitch!'

'But I hope you care about what I think?' I replied just a tad self-righteously.

'Nicholas, I think it is time to return to our former arrangement where I *never* discuss business decisions with you,' Anna said quietly.

'Shit, darling. Not trees!' I lamented, sensing I had been defeated. 'Leave the big old jungle monarchs alone. Some have been standing tall since Cornelis de Houtman reached the Spice Islands in 1596.'

Anna looked impressed. 'How do you know about him?'

'Probably the bishop; my mind is full of that sort of crap. Anna, those big trees have been standing forever,' I said, returning to the subject.

Anna shrugged. 'I can't save the forests nor can Budi. The deal involves several generals and Tommy Suharto himself. If we withdraw, the Malaysian Chinese will take up our concession quick as a flash.'

'That's what the drug peddlers always say – if we don't do it, someone else will,' I shot back.

Anna sighed, visibly impatient. 'The Suharto family and the generals just see cash, and in Borneo it's growing on trees.

Besides, the deal is already done, Konoe Akira introduced me to Komatsu and six D15 bulldozers and machinery have already been shipped from Japan.'

'What are you saying? If rape is inevitable lie back and enjoy it?' I spat.

'Nick, I didn't hear that! I don't have to justify my actions!'

'Oh yes we do, darling. In the end we all do.'

Anna turned on me, now very angry. 'What sanctimonious crap! Your problem, Nick, is you've been so busy fucking the Green Bitch that you've forgotten how the *real* world works!'

It was the first time I had seen her on the defensive.

CHAPTER FIFTEEN

'Nick, I love you.
I always have, always will.
But I don't want to be taken for granted ever again,
to be a convenient arrangement.
A handbag.'
Marg Hamilton, Beautiful Bay

ANNA'S LITTLE SIXTY-SECOND make-up-your-mind surprise about Marg on our last night in Japan didn't result in our slipping quietly into bed together next time Marg visited Beautiful Bay. We'd always been the best of friends and had grown even closer since Rob had died so tragically, but now, even though Marg had confessed that she felt about me much as I did about her, suddenly everything was about to change. From the moment I had said yes to the ticking of the second hand on Anna's watch, she never mentioned the subject of my sleeping with Marg again and was obviously waiting for me to make the next move.

Allow me to backtrack for a little. Marg was due to come and stay at Beautiful Bay two weeks after I arrived back in Port Vila from Japan. I'd said goodbye to Anna in Melbourne, where she said she needed to finalise the Nauru House property deal. She wouldn't be able to visit the island for a month, she said, and we agreed it was not a bad idea. We'd been through a fair bit together and a period of separation was probably good for both of us.

Marg called once each week as usual and said more than once that she wanted to discuss something rather important with me but would wait until she visited. It wasn't hard to guess what this might be and so I rehearsed and rehearsed. I mean, how do you tell one strong-minded woman with a healthy ego that another strong-minded woman has given you permission to take her to bed? How the hell was I going to put it to Marg?

I rehearsed hundreds of beginnings in my head, some more pathetic than others: *Darling, I have wonderful news . . . Darling, I have something to tell you . . . Darling, in Japan Anna . . . Darling, remember our discussion . . . Darling, I've given it a lot of thought and . . . Darling, things have changed . . . Darling, what would you say if . . .* Or my personal version of the usual macho crap: *Okay, Marg, get your gear off. Let's rumble, baby!* That's if I could even think up a *my* version, which of course I couldn't. I love the idea of women too much to be rough or crude, to slap them around verbally or otherwise, even though Anna still enjoyed a good spanking. I'm laughing to myself now; I couldn't even *imagine* spanking Marg, but I did try to imagine her responses: *Gee, tell Anna thanks, Nick. It's been a long flight, let me take a shower. Ha, ha, ha, isn't it lucky I bought new undies. Give me half an hour and I'll expect you. Don't knock, just come in, darling.* I don't think so! Marg, just like Anna, would want conditions, rules. She wasn't going to play second fiddle. There would be no pecking order.

When I was eighteen Marg had invited me into her bed and delightfully, beautifully and lovingly taken my virginity and thereafter taught me the ways of pleasing a woman. In the glorious days and weeks that followed, she repeatedly drew me into her bed, but always on her terms. I was never under any illusions about who was in control. She wasn't likely to allow me to turn the tables on her twenty-eight years later.

So you can see, standing on the tarmac waiting to embrace Marg as she came down the steps from the plane at Port Vila, I might have been the old grinning Nick on the outside, dead pleased to see her, but inside I was a mess.

We kissed and embraced as we always did, but neither of us said much until we were back in the ute.

'How was Japan?' she asked.

'Great. Anna and I bought two freighters practically for the price of one,' I laughed.

'Anna? I wasn't aware she was an expert on boats?'

Oh god, I'd put my foot in it already. 'Not boats – business. She proved to be a tremendous help in the negotiations. In fact she was responsible for my ending up with two ships.' Knowing it was probably foolish, I told Marg the story of the negotiations with the two Mitsubishi executives. 'I was ready to knock their heads together and storm out but Anna turned the tables so that we ended up with two freighters for the price of one.' I laughed. 'In retrospect it was hilarious,' I said. Thinking, *Any moment she's going to ask me how things went with Anna's nemesis, the Japanese general.* Like Anna, Marg never forgets anything and her questions go straight for the jugular.

'Very amusing. Clever gal,' Marg said, adding crisply, 'How fortunate that you took her along.'

Here it comes! We were approaching the gates of Beautiful Bay. 'Well, here we are. I'll get cook to bring a pot of tea to your room while you unpack. She's baked a cake.'

We entered the long driveway. 'Anna's trees look good. I don't believe I've ever tasted a persimmon.'

'I'll see if the gardener can find you a ripe one. They're a bit of an anticlimax really – look great but taste a bit dull.' I laughed. 'If fruit were personified a persimmon would be a really good-looking redhead with nothing much to say for herself.'

Only a few more yards to go before the servants waited to greet us. 'Will you take an afternoon nap?'

'Lovely.'

'Drinks at the usual time on the verandah,' I said, drawing up beside the house where Ellison, cook and the two housemaids, in freshly laundered uniforms, were lined up. The youngest maid, shy little Francina, was clutching a lei of frangipani blossom. For the first time she'd been given the honour of placing it over Marg's head. She was trembling, knowing grandfather Ellison would be watching her, his stern patriarchal eye on the latest family member of the countless who had already served somewhere amongst the shipping company's widely scattered staff.

'Welcome, Missus Marg!' they all chorused as I turned off the ignition. I'd made it safely home without a major conversational disaster. The next hurdle would be drinks on the verandah overlooking the bay at six o'clock. It was a half moon waxing tonight, but as it was the dry season, cool with little humidity, the stars would be splendid. I could only hope they were lined up correctly for me.

Marg emerged at six o'clock, showered and freshly made up. She'd done nothing about the grey streaks in her lovely chestnut hair, and if Anna was still beautiful, Marg was what you might call a very handsome woman. Even the tiny crow's-feet at the corners of her eyes when she smiled were attractive and at fifty-four her figure was remarkable. She was barefoot, her toenails manicured and painted in a natural colour, and wore tailored white shorts that reached just above her knees and a blue T-shirt.

I mentally slapped myself as I caught myself wondering what her breasts were like out of a bra. If they looked as good as her long, lovely legs they'd be in great shape, I decided. Funny, Anna and Marg often wore the same shade of blue. Marg had worn a dress almost exactly the blue of her T-shirt on the first day I'd met her in Fremantle. Strange how you remember the little details in your life, while often forgetting some of the more important events.

Marg plonked herself down on one of the big comfortable batik-cushioned rattan chairs and I handed her a gin and tonic. 'Thank you, Nick.' She held the glass still, the late afternoon light showing through the slice of lime. She was looking out across Beautiful Bay to sea where the sun was slipping behind the horizon, as it does in the tropics in just a couple of minutes. 'Oh, I do so like it here,' she exclaimed. 'I hope I shall always be able to come back.'

Here it comes! 'What do you mean? What's to stop you, darling?' I asked, trying to keep my voice calm.

Marg turned to look at me. 'Nick, I want you to be the first to know that I've baked my last batch of scones. I will never fill another sausage roll, run a tombola or attend another naval cadet passing-out parade. I've been to my last garden party at Government House, and I will never again sit through one more war veterans' dinner with Rob's medals dragging my bosom down to my waist. It's almost five years since he died, and from now on I'm no longer the dead admiral's wife, no longer general factotum to all things navy past and present. I'm Marg Hamilton, single, and in charge of my own destiny.'

You could have knocked me down with a feather (nice cliché that). It wasn't what I'd expected, but it was quite an opening speech. 'That's the second resurrection I've witnessed in a month,' I said, thinking of Gojo Mura.

'Resurrection? Call it what you may, I'm no longer the admiral's wife, widow or navy charity worker. I'm Marg Hamilton and I'm going to Tasmania.'

'Tasmania!' I cried in alarm. 'Why on earth?'

'I knew you'd say that, Nick,' Marg replied. 'Well, for a start, when you decide on a new life the first requirement is to move as far away from the old one as you can, but I still want to be close enough for the kids and the grandchildren to visit occasionally.'

'Yeah, but is that a sufficiently good reason to bury yourself alive after you've just been resurrected?'

'Tasmania is a perfectly lovely, vibrant place. You'd be surprised.'

'You can say that again. It's still got one foot in the last century and a mindset in the one before that. The ghosts of convicts past haunt the streets at night and I'm told they're just a tad insular and conservative. Isn't it true that the convict descendants are timber-getters who live in the deep dark forests? And you know what happens when people forget who their cousins are . . .'

'Nonsense,' Marg snorted. 'I've met the governor and he's a perfectly nice man. Besides I have relatives there, several cousins in fact, and they are *not* chinless wonders.'

'Oops!'

Marg laughed. 'The Babbages, they're on my mother's side, *and* just so you know, Nick Duncan, they're practically landed gentry and one of them was knighted several years back. Their forebears were the recipients of a land grant as free settlers in the mid-1820s.'

'Have you met them?'

'Oh, yes. Aunt Nettie and Uncle Bob – Sir Robert in polite parlance. They rather liked the idea of having an admiral as well as a knight in the family and visited us once or twice in Sydney, and the kids spent a holiday with them when they were teenagers.'

'You've visited yourself?'

'Yes, on only one occasion, when Rob sailed in the Melbourne to Hobart yacht race. New Hope, their rather grand estate, is twenty miles from Hobart. The homestead, a replica of an English manor house, was built over a hundred years ago. They're awfully keen for me to come over.'

'What? To live with them?'

'Good gracious no! He, Uncle Bob, now dead, was grossly fat and proportionally pompous, and she, Aunt Nettie, is very conscious of her status and requires to be addressed as Lady Babbage by the housekeeper and the farmhands. Various other members of the family also live on the estate and struck me as being a rather rural lot, shotguns and horses, dogs for retrieving dead birds and bunnies.'

Having delivered this scathing but as usual honest opinion of her Tasmanian relatives, Marg went on to say, 'A nice Hobart estate agent has found me a lovely Georgian terrace house in Battery Point.' Then, just in case I had missed the point she said, 'You do know that Hobart has the best Georgian architecture outside of Great Britain, don't you?'

I laughed. 'Well, as a matter of fact I do, compliments of a conversation with my father who, after the war, was offered a bishopric in Tasmania but chose to remain in the islands. He claimed that he'd rather preach to primitives than to degenerates.'

'Nick! He didn't say that! You made that up.'

I laughed. 'No, of course he didn't. What he did say was that Hobart got caught in a time warp and missed most of the Victorian era and just kept building in the Georgian manner long after it was no longer fashionable elsewhere.' Then, lest she thought I was having another crack at the island, I hastily added, 'Good thing too. Much nicer than those neo-Gothic Victorian monstrosities you see in Sydney.'

'Battery Point is lovely and looks over the entire sweep of the Derwent River with Mount Wellington rising up behind it, usually snow-covered in winter. Such a pretty place.'

'Marg, are you sure this is a good idea?' I asked again, adding, 'I'm sorry about what I said. I've never been to Tasmania and so I have no right to comment. I hear it's beautiful,' I added, thus once again damning it with faint praise. 'But, darling, it may be pretty, but isn't it rather isolated?'

'And the New Hebrides isn't?'

'That's different. I work from here and, besides, I love the tropics. But what will you do in Hobart? If there's snow on the mountaintop it's going to be bloody cold in winter. Are you sure you want to retire and spend the rest of your days so close to Antarctica?' I said, borrowing again from the bishop who'd mentioned this as part of his refusal, pointing out that only the Falklands were closer to the permanent ice.

'Retire! Of course I'm not going to retire! How ridiculous! I intend to go to university. I shall take an arts degree in political science.' Marg was so affronted by my suggestion that she had almost spilt her drink.

I apologised. 'Bad choice of words, but one doesn't think of Tasmania as a place to start a new life.' Then I added clumsily, 'Even less a career in politics.'

'God, you can be tiresome sometimes, Nick Duncan. The University of Tasmania is one of our better tertiary institutions and I intend to have a career that *involves* politics.'

'Marg, I'm confused, I can't ever remember you taking the slightest interest in politics.'

'That's why it's an entirely new career, silly. But you're right. I don't want to be a politician. I want to be myself again.'

I grinned. 'Marg, if I may say so, you've always been yourself.'

'Only as much as men have allowed. Nick, you're an Australian male, sometimes a fairly sensitive one, but still typical of the breed. By the way, I don't suppose you've read the book I sent you?'

'Ah, well, er . . . no. We've been in Japan,' I protested.

'I sent it five months ago,' Marg pointed out.

I recalled picking it up at one stage. It was by an American writer and was called *The Feminine Mystique*. I remembered thinking I'd had my fill of feminine mystique for a while as I put it down again. 'Sorry, I'll get around to it,' I promised.

'Well, it's about women having the same rights in society as men,' Marg explained.

'Don't they? I know a couple of bossy women who qualify,' I chaffed.

Marg missed the humour and rebuked me. 'That's crap, Nick!'

'Well, yes, I suppose it is,' I admitted, thinking of Anna and Stan McVitty and how she'd suffered at his patronising hands. 'You'll have to explain, I'm *only* a male.'

But Marg was suddenly in no mood for banter. 'I started out in Naval Intelligence where, despite the traditional bias against my gender, my own intelligence counted for something. Put bluntly, Commander Long, the autocratic misogynist who ran the Australian Naval Intelligence Service, couldn't afford to ignore me,' Marg went on.

I remembered meeting Commander Long, a strange, abrupt man who often spoke in monosyllables. 'Yeah, scary bloke,' I chipped in.

Marg ignored my remark. 'There was a war going on and they needed all the grey matter they could muster. If you look dispassionately at what I achieved, had I been a male I would certainly have been promoted to the rank of captain and encouraged to make the navy my career after the war. But I was a woman, wasn't I? I'd married a commander, a bright enough bloke who did decide to continue in the navy.' Marg paused. 'Nick, I've never said this to anyone before, but it's important to this discussion. Rob Rich would never have made it beyond commander without me; he lacked the drive, the ambition and, dare I say it, the brains. My post-war naval career simply became his. On the surface I was a wife and a mother, but let me tell you what I heard in the officers' mess from one of his fellow officers a bit the worse for wear: "Bloody Rob Rich! Lucky he's got a great-looking sheila on his arm. She won't do the bugger's promotion prospects any harm, let me tell ya. Admiral can't take his eyes off her tits." I was Rob's good-looking handbag who could hold a conversation on navy matters with an admiral and who boasted as many service medals on my motherly breast as most of them. I was, in navy parlance, Rob's major asset, the well-manicured hands pushing him in the small of the back. But still the hands that washed the dishes, changed the dirty nappies, cooked and cleaned and drove the kids to school.' Marg smiled. 'It's all so predictable. As a woman you begin by taking the back seat as a wife and you end up taking the back seat in life.'

'Marg, I had no idea. You've never spoken about any of this.'

'Nick, don't get me wrong, I loved being a mother. I have two loving kids, an adorable grandchild from each, and like thousands of capable and bright women I did what was expected of me. But once your womb comes into play it's all over. When Rob died I immediately became the admiral's widow, a new persona with a slightly different job. Rob was dead, I was alive, but in his memory I was expected to play a new and as usual subservient role. I became the sausage-roll queen, the highlights of my life the next fete, garden party, veterans' dinner, cadet passing-out parade, and so on. I could see myself getting a medal for my ten-thousandth sausage roll and composing a nice humble thank-you speech to acknowledge the honour!'

I laughed at the thought and accepted her empty glass and began preparing a fresh drink. 'So what caused the epiphany?' I asked, adding fresh ice and reaching for the gin.

'You did.'

'Huh?'

'Our conversation before you and Anna left for Japan.'

'Marg, I wanted to talk to you about that,' I said hastily.

'No, let me finish, Nick. The week before I came up to see you, I lay in bed thinking. Not for the first time, mind you. I was fifty-four years old, I'd kept my figure – I can still turn a few male heads walking down the street – yet I hadn't felt the arms of a man around me for five years and in the last few years Rob . . . well, you know how it is with marriage. I was playing the role of Rob's widow and hating it. But unless I remarried it was all over, my role was defined, set in aspic. And the thought of being married again was too ghastly a thought to entertain. Besides, the only man I'd ever loved, apart from the first few years with Rob before he became imbued with his own glorious image, was all too briefly you. I knew about Anna's problem, of course. I also knew how you felt about me – you'd never stopped sulking about my marrying Rob.'

'It wasn't sulking. I was in love with you!' I protested, handing her the drink.

'Thanks,' she said absentmindedly, accepting the glass. 'Well, anyway, in the true manner of an Australian woman I came up with a compromise. You and I would get together for mutual tenderness. Anna was a part-time partner who spent a week a month with you. I was your cherished female friend who now spent a week a month at Beautiful Bay and who, like Anna, shared a history with you. What, I reasoned, was the difference? We would share you, but obviously play different roles.' Marg stopped and smiled. 'But for once in your life you were smart enough to see it wouldn't work, that your loyalty lay with Anna. When you told me you'd given up your scattered surrogates, I knew it couldn't happen. Then shortly afterwards, when I finally came to my senses, I realised that I was desperate to change my life and in the process had lost my judgment.'

'Marg, whoa! Can I say something?'

'No, not until I'm finished. Please, Nick.'

'Sure.'

'So that was when I had what you call my *epiphany*. I realised that Betty Friedan was right and Bob Menzies with his bushy eyebrows and smug superior father-of-the-nation expression was wrong.'

'Betty Friedan?'

'The book I gave you.'

'Oh, yes, sorry. Is this what they're calling women's liberation?'

'Well, men are calling it that; women refer to it as the feminist movement.'

'There's a difference?'

'Of course! Liberation suggests something males are going to have to be persuaded to do for women; the feminist movement is what women are going to do for themselves. We don't need permission.'

'Hang on, Marg. Anna has never asked permission from a man. In fact, just the opposite, she uses me as a measure of what *not* to do. And you are never short of an opinion, darling . . . I don't see you getting pushed around all that much.'

'It's not about personality, about asserting oneself, it's about closed doors, doors that have a welcome mat laid out for men but any woman wanting to enter has to charge it with a battering ram. How many women are in parliament at present? Let me tell you. Two in the Senate, none in the House of Representatives. How many have there ever been? Six! And yet we're half the population! Why do we get less pay than men for doing the same job? If Rob could make admiral, then, intellectually speaking, I should be head of the armed forces.'

I sighed. 'Marg, you know as well as I do that that's never going to happen. It's all about having babies. You can't have the prime minister or the head of the navy wet-nursing during a debate in the house or while conducting an operations briefing. I don't mean that literally, of course, but that's the whole male mindset.'

'Why does it always come back to the womb?' Marg lamented. 'But you're perfectly right, Nick. It's going to take a long time to change, but that doesn't mean it isn't high time we started.'

'Bravo! Is that why you're going to study political science in Tasmania? Will you go into politics? Why not start at the State level? The door to the House of Assembly probably isn't too sturdy to batter down.'

'God, no, I told you, not a politician! How to lose friends and influence nothing! No, Nick, the feminist movement isn't just about being an equal part of the male world. It's about challenging the system and coming up with new and better solutions. There are new doors to open, not simply old ones to batter down.'

'Jesus, Marg, how many lifetimes have you got?'

'Nearly half of one, I hope.' She laughed. 'I have every intention of becoming a very forthright and cantankerous old woman.'

'So, let me ask you again. What will you do with this new life as Marg Hamilton?'

She looked at me, almost appealing to me to help. 'Nick, I *think* I know. In the last year I've read two books that have made me question a whole lot of things. Things are happening in America, Europe, even I suspect here.'

'One of them being this Betty Friedan?' I suggested.

'No, I read that four years ago, not long after Rob died. Rachel Carson's book *Silent Spring* had a big effect. She writes about the fact that we are drowning the environment in dangerous insecticides that are killing everything. She tells, for instance, how DDT persists in the environment, poisoning indiscriminately every living thing with which it comes into contact. Then shortly afterwards I read Paul Erlich's *The Population Bomb*. The two books taken together make it plain that we're destroying planet earth. We're like a cancerous growth invading the precious tissue of Mother Nature. We are killing the means of sustaining ourselves; the earth, our host, is being poisoned with our wastes; our exploding human population can't be sustained, and while we populate, everything around us perishes!'

'Hang on, Marg, I still don't see why you're off to Tasmania.'

Marg ignored me. 'That's the third thing that happened. Shortly after you left for Japan *The Age* ran an article – no that's wrong, they ran a comment, a couple of columns – on the subject of the Tasmanian Hydro-Electric Commission and its plans to flood a large part of the south-west of Tasmania, including the iconic Lake Pedder. Apparently there had been local protests in the past but I was unaware of them.'

'Lake Pedder? Never heard of it! Why is it iconic?' I interrupted.

'They plan to flood a wilderness area, which includes the lake, with eighteen times the volume of Sydney Harbour that includes the lake which would have disastrous effects on the environment, on already threatened animal species and plants unique to the area. The lake, high up where the button grass grows, is also seemingly very beautiful and primordial, though not easy to get to and so is entirely pristine. *The Age* wanted to know what was so important about a lake few people would ever see and referred to the protesters as a mixture of long-haired hippies in need of a shower, university students in need of a cause and middle-aged women in twin-sets and pearls with nothing better to do with their time.' Marg chuckled. 'Well, I guess that was me. Menopausal, midway through life and searching for a cause.'

'So, the rebel has found her cause, eh? The new feisty Marg is on her way.'

'Well, hardly. I have no idea where it will all lead. But everything seemed to fall into place. The tone of the piece in *The Age* was so impossibly pompous and complacent and, well . . . wrong. I felt it was time for a new start. The protesters, who it seems are still at it on behalf of Lake Pedder, made me realise that there are people who care and that I also care.' Marg hesitated, then burst out, 'I am going to try to do something that I believe is important. With Friedan, Carson and Erlich as my guides. I'm fifty-four, fit, there's nothing wrong with my brain, in fact it's better than ever, and I've made up my mind.' She paused. 'What do you think?'

I was silent for a while, thinking about what I should say. 'Marg, the first word that comes to mind is "bemused", but it's much too tame. Will "gobsmacked" do?'

'Nick, it's important I have your opinion.'

'That makes a nice change. Anna usually asks for it only so that she can do the opposite.'

'Well?'

I laughed. 'Marg, what have you got to lose? Darling, you've got both my hands, chipped and callused, in the small of your back. Go out and make trouble. But have you got the practical aspects worked out?'

'Thank you, Nick, darling. While you may not think so, your opinion is very important to me.' And she began to reel off her plans. 'I've taken stock of things as they are. If I sell the house in Point Piper and buy another, much cheaper, but just as nice, in Hobart, and invest the money I have over in something safe, then together with Rob's navy pension I can afford the fees to go to university and still live reasonably well. The degree is so that at least I will be well-informed and nobody can look at me with that "What would you know, you're *only* a woman?" look that men, particularly state politicians and navy officers, seem to cultivate as a necessary part of their persona.' Marg chuckled. '*And*, as an activist for the environment I qualify in all categories except youth – I'm a student and a middle-aged female protester, I even have a set of pearls and I can always buy a twin-set, my hair is already long and I'm prepared to go without a shower once or twice, always providing I've got a deodorant stick in my handbag.'

'When? When will all this take place?' I asked, enjoying her enthusiasm.

'When? Well, just as soon as I get back to Sydney. The house has been put up for sale, it goes to auction the week after next. I told you I think I've found a house in Hobart and when mine is sold I'll go over and have a look at it. If it's not suitable, I'll find something else. After that it's come home, pack up, get back to Hobart, settle in and enrol as a mature-age student at the beginning of next year.'

'And that's a very good reason why you can't come here once a month in future?' I said, stating the bleeding obvious.

She smiled. 'Yes, but I can for some part of the university vacations. If you'll have me?'

'Of course, you'll always be welcome at Beautiful Bay.' I grew serious. 'We'll always be mates, come what may,' I said, a tad sentimentally.

I accepted her proffered glass and started to prepare Marg's third gin and tonic – two was usually her limit. She was silent while I sliced a fresh lime, added ice, gin, tonic, and handed it to her. Frankly, I didn't really know what to think, what to say other than to encourage her. I must admit surprise though; I'd always thought of both Marg and Anna as liberated women, but she'd made me see that there clearly was a huge flaw in my male perception. However, one thing was certain. Nick Duncan's future sex life had reached a sudden hiatus. Can't say halt – Anna was still a remarkably skilled practitioner of the art of 'anything but'.

'Nick, you wanted to say something. I apologise, but I really wanted to get everything off my chest. Thank you for listening so patiently. Now, what was it, darling?' Marg asked.

I grinned in an attempt to appear casual, unconcerned. 'No . . . nothing, it wasn't important. Honestly.'

It was the word 'honestly' that did it. Marg went for the jugular. 'What happened in Japan?' It was more than a question and just short of a command.

'I told you, we bought two freighters.'

'Don't be a smart arse, Nick. The Japanese general and Anna?'

'It was a furphy. They ended up good friends, business associates.' While I didn't think the world had anything against tuna fishing, my instinct told me not to elaborate.

'And the vaginismus?'

'Ah, still there,' I shrugged. 'Anna now thinks that he wasn't the cause.'

'Oh, Nick, how sad! For her . . . for you! Does she have any insight into what it may be?'

'None whatsoever, not the foggiest,' I replied, using the silly expression to lighten the implications.

Marg wasn't fooled. 'So, what now?'

I shrugged again. 'Life goes on.'

'But it doesn't. It changes things . . . dramatically.'

'How?' I asked.

'Well, you had hopes that things would change. You gave up your previous arrangements . . .'

'Yeah, just as well . . . Time I grew up.'

Marg was silent, staring into her glass. The stars were out. It was a bright night, despite the half moon. Lights twinkled across the bay. Then she said, 'Nick, you and I . . .'

'No, Marg, I understand.'

'Darling, I'm starting a new life. Intimacy with you, a relationship other than friendship, isn't possible now. It would be going backwards. Back to where I was. You do understand, don't you?'

'Yes, of course,' I said, not sure I believed myself. At least I didn't have to tell her I had Anna's permission.

'Nick, I love you. I always have, always will. But I don't want to be taken for granted ever again, to be a convenient arrangement. A handbag. Pillow partner. Perhaps later, when I've got my new life underway, when I know who I am, what I want. Then perhaps something meaningful?' Marg came over and sat on the arm of my chair and leaned over and put her arms around me and kissed me. 'Nick, Nick, Nick,' she whispered softly. I could feel her beautiful breasts pressed against me. Nothing had changed. Marg was still doing things on her own terms. It was only that they were bigger, more important terms than sharing her bed.

Shit!

And that's pretty well how all the trouble began. As a first-year mature-age student Marg gravitated to the more serious-minded and radical students and faculty members, many bitterly opposed to the pro-development Tasmanian establishment and the new Liberal government headed up by Angus Bethune. It came as no surprise when he continued the Reece Labor government's support for the Hydro-Electric Commission and the massive damage they were causing to the wilderness areas, to be epitomised by the drowning of the exquisite Lake Pedder. Let me remind you about the early seventies, when 'the times they *were* a-changing', as Bob Dylan said. Vietnam had radicalised many Australians, just as it had many Americans. The war didn't make sense even to quite conservative families. The idea that your son, still too young to vote, could be sent to fight and possibly die according to the tumble of a lottery ball angered a lot of people who might normally have counted themselves as patriots rather than protesters. Furthermore, since 1968, European and American campuses had been convulsed by protests, often violent, from student activists seemingly protesting against everything. The rage of the world's young against the reactionary forces that ruled the world was finally being expressed, and, almost too late, it had reached Tasmania, where it met head-on one of the most reactionary and conservative organisations of them all: the Hydro-Electric Commission. The acrimonious, doomed and often bitter campaign to save Lake Pedder would divide families, friends and whole communities in Tasmania.

Almost at once, Marg joined the Save Lake Pedder National Park Committee. One of her first political acts was to take the train with fellow students to Launceston, where they joined others to visit all the public toilets in town to write 'No Dam!' on every single sheet of toilet paper, then roll them up again. They were to learn that not all publicity is good publicity. The forces ranged against them had a field day. Some examples from the local wags: *A real bummer. I wipe my arse on the protesters. A shithouse idea. A heap of student crap.* And so on. The students tried to respond with: *Damming Pedder stinks. Pedder – another shitty idea from the state government. The Hydro is talking crap as usual.* But the general consensus was that conservative forces had won the day, especially when the Hobart *Mercury* came out with the headline, *A protest not worth the paper it's written on.* It was all pretty childish stuff but it seemed to do more to entrench opposition attitudes than change them.

Long before she graduated with honours Marg had found her true vocation: environmentalist–troublemaker. The war for the forests, rivers and lakes had begun and the first of the battlelines were drawn along the scalloped white beach of Lake Pedder. It was here that she enthusiastically began her career as a tree hugger; river rescuer; guardian of lakes; opposer of dams, bulldozers and chainsaws; and mortal enemy of the all-powerful Tasmanian Hydro-Electric Commission.

I had gone down to Tasmania in 1971 to see Marg after she'd badgered me to attend a protest meeting to be held in Hobart. I agreed only because it was a good excuse to see her.

Anna had never again brought up the subject of my sleeping with Marg. Strangely, it was never the prospect of sharing a partner that created the antipathy between the two women, but rather how they saw each other's lives and values: the fierce and fanatical environmentalist and the rapacious plunderer of the planet – Green Bitch versus Princess Plunder.

I never returned to my scattered surrogates and while I can't say it was perfect or that I didn't retain a strong desire for Marg, life, even with its sexual compromises, was tolerable. In the moral sense I was the guilty party. I never gave up hoping Marg would change her mind. But if I had any carnal thoughts during my first visit to Tasmania, Marg definitely had other things in mind. She was entirely preoccupied with the protest over the damming of Lake Pedder and was anxious to have me meet her new friends.

While there were too many of them to recall all their names, some I met on that first visit became stalwarts of the conservation movement. There was feisty Helen Gee, who had the distinction of having been called a communist ratbag in parliament; Olegas Truchanas, one of the finest nature photographers in the world, who was later tragically drowned canoeing on the Gordon; Peter Sims, a fifth-generation Taswegian who had, along with the redoubtable Jessie Luckman, been involved in the conservation movement for at least a decade. I also met Brenda Hean and Max Price, who died soon afterwards when the Tiger Moth in which they were flying to Canberra to skywrite 'Save Lake Pedder' above the Federal Parliament crashed. While I am not one for conspiracy theories, they had, as a matter of record, received several threatening phone calls and Price's Tiger Moth had, on a previous occasion, been tampered with while in the hangar.

There were of course many others as brave and true who

fought and suffered greatly for their beliefs. Tasmania is a small island with a close-knit population. The fight against the Hydro-Electric Commission's projects and the battle to save the Tasmanian wilderness and old-growth forests has left deep divisions. To this day families are divided and communities split. Many of those conservationists who took the side of nature have paid a heavy price in their social, working and family lives, but also, it must be said, those who sided with the Hydro and logging interests have not come through unscathed.

Making a stand for the environment wasn't and isn't for wimps; these were and still are the bravest and truest of our green warriors. When the saints finally come marching in, it won't surprise me to see that Brenda Hean and Max Price are the official flag-bearers, with Olegas Truchanas the photographer for the *Resurrection Bugle*, and Bob Brown will be giving the celestial newspaper his scathing opinion on the clipped box hedges of the Anglican suburbs of Heaven, while the other true greens will all be marching with chestfuls of campaign medals in the front line.

But, of course, all of this is with the benefit of hindsight. At the time I was at best ambivalent. I supported Marg more for her resolution to change her life than for her chosen cause, which meant that I wasn't entirely apathetic or uninterested but rather what I considered at the time 'sensible and fair-minded', pretty much the same thing, if you consider it in any depth.

This doomed wilderness, euphoniously named the Middle Gordon Scheme, was first proposed by the Labor Premier Eric Reece, known as 'Electric Eric', who came to power in 1958 and described the area to be dammed as 'worthless land that only contains a few badgers, kangaroos and wallabies and some wildflowers that can be seen elsewhere'. This just about sums up the prevailing attitude and appalling ignorance of the premier and his government about the state's flora and fauna. Moreover, the Liberals who came to power in 1969 were no better informed, although it should be mentioned that one lone MP, Louis Shoobridge, a scion of one of the old landowning families, was the only member to protest against the damming of Lake Pedder.

I arrived in Tasmania three days before the November Lake Pedder protest meeting, after first stopping off in Melbourne to see Anna and the site – now cleared – for Nauru House, the building of which was due to begin the following year. The Melbourne *Herald* had discovered who the genius was who'd put the real-estate deal of the decade together and Anna was suddenly being taken very seriously by the big end of town.

Marg had urged me to bring my hiking boots, gear, rucksack and sleeping bag, and from her friends she'd borrowed two single tents (not a promising sign) and a rather beaten-up Toyota four-wheel drive. We spent the first part of the evening at a pub meeting Marg's friends but she'd warned of an early start and a long day's walk so we left around eight. Marg made a light supper – ham omelette, toast and tea – and I was in bed in her spare room by about half-past nine, only to be wakened just after four in the morning by the dead admiral's resurrected wife dressed in hiking gear and assuring me that I had plenty of time to get ready but we would need to leave in fifteen minutes on the dot. 'You don't need to shave, Nick.'

'What about going to the dunny?'

'Well, yes, okay, but hurry,' she laughed.

We drove north along the Midland Highway, turning off to Bridgewater then heading along the Strathgordon Road through Maydena along a well-graded gravel road built to service the Hydro-Electric Commission projects. We left the Toyota at a muddy clearing off the road and, humping our backpacks, set off into what looked like an impregnable tangle of dark vegetation filling every inch of the space in the temperate rainforest where the trees rose no higher than forty feet. The path was narrow, muddy, dark and slippery and the vegetation kept snatching at my rucksack as if determined to close up the puny path humans had scratched and hacked through it. I'd never witnessed bush as dense and the fact that even this narrow path existed at all seemed remarkable.

I was accustomed to hiking in tropical jungle where the canopy prevents sunlight penetrating to the floor so that, with the exception of vines and creepers, the surface is almost free of undergrowth and progress is relatively easy. The track Marg and I were following was going to make it a very long hard day, and despite the early-morning chill I was soon sweating profusely. 'Christ, how long does this go on?' I called to Marg.

'If you were younger and fitter it would be about four hours but we should be there before nightfall,' she replied.

'Thanks for the ego boost,' I called back.

'Count yourself lucky, darling. One of the ironies of this situation is that by putting the track through to Maydena the Hydro people have reduced the hike to Pedder and back to two days. It's much easier to make protest visits now. The old way was a three-day slog through rainforest and over the high peaks and you needed to really know your onions to complete it.'

In the pub the previous evening Helen Gee had assured me that I would enjoy the hike, which she described as following a well-defined path. She mentioned several pleasant watercourses and a few easy rocky ridges with most of the trail winding through rainforest. 'You'll love the button-grass plateaus,' she'd commented.

'I'm looking forward to it,' I'd replied with enthusiasm. 'I'm pretty fit. Not long ago I spent a week or so wandering in the beech forests in the foothills in Japan,' I'd told her confidently.

'Well then, you'll have no trouble at all, Nick,' she'd assured me, smiling, I now realised, in a rather knowing way.

While Helen's description of the terrain was, technically speaking, correct – there were certainly trees, streams and rocky ridges – these were *not* sylvan beech glades with winding mossy paths well-trod for a thousand years, gently gurgling brooks, hot springs and leaf-carpeted foothills. The forest was choked with a vicious, tearing, angry tangle involved in an all-out wrestling match with us; the thundering streams threatened to carry you away with the first misstep; and the towering ridges resembled the jawbones of dinosaurs.

By late afternoon I'd been flayed alive by undergrowth with a clearly malevolent intent, slipped on my arse countless times, slid uncontrollably down muddy slopes grabbing onto tree roots and stumps until my hands bled, been scratched and cut wherever my skin was exposed (later I would discover that half the blood in my body had been sucked from it by leeches the size of bananas), puffed, panted, gasped and groaned. Finally we emerged onto a high button-grass plateau and faced one last steep razorback ridge.

By this time I was well and truly bent, buggered and totally be-wildernessed. Marg had left me for dead and seemed still to be in remarkably good shape. Moreover, her resolute cheeriness was giving me the veritable screaming shits.

'One last little climb, darling!' she called, as if this were some Sunday-school picnic paper-chase we had a good chance of winning if only I'd move my fat backside a bit faster.

The final climb up the last ridge damn near did me in for good. I reached the top and stood gasping, bent over with my hands on my knees, panting like an ageing bull-mastiff. Finally I looked down into the valley below.

Oh shit, oh glory!

Okay! Perhaps there are glacial lakes somewhere in the world, probably New Zealand or Switzerland, Italy or Norway, that are more beautiful in the accepted azure-blue, surrounded-by-snow-capped-mountains, picture-postcard sort of way. But Lake Pedder hadn't taken any cues from these archetypical vistas. It was startlingly different in the way a woman, whether blonde, brunette, redhead, dark, fair, sloe-eyed or wide-eyed, can be beautiful and yet not conform to any cultural paradigm of beauty, but is simply a new definition, an original, who, having imitated nothing, somehow epitomises everything.

Lake Pedder was a one-off. From where I stood, even in the late afternoon with the light still good, the water appeared as black as polished anthracite, a mirrored surface that stretched five kilometres or so, surrounded by ragged, plain-faced saw-toothed mountains. Above it was a sky of roiling, towering cumulus, all of it duplicated on the mirror-still surface. I have never seen nature reflected in quite so precise a way, the reflection more perfect than the wider reality, for it was completely contained, one end sharply defined by scalloped white sand. It was the absence of detail that struck me. It was as if the original artist had rejected every distracting element, eliminating the minutiae of trees and grass and sudden outcrops of rock, the myriad devices of landscape that serve to distract the eye. Every component existed for a single purpose, to maximise the dark surface of the lake and to call one's attention to its primordial beauty. It seemed impossible that this purity of vision was due to be swamped with the dishwater contained in a man-made cement basin, a fat-bottomed frau to replace an astonishingly beautiful nymphette.

I saw at once the ugly face of humankind hell-bent on profit, using the self-righteous catchcries of cheap electricity and jobs for workers as an opportunity for tawdry profit. These rapacious and vainglorious men, oblivious to the wonderful gift of purity and joy we had been granted forever with this ancient lake, were spitting into the face of God.

That Lake Pedder would disappear was akin to a terrorist taping the ceiling of the Sistine Chapel with sticks of dynamite strung with cordtex and then announcing that it was being blown up in the interests of jobs for plaster workers and artists on the dole. The late James McQueen said it more eloquently than ever I could: '. . . the river was not just a river, for me it is the epitome of all the lost forests, all the submerged lakes, all the tamed rivers, all the extinguished species. It is threatened by the same mindless beast that has eaten our past, is eating our present and threatens to eat our future: that civil beast of mean ambitions and broken promises and hedged bets and tawdry profits.'

People simply don't and won't ever switch on the light with the thought, 'Oh God, there goes another natural wonder!' Hydroelectricity was the perfect answer for Tasmania's politicians, and Marg's mob bleating about a coffee-coloured lake in the high scrub was never going to win the hearts and minds of voters.

There is very little doubt that if the Franklin–Gordon schemes had been proposed in the earlier post-war period of national euphoria and adulation of bulldozers and cement, it would have happened with a loud fanfare from both federal and state governments.

Moreover, if we think those were the bad old days, the fight to ban the exploitation of Tasmania's old-growth forests continues, and politicians and profiteers are *still* using the same specious arguments about jobs and unemployment. Tasmania has a history of old-growth timber extraction for pulp and paper mills that began back in the late 1930s. That 'civil beast of mean ambitions and broken promises and hedged bets and tawdry profits' is alive and well and making huge profits exporting woodchips to Japan. And yet, for every Tasmanian timber worker who loses his job, there are two jobs waiting in the tourist industry. It is simply a matter of willingness and a little training on the job.

Marg and I erected our tents at the back of the quartzite beach that had seemed white from the top of the ridge but turned out to be a lovely pink colour and as fine as talcum powder. The sun was setting across the lake as Marg prepared supper and I removed my boots and socks and started to locate the banana-sized leeches – well, perhaps not quite that big, but still big buggers – freeloading on my blood. Marg laughed, 'Good thing you're a large fellow, Nick, or you'd be bones rattling around in a bag of skin by now.'

'Are you quite sure it's a good idea to save this lake? The amount of human blood lost could be considerable,' I kidded, knowing, of course, that what I'd just seen was worth every bloated bloodsucker that had come along for a free feed and a ride. Marg, of course, had foreseen this additional blight and handed me a small saltshaker. I knew from the jungle that a little salt will make a leech drop off, taking what seems like half a cup of blood with it, but at least it won't itch for a week. Of course, I hadn't thought to bring my own supply of salt.

Marg had also brought a vegetarian stew, which she was heating on the spirit stove she'd lugged all the way in – we were well above the tree line and there wasn't a stick of wood available to make a fire. We talked as we ate, arguing in a lethargic way about some of the issues I've just mentioned, but it was fairly pointless. Marg was committed to a single cause and I wasn't prepared to support the opposition with any real enthusiasm, let alone vehemence. The vegie stew was bloody awful but I was hungry and almost licked my plate.

We were both dog-tired, never a good time to squabble or get tetchy, so I changed the subject and asked, 'How are the landed gentry, your cousins and the ancient titled aunt?'

Marg pulled a face. 'I've been ostracised.'

'Oh?' I pointed to the lake. 'Because of this?'

Marg nodded. 'Banished is a better word. Three months ago I was summoned to Sunday lunch with nine cardigan-clad senior members of the family. It was eaten in almost complete silence except for an occasional "Pass the salt, please." Nick, you should have seen their faces, munching away. The only noise was the clack of dentures and the loud mastication of the overcooked roast beef, or an occasional clearing of the throat.

'After lunch I was commanded by the dowager Lady Babbage to wait in a small anteroom until I was summoned. Another fifteen members duly arrived after lunch in a rattle of cars and trucks and all assembled in a large room they refer to rather grandly as the ballroom, where I believe folk-dancing took place in the old days.

'A maid then came to fetch me and I was led into this huge room where all twenty-three members of the Babbage family, male and female cousins, second cousins, wives and maiden aunts, were assembled behind a chaise longue as if posing for a family photograph, all wearing their Sunday best in preparation for my banishment back to the mainland. The old dragon, attired entirely in black as if, like Queen Victoria, in perpetual mourning for Prince Albert, was seated alone on the chaise longue, visibly smouldering. The room fell silent as I entered.'

Marg then described the whole comic opera, how the ninety-year-old Lady Babbage, the erstwhile Aunt Nettie, widow of Sir Bob 'Bulldozer' Babbage, the first deputy chairman of the Hydro-Electric Commission and a long-term member of the Legislative Council, sat ramrod straight, gripping the walking stick in both hands, the tip resting between her black lisle-stockinged legs.

'Glaring at me she commanded me to sit in a lone straight-backed chair facing her and the remainder of the family. Then rapping her cane several times on the magnificent polished hardwood floor she barked, "We shall have silence!" even though no one had uttered a word since I'd entered the room.

'By this stage I'd worked up a head of steam. At rallies I had grown accustomed to being yelled at by rednecks, drunks, angry workers and their wives but this was my own family. I sat down, trying to appear composed, even unconcerned. Then, remembering the admiral's technique when dressing down a group of young naval officers, I looked over the silent assembly carefully, taking in each member, and announced, "Right then, let the inquisition begin!" The old witch didn't bother with any polite preliminaries.

'"You are a disgrace, child! You will leave Tasmania at once! We simply will not, cannot have the Babbage name sullied, dragged in the mud, as you have so heinously done! Your name has appeared in the Hobart *Mercury* with several other communists and leftwing agitators from the university. Who on earth do you think you are? What on earth do you think you are doing? You may have been an admiral's wife but you have absolutely no right to come over here to make trouble. We know what's best for Tasmania and we know what's *not* best for it! We have spent five generations protecting Tasmania from people such as you. My dear departed husband, Sir Robert, spent his life serving this island. You have been here five minutes and have the temerity to tell us how to run our affairs! I will not have it! I shall write to the *Mercury* and tell them that we do not share your views and will have nothing further to do with you! That you are a disgrace! Now, what have you to say before you pack your things and leave Tasmania?"'

Marg, completing the old lady's tirade, laughed and in an almost admiring voice said, 'It was an amazing performance, straight out of *Bleak House*. You were right, Nick, some families on this island are still in the nineteenth century. I swear, she didn't draw breath once.'

'I can't believe it. As you say, it's straight out of Charles Dickens. How awful for you!'

'I suppose I should have been amused – in retrospect it's very funny – but I was mad as hell, Nick. How dare the old shrew! So I'm ashamed to say I gave her the full admiral's-wife treatment. I took them all in, lingering a moment on each face. Two grossly overweight men I recalled sat on the board of the Hydro-Electric Commission and were champions of dams and hydroelectricity, and several others were members of the Tasmania Club, a bastion of conservatism, bigotry and class prejudice. All the men had doubtless attended the Hutchins School, the women St Michael's Collegiate. I must say, seen en masse like this, the Babbages were not a particularly prepossessing lot, and I realised that all the men shared a remarkable genetic characteristic – very large sticking-out ears. The light from a stained-glass window behind them shone through these flapjack-sized lugs, so that each possessed a pair of bright red stoplights, one on either side of a brow that protruded so far over their eye sockets as to hide their eyes. "Stop! Do not proceed until this blithering idiot has passed!" the stoplights seemed to command.'

Marg, having completed her family inspection, leaned back in her chair and crossed her legs, an affectation she told me she'd learned in response to endless squabbles between naval wives at meetings. 'Sit back, half close your eyes, cross your legs, look bored and relax. People fight to be noticed, not to be ignored.'

Finally, turning her attention to the old woman, and with a calm she claimed she didn't feel, she announced, 'Ah, the blithering, blathering, barking Babbages! Fortunately I was born a Hamilton and not a Babbage and take after that side of my family, so I have not been subject to the results of five generations of inbreeding with the unfortunate physical and mental results so readily apparent in this room. I happily divorce myself from all of you.'

I chuckled. 'I can't believe you said that! That's almost as bad a monologue as your Aunt Nettie's!'

Marg sighed. 'It's the kind of pompous archaic language you're forced to use on such occasions. I'm afraid there's more to come. I rose imperiously, chin up, shoulders squared, and walked towards the door, where I paused and said in my plummiest tones, "Furthermore, I shall not be leaving Tasmania until I've helped to save this beautiful island from being destroyed by the likes of you lot, the cretins and the barking mad!"'

I laughed. 'Bloody lucky you weren't lynched on the spot. Did you run for your life?'

'Oh, far worse than that!' Marg grinned. 'I was forced to walk the twenty miles back to Hobart. No hardship really. I'm fit as a fiddle.'

'I hadn't noticed,' I laughed.

'Fortunately I was wearing my sensible shoes and, anyway, a farmer with a truck full of pigs stopped and gave me a lift ten miles from town, a definite improvement on the company I'd so recently been keeping. A pity really – another ten miles of walking along quietly fuming and I'd have composed several quite brilliant and witty soliloquies to the blithering, blathering, barking Babbages. The mind never moves quite fast enough when it's needed for withering and scathing responses,' she observed.

'I don't know about that,' I replied. 'I don't suppose the Babbages will soon forget the withering and scathing they received at your hands. I only wish I'd been a fly on the wall. You always look sexy when you're angry.'

'Sexy? I'm fifty-five!' She looked down at her boots and socks, khaki shirt and over-large shorts. 'Positively the belle of the ball,' she laughed.

'You look terrific, Marg.' She did too! She'd lost at least a stone and a half in weight, her hair was cut in a neat bob, she still possessed bosoms to make any man drool and in high heels a pair of legs you'd happily follow five city blocks in the opposite direction to the one you had originally intended taking. My great fear was that with all these weekend wilderness ventures in climbing boots and rucksack, she might abandon displaying possibly the best legs in stilettos in Australia. Marg, if no longer the beauty that Anna still remained, was nevertheless a great-looking woman at the height of her sexual powers who would turn the head of any man over the age of thirty. I lusted after her almost as deeply now as when, as a Naval Intelligence officer in Fremantle, she'd first helped herself to my virginity.

'Nick, you're not thinking of —? No, of course not!'

'Why not? It's eighteen months since you went into the wilderness to find out what you stood for and who you are, and you seem to have that pretty well sorted out.'

Marg laughed. 'Thank you, I hope you approve.'

'Only if you never give up wearing stiletto heels,' I grinned, attempting to lighten the moment.

'Well, perhaps not for a while anyway. Although my sensible years are not *that* far off, I suppose.' She gave me a forthright look as only Marg can, its meaning unequivocal even though she hadn't said a word. 'Nick, I've got two years to go to get my degree.'

'I know, but no harm in having a round of preliminary talks. Never know your luck in the big city . . . er . . . wilderness.'

Despite herself, Marg laughed. 'And Anna? She must be accustomed to having you to herself by now?'

'Oh, she's agreed,' I said airily, with a flick of the wrist.

'She's what?' Marg exclaimed, surprised. 'She's a part of these preliminary talks?'

'Well, sort of. We've had a long talk.' I didn't see any point in telling Marg this was months ago in Japan.

'And?'

'Her vaginismus . . . the situation hasn't changed.' I was skating on thin ice.

'But I have!' Marg said firmly. 'Besides, I thought I'd made it perfectly clear?'

'Yes, you did at the time, but you left the door slightly ajar. You said, and I recall precisely, "Perhaps later, when I've got my new life underway, when I know who I am, what I want."'

'You remembered that?' I could see she liked the fact.

I grinned boyishly. 'Etched with a red-hot poker into my mind.'

'You're a bastard, Nick! Nothing changes. I told you before, I'm not going to be the surrogate fuck next door.'

The use of the 'f' word I took to be part of her student and feminist emancipation but I could sense a slight softening. 'Hardly. You live here, Anna is in Melbourne and I'm at Beautiful Bay.' Then, taking a big chance I said, 'I'd be your university vacation bonk.' I realised at once that it was a cheap shot.

Marg pressed her lips together, a sure sign that she wasn't

pleased. 'Am I supposed to feel grateful, Nick?'

I suddenly realised just how stupid the remark was. Should Marg refuse me she would naturally be reluctant to come to Beautiful Bay in future. I reached out and touched her arm. 'Marg, I guess I'm tired. That was a very stupid thing to say. I'm sorry if I offended you,' I said, crawling like a salamander from a pond.

Marg pulled away. 'Nick, what you've just asked is outrageous! It's also insensitive, disloyal and shameless!' She paused, then grinned. 'I'll think about it.'

My relief must have been obvious. 'You will?' I exclaimed, not sure I'd heard correctly, in my mind still copping the adjectival flak.

Marg gave me a reproving look. 'Nick, let's get things straight from the start. You're staying in your own tent tonight and there isn't any room in my sleeping bag. When we get home tomorrow night don't lie awake waiting for a knock on the door. I need time to think about all this. It comes as a bit of a shock.'

'How long do you think this thinking will take?' I said, grinning cheekily, knowing that a bit of crawling to the opposite sex never goes astray.

'It needs considerable thought, and besides, first I'll have to speak to Anna.'

CHAPTER SIXTEEN

*'Nick, we have to believe that
political movements are like the rivers we're
trying to save, first a trickle, then a rill, then a
creek and perhaps finally a roaring river.'*
Marg Hamilton, Tasmania

THE PROTEST MEETING I'D come to Tasmania to attend at
Marg's behest was the day after we'd returned to Hobart, feeling
stiff and sore from the walk to Lake Pedder. While I wasn't yet
a convert to the cause, I was beginning to see that saving the
magnificent Lake Pedder for future generations was not to be
dismissed as mindlessly as the opposition seemed to be doing.

Milo Dunphy spoke first, angry and disappointed at the
adamantine refusal of the state government to consider saving
even the unique pink quartzite beach, which could have been
done relatively easily. It was clear that the Hydro people wanted
to show the students and other upstarts that they and their
resistance were inconsequential. It almost seemed as though
drowning the lake was as much to teach the recalcitrants a
damned good lesson as anything else.

Dunphy, an articulate and reasoned speaker and far from
the rabblerouser he was claimed to be, delivered an intelligent

speech over a scratchy microphone to a captivated crowd who cheered loudly and frequently. He encouraged the protesters to be more professional in future campaigns (writing on toilet paper just meant the message went down the gurgler) and reminded them that this was not the end but only the beginning. Never give up the fight, he urged.

No observers from the government or opposition attended except Louis Shoobridge MLC, whose voice crackled, squeaked, whistled and frequently disappeared altogether as he tried to tell us over the loudspeakers what we already knew – that his colleagues in state parliament were a bunch of irresponsible reactionaries, no-hopers and opportunists. He once again confirmed that the Hydro-Electric Commission was ruled by a bunch of anti-conservation nabobs who were a law unto themselves and answerable only to the devil. The lone politician received the second biggest cheer of the day. I guess one member of state parliament on the side of the angels is better than none.

Perhaps these remarks in the white-hot atmosphere of the Lake Pedder crusade were to be expected, but in hindsight the state politicians of the day were merely falling into line with the prevailing pro-development ethos. I don't think they were wicked or evil or even vindictive; they simply saw the Tasmanian wilderness as a God-given resource for the good of humankind. They were pragmatists who pointed out that unless the abundant rivers were tamed and harnessed, all that water would empty uselessly into the sea. Water that gurgled through gullies, over rocks and through ferny creeks, that tumbled into rivers and flowed silently through giant eucalypt forests, serpentining along valleys, could only have one possible use, couldn't it, and if it was wasted, how bloody stupid was that?

The island's reactionary forces were quick to condemn as

futile this gathering to protest over Pedder. Or to paraphrase the countless long-winded speeches in state parliament, newspapers and the halls of Hydro, it was the work of a bunch of radical students causing an unnecessary fracas over a few acres of ponds, scrubland, a handful of ubiquitous marsupials and a bunch or two of common wildflowers.

It was obvious to me that it was already too late to save Lake Pedder, and after the meeting it was clear from the bitterness of failure on many faces that others realised that all their efforts had come to naught.

The protest meeting seemed to me to be a call to arms and a warning about the ever-present dangers of the short-sighted Tasmanian government and hydra-headed Hydro. It was, in fact, the beginning of the world's first Green movement.

After the rally, we went with Marg's friends to a barbecue in a beachside park near the Wrest Point Riviera Hotel owned by Federal Hotels, who had applied to the state government for the first casino licence in Australia. This proposal brought out an entirely different but almost equally vociferous protester. The deep leather armchairs of the Tasmanian Club were filled with old duffers and establishment types who, urged on by their wives, all of whom had sided with the Hydro over Lake Pedder, waved their fists and demanded that the plans be scrapped. They were furious at the audacity of the government, loudly proclaiming that, with the advent of a casino, the state would be overtaken by mafia gangsters and white trash would invade from across Bass Strait.

Despite the bitter disappointment at failing to save Lake Pedder, the barbecue was an upbeat affair attended by many of the locals as well as several hundred out-of-town protesters. The partygoers must each have drowned their sorrows in a half cask of wine or a sixpack of Cascade, which didn't help when the pubs closed at ten and a hundred or so gatecrashers, the roughneck supporters of the Hydro scheme, descended on us.

I was returning from talking to some of the locals when I heard, 'Hey, lady, your name Marg Hamilton?'

Marg's 'Yes?' was uncharacteristically nervous, and I soon discovered why.

'Bitch! I've got a message from your family!'

I don't remember a great deal more after that, except that I looked around to see a man holding Marg by her hair, a broken beer bottle poised above his shoulder, seemingly about to stab her in the face. She screamed, and the next thing I recalled was sitting in a police paddy wagon with my right hand hurting like hell and the siren of an approaching ambulance ringing in my ears.

The following morning I was arraigned before a magistrate and charged with causing grievous bodily harm. It seems that despite the drunken state of most of us, there were several reliable witnesses who had seen the incident and testified that I had responded to an unprovoked attack on Marg. Apparently I had lifted the bloke with the broken bottle above my head and thrown him against a stormwater pipe, breaking his left shoulder, arm and pelvis. Another guy who'd tried to take me on had his jaw broken in three places, although I don't remember either incident, just the scream from Marg and then finding myself in the police paddy wagon.

The bottle was tendered in evidence, and Louis Shoobridge, who'd been sober and whose testimony couldn't be easily dismissed, was called as a witness. Unusually and to everyone's surprise, the police sergeant who attended that night was more than even-handed, corroborating the politician's evidence in his report.

I was fined a hundred dollars for being drunk and disorderly in a public place and released on a good-behaviour bond, but not before the magistrate lamented at length about how most of the trouble over Lake Pedder and the Hydro-Electric Commission was fulminated by irresponsible and ill-informed students and mainlanders, of which I was a prime example. Clearly he believed that both were a blight on the landscape. He went on to say that it was high time mainland people realised that Tasmania knew what was best for its own welfare. I took a quick look at his ears but they were small and snug against his head. Having thus delivered his lecture he dismissed me and wished me a speedy return across Bass Strait.

Alas, the incident made the Hobart *Mercury*, where Marg Hamilton's name appeared once again, I have no doubt confirming the judgment of the recently scathed and withered, blithering, blathering, barking Babbages, who had demanded her transportation to the mainland.

While I packed my gear to return to the islands, Marg didn't say much, but her smiling and gorgeously unmarred face suggested that the date of the renewed liaison between us might have been brought a little closer. Certainly my chances hadn't been harmed by the drunken incident in the park. At the thought of bedding Marg once more, my dislocated thumb suddenly seemed a small price to pay.

We said our farewells just before I boarded the TAA flight to Melbourne, and she kissed me lovingly. 'Nick, thank you for coming, it was wonderful.' She touched her face. 'And thank you for this. It may not be beautiful, but I like it the way it is.'

'It's a lovely face, darling, and I like it better than ever.' Being Marg, she'd made no mention of the *when* question. I turned and started to walk across the tarmac towards the plane.

'Nick!' she yelled. I turned back. 'Tell Anna I'll phone her. It would appear that we have something in common and that we need to talk about him.'

Marg and Anna may have decided to have me in common but in the years to come I sometimes wondered how central I really was to their lives, and whether each of these two strong and determined women clung to me so tightly simply as a matter of principle because each didn't want to let the other have me. Or was it possible that Anna, who always loved a challenge, had agreed to share me with Marg so that the rivalry between the two of them became an even contest? I could do nothing about the real antagonism between the two of them and so I seldom, if ever, raised the subject, but their passionate pursuit of opposing goals was a different matter. Each hated the other for what she represented and I was to become a sort of perpetual trophy which they exchanged when they imagined that one of them had temporarily trounced the other.

Some of the protesters found the strain of defending Lake Pedder and the forests too hard on their family, jobs and lives and, worn out, retired from any further involvement in the conservation movement. They had become convinced that the opposition, a combination of big business, the state's political elite and the rapacious and arrogant Hydro, couldn't be defeated. But Marg, while bitterly disappointed at the outcome, was, if anything, strengthened in her resolve. She knew with absolute certainty how she was going to spend the remainder of her life and she set about preparing for the difficult times ahead. 'Nick, we have to believe that political movements are like the rivers we're trying to save – first a trickle, then a rill, then a creek, and perhaps finally a roaring river.' Marg had not lost her spirit and lived to fight another day, another year, another decade.

It had become apparent to the activists that the politics of the environment were too important to be left to the pragmatism of politicians. The 1972 Tasmanian state elections were coming up and it was decided by the remaining Pedder protesters to form a new political party to be called the United Tasmania Group to contest it. The world's first Green political party had emerged. Its birth was met with hilarity and ridicule in political circles, from the vast majority of the Australian public and certainly the media, who, after the loss of Pedder, had almost entirely lost interest in the environment movement.

Marg immediately became a member of the new party and threw herself into the organisation, so much so that she very nearly failed to get the marks required to do an honours degree. There had been some talk of her standing as a candidate but it was decided that she was too valuable as an organiser. Besides, as a mainlander until recently, her chances were too small with the locals.

The new party failed to gain a seat but surprised everyone when they lost by a mere handful of votes. It proved that while many Tasmanians were reluctant to come out and publicly protest, they nevertheless objected to the drowning of Lake Pedder and didn't want any more damage done. It also proved that it wasn't only the ratbags who cared about trees and rivers.

The last hope to save Lake Pedder disappeared when Gough Whitlam, elected in 1972 after the famous 'It's Time' election campaign, decided it wasn't time to help in Tasmania. A year into office he was not prepared to jeopardise Labor's chances in the coming state election or risk antagonising the federal Labor members in the island.

Marg's war career had been as a Naval Intelligence officer and she had earned a considerable reputation for her ability to infiltrate, in particular, the American Naval Command in Australia, an essential and covert task if the Australians were to know what their Yankee allies were planning in the Pacific before, as often happened, they were officially and often belatedly informed. She'd also guided a naval officer, no more intelligent or bright than his fellow officers, to the rank of admiral, a considerable exercise in guile, sagacity, opportunism, anticipation and long-term planning. Now, as a student, she began with a hard core of friends to quietly build a network that could infiltrate the memberships of the state Labor and Liberal parties, the government bureaucracy and the Hydro-Electric Commission. The concept of planting moles is not new to espionage but to be effective it needs time. And while information from an insider is important for planning it can't be openly used. What was needed was a weapon that could be wielded in the political arena in the cause of the rivers and the trees.

Over the next ten or so years, as Anna was building a business empire that was to make her the richest self-made woman in Australia, I watched as not very much seemed to be happening in Tasmania, even though Marg was always inordinately busy. She talked constantly about the need to become more radical, to use civil disobedience and to try to inform and change public opinion. I was wary of the first tactics and sceptical about her chances of changing public opinion and often felt that she was wasting her time. She was certainly committed and enthusiastic and, of course, when it came to trees, I was very much on her side.

There was no point and little chance of dissuading her; it would have been easier to move the Rock of Gibraltar. But I often concluded a discussion with the words, 'Marg, please, just don't do anything stupid and get yourself arrested.'

'Oh, but I probably shall,' she'd always reply. 'We simply have to make our presence felt.'

I'd sigh heavily. 'I can already see the newspaper headline – *Admiral's Widow Jailed!* Rob will turn in his grave and the navy establishment won't be at all pleased. But you can count on me to post your bail, darling.'

'Don't you dare, Nick! A stint in jail is essential. The only thing politicians understand is public pressure – Mahatma Gandhi, Martin Luther King. I'm not suggesting a comparison but arresting an admiral's widow is always going to be news.'

'That's what I'm afraid of. The public doesn't seem overly excited. They'll write you off as a silly old menopausal moo. You know what people are like, distracted and generally apathetic. If it isn't football or cricket it isn't news. They're not exactly shitting their britches in Canberra or Hobart either.'

'Well that's just too bad and thank God my menopause is largely over. I Am Woman!' Marg laughed, quoting the title of a song made famous by Helen Reddy.

While the Greens still failed to gain a seat in the subsequent Tasmanian elections, Marg assured me that they'd been hugely encouraged by their campaign and it was only a matter of time before the trickle became a runnel and then a creek. Even Marg didn't dare refer to the prospect of a river in her earlier metaphor.

To support the nascent political party two new organisations were formed during this period: the South West Action Committee immediately after the elections, and in 1976 the Tasmanian Wilderness Society, the organisation Marg believed would lead them to the radical and confrontational stand she felt certain had to become a part of the movement. Marg was wildly excited about this last group, which had grown out of the experiences of a shy young Launceston doctor named Bob Brown. Dr Brown was known as a pleasant, mild-mannered man who wasn't one of the original Pedder firebrands, although he'd shown support quite early over the issue of Lake Pedder when he paid for and placed a large advertisement in the

Australian newspaper. His interest in the lake was coupled with a search for the Tasmanian tiger and in this endeavour he'd fallen in with the Launceston Walking Club, joined the Tasmanian Conservation Trust and was encouraged to become a member of the United Tasmania Group where Marg had first met him. His involvement at first was as an enthusiastic bushwalker sympathetic to the cause.

This all changed when, in a conversation with a friend, local forester and adventurer Paul Smith, he'd expressed some doubts about the possibility of saving the south-west wilderness. Smith had immediately challenged him to raft the Franklin with him and to see the area for himself. Smith explained that the river had only been successfully navigated twice by pioneering adventurers and in both cases it had proved a hazardous experience. 'It'll be heaps of fun,' Smith concluded, downplaying the danger involved in the proposed adventure. The young doctor, never one to back away from a challenge, accepted, unaware of what he was in for. Like most Tasmanians, he knew almost nothing about the river.

When Smith and Brown returned after successfully navigating the Franklin and on more than one occasion having come close to losing their lives, the young doctor knew he would never see things in the same way again. Smith and Brown, two of the commonest names in the lexicon of English names, were about to change forever the direction of environmental protest. Smith for his initial enthusiasm; Brown because he'd been born again as a devotee of the pristine rivers, lakes and forests of his adopted state. As a doctor he'd dedicated his life to healing the sick, but now he re-dedicated it to preventing the wilderness from being destroyed, to keeping it, above all things, healthy. He had become a fierce guardian of trees, lakes and rivers and the abundant life that depended on them.

He later described the experience as if it had indeed been an epiphany by declaring how he found himself 'fused into the inexplicable mystery of nature'. Several weeks after his return, on the last Saturday in June 1976, sixteen people, a hard core of true believers, met at his house in Liffey and formed the Tasmanian Wilderness Society, Marg, of course, being one of them.

Although, to her chagrin, Bob Brown didn't stand as leader, pleading he still had a medical practice to run, Norm Sanders, a Pedder veteran, became the director until Bob Brown finally took over when Sanders resigned to stand for the Democrats in state parliament.

Brown was the right person at exactly the right time. What is the expression? Oh, yes: 'Cometh the hour, cometh the man.' He was young, had the status of his profession, was unattached with no family ties to consider, hadn't been beaten down by the Lake Pedder failure and finally wasn't subject to the social pressures of the old guard or tainted by any previous activism.

It was difficult to call the young Dr Brown a ratbag: he was a member of the medical profession, dressed in a suit and tie for media interviews and spoke quietly and reasonably. In one interview broadcast nationally in 1980 he hadn't lambasted the state government or the Hydro-Electric Commission, both of whom had gone out of their way to discredit him. He simply declared, 'Within a few years, the wilderness areas of the world – and there are only a few left – will be gone. We have a chance to save this one in Tasmania, not so much for this generation but for the future, and not just for Australians but for mankind.'

Marg had obviously fallen under the spell of the young doctor and during one of our nightly phone conversations she said, 'In him we seem to have someone who can make the mainland sit up and take notice, someone whose voice isn't drowned out by the clatter of politics. People are beginning to see that this is no longer a parochial problem in a state where the politicians are a bunch of reactionaries; they're starting to realise it involves us all.'

'Hey, wait on, it isn't all political clatter down there. Didn't I read somewhere recently that your Labor premier Doug Lowe proposed a compromise? Some of the Franklin River could be saved? Isn't that a sign that things might be changing?'

I could sense Marg's sniff of derision on the phone. 'Like all compromises, both rivers would be wrecked and the politicians would claim as usual that they had made everyone happy. I wrote a letter to the editor of the Hobart *Mercury* pointing out that two half rivers don't make a whole ecosystem. To my surprise they printed it and Norm Sanders, the Australian Democrat, read it out in parliament.'

'Yes, sure, but at least it indicates some ambivalence, a crack in the armour —'

'Crack? Not even a tiny dent!' Marg snapped, but then immediately calmed down. 'But, I admit, Lowe's a cut above the rest of the scoundrels. He passed me in the street several days ago and stopped briefly and gave me a pat on the shoulder, then said softly, "Brave girl, keep up the good work." I couldn't believe my ears! He's even come out and said . . .' Marg paused. 'Wait, I have the clipping right here on my desk.' Moments later she started to read. '"*The Hydro-Electric Commission is an engineering organisation . . . it is not a socio-economic planning body. Previous governments may have been satisfied with a cursory perusal of the Commission's recommendations followed by an automatic stamp of approval. This is not my style.*"'

'There you go!' I exclaimed. 'You have a friend . . . well, at the very least, not necessarily an enemy.'

There was silence on the other end. Then Marg, not without a tincture of drama in her voice, announced, 'Last night in a late sitting of the Labor Party caucus, Doug Lowe was deposed as leader by the majority pro-dams faction in the party. They elected Harry Holgate, whose support for the Hydro is almost as vociferous and one-eyed as that of the leader of the opposition, Robin Gray.'

'Oh dear, as bad as that?' I said, the egregious Gray being at the top of Marg's hate list. 'Pity, Lowe sounds like a good man.'

Marg laughed. 'About as good as they get around here, which isn't saying a great deal.'

'Marg, you're beginning to sound like a politician.' Which, as it subsequently turned out, proved prophetic. Doug Lowe resigned from the Labor Party and sat as an independent with Mary Willey, also ex-Labor, and Norm Sanders. Norm Sanders then brought a motion of no confidence against Harry Holgate's now minority government and, supported by the other two and the opposition, the Labor government collapsed and an election was called for the 15th of May 1982.

Bob Brown proposed to stand and asked Marg to do so, too. She called me at Beautiful Bay, her voice excited. 'Nick, Bob has asked me to be a candidate for what's to be known as the Tasmanian Greens; it's a new party we're forming. What do you think?'

'Brilliant!' I exclaimed. 'But what about the United Tasmania Group?'

'Mostly the same people, same purpose, different name – United Tasmania Group is simply not specific enough. Besides, Tasmania is anything but united behind our cause; we want people to know exactly what we stand for.'

'Yes, sure, but won't that leave you open to being accused of being a one-issue political party?'

'Well, yes, but the Libs and Labor are also electioneering on one issue – jobs for workers. Now that they've decided to dam the Franklin and the Gordon, there aren't any other issues, except a few strictly parochial ones, and they won't be ones we'll be contesting. Everyone knows it's pretty well a revolving door between the two parties. At least we stand for something different.'

'Well, yes, but *they're* standing for food in the mouths of their children and *you're* standing for a couple of rivers and a bunch of trees. Different, yes, but is it a significant difference? I mean, to the voter?'

'Nick! That's not fair! They're two stunning rivers and the old-growth forests can never be brought back . . . well, not in several lifetimes anyway.'

'But paying the bills is in *this* lifetime,' I insisted. 'Don't get me wrong, darling, I'm on your side. But food on the table, shoes for the kids will always be an issue. People haven't got around to making trees a priority in their lives. They seem to be in abundance, everywhere they look! And who cares about two rivers nobody'll ever visit?'

'What are you saying? It's hopeless, that I shouldn't stand?'

'Of course not, you *must*. I'm proud of you, but you're in for a rough ride, my girl.'

'Nobody said it would be easy. I take it I have your blessing, then? I'm . . . We're going to need campaign funds. We're holding fetes, raffles, that sort of thing, but it won't be sufficient. We have to print pamphlets, posters, pay the postage for thousands of letters . . . it's going to cost a fortune.'

'I see. When Anna calls later today I'll ask her to back you with the ingredients for two thousand sausage rolls,' I joked.

'Nick, that's not in the least funny!' Marg scolded, then laughed.

'How much?'

A moment's hesitation. 'Five?'

'Hundred?'

'Thousand. We won't waste a penny, I promise,' Marg said in her most compelling voice.

'Yeah, okay. But Anna won't be pleased that I'm supporting you,' I added.

'How could she possibly know?' Marg shot back, then, 'Nick, you wouldn't . . .'

'No, of course not! However, you two always seem to know what the other is up to. Don't these donations have to be declared to the electoral office?'

'Yes. I never thought of that. But surely she wouldn't think of that, would she?'

'Look, I shouldn't be doing this. I try very hard to follow the rules the two of you made, but I'm also having some ongoing personal difficulties with Anna and trees.'

'You mean Princess Plunder raping the forests of Borneo?'

'Oh, you know about that?' I said, astonished, not yet aware of her connections with Roger Rigby, her intelligence contact in Canberra and ex-colleague in Naval Intelligence during the war.

'Of course!'

'How?'

'It's not important, and besides, you're breaking our rule,' Marg reminded me, forcing me to silence.

'Right, tell you what. Tell your mate Bob Brown to expect a cheque. If Anna looks up the electoral donation lists I can work my way out of a donation in my name to him – personal conscience, general concern, that sort of thing.'

'Oh, I do love you, Nick,' Marg said. 'You will be especially rewarded next time I visit Beautiful Bay,' she promised, but then added, 'But you do understand that with this election, I may not be able to keep to the Beautiful Bay schedule each month, at least in the next little while.'

'Oh well, I guess I'll simply have to spend a little more time with the soap in the shower,' I joked.

'Nick Duncan, that's naughty! You mean you won't know me from a bar of soap?' she replied cleverly.

Marg and I hadn't resumed our former intimacy straightaway. The Calendar of Nick's Joy didn't come into regular use until Marg had graduated with honours. This proved to be a good thing, as it seemed to help Anna to adjust to the new arrangement.

I was to learn in snippets over the years what transpired during Marg and Anna's telephone call about sharing yours truly. It seems they quite quickly decided they could make it work using the calendar idea. After this decision it would appear that most of their conversation concerning me involved whether they could endure my numerous shortcomings, a subject they constantly returned to whenever I failed to please them in the years that followed. They would allude to this original telephone conversation with statements such as, 'We discussed this highly annoying (vexing, irritating, alarming, unfortunate, tedious, cunning, duplicitous, selfish, vainglorious) aspect of your personality at some length, Nick. Our sincerest hope at the time was that it wouldn't play, as it disappointingly now has, a part in our future relationship.' That is, of course, a paraphrase of several hundred different statements that meant roughly the same thing. If I were to string all the accounts of my shortcomings together, the phone call must have lasted several weeks. Moreover, these conniptions, spats, quarrels, dummy spits, call them what you may, seemed always to end with roughly the same sentiment from both women: 'Well, what can I expect? After all, you're only a man.'

While I might only have been a man, I was *their* man, and one rule was inviolate. Marg had suggested it, and Anna had agreed at once: if ever it was discovered that a third woman had entered my life, no matter how fleetingly, both of them would leave me immediately. I was involved in a female duopoly I didn't dare abuse. Had I ever done so, I hasten to add, it would have been a case of greed and not need. Marg and Anna between them were enough in every sense to satisfy any imaginable desire, carnal or otherwise, I might have, except occasionally for an hour or two of peace and quiet, when one of them had a particularly loudly buzzing bee in her bonnet about the other. Two women in any man's personal life is a double armload of problems; I cannot imagine the extra burdens a third might bring.

When Marg had come to Beautiful Bay that first time after the agreement to share what was laughingly known as my body – I have to be frank, and crude – I was shitting myself. Thirty years is a long time between drinks, so to speak. Marg had taken my virginity at the age of eighteen after I had promised it to Anna, then sixteen. Anna and I had solemnly and tearfully agreed as we parted company on the wharf in Batavia in 1942 that no matter how long it might take to consummate our love we would wait for each other, until the war ended or, if necessary, until the end of time. I recall feeling only momentarily guilty as Marg's tongue entered my eager mouth for the first time and it became obvious that she was about to steal something I suddenly regarded as having no value to me whatsoever and, in turn, she was about to reward me with an experience of tremendous worth.

In fact, I had simply capitulated at the first deep kiss from another woman and broken my solemn promise to beautiful Anna with alacrity and not a twinge of conscience. In such moments the one-eyed snake rules supreme and I would be a hypocrite to pretend that I regretted my unfaithfulness for a moment. If ever a young lad was blessed with a loving, generous and exquisite plundering of his manhood, then it was Nick Duncan at the hands of Marg Hamilton.

I confess that in the glorious process Marg did take all the initiative, doing and directing while I happily performed whatever muscle work I was instructed to perform. Left to me it would have been all mumble, fumble and grope and I would have had no idea how to go about seducing her.

In the few weeks that followed I was her eager pupil and if I managed to gratify her, the plot, the plan and the peak of perfection reached was all under her control. By the time I went to Melbourne to join the navy, Marg had taken me from ingenue to someone with a small degree of competence in bed.

More importantly she had inculcated in me the notion that loving sex is not complete until both partners are equally gratified. I was also helped to understand that gratification usually took a lot longer for a woman than it did for a man and should be regarded as a serious undertaking as well as a joyous task.

I have been fortunate with the women in my life, but I honestly felt that none of my experiences had compared with the sheer exuberant joy of sexual intercourse with Naval Intelligence Officer Marg Hamilton. Perhaps I should change that to *loving* sexual intercourse because there is a difference, no matter how skilled the partners. Or so, thanks to my early instruction from a good woman, it has always seemed to me.

And now, on a bright moonlit night at Beautiful Bay, thirty years after that glorious first experience, I found myself at the age of forty-eight about to face my old lover again and, despite all my subsequent experience, I was absolutely terrified.

The love, the lust and the longing seemed suddenly to be overtaken by a fear that after three years of relative celibacy I would fail to have an erection or, worse still, that I might suffer from premature ejaculation. On the surface, this seemed patently ridiculous. I continued to respond to Anna's generous mouth and clever hands as eagerly as ever, but then I told myself that bringing Anna the gratification she sought was an entirely different skill from what I believed Marg would require. Heavy petting followed by a spanking wasn't quite how I saw myself bringing Marg to the point of ultimate satisfaction. I became convinced I'd be rusty and clumsy, over-anxious and in need of specific instruction – a terrible disappointment in bed. Or, to put it into male parlance, a dud bash.

After all my talking and cajoling Marg would expect me to be a regular gigolo or, at the very least, after all my experience with my so-called scattered surrogates, a highly competent lover. It takes a woman to tell a man if he's any good in bed and while my surrogates had always been generous in their praise, perhaps they had been bolstering my ego. Maybe Nick Duncan wasn't the lover they'd always made him out to be.

Throughout all this, it never occurred to me that Marg might also be experiencing her own sexual angst. She'd hinted, that first time at Beautiful Bay when I'd rejected her generous proposition, that except for the first half-dozen years with Rob Rich, the boudoir hadn't played an important part in their relationship. Though there would have been nothing to stop her having an affair after he'd died, she told me she'd been virtually celibate. Later I would recall something she'd said that was very poignant, particularly if, like Marg, you'd always been a head-turner, accustomed to being noticed whenever you entered a room. 'Darling, you can take all the care in the world with your figure and your grooming, but a woman over fifty goes from being noticed and admired to being practically nonexistent, from turning heads to turning invisible.' I hadn't taken into consideration her own anxiety that, at fifty-six, Marg might also have been feeling anxious. I guess men are entirely self-obsessed in their anxieties and so I imagined Marg, horny as hell, raring to go, wanting me as explicitly and lovingly and demandingly as when we'd both been young but with me unable to perform, slack as a salamander, failing her, falling down on the job. As one gets older the one-eyed snake's power is often undermined by the brain; perhaps this is nature's revenge for the many times the cautioning brain has been overruled and disregarded in the past.

Marg had asked to be excused from dinner and Gloria the cook had taken a tray – scrambled eggs and toast and a pot of tea – in to her.

I ate very little and was scolded by cook, then she'd giggled. 'Masta emi needim plenty kai-kai long dis time. No good yufella weak tumas tonight.' I have no idea how women know these things; after all, Marg was a frequent visitor and the servants would have known there had been no hanky-panky between us. When I thought about it, Gloria had as good as given me her approval, unusual because she was a Seventh Day Adventist and regular churchgoer who sang in the choir and was strict on moral rectitude. How could she possibly have known that Anna and I practised unorthodox sex? But she must have done, because normally when she disapproved of me, I might have expected burnt chops, lumpy mash and a generous serving of stony silence.

After dinner on the big frightening night, I repaired to the verandah as usual, though this time somewhat nervously, where cook had placed cheese and biscuits, a fresh sliced lime and ice before retiring for the night to the servants' compound. I mixed Marg her usual gin and tonic and poured myself a brandy and sat down to wait. As I said earlier, the tropical moon was the full James Michener and you could clearly see *Madam Butterfly* rocking in her mooring at the bottom of the garden. We'd been sailing that afternoon and had come back at sunset, when Marg had declined afternoon tea or a drink or dinner. Seeming tired and happy she had retired to her room for a nap.

When she appeared with a soft swish of silk she was wearing a simple low-cut dress in the azure blue that both Anna and Marg mysteriously chose as their favourite colour. Marg always changed and brushed up prettily for the evenings, but like everyone else at Beautiful Bay, she normally went barefoot in the best tradition of the islands. Marg had once laughingly remarked that days before leaving Tasmania for Beautiful Bay, she'd leave a note on the fridge – PAINT YOUR TOENAILS! Now she swept onto the verandah with her bobbed chestnut hair catching the light, the silver streaks untouched and very attractive, her make-up perfect so that her eyes, heightened by the careful use of eye shadow, appeared brilliant. Her tall figure, lightly tanned and slightly muscled from bushwalking, gave her the appearance of a much younger woman, and if her breasts were somehow cunningly up-holstered to appear firm and true, nothing showed through the thin silk except the suggestion of her nipples and they looked perfectly wonderful. But it was her long, tanned, shapely legs and her feet encased in a pair of light grey court shoes with stiletto heels worthy of a stilt dancer that set my heart pounding and sent a flush of tumescent heat to my thighs. So much for post-fifties women being invisible. Had I been required to get to my feet thirty seconds after her entry it would have proved highly embarrassing.

'Marg, you look wonderful!' I exclaimed.

'A girl does the best she can,' she laughed, sitting down in a swirl of silk, her magnificent pins brought together and to one side so that the elegant shoes touched.

'No, no, I . . . I . . . er, mean it, the shoes . . . legs . . . ah . . .' I involuntarily glanced at her breasts, '. . . everything,' I stammered stupidly, handing her the gin and tonic.

Marg smiled at me fondly. 'Thank you.' Then she said, 'Nick, do you remember the first time?'

'As if yesterday, encoded into my every synapse.'

'You were so impossibly young and beautiful, a boy so innocent, tall, bronzed, skinny as a rake, entirely delectable and furthermore completely unspoilt, oblivious of the hero you were. You'd seen the horror of a brutal massacre on a lonely beach and sailed virtually single-handed across the Pacific, and even though you'd showered, I recall your skin tasted of salt and of the sea. I simply couldn't wait to have you all to myself.'

I glanced down at my clearly defined paunch. Fortunately my arms were suntanned from sailing, which concealed the first signs that the once ropey forearm muscles and biceps were not worked as hard loading cargo as they had once been. I possessed only a shaving mirror in my bathroom, so looking down when I came out of the shower was no way of assessing my physical condition and, besides, it did nothing for my old fella. But skinny I definitely was not, nor innocent, nor a hero. I took a gulp of brandy, conscious of the warmth suffusing my body. Brandy was a stimulant, wasn't it? I knew I wasn't going to suffer from brewer's droop. Fortunately trousers are equipped with zips, otherwise my fly buttons would have been pinging off the ceiling. Anna would sometimes joke in bed, 'Nicholas, is that a gun in your pocket, or are you just pleased to see me?' But I am ashamed to admit that, just like the first time I lay with Marg, Anna never entered my mind.

I grinned. 'I still lie in bed some mornings and think of those glorious three weeks with you in Fremantle. It was as if I hadn't reached land in *Madam Butterfly*, but had drowned in the last big storm and gone straight to heaven,' I said, trying to sound vaguely in possession of my wits. *C'mon, Duncan, it's only sex!* But it wasn't.

Marg laughed, then rose and kissed me on the lips. 'Nick, come, darling, it's been too long. One admiral, two children, twenty-nine years and fifty-one weeks.' She reached out and took my hand.

We entered her bedroom, a large room like all the bedrooms at Beautiful Bay, except for my own – I preferred a very small room, not much bigger than a monk's cell. It had nothing to do with self-denial, but I'd spent so much of my life sailing or on freighters that I'd become accustomed to sleeping in a small space and liked a bedroom that wasn't much bigger than a ship's cabin.

Marg had left the curtains open so that the moonlight streaming in made it unnecessary to switch on the light. To my surprise she simply pulled her dress over her head and in the soft light stood naked before me, neither bra nor panties in evidence, the divine V of her pubic area clipped close but not shaved as it had been when we'd first made love.

Still in her stilettos (corny perhaps, but just about every man's fantasy) she was simply beautiful as she moved up to me and kissed me lightly on the lips, adding just the tip of her tongue, a suggestion of things to come. Then she slid down, her hands on either side of my body until she was on her knees, where she unzipped then unbuckled and in a single movement pulled every encumbrance but one down to my ankles. As I was barefoot it was a simple matter to step clear and then to pull the cotton shirt over my head. It seemed to take only moments before I stood naked and rampant, looking down at her lovely neck, strong shoulders and back, the sharp tuck of her waist and the elegant curve of her thighs. She was even lovelier than I'd imagined. Marg reached out and took me in her fist, giggling as she did so. 'Nick, I've waited a long time to have the man I've always loved finally back within my grasp.'

'Keep doing that and your grasp will come to a sticky end,' I laughed.

Marg chuckled with delight, any tension between us gone; we were back where we'd been so very long ago and her mouth slipped over me and the loving began. Sex with Marg was delightful fun, playful and arousing, but soon she pulled away and announced, 'Nick Duncan, I want everything and I want it now!' I drew her to her feet, picked her up and placed her on the bed where she raised her shoes towards the ceiling. 'Last look,' she said, kicking them off, then, spreading her gorgeous legs wide she murmured, 'All's fair in love and war. One mouth deserves another.'

That was the wonderful thing about making love to Marg – it was exuberant, vigorous, soft and hard, joyous, open, demanding and funny, and we talked between the groans and moans and laughed a lot. When I finally entered her she was surprisingly and gorgeously tight. 'Marg, this is a nice surprise! You've had two kids . . .'

'Exercises,' she gasped. 'Oh God, that's so good!'

'Exercise? What, bushwalking?' I said, laughing.

'No,' she gasped. 'Exercises with an "s". Harder, Nick, oh yes, yes, that's lovely.'

'What, pussy exercises?' I laughed again. Marg was obviously enjoying herself, thrusting and gripping me tightly, using her pelvic muscles skilfully. Thankfully I felt I still had a fair safety margin before I exploded. The great advantage of the subtle non-penetrative loving I'd been receiving for so long was that control for long periods was what heightened the ultimate experience and I had been expertly tutored.

'Oh, a dildo!' she gasped. 'Oh! Oh! I'm going to come. Now! Now! Hard! Nick, Nick! Bastard! Hard!' she screamed.

'Dildo, eh!' I roared. 'Here, take this then, bitch!' I shouted in mock arrogance, then joyfully got my back stuck into pleasing her.

After this we made love several times, easily and happily exploring, getting to know each other, her wonderful breasts, the sudden delicious curve of her hips, her thrust and grip, the tenderness of her mouth and lips, the soft folds of her labia, her arms and legs folded about my body, the laughter and joy of the way of a man with a maid, of a girl and a boy (good love always seems young). Making love with Marg was, as it had previously been, a sharing between two people with a single purpose, each to please the other, but at the same time with the self-serving reward of maximum personal pleasure. This time, though, I'm happy to say, I needed a great deal less specific instruction.

Afterwards as we lay back in each other's arms, a soft kiss of air from the ceiling fan cooling our naked bodies, moonlight streaming through the French windows, a whiff of frangipani blossom carried on the hot tropical night, I couldn't resist the question contained in the word. 'Dildo?' I said.

Marg disentangled herself and, leaning on her elbow, kissed me on the nose. 'A girl has to do what a girl has to do.' I was silent, not quite knowing how to react to so open and honest a response. 'Why? You don't approve?' she asked.

'No, no,' I hastily assured her. 'I most certainly do! The

results of the exercises with an "s" are truly remarkable and I'm a very grateful recipient.'

'Oh, it wasn't all pleasuring,' Marg said.

'There is a downside to a dildo?' I asked. 'Isn't the standard joke that using one a woman meets a better class of lover?'

Marg smiled, the joke obviously not new, and then replied equally flippantly, 'Nick, the only downside to a dildo is that it doesn't put out the garbage.'

The old forthright Marg Hamilton was, I decided, much better than Mrs Rich, the admiral's wife. 'I can't say that does a whole lot for my ego,' I laughed.

'It's all about the transition from sausage-roll queen back to Marg Hamilton. Rob and I had an indifferent sex life after the kids came, you know, the obligatory birthday and Christmas bonk, the full ho-hum. He had his career, I had my career, and also the kids, school, sport, a man who needed constant reassurance and direction. Bed was a debate, not a delight. In short, ours was what so many marriages seem inevitably to become.'

'Marg, whenever we met, you always seemed so upbeat, a successful woman and wife, with lovely children, well in control of your destiny, the future . . . it was almost scary.'

'Now that I think back on it, it was scary, though in part I was to blame.'

'Oh?' I said, surprised. 'I wouldn't have thought so.'

'Nick, child-bearing makes a mess of the parts that count with a man. We go from tight to sloppy, breasts sag after breastfeeding, tummies don't tuck back quite as tightly and we tell ourselves – that is, if we think about it at all – well, that's life, having kids, the physiology of marriage, the body beautiful sacrificed for a higher cause. I did, and so Rob, who wasn't the rampant stallion type to begin with, gradually lost interest in me.'

'And so you found another way?' If this wasn't exactly a romantic post-coital conversation, it was pleasant to be reacquainted with the original 'tell it how it is' Marg.

'Of course not!' Marg protested. 'I simply felt unwanted, unloved, taken for granted, resentful, the admiral's factotum, the whole sad-sack story.' She paused. 'But then Rob had the accident and the kids were flying the coop and I was suddenly on my own, in a sense my own responsibility.'

'Yeah, the sausage-roll queen,' I said sympathetically.

'Yes, well, you know all that and the denouement, the return to Marg Hamilton. Part of the way back was to resume control of my body.' Marg paused, leaned forward and kissed me on the forehead. 'I couldn't bear to think that it was all over for me, that I'd had all there was and the rest was simply growing plump and what women laughingly refer to as "comfortable", when carrying any extra weight is patently anything but. So I started to lose weight and to tone the pubococcygeus muscle, or the PC muscle, with vaginal-tightening exercises.'

'I don't suppose I should ask, but is that done with a . . . you-know-what?'

'You probably don't want to know, Nick, but seeing you've asked, it's done by tightening and pulling on the band of muscle that stretches from the coccyx to the pubic bone, as if you are trying to resist the urge to pee or fart.'

We both started to giggle. 'Useful if you're caught short in the middle of a good movie?' I managed.

'Don't joke. One of the benefits is that it reduces the risk of urinary incontinence, not uncommon in women my age,' Marg replied.

'It suddenly occurs to me that this conversation isn't all that romantic,' I said, 'but it's stuff men don't know anything about and it's bloody interesting. But if I may be persistent, we still haven't come to the . . . er . . . offending item.'

'Ah, the dildo,' Marg proclaimed. 'Well, I have a very sensible gynaecologist, who fortunately for me is a woman of my age and a very practical one. One of the PC-tightening exercises she recommended involves a Kegelmaster – not dissimilar to a dumbbell – you use it by tightening against it as it tries to . . . well, fall out. My gyno simply said, "Marg, a dildo is just as effective and a lot more fun; I personally recommend it."' Marg giggled wickedly. 'One should always take one's doctor's advice, don't you think, darling?'

'Nice,' I said, genuinely pleased that she'd confided in me.

Marg jumped on top of me and said, 'Darling, shall we benefit just once more from the results of the modified Kegelmaster?'

'Oh, okay, if you insist,' I laughed, 'but you have to promise to be gentle.'

I guess, as they say in the vernacular, I was double dipping. (Oops! Under the circumstances quite the wrong expression.) Anyway, having a bet each way. But the two glorious women in my life approached the act of making love so entirely differently that it was as if I was taking pleasure in two essentially different experiences: the exquisite subtlety and knowledge of the male erogenous zones that Anna possessed, and the joyous exuberance of Marg's approach to lovemaking. In return, I think I learned to satisfy the desire of each in a completely different manner.

Marg won her seat in the May 1982 state election on a count back, ten votes separating her from her Liberal rival, while Bob Brown in the neighbouring seat of Denison missed out almost as closely. This was almost certainly due to the perfidious campaign Robin Gray's Liberals ran against him where they letterboxed every house in Denison with a copy of an article that had appeared in the *Launceston Examiner* many years previously with the headline '*Doctor admits he's gay!*', making sure that everyone in the electorate knew Bob Brown was homosexual.

It is not unusual for the Libs and Labor to give a new member from either side some time to settle in, but the first member of the new Greens party enjoyed no such luxury; both traditional opponents lined up to be the first to chew her up and spit her out.

The very idea that sufficient Tasmanians existed to elect a member of a new political party that stood for trees and rivers was totally abhorrent to the old guard, particularly in the year when the infrastructure was just about in place to build the first dams to flood a large part of the state.

These dams would effectively submerge over a third of Tasmania's south-west wilderness. On any map in any nation it was a sizeable area to change forever, to simply swallow in one great greedy gulp. Planning had been furiously underway since October 1979 when the multi-million-dollar scheme to build a 296-megawatt hydroelectricity project was announced.

However, in this period the Wilderness Society hadn't been idle either. Active membership had grown from the sixteen original members to two thousand nationally and the movement to save the Franklin and Gordon rivers was now on a much firmer base. If it had not yet attained a powerful head of steam, it had at least given off several good puffs, noticeable on an expanding national horizon.

At the Federal Labor Conference in July, the New South Wales premier Neville Wran, a powerful figure in the Australian

Labor Party, together with his wife Jill, came out strongly against the building of the dams and, mainly due to their efforts, Federal Labor adopted as policy the no-dams case.

This certainly counted as a significant win for the movement, but as Labor was still in opposition, as far as Robin Gray, now Liberal premier, was concerned, it was a toothless tiger and he simply thumbed his nose at Federal Labor.

Marg was a single flea on the hide of the Hydro monster and with both sides so closely aligned to the Electric Kremlin, as the Hydro-Electric Commission had been dubbed by some wag in the Wilderness Society, she simply became an object of derision, the daily joke in the House.

Marg would often call me at the end of a difficult day and burst into tears, but I don't think she ever for one moment lost her resolve. The battle-hardened Wilderness Society was not easily thwarted and in a series of mass rallies they collected forty thousand signatures on a 'Save the Rivers' petition, presented it to state parliament and quite noticeably tweaked political noses.

This must have had some real effect, because Russell Ashton, the head of the Hydro-Electric Commission, showing the typical autocratic arrogance of the Electric Kremlin, declared, 'If the parliament tries to work through popular decisions we are doomed in this state and doomed elsewhere.' So much for democracy at work and, of course, the premier Robin Gray decided to heed this self-serving advice.

This time Marg couldn't take it on the chin. Forty thousand Tasmanians simply couldn't be dismissed or ignored as ratbags, she maintained in a speech to the House that was accompanied by the jeers of both Liberal and Labor. I recall how on one of her now daily phone calls she could barely contain her anger. 'Nick, it's not the derision of the politicians – I'm one of them now and I suppose I have to accept what's coming to me – it's the bloody-minded arrogance of the Hydro. They really think they're omnipotent and can do as they wish.'

'Well, my dear, it seems as though they can,' I replied.

'It isn't even an issue that will be decided at an election,' Marg fumed. 'The opposition has the same point of view and that's why they got rid of Doug Lowe. The Franklin–Gordon doesn't even get debated! We spent the entire session today discussing the price of potatoes!'

But Marg wasn't completely right. Doug Lowe, before he'd been deposed as the Labor premier, had proposed to Fraser's federal government that the south-west wilderness area, incorporating the Gordon and Franklin rivers, be submitted for World Heritage listing. Fraser agreed. With an election looming, he was keen to neutralise conservation as an issue, now that Federal Labor had taken up the no-dams issue.

At the time the World Heritage gesture was seen as futile in the face of the absolute determination by both sides of state politics to proceed with the damming of the rivers, but it would later come to be regarded as the one critical action that saved the wilderness. It also showed that men of conscience and independent thought such as Doug Lowe can still occasionally be found in politics, even if their chances of success are minimal.

Marg, echoing the Wilderness Society, seemed to think the heritage listing wasn't going to make a huge difference. 'It's just politics,' she asserted. 'Local Labor won't take any notice but at least it put us on the international agenda and gave me a rare moment of satisfaction in parliament.'

'So what does that tell you?' I asked.

'That we've got to go outside Tasmania? Even outside Australia? Yes, we know that. It's not about the local pollies and the Hydro – they're never going to change. All our efforts must be directed at Canberra and overseas. Australia must be made to look foolish and backward in the eyes of the outside world.' She paused. 'But our rejection of Doug Lowe's original compromise to save some of the wilderness isn't helping at the moment. The mainlanders don't understand that it's a complete ecosystem and can't simply be halved. They, the media, think Lowe's compromise was a reasonable suggestion and we should have accepted it while it was available. Now it no longer is. But we're fighting back. Yehudi Menuhin helped by launching a booklet that set out the whole issue and it seems to have been a great success. He knows everyone who is anyone, not just in Australia, and we're hoping that will have some effect.'

I didn't comment that there was something very funny about one of the world's greatest violinists in a sense fiddling while Rome burned. I simply couldn't see a truck driver from Strahan, the town chosen as the launching point for the Franklin River project where unemployment was three times the national average, getting too excited by the violinist's contribution or the booklet. These glossy brochures always seem to bolster the spirits of the converted and arouse the suspicions of the doubters. (Where did the money come from to print that?) It's a curious paradox that in Australia protesters have to be seen to be battling without resources to be considered legitimate. Nearly two hundred years of battler versus squatter seem to have conditioned us so that a well-organised and properly financed protest is generally regarded with considerable suspicion. Printed placards don't work; it's always crayons on cardboard and silly chants against seemingly well-organised arrogance and indifference – rags versus riches.

'We've also invited David Bellamy to come over. We're crossing our fingers he'll agree,' Marg went on.

'Who's David Bellamy?' I asked.

'God, Nick, you're hopeless! Only one of the world's best-known conservationists! He has a program on the BBC that's watched all over the world by tens of millions of viewers.'

'That's good,' I said, not knowing if it was. Outside pressure is fine, but actual interference from elsewhere sometimes alienates more than it helps.

'We're planning a blockade when the bulldozers start coming. Thankfully we have quite a lot of lead time. Our intelligence tells us the Hydro can't really get underway until early 1983. Hopefully Bellamy will come. If he does there will be worldwide publicity. Nick, you'll be happy to know it's non-violent, but the time has come for direct confrontation. We're planning several rallies in the lead-up and a lot more signatures.'

'No doubt they'll be as effective as the last lot were,' I said, then immediately wished I hadn't.

Marg sighed and sounded uncharacteristically discouraged. 'Nick, we're learning, watching what's done overseas. It's all about pressure. Bob Brown says it's about never taking your foot off the pedal, never letting the opposition relax.'

'I must say, they don't appear over-agitated at the moment.'

'No, I agree. But Malcolm Fraser and the Libs look as if they're on the way out and if Labor gets in they're our big chance. It's not Gough Whitlam this time, and Bob Hawke, the union leader, looks like challenging Bill Hayden for the leadership, but both of them are on our side. And in the meantime we must be seen to be applying the pressure, making a noise, being noticed, doing things. David Bellamy, Yehudi Menuhin, world figures like that can't be ignored.'

But it seemed they could. A poll showed sixty per cent of Tasmanians were against the Franklin River project. In an attempt to refute this statistic Tasmania held a deeply flawed referendum where it wasn't possible to formally vote against the Hydro scheme, and yet almost forty-five per cent of voters voted informal and wrote 'No Dams' on their ballot papers, but this still didn't make the slightest difference. In the history of state politics, Labor and Liberal have never been so totally united on a single issue while both deliberately ignoring the wishes of their constituents.

Two months after Marg was elected, on the 22nd of July 1982, the Hydro-Electric Commission began to build the roads into the Franklin. At 11 p.m. on the 14th of December, both the Franklin and Gordon rivers and the south-west wilderness area received World Heritage listing. It was also the first complete day of the blockade, but I'm getting ahead of myself.

Despite all the outside pressure, which even included the Fraser Liberal government offering Robin Gray five hundred million dollars to stop the project, he instructed the bulldozers and the police to move in and passed a law through state parliament making protest at the construction site illegal. The eternal battle, Mother Nature versus human nature, was about to begin with the odds stacked hugely against the rivers, the lakes and the forests, where the whine of the chainsaw cutting a swath through the tall timber was drowning out the birdsong.

And on the domestic front, a wilderness would become the battleground for the real contest between the two women in my life. It would not be over me that they fought, but over trees – Princess Plunder and the Green Bitch, the two in direct opposition for the first time, the one tearing down the forests of Borneo, the other fighting to save the trees. Later of course it would be tuna fishing and whales, the extinction of species due to lack of habitat or river pollution, carbon emissions and the atmosphere. I often wondered what might happen if ever I disagreed with one or the other violently and issued her with an ultimatum, that is, either me or the particular pursuit I objected to. I had serious doubts that I'd survive the challenge.

I realised that the rule Anna had made in Japan – that I was not to speak to one about the other – was going to be a very important factor if I wished to have a peaceful as well as a sexually fulfilling life. If I accepted the negative barrage of words from each about the other without passing them on, then the triumvirate had a chance of surviving. Although I realised as time passed that each seemed to know what the other was doing most of the time and would sometimes come up with information that was news to me. Anna, I suspected, paid someone to keep an eye on Marg, though she never admitted it. Marg, as usual, went to the horse's mouth. Her erstwhile boss in Naval Intelligence during the war, when she'd been stationed in Fremantle, was Lieutenant Commander Roger Rigby, who was now head of Australian Intelligence based in Canberra, his main responsibility being Shoal Bay near Darwin, the monitoring station responsible for close surveillance of Indonesia and its rulers.

Anna now had investments in all Australian states and territories, for instance, she owned significant real-estate interests in the Melbourne CBD and at least two major parking stations in the CBD of every Australian capital city. She also owned more than a dozen franchised fashion label boutiques in Hawaii and on the west coast of America, and a fifty per cent share of a high-fashion workshop in Paris.

Miss Sparkle, who had passed away in 1973, had left Anna a number of blue-chip investments in major Japanese companies and twenty-five pachinko bars in Tokyo, plus – surprise, surprise – a one-third share of the Jade House. These last two assets were overseen by *Fuchida-san*, who had forged a great friendship with Anna on her frequent visits to Japan. But by far her major capital investments and enormous profits were coming out of Indonesia where she was partnered by Budi, who by 1975 had achieved the rank of major general and been appointed head of the army's legal department.

It was this Indonesian aspect of Anna's life that Marg could monitor through her old mate, Roger Rigby. 'Princess Plunder can't make an indecent move without my knowing,' she'd boast as she expanded on the subject of Anna on her week-long visits, just as Anna held forth about the Green Bitch on her visits. They were obsessed as well as fascinated by each other. The depth of knowledge each possessed of the affairs of the other constantly surprised me, and there was little doubt that it added extra spice as well as spite to their lives. The extent of their enmity and the lengths to which each would go to destroy the other was to be revealed in the future, but back then I was blissfully unaware of what lay ahead.

CHAPTER SEVENTEEN

'Five of our blokes are killed
and our prime minister is full of
mealy-mouthed words of regret
but taking bugger all action
to discover the bastards who did the killing.
Crossfire my arse!'
Nick, on the Balibo Five

ON THE 12TH OF DECEMBER, two days before the blockade was due to start, Marg had moved to Strahan in the somewhat battered but indestructible Toyota we'd used on our original trip to Lake Pedder. She'd fallen in love with the old heap, with its diesel engine that refused to die, so when I left for the mainland I bought it for her from the friend who'd owned it. Now she resolutely refused my offer to replace it. 'Buy me a new battery instead, Nick. Sometimes the old bloke won't get out of bed and start on a cold morning.'

Marg had sounded tired but elated when she phoned that evening. 'Nick, we've arrived!'

'Where are you staying?' I asked.

'In an old customs building that belongs to Parks and Wildlife. It's vacant and close to the town centre, thank God. People are pouring into town from everywhere – a lot of mainlanders, young people – the first lot have already left for the campsite on the Gordon. I'm told they're going to be sick as dogs crossing the harbour.'

'Marg, you're going to be okay, aren't you? You won't do anything silly?'

'I'm not allowed to, Bob Brown's instructions. The media comes first. I've got to keep my nose clean.'

'Remind me to send him another cheque,' I laughed. 'Let the kids do the getting arrested bit. Tell me, what are the townspeople like?'

'Haven't really had time to find out. Although I was briefing a TV crew from Melbourne who'd come two days early to get background footage and interview the protesters who are already here. We were standing out of the rain under a fish-and-chip shop awning this afternoon and a woman came out wiping her hands on her apron, obviously the proprietor. "All yer do is film the greenies, the filthy greenies. Youse never even think about the people of Strahan!" she shouted at us.

'So the TV reporter said, "Come on then, give us a comment, madam," to which she replied, "I just bloody did!" The TV man pointed at his cameraman. "Here, directly to camera."

'The woman put her hands on her hips, unaware that the camera was still on. "If me husband was here he'd give yiz a comment orright – a boot up the whatsit! Lemme tell yiz, youse'd be walking real strange for the next few days, mate."

'"So, where is he, your husband?" the reporter asked.

'She glanced down at her watch. "Probably down the pub trying ter buy more fish from the fishermen." She gave an impatient sigh. "Look, I ain't got time to stand around. There's lotsa strangers in town gunna need feedin' ternight."'

Marg laughed. 'It's going to air tomorrow night. I'm not

sure Bob is going to approve. I think he wants a bit of spit-flecked acrimony, not a good laugh on nationwide television.'

Marg had been assigned to help the team coordinating the media, the most essential aspect of the blockade, in fact, the primary reason for it. Maintaining the momentum for the nation's radio, television, newspapers and magazines was critical. A blockade that isn't national news is simply a waste of time and effort.

The activists had learned from their failures with Lake Pedder. They now knew better than to appeal to parliament and the local media, and had concluded that peaceful confrontation was their only hope of involving the mainland media. And they needed their involvement to galvanise national opinion, especially as the blockade was to start on the 14th of December, the day the World Heritage Committee would announce its decision on the application to list the south-west wilderness area. They were gambling on a positive outcome. The Federal Parliament would be in recess and there would be the usual paucity of news over the Christmas period. If all went well, the blockade could be front-page news.

On the evening of the 14th of December, Marg phoned again, sounding elated. 'Nick, it went brilliantly today! Over fifty of our people have been arrested and we managed to get the media across the harbour in some abalone fishermen's boats! Bob Brown flew over the river with Norm Sanders and radioed in to say that what took place upriver looked like a cross between a navy battle and a regatta. There were dozens of our little red and yellow rubber inflatables filled with protesters holding banners and waving flags, and police launches like sharks hunting for mackerel, trying to get to our inflatables, dodging between the media and the tourist cruise boats.'

'What are they arresting you for? I mean, it's a peaceful

protest, isn't it?'

'Yes, of course, no resistance is offered. They arrest us for trespassing. It goes like this: "If you do not leave immediately I will arrest you for trespass." We then say, "This is a national park and I am entitled to be here." Then the cops say, "You are under arrest." We signal our whereabouts for the media boats and then obligingly climb up onto the deck of the police launch chanting slogans.'

On the first day the police launches were up the Gordon near the dam site and made their arrests there, but the number of protesters arriving had taken them by surprise and police now began to arrive in Strahan and Queenstown in much greater numbers.

Marg's voice on the phone began to sound increasingly concerned. 'Nick, there are police everywhere you look. This is a town that usually has one policeman who spends most days with his feet up on his desk. Today a hundred and fifty moved into the district. There are police boats on the harbour and everyone's looking grim-faced. I tried to talk to three young uniformed lads today who looked nervous enough to bolt. "This is a peaceful blockade, why are you here?" I asked them. "Dunno, lady," one said. "Just told," another mumbled. Then a sergeant came up. "What's going on?" he asked. "I was just telling your men this is a peaceful protest, sergeant," I said, giving them my most winning smile. "Then keep the peace and move on, lady," he instructed.

'Remembering Bob's caution to keep my nose clean, I turned to go and he called, "You tell your mob if they want trouble we'll be waiting."

'I couldn't help myself. "Sounds as if you can't wait, sergeant."

'"Move on, madam!" he said with a flick of the wrist.

'I'm afraid I lost my patience. "My name is Marg Hamilton and I'm a member of parliament and I can't say I like your manner, sergeant. What is your name, please?" I used my crisp admiral's-widow voice and took a notebook and pen from my handbag.

'"Docker, madam, Sergeant Danny Docker. Our orders are direct from the premier. Perhaps you'd like to take it up with him, madam?" Whatever else he was, Sergeant Docker wasn't stupid or lost for a rebuttal and I guess he won that round handsomely,' Marg admitted. 'Besides, I shouldn't have used that "do you know who you're talking to" pathetic bullshit, Nick.' Then she added, 'And now it's raining!'

As the blockade wore on, and the weather didn't improve, I could hear the weariness in her voice. It was much the same routine – welcome the press, arrange transport across the harbour and up the Gordon to the protesters' camp or see that they were present if anything was happening in town, attend the magistrate's court in Queenstown each night, then, exhausted, call long distance to Beautiful Bay.

Marg was getting to know the townspeople and often expressed her sympathy for them. 'Nick, it's basically a working-class town, miners, lots of men who are pretty much unskilled. The Mount Lyell copper mine, the biggest employer around here, has closed down most of its operations because the price of copper has fallen through the floor. For the locals it's a disaster. Strahan now has twice the unemployed of the rest of Tasmania.'

'Hmm, not the best situation to find yourselves in. Are they making it difficult for you?'

'Nothing we haven't been told to expect and in some ways better than the anti-dam rabble we often had to put up with at rallies when we were protesting Lake Pedder. You know, the usual shouting out in the street, some of the young blokes, from Queenstown mostly, wanting to start fights. We dare not go into the pub. But the older townsfolk are not too bad. You get accustomed to being served silently in the shops, but then again, they realise we're bringing income into the town.'

'I must say I can see where they're coming from. They're depending on the Hydro work and you're threatening it. How many jobs are involved?'

'Four hundred and fifty at the dam site, and of course the Hydro also brings ancillary jobs to Strahan.'

'Marg, for these people it probably seems that the ingredients for happiness have arrived in the nick of time: food on the table, shoes for the kids, a beer or two at the pub after work, a bet at the TAB and the ability to meet the monthly payment on the truck or the washing machine.'

Marg laughed. 'Very eloquently put, Nick. Whose side are you on anyway?'

'People have to live, Marg.'

'Of course, and it's not all one-sided in the town either. The local population is divided between those who believe it's necessary to destroy some of the wilderness and the rivers to put food on the table and those who want it kept for the growing tourism trade. One of the pro-dam councillors put it rather neatly in this morning's paper: "These jobs are here and now, guaranteed. Must we bet on keeping the wilderness for the potential welfare of strangers?"'

'Oh, I hadn't realised there was a tourism issue.'

'Strahan is one of the gateways to the south-west wilderness. Last year it attracted sixty thousand tourists.'

'That's pretty impressive, but I don't suppose tourism supplies too many jobs for people who earn their living by working from the neck down.'

'Nick, that's a bit harsh! But the truth is that at best the dam work is short term and when it's built the town will be back in the doldrums, but tourism can only grow and make more jobs. Of course, the government claims the dam will attract the same number if not more recreational tourists and will become a sort of Tasmanian lakeland – yachts, motorboats, fishermen, weekenders. It's a lot of hooey, of course, and besides, not what the wilderness is all about.'

'But from the Hydro's viewpoint they've chosen the perfect town as their entry point. They've relieved the unemployment situation and frustrated the protesters. The construction site is very difficult to get to and so it's going to be relatively easy for the police to keep the wilderness activists in check and, moreover, dampen the enthusiasm of the media and discourage them from prolonging their visit.'

'All too true,' Marg said ruefully.

But as Marg's nightly calls indicated, there was no dampening of the spirits of protesters, who kept arriving in the town from the mainland, surprising everyone by their sheer numbers, including TAA and Ansett who had to put on extra flights. Most of the protesters were young, but many were older middle-class people who were determined to add their voices to the protest and stoically put up with the appalling mud, the constant rain and the primitive conditions.

'Nick, people keep surprising me. A more miserable experience would be difficult to find. Most of the time they're soaked, cold and violently seasick with almost every harbour crossing. At night they sleep in muddy conditions in wet sleeping bags. If ever a protest called for courage, dedication and persistence it's this one. Yet spirits are high and people are laughing.'

Bob Brown, as head of the Wilderness Society, was the logical spokesman for the activists, who were not all 'greens'.

There were hippies from Nimbin, housewives, teachers and pensioners, students from all over Australia making a stand during their uni vacation, and working professionals who gave up their Christmas holidays.

While the protesters could get to Strahan by road, the trip to the dam site from the town began with the notoriously rough crossing of Macquarie Harbour. Once they reached the other side they still had to travel by boat up the Gordon River to the proposed protest camp near the dam construction site.

It was here that local Strahan tour operator Reg Morrison stepped up and announced he'd donate the use of his boat, the *J. Lee M*, together with fuel and crew. 'If you bring the people I'll run 'em for ya. I'll provide all the transport.' He and his skipper Denny Hamill ferried most of the blockaders across the harbour and up the river to the protest site.

Marg often talked about Reg, whom she referred to as 'the salt of the earth'; he had founded tourism on the Gordon River, taking tourists up the river after the war, and he had been on a one-man crusade to save the south-west wilderness for years. 'Damming the Franklin and the Lower Gordon would be like cutting off my arms and legs,' he'd once told her.

'Nick, he's everything good about being Australian, a man of conscience who stands to lose everything by siding with us. He's rough-hewn, weather-beaten and softly spoken and he hasn't had a lot of education – he's one of those men who you wouldn't notice in a group. Yet faced with something he believes in, he becomes an intractable and formidable foe. I just love him! The template for Reg Morrison was forged at Gallipoli and Pozieres and the killing fields of France.'

I laughed. 'Well said, darling. Any man would be happy with those words as his epitaph. Nice to know you've made a friend in the town.'

Marg went on to say how Reg Morrison had known and worked the river since he was a boy of seven, following his father, who once ran a small pining gang, and made a simple living from the river.

'Bob Brown likens him to the Huon pine because they're unique to the south-west wilderness. The analogy is perfect. The Huon pine looks unpretentious to say the least, gnarled and wind-battered, misshapen and usually covered in lichen, but its core wood is beautiful. It's self-oiling, it never cracks and will last indefinitely. Logs found in the river, still in perfect condition, have been shown to be ten thousand years old. There's one near the River Camp called the Lea Tree that's over three thousand years old! Can you imagine, Nick? It was already a thousand years old when Cleopatra met Antony and they sailed down the Nile together.'

Decades later, a conservationist writer described Reg in these words:

Reg Morrison loved the river and couldn't imagine its runnels and ferny creeks, the wide bends and sudden twists, the rapids with their rocky roar, the quiet sylvan stretches of calm water, the waterfowl and platypus and windblown beds of rustling reeds, the essence of the glorious Gordon, all gone forever. He couldn't bear to see the beauty of the valley lost, turned into a giant and turgid pond, the so-called national park a playground for Sunday sailors, where the high cry of eagles would be replaced by the raucous roar of outboard motors and sudden snap of sails tacking to a breeze that swept across the drowned and desolate waterscape, all in the name of a few extra megawatts of electricity to run the mix-masters and those weapons of mass distraction, the television sets of the nation.

Bob Brown contends that without Reg Morrison the blockade would never have got off the ground. Reg was the first to stand up for the rivers and the south-west wilderness, and this simple self-effacing man became the whole difference; he demonstrated the power of one man's persistence and sacrifice. Reg Morrison earned his colours by transporting the protesters up the river to the camp, as close to the dam construction site as the police – determined to keep them as far away as possible – would allow.

Marg and other workers found a second important friend in Strahan, all the more surprising as he was the town and district warden. Harry McDermott allowed the protesters the use of the council-run camping ground near the town centre, known as Peoples Park. Later they were forced to move to a larger site on the outskirts of town organised by Harry and donated by the son of a sympathetic councillor. It became known as 'Greenie Acres'. Without these two men, the blockade would have been almost impossible.

In the same article on the blockade the writer concluded:

Without Reg Morrison and Harry McDermott, the blockade would have been well nigh impossible. Such quiet and largely unsung men and women who give our nation its essential character are seldom recognised as heroes and receive few of the glittering prizes, unlike the highly profitable companies who are still actively destroying the wilderness and turning the old-growth forests into minced wood and money while spouting the same greedy, self-serving and duplicitous twaddle about jobs for workers. These are big corporation men who blithely face the TV camera and talk of building a pulp mill they assert will do no ecological harm when each day it empties 60 000 tonnes of polluted effluent, the detritus of destruction, into Bass Strait.

Some of the nation's superannuation funds happily buy shares in these logging companies and see no paradox when they boast that they are growing a safe and secure future for their clients.

But at the time, much of the local media was less than sympathetic. The Hobart *Mercury* gloomily predicted: 'The movement increasingly resembles a mortally wounded beast that just won't lie down and die.' The paper almost gleefully swallowed anything fed to it by premier Robin Gray and turned it into headlines: 'Protests by greenies could provoke bloodshed! Unions call for a State of Emergency to prevent greenie harassment! Violence of some kind seems inevitable at this indefensible blockade.'

It was obvious local media could not be relied on for unbiased and even-handed reporting. Even the venerable local ABC radio station seemed to forsake its usual fair-minded approach by allowing a lot of time for pro-dam comment of the 'They're taking our bread and butter!' variety. Truth was an early casualty. Despite the peaceful behaviour of the protesters, carefully managed by the organisers, the warden of Queenstown broadcast a typical and widely held opinion: 'The protesters' half-truths and platitudes are like that of Hitler before the war. If there's bloodshed, which is not unlikely, the responsibility will rest with the Wilderness Society.'

Communication was never going to be easy for the protesters. Marg was part of an initial team of four media coordinators, although later there would be others. With her were Pam Waud and Cathie Plowman, two extraordinarily dedicated and competent women, and Geoff Law, a young bloke mature beyond his years with a very black beard reminiscent of the nineteenth-century cricketer W.G. Grace that belied his tender age and made the cops instinctively suspicious of him.

The team spent most of its time organising the media, for whom they were able to set up a media centre in the middle of town.

Accommodation for the protesters proved to be the real nightmare. Marg would often say how guilty she felt that the media team were housed in an old customs building and were able to stay warm and dry at night while the protesters arriving in the incessant rain were forced to camp. Conditions generally called for a fair bit of character and determination, but toilets were dug and kitchens constructed of canvas. And the Town Camp was described by the protesters as sheer luxury compared to the River Camp, which was closer to the dam site on the Gordon. Some of those returning from the River Camp would go down on their knees and kiss the ground at Greenie Acres.

Keeping the camps clean in such bad weather was difficult. Marg told me that Bob Brown had expressed real fears of an outbreak of dysentery or a flu epidemic. He'd set up a rigid routine for maintaining hygiene in the public areas of the camps and there were a great many veteran Tasmanian protesters who volunteered to do latrine duty and other unpleasant tasks. Without them disaster would almost certainly have befallen the campsites.

Marg was one of the people responsible for communication between the two camps. Norm Sanders, fellow member of parliament and first director of The Wilderness Society, had helped set up a radio shack at the River Camp so that the two protest sites could communicate with each other, although the frequency was often jammed by the police.

Bob Brown briefed the media team at length. He started by saying, 'Marg, they're not going to be targeting you and Norm. Robin Gray isn't stupid. He knows that if they arrest Marg Hamilton and Norm Sanders, the subsequent publicity would be very good for us. Imagine, two MPs thrown into jail!

Provided you keep your noses clean, you'll both be left alone. This is very important. The whole blockade hinges on media participation, so getting reporters across the bay to the River Camp is paramount.'

He turned to Geoff Law, Cathie Plowman and Pam Waud. 'You three are going to cop the most flak, so be careful, but don't be surprised if they come after you. What's more, the media are going to be in a pretty foul mood after the trip to the River Camp if we get the rain they're forecasting. As you know, it's horrific. They're going to be violently seasick and thoroughly miserable by the time they go across the harbour and upriver, so they won't be keen to make daily trips. Nobody likes to throw up for several hours a day. In fact we may only get one go with each media contingent we send over. Your job is to see they get something meaty to chew on when they arrive and something even bigger when they get to the River Camp.

'We're going to call these media events DMEs – Daily Media Events. I want at least one major DME each day if possible. Pam, Cathie and Geoff will be on the front line but they'll coordinate everything with you, Marg, whenever possible, to get the maximum effect. Marg, you will make sure the media are always present at the scene and sent home with the right message. This is public relations at a very high level; you're the indefatigable smile, the "nothing is impossible" person. You can be sure they'll research your society background, and the "admiral's widow turns greenie" is a nice angle. "Charming, smiling, never ruffled admiral's wife turned greenie" is an even better one.'

He paused, then said, 'Now, we can't guarantee Pam, Cathie and Geoff won't be arrested and so it may eventually come down to you, Marg. Every day we don't get something on the national news that demonstrates the contrast between the peace-loving and caring protesters and the brutal, heavy-handed authorities is a step closer to failure. Remember the first rule in reportage – no picture, no story.

'The essential thing for you all to remember is that the chief perpetrators are not the police, they're Robin Gray, who sent in the police, and Russell Ashton, the Commissioner for the Hydro.' Bob grinned. 'Fortunately neither is ever short of an acrimonious comment and they can be guaranteed to keep their end up very nicely. The more they shout, rave and gesticulate, the better.'

The media group obviously did their job well and every day there was at least one good piece in the leading papers, or on the TV and radio stations in the capital cities. I'd get the Brisbane papers twice a week but, of course, my personal news came via telephone. Weary, wet and miserable at having to stay out of trouble by not actively joining the protesters, Marg would call me reverse charges long distance from a private phone in the home of a local sympathiser in Queenstown, where each night in the rain she would drive, following the police paddy wagons that transported arrested protesters to the late sitting of the magistrate's court. She'd wait until the magistrate offered them bail on condition they didn't return to the dam site, they would duly refuse to comply and then they'd be carted off to Risdon Prison, a long ride in the dark, to arrive near Hobart often in the early hours of the morning.

Even though my long-distance phone bill could have purchased one of the smaller Pacific Island nations, there were a few calls that are worth repeating. The first, of course, came a day or two before the start of the blockade when Marg was bubbling over with excitement. 'Nick, Bob arrived with

Professor Manning Clark in a plane chartered by Dick Smith!'

'Electronic Dick,' I laughed. 'Perhaps not the subtlest slogan for a guy who sells electronic gear, but I'm told the geeks love it. He has it painted on all his vans.'

But Marg wasn't listening, too anxious to tell me her news. 'They've been told on the grapevine to expect good news at 11 o'clock tonight.'

'What, Robin Gray is going to capitulate? I'd have thought he would wait until the stroke of midnight.'

'Have you been drinking, Nick?' Marg asked, suddenly stern.

'No. Just the usual Scotch after dinner.'

'Of course he's *not* going to capitulate!' Her voice grew excited again. 'But maybe, perhaps, possibly, something almost as good. Guess what? The World Heritage Committee is going to give the south-west wilderness area, including the two rivers, World Heritage status.'

'But I thought that wasn't a big deal, in terms of, you know, changing anything?'

'It wasn't, but now it could be! Fraser has been told by the High Court that he can stop the dams, but he doesn't think it's an election issue, so he's doing nothing.'

'No, of course not. He doesn't want to tread on dear little Robin's toes.' Marg's hatred for Robin Gray was becoming infectious.

'Manning Clark says if Hawke can oust Hayden as leader, then Labor are a very good chance to defeat the Fraser government. If that happens, Hawke, who Clark says is a great mate of Neville Wran's, has agreed – No Dams!'

'A fair number of "if"s there, darling,' I cautioned.

'Yes, I know, but don't you see, we *have* to make the damming of the Franklin a national election issue!'

Marg, weary but excited, called again late on the 17th of December. 'Nick, they've arrested Bob Brown!' she shouted.

'Where?'

'The riverbank at the camp for the police and hydro workers.'

'Did you get the press there?'

'Yes, both TV and newspapers.'

'I'll put the short-wave radio on to Radio Australia tonight,' I said. 'I guess it's going to be in all the headlines tomorrow.'

'I've just come from the court in Queenstown. By sheer luck there just happened to be a TV crew there with cameras. He was arrested on the riverbank by a young policeman visibly shaking in his boots. Bob put his hand on his shoulder and said calmly, "Don't worry, mate, it'll be okay."'

'What happened in the court, I mean with the magistrate?'

'Oh, the usual, there were about forty of our people appearing with him, mostly women. The usual offer and refusal of bail, then a three-week sentence passed, the only difference was that the magistrate threatened to throw the TV people and the press out of the courtroom and, of course, it means Bob and the others will be spending Christmas in Risdon Prison. Much clapping from locals jamming the courtroom when the magistrate pointed this out, quite unnecessarily.'

'Silly move! Having them spend Christmas in jail won't do any harm to your publicity.'

'Nick, I feel so guilty.'

'Guilty? Why?'

'I'm sleeping in a dry sleeping bag with a roof over my head, while others are getting arrested. I'm supposed to keep my nose clean, but right now, Bob and my friends are sitting jammed into the back of a dark paddy wagon for a five-hour trip over the mountains to Risdon Prison.

I should be with them. It's only three days in and I'm tired of smiling and being unflappable and charming. Most of the media are great but some can be real pigs, and then there's the bloody rain!' Marg started to cry quietly.

'C'mon, be a brave girl now, darling. Bob's chosen the four of you in media relations because he knows you'll come through for him, for the movement. Remember, with no incidents for the camera and no arrests there's no news.' I laughed deliberately. 'Fat lot of good you'd be doing sitting on your bum in the dark in the back of a paddy wagon.'

'Suppose,' Marg choked. 'Today a TV reporter said to me, "Look, lady, we're not going out again in the rain to throw up on that bloody harbour. Why don't you get off your arse and stage a demo somewhere dry? What you're doing is all phoney bullshit for the cameras anyway. I've had my fuckin' Christmas holidays cancelled because of this drop-kick place. It's the least you could do!" I had to smile sweetly and say, through gritted teeth, "Queenstown Magistrate's Court tonight at eight o'clock. There are bound to be arrests." Of course I didn't know it would be Bob in court and when it was all over the little shit came up and said, "You're good, lady, you ought to get a job in TV!"'

On one of her calls Marg expressed some dismay at what she referred to as 'ferals'. These were young protesters from the Nimbin and northern rivers area of New South Wales, where they'd excluded themselves from society and taken up living in loose-knit communes in the eucalypt forest where they grew their own food and marijuana. Marg was unimpressed. 'They've come down to Tasmania to add their weight to the blockade, which is all very well, but they're unwilling to accept the rules of peaceful protest,' she lamented. 'Nick, they live in the forest in small camps of their own close to the River Camp. Quite alarming really. They wear their hair in dreadlocks and walk around naked or with very little clothing and paint their faces and bodies and refer to themselves as Aboriginals.'

'Have you talked to them, asked them to comply with the same rules as everyone else? Sounds like a bunch of lost kids showing off.'

'If they are, it's very disruptive. The police can't catch them in the forests and of course they're blaming us when the ferals jump onto bulldozers and risk their lives doing stupid things. Sooner or later one of them is going to be killed.'

'Can't you disassociate yourself from them?' I asked.

'Well yes, of course, in some ways, but they're here to protest and we feel we have to try to contain them and support them by offering them food and medical help.'

Later she sounded less supportive. 'Several "ferals" have come into camp with gastroenteritis looking for a doctor. We're terrified of an epidemic spreading through the River Camp,' Marg said, adding, 'They're completely wild! Yesterday a bulldozer driver refused to stop and one of the ferals was very nearly injured – the bulldozer stopped inches from him. The driver got down and dragged him into the forest then reported the incident to the police. The police have been around again to say they're our responsibility and when they come into camp we're to hold them for arrest. Of course, we can't do that.'

'No, of course not. Pity, they're spoiling it for the rest of you in the eyes of the media. You know how Joe Public loves to hate them "marra-jew-anna smokin' hippies",' I observed.

'In fact, the bad accident waiting to happen is likely to be caused by the police,' Marg noted, then explained. 'They use their launches to ram the rubber rafts, knocking us into the water and often enough under their launch. This has happened on several occasions and our people only escaped serious injury by diving away from the propellers!'

Over the weeks of the blockade Marg's nightly reports featured distinguished visitors and arrests: Claudio Alcorso, a prominent Tasmanian industrialist and his wife Lesley were arrested; Don Chipp, founder of the Australian Democrats, visited and made a speech and wasn't arrested; Peter Cundall, who was to become a star for the ABC, refused to take a neutral stance and addressed a large group of protesters but wasn't arrested.

Finally, two days before Christmas, Norm Sanders resigned from state parliament in protest over the government's actions in relation to the Franklin. Then, on New Year's Day 1983, *The Australian* newspaper voted Bob Brown Australian of the Year. The local media took the news badly, pointing out that he was a criminal in prison. But worse was to come for the government, friendly local press and radio. With Norm Sanders' resignation from parliament, Bob Brown was declared the new member for Denison in the state parliament, having been the runner-up to Norm Sanders in the last election.

The rain continued deep into January but the winds of change were beginning to blow the storm clouds away, starting with a breeze and turning into a big gust. Finally the sun seemed to be coming up over the political horizon.

The rain stopped at last, and on the 4th of February Malcolm Fraser announced a federal election. On the same day the Federal Labor caucus voted Bill Hayden out as leader and elected Bob Hawke, who hours after he'd been elected to the leadership declared that a Labor government would stop the dams.

The day after Bob Hawke was elected to the Labor Party leadership, the Wilderness Society held what they termed the 'Rally for Reason' in Hobart, attended by twenty thousand people – at the time the largest environmental protest in

Australia's history. The cracks were beginning to show in parliament and for the first time the Hydro-Electric Commission realised that they were no longer in total control.

Then, at precisely the right time, the biggest arrest of them all was made in a public relations coup that practically flipped Robin Gray's government onto its back. Marg virtually screamed down the phone to Beautiful Bay: 'Nick, today they arrested David Bellamy! It's going to be front-page news all over the world! We've already got our election issue with Bob Hawke, but this is the clincher we needed! Bellamy's BBC wildlife program is watched by millions – it's huge here as well; practically every Australian will now know what's happening.'

'Congratulations! Who did you bribe in the police force? That was a very, very stupid thing for the cops to do,' I shouted back happily.

Marg burst into laughter. 'You'll never guess. Remember the police sergeant who was rude to me, Sergeant Danny Docker? He ordered Bellamy's arrest!'

'There is a God in heaven,' I laughed. 'But surely they'd release him immediately?'

'No! They've carted him off to Risdon! Isn't it marvellous? The magistrate even gave him a stern rebuke in front of camera,' Marg chortled.

When Bellamy was released, the world's television cameras were focused on the gates of Risdon Prison. But, of course, by this time it was a public relations disaster of the highest magnitude and the Tasmanian Liberal government became the laughing stock of the nation, its members regarded around the globe as ignorant pariahs. Marg, as the member for the Greens, along with the new member Bob Brown and the Wilderness Society, was seen to have given the state Liberal government their comeuppance. Marg especially, as the maverick parliamentarian, was to learn that the notion that revenge is a dish best eaten cold is practically an oath taken upon entry into parliament. They were lying in wait for her to make a mistake.

From that point it was all relatively smooth paddling for the environment movement. Bob Hawke was elected in a landslide on the 5th of March and his first words to the nation as prime minister were, 'The dam will not be built.'

Marg was over the moon, of course. 'Nick, Robin Gray, recalcitrant as ever, allowed himself to be photographed in Queenstown wearing boxing gloves! He announced that work would continue on the dam and vowed that he intended fighting the government all the way to the High Court.'

'Don't count him out, darling. He will have taken the best advice.'

'Nick, they couldn't, could they?'

'Win the case? Anything could happen. After all, the law is above politics.'

'I couldn't bear it. I just couldn't bear it. Imagine if the shit won his appeal!'

But Gray was a flea fighting an elephant. Gareth Evans, the Minister for Foreign Affairs, arranged for RAAF F-111s to fly over the river and the dam construction site, photographing the destruction, in the process earning himself the nickname 'Biggles', which would dog him for the remainder of his political career. The photographs were released to the media, and Marg faxed a set to me, declaring, 'Nick, Australians are furious, and a great many Tasmanians have confessed to me personally that they feel ashamed and humiliated by the havoc caused in their names. They've promised to vote Greens at the next election!'

'I don't think that's going to make Gareth Evans very happy,' I said.

The High Court began sitting on the 31st of May 1983

and on the 1st of July, by the margin of a single vote – four to three – upheld the right of the Commonwealth to enforce its foreign affairs power and stop work on the dam to preserve forever the World Heritage area. When I heard the decision on the radio and shortly afterwards got the ecstatic call from Marg I was once again reminded how one person can make a difference. Had Doug Lowe, who was dumped as Tasmanian premier by his Labor colleagues, not initiated the request to the World Heritage Committee, the High Court would almost certainly have been forced to side with the Tasmanian Government. One man or woman, one action of conscience, and our national attitude to the environment changed forever. Of course, it was not just a single action, but a pivotal one amongst the many by people such as Bob Brown, David Bellamy, Peter Cundall, the late Don Chipp and Professor Manning Clark. There were many who laboured over the years for the trees and the rivers, among them Helen Gee, Geoff Law, Pam Waud, Cathie Plowman, Norm Sanders, Reg Morrison, Denny Hamill, Harry McDermott, and the countless men and women who went with and before them; Olegas Truchanas, who lost his life to the river; Brenda Hean and Max Price, who also lost their lives for the cause; Peter Sims, Jessie Luckman, Milo Dunphy, Louis Shoobridge and the many other unsung heroes who gave everything for the movement and often suffered the enmity and scorn of their families and friends. We owe them all a debt we can only repay by remaining vigilant, angry and vocal. Even today the old-growth forests of Tasmania are being plundered, sawn, minced and spat into ships' holds to be sent to Japan to be turned into unnecessary miscellanea.

The Tasmanian Government received $200 million from the federal government as compensation for halting the dam, and in an extraordinary gesture of spite and hubris spent it on small and unnecessary dams on several rivers not included in the World Heritage area. Some of the pro-dam workers at Warners Landing, near the site of the blockade, took out their frustrations on the Lea Tree: drenching the three-thousand-year-old Huon pine in diesel, they set it alight, burning it to the ground. On the blackened stump they left a painted sign: FUCK YOU GREEN CUNTS!

I recall how I reacted when Marg told me what they'd done to the Lea Tree. 'Jesus! Haven't they learned anything in two hundred years?' I yelled. 'They're still carrying the mindset of their forebears! How could anyone burn a three-thousand-year-old tree to the ground, leaving behind their triumphant signature in the form of a crude and ignorant sign?'

'Nick, it's only a few ingrates. Tasmanians are, generally speaking, a very nice bunch.'

'Like the Babbages?'

'Nick, you're being unreasonable! You know they're only another exception at the other end of the social strata. There are plenty of both kinds on the mainland. Stop being cross with Tasmanians.'

'I'm not cross with Tasmanians!' I protested. 'I'm cross with humankind!'

'God, you can be a pompous prick sometimes, Nick!' Marg replied. And that's all the thanks I got.

The postscript to the proposed damming of the Franklin–Gordon rivers and near destruction of the south-west wilderness came in 1987 when Sir Geoffrey Foot, Associate Commissioner of the Hydro-Electric Commission, by now a toothless tiger, admitted that the power forecast for the flooding of the Franklin–Gordon had been 'too optimistic', all but admitting that the entire project would not have been economically viable and was unlikely to recoup the initial investment.

Marg returned to her duties as a parliamentarian, her attention switched to logging and, in particular, to all creatures great and small, the ultimate victims of the destruction of natural habitat. But now she was striking at the very soul of Tasmania. Logging the old-growth forests has been a birthright for some rural Tasmanians since their forebears had been sentenced for the term of their natural lives to the vicissitudes of life on one of the most pristine and beautiful islands on earth. These poor wretches were never to return to the excremental hovels in the vile city slums from whence they came. With not much call for their previous occupations of purse-snatching, robbery with violence, horse-stealing, forging, prostitution and crimes against the Crown, they took to chopping down trees for a living.

Some of these early timber-getters stuck to the axe and cross-cut saw, but all finally arrived at the petrol-driven chainsaw and bulldozer. Sharp teeth and brute force brought to bear on the old-growth forests allowed them to prosper mightily and become powerful in the land. Foremost among these pioneer woodsmen were John and Thomas Gunn, both respectable settlers and initially builders, who saw the potential of the abundant natural resource and the cheap labour available to harvest it. They founded their timber company in 1875, twenty years after the last convict was transported to the island, thus creating the slogan 'Jobs for timber workers', still beloved by Tasmania's politicians and dusted off at every election.

Today Gunns, a public company, can be said to rule over the tall timber of Tasmania; Marg had found herself a formidable and uncompromising enemy every bit as determined to have its own way as the once recalcitrant Hydro-Electric Commission. It is perhaps of passing interest to note that the notorious Robin Gray, retiring at last from active politics, but not before it was revealed that he'd held back $10 000 of election donations stashed in his freezer, now sits on the board of Gunns Limited.

As Marg repeatedly told me, the company has about 1500 square kilometres of plantation timber and is Tasmania's largest private property owner. It has become the largest woodchipper in the southern hemisphere and is now one of the largest loggers of old-growth forest in the world.

Marg was well aware that while I was prepared to listen to both my partners' scorn, the one for the other, I had also sworn not to transmit the invective and judgments, although I had reason to believe that both women had come to secretly regret it. They both longed to have a conduit for their spleen and each worked assiduously to get me to make them the exception.

I had long since learned that what may seem to be gossip to many men is essential information to many women. I call it bitchery, they regard it as vital intelligence. Neither woman did things by halves and in their own spheres they thought big and acted even bigger. As each developed their personal power base, their antipathy and scorn for each other increased. 'Anything you can do I can fundamentally oppose' seemed to be the rule by which they played. I sometimes wondered if the Green Bitch and Princess Plunder were reassured that they were on track by the degree of opposition they received from each other, a little like the way they used my taste as a guide to their shopping – they never bought anything I liked.

If I may be presumptuous for a moment, I came to think that both sought my approval for different reasons. Anna, naturally secretive, needed the constant reassurance that I loved her, while Marg, who was a determined proselytiser, confident of her objectives, simply took my love and affection for granted and thought I must be secretly on her side. In the matter of hydroelectricity I was always able to be ambivalent; after all, progress and energy march hand in hand and it's possible, especially with the threat of global warming, to put forward an argument for hydroelectricity. But in the matter of trees she was probably right. More cardboard boxes, low-grade paper and toothpicks do not advance the progress of civilisation.

While I kept to my side of the bargain and seldom if ever passed on from one to the other the information they shared with me, they constantly surprised me by how much they knew about each other's current activity. Marg would sometimes tell me stuff about Anna I didn't know myself, while Anna would do the same, neither losing an opportunity to belittle the efforts of the other.

I discovered that for both the new facsimile machines that were rapidly replacing the telex network were vital. Anna had installed one of these at Beautiful Bay and of course another in her Melbourne office and no doubt elsewhere, while Marg had the use of several in Parliament House.

To know what she knew about Marg, Anna obviously had someone in Tasmania spying for her, while Marg, of course, had her old Fremantle mate, Roger Rigby, head of the Defence Signals Directorate in Canberra, who kept an electronic intelligence eye on Indonesia from their listening station at Shoal Bay near Darwin. They followed the careers of the Indonesian military, including, I have no doubt, Major General Budi Til, head of the army's legal department. While they were obviously more interested in his military career than in his civilian activities, they nevertheless collected information on both, aware that the two were often closely aligned. As Budi's commercial interests in the archipelago closely mirrored those of Anna's, Marg had no problem spying on her.

Once she was ensconced in parliament and had her teeth well and truly fastened onto the activities of the local logging industry, Marg turned her interest to logging in the forests of Indonesian Borneo and, as I indicated earlier, on the consequences of deforestation for all creatures great and small. In 1984 the first of many pictures arrived at Beautiful Bay via fax. It was a gruesome image of five headless orangutan corpses, behind each of which stood a smiling forest worker holding up the head of the creature that lay sprawled at his feet. The caption read: *This was done by one of Anna's logging gangs(ters)!* There was no doubting the veracity of the information – in the background stood a bulldozer, on the door of which was painted *TT* with the words *Til Timber* directly under the initials. Anna always loved twinned letters.

I waited with some real trepidation for that evening's phone call and I was right to be apprehensive.

'Nick, did you get my fax this morning?'

'Yes, darling, awful. Very regrettable.'

'Is that all you can say?'

'Well, really, there's nothing one can say. It's bloody awful, heinous!'

'Nick, it's got to stop!'

'Marg, you know the rule.'

There was silence, then she screamed down the phone, 'Fuck the rule! If you don't stop it I will!'

'Now, Marg, careful, darling.'

'Careful! No, Nick, *you* be careful! And don't call me *darling*! Not today!'

'If I break the rule Anna will demand the same rights. You know that.'

'Ha! What can she do?'

'Marg, Anna is a very powerful woman.'

'And I'm a member of parliament and not without some influence. That's bullshit, Nick, you're trying to squirm out of this!'

While it was an unfortunate choice of word, I ignored it. 'If I am it's for the sake of you both.'

'Both of us! I don't care about both of us! Fuck her! Fuck you! I care about those poor hapless creatures!'

Marg in her student days would occasionally use the 'f' word in the pejorative sense, but never like this. I sighed, attempting to remain calm. 'I'll talk to her, pretend I got the information elsewhere. I can't believe she'd tolerate this kind of thing going on if she knew about it. Besides, she'd know they're protected animals in Indonesia.'

'Nick, don't patronise me! Of course she'll play ignorant, cry crocodile tears, promise to have the timber workers involved arrested. She's not stupid!'

'Well then, what else can I do?'

'She's got to stop logging! She has a major concession that covers two-thirds of the remaining orangutan habitat!'

'Hey, wait on, she's not going to do that,' I protested.

'She'd better!' Marg threatened.

I tried to defuse the situation a little. 'How come you know all this?' She was right, but I was the only one outside Indonesia who could know the extent of Anna's timber concession.

'Never mind, just let me say there's more where that came from.'

'Marg, be sensible, Anna won't brook any interference from me. She never has, why would she now?'

'If she doesn't . . .' Marg stopped short.

'What?'

There was an audible sigh on the line. 'Tell her, then it's all over between the two of you,' she said calmly. 'Nick, if you're associated with her and anything comes out, your own reputation will be at stake. You'd be better off getting her out of your life.'

It was my turn to be angry. 'How dare you! Apologise immediately!' I shouted, her sheer effrontery leaving me shaking with rage.

There was silence, then in a bright voice that didn't deceive me for a moment she said, 'Okay. I apologise but —'

'You're going to put our relationship, you and me, on the line?' I suggested, still bloody angry.

'Certainly not! I'm not the one who's slaughtering God's innocent creatures! Why should I be punished?'

'Jesus, Marg, you can be an obdurate bitch!'

'I resent that, Nick! Let me tell you about these remarkable simian creatures. In that photograph are two mothers, each with an almost grown child, in orangutan terms, teenagers. The fifth is an old man, though probably not the father of either child. The orangutans are the last of the great apes surviving outside of Africa. Already logging has killed off one-third of them. Eighty per cent of the forests in Indonesian Borneo have been destroyed – that's the biggest area in which they're found – and Anna has almost two-thirds of what remains!'

'How do you know all this?' I demanded.

'Nick, don't interrupt! Orangutans live social lives, with the mother caring for the child for longer than with any other creature in nature apart from ourselves. They have the intelligence of a five-year-old child. Would you wilfully murder a child of five? What you see in that photograph are five separate murders in three different parts of Anna's concession! Anna's timber gang are actively hunting them down and killing them. The vile bastards are going to eat them!' Marg began to cry.

I waited a moment or two. 'Please don't cry, darling,' on this occasion the 'darling' going un-challenged. 'I'll talk to Anna, that much I *can* promise. But please don't pin your hopes on it. That timber concession is worth tens of millions and there's a kickback to the President's family. And then she'd have to get Major General Budi Til to agree, it's not only *her* decision.' I was conscious of breaking the rule and telling her about Anna's business affairs.

'That evil bastard!' Marg spat. 'Anna better watch it with him.'

'What do you mean by that? She's known him since he was a kid! She paid for his education, put him through university. He's like a younger brother to her. They're business partners; he'd never turn on her.'

'Maybe he won't have to.'

'Ferchrissake, Marg, what are you trying to say?'

'East Timor.'

'East Timor? What, the invasion by Indonesia? That was 1975, nine years ago. It's old news.'

'Watch this space.'

'What's that supposed to mean?'

Marg ignored my question. 'Nick, you have to decide. You've been sitting on the fence too long! I don't care how you do it, but the endgame is Anna stops logging and leaves the jungle for the orangutans!'

'Marg, that's completely unreasonable and you know it!' I protested, almost shouting down the phone. 'I may get her to save some small part for them, but not the whole concession. Even if she could – and she can't – she'll never agree.'

'Nick, as it is, what's left is not really enough, but at least it's habitat. In Indonesia, Malaysia and Brunei there was a total of 123 000 000 hectares of habitat, of jungle; now there's only thirty per cent of it left, and nearly twenty per cent is Anna's timber concession. She has to save all of it! Every inch!' I could hear a bell ringing in the background. Then Marg said, 'I have to go. The bells have gone for a special evening sitting of the house. Oh, by the way, I have more photographs, but I'll hold them until I hear from you. Love you, darling.' With this she rang off.

I walked onto the verandah and poured myself a stiff Scotch. A squall was passing through and the bay beyond was invisible behind the driving rain belting down on the tin roof. Marg's phone call was, of course, perfectly timed. Anna was due to arrive in the morning and I hadn't any idea how I was going to approach her. I knew I hadn't a snowball's hope in hell of getting her to drop the Borneo timber concession, much less preserve it intact as pristine jungle. I knocked back the Scotch in two gulps and poured another with a heavy hand.

Marg was being both arrogant and unreasonable to the point of near insanity. The threat that she had photographs she'd release to the press was going too far. On the other hand, Marg was a fanatic. So was Anna, and going too far with both of them was pretty well how they habitually operated. While they had different objectives they shared a similar mindset and were equally stubborn.

I told myself this wasn't the Franklin River and democracy at work; this was Indonesia, where nobody gave a tinker's cuss for the creatures of the jungle. In theory they were protected, but this was merely window dressing for the West; in practice nothing was done. Trees, habitat, river systems, wild creatures – they were all up for grabs. Nobody thought about the future, it was all about money, millions upon millions of dollars.

And then a crazy 'what if' thought struck me. Maybe Anna did have sufficient money to buy the concession outright, then just as quickly I dismissed the thought as absurd. But no other idea occurred to me and I started to wonder what might be involved.

She could work out the ultimate value of the timber in

advance, then forgo her share of the profits, and she might be able to persuade Budi to do the same. He could hardly refuse. After all, he owed her everything. Then she could pay the usual percentage raked off by the Suharto family, probably not much more than ten or fifteen million dollars. It was a big ask, a huge ask, and I didn't like my chances, but it was the only way I could think to go. I could probably give her a couple of million dollars towards the settlement with the President's rapacious family, maybe a little more. I decided to call my accountant first thing in the morning.

Suddenly I felt resentful. 'Fuck, Marg!' I shouted into the din of the rain on the roof. Wasn't winning the Franklin enough? But I knew she was right in one respect. I could no longer sit on the fence. It was now constructed of barbed wire and if I had any balls it was time to choose the side on which to make a stand before I was deservedly emasculated.

A little later I began to think about what Marg had said about Budi and Timor. I recalled speaking to Anna just a few days after Indonesia's invasion of the tiny country when the five Australian journalists were shot. It had reminded me painfully of the assassination of the Australian sailors on the beach in Java. It was an image that has never left me. For weeks after the deaths of the Balibo Five I'd wake up screaming, the whole Java beach thing replayed in a nightmare, but this time, with the sailors, were the five journalists, their bodies riddled with bullets and blood pumping from their throats.

Anna had been in Indonesia the week it happened and I was anxious to question her about the incident. She arrived on the island during the afternoon, and we were soon, as usual, drinking champagne on the verandah before dinner. 'How are the Indonesians reacting to the invasion of East Timor and the news of the five journalists killed? What do you think really happened?' I asked.

'What the news report said – they were caught in crossfire between the two sides.' She sipped her champagne. 'As for the locals, I don't think the deaths caused much of a stir. Violent death is pretty commonplace in their society. Last week the price of cooking oil went up; to them that's the truly tragic news.'

'Jesus, it's a weird world! But I guess you're right – if it isn't happening to us, we don't care! But you can't help thinking it's rather strange. The journos were not all from the same media organisation. Bloody strange that they should all be in the same spot at the same time.'

Anna shrugged. 'Bad luck, I guess. Balibo is not a big town and it's built in the Portuguese style more or less around a large square. That's where most of the fighting took place. It would be quite logical they'd be found there. It's horrible . . . their poor families,' Anna concluded.

'You've been there? Balibo?'

'No, Budi has . . . is.'

'There now, as we speak?'

'Well, perhaps not now, not at this moment, but after the incident. He's head of the army's legal department; there's going to be an inquiry into the deaths,' Anna explained.

'Inquiry or the usual whitewash?'

'Nicholas, Budi is a good lawyer!'

'Yeah, but working for a bad country.'

'That's not entirely fair. We don't know what happened.'

There was no point in continuing along this line. 'You speak to him regularly. Why are the Indonesians so keen to take over East Timor?'

I asked. 'It's an impoverished agrarian country, has no strategic importance and produces bugger all that Indonesia doesn't possess in spades anyway. You would think it will prove a millstone around their neck rather than an asset.'

Anna laughed. 'Well, I don't have to ask Budi for the answer to that one – the Indonesian newspapers are full of it, have been for months. It's Fretilin, the home-grown communist group who have become a force in East Timor. Indonesia – well, the Suharto regime – is paranoid about the communists. Look what they did to their own! They're afraid it'll start to spread from East Timor and create trouble in the region.'

'Anna, that's bullshit. Indonesia has the biggest army in Asia after China, they couldn't possibly be concerned.'

'Well, the invasion seems to have pleased America and that's important to Indonesia. Besides, Australia isn't exactly rushing to condemn the invaders, either at home or at the United Nations. Or, it seems, make too much of a fuss over the five dead journalists.'

'Precisely. That's what worries me. It's a Labor government and Whitlam is running for cover. Talk about prevarication. Richard Woolcott is bending over backwards toadying up to Suharto – the back of his ambassadorial head is practically touching his heels. I just don't get it. Five of our blokes are killed and our prime minister is full of mealy-mouthed words of regret but taking bugger all action to discover the bastards who did the killing.' I sniffed in disgust. 'Crossfire my arse!'

Anna proffered her empty glass. 'Thanks, Nicholas, the third glass is the one that makes me relax.' I poured the champagne and, accepting it, she said almost casually, 'It's the oil.'

'What oil? There's been nothing about oil in the Australian papers.'

She laughed. 'Nor in the Indonesian ones. Of course not! It's the very last thing either country wants to talk about but it's the unspoken reason for everything.'

'You mean the death of the journalists? Is that why no one is making an official fuss?'

Anna shrugged. 'Possibly.'

'How do you know all this? Budi?'

Anna pouted and shrugged again. 'How else?'

'This oil, is it a lot? What does Budi know about it?'

'As it happens, quite a lot. Remember he's the army's top legal man. And yes, the ocean floor deposits are huge.'

'Let me guess, the oil is in East Timor's territorial waters.'

'And a small part of it in our own. No prizes for obvious conclusions, Nicholas.'

'Ah, I see! Stupid me. Fretilin, the communists, won't cooperate but Indonesia will?'

'Well, yes. They, the Indonesians, are prepared to give us a more equitable share.'

'Of a commodity they don't own!'

'But now control. Yes, they gain and we gain. We don't make more than a token fuss with the UN and everyone's happy.'

'Except the people of East Timor who get bugger all. Shit, that's unfair!'

'Nicholas,' Anna said reproachfully, 'get real. You've been around long enough and you've seen enough in the islands to know what goes on. Only, with the big countries, the grubby commercial realities are all dressed up in sanctimonious crap about freedom and regional security. The free world will never have a better scapegoat than communism. *There's a red under every bed* still works as a scare slogan. Both countries should pay Fretilin a bonus for supplying the perfect excuse for an invasion. There's certain to be an Order of Australia coming up for Ambassador Woolcott as soon as the fuss dies down. Our good man in Indonesia,' Anna laughed.

We were silent for a while then I asked, 'Anna, this oil. You and Budi, you're not . . . ?'

Anna drained her glass. 'Of course not! It's much too early yet. Burmah Oil haven't completed mapping the extent of the find.'

CHAPTER EIGHTEEN

'Every two minutes a woman is raped in the world!
Every two minutes! That's 263 000 reported cases, and
it's estimated only sixteen per cent of rapes are reported.
When you extrapolate from that, every twenty
seconds a woman or a child is being raped
somewhere in the world!'
Anna Til

IT WAS NINE YEARS since Anna and I had talked about East Timor, but in retrospect, Marg's telephone call was nicely timed to coincide with a resurgence of bad publicity about what was now referred to as the murder of the five journalists in Balibo by the Indonesian forces. While nothing could be proved – no country had yet instigated an independent inquiry into the deaths – it was impossible to ignore the many rumoured eyewitness accounts maintaining that it was a deliberate assassination carried out by Indonesian military forces. This was certainly the opinion of most thinking Australians.

I had been pretty angry at the time and still believe that, as a country, we behaved in an unconscionable manner. When Britain deserted Australia in 1942, leaving us open to invasion by Japan, the Australian people felt betrayed, and now we were watching another even smaller country being trounced by a much larger power. It is no different to watching your neighbours being murdered and their home being trashed while you sit by and do nothing.

In fairness, the Whitlam and the caretaker Fraser governments couldn't have done much to stop the Indonesian invasion of East Timor. While the Indonesians deliberately flouted international law, nobody, least of all the Americans, was interested in coming to the defence of a new 'communist' island state or challenging an invading anti-communist Indonesia whom America regarded as a good friend. Australia simply lacked the necessary military might, quite apart from the political will, to launch a military operation to halt the invasion of the fledgling independent state.

To my mind, our refusal to take a strong political and diplomatic stand against Indonesia's actions was gutless and morally reprehensible, a cynical decision, although politicians will always claim it was pragmatic. We didn't even take the matter to the United Nations, the organisation supposedly set up to resolve such issues.

One of the major reasons was that we were greedy. We understood that, with a proverbial diplomatic nod and a wink, Indonesia would agree to Australia getting the lion's share of the vast, newly discovered Timor Sea oil and gas reserves – a far greater share than we were entitled to under international law or special treaty – so long as we acquiesced to the annexation of a tiny, newly independent nation.

The Australian Government's cowardly acceptance that the deaths of the Balibo Five were an accident of war when they were so obviously blatant murder, and the craven refusal by successive Australian governments to condemn the murders meant that nine years later the issue still refused to go away; in fact the greed, cowardice and duplicity of all three

Australian governments became more and more evident as time went by. The repeated atrocities – some observers called it genocide – against the population of East Timor continued to keep the issue on the front pages.

To put the losses of the East Timorese in perspective, Australia in all its wars to this point has lost a total of 102 807 service people. East Timor, in the short, vicious and unequal war with Indonesia and its subsequent struggle over the past nine years, had lost 200 000 people! Almost one in three Timorese lost their lives, while we calmly looked on, and continue to do so.

Indonesia was on the nose big-time, and Marg's threat to expose Anna's destruction of old-growth forests in Indonesian Borneo, taken together with the heart-rending photos of the cruel deaths of the orangutans and the threat of their extinction, was perfectly timed and had all the ingredients of a major journalistic coup.

Of even more concern was Marg's hint that she possessed new material on East Timor and that Budi might be implicated. If this was about the Balibo Five, then Anna was, technically at least, in the clear. But if it concerned East Timor oil . . . Nine years previously Anna had hinted to me that she and Budi might become involved, which for Anna was shorthand for certainty. She would, I knew, by now be in it up to her neck. Anna was a long-term planner who could sniff out money long before anyone else caught the faintest whiff.

Anna's association with Budi wouldn't be hard to uncover. If he was somehow implicated in the deaths of the Balibo Five, as well as being in on the oil deal, her involvement with him could lead to all sorts of conclusions being drawn. Major General Budi Til was head of the military legal department, married to one of Suharto's cousins and known to be among the powerful and mega-rich (read corrupt) generals in the president's inner council. Add to this their destruction of the jungle and the great apes story and Australia's richest self-made woman had nowhere to hide. She would be seen as totally corrupt. Once it was known that she had been born in Java and was half Javanese, she would be regarded as one of them. There was a lot of loose ends, but an imaginative journalist wouldn't have too much trouble tying them together, and once knotted, there was enough rope to hang Anna Til, the woman with the same surname as the notorious major general. No doubt just another coincidence? Ha! Ha! The Sunday tabloids would have a field day.

That's the trouble with a couple of stiff Scotches on an empty stomach – you start to speculate, then make connections, then draw conclusions. Cook called me in to dinner and I found I'd lost my appetite, even though shepherd's pie is a favourite.

I picked Anna up from the airport the following day but decided not to broach the subject with her until champagne hour. I'd also decided to refer to the oil first, because it wasn't connected directly with Marg, unlike the deforestation and the orangutan photograph. With luck I could fudge it and say I'd heard it elsewhere. I knew that, no matter how much I denied it, if I led with the photograph she'd instantly know Marg was involved and from that point on any possibility of finding a solution would be lost.

These days Anna's time at Beautiful Bay was less about relaxing and more about work. I was lucky if we got two days free to go sailing. She didn't seem able to relax and was losing weight. For the first time since we'd known each other her incredible eyes seemed to lack some of their former lustre, and sometimes, when she thought nobody was looking, I'd see her slightly slumped with her eyes closed, gripping the arms of her chair. Anna was obviously under a fair amount of stress but if I brought it up she'd laugh. 'Part of the business, Nicholas; it goes with the territory. But really, darling, I'm fine, it's just that the past three weeks have been busy.'

I'd long since given up hoping that her one week a month at Beautiful Bay would allow her to relax and for a few days forget about the empire she was building. I had gradually learned that making money in very large amounts was an obsession like any other and that it had nothing to do with never having enough or even with security. It was a psychological need and an addiction. Her substance abuse was no different; Anna was never going to kick her heroin habit and she'd long ago giving up trying. Asking her to stop increasing what was already a vast fortune in order to smell the roses was equally pointless.

Rather than have her working all day in her bedroom, I'd built her an office next to my own so that we could share the filing facilities, fax and phone lines, and if anything came in for her while she was away, I'd fax it to her office in Melbourne then file it without reading it, or I'd re-direct callers to her office. While always maintaining what I hoped was a healthy curiosity about how the world works I've never been a stickybeak. If Anna didn't care to tell me what she was up to, as was usually the case, I didn't want her to think I was a snoop. There was also the fact that Anna's financial affairs were all transacted through Port Vila, not only because it was a tax haven, but also because government administration was pretty lax and unlike the Australian Tax Office or Corporate Affairs, there would be no one looking over her shoulder.

But now I realised that all along, Marg (perfidious woman) must have been taking the opportunity to rummage through the documents in Anna's filing cabinets. I'd have to speak to her, for if Anna, who was by nature secretive, discovered that she couldn't trust me to maintain her confidentiality, it would lead to a major breach of faith between us.

Anna maintained a suite of offices in Melbourne with a staff of seven dedicated women who took care of things, knowing exactly what to do when she was away. As an interesting aside, these seven employees were all ex-Madam Butterfly dominatrices. As they grew older, the rigorous physical effort required for some of the discipline routines of bondage became more difficult, so Anna paid for the women to be re-trained. They continued to earn the same salaries they'd made in the bondage house, which was greatly in excess of a normal clerk's wages, but then the work they did was greatly in excess of that of a normal clerk. They also had generous superannuation and their mortgages were all paid out.

While this was kind and generous it was also practical. Her staff were accustomed to keeping information about their clients to themselves. Anna demanded and received absolute loyalty, probity and secrecy in return for her largesse. They not only loved her but also, I felt certain, would willingly have committed perjury for her and happily gone to prison with their mouths still firmly shut. I felt sure they would have worked for a bed and a meal, if necessary. They were at her beck and call twenty-four hours a day and if they possessed lives of their own they could only lead them once Anna's needs had been satisfied.

I had dubbed them the Secret Seven, and while they all treated me with the utmost respect on the phone and when occasionally we met in Anna's offices, I knew better than to ask them even the smallest detail about her business. More than one financial journalist, TV current-affairs producer or tabloid gossip columnist had tried to crack the Secret Seven but to no avail; Anna Til remained a closed book, each page seemingly glued to the next. The exception might have been Marg. Just how much she knew of Anna's affairs I couldn't say, but certainly, as far as Indonesia was concerned, obviously she knew more than I'd like to think.

That evening, I poured Anna a glass of champagne and myself a Scotch (I keep a clearer mind on whisky, or so I tell myself). As I handed it to her she said, 'Yummy, thank you, Nicholas. Now, what's wrong? You've been like a bear with a sore head all afternoon. C'mon, out with it.'

It was pointless denying it. Anna could sense the twitch of a single synapse. 'Can we talk, darling?' I said, attempting a grin.

'Of course, always providing you don't want the details of my bank account,' she laughed.

'No, it's about an anonymous call I received two days ago,' I lied.

'What about? Me?'

'Only indirectly. It was about your mate, Budi.'

'So, what about him?'

'Well, as you may know, the conspiracy about the Balibo Five has blown up again.'

'Yes, it's in all the papers. I was unaware that Budi had been mentioned.'

'No, I don't think he has, but the voice on the other end of the phone suggested that he was about to be.'

'Oh? Did he give any details?'

'No, just referred to the media and said, "Watch this space."'

Anna took a sip from her glass. 'Nick, are you telling me

everything you know? I sense you're not.'

I guess Anna dealt with duplicity a lot more than I did and had a finely tuned ear for a lie – either that or she was bluffing – but except for saying the call was anonymous I'd stuck to the truth . . . so far. 'I think I resent that,' I replied evenly.

'Sorry, Nicholas,' Anna said hurriedly. 'I don't mean to offend you. Was the voice Australian or Indonesian?'

'Australian.'

Anna seemed to relax a little. 'Aha. There's been a reporter from the *Fin Review* snooping around. Two of the girls have been approached in the coffee shop in our building. He's probably chancing his arm, knowing your connection with me. His name is Peter Yeldham, the one investigative reporter no one in the financial community wants sniffing about. He's a hard-evidence man and doesn't deal in speculation, but he also never lets go. A certain titled millionaire in Sydney is said to have tried to pay him off once and Yeldham simply reported the bribe in the piece he wrote linking the knight of the realm to serious corruption in the transport industry.'

'Who would sool him onto you? Stan McVitty?'

'He'd be awfully silly if he did, but that's unlikely. This is obviously about Indonesia.'

I wasn't quite silly enough to ask Anna if she had anything to hide, but ventured, 'Is that anything to worry about?'

Anna laughed. 'In business there's always something to worry about, Nicholas.'

'No, Indonesia, is there something specific?'

'Well, no, I don't think so. Business is good, the clothing factory is doing extremely well . . . no, I don't think so,' she repeated as if she was reconsidering the question. 'You yourself know that business in Indonesia is always done in partnership, usually with a general. Budi's involvement is by no means unusual, every financial reporter would be aware of that.'

It wasn't yet time to bring up her timber concession. 'Anna, nine years ago, right here, drinking champagne, we talked about the murders of the five journalists in East Timor and you told me the invasion was all about the oil that had been discovered on the continental shelf, most of it in East Timorese territory. You hinted that maybe you and Budi might get involved, but said it was still much too early . . .' I paused before asking, 'Are you?'

'Am I what?'

'Involved in the Timor Sea oilfields?'

Anna handed me her glass. 'Nicholas, always what amazes me, it is your memory, it is so *goed*.'

Anna was suddenly very upset, unaware of the slip in her syntax, or her reversion to the Dutch of her youth. I'd hit the jackpot, but the last thing I needed was a quarrel. I needed her to come clean, not to burst into tears and to protest and obfuscate. Anna was pure titanium in business, but there was a secret Anna I'd met in Batavia in 1942 who was still vulnerable, who could still be reached under all the hammered-down protective layers with which she had surrounded herself. I filled her glass and handed it to her, the surface bubbles still popping. Her hand shook slightly as she accepted it. 'Darling, you know it goes no further. Just occasionally it helps to talk about things,' I said as gently as I could.

Anna turned away from me, leaning on the verandah railing and looking over Beautiful Bay. She remained silent for some time, then sighed, turned and, with her back against the railing, asked with a determined toss of her head, 'Nick, what is it you want to know?'

The use of Nick rather than Nicholas warned me that she had not yet quite regained her composure. 'Anna, you're angry. We can leave it right here if you wish.'

There was a moment's hesitation, then she said, 'No, Nicholas, what is it you want to know?'

'Was Budi involved in the mur . . . assassination of the five journalists?'

'Yes.'

'Jesus! How?'

Anna downed half a glass of champagne in one gulp. 'The Suharto government isn't stupid, Nicholas. There had to be a risk assessment, a legal opinion, that's why Budi was in East Timor. There was much too much at stake for the world to see what was going on. The journalists had seen too much; they had to be silenced.'

'Sure, legal opinion, risk assessment, that makes sense, but he wasn't the general actually in command, was he?' I was desperately clutching at straws.

'You should know by now that it doesn't work like that, Nicholas. We, Budi and I, weren't the only ones who wanted a share of the oil revenue.' Anna shrugged. 'This was a way to make sure we were first in line after the Suharto family.'

'He gave the order to kill them?'

'Yes.'

'The direct order?'

'Yes.'

'How much is involved?' I was deeply shocked.

Anna drained her glass. 'It could be worth six billion dollars to us, Nicholas.'

'Fuck!'

'Then there's the natural gas,' she added calmly.

'Not just oil?'

'No, you could add half as much again for the natural gas. There's also the supply and support contracts.'

I was silent, shaking my head. Anna handed me her glass,

the champagne bottle half empty. 'If you add in Roger East, the Australian journalist murdered by them in Dili, that's a billion dollars for each life,' I said. My hand was shaking as I poured the champagne.

'Nicholas, wouldn't you kill someone for a billion dollars?' Anna asked.

'No! I can't spend what I've got. No! No! No!'

'That's not the point,' Anna said softly, as if speaking to herself.

I handed her the champagne. 'Anna, if what's-his-name, Peter Yeldham, gets hold of this, you're history! The implications are too terrible to contemplate.'

'Nicholas, you're getting too far ahead of yourself. How could he? He won't get any stuff on Budi from me or from the Indonesians. The oil thing is still years away, twenty at least. We won't earn a cent until then. Right now there's only red and green areas marked on a map of the ocean floor and none of them has my name on it or his.'

'Anna, in twenty years you'll be seventy-eight! You've got to live with this! What on earth's the point?'

'The endgame,' Anna replied calmly.

'I don't understand.'

'Nick, no woman in modern business history has ever become a multibillionaire through her own efforts, starting from scratch.'

'That's important?'

'You're damn right it is. It's revenge!'

'Uh – against who?'

'Men!'

'Me?'

'No, of course not! I love you, Nicholas, but there is always an exception and it *doesn't* prove the rule. I have to avenge my mother, who was raped by my father and lost her life for lack of medical attention when I was born. He, the bastard, murdered her!

'Every two minutes a woman is raped in the world! Every two minutes!' she cried. 'That's 263 000 reported cases, and it's estimated only sixteen per cent of rapes are reported. When you extrapolate from that, every twenty seconds a woman or a child is being raped somewhere in the world! Men mostly get away with it, not just young louts, thugs and brutes, but fathers, uncles, lawyers, doctors; respected men escape justice because most judges are men. Who knows how many of the men sitting in judgment are guilty, or for that matter the defence lawyers! Throughout the world ninety-five per cent of rapists get off scot free! Even in Australia it's seventy-five per cent! One in every three women in our own country is sexually abused as a child. In Saudi Arabia if a woman has been raped she is accused of being a temptress and beheaded!'

'Whoa! Wait a cotton-pickin' minute, darling. What has being a female billionaire got to do with revenge?'

'Hear me out,' Anna said. I don't believe I'd seen her this worked up since my attempt to kidnap her on *Madam Butterfly* all those years ago. 'First Konoe Akira attempted to steal my mind, but in fact he gave me something invaluable; he gave me strength. He taught me that I had the power to protect myself. That I didn't have to be another male conquest. He is the one man beside yourself, Nicholas, who gave me anything. And you? You gave me love.'

'But wait a minute, when you were sixteen, a virgin, you didn't have these thoughts. At the time you said I was the first man in your life, that we'd wait for each other. I remember we discussed our fidelity.'

'Yes, but it was only in Tjilatjap that I discovered the

circumstances of my birth from my drunken and dying father. He told me the story not out of deep regret for what he'd done – he'd effectively killed my mother – but because my mother's people had destroyed his life by castrating him. For once a rapist had been punished.' Anna paused, attempting to calm down, then said, 'Then I read in his will he had left nothing for me, not a brass razoo. I had bad blood! That, but more especially the knowledge that I was the child of a rape victim, shocked me deeply and, as it's turned out, permanently. That was at exactly the same time as I came under Konoe Akira's influence. He had *Korin-san* teach me the techniques of female domination and through male bondage he gave me power, the power never to let a man simply take my body, plunder me, treat me as if I was a worthless piece of shit.'

'But, Anna, what about a man who loves you? Me, for instance?' I thought guiltily of how quickly and happily I had betrayed her when I'd first met Marg. The eternal curse of the one-eyed snake.

'Please, Nicholas, let me finish,' Anna demanded. 'I'm never going to say this again . . . to anyone. When Colonel Takahashi, that repulsive *kempeitai* pig, tried to force me to have sex with him in the Nest of the Swallows, I was going through the motions, the sexual foreplay *Korin-san* had so diligently taught me, when my mind went haywire and flipped inwards. I saw my father in the nude, not as a young man, but as a huge, bestial bloated man, the broken veins on his bulbous whisky nose, the snorting, the snot covering his upper lip, his huge repulsive body heaving as it had been just before he died from the effects of alcohol and diabetes. But he wasn't dying, he was raping my tiny mother, and then just as suddenly I was in the process of being born, forcing my way out, rupturing her cervix, too big to pass through, with blood everywhere as she screamed and screamed, dying in agony.' Anna was shaking as she looked at me. 'The blood belonged to that Japanese scum I'd stabbed to death.'

I rose from my chair and took her in my arms. 'Darling, you don't have to do this. Enough! It's enough!'

She pushed me away. 'No, I do! I have to.'

I moved to stand at her side, leaning with my back against the railing.

'No, Nicholas, sit. I need to see you. I need to explain,' she commanded.

'Anna, you're upset,' I said, moving away toward my chair.

'Of course I'm fucking upset!' she yelled furiously, losing control. '*Jesus-Christus*, sit down, Nick!'

'Your vaginismus!' I said, too loudly.

It was as if the word took all the wind out of her. 'Yes. Every time you tried to penetrate, the scene came back, exactly the same, the rape, me being born, my mother dying in a scream of agony! I thought it might be you, my daring to love you, that was my punishment.'

'Darling, how long have you known this was the cause of your vaginismus?'

'A long time.'

'And you did nothing about it, saw no one?' I was trying to conceal my sudden anger.

'Nicholas, please don't be angry. I'm sorry, I couldn't, I mean, I didn't *want* to. It became my reason for revenge, that and the money.'

'Forgive me if I'm stupid, but I don't understand. The money? What the fuck has that got to do with it?'

'Men! Don't you understand? It's all about power! Young blokes rape women by using force, it makes them feel powerful. They take them then discard them, sick fathers or uncles or family friends do it to their daughters, nieces or their friends' children and it gives them a sense of power. And the daughters, nieces or friends' children are destroyed, often forever. Older men get their power through money. In the male world power is everything and money buys it, buys ego. What they can no longer take with their loins, their threats and their fists, they now take with their money. Nothing is as exhilarating in the male world as money, simply because it's the thing other males respect the most and will bring a beautiful woman to her knees to perform fellatio. But for those who can't do it with money, there's always rape! Do you know why my father raped my mother?'

'Yes, you told me.'

Anna ignored my reply. 'Because his cock was too small! He was terrified a Dutch girl would laugh when she saw his pathetic little willy, so he raped my mother, a native girl he could discard, throw on the scrap heap, just so he could feel powerful! His teeny-weeny little prick may have been small, but hooray! It was still capable of murder!'

I wanted to contradict her, to protest that men were not all like that, that I'd never even contemplated raping a woman, that I'd have given anything to have kids with her. I recalled the time ten years previously when Marg underwent her metamorphosis and got Helen Reddy'd and went from admiral's widow to roaring '*I Am Woman!*' I confess I thought at the time she was going somewhat over the top, but I understood her frustration. But, Jesus, that was nothing compared to this, to Anna now.

'I had no idea, darling. But does rape and money have to affect you like this?'

It was a badly phrased question. 'Affect me like what? Both have *affected* my entire adult life, Nicholas. I'm going to put it as crudely as a man would, in male language so you understand. What's more, I don't apologise. No male has or ever will enter my cunt! Since those imbeciles in Japan, no male has ever harmed me. No man will ever bully me, or intimidate me, or slap me around, or compromise me, or threaten me, or force me to flatter him or appeal to his ego as millions upon millions of women are forced to do every day. I smile and scowl of my own volition. I don't care what any male on earth thinks of me except for you, and even then I don't care all the time. I intend to be the one woman on earth who started with nothing and never became a victim. No male on earth possesses enough money to buy a single compliment formulated by me to please him. It is I who have the power, not only the virgin power, but all the fucking power to bully, to enforce, to bribe, to corrupt, to get my own way! I may not care to use it, but I've got it, or most of it, and when I'm worth several billion, I'll have it all. The first woman to take men on in their own terms and win!'

'Anna! You can't win! Never! They'll just think of you as a dyke, a ballbreaker!' I cried rather lamely.

'What do I care? I know more about their balls than they do, and I know how to break them, too. I'm one of the world's best dominatrices. I know all about their pathetic little male perversions, and believe you me, no male exists without one, and the richer and more powerful the more pathetic they are. On the outside he's the big bad wolf, on the inside he wants to wear a nappy, shit in it, then rub it all over himself while I scold him and he ejaculates!'

Cook came out and called us in to dinner. I rose and took the champagne bucket with me. Anna's glass was empty again and I estimated there was one glass left in the bottle. We walked silently towards the dining-room table, the only noise our footsteps and the rattle of what remained of the ice cubes in the melted water. We'd come a long way from the subject of Budi and his implication in the murder of the Balibo Five, now confirmed by Anna. In fact, we'd simply come a long way full stop. But I wasn't sure where the last bit had taken us or how to continue.

Cook placed avocado halves filled with tiny harbour prawns marinated in fresh lime juice and coconut in front of both of us and I topped up Anna's glass with the last of the champagne. I was aware that she'd had too much to drink, in fact, three glasses was usually her limit. She only drank when she was at Beautiful Bay, knowing it was the one place she could let her hair down, although I don't believe I'd ever seen her quite this inebriated; her face seemed unusually flushed.

What she'd just told me I realised wasn't merely the drink talking, it was something she wanted to say and the champagne had allowed her to say it. I was deeply shocked as well as saddened, even angry, at the reasons behind her vaginismus, and that, by attempting to force myself into her, I had caused the return of such horrific hallucinations. In the act of loving her I had filled her with unspeakable terror.

I had always known Anna to be a deeply troubled soul – how could she not be? – but I could never have guessed to what extent. I hadn't understood how she felt about men, rape and the symbolic and actual power of money. Perhaps it wasn't normal, yet nobody could call her insane. You could say she was mentally unbalanced, but she was no more so than the male power moguls with whom she saw herself competing, and their behaviour was accepted without question.

I momentarily asked myself how all this affected me, then immediately dismissed the thought for another time. One thing was certain – if Budi was exposed as the general who had ordered the murders in return for a share of the Timor Sea oil revenue, and then her connection with him was brought to light, the effect on Anna would be disastrous. It would mean she had been eliminated from the endgame. In her mind she would have been cheated of the triumph of being the single woman in history who took on men at their own game and on their own terms and beat them. Instead there would be ignominy and abject defeat. She would think she had failed not only herself, but also her gender. The independent and untouchable woman would become a disgraced and corrupt one, the ice maiden who was prepared to condone murder to achieve her objectives. She would have left herself open to the slings and arrows of an outraged world and the laughter of her male competitors as well as the scorn of every woman alive. Even though she would still possess a vast fortune she would see herself as a loser. Anna played by the same rules as men, where the winner takes all, but when men fail, the world allows them to fold their tents and slip silently into the night; her punishment would be different, infinitely harsher, because she was a woman.

I wanted to say something kind and instead put my foot in it, but at least it served to change the tempo, ameliorate her anger. 'Anna, I want you to know that I would have regarded it as a great privilege to have had children with you.'

Anna smiled, but not happily. 'Nicholas, what would have happened if we'd had a girl?'

I was shocked. 'You can't mean . . . her and me . . . rape?'

'Nicholas! Of course not! Darling, how awful. What I meant was how would I cope? I would be so protective of her I would totally destroy her life.'

'But you adore Saffron.'

'Yes, but she's not mine and with Joe as her grandfather she's a pretty grounded little twelve-year-old. When are the school holidays? I'm high as a kite on champagne – I can't think straight. Can you have her to stay on the week that I'm here?'

'Of course. Her parents want her to go to boarding school in Sydney in a year or two. She's pretty bright and can't get the schooling she needs in New Guinea.'

'Oh good! She can fly down to Melbourne on the weekends. I'd love that. But why can't she go to school in Melbourne?'

'It's got something to do with Uncle Joe scholarships. He has several of the really bright island girls at Presbyterian Ladies' College in Sydney and he thinks it will be good for Saffron to have her own people with her to keep her grounded. He doesn't want her growing up to be a toffee-nosed little madam. He was going to speak to you about letting her come down to you on some weekends.'

'Every weekend, I hope. I love that child,' Anna said happily.

I was grateful that we'd been reduced to small talk but conscious that what had been said, momentous as it was, hadn't actually advanced my plan to get to the Borneo timber concession and the survival of the great apes.

Cook brought in the roast and I was preparing to carve when Anna put down her napkin and rose from her chair. 'Nicholas, I don't feel well. Too much champagne. Please excuse me from the rest of the dinner, darling. Tell cook the shrimp marinade was delicious.'

I jumped to my feet. 'Let me see you to your room . . .'

She gave a little smile. 'Sweetie, I'm not that pissed. I think I might be able to find my way, but thank you.' Slightly unsteady on her feet, she came over and kissed me lightly on the forehead.

'Goodnight. Hope you feel better in the morning,' I replied, watching, concerned, as she turned and walked away then suddenly stopped. I caught her slim image in the hallway mirror – it was true, she was losing weight – and she had her right hand clasped to her left breast, her eyes tightly shut in what was clearly a grimace of pain. 'You all right, Anna?' I asked. 'Shall I call someone?' Meaning a doctor.

'No, no . . . I'm fine, a bit of indigestion, that's all,' she answered, then moved on down the hallway towards her bedroom.

I ate almost nothing and when Cook brought dessert I sent it away with a gesture of impatience. 'Masta no feel gud,' she said, removing the pudding. I poured myself another Scotch, telling myself it was the last for the night, but as it was only half-past eight I knew it wouldn't be. I went out and sat on the verandah, not knowing whether to feel angry, sad, frightened for Anna or all these things together. But underneath these feelings was a slow fuse of anger because she'd known the cause of her vaginismus and had chosen to do nothing about it. I felt sad that I'd been denied her children while it was still possible, and fearful that if her tightly constructed world came apart I'd lose her. Typically, my initial concerns were all about me, whereas it wasn't me who was standing on the edge of a precipice, it was Anna.

Through all her suffering she'd somehow held herself together in a world she thought of as rotten to the core and formulated her own search for justice in a peculiar and personal endgame. But now I found myself critically involved in the outcome. I reasoned that she couldn't possibly have stopped the deaths of the five journalists, and furthermore she'd seen so much gratuitous death under the Japanese, so much violence that went unpunished, that it was bound to have affected her. On several occasions she had come perilously close to a violent death herself. As a nineteen-year-old, the year everything had changed for her, she'd seen the severed head of her beloved Til, the humble trishaw driver and homespun philosopher, stuck onto the front gatepost to intimidate her in preparation for her own rape by the Japanese commoner *kempeitai* colonel, Takahashi. No doubt afterwards he would have killed or discarded her in a show of neurotic contempt for his predecessor, the nobly born Konoe Akira.

Given her circumstances and mindset, which she'd just outlined for me, gaining financially as a consequence of a tragic event over which she had no control was something she could live with, whereas I, with my comparatively sheltered life and putative Anglican background, might have reached a different conclusion.

Marg had quite correctly insisted that I could no longer sit on the fence, be ambivalent, play moderator between the two of them. I had to choose where my conscience lay. I cared about trees, I cared about the great apes, I cared about justice for the five men who'd died and I cared about the 200 000 Timorese men, women and children who had lost their lives. To be honest, in the case of the environment and the orangutan, perhaps not to the extent Marg cared, but the dreams of the slaughter of the nine sailors jumbled up with the Balibo Five had been haunting me in nightmares for nine years. One of the two women I loved stood to gain hugely from the tragedy and as a consequence the other was threatening to destroy her. The outcome, I felt certain, would be that I would lose both Anna and Marg.

Moreover, Anna considered herself quite safe from discovery in terms of the Timor Sea oilfields. She had shown enormous trust in me by revealing Budi's guilt and the reason for it, knowing rightly that I would never betray her. But therein lay the problem. She'd only told me because she felt safe from Peter Yeldham, the never-give-up *Fin Review* reporter. I had the task of revealing to her that she wasn't safe by any means. I was now convinced Marg had spoken to him or he to her. Her 'watch this space' threat was real. I had somehow to get Anna to sever her ties with Budi and the oil deal and furthermore abandon her timber concessions for the sake of the orangutan. It was going to be a long week.

It was just before nine when I decided I needed to know exactly what Marg knew. I was making too many suppositions, too many leaps in the dark. I'd call Marg in Tasmania rather than wait until she called me in the morning. When Anna was in residence Marg called in the morning around seven-thirty because I'd told her Anna didn't rise until around ten, a habit she'd formed when she'd worked the late nights required at Madam Butterfly. I'd usually take the call in my office because sometimes the line was so bad I'd be forced to shout and I didn't wish to disturb Anna. Marg was an early-to-bed and early-to-rise person and with luck I might just catch her before she retired for the night.

Marg answered in a curt voice and after I'd said good evening she ticked me off. 'It's late, Nick. I was just about to go to bed. My hands are all sticky with face cream.'

I apologised then said, 'Marg, the journalist you spoke to from the *Fin Review*, was his name Peter Yeldham?'

There was the slightest pause, then, 'I didn't say I'd spoken to a journalist.'

'You as good as did. You spoke of Major General Budi Til and East Timor and said watch this space. That's tantamount to saying you were going or had gone to the press. Marg, I have one or two questions. How did you know about the timber concessions or for that matter about Anna's business association with Budi Til? And how were you able to connect him with East Timor?' I asked, then added, 'You didn't get any of this information from me.'

'From Anna's files, of course,' Marg answered blandly.

'Yeah, I thought so. Marg, that's reprehensible.'

'All's fair in love and war, Nick.'

'It's unconscionable and underhand and sneaky.'

'The first two perhaps, but not the third. I always did it with her office door open and in broad daylight,' Marg replied without a scintilla of regret in her voice.

'How would you like it if I told Anna?'

'You can't, that's our agreement,' she snapped.

I realised I was getting away from the reason for my call. 'You ought to be bloody ashamed of yourself, Marg.'

'Oh, don't be so pompous, Nick. You of all people! You know my background is in intelligence. Old habits die hard.'

It was pointless continuing, Marg wasn't going to show the slightest contrition. 'Yeldham? Did you speak to him?'

'Yes, as a matter of fact I did.'

'About Anna?'

'Yes, of course.'

'Not yes of course! What did you discuss?'

'He told me he was doing an article for the *Financial Review* about women and money. As Anna was Australia's richest woman – I think he said richest self-made woman – he was trying to build a profile. He said he'd gone to Melbourne, to her office, and had been given short shrift. Could I help join the dots so to speak.'

'And you agreed?'

'Why not?'

'You know Anna keeps a tight lid on her affairs.'

'No, Nick, I don't. All I know about her affairs is from

reading her files at Beautiful Bay.'

'How did he contact you in the first instance?'

'Nick, that's a silly question. I'm a politician, I'm not exactly hard to find and your relationship with us isn't an official secret.'

'I mean, what did he say about Anna to interest you?'

'Nothing, he simply mailed me the photographs of the orangutans with a note attached that said, "Note the name on the bulldozer cabin. Would you like to comment? I'm doing a piece on Anna Til", together with his name and a Sydney phone number. I took the pictures home and every time I looked at them I grew more and more angry. When I got to my office in Parliament House the next day I called him and said, "Yes." As it turned out I wasn't a great help. In fact he told me more than I knew myself.'

'Like what?'

'Well, he knew about the clothing factory, military uniforms and kids' pyjamas, the KFC involvement, the property holdings and, of course, the timber concessions. He wanted to know what I knew about Major General Budi Til, Anna's partner in all these undertakings. I had to tell him that I knew nothing other than that I'd seen his name on various documents. He then told me he was one of the generals who were implicated in the invasion of East Timor.'

'Of course he did. Marg, there's nothing in there that any competent journalist couldn't find out for himself. To do business in Indonesia Anna would have to have a local partner, preferably a general. Anna's not going to get out of bed for that exposure. There's nothing there to frighten her, she'll call your bluff.'

'I know, so I told him about the oil.'

I feigned ignorance. 'What oil?'

Marg switched to her intelligence-officer-briefing voice.

'That's one of the major reasons Australia stood by and watched East Timor being crushed. The Timor Sea has huge oil and natural gas deposits. The Indonesians wanted Timor's oil and because the boundary between Australia and East Timor isn't settled they offered to be generous in the ongoing negotiations, giving us a much larger slice of the oil reserves. In return Australia would keep quiet and not make a fuss if they annexed East Timor.'

'Oil? Are you sure?' I asked, shocked that she knew.

'Yes.'

'How the hell do you know all this? Let me guess, your friend in Canberra, Roger Rigby.'

'Nick, I'm not at liberty to say,' Marg said crisply.

'But why would he do that? He'd be charged under the *Official Secrets Act*, they'd put him in jail and throw away the key. Worse still, he'd lose his pension.'

'I didn't say it was him. But it's all going to blow up and the government can't do a thing to stop it.'

'And that's why Roger told you? How? How is it going to blow up?' I asked, suddenly fearful for Anna.

'Nick, I didn't say it was him. Apparently somebody who was at Shoal Bay, the radio intercept post near Darwin, during the invasion of East Timor is about to die of cancer and he wants to clear his conscience. He knows the game and how to play it and has a set of the transcripts of the intelligence intercepts that show the Australian governments have been lying through their teeth about East Timor. He's released details to Reuters and other international media organisations. The cat has been let out of the bag, or if you'll excuse the French, as my contact put it, "We can't put the shit back in the goose this time." He was only telling me what the whole world is about to find out.'

I tried to gather my thoughts. I needed to know if Marg

had any more details. 'Hang on, so what? The conspiracy, if it's about oil, is between us and Indonesia. What's that got to do with Anna?'

'I didn't say the exposure was *only* about the government's grubby oil deal; all I said was that I told Peter Yeldham about the split-up of the oil in Australia's favour. As a matter of fact he had heard rumours for years and wasn't that excited about it. There's no hard evidence the media can get onto and both governments simply deny, deny, deny.'

'So, what's the exposure about if it isn't *only* about the oil?'

'It's what I hinted to you last time we talked. It's about Major General Budi Til. Australian intelligence overheard the Indonesian army planning the murder of the Balibo Five. He's the general who formulated it and issued the orders to kill them all. They did it to cover up the Indonesian army's invasion of the area around Balibo. He was also implicated in the death, a little later in Dili, of Roger East, the Australian correspondent.'

'You mean we knew *before* the murders happened?'

'Yes, despite denying it for nine years, the Australian Government knew precisely what happened to the five journalists. They knew when, where and by whose command, before it took place! The Indonesian army heard from their Timorese sympathisers that there were five journalists in the village, the army radioed for instructions and Major General Budi Til instructed the nearest army unit to go in and assassinate them.'

'Jesus!' This was something I didn't know. Anna was even closer to being in big trouble.

Marg was still in intelligence-officer mode. 'As you possibly know from your own time in radio intelligence with the marines and elsewhere, the last thing you want your opponent to know is that you have the capacity to eavesdrop on their top-secret conversations. From the end of the war until 1977 Canberra didn't even allow any reference in the press to the existence of what's now the Defence Signals Directorate.'

'Where Roger is the director?'

Marg gave an audible sigh. 'Yes, Nick. I've told you that previously. Now, please stop probing for my source. You're insulting my intelligence.'

'And so the government was prepared to wash its hands of the five journalists to keep this knowledge from Indonesia?'

'Nick, you should know that will always be the case – "for the greater good" and all that twaddle.'

'Do you know any more about Budi . . . er, Major General Til?'

'As a matter of fact, yes. Major General Budi is also the commander of a counter-intelligence unit that has been responsible for the torture and killing of eighty-two Timorese resistance fighters and the wholesale slaughter of civilians in reprisal raids by units of the Indonesian army under his command. The Indonesians won't release him to an international tribunal to face charges, of course, but if he'd been a German or a Japanese general in 1945 he would certainly have been hanged.'

'And Anna is his partner in several business enterprises, so it's guilt by association? Is this the basis of your threat – that if she doesn't give up the timber concessions you'll reveal the relationship between her and the man responsible for the murder of the Balibo Five?' I asked pointedly. Then, not waiting for her to answer, I let her have it. 'Marg, Anna is one tough cookie. She won't like the news about her business partner, but it won't make her back off. *She* isn't guilty of war crimes! It's bad for Budi Til, but it's not necessarily a disaster for Anna. You may be certain she'll call your bluff.'

Marge laughed. 'Nick, I saved the best for last. This vile little murderer was rewarded for his deeds with a small part of the future oil and natural gas concessions and Anna is a fifty per cent partner! My contact says when it comes into production their part alone will be worth billions and so Anna will be shown to be a direct beneficiary of murder and genocide in East Timor.'

My heart sank. Marg knew. 'Holy shit! Is this all going to be released? Anna is a part of the exposure?'

'No, Anna's involvement is not known . . . yet. It was told to me separately by my contact. Now, you tell her, Nick, that she has one week. Seven days! I believe the exposure of Major General Budi Til will break in the next couple of days. You tell Princess Plunder that if the timber concessions she holds are not left intact as habitat for the orangutan, and I mean every inch of it, I tell Peter Yeldham and he prints the pictures and the story about Australia's richest self-made woman and how she goes about her business! It's a story that's bound to be syndicated throughout the world.'

'Marg, you wouldn't. You'd destroy not only Anna, but all three of us.'

'Watch me, Nick. I don't give a shit about Anna and the oil, but I do about the great apes. It's got to stop somewhere and if I don't do it, it will be on my conscience until I die. I'm not going to stand by and allow these gorgeous creatures to become extinct, which at the present rate will happen by the year 2015! If it destroys our relationship, and God knows I love you, Nick, I have to take that chance! Now, if you don't mind, it's past my bedtime.'

So, of course, I had another Scotch and then another and followed it up with a near sleepless night. I decided I had no choice. I was going to have to confront Anna in the morning and stand by while the excrement hit the rapidly rotating blades, as they say in the classics.

The following morning – the usual tropical extravaganza, various shades of blue with a sharp bite of green between sea and sky – I waited until after breakfast, which consisted of a single slice of dry toast and a glass of orange juice for Anna, then suggested, 'Darling, it's a beautiful day. Why don't we take *Madam Butterfly* and sail to Coffee Scald? I'll get Cook to pack a cold chicken, a salad and a bottle of chilled wine for lunch, shall I?'

'Wine? God no, Nicholas! Tell her a bottle of soda water and a packet of crackers for me. I must be getting old – my head feels as though it's been inside a voodoo drum all night.'

'Take it easy, have a couple of hours in the hammock under the big old native fig in the garden. It's dark and cool under the canopy. What say we leave about eleven-thirty? There's a nice following breeze this time of the year – we'll get there about one-thirty. You're bound to feel a little better by then,' I said optimistically. 'Nothing like a bit of a breeze and the open sea for a hangover.'

At one-thirty when we arrived at Coffee Scald it was hot as hell and I rigged a beach umbrella while Anna laid out lunch on a blanket, then we went for a swim. Strangely she wore a bikini top, but not the pants, which was unusual because we usually swam in the nuddy and Anna wasn't exactly big breasted. If she was becoming self-conscious of her breasts drooping I certainly hadn't noticed; as far as I was concerned, at fifty-eight she still had the figure of a young woman, although she was just a tad too thin. We dressed in shorts and T-shirts by which time Anna pronounced herself hungry and headache free.

'Eat a good lunch, darling, you need to put on a kilo or two,' I observed. 'I could see your ribs clearly as we were swimming.'

Anna laughed. 'Don't be ridiculous, Nicholas, a woman can never be too rich or too thin. I guess I've been travelling and working a bit too much lately. There's a world shortage of high-quality long-fibre cotton and I was in Egypt last week trying to negotiate supplies. The cotton merchants were giving me the run-around. Egyptian men still see women as a cross between a mule, a cook and a begetter of sons; they have few rights and are sent packing if they have the misfortune to bear more than one girl child. Budi usually does the trip but he couldn't go on this occasion; some urgent government business cropped up. The Egyptians respect him as a fellow Muslim and a general to boot. With my attitude towards men, misogynists in particular, it's been a difficult few days.'

Anna sat cross-legged on the blanket. She reached forward and tore off a chicken leg and helped herself to salad and a cold roast potato left over from last night's scarcely touched roast, placing the plate in her lap and eating hungrily but still somehow elegantly with her fingers. I poured her a glass of chablis and she placed it beyond the edge of the blanket, digging the base and stem slightly into the dry sand.

'Anna, I'm glad you brought up Budi. There's something I need to say.'

'Oh dear. About last night – too much champagne, too little discretion.'

'Not at all, I was honoured that you chose to tell me.'

'Nicholas, I've always wanted to. I don't share much with you that's business, but lately I've been conscious that perhaps, as the person I love the most in the world, you really ought to know a little more about what's going on. I'm not sorry about last night.'

'Anna, please don't. The problem I have at the moment is that I know rather too much of what's going on in your life. Perhaps even more than you do. Last night helped clear up several things in my mind and it's the primary reason we're here.'

'Oh? What can you possibly mean?' Anna, holding the chicken leg poised, grinned. 'I hope you're not going to try and kidnap me again?' She'd played it for a laugh but suddenly noticed my expression. 'What's wrong, Nicholas?' she asked, her expression now serious.

'Darling, I think you're going to be involved in a spot of serious trouble that concerns you and Budi. I'm afraid I have to break our agreement. The information comes from Marg.'

'The Green Bitch? It can't be good news,' Anna said, frowning.

'It isn't. But first you should know where I stand. I've made my position clear to you on more than one occasion.'

Anna said quickly, 'Nicholas, there's no way —'

'Please, Anna, just hear me out without interrupting, then you can decide for yourself what to do,' I pleaded.

Anna put down her plate and reached for the glass of wine, lifting it to her mouth and taking a small sip. 'Go ahead, I'm listening.'

I spent the next twenty minutes outlining the situation to Anna, ending with Marg's ultimatum and then saying, 'I realise you're caught between a rock and a hard place, darling, but if your oil and gas partnership with Budi comes out there'll be no endgame for you. The media are going to hang you out to dry. But there's worse.' I reached into the back of the picnic basket for a plastic bag, broke it open and withdrew a large manila envelope. I handed her the picture of the five beheaded apes. 'Peter Yeldham is syndicated throughout the world. If this photograph gets out, and Marg says she has more, it's all over for you, Anna.'

Anna wiped her hands and took the photograph. Moments later, while her expression didn't change, her hand started to shake. Then her eyes filled and a single tear escaped and ran down her cheek. I shall never know whether the tears that followed were out of compassion or rage. She handed back the photograph. 'The bitch! She wouldn't hesitate, would she!' she spat.

'No, Marg is a zealot. She doesn't make threats unless she intends to carry them out. She feels very strongly about the great apes. The oil information, your sharing it with Budi, is also well founded. It very likely comes from Roger Rigby, who was with her in Naval Intelligence during the war and now heads the Defence Signals Directorate in Canberra. It's kosher all right.'

Anna sniffed and knuckled away the tears. 'Where did she get that photograph?'

'Peter Yeldham.'

'Nick, she's trying to make a fool of me. If the photograph comes from Yeldham, then he obviously possesses the negatives. If we comply with Marg's wishes and in return she doesn't tell him about our oil and gas deal then Yeldham still has a good story, though a different one. He simply goes ahead and prints the photographs and I'm well and truly discredited. Not perhaps as badly as I would be over the oil deal, but I'm total mud in the media from then on.'

'Whoa, not so fast, Anna, now listen carefully.'

'I always listen carefully, Nicholas,' Anna snapped.

'I don't know whether Marg didn't see this obvious problem or has a separate agreement with Yeldham . . . or perhaps didn't think it through.'

'Separate agreement my arse! She's been in intelligence and she wouldn't miss a detail like that! She'd know Yeldham had the negatives.' Anna emulated Marg's slightly posh accent, '"Oops, so sorry, Nick, Peter Yeldham gave me his word he wouldn't publish!" Or better still, "Oh, Nick, how careless of me not to think it through."' Anna looked directly at me. 'The Green Bitch will be hugging herself with glee. She's off the hook and Yeldham publishes anyway! Double whammy!'

'Are you quite through, Anna?' I demanded. 'Will you just listen and let me explain? We've got one photograph, you can bet it's the best one, the most incriminating of them all. Marg has the others, or so she says. Okay, we've got a week before Peter Yeldham runs his piece. He has to wait until Budi is exposed over Timor, that way he gets maximum mileage worldwide with a follow-up story.

'But that's not what happens. Tomorrow we contact the features editor of The Australian, Melanie Griffith, and tell her that Marg Hamilton, the Green politician in the Tasmanian state parliament, has sent you this picture and asked you to authenticate the name on the door of the bulldozer in the background.

'Of course, you know nothing about the killing of the apes and you're horrified! You and your business partner are so mortified that you have decided to cease operations immediately. You've decided to keep the jungle environment pristine and to create a national park under the auspices of the World Wildlife Fund as a permanent gift to the people of Indonesia.' I paused and looked directly at Anna. 'So far any questions?'

'No, go on.'

'Well, here's the tricky bit. You have to get Budi to persuade President Suharto to announce that the Indonesian Government is determined to protect its orangutans and declare the new national park a safe habitat for these magnificent great apes. That hunting or killing one will earn the severest penalty possible under Indonesian law. Do you think he can do that?'

Anna was silent for several moments. 'No, it won't work. Budi can't be, as you suggest, the one who explains it to the president or the council, which is more likely. The Australian Government is bound to have let them know that they've both been sprung over the five journalists and that Budi is implicated. If he comes up with the gift to the nation idea they'll see him as weak. So will Suharto.' Anna looked directly at me. 'Weakness isn't tolerated among the generals. Besides, nobody in Indonesia would give up a concession worth a hundred million American dollars for a bunch of breast-beating apes and the good of the common people. In fact, it would be taken as sign of profound weakness. Remember, Budi is a member of the president's family through marriage; he must continue to look strong, be strong, resist, and accept the protection of his president, who will cover for him when the story breaks.'

'You mean the president will take the rap? That wouldn't happen in our society. A Western prime minister would throw him to the wolves.'

'It's not the Indonesian way. Suharto will brazen it out. He won't publicly say anything himself. The army will simply deny they were involved, say the radio signals were a set-up by the Fretilin terrorists to implicate and compromise Indonesia. They have sworn witnesses to this effect, etc., etc., blah, blah, blah. With the rest, they'll talk up the communist menace, the atrocities committed by Fretilin, Indonesians persecuted by Timorese, that sort of thing. Then they'll insist Budi was just doing his duty. Budi will stay out of the whole thing, go on sick leave or resign as a noble gesture. Later, when things calm down, he'll be appointed to something worthwhile, probably as a judge in the high court.'

'But no such protection will be forthcoming for you, Anna. The Australian media and the wire services are going to have a field day with the business partner of the Butcher of Balibo who allows the murder of great apes threatened with extinction and who plunders the environment for profit!' My beautifully formulated solution had suddenly gone up in flames. 'So, in fact, Budi dares not give up his timber concession, is that right?'

'Pretty well.'

I thought for a moment. 'Okay, you're horrified when you see the photographs and you sell your share to Budi. It's not great but it's better than doing nothing.'

'So, the Butcher of Balibo can continue killing the great apes and destroying their natural habitat? That's really going to make me look good in the eyes of the media,' Anna snorted.

And then her face lit up and she clapped her hands. 'Got it!' She started talking rapid-fire, ticking off decisions on her fingers. 'Okay, I buy Budi's share of the concession, I don't have to find the money, it's only a paper transaction anyway. We then backdate the sale two years – that's easy enough to arrange in Indonesia. So now the concession has been in my possession two years, long before anyone knew, least of all myself, that the atrocities were ordered by Major General Budi Til.

'I then receive the photograph from Marg Hamilton. I'm horrified and want to do something meaningful apart from having the killers of the apes arrested. I'm an Australian citizen with several businesses in Indonesia and so I decide to offer my timber concession as a gift of gratitude to the nation as permanent habitat for the apes and all the other jungle creatures.

'That is, if my dear friend the president's wife, Siti Hartinah Suharto, after whom the national park will be named, will get him to agree to protect the orangutan. The habitat is a gift from Australia to Indonesia. The permanent protection of the orangutan is a gift to the world from the wife of the Indonesian president. It's the story of two powerful women and a generous and wise man, all of whom care tremendously for the environment and for the continuing existence of the great apes. A gesture of friendship, hands held across the sea.'

Anna caught her breath. 'Budi is now completely out of the picture and there is no link to the oil or the Balibo Five.' She leaned back, grinning. 'That's the story *The Australian* newspaper gets and later Melanie Griffith will be invited to meet Madame Suharto at the ceremony to hand over the national park to the nation.' Anna looked pleased with herself. 'Finally, Peter Yeldham has his pictures, but no story to tell.'

'Brilliant! Absolutely brilliant! Will Mrs Suharto do it?'

'Of course, she's a good friend. She'll love the idea, so will he. Siti Suharto National Park has a nice ring to it, don't you think?' Anna said, smiling.

'What about the rake-off, the ten per cent the Suharto family is owed from the concession? That's around ten million American, isn't it? I can let you have two million of it if you're in trouble. You don't have to pay it back.'

'Thank you, Nicholas, that's lovely of you.' Anna smiled benignly. 'Damn good thing Kevin looks after the money. You're as bad as Joe with his scholarships. You're never going to be a really top businessman, Nicholas. But I can find the money. Besides, it depends very much on how the president feels. If he really likes the goodwill gesture between his wife and myself and between our two countries, as I'm pretty sure he will, the debt could easily be cancelled. I know he's fond of me and he can be very generous.'

'What about Budi? Will he go along with all this?' I was trying hard not to show my revulsion for Anna's business partner, who in any language could only be seen as a mass murderer. He'd come a long way in the wrong direction since, as an eager teenage freedom fighter, I'd shown him how to set up an effective ambush. Which was somewhat ironic, since he'd just been very effectively ambushed by my own people.

Anna, as if reading my thoughts, now said, 'Nicholas, I know it's hard for you to understand, but Budi is an honourable man. He owes everything he's gained in life to me and he's also been a critical part of my life. He, *Kleine* Kiki, Mother Ratih and her brother Til, both now dead, are my real family. Without Budi and his mother and his Uncle Til, whom the Japanese beheaded to intimidate me, I simply wouldn't be here.' Anna shrugged. 'I know you think he's turned out to be a monster. But like most of the generals, they're only where they are because they committed themselves to Suharto when he deposed Sukarno and decided to destroy the communists among his own people. They've all got blood on their hands. God knows how many of their own people they've killed – certainly half a million, some estimates put it at a million, some even more. There are no innocent generals or people who are in senior positions in government. They're all equally guilty.

'Budi may be everything you think he is, but I trust him with my life and he trusts me. Our relationship goes back almost as far as we do, you and I. He was a bright thirteen-year-old peasant boy who took me home to his mum when I was sixteen. They all risked their lives to protect me.

Til lost his life doing so. These are bonds that can't ever be broken.'

'Christ, it's a fucked-up world!' I said, shaking my head.

'It's the only one I understand,' Anna said phlegmatically, tossing the remaining wine in her glass into the sand. She stood, looking beautiful in her familiar blue T-shirt and white shorts, but despite her gear her demeanour was suddenly all business. 'We'd better get going, Nicholas, I have to catch the plane to Perth tonight and then on to Jakarta. You'll have to call the *Australian* and set up the interview with Melanie Griffith in three days' time. Will you call the Green Bitch and tell her I'll let you know next Monday what I've decided to do? If she asks how I reacted, tell her I was furious but say nothing more. I'll take the *Australian* interview on Thursday. That means the story can break over the weekend. See if bitch-face in Tasmania can stall Peter Yeldham and get a little more time, even one more day; I'd be most grateful. No, I wouldn't, I hate the slut!'

Quite how Anna managed to get the fundamentals in place in less than a week I'll never know. The final details would take months but by the time she did the interview with *The Australian* newspaper she was, on paper anyway, squeaky clean, and she'd obtained the president's wife's delighted cooperation. While the legislation dramatically increasing the penalties for killing or injuring orangutans would take some time, she had Suharto's agreement in principle and his permission to make the announcement. The matter of the ten million American dollars hadn't yet been raised.

The exposure of Major General Budi Til as the Butcher of Balibo and the Australian Government's cover-up happened the day after our visit to Coffee Scald and occupied the headlines all week, with Gough Whitlam and other government leaders denying any prior knowledge from intelligence sources of events as they unfolded in East Timor, a statement I've always found very difficult to believe. The Indonesian way was to stonewall; ours was to run for cover.

By the weekend Melanie Griffith's well-crafted piece came out about the love and care of two strong women for the environment and the world we live in, an example of how, while men are duplicitous, greedy, dishonest, suspicious of each other and quarrelsome, women, regardless of creed or colour, can get together to heal and to nurture. It was the first piece of good news about the two errant countries all week, made all the more poignant by the horrendous picture of the two beheaded mothers with their dead children and the old grandpa orangutan. Later that year, Melanie Griffith would win a Walkley Award for newspaper feature writing. Anna had gone from sinner to saint and Marg was furious, even though she had achieved her purpose and won a momentous victory for the Greens movement, she could speak of it to nobody nor receive the credit for taking such an important step to save a member of the great ape family from extinction. That accolade would forever belong to Anna.

I foolishly congratulated Anna when next she was at Beautiful Bay. 'A veritable masterstroke, darling! A public relations coup! Brilliant!' I said, raising my champagne glass.

Anna paused, looking down into her own glass. 'Yes, isn't it amazing how much publicity you can buy these days for fifty million dollars.'

I felt like a real idiot, because it hadn't been my money. I'd carelessly forgotten that this was the amount she stood to make as her share of the timber concession. 'Christ, I'm sorry, sweetheart, that was pretty gauche.'

Anna smiled. 'That's okay, Nicholas, money *is* everything, but even so, it may surprise you that it's nice to be liked and openly admired. I've received several hundred letters from women congratulating me, young women in particular, who say things like "Way to go!"' Anna grinned. 'One said, "Beauty, brains and money! My idol!"'

'Hmm,' I ventured, not offering an opinion.

'Nicholas, I know what you're thinking, but at least it shows an attitude that has been missing in women for too long. This generation thinks they can compete in a male world – surely that's a good sign?'

'Well, I suppose . . . yes, maybe. It'd be nice if she'd added integrity to beauty, brains and money.'

'Integrity!' Anna cried, plainly incredulous. 'Nicholas, it's the very first word dropped from out of the boardroom window onto the street twenty storeys below!'

'Yeah, pity.'

'Get real, darling, it's *all* about money. Everything is!' I guess Anna hadn't changed.

'Perhaps so,' I said pompously. 'Money isn't a lot of help if you don't have your health, though.' It was a pretty puerile response, one of those silly platitudes nobody should be caught dead saying. I expected Anna to dismiss it with a flick of the wrist and the silent sneer it deserved, but she seemed to be examining the bubbles rising in her glass very closely. She turned slowly and looked directly at me, then speaking quietly, said, 'Nicholas, funny you should say that. I have breast cancer.'

When you love someone there are some words in any

language that chill you to the bone, and *cancer* is probably the worst of them. The weight loss, the time she stopped and clutched her breast in obvious pain shortly after she'd deserted the dinner table, the falling asleep in her office chair. My shoulders slumped. 'Oh, Jesus Christ, no!' I cried.

It was to be a costly time for Marg, too, but in a quite different sense. Months after Anna's elevation to the top of the feminist popularity poll as an inspiration to a new generation of young women beginning to flex their gym-toned muscles and sharp minds, on her evening call Marg mentioned casually, 'Strangest thing happened today, Nick. I carelessly left my handbag in Mr Grumpy while I went into the post office to retrieve a parcel, a pair of hiking boots I'd sent to Paddy Pallin in Sydney to be re-soled. I wanted the original New Zealand manufacturer's rubber soles. The post office was busy and I must have waited nearly twenty minutes for the parcel. When I returned, Mr Grumpy had been broken into and my handbag was open, but when I looked, nothing had been taken, the contents of my purse, all the money, chequebook, bankcard, the nice pen you gave me, they were all there. It was a complete mystery. I looked about thinking I might have disturbed the would-be thief but mine was the only vehicle around and there was nobody about.'

'Your lucky day, I guess. Any damage? Did they break a window?'

'No, they jemmied the front passenger door, but it still closes, sort of.'

'I wish you'd let me get you another car, you can have a similar one, just updated,' I offered for the umpteenth time.

'Don't be ridiculous, Nick, I couldn't bear to part with Mr Grumpy. Besides, I had the front seat re-covered last week. It was down to the cotton lining and you could see the shape of the springs underneath.'

Then a week later Marg began her call excitedly with, 'You'll never guess what he stole, Nick!'

'Stole? Who stole?' I'd entirely forgotten about the great Mr Grumpy heist.

'A pair of earrings! Clip-on frogs! Green Tree Frogs! They're only the size of my fingernail. I mean, the babies in actual life. I'd been wearing them the previous evening to a fundraiser for The Wilderness Society. The clips were a wee bit tight and I'd taken them off and popped them into my bag on the way home. They have absolutely no value whatsoever. I bought them for five dollars at the Sandy Bay chemist. But I rather liked them and thought I might wear them to parliament, so I went to my handbag this morning and, well . . . they were gone! He took my frog earrings! Isn't that bizarre?'

'Sounds more like a female thief,' I remarked.

'Nick, girls don't jemmy car doors open,' Marg said in her practical voice.

'Darling, she could have opened Mr Grumpy with her teeth,' I laughed. 'Sorry about your frogs.'

'Oh, I can get another pair. As a matter of fact I nearly chose a Corroboree Frog, black with brilliant yellow squiggly stripes. I'll get a pair of them this time. Since the blockade and after visiting the River Camp so often, I've become rather fond of frogs. Did you know, Nick, several species are facing the prospect of extinction?'

'Marg, I'm glad you've solved the mystery of your earrings. Have you considered that the car thief was gay?' I said quickly in an attempt to avoid a lecture on the demise of Freddo the

Frog and all his croaking mates.

Two weeks after the solution to the 'Missing Frogs in the Handbag Mystery', Marg's nightly call came rather later in the evening than usual. This happened occasionally when the house was sitting late. The servants had all retired and I answered the phone myself.

'Hello?'

Silence.

'Hello?' I said again.

There was a loud sob.

'Who is it?' I asked. I'd been expecting it to be Marg, but Marg didn't do a lot of sobbing, especially on the telephone.

'Nick, I've just resigned,' Marg said in a tearful voice.

'What! Whaddaya mean?'

'From parliament,' she sobbed.

'Whoa! Slowly, sweetheart. What on earth for?'

'Having Gunns and Norths shares,' she gulped.

'Huh, come again?' Gunns and Norths are the two main companies logging the old-growth forests in Tasmania. I knew this because Anna had bought a whole heap of stock in both, I suspect just to spite Marg. ('Why shouldn't I? They're on the share market and highly profitable, Nicholas.')

'Remember the Mr Grumpy break-in?' Marg sobbed.

'Yeah . . . you lost your frog earrings.'

Marg sniffed and then blew her nose and seemed a little better. 'Two cheques and a deposit slip were taken from my chequebook that day, from the middle, the stubs removed as well. Of course I didn't notice. Who would?'

'Of course not. What happened, they rob your cheque account?' I asked.

'No, Nick, they deposited $18 000 in cash into my bank account and the cheques were used to withdraw that total to pay for the shares – $11 000 to Gunns, the balance for the Norths shares.'

'Hey, c'mon, mysterious cash deposits? Everyone will know it's a set-up,' I comforted her, then added, 'What about the phoney signatures?'

Marg's voice was almost normal. 'Nick, I'm always getting cash donations from supporters who don't want their families or bosses to find out. The signatures are expertly forged – my signature isn't all that complicated – the forged versions almost fooled me.'

'Have you been to the police?'

'Of course.'

'No, I mean when they broke into Mr Grumpy.'

'No, of course not. What, tell them I lost a five-dollar set of earrings?'

'I see your point. That blows the cheque robbery. Surely they'll realise it's unusual for you to buy shares, particularly with your outspoken views about both companies?'

'Nick, I've been dabbling in shares for years. It's a hobby, not a vocation, but I usually end the year a few dollars ahead. But both transactions are bigger than I'd ever venture. I've got my super but you know I don't have that kind of money to throw around.'

'Okay, now tell me exactly what happened in parliament.'

'During question time earlier this week the attorney-general stood up brandishing a sheaf of papers showing that I'd bought the shares. He claimed that they'd been sent to him anonymously.'

'Wait a moment, you must have questioned that.'

'Well, of course, but they were ahead of me. They'd had the signatures on the cheques authenticated by the police and the bank, who both validated them, checking them against legitimate cheques I'd written out in the past. He even had a certificate from a handwriting specialist the police use all the time in Melbourne!'

'So, then you resigned? Do you think that was a good idea?'

'Nick, I took legal advice. They went through everything with me again. Because I didn't report the original theft to the police I had no case, they said. I can sue to clear my name, but the circumstantial and actual evidence is overwhelming; the chances of losing are pretty high. Even if I eventually win, it will be far too late to clear my name.' Marg started to sob. 'For the next two days, every time I entered parliament both sides stood up and booed and the attorney-general immediately rose and demanded my resignation. Today I had no choice. Bob Brown spoke up for me and they howled him down as well. "You in this too, Bob?" some idiot called out.'

'Hey, wait on. Didn't you show the police where the two cheques had been razored out of your chequebook, stubs and all?'

'Nick, what would you do if you were trying to remove any evidence of a cheque you'd written?'

'Yeah, I can see your point. Marg, now you get yourself the best barrister in town. Don't worry about the money, I'll take care of it.'

'Thank you, Nick, but even if I do, it will be much too late. I'm finished in Tasmania.'

'Hang on, Marg, your friends will know you've been set up. There's lots of other things you can do in the movement.'

'Oh, Nick, it's not quite like that. Some agree I should stay and fight. Bob does, but most disagree. We're going after Gunns and Norths cutting down old-growth forests, they're our next really big fight. Most agree my remaining would simply distract from the issue. Now the so-called evidence has gone public – it's in all the newspapers, on the local radio, TV – the local media are not being kind, and the two companies are free to use it to lampoon and ridicule the movement. Even Bob agrees that's likely to happen. And there's a fair bit of jealousy in the movement, with some people seeing me as a born-again silvertail from the capitalist system they deeply despise. It came out on the radio that I have a large portfolio of shares. I guess they've never had two bob to rub together, so that's enough to make them suspicious of me.'

'Marg, I'm so sorry. So *very* sorry. What next, darling?'

'Oh, Nick, will you come over and help me pack? Put my lovely house on the market? *Please*, darling,' she pleaded.

I hesitated. While I'd agreed that Marg could call me every evening, after what she'd done to Anna I'd put a moratorium on seeing her or her coming to Beautiful Bay for six months. It was my way, not a very strong protest, I admit, of letting her know that she'd gone too far. 'Of course,' I said, feeling a real weak shit.

I put down the phone. 'Anna, Anna, Anna, you little bitch!' I said to myself, heading straight for the drinks cabinet and the Scotch bottle. Anna had appeared on the cover of the latest *Time* magazine and my copy had arrived earlier in the day. She was the cover story, the richest self-made woman in South-East Asia and Australia who had given a hundred-million-dollar gift to save the great Asian apes from extinction. I picked up the magazine from the coffee table. Anna looked out at me, still a radiantly beautiful woman. I hadn't noticed earlier, but now I saw them. She was wearing a pair of five-dollar Green Tree Frog earrings.

GAME OVER

1993–2000

MARG, EVER THE ZEALOT, moved back to Sydney and soon became a vocal spokeswoman on the subject of oil, fish, timber, coal, minerals, the pollution of rivers and the sky, and other big environmental issues. She was the number-one troublemaker pitted against the big companies and governments, local and international. She referred to them as 'The Principal Plunderers' and I often wondered whether this was a variation on Princess Plunder, just to remind her constantly who the enemy was.

Her speech to the United Nations Earth Summit had made her a national identity and her nickname, 'The Termite', was taken seriously in the bastions of power; she could undermine the most carefully prepared government or corporate plans to conceal the signs of planet plunder. Moreover, a fuss made by her was usually taken seriously by media slowly becoming conscious of the environment issue, even though most of Canberra disputed climate change and the melting of the icecaps as scientific scaremongering.

Marg Hamilton on the warpath was to be taken very seriously by one and all, and many a politician or company chairman knew to batten down the hatches when Marg Hamilton was on the case. As a testimony to her impact she probably appeared in more newspaper cartoons than any other woman in Australian history.

I had employed the eminent Sydney barrister, John Robertson, to investigate the chequebook scandal and the shares bought in her name in Gunns and Norths. He eventually cleared her name when a Melbourne forger was arrested on another charge and admitted to being paid five thousand dollars by an unknown person to forge Marg's name on the two cheques. Nevertheless, her demise from the Tasmanian Parliament still proved a handy instrument with which to bludgeon her under parliamentary privilege during debate in parliament.

I should also be completely honest and say that at times I also found her pretty heavy going; Marg in full flight can make your average busybody appear to be in a coma. But as she grew older, more and more she turned to the fight against the extinction of all creatures great and small. She had joined the board of Taronga Zoo and was a committee member of the Taronga Foundation and became an expert on the extinction of frogs.

She'd long since worn out the five-dollar Sandy Bay chemist earrings of the Corroboree Frog she purchased to replace the Green Tree Frog ones stolen by Anna and I'd since replaced the little black and yellow striped frog with a pair carved out of tektite, the squiggly stripes formed with gold. These she wore every day of her life and when they sparked a casual comment, as they invariably did, to the eventual regret of the enquirer, she launched into the story of the little frog only found in the upper reaches of Kosciusko National Park and threatened with imminent extinction. Having completed her set piece she'd extend her hand, then smilingly demand, 'Now, please give me the smallest note in your wallet to help save this dear little frog.' It never failed to work. The hapless recipients of Marg's little lectures were pleased to pay in order to make their escape. Marg would often boast that, using the Corroboree Frog earrings, she raised ten thousand dollars a year for the zoo's research into endangered species. I guess you get the idea of the formidable old hen she'd become. A well-known Hungarian shopping-centre magnate and philanthropist referred to her as 'Dat Mrs Termite vid da earring'. Every time he saw her coming he'd throw up his hands and shout, 'Please, no lecture!' and hand her a hundred-dollar note.

Anna – oh, how very much I miss her – fought her cancer like a tiger to the very end. Almost every day since her death in late 1993 I recall the evening she told me about it. There are moments in your life that are captured completely in your mind, every detail frozen in perpetuity. Dusk falling; a sliver of moon on the horizon just showing through the gloaming; the bay like a millpond; *Madam Butterfly* perfectly still, not even the slightest rocking of her mast; the evening chorus of birds in the garden preparing to bed down for the night; the lazy wing-beat of a giant fruit bat as it swoops over the native fig tree preparing to feast on the tiny fruit; Cook singing in the kitchen, a hymn, her sweet voice coming from far away; my pathetic statement about health being more important than wealth, a single letter of the alphabet separating the two words. Then, like a sudden, unexpected bolt of lighting, Anna saying she had cancer, marking the end of my brilliant world.

She had sought a diagnosis too late, the trouble being that it was inflammatory breast cancer, one of the worst types because there is no lump, the usual early-warning sign women are taught to look for. This is because the cancer forms in the dermal lymphatic system under the skin and cannot be detected even by mammogram or ultrasound. Anna, feeling no lump, had simply ignored the pain, putting it down to stress, indigestion, perhaps a small infection, which she'd unsuccessfully self-medicated with antibiotics without going to the doctor. Finally she'd simply soldiered on. I recall her words when later she was explaining all this to me, her voice carefully matter-of-fact. 'Because of the delay, it's spread to the lymph nodes under my arms.'

'What does that mean? Is that bad news?' I asked fearfully.

'Not great. Usually by this time it's spread throughout the body.' Anna paused and smiled. 'But you'll be happy to know they're optimistic they can treat it when it's only gone this far.'

I was to find out that the word 'treat' has a qualified meaning with this type of cancer, rarely indicating that it leads to a cure. In Anna's case it was only a matter of time before she died and no doctor we saw seemed prepared to guess how long that might be. The usual reply, 'Six months to ten years if we do everything right', wasn't a great deal of help.

Anna started the usual course of chemotherapy, and even completely bald she was still beautiful. She refused to wear a wig. I damn near burst into tears when she said, 'Nicholas, I don't need to hide anything anymore.'

Then came the second great crisis when she told me tearfully, 'Nicholas, they want to cut off my breast.'

'Darling, you have to listen to them, they're only trying to help.' I smiled sympathetically. 'You mean far more to me than your breasts, however beautiful, and afterwards you can have those implants and get nice new ones with the nipples pointed to the moon.'

This didn't go down well. 'Nick,' always a warning, 'it's my body! No one is going to violate it. Only you may touch it. Nobody else, you hear? Not for any reason!' Not even to save her life.

I thought of her vaginismus and how she had resisted treatment. I now realised that Anna's entire body was her temple; she not only forbade entry to it, but also it couldn't be changed, the structure was to remain intact, exactly as it was; only age would alter it.

And then Anna's long exhausting fight to stay alive began. At first she seemed to get well and was almost her old self. For the next six years she started to put her affairs in order and spend a lot more time at Beautiful Bay, except for the one week a month Marg visited, when she would go to Melbourne and attend to a business virtually run by her dedicated staff.

Mostly she remained at Beautiful Bay, with an occasional trip to Japan or Indonesia. I worked less and less, wanting to spend as much time as possible with her. Often I'd sit near her, cataloguing my enormous collection of butterflies so that they would be in good order for the museum. Anna never forgot the Clipper I'd given her all those years ago. Sometimes we'd sail for a couple of weeks on end and have a lot of fun together. Other times it was the simple stuff she'd never had time to do – go to the movies, a local dance, have parties, cook, visit Joe and Lela, spend all the time she could with Saffron when she was home from school. The two of them would sit in the garden for hours talking; Saffy was the little girl Anna had never had, and seemed to worship her.

Then her remission ended and she grew steadily weaker. Saffron wanted to delay going to university to care for her but Anna insisted that she go. 'Saffy, remember, we have plans,' she'd say. During her last three years, when she became increasingly ill, she'd spend all her time when she was well enough writing. On one occasion I'd found her in tears in front of her Mac, and said, 'Darling, you're tired, can't you leave that for a while?'

'No! I'm running out of time, she must know *everything* before I die!'

'Who?'

'Saffy, of course.'

'What, your life's story?'

'Pfft! Of course not! Who cares about that? Money. She must know about money.' She wouldn't explain any further, but every day she'd print out what she'd written and lock it in the safe. Not that I would ever have looked at it. Saffron and Anna were a private duo and I was happy that the beautiful youngster took Anna's mind off her own increasingly intense pain.

Two months before Anna passed away she handed me a very large envelope she'd sealed with red sealing wax and imprinted with a stamp that carried her Dutch family coat of arms. I had never seen her use it before.

'Nicholas, this is for Saffron. You must give it to her on her twenty-second birthday.'

'Not her twenty-first?' I questioned.

'No, she will finish university, graduate and have her twenty-first birthday – for that I have arranged the Visa card. Then you must let her have a year to travel, find herself. Then on her twenty-second have a big party and give her this envelope. She has been enrolled at MIT and the London School of Economics – she will choose which one she wants. After that,' she indicated the envelope, 'these are her instructions.'

Sick as Anna was, I felt the need to object. 'Anna, you can't control the girl's life; she may not want to do as you instruct.'

Anna looked at me. 'That is for her to decide. There are instructions in there if she doesn't . . .' Anna paused. 'But she will,' she said with total conviction.

Anna rapidly declined. She was now permanently

bedridden, with a buzzer next to her bed, a nurse who slept in the room next door and a doctor who visited twice a day to administer morphine. She was mostly in a semi-coma with only brief moments of lucidity and couldn't possibly manage to inhale the heroin even if I prepared it for her. If she wanted to call me she pressed the buzzer twice.

Then in the dry season, on the 5th of April 1993, when the persimmon trees were bursting with fruit, great golden orbs hanging on the twisted leafless limbs, at two in the morning the buzzer woke me.

I stumbled into Anna's bedroom. It was the first time in two days she'd been sufficiently lucid to use the buzzer. The nightlight was on and incredibly she'd managed to sit up. 'Come and hold me, Nicholas,' she said in a whisper, 'one last time.'

I crawled into bed, careful not to hurt her. Then I gently took her tiny body into my arms. 'Who would have thought that the brightest star in all creation was the first one I ever caught.' She smiled a little, then whispered, 'Thank you. Thank you for everything, my beautiful man. I only ever wanted you.' And she died in my arms.

Fifteen hundred islanders came to her funeral feast at Beautiful Bay. They came from every part of the Pacific – administrators, politicians, teachers and common people, hundreds of them, recipients of her and Joe's Uncle Joe Scholarships. Joe started to make a speech and then broke down. Kevin, with a cigar in his mouth, kept telling anyone who would listen, 'She was one helluva dame!' Saffron, only fourteen, organised the island children to plant the remainder of the persimmon trees, seeded in the propagation shed by Ellison the previous wet season.

That is, except for one robust seedling. It is traditional in the islands to bury a loved one in the garden, but as usual Anna had other plans. After the great feast I had her coffin placed on *Madam Butterfly* and sailed single-handed to Coffee Scald Island. Ellison had gone out the previous day in the motorboat with three strong island lads, his grandsons, and they'd dug her grave through the coral on the topmost knoll.

They'd gone ahead after the feast and were waiting for me as the sun started to set and Ellison waded in and pulled *Madam Butterfly* into the shallows. The three young men, Ellison and I carried her coffin up to the knoll and lowered it into the grave. Then they returned to the beach and left me there.

I said the same prayer I'd learned standing beside my father at countless native funerals. The one I'd said for the ten sailors all those years ago on the lonely beach in West Java.

"I am the resurrection, and the life", saith the Lord:
"he that believeth in me, though he were dead,
yet shall he live: and whosoever liveth and believeth in me
shall never die . . ."
For I am persuaded that neither death, nor life, nor angels,
nor principalities, nor powers, nor things present, nor things to
come,nor height, nor depth, nor any other creature,
shall be able to separate us from the love of God,
which is in Christ Jesus our Lord.
Earth to earth; ashes to ashes; dust to dust;
in the sure and certain hope of resurrection to eternal life.
Amen.

Ellison returned with his grandsons and filled Anna's grave, then they departed and Ellison returned with a watering can filled with fresh water and I planted the last of the persimmon trees where my darling Anna rested for eternity. I watered it in and handed the can back to the old man who had been at my side almost every day of my life for over fifty years. He turned to me and said, 'Yumi everywan kum ia today for say tang yu for life long missus blong yumi. Mifella everyman missim hem tumas and mifella everywan lak tellem sori tumas long masta Nick.' [*We are here today to give thanks for the life of our mistress Anna. We will miss her very much and we would like to tell Nick we feel sorry for him.*]

Then Ellison left me and I heard the motorboat departing. It was dark by now and I spent the night with Anna. Dawn came in a brilliant splash of light and I had no more tears to give my beloved. I waded through the shallows and hauled in the anchor and set sail for Beautiful Bay.

And now, let me tell you about my beautiful godchild, Saffron, returned from Europe for her twenty-second birthday. Marg came over to Beautiful Bay, as well as several of Saffron's school and university friends from the islands and from Sydney. Joe and Lela, of course, and Saffy's dad and mum, Joe Junior and Francis. We gave her a lovely party at Beautiful Bay and then, late in the evening, I drew her aside and handed her Anna's envelope.

'What is it, Uncle Nick?' she asked, taking the plain brown manila envelope and examining the inappropriately elaborate red seal.

'I don't know. Your Aunty Anna instructed me to give it to you on your twenty-second birthday. Perhaps you should wait until tomorrow to read it. It took her weeks to compile.'

When Saffron came to breakfast the following morning she was puffy-eyed and said she had read all night. 'Uncle Nick, I'm overwhelmed; it's going to take weeks for me to digest. But she wants me to go to MIT near Boston or LSE in London.'

'Yes, that much I know. What do you think?'

'London,' she said without hesitation.

'You mean you agree to go?'

'Of course.'

'And?'

'That's the frightening bit. She has placed nearly a billion dollars in a Swiss account in the name of a foundation she's called 'Women Against Rape'. She wants me to run it – the foundation. One of its major purposes is to supply legal fees to support any woman who has been raped to bring a case, anywhere in the world. The interest on the billion dollars is to be for these legal fees, as well as for refuges, shelters, counselling and support. Then she says in 2005 or thereabouts there will be income starting to come from an oil and gas interest she has in the Timor Sea. I'm to go to Indonesia soon to meet Justice Budi Til to be briefed. This second lot of money, when it comes on stream, is to be used for the rehabilitation of women who have suffered as a consequence of rape.'

'Whew! How do you feel about that, sweetheart? You don't have to take it on, you know.'

'Yes, Aunty Anna says it's my call.'

'Well?'

'She's left a hundred million in a separate account. She says if I don't want to do the foundation, then she expects me to turn the hundred mill into a billion by the time I'm forty; anything less would be an insult to her memory.'

I laughed. 'Either is an awful lot of responsibility for a twenty-two-year-old.'

'Oh, I'll do both. Aunty Anna has been training me all my life, until she died, I mean.' Saffron was suddenly sombre.

'Saffy, you've got a couple more years in which to take your masters degree, or more if you want to take a doctorate, plenty of time to think about it.'

'Yes,' she said, 'but I won't change my mind.'

'The second lot of money, it won't be forthcoming. The United Nations have taken over East Timor and when they get independence the oil reverts to them and only a bit to us.'

Saffron sighed. 'You'll never make a businessman, Uncle Nick. Aunty Anna took her percentage of the oil and gas fields and split it among the various international oil exploration companies bringing the field into production. She exchanged it for shares in each of them. She doesn't own any Indonesian oil but she does own an awful lot of shares in Royal Dutch Shell, British Petroleum, Exxon, Phillips Petroleum and others. The oil income is perfectly intact, I accessed her numbered account in Switzerland early this morning; there's already a couple of hundred million in the second account.'

'Why do I bother? Anna could always sniff money and make plans years ahead of anyone else.'

'Yes, you have to plan before anyone else has started to think or act, that's her first rule. "Saffy, think hard, very hard. Then act hard, very hard. Then never regret anything you've done." That's her mantra,' Saffron said, with all the assurance of her BA in economics and twenty-two years.

And that leaves yours truly and Dr Tony Freeman, at whose suggestion I have written all this. In the time it's taken, almost two years, the nightmares have persisted, in fact, if anything they have grown worse. I'm shit scared of having another one. I hate them, hate revisiting the battlefield in the phantasmagoria of a dream, double-tapping my Owen as the bastards advance, a Jap soldier getting close enough to lunge at me with his ridiculously long bayonet, parrying his thrust, reaching for the blade I keep secreted in my boot, coming in under his heart, seeing him sink to his knees, me staring down at the surprise on Anna's beautiful young face as my wrist twists and the knife slices through the main artery from her heart. Then waking in the dark screaming, clutching the pillow, thinking I have Anna in my arms with blood running from the corner of her beautiful mouth.

I sent Tony Freeman what I laughingly called my manuscript. The note attached simply said: '*Tony, don't know if this will help any. But if and when you can be bothered to read it, yes, I'd like very much to see you. Nick Duncan.*'

He called me at Beautiful Bay a week later and was kind enough to say it was a remarkable document of a man's remarkable life.

'Fortunate life,' I replied.

'Nick, I have a suggestion. I'm due some holidays. Why don't we return to Bloody Ridge together, work this thing through on the spot?'

'Tony, how long have you got?'

'Well, stretching it, two weeks.'

'Would you consider coming over to Beautiful Bay and sailing to Guadalcanal on *Madam Butterfly*?'

He paused for a millisecond. 'Got me, you bastard,' he replied.

God knows I've spent enough time in Honiara over the years but I've never been back to Bloody Ridge. I would get out of the plane and scurry across the wet tarmac, knowing that if I looked over my shoulder the low rise would be just behind me, just over a mile away.

There was no particular reason I told myself, I just hadn't. Why revisit the past? Which was bullshit, of course, I realise now it was what is called *avoidance*.

Tony explained when we'd been talking out at sea. 'Nick, the reason you return to places where bad things happen is to attach the feelings you have, the feelings and emotions causing problems. We need to attach them to the place and time the traumatic events took place.'

I moored *Madam Butterfly* off the Point Cruz Yacht Club and we dealt with the customs and immigration formalities. Our local manager met us as we came ashore with one of the company's four-wheel-drive Toyotas and we set off directly. It wasn't all that long and I realised we were bumping up the potholed path to the ridge where I'd been all those years ago in September 1942.

We reached the low crest and, looking back towards the airfield, I was reminded how important this strongpoint had been. If the Japs had overrun us here the airfield and the battle would have been lost.

In the valley before the ridge I remembered the huge pit and the Jap soldiers being bulldozed into a mass grave. I realise I can barely remember where it was. The years had blurred the contours, and the long grass, like sheets over battles past, had covered everything. Even the foxholes were only just recognisable, as many had collapsed and slowly filled up again over the years.

Standing near the top of the ridge, looking down the valley, there were no screaming Jap soldiers, just the grass waving gently in the light breeze. The imagined crump-crump of artillery was replaced by a soft distant rumble behind Mount Austen, where the usual afternoon thunderstorm was brewing within the roiling cumulus.

My legs suddenly felt weak, and slumping down on a small ledge I just sat there feeling numb. Instead of the horrifying screams of banzai charges and men dying, all I could hear was the rustle of the grass kissed by the breeze. Somewhere behind me two children were shouting at each other, playing on the top of the battlefield, oblivious to the several thousand invisible bodies over which they were running.

It was all gone. All past tense. There was nothing here, just a low rise overlooking the airport. All the caterwauling ghosts and howling demons had disappeared, only the memories remained. As I sat silently beside Tony a lot of things seemed to drain away from me.

Nick Duncan of the fortunate life had survived, while so many had not. That was just the way things were. *Vale* sweet spirits for whom the sun will never go down. Then, I don't know why, I knew the nightmares were over. There would be no more battles while I slept. I could rest in peace and dream of holding sweet Anna in my arms.

List of Sources

Armstrong, Lance, *Good God, He's Green*, Pacific Law Press, Hobart, 1997.

Brown, Bob, *Memo for a Saner World*, Penguin Books, Melbourne, 2004.

Buckman, Greg, *Tasmania's Wilderness Battles*, Allen & Unwin, Sydney, 2008.

Gee, Helen, *For the Forests*, The Wilderness Society, Hobart, 2001.

Henton, D. & Flower, A., *Mount Karwe Gold Rush PNG 1988–9*, Mt Kare Gold Rush Cotton Tree, Queensland, 2007.

Jones, Richard, *Damania*, Jones-Fuller Bookshop (publishing division), Hobart, 1972.

Kingsbury, Damien, *The Politics of Indonesia*, Third Edition, Oxford University Press, Melbourne, 2005.

Law, Geoff, *The River Runs Free*, Penguin Books, Melbourne, 2008.

Lohrey, Amanda, 'Groundswell: The Rise of the Greens', *Quarterly Essay*, Issue 8, Black Inc., Melbourne, 2002.

MacQuarrie, Hector, *Vouza and the Solomon Islands*, Angus & Robertson, Sydney, 1946.

McQueen, James, *The Franklin: Not Just a River*, Penguin Books, Melbourne, 1983.

Newton, M. & Hay, P., *The Forests*, Matthew Newton, Tasmania, 2007.

White, Osmar, *Time Now, Time Before*, William Heinemann, Melbourne, 1967.

Acknowledgements

While we are always aware of the writer, a story usually has a large invisible group of helpers – not just the professional team that works behind the scenes, but the unpaid help of mates and the kindness of strangers. Without their knowledge my own work would amount to a very slim and inaccurate volume. I thank them all.

Neil and Barbara Crowther, Luganville, Vanuatu; Gayle Stapleton, Port Vila, Vanuatu; Greg and Lorraine Woon, Yarramalong; Trevor Kanaley, Pacific Islands and Canberra; Senator Bob Brown, Hobart; Helen M. Gee, Hobart; Geoff Law, The Wilderness Society, Hobart; and Peter Thompson, presenter of *Talking Heads*, ABC television.

Guy Cooper, the inspiring Director and Chief Executive of the Taronga Conservation Society Australia, incorporating Taronga Zoo and Taronga Western Plains Zoo; Dr Peter Harlow, Manager of Herpetofauna, Taronga Zoo; Linda Newton, Major Gifts Manager, Taronga Foundation; Michael McFadden, Supervisor of Herpetofauna, Taronga Zoo; Joanne Kee and Suzie Galwey, Research and Conservation Fundraising, Taronga Foundation.

John Olsen, artist and painter of frogs and all things beautiful.

Dr Niall Doran, Coordinator, BookEnd Trust, Tasmania.

Yasuko Ando, Japan, and 'Toshi', owner of Toshi's Japanese Restaurant, Mittagong, NSW.

Those who read every chapter as it came off my computer and advised and added and sometimes even disagreed, and those who picked up the phone when I called for help and then gave it unstintingly: Adam Courtenay, Tony Crosby, John Forsyth, Dr Tony Freeman, Alex Hamill, Marg Hamilton, Celia Jarvis, Christine Lenton and Dr Irwin Light.

Elizabeth Marantz, Melbourne, who so very kindly gave me the inspired title, *Fishing for Stars*.

Now for the daily and heavyweight working division:

My full-time researcher Bruce Gee, who was available at any hour of the day or night, seven days a week and never failed to find the information I needed, to advise, to suggest and even outline what we came to call 'possibilities' – his suggestions on what might happen in the narrative. Bruce was both indispensable and invaluable, his input always cogent and insightful – I simply cannot thank him sufficiently.

Teacher and noted grammarian John Adamson (Sir!), who read and then sternly marked every chapter and sometimes despaired at my grammatical incompetence. It took me sixteen books to learn that you can't fool around with grammar while Mr Adamson is looking over your shoulder. At times it was bloody infuriating but I sincerely believe the book is all the better for his insistence.

She who must be obeyed, my editor, Nan McNab, who was unfailingly helpful, persistent, correct, polite but tough, thoughtful, insightful and at times when I disagreed, annoyingly, she would mostly turn out to be correct. Turning a chapter inside out and asking an author on a tight deadline to rewrite is very dangerous work. Nan managed it on several occasions with aplomb. These are all the ingredients needed in a great editor. Good books are invariably made better by good editors whereas bad ones are the author's fault.

My executive editor at Penguin, Rachel Scully, who rides shotgun, makes intelligent and insightful suggestions and has to make it all happen on time – but, at the same time, never appears to panic or impose her will or scream ancillary in sheer frustration and who must answer to those above who only care about telling the trade that yes, there will be a book this Christmas. Rachel, you epitomise a good publisher.

Here are the Penguin Family who care and nurture my career as a writer, the unsung heroes who have been involved with this book and others: managing editor Anne Rogan, who fields at first slip and gets everything going that comes under the name of final production, Jessica Crouch, Deb Brash, Allison Colpoys, Gabrielle Coyne, Bob Sessions, Julie Gibbs, Dan Ruffino, Sally Bateman, Anyez Lindop, Gordon McKenzie, Sharlene Vinall, Abigail Hockey, Beerley Waldron, Erin Langlands, Mary Balestriere, Ian Sibley, Peter Blake, Louise Ryan, Peg McColl, and typesetters Lisa and Ron Eady.

Then comes the ancillary help, the healing hands and the exercise program that keep me tapping at the keyboard: Penelope Piccione, my massage therapist, who heals my hurts, and Erin Walsh and Jodie Iliami, my fitness instructors, who, three times a week in the gym, make brand-new pains to make me stronger to endure the pain that Penny heals. All were indispensable.

Finally, and principally responsible for the successful outcome of this book, is Christine Gee, my beloved partner. Living with a writer can be hell.

It takes food, comfort, patience, encouragement, and sometimes just a glass of wine at six in the evening, and being there and looking gorgeous when I am feeling ragged. Christine also works closely with me in managing our professional interests with integrity and an unwavering commitment for which I am hugely grateful. Also nobody does all of these things with more panache and love than this truly extraordinary woman, the Queen of Werrington Street.

Then there is the support staff, Princess Cardamon the Burmese, and Mushka, the stray cat, who took weeks to encourage out of the bush. Both spent most of the day importantly asleep on my desk. And of course Tim, the dog of dogs, who doesn't feel secure unless he is no more than a metre away from me and who has a snoring problem. They are my writing family who keep 'my paws' on the ground and couldn't care less if I write well or badly so long as they are with us and get fed on time.

Epilogue for Frogs

In the mossy folds and runnels of the highest mountain springs in the upper regions of Kosciusko National Park, just below the snow melt, there used to live a small yellow and black frog hardly anyone has seen or heard or would probably miss if it became extinct. Its name is Corroboree, a word that, if you say it quietly to yourself, sounds like water running over rock. There are as few as fifty Corroboree frogs remaining alive in the wild and they are about to disappear forever – and 'forever' is just another word for eternity. But there may be some hope we can save this tiny little snow and wind and high- mountain frog. That is, if you should decide to help.

Okay, why should you? Good question. Australia has 219 frog species, of which eight have become extinct in the past thirty years and a further twenty-seven species are about to croak for the last time. Frogs not only make the night sound like a beautiful place, but they are an early-warning system that tells us things are taking a wrong turn in the environment. They are nature's equivalent of the canary in the coalmine. Save them and we begin to save ourselves.

The Taronga Conservation Society Australia is working around the clock to save little Corroboree, who, by the way, isn't much bigger than your thumbnail. Not just this little high-mountain fellow, but also the twenty-seven other endangered species. The trick is to breed them at the zoo and then to release them back into the wild. Captive husbandry and breeding is their only hope of survival. And, of course, there is little point in doing this unless we can make their natural habitat a safer place. At Taronga Zoo both are being undertaken and we believe, with your help, that we can eventually win the battle to save these tiny frogs.

Now, will you consider popping a cheque or money order in an envelope and sending it to the Taronga Foundation at PO Box 20, Mosman, NSW 2088 Australia? Or you could make a donation online (it doesn't have to be a whopper) at www. taronga.org. All donations $2 and over are fully tax-deductible, so don't forget to include your name and address for your tax-deductible receipt.

Ribett, ribett – that's 'thank you' in frog.

Bryce Courtenay

PS If you read my book in years to come, don't think it's all over bar the croaking – this is a long-haul project and needs your help now and in the future.